P9-EDA-738

THE WALKING DEAD ™

BOOK SIX

a continuing story of survival horror.

created by Robert Kirkman

image comics presents

The Walking Dead

book six

ROBERT KIRKMAN
creator, writer

CHARLIE ADLARD
penciler, inker, cover

CLIFF RATHBURN
gray tones

RUS WOOTON
letterer

SINA GRACE
editor

Original series covers by
CHARLIE ADLARD & CLIFF RATHBURN

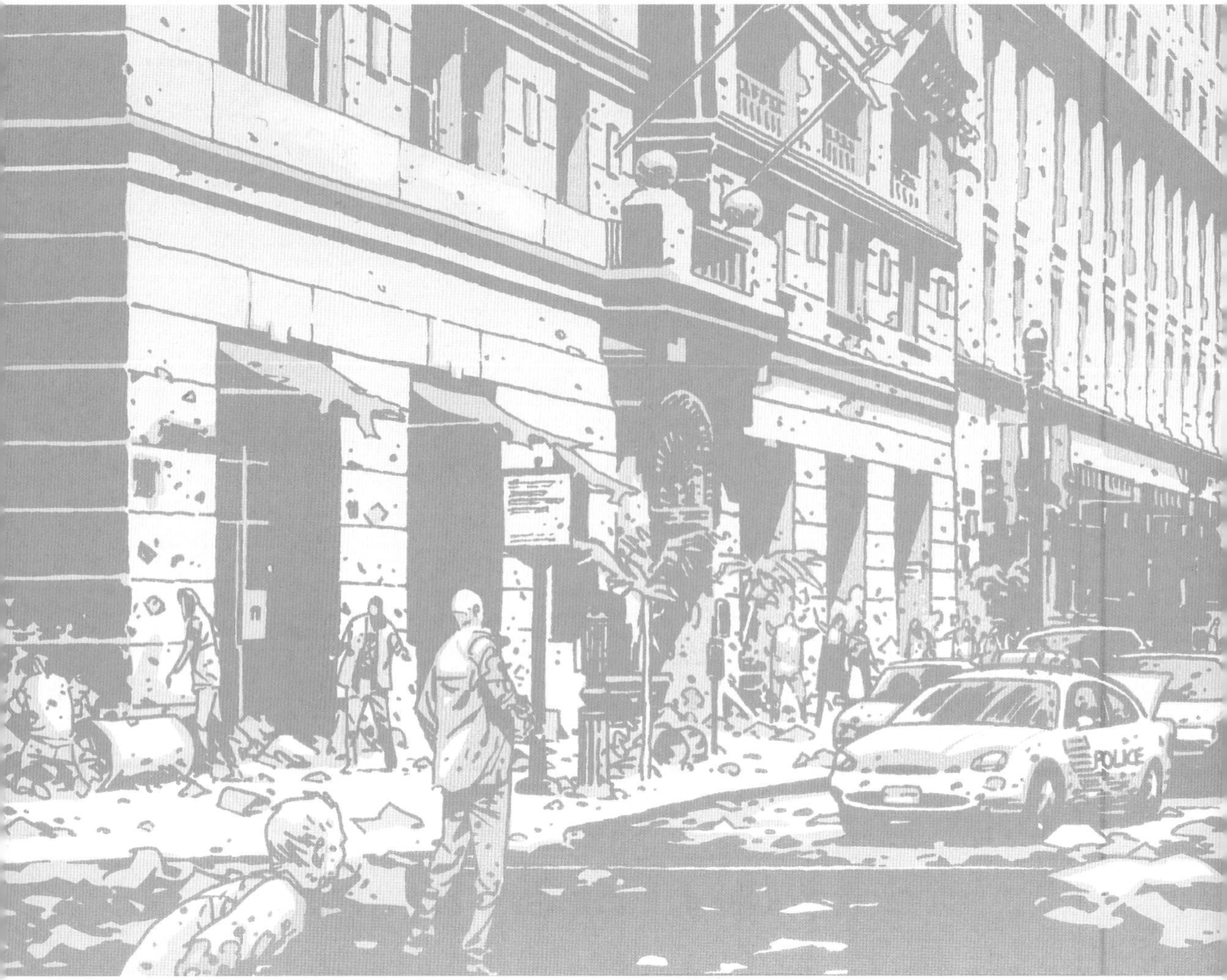
POLICE

SKYBOUND

www.skyboundent.com

Robert Kirkman
chief executive officer

J.J. Didde
president

Sina Grace
editorial director

Chad Manion
assistant to mr. grace

image

www.imagecomics.com

Robert Kirkman
chief operating officer

Erik Larsen
chief financial officer

Todd McFarlane
president

Marc Silvestri
chief executive officer

Jim Valentino
vice-president

Eric Stephenson
publisher

Todd Martinez
sales & licensing coordinator

Betsy Gomez
pr & marketing coordinator

Branwyn Bigglestone
accounts manager

Sarah deLaine
administrative assistant

Tyler Shainline
production manager

Drew Gill
art director

Jonathan Chan
production artist

Monica Howard
production artist

Vincent Kukua
production artist

Kevin Yuen
production artist

THE WALKING DEAD, BOOK SIX. First Printing. Published by Image Comics, Inc., Office of publication: 2134 Allston Way, 2nd Floor, Berkeley, California 94704. PRINTED IN CANADA. ISBN: 978-1-60706-327-8

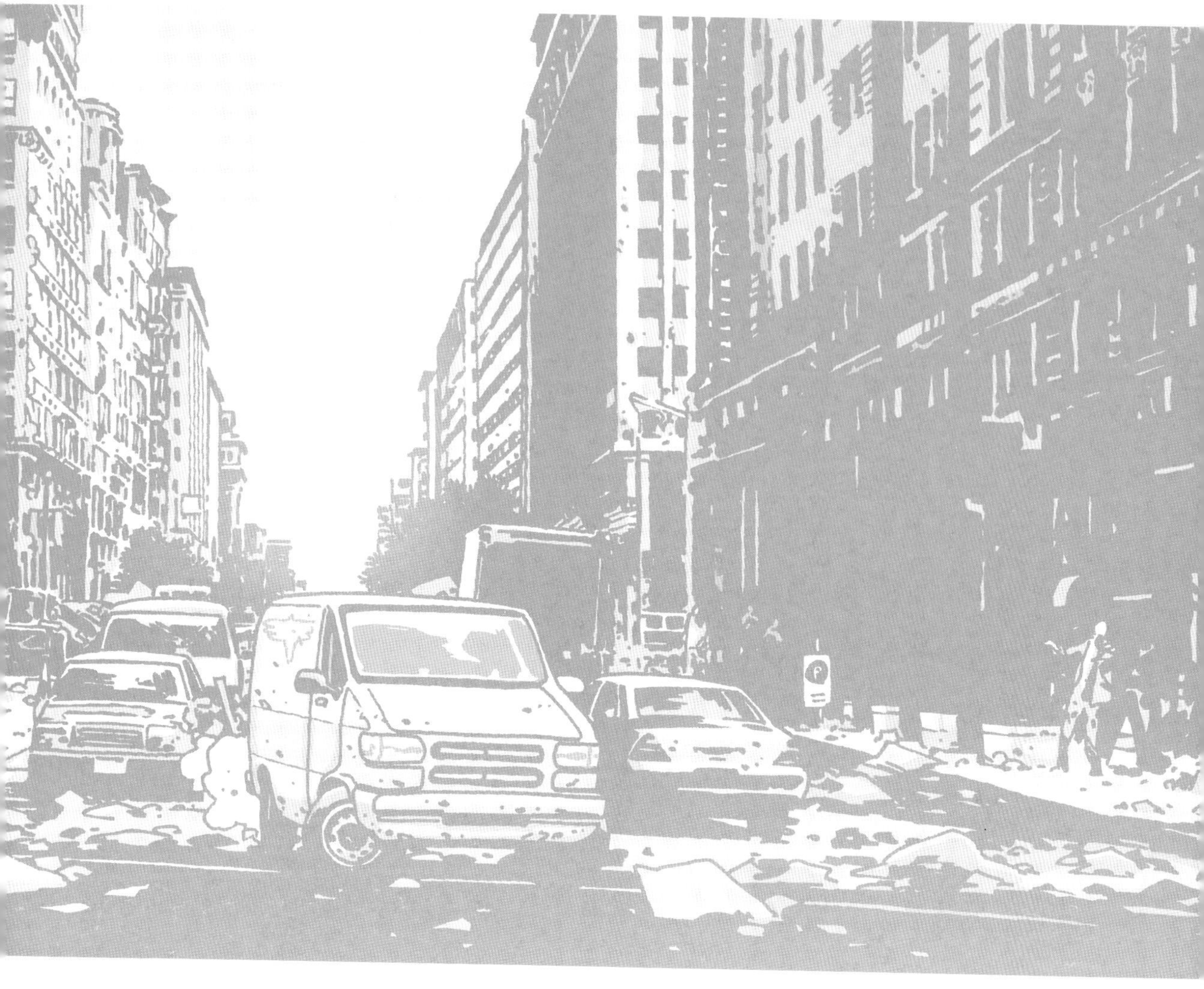

Chapter Eleven:
Fear The Hunters

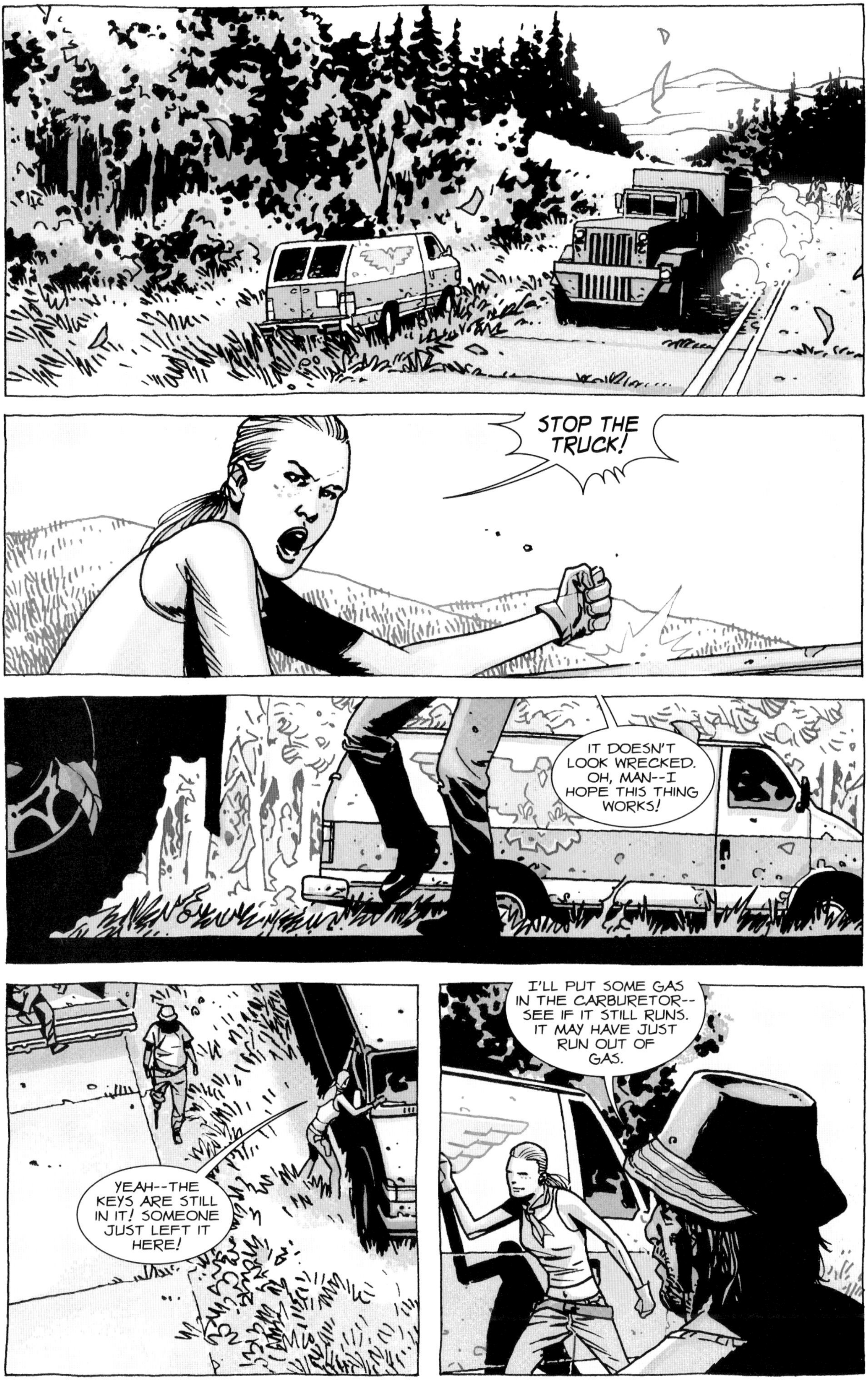
STOP THE TRUCK!
IT DOESN'T LOOK WRECKED. OH, MAN--I HOPE THIS THING WORKS!
YEAH--THE KEYS ARE STILL IN IT! SOMEONE JUST LEFT IT HERE!
I'LL PUT SOME GAS IN THE CARBURETOR-- SEE IF IT STILL RUNS. IT MAY HAVE JUST RUN OUT OF GAS.

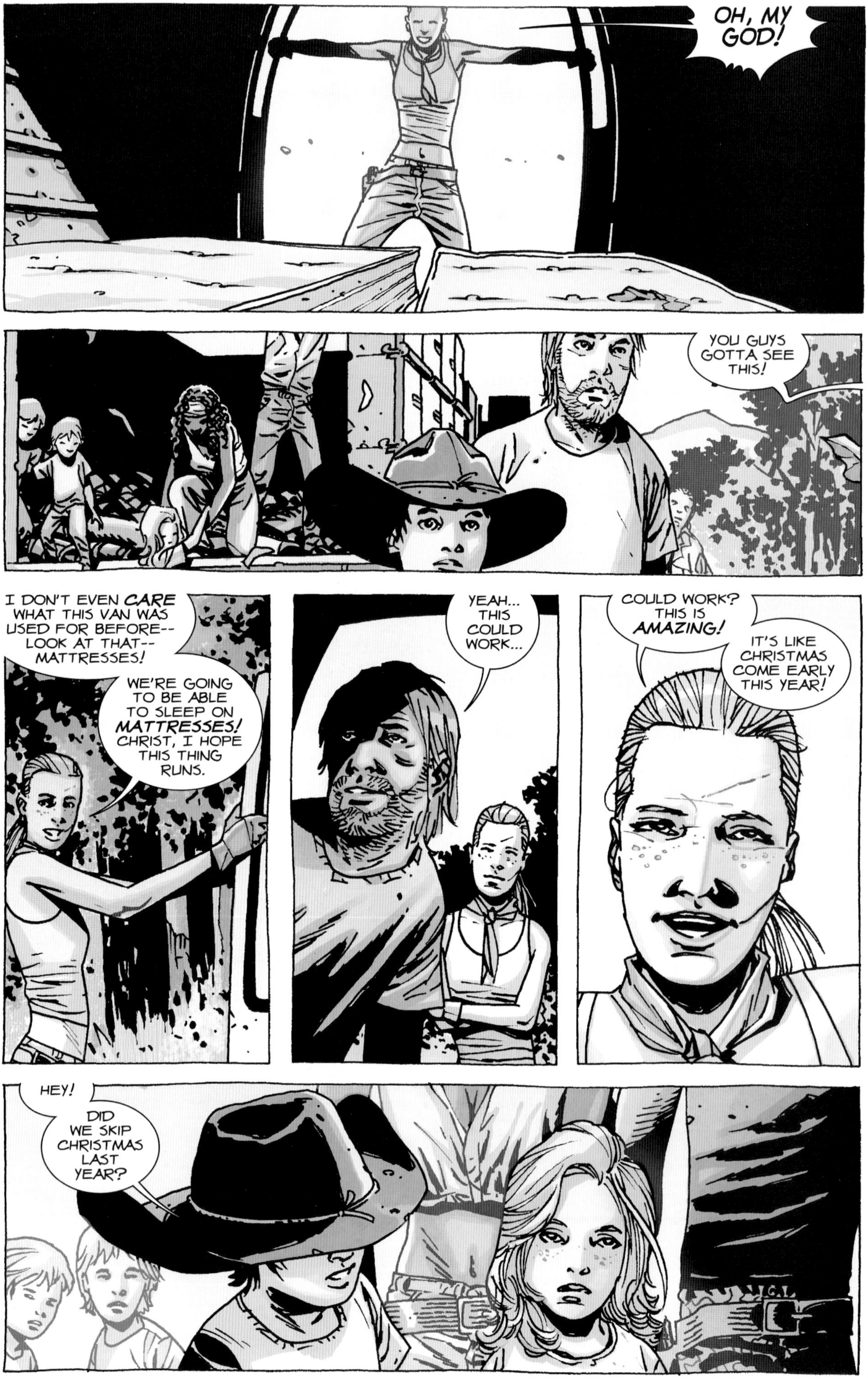
OH, MY GOD!
YOU GUYS GOTTA SEE THIS!
I DON'T EVEN CARE WHAT THIS VAN WAS USED FOR BEFORE-- LOOK AT THAT-- MATTRESSES!
WE'RE GOING TO BE ABLE TO SLEEP ON MATTRESSES! CHRIST, I HOPE THIS THING RUNS.
YEAH... THIS COULD WORK...
COULD WORK? THIS IS AMAZING!
IT'S LIKE CHRISTMAS COME EARLY THIS YEAR!
HEY!
DID WE SKIP CHRISTMAS LAST YEAR?

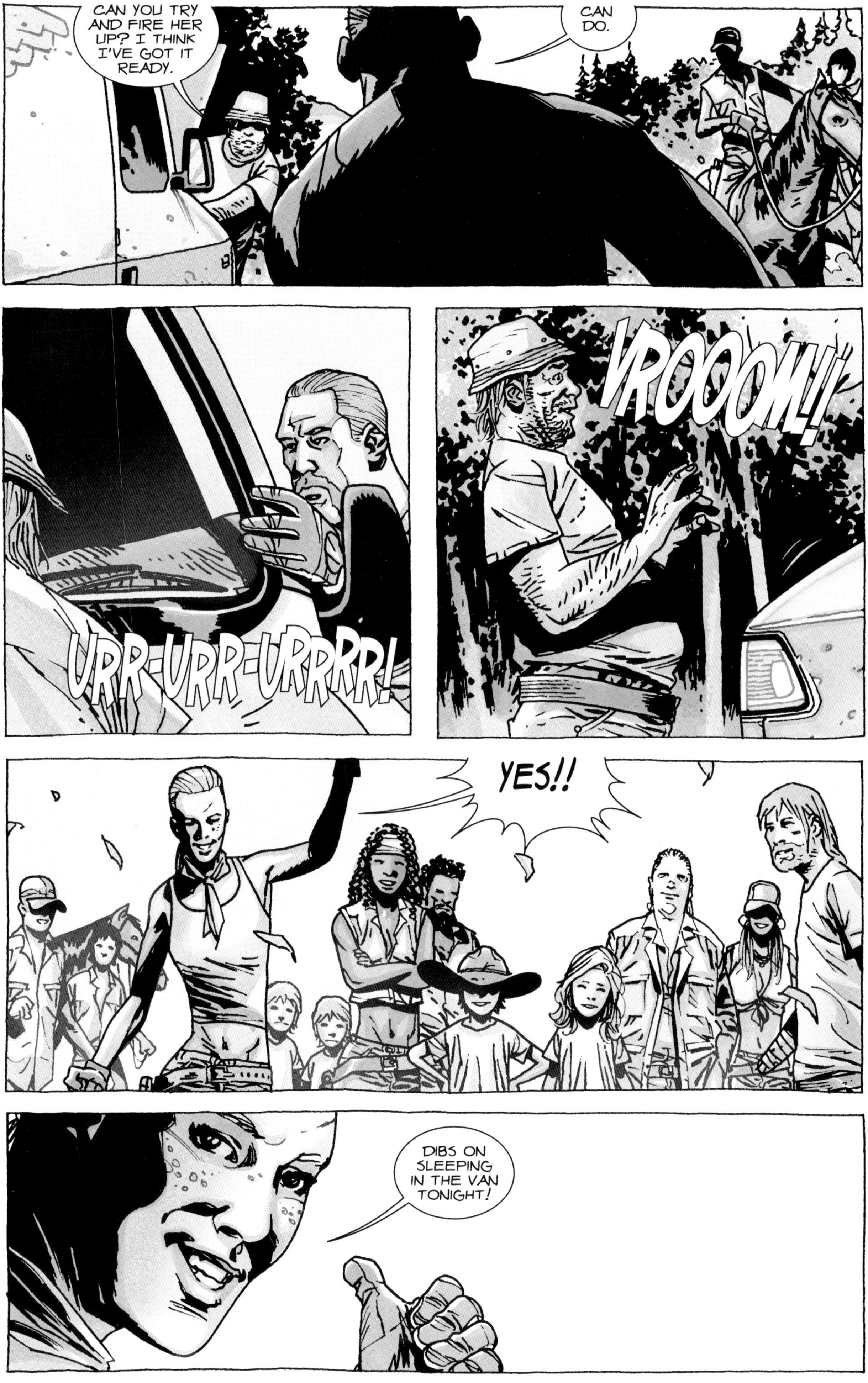
CAN YOU TRY AND FIRE HER UP? I THINK I'VE GOT IT READY.
CAN DO.
URR-URR-URRRR!
VROOOM!!
YES!!
DIBS ON SLEEPING IN THE VAN TONIGHT!

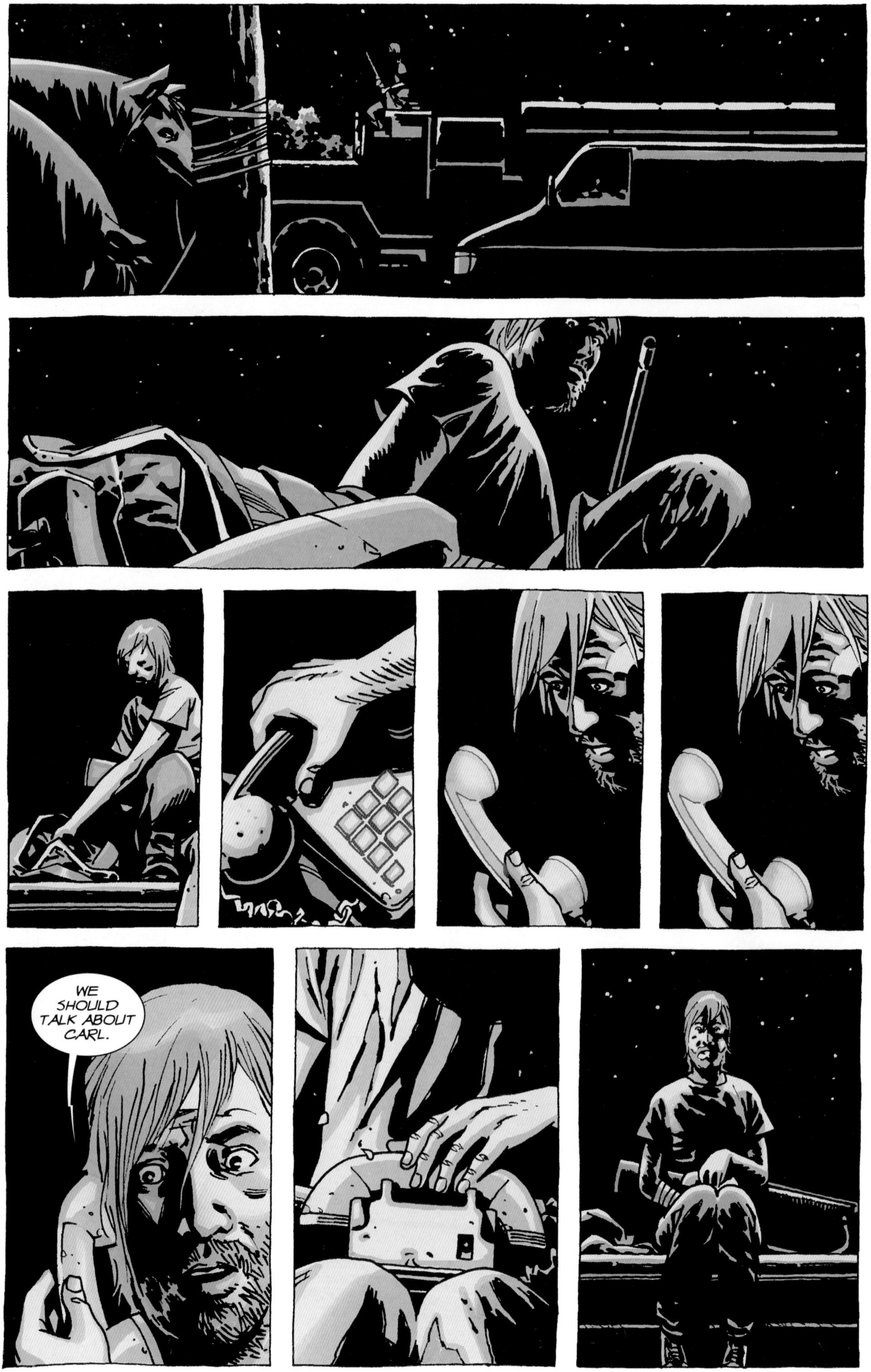
WE SHOULD TALK ABOUT CARL.

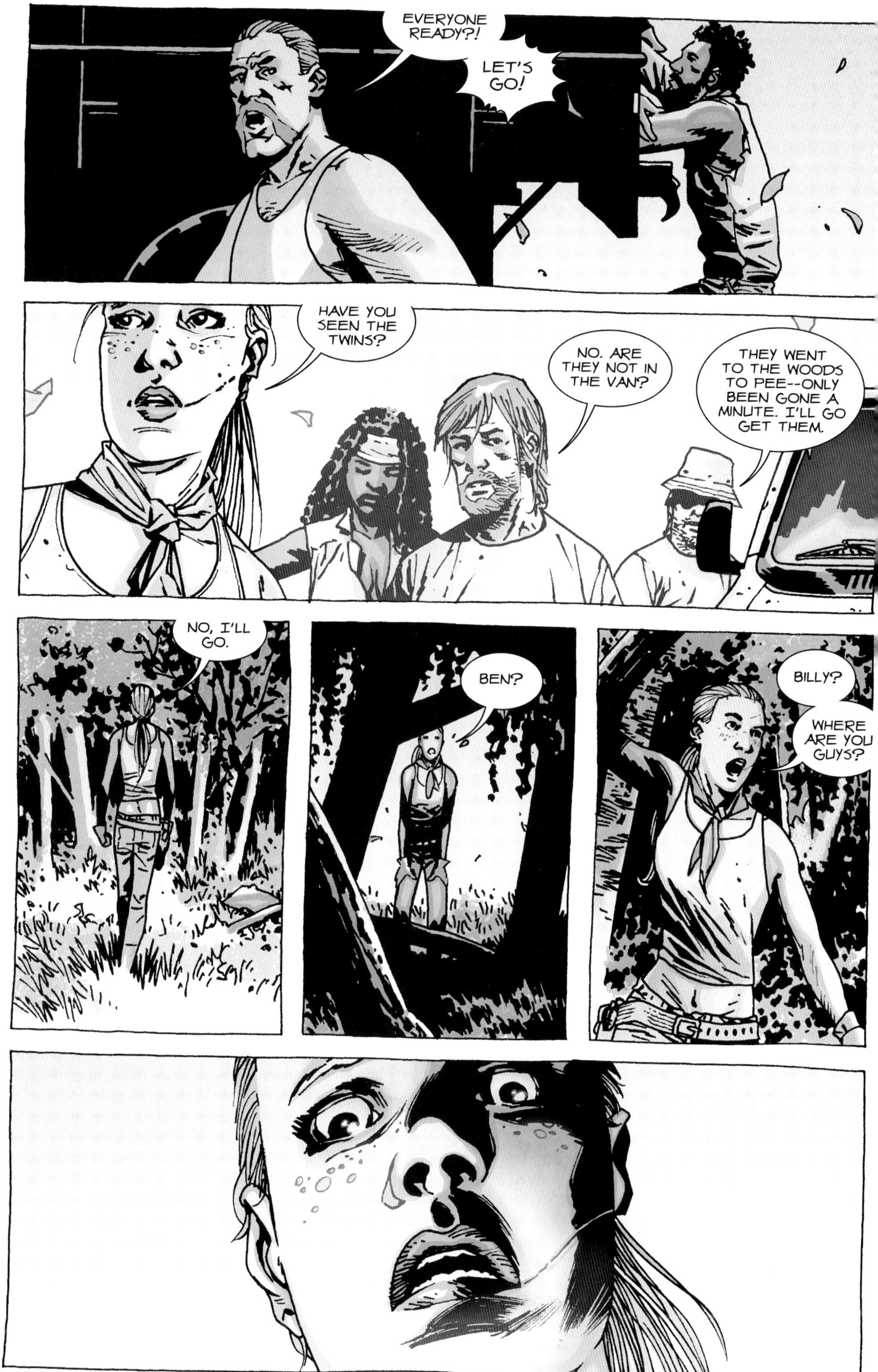
EVERYONE READY?!
LET'S GO!
HAVE YOU SEEN THE TWINS?
NO. ARE THEY NOT IN THE VAN?
THEY WENT TO THE WOODS TO PEE--ONLY BEEN GONE A MINUTE. I'LL GO GET THEM.
NO, I'LL GO.
BEN?
BILLY?
WHERE ARE YOU GUYS?

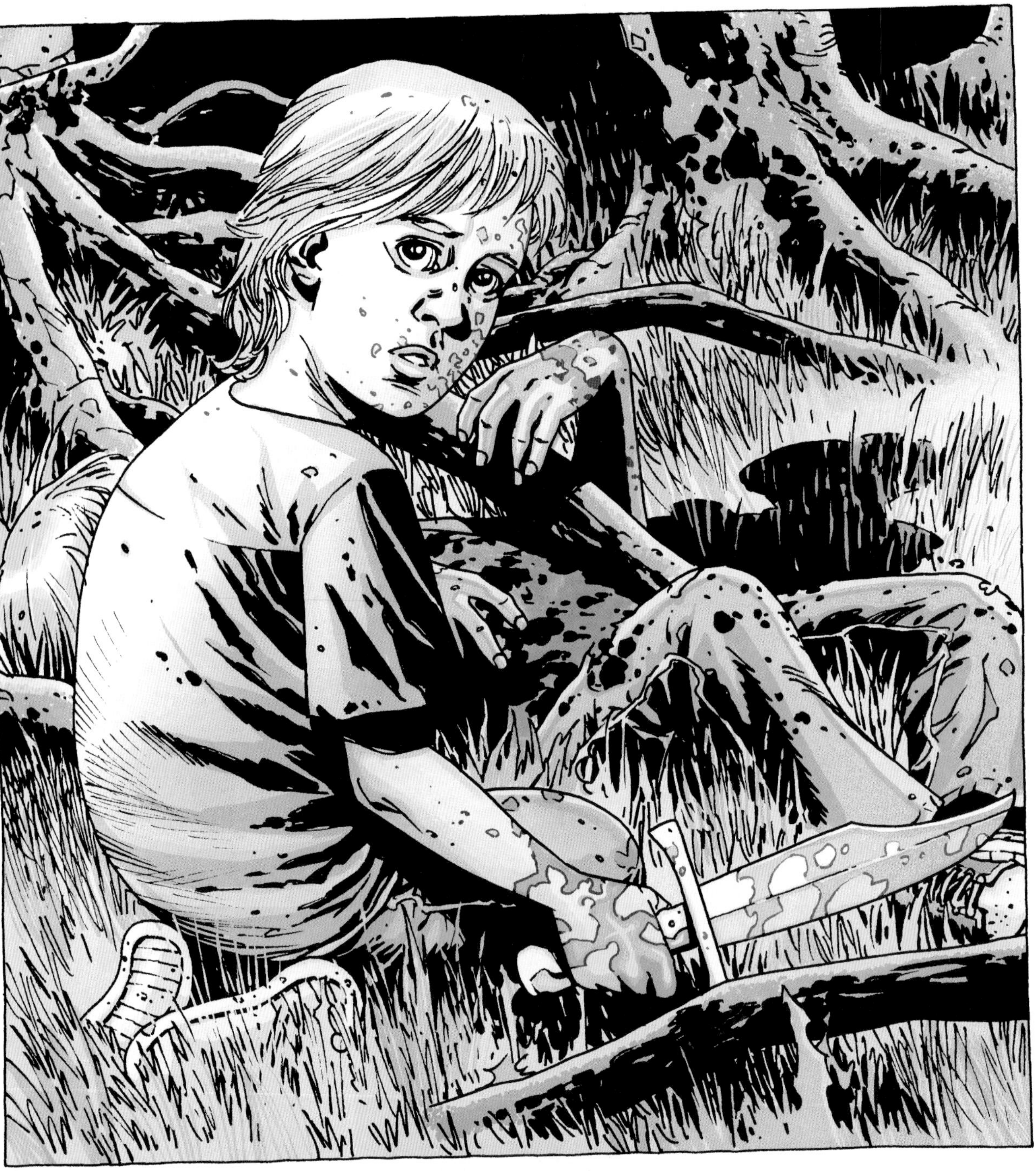

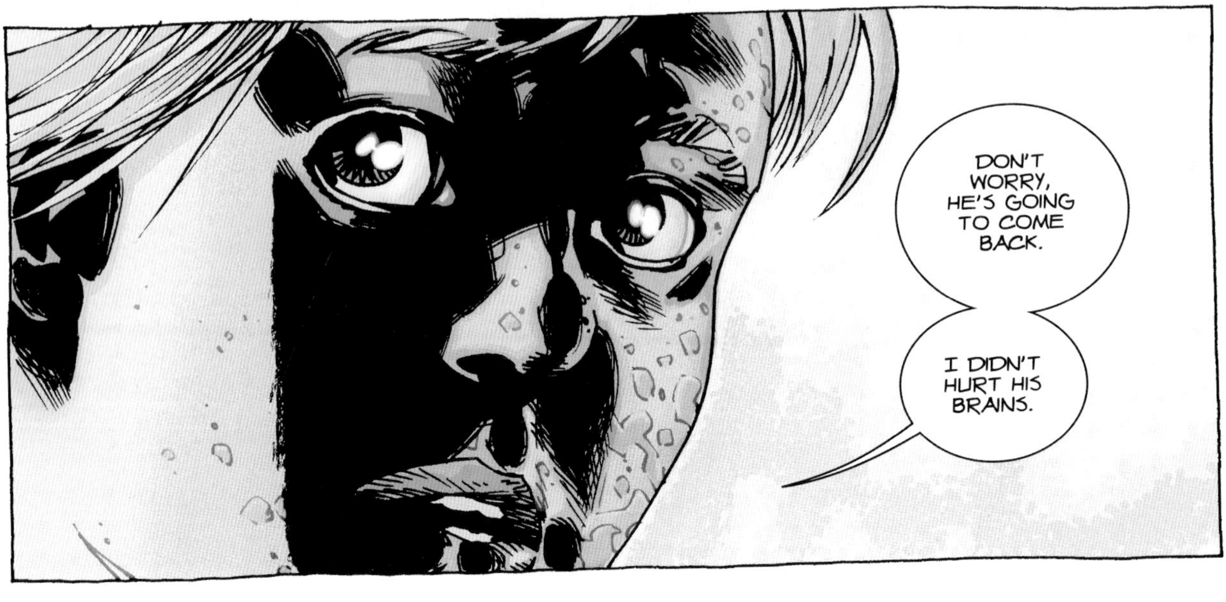
DON'T WORRY, HE'S GOING TO COME BACK.
I DIDN'T HURT HIS BRAINS.

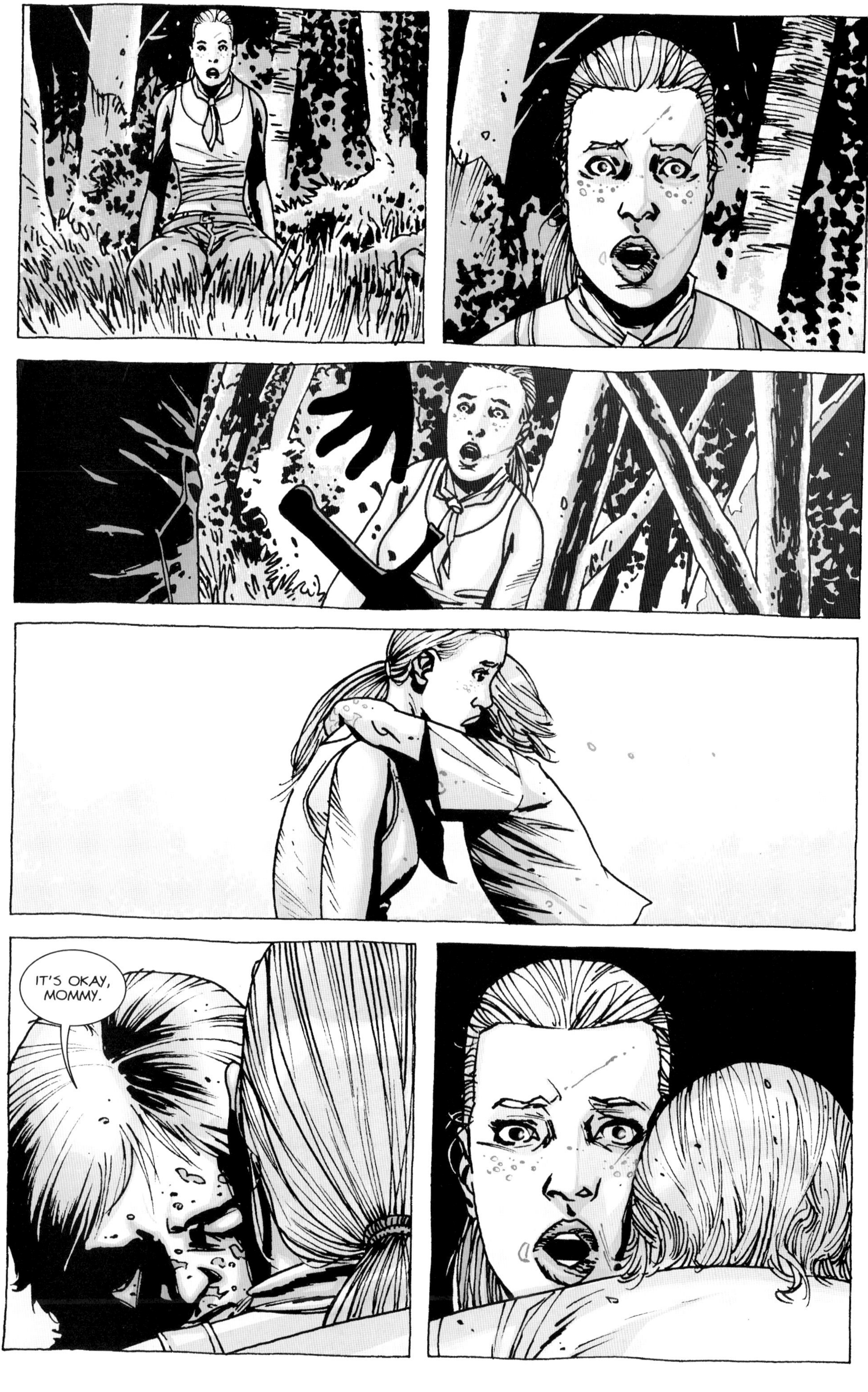
IT'S OKAY, MOMMY.

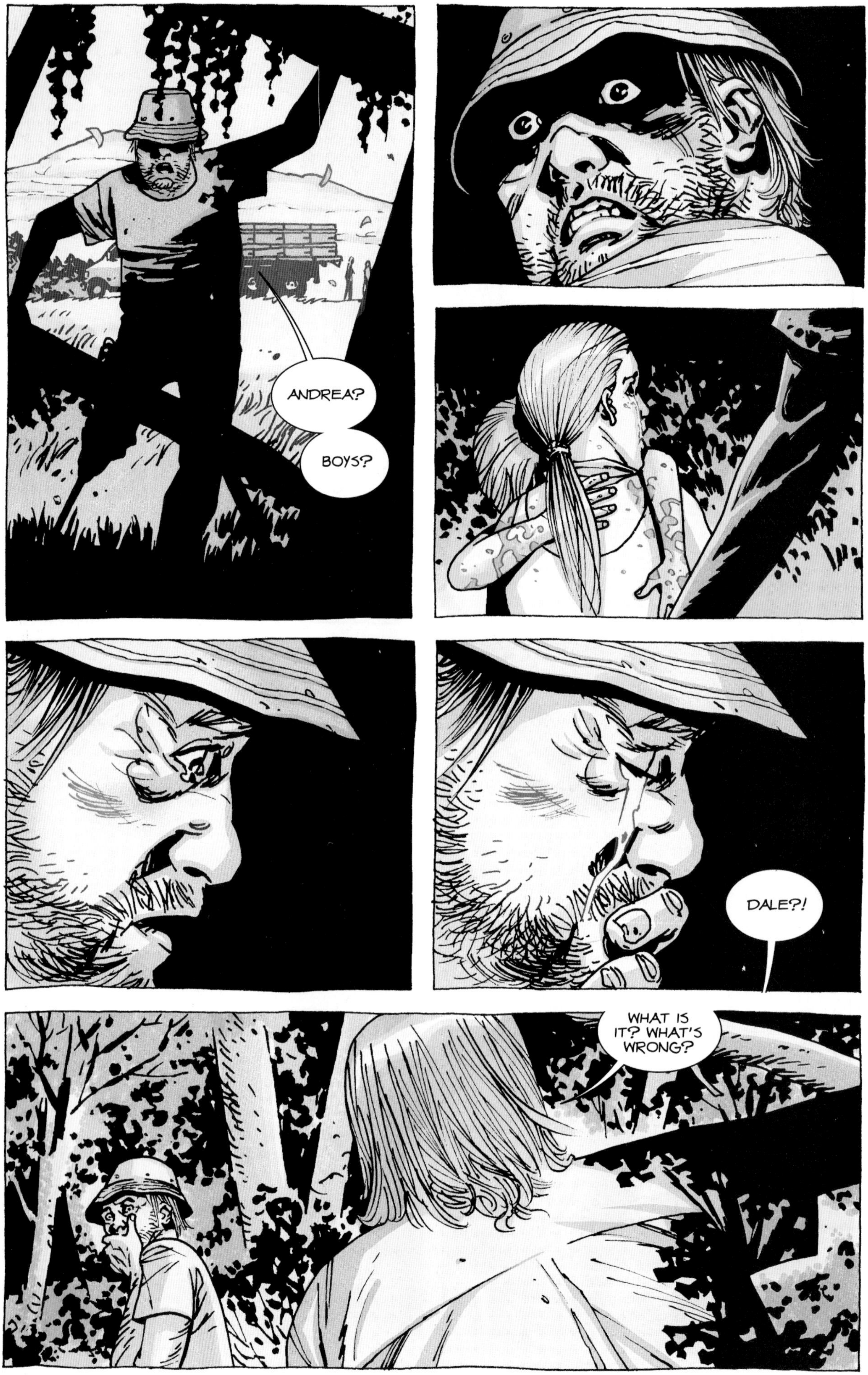
ANDREA?
BOYS?
DALE?!
WHAT IS IT? WHAT'S WRONG?

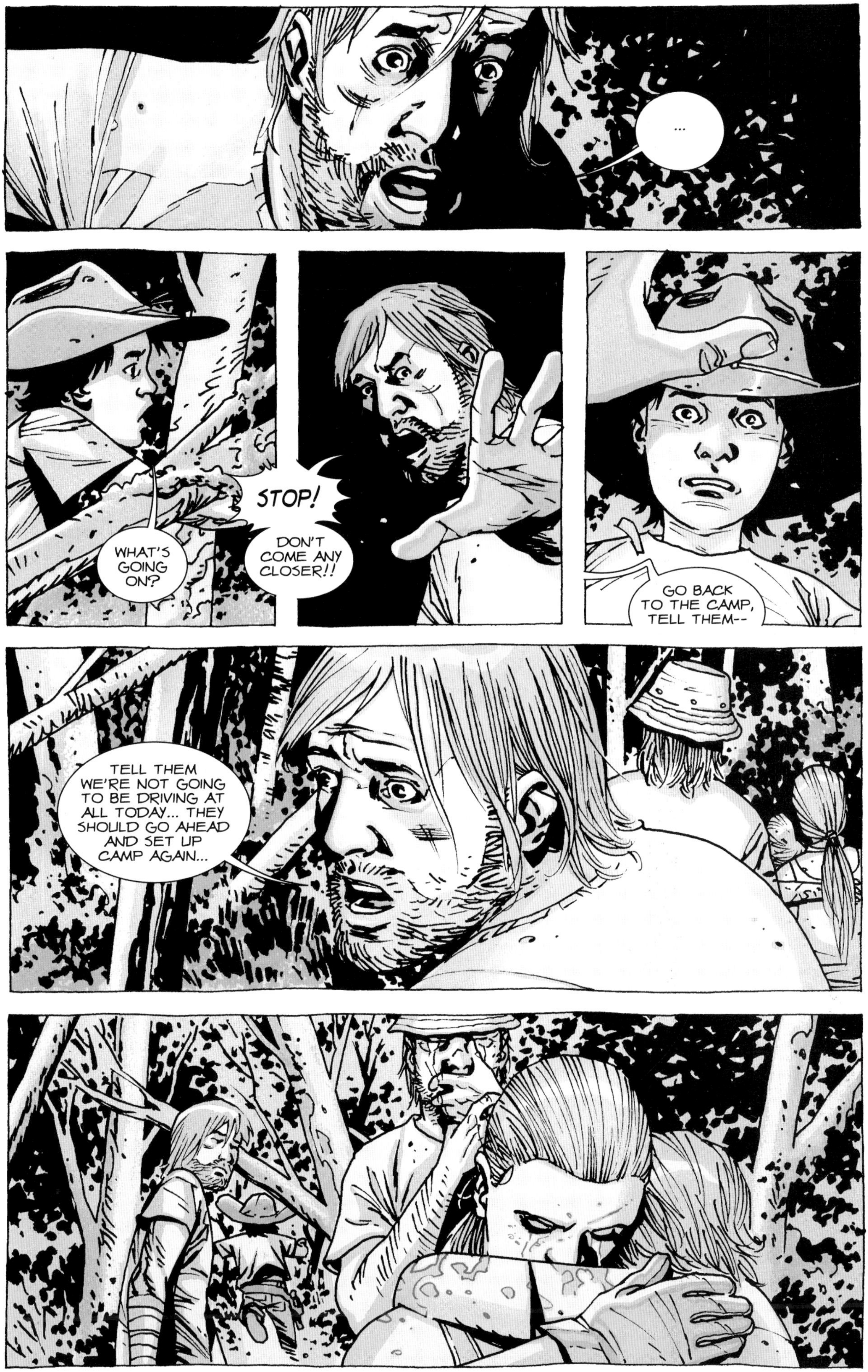
...
WHAT'S GOING ON?
STOP!
DON'T COME ANY CLOSER!!
GO BACK TO THE CAMP, TELL THEM--
TELL THEM WE'RE NOT GOING TO BE DRIVING AT ALL TODAY... THEY SHOULD GO AHEAD AND SET UP CAMP AGAIN...

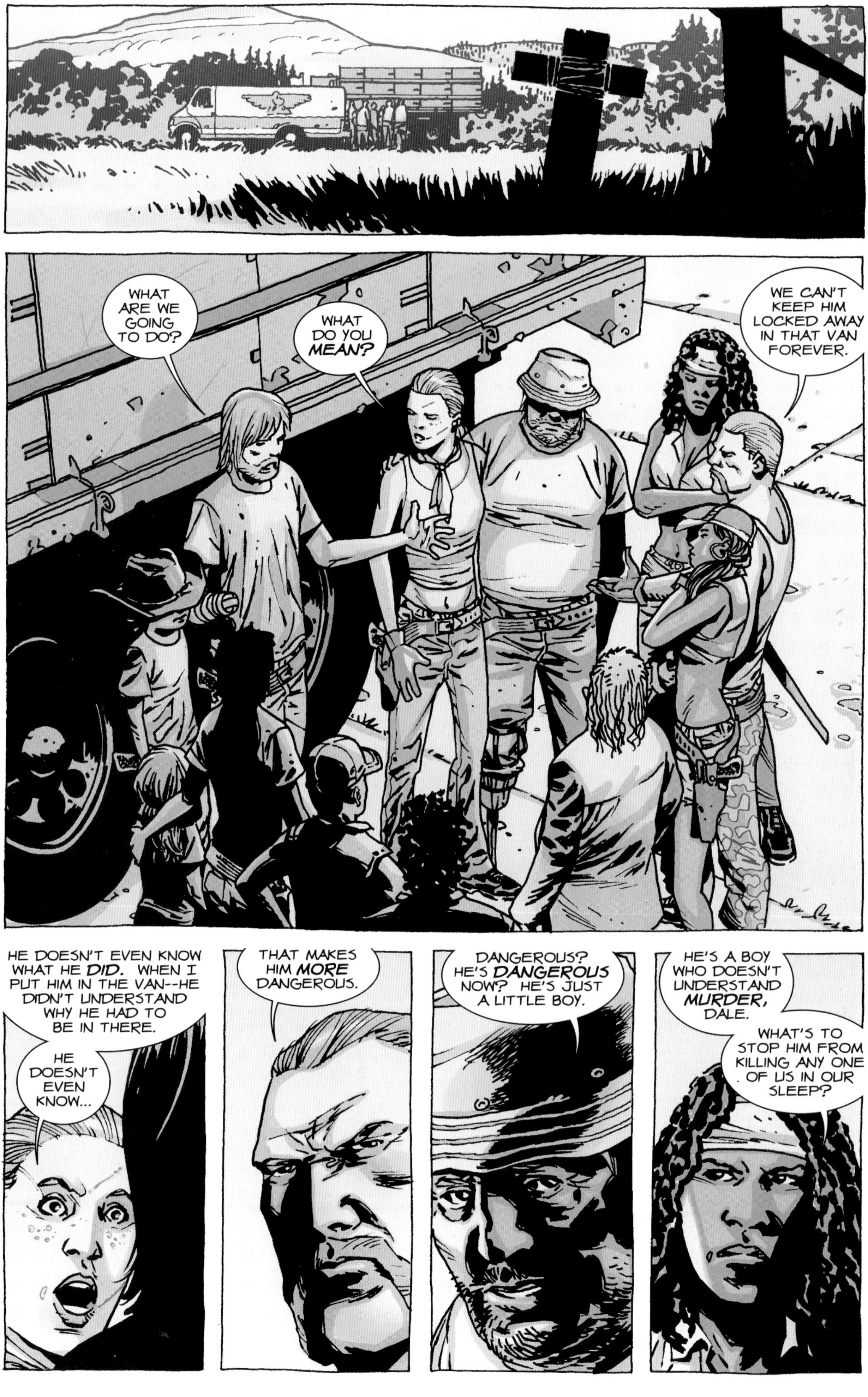
WHAT ARE WE GOING TO DO?
WHAT DO YOU MEAN?
WE CAN'T KEEP HIM LOCKED AWAY IN THAT VAN FOREVER.
HE DOESN'T EVEN KNOW WHAT HE DID. WHEN I PUT HIM IN THE VAN--HE DIDN'T UNDERSTAND WHY HE HAD TO BE IN THERE.
HE DOESN'T EVEN KNOW...
THAT MAKES HIM MORE DANGEROUS.
DANGEROUS? HE'S DANGEROUS NOW? HE'S JUST A LITTLE BOY.
HE'S A BOY WHO DOESN'T UNDERSTAND MURDER, DALE.
WHAT'S TO STOP HIM FROM KILLING ANY ONE OF US IN OUR SLEEP?

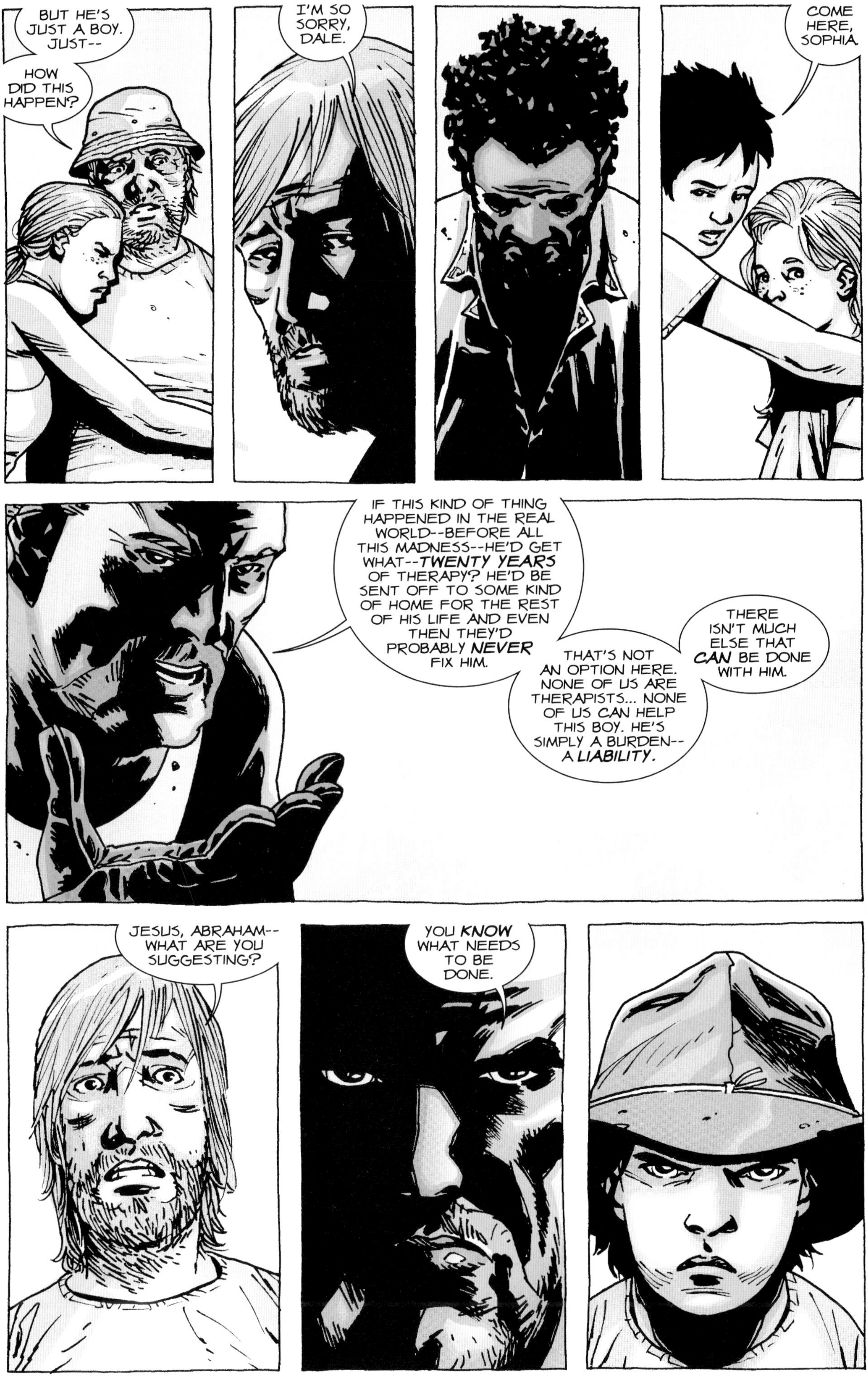
BUT HE'S JUST A BOY. JUST--
HOW DID THIS HAPPEN?
I'M SO SORRY, DALE.
COME HERE, SOPHIA.
IF THIS KIND OF THING HAPPENED IN THE REAL WORLD--BEFORE ALL THIS MADNESS--HE'D GET WHAT--TWENTY YEARS OF THERAPY? HE'D BE SENT OFF TO SOME KIND OF HOME FOR THE REST OF HIS LIFE AND EVEN THEN THEY'D PROBABLY NEVER FIX HIM.
THAT'S NOT AN OPTION HERE. NONE OF US ARE THERAPISTS... NONE OF US CAN HELP THIS BOY. HE'S SIMPLY A BURDEN--A LIABILITY.
THERE ISN'T MUCH ELSE THAT CAN BE DONE WITH HIM.
JESUS, ABRAHAM--WHAT ARE YOU SUGGESTING?
YOU KNOW WHAT NEEDS TO BE DONE.

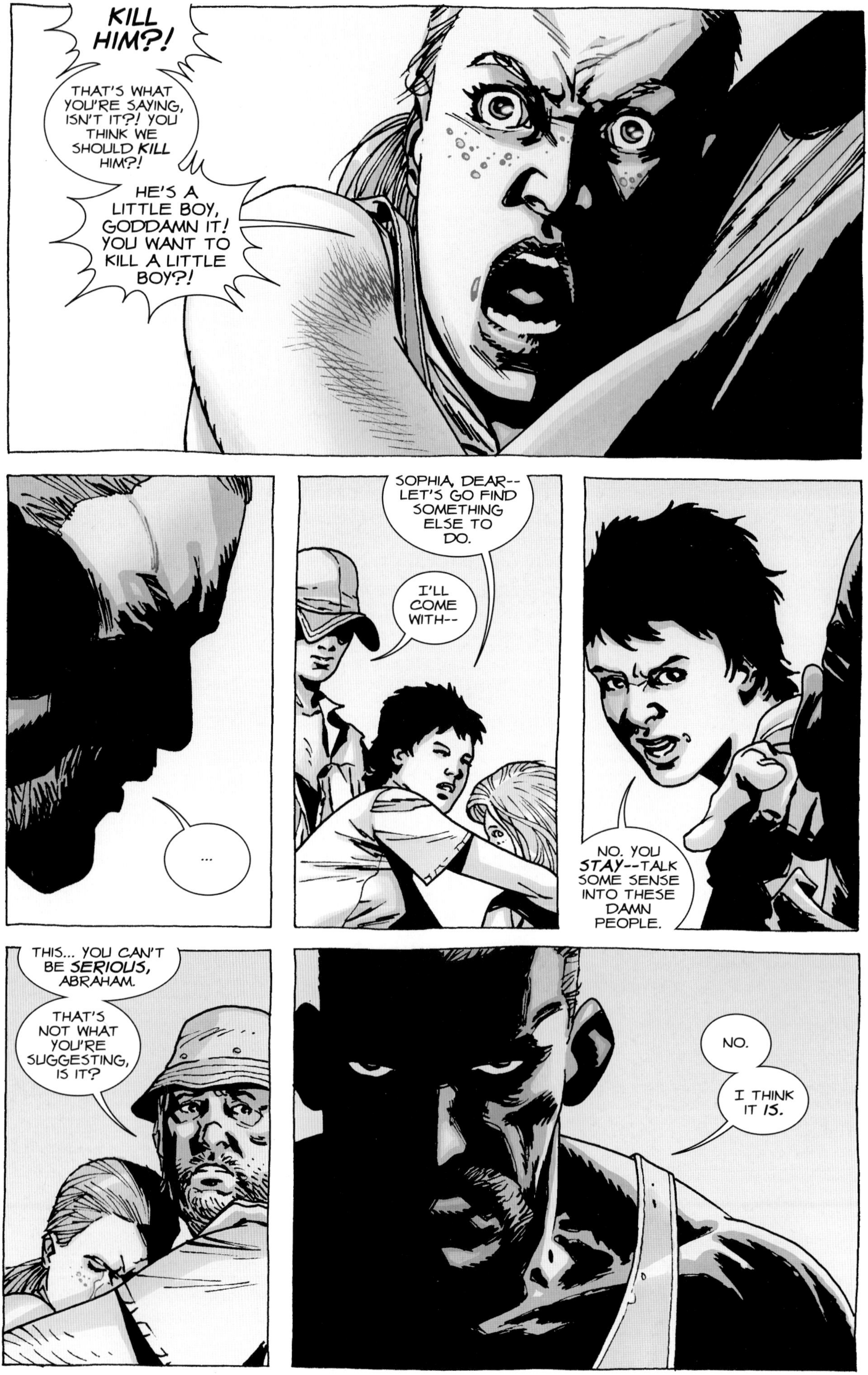
KILL HIM?!
THAT'S WHAT YOU'RE SAYING, ISN'T IT?! YOU THINK WE SHOULD KILL HIM?!
HE'S A LITTLE BOY, GODDAMN IT! YOU WANT TO KILL A LITTLE BOY?!
...
SOPHIA, DEAR-- LET'S GO FIND SOMETHING ELSE TO DO.
I'LL COME WITH--
NO. YOU STAY--TALK SOME SENSE INTO THESE DAMN PEOPLE.
THIS... YOU CAN'T BE SERIOUS, ABRAHAM.
THAT'S NOT WHAT YOU'RE SUGGESTING, IS IT?
NO.
I THINK IT IS.

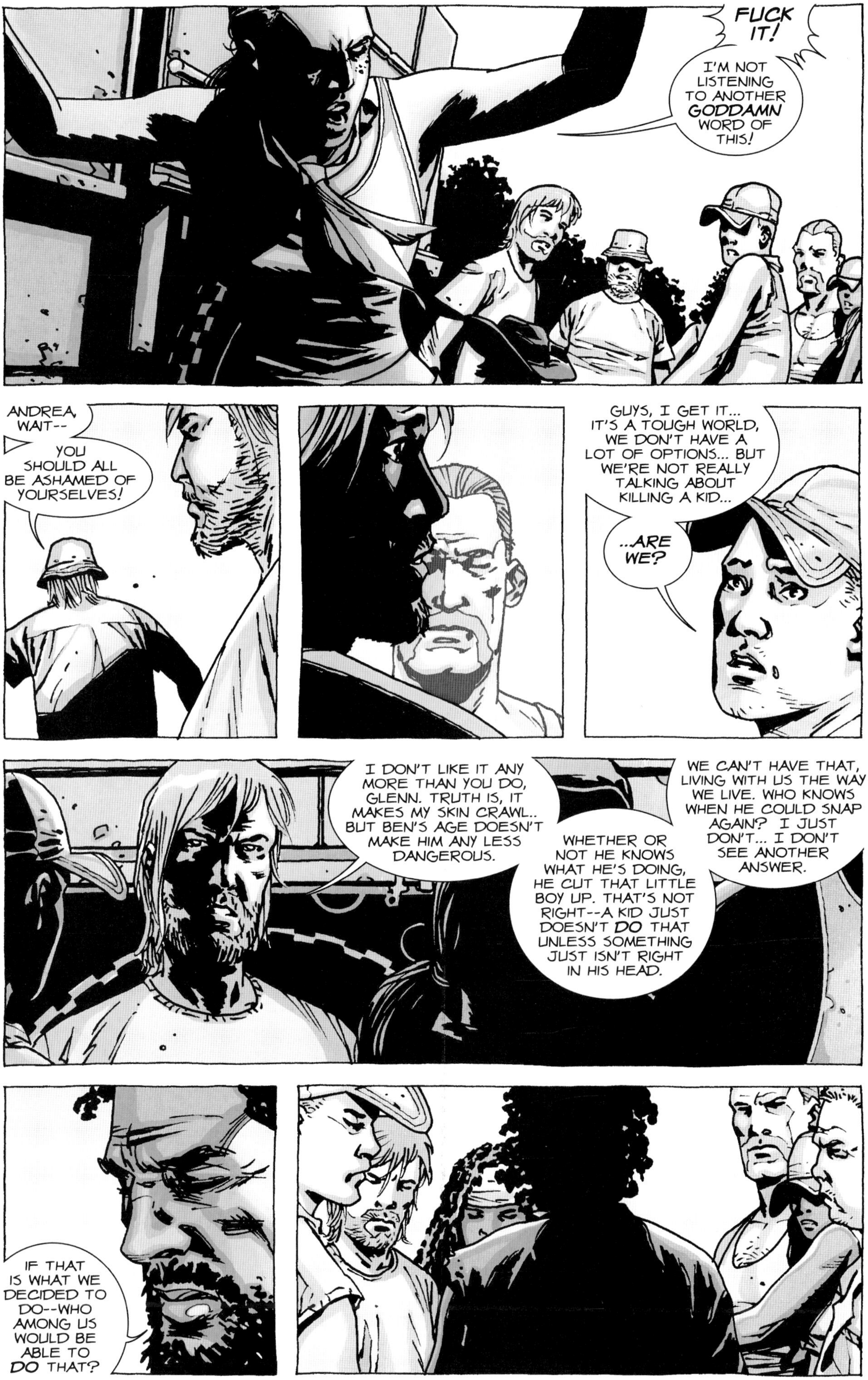
FUCK IT!
I'M NOT LISTENING TO ANOTHER GODDAMN WORD OF THIS!
ANDREA, WAIT--
YOU SHOULD ALL BE ASHAMED OF YOURSELVES!
GUYS, I GET IT... IT'S A TOUGH WORLD, WE DON'T HAVE A LOT OF OPTIONS... BUT WE'RE NOT REALLY TALKING ABOUT KILLING A KID...
...ARE WE?
I DON'T LIKE IT ANY MORE THAN YOU DO, GLENN. TRUTH IS, IT MAKES MY SKIN CRAWL.. BUT BEN'S AGE DOESN'T MAKE HIM ANY LESS DANGEROUS.
WHETHER OR NOT HE KNOWS WHAT HE'S DOING, HE CUT THAT LITTLE BOY UP. THAT'S NOT RIGHT--A KID JUST DOESN'T DO THAT UNLESS SOMETHING JUST ISN'T RIGHT IN HIS HEAD.
WE CAN'T HAVE THAT, LIVING WITH US THE WAY WE LIVE. WHO KNOWS WHEN HE COULD SNAP AGAIN? I JUST DON'T... I DON'T SEE ANOTHER ANSWER.
IF THAT IS WHAT WE DECIDED TO DO--WHO AMONG US WOULD BE ABLE TO DO THAT?

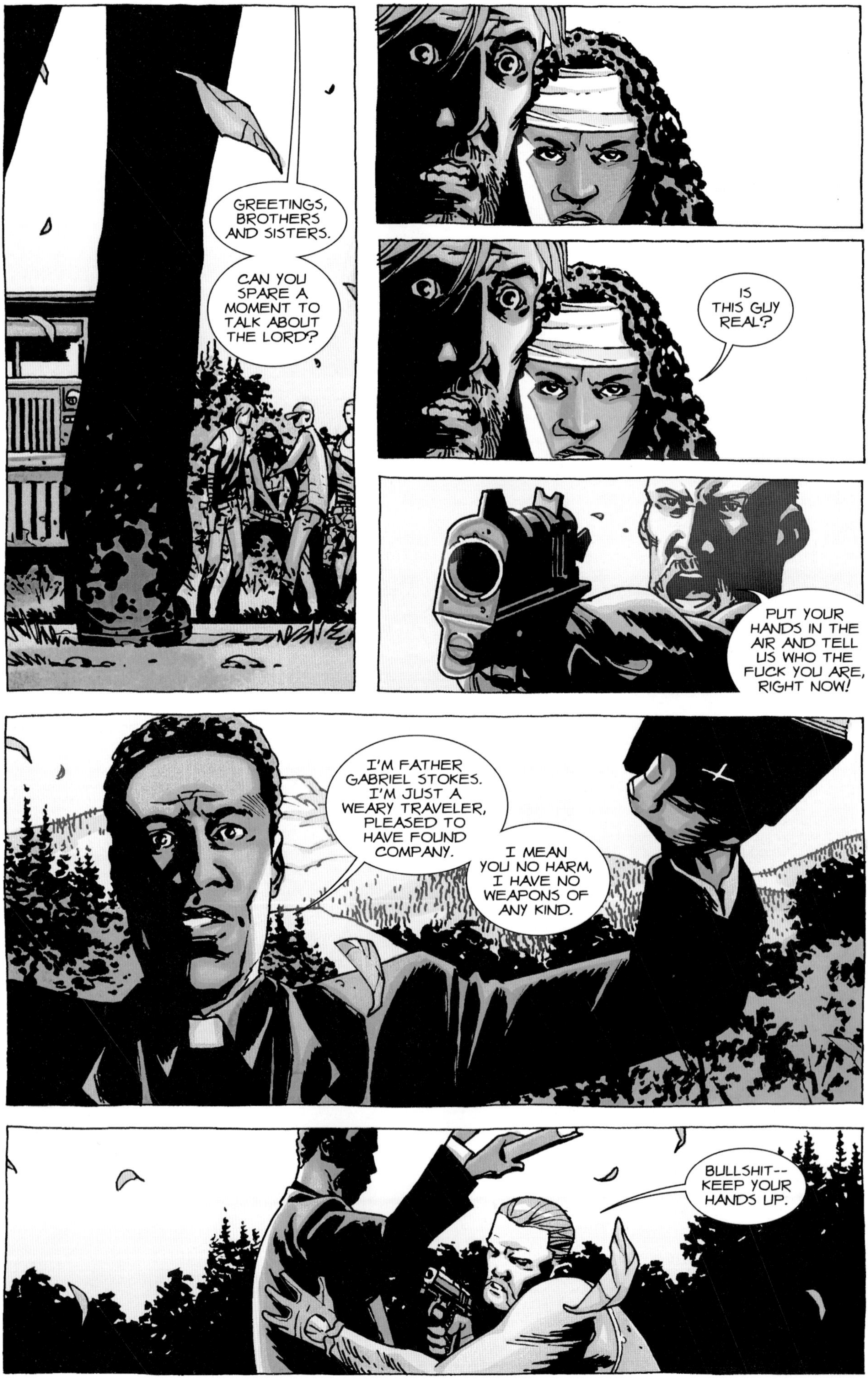
GREETINGS, BROTHERS AND SISTERS.
CAN YOU SPARE A MOMENT TO TALK ABOUT THE LORD?
IS THIS GUY REAL?
PUT YOUR HANDS IN THE AIR AND TELL US WHO THE FUCK YOU ARE, RIGHT NOW!
I'M FATHER GABRIEL STOKES. I'M JUST A WEARY TRAVELER, PLEASED TO HAVE FOUND COMPANY.
I MEAN YOU NO HARM, I HAVE NO WEAPONS OF ANY KIND.
BULLSHIT-- KEEP YOUR HANDS UP.

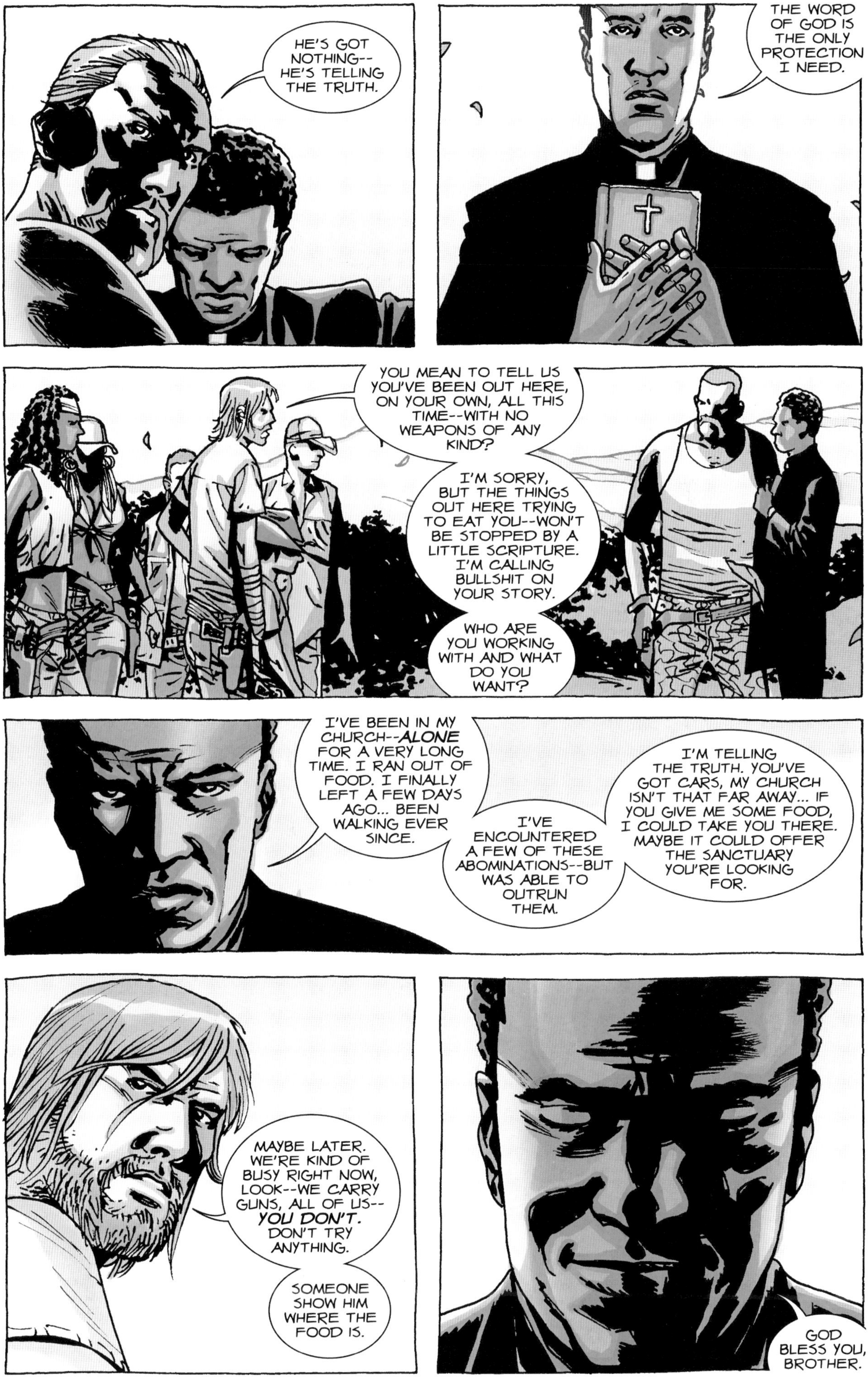
HE'S GOT NOTHING-- HE'S TELLING THE TRUTH.
THE WORD OF GOD IS THE ONLY PROTECTION I NEED.
YOU MEAN TO TELL US YOU'VE BEEN OUT HERE, ON YOUR OWN, ALL THIS TIME--WITH NO WEAPONS OF ANY KIND?
I'M SORRY, BUT THE THINGS OUT HERE TRYING TO EAT YOU--WON'T BE STOPPED BY A LITTLE SCRIPTURE. I'M CALLING BULLSHIT ON YOUR STORY.
WHO ARE YOU WORKING WITH AND WHAT DO YOU WANT?
I'VE BEEN IN MY CHURCH--*ALONE* FOR A VERY LONG TIME. I RAN OUT OF FOOD. I FINALLY LEFT A FEW DAYS AGO... BEEN WALKING EVER SINCE.
I'VE ENCOUNTERED A FEW OF THESE ABOMINATIONS--BUT WAS ABLE TO OUTRUN THEM.
I'M TELLING THE TRUTH. YOU'VE GOT CARS, MY CHURCH ISN'T THAT FAR AWAY... IF YOU GIVE ME SOME FOOD, I COULD TAKE YOU THERE. MAYBE IT COULD OFFER THE SANCTUARY YOU'RE LOOKING FOR.
MAYBE LATER. WE'RE KIND OF BUSY RIGHT NOW, LOOK--WE CARRY GUNS, ALL OF US-- *YOU DON'T.* DON'T TRY ANYTHING.
SOMEONE SHOW HIM WHERE THE FOOD IS.
GOD BLESS YOU, BROTHER.

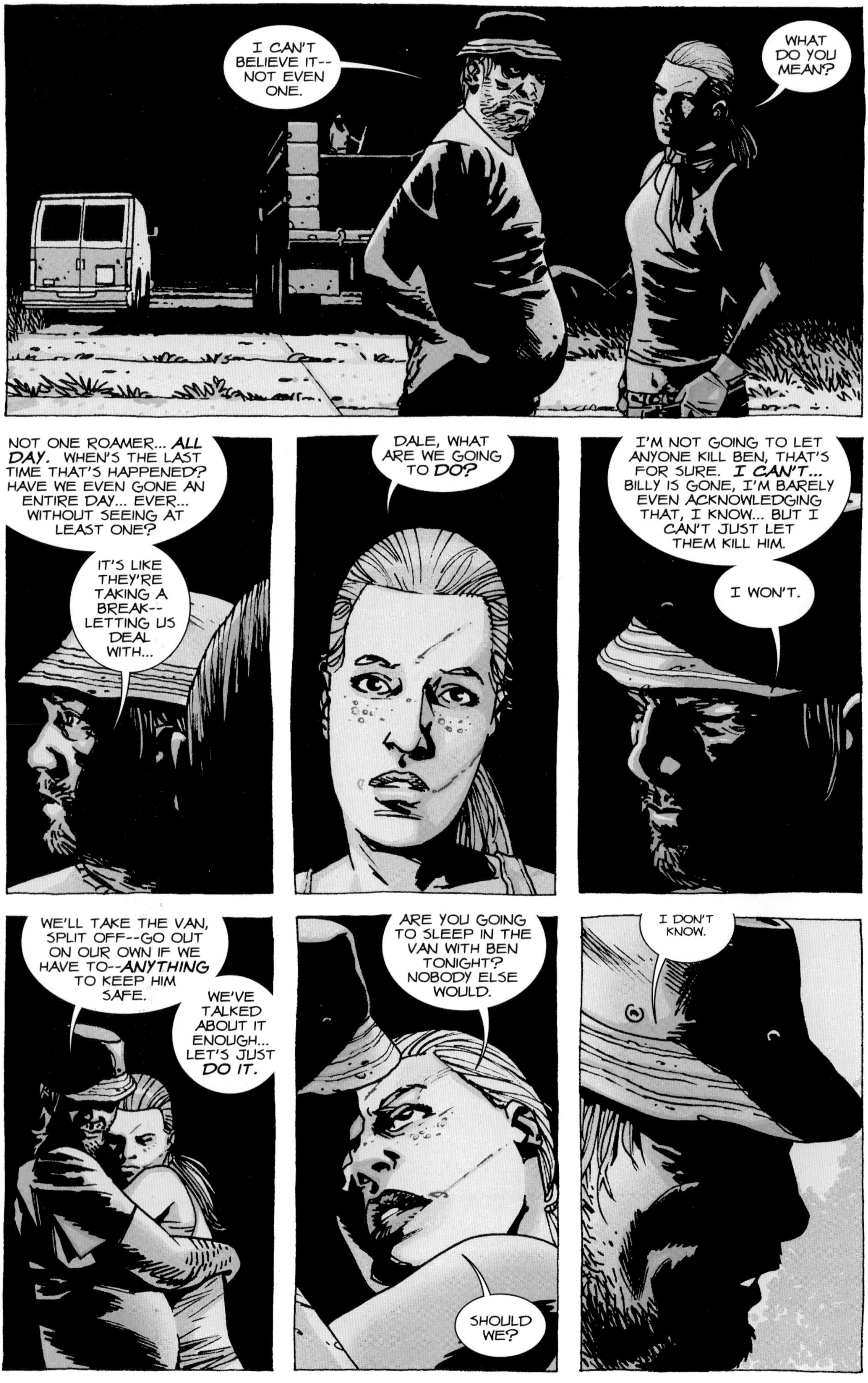
I CAN'T BELIEVE IT-- NOT EVEN ONE.
WHAT DO YOU MEAN?
NOT ONE ROAMER... ALL DAY. WHEN'S THE LAST TIME THAT'S HAPPENED? HAVE WE EVEN GONE AN ENTIRE DAY... EVER... WITHOUT SEEING AT LEAST ONE?
IT'S LIKE THEY'RE TAKING A BREAK-- LETTING US DEAL WITH...
DALE, WHAT ARE WE GOING TO DO?
I'M NOT GOING TO LET ANYONE KILL BEN, THAT'S FOR SURE. I CAN'T... BILLY IS GONE, I'M BARELY EVEN ACKNOWLEDGING THAT, I KNOW... BUT I CAN'T JUST LET THEM KILL HIM.
I WON'T.
WE'LL TAKE THE VAN, SPLIT OFF--GO OUT ON OUR OWN IF WE HAVE TO--ANYTHING TO KEEP HIM SAFE.
WE'VE TALKED ABOUT IT ENOUGH... LET'S JUST DO IT.
ARE YOU GOING TO SLEEP IN THE VAN WITH BEN TONIGHT? NOBODY ELSE WOULD.
SHOULD WE?
I DON'T KNOW.

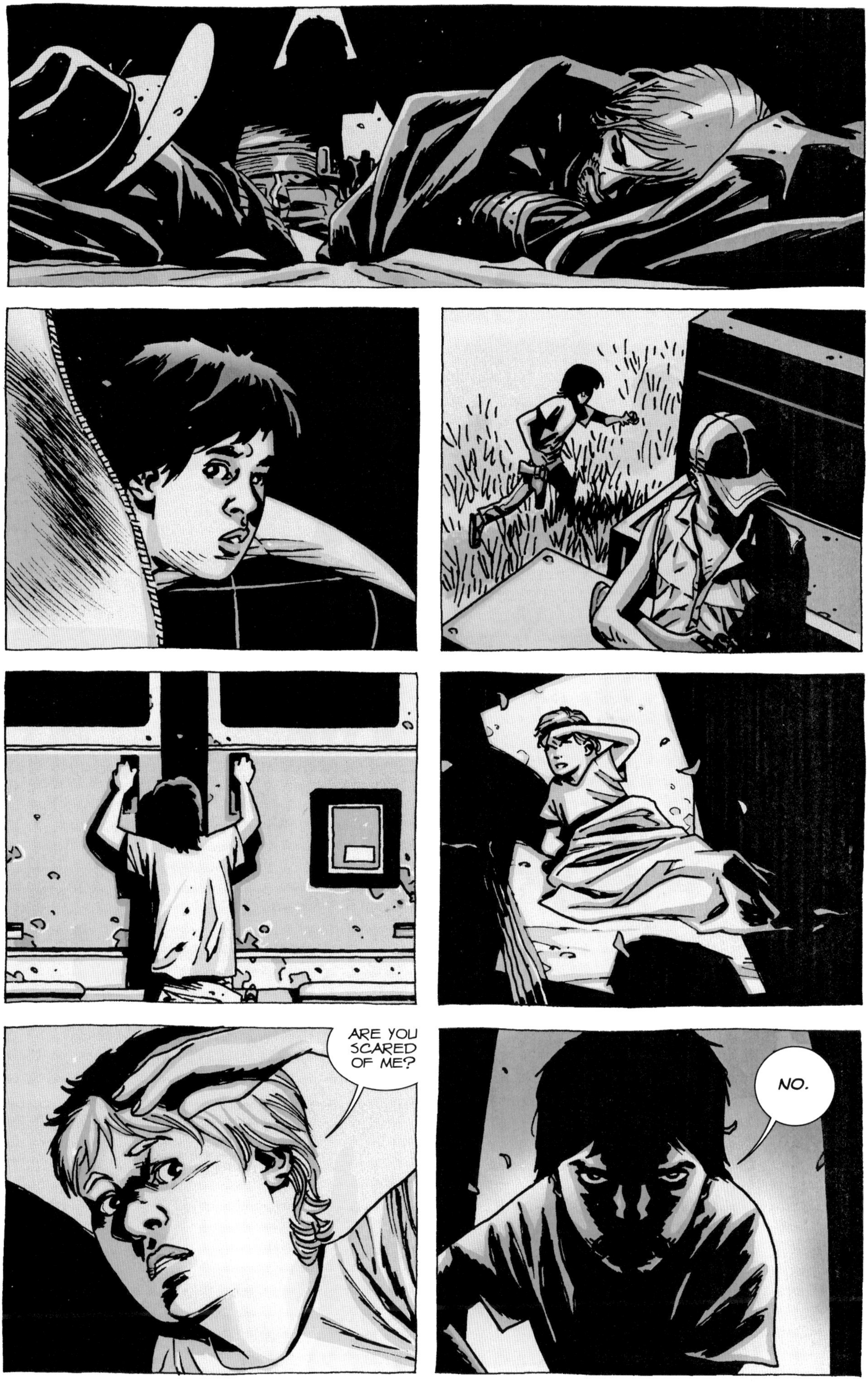
ARE YOU SCARED OF ME?
NO.

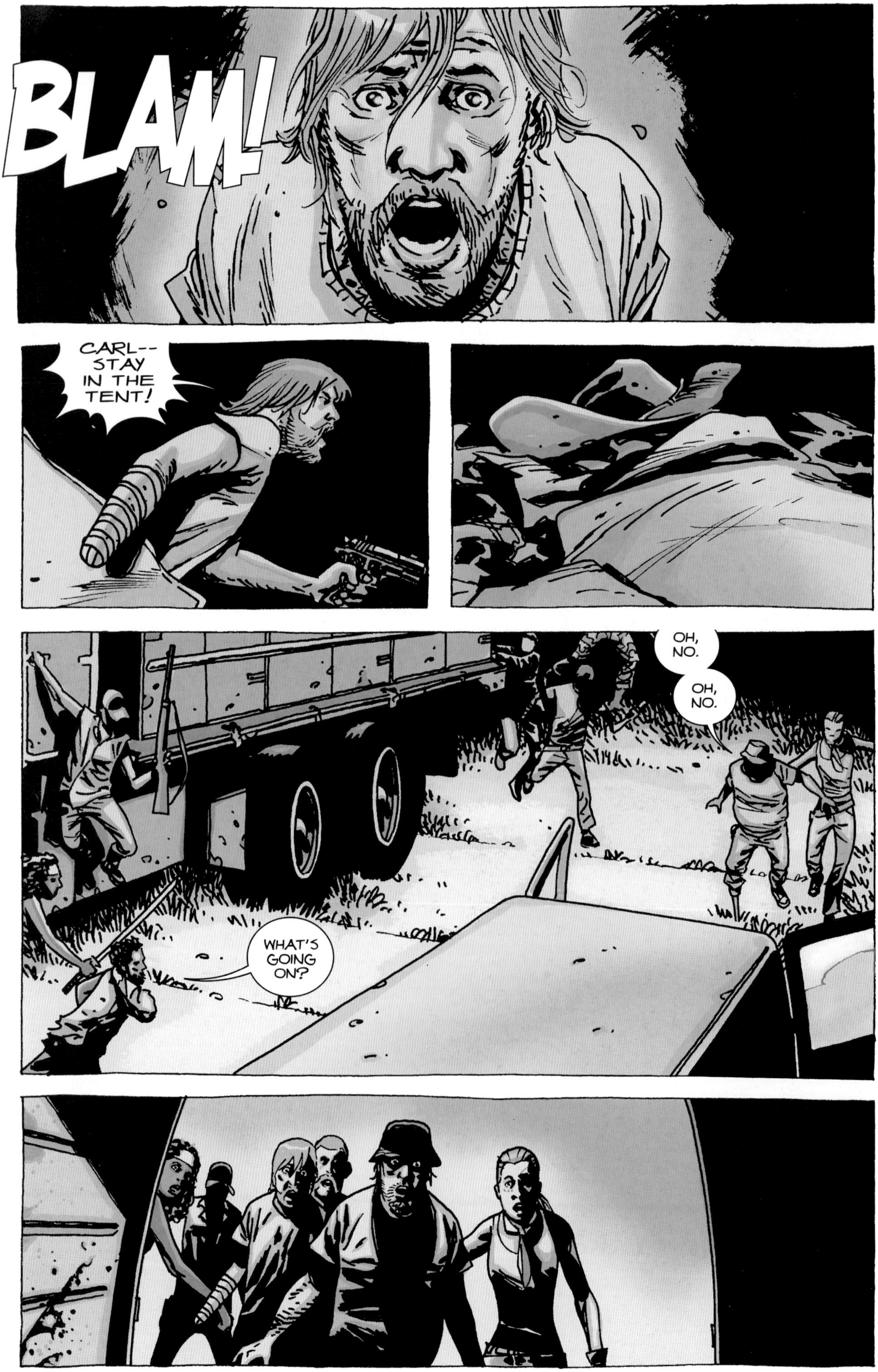
BLAM!
CARL-- STAY IN THE TENT!
OH, NO.
OH, NO.
WHAT'S GOING ON?

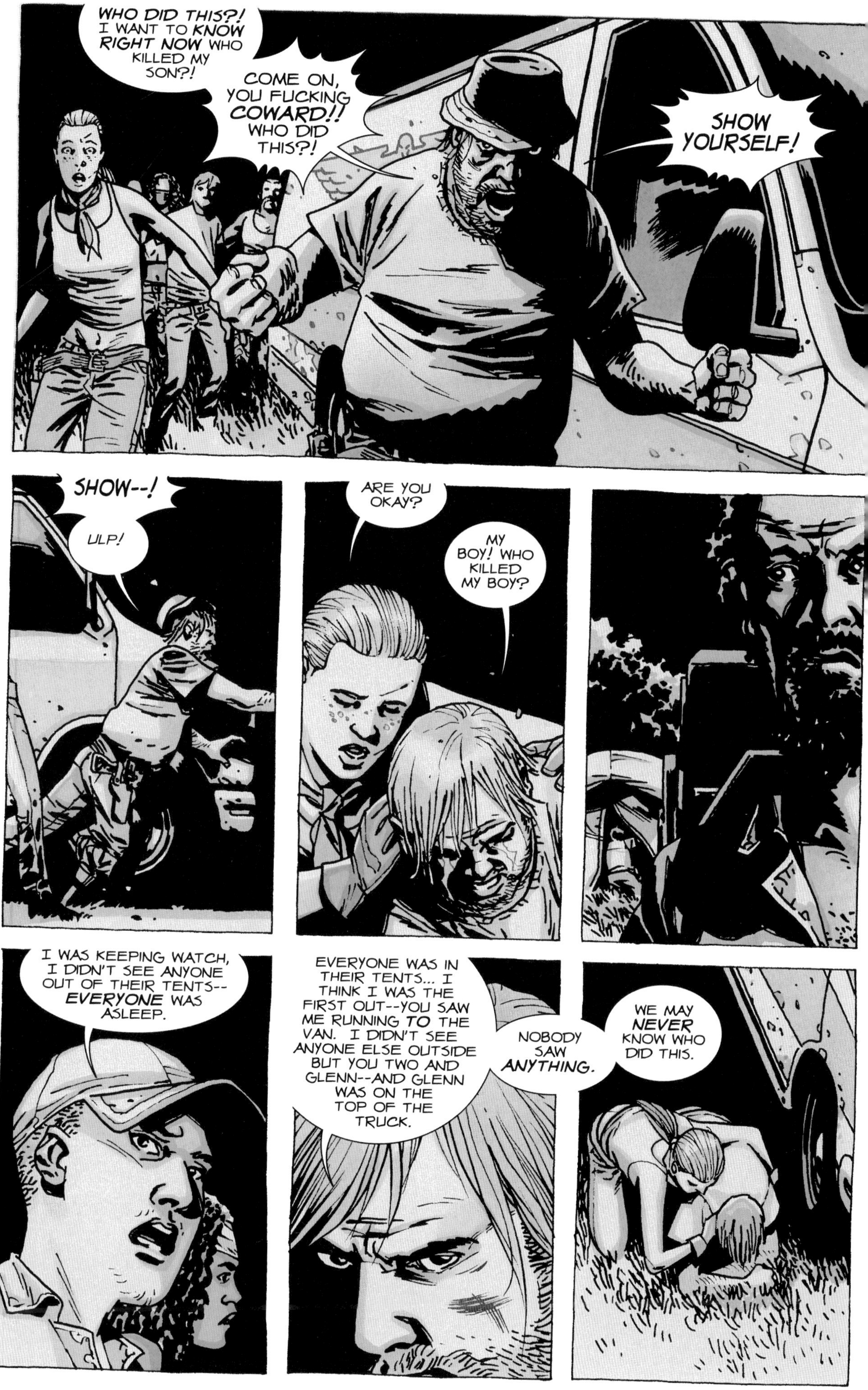
WHO DID THIS?! I WANT TO KNOW RIGHT NOW WHO KILLED MY SON?!
COME ON, YOU FUCKING COWARD!! WHO DID THIS?!
SHOW YOURSELF!
SHOW--!
ULP!
ARE YOU OKAY?
MY BOY! WHO KILLED MY BOY?
I WAS KEEPING WATCH, I DIDN'T SEE ANYONE OUT OF THEIR TENTS-- EVERYONE WAS ASLEEP.
EVERYONE WAS IN THEIR TENTS... I THINK I WAS THE FIRST OUT--YOU SAW ME RUNNING TO THE VAN. I DIDN'T SEE ANYONE ELSE OUTSIDE BUT YOU TWO AND GLENN--AND GLENN WAS ON THE TOP OF THE TRUCK.
NOBODY SAW ANYTHING.
WE MAY NEVER KNOW WHO DID THIS.

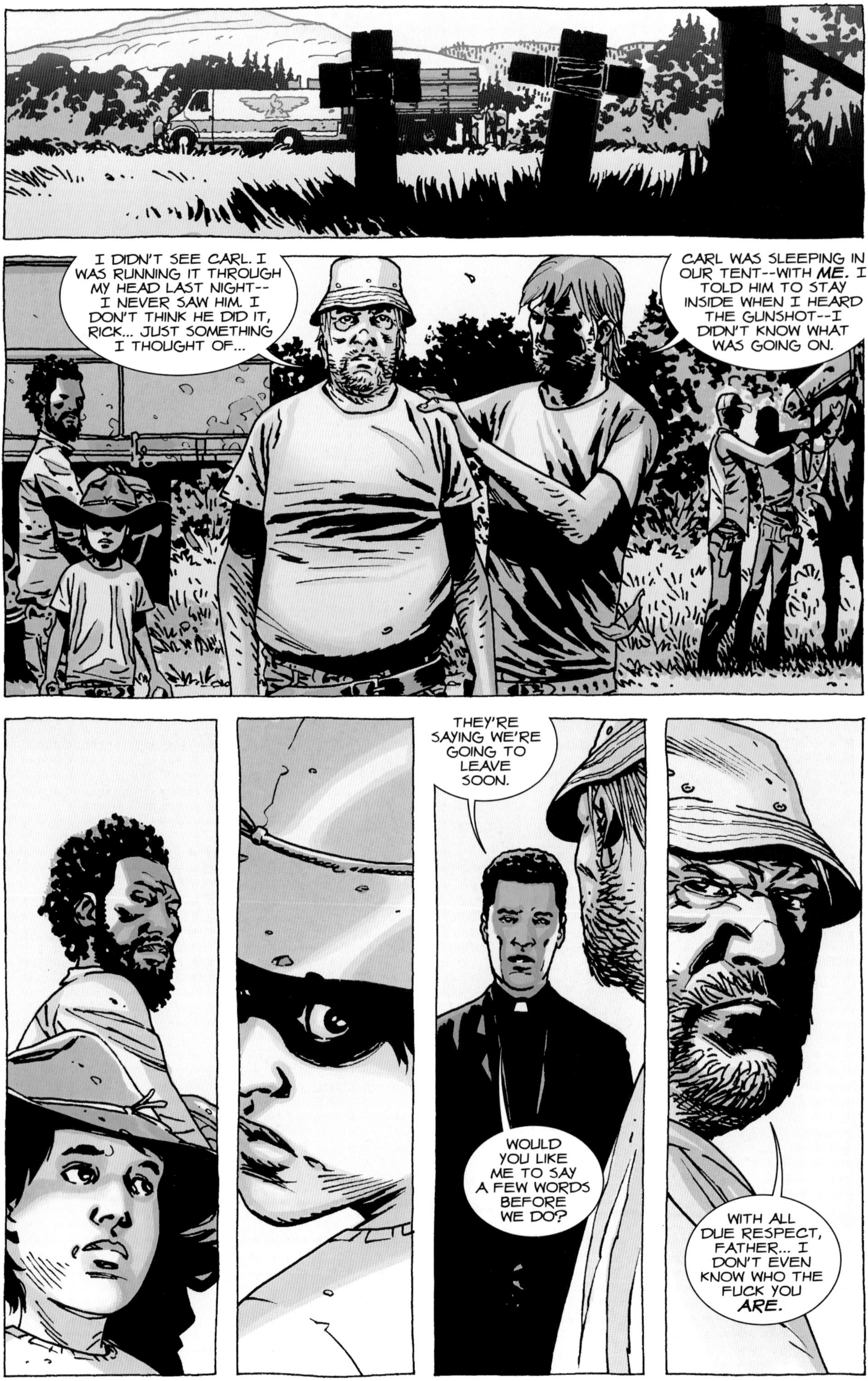
I DIDN'T SEE CARL. I WAS RUNNING IT THROUGH MY HEAD LAST NIGHT-- I NEVER SAW HIM. I DON'T THINK HE DID IT, RICK... JUST SOMETHING I THOUGHT OF...
CARL WAS SLEEPING IN OUR TENT--WITH ME. I TOLD HIM TO STAY INSIDE WHEN I HEARD THE GUNSHOT--I DIDN'T KNOW WHAT WAS GOING ON.
THEY'RE SAYING WE'RE GOING TO LEAVE SOON.
WOULD YOU LIKE ME TO SAY A FEW WORDS BEFORE WE DO?
WITH ALL DUE RESPECT, FATHER... I DON'T EVEN KNOW WHO THE FUCK YOU ARE.

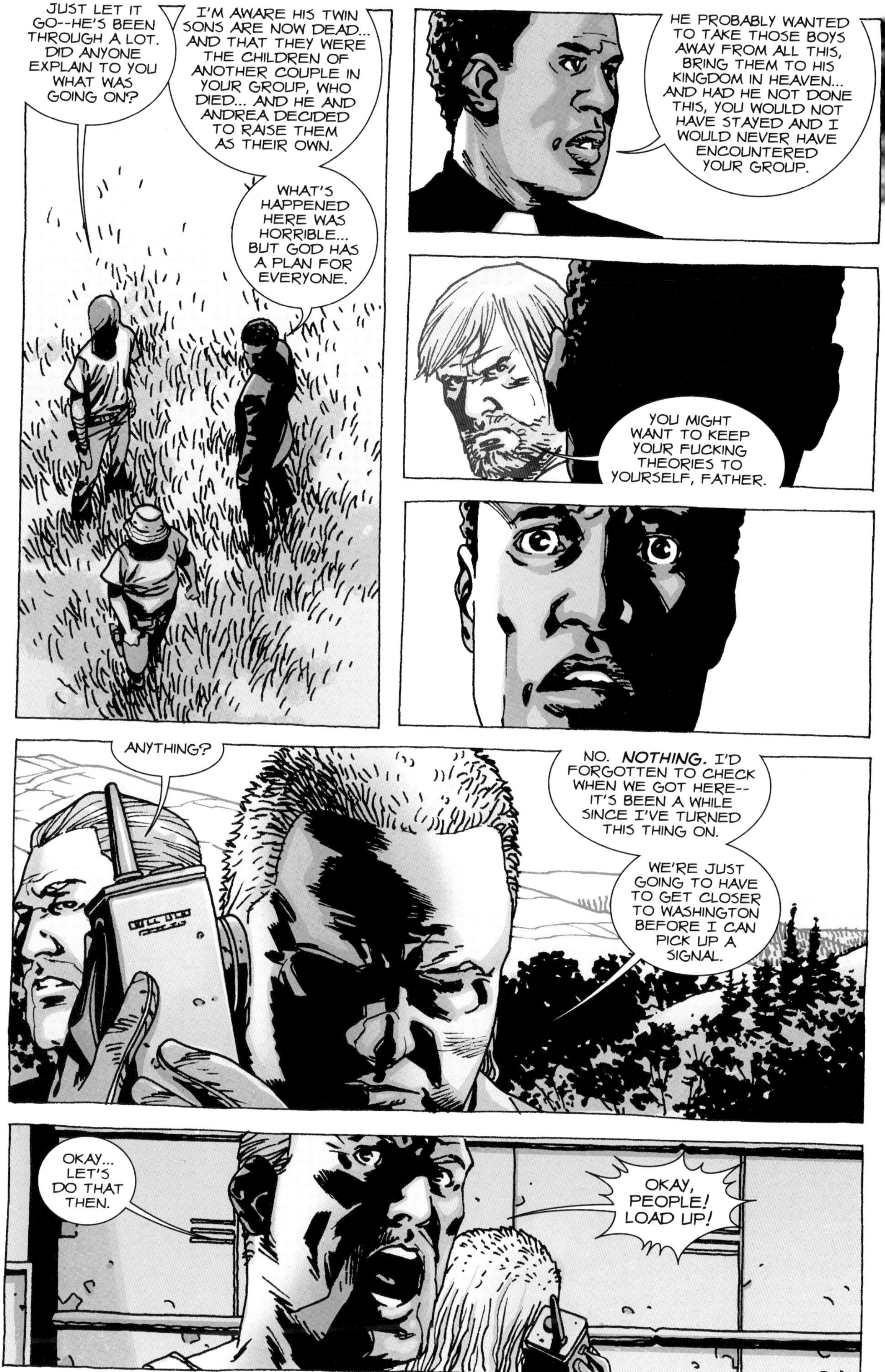
JUST LET IT GO--HE'S BEEN THROUGH A LOT. DID ANYONE EXPLAIN TO YOU WHAT WAS GOING ON?
I'M AWARE HIS TWIN SONS ARE NOW DEAD... AND THAT THEY WERE THE CHILDREN OF ANOTHER COUPLE IN YOUR GROUP, WHO DIED... AND HE AND ANDREA DECIDED TO RAISE THEM AS THEIR OWN.
WHAT'S HAPPENED HERE WAS HORRIBLE... BUT GOD HAS A PLAN FOR EVERYONE.
HE PROBABLY WANTED TO TAKE THOSE BOYS AWAY FROM ALL THIS, BRING THEM TO HIS KINGDOM IN HEAVEN... AND HAD HE NOT DONE THIS, YOU WOULD NOT HAVE STAYED AND I WOULD NEVER HAVE ENCOUNTERED YOUR GROUP.
YOU MIGHT WANT TO KEEP YOUR FUCKING THEORIES TO YOURSELF, FATHER.
ANYTHING?
NO. NOTHING. I'D FORGOTTEN TO CHECK WHEN WE GOT HERE-- IT'S BEEN A WHILE SINCE I'VE TURNED THIS THING ON.
WE'RE JUST GOING TO HAVE TO GET CLOSER TO WASHINGTON BEFORE I CAN PICK UP A SIGNAL.
OKAY... LET'S DO THAT THEN.
OKAY, PEOPLE! LOAD UP!

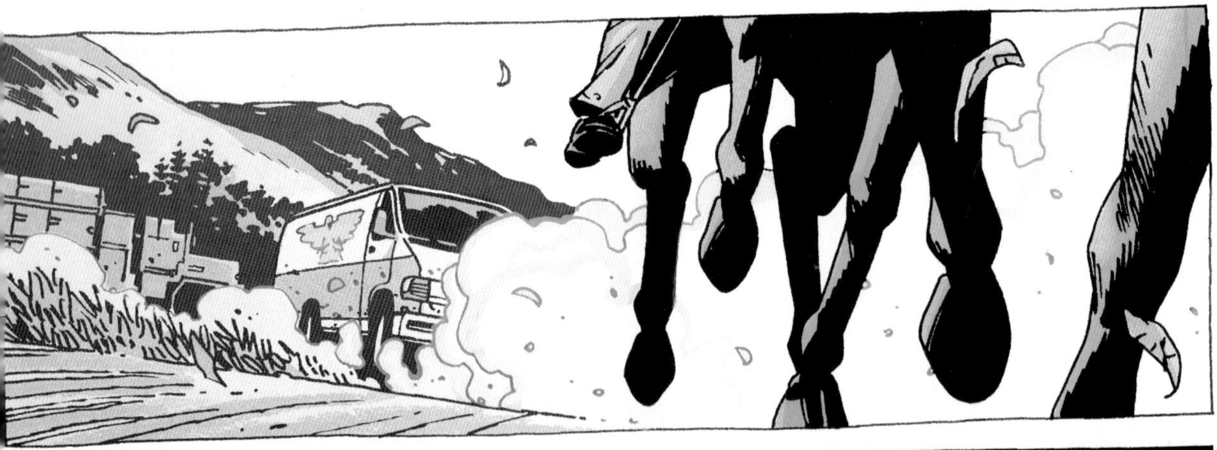

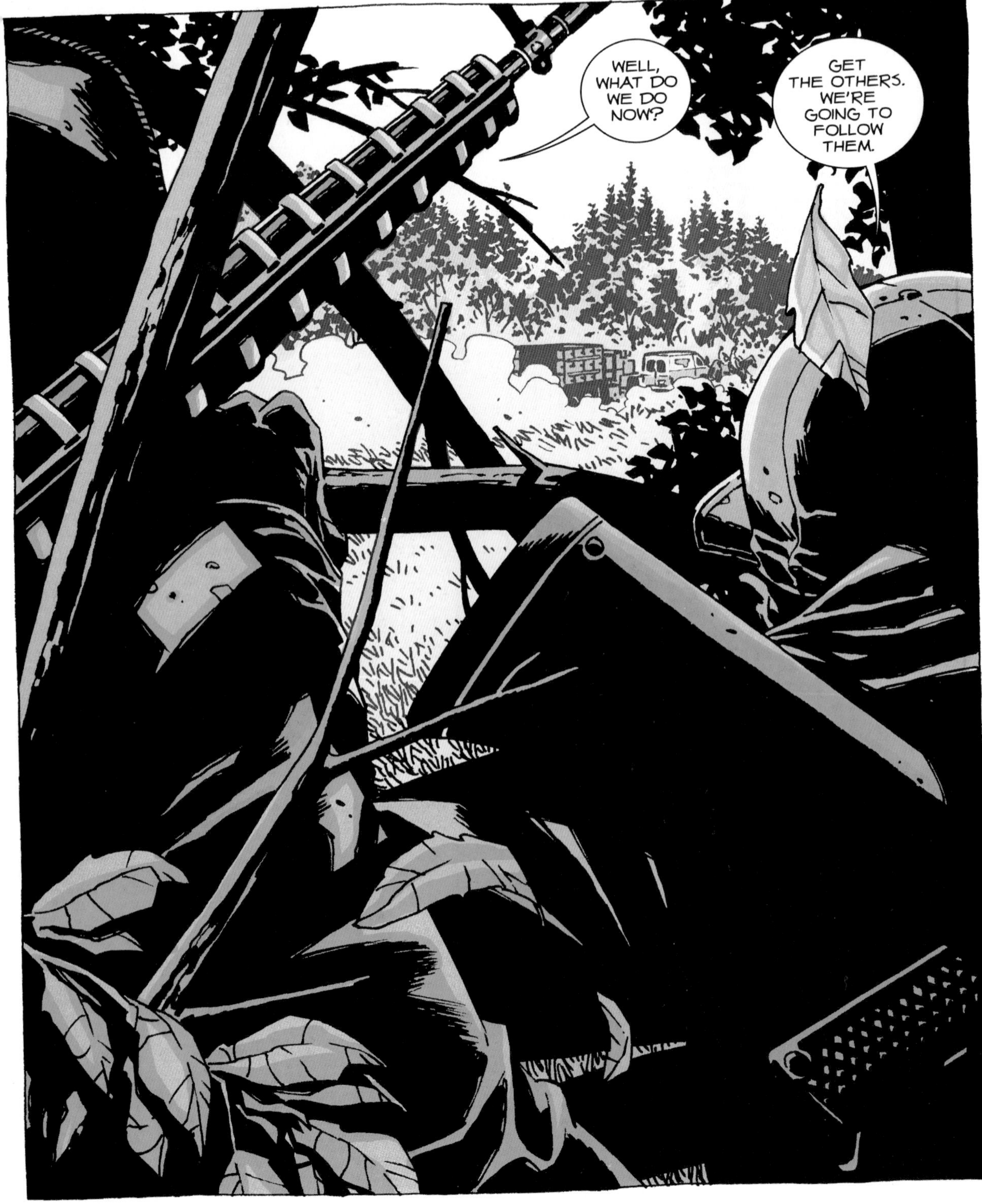

WELL, WHAT DO WE DO NOW?
GET THE OTHERS. WE'RE GOING TO FOLLOW THEM.

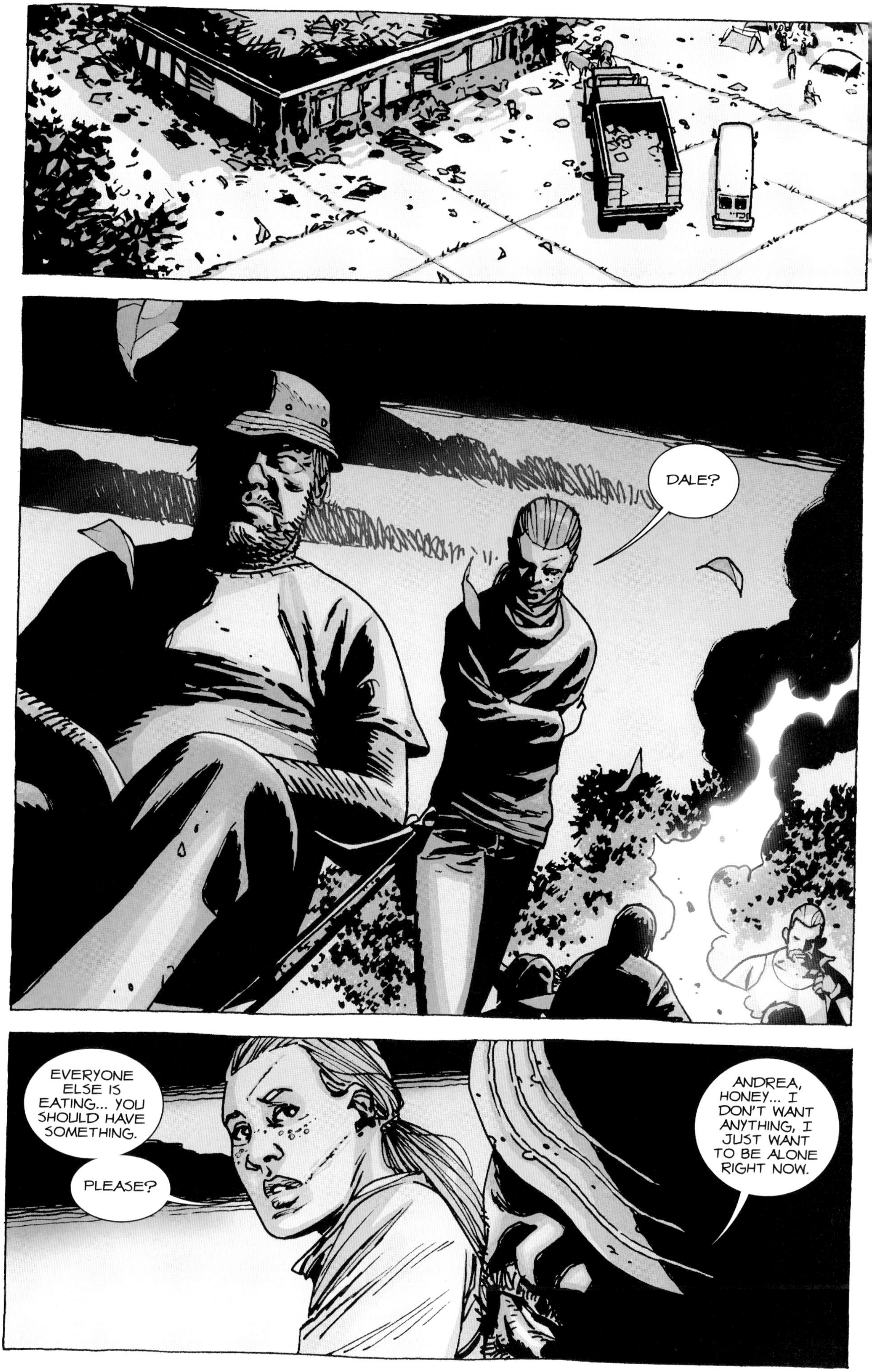
DALE?
EVERYONE ELSE IS EATING... YOU SHOULD HAVE SOMETHING.
PLEASE?
ANDREA, HONEY... I DON'T WANT ANYTHING, I JUST WANT TO BE ALONE RIGHT NOW.

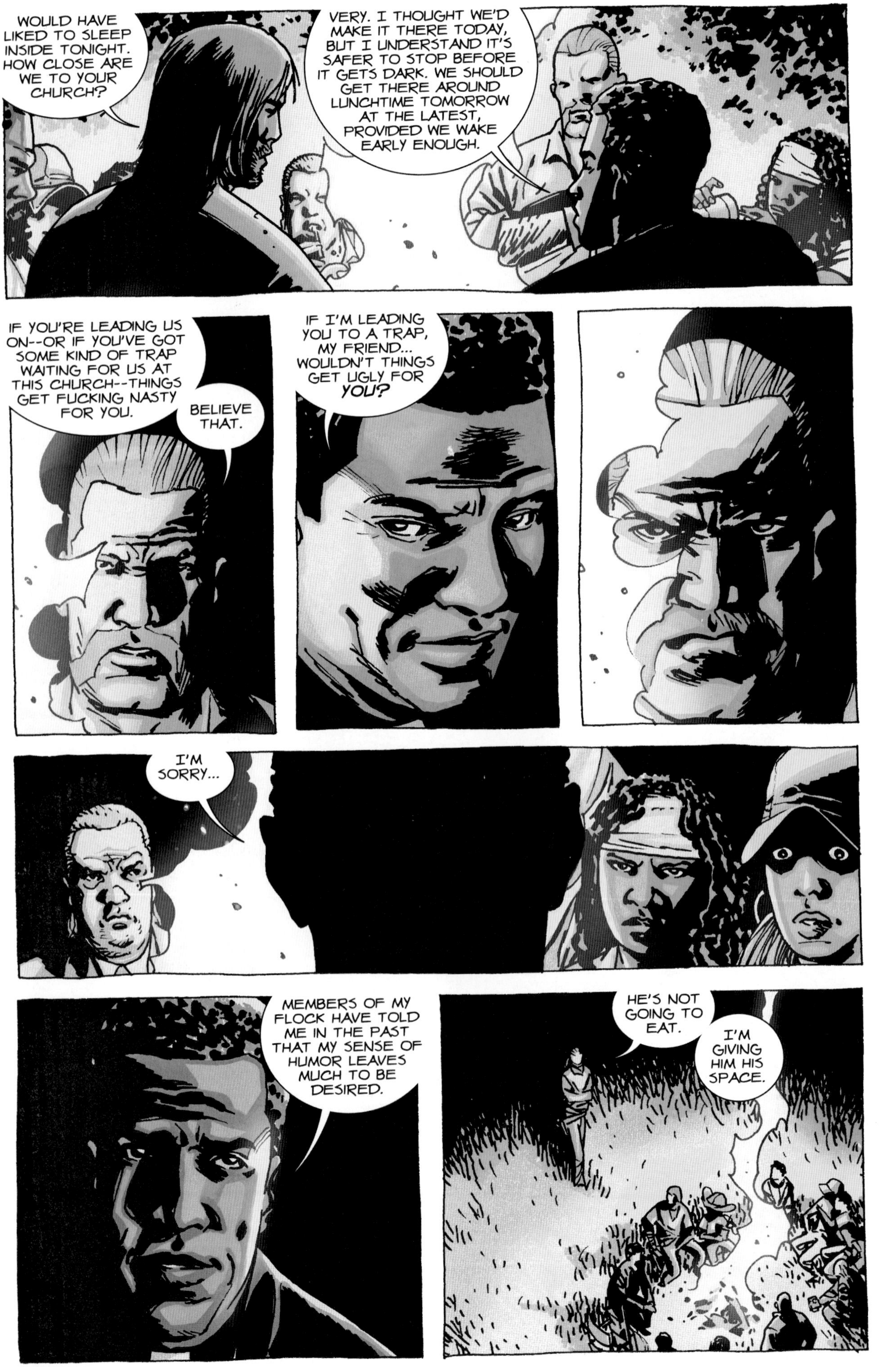
WOULD HAVE LIKED TO SLEEP INSIDE TONIGHT. HOW CLOSE ARE WE TO YOUR CHURCH?
VERY. I THOUGHT WE'D MAKE IT THERE TODAY, BUT I UNDERSTAND IT'S SAFER TO STOP BEFORE IT GETS DARK. WE SHOULD GET THERE AROUND LUNCHTIME TOMORROW AT THE LATEST, PROVIDED WE WAKE EARLY ENOUGH.
IF YOU'RE LEADING US ON--OR IF YOU'VE GOT SOME KIND OF TRAP WAITING FOR US AT THIS CHURCH--THINGS GET FUCKING NASTY FOR YOU.
BELIEVE THAT.
IF I'M LEADING YOU TO A TRAP, MY FRIEND... WOULDN'T THINGS GET UGLY FOR YOU?
I'M SORRY...
MEMBERS OF MY FLOCK HAVE TOLD ME IN THE PAST THAT MY SENSE OF HUMOR LEAVES MUCH TO BE DESIRED.
HE'S NOT GOING TO EAT.
I'M GIVING HIM HIS SPACE.

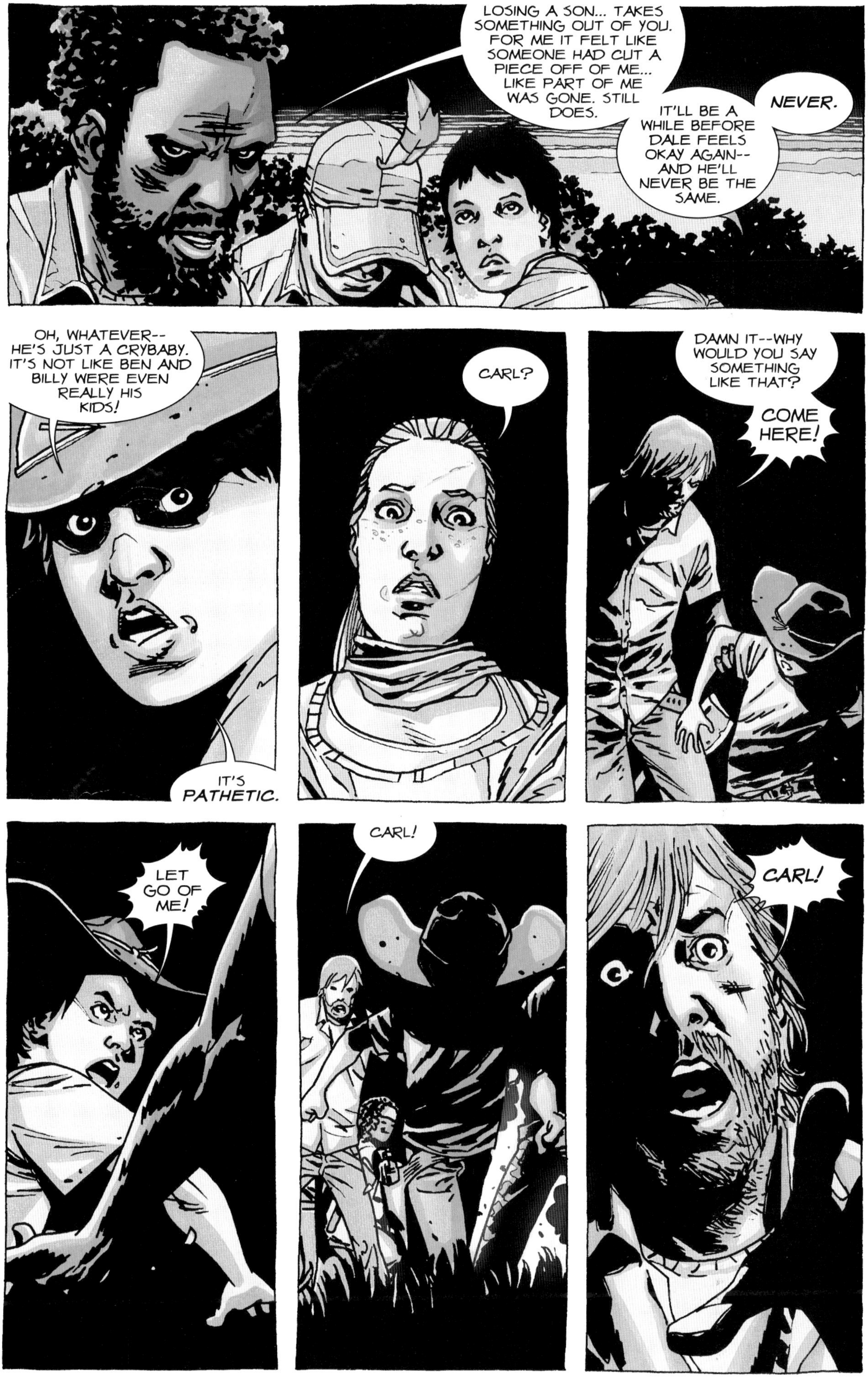
LOSING A SON... TAKES SOMETHING OUT OF YOU. FOR ME IT FELT LIKE SOMEONE HAD CUT A PIECE OFF OF ME... LIKE PART OF ME WAS GONE. STILL DOES.
IT'LL BE A WHILE BEFORE DALE FEELS OKAY AGAIN-- AND HE'LL NEVER BE THE SAME.
NEVER.
OH, WHATEVER-- HE'S JUST A CRYBABY. IT'S NOT LIKE BEN AND BILLY WERE EVEN REALLY HIS KIDS!
IT'S PATHETIC.
CARL?
DAMN IT--WHY WOULD YOU SAY SOMETHING LIKE THAT?
COME HERE!
LET GO OF ME!
CARL!
CARL!

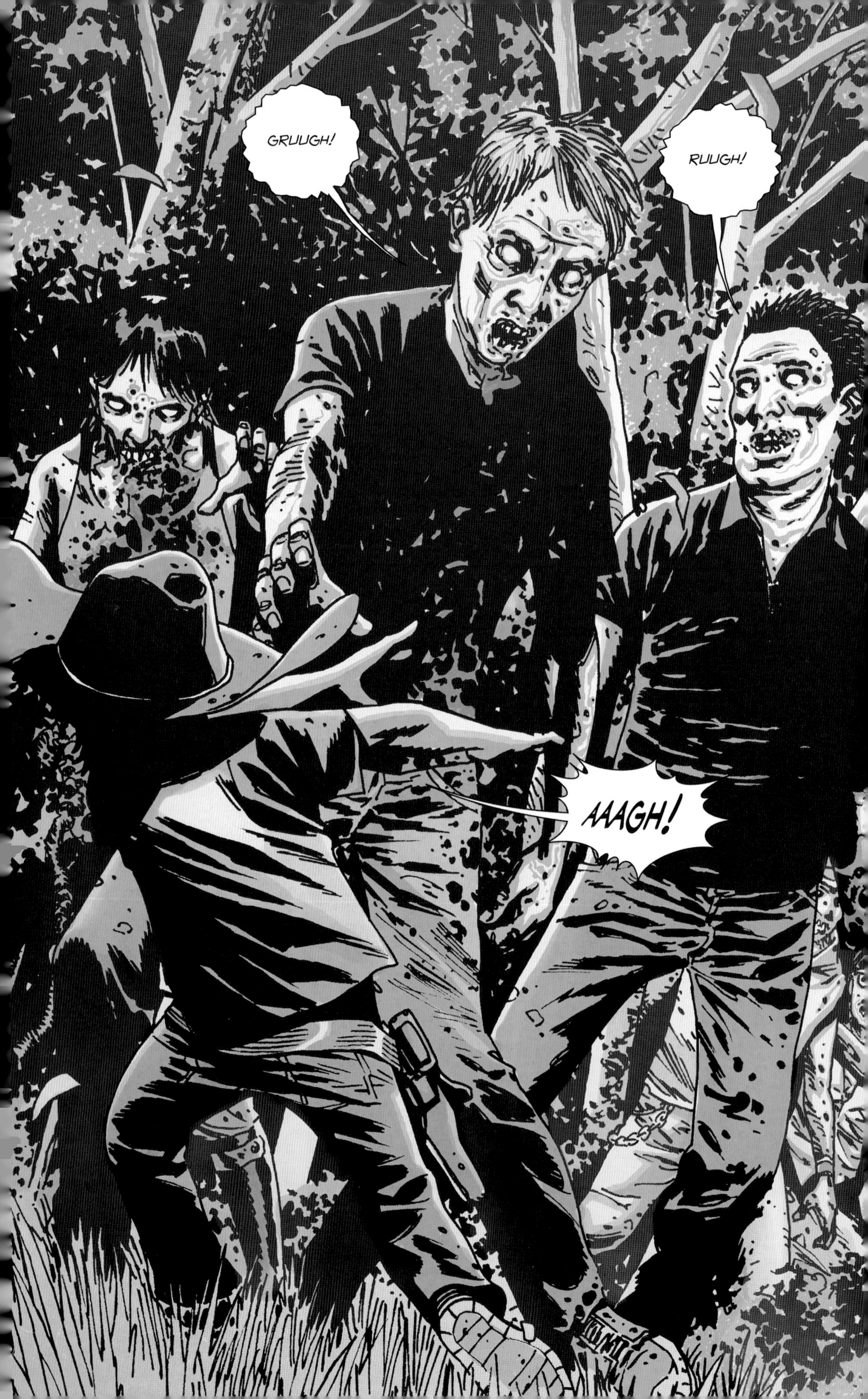
GRUUGH!
RUUGH!
AAAGH!

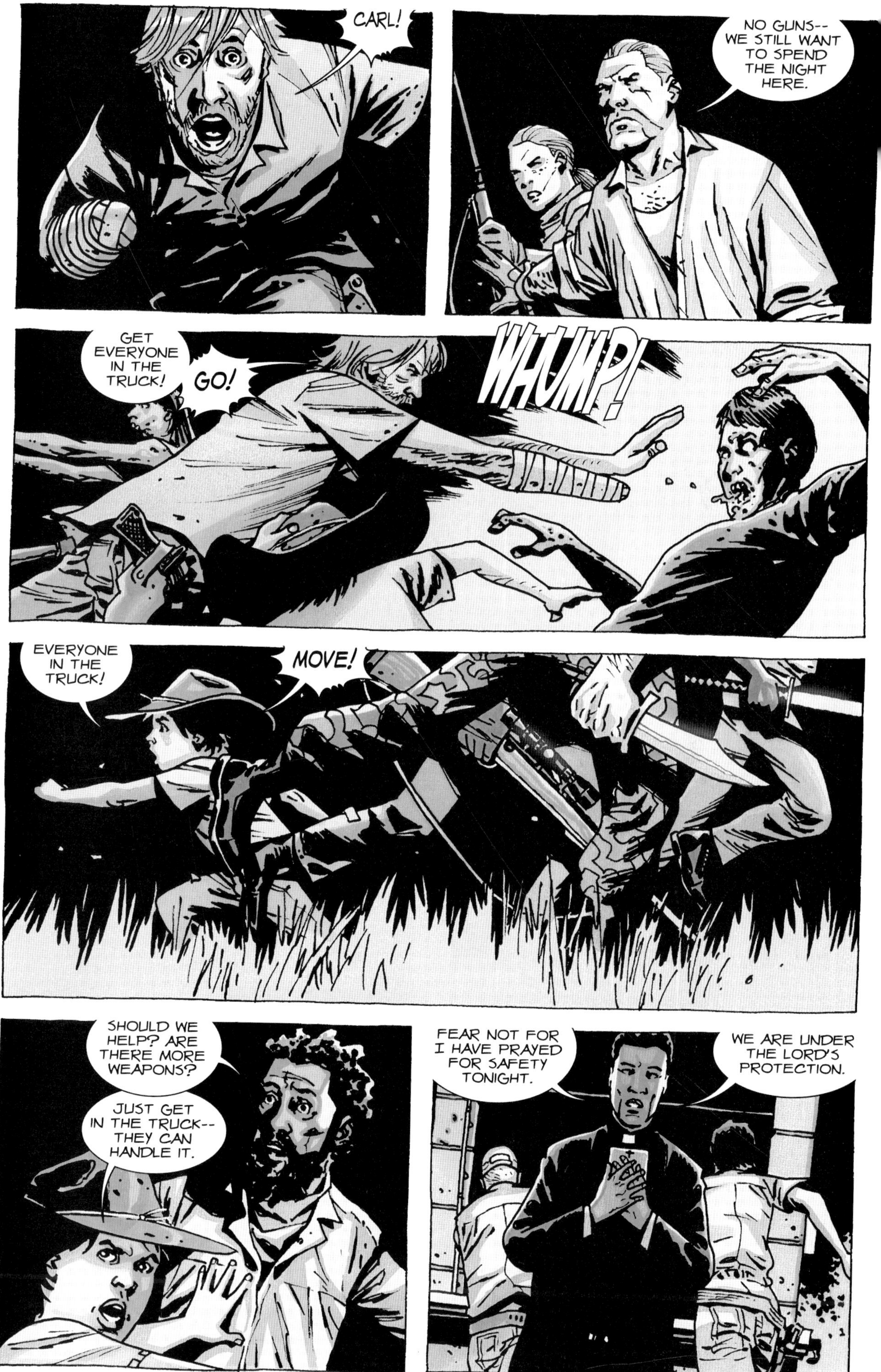
CARL!
NO GUNS-- WE STILL WANT TO SPEND THE NIGHT HERE.
GET EVERYONE IN THE TRUCK!
GO!
WHUMP!
EVERYONE IN THE TRUCK!
MOVE!
SHOULD WE HELP? ARE THERE MORE WEAPONS?
JUST GET IN THE TRUCK-- THEY CAN HANDLE IT.
FEAR NOT FOR I HAVE PRAYED FOR SAFETY TONIGHT.
WE ARE UNDER THE LORD'S PROTECTION.

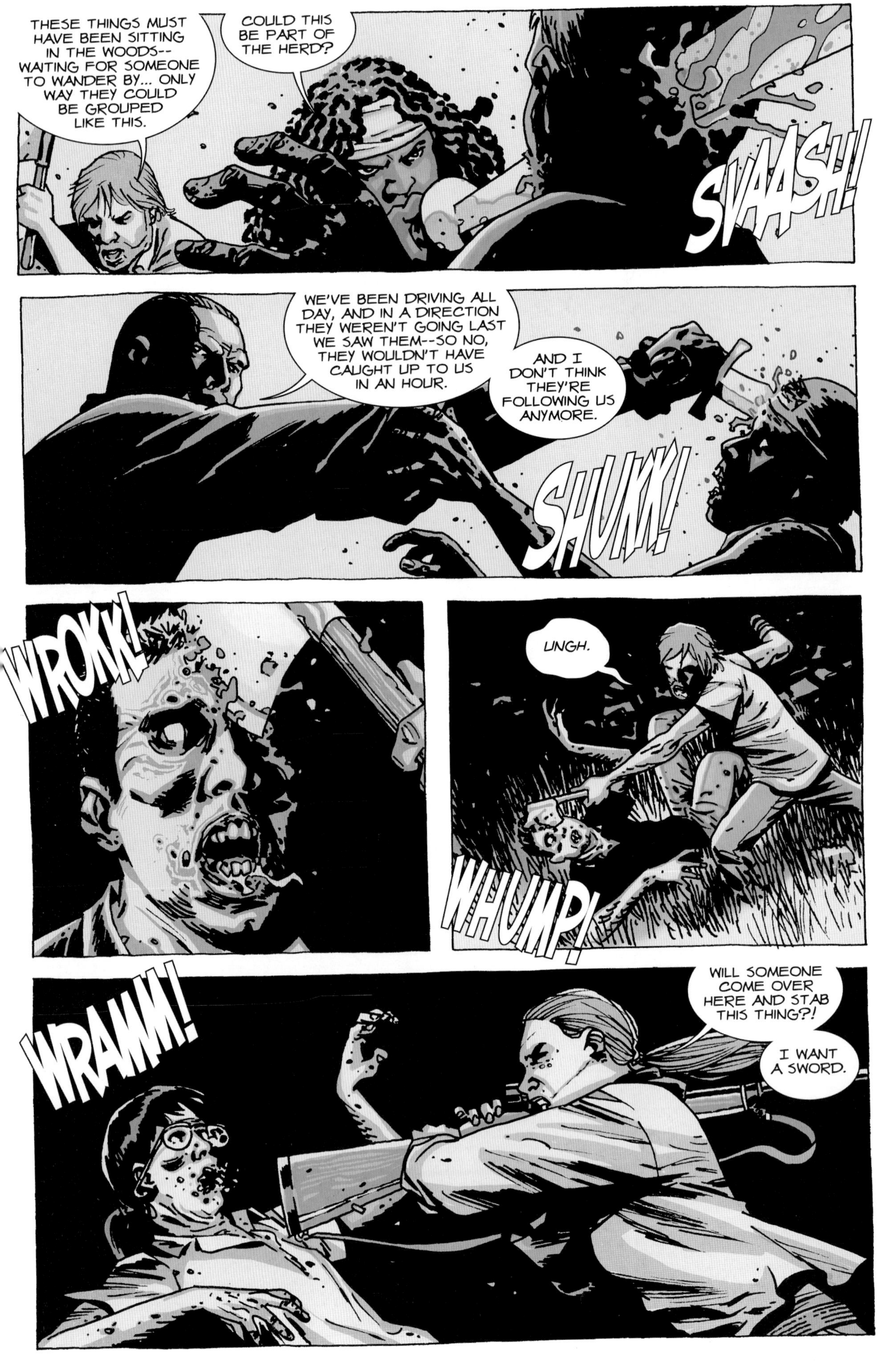
THESE THINGS MUST HAVE BEEN SITTING IN THE WOODS-- WAITING FOR SOMEONE TO WANDER BY... ONLY WAY THEY COULD BE GROUPED LIKE THIS.
COULD THIS BE PART OF THE HERD?
SVAASH!
WE'VE BEEN DRIVING ALL DAY, AND IN A DIRECTION THEY WEREN'T GOING LAST WE SAW THEM--SO NO, THEY WOULDN'T HAVE CAUGHT UP TO US IN AN HOUR.
AND I DON'T THINK THEY'RE FOLLOWING US ANYMORE.
SHUKK!
WROKK!
UNGH.
WHUMP!
WRAMM!
WILL SOMEONE COME OVER HERE AND STAB THIS THING?!
I WANT A SWORD.

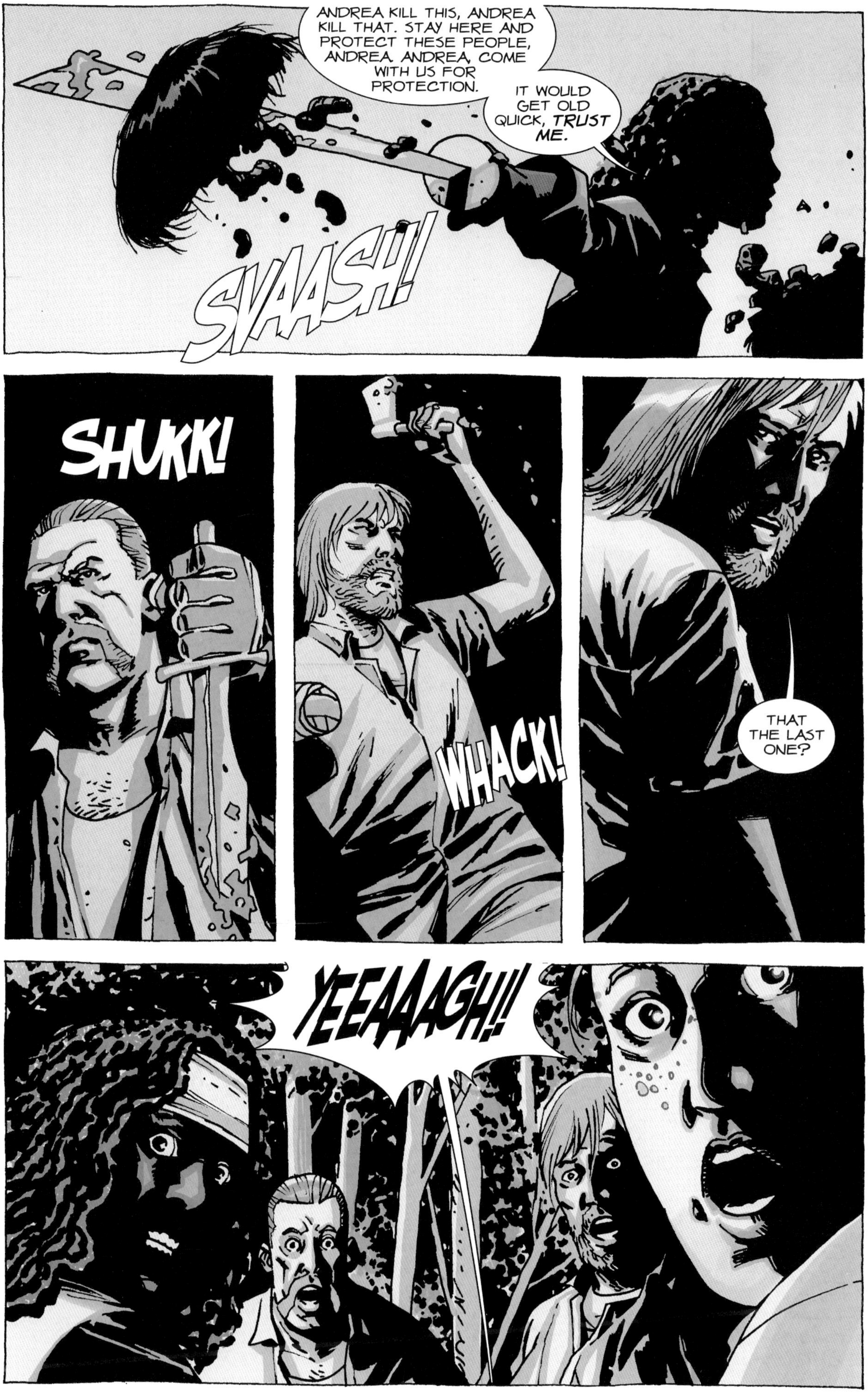
ANDREA KILL THIS, ANDREA KILL THAT. STAY HERE AND PROTECT THESE PEOPLE, ANDREA. ANDREA, COME WITH US FOR PROTECTION.
IT WOULD GET OLD QUICK, TRUST ME.
SVAASH!
SHUKK!
WHACK!
THAT THE LAST ONE?
YEEAAAGH!!

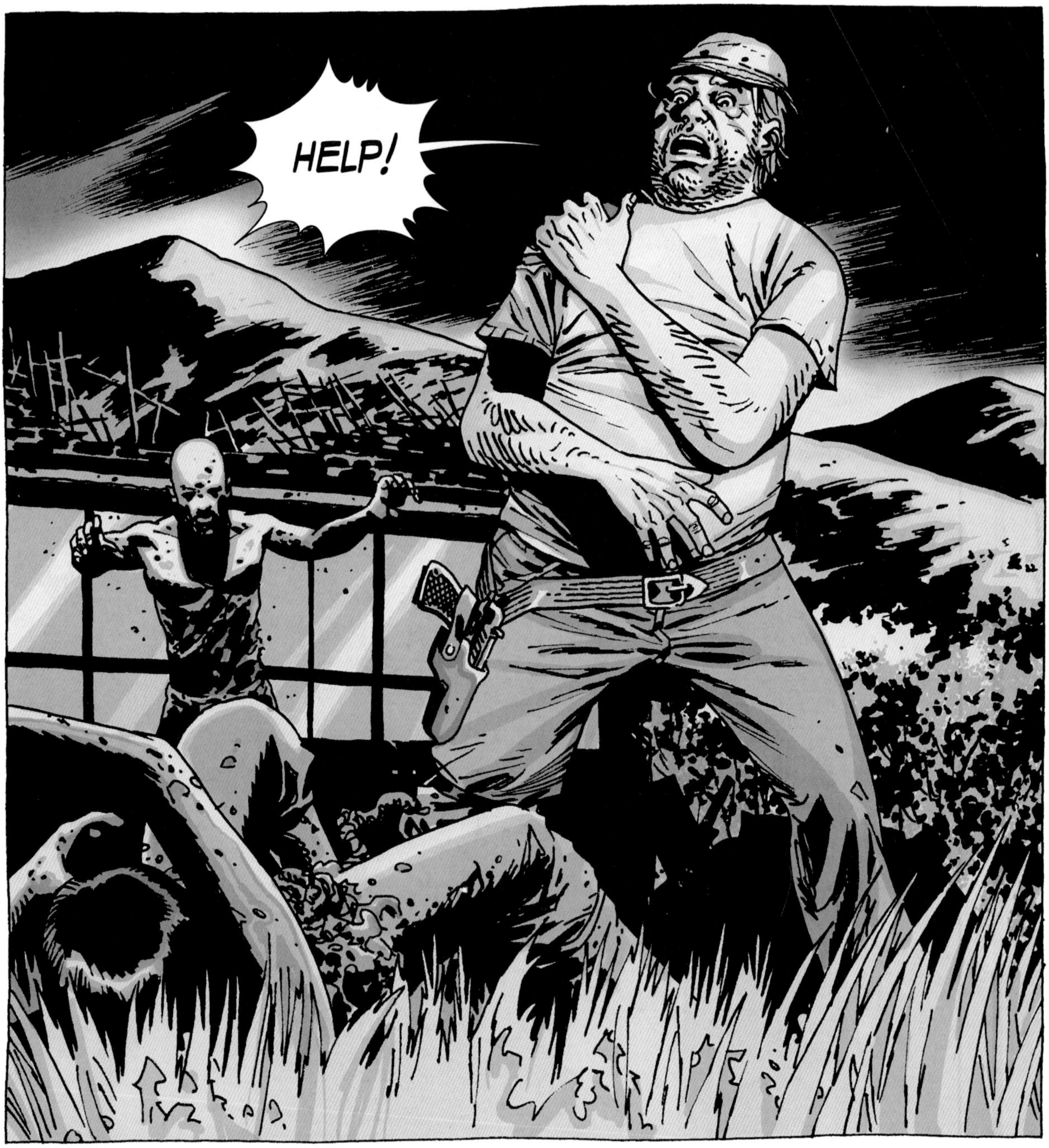
HELP!

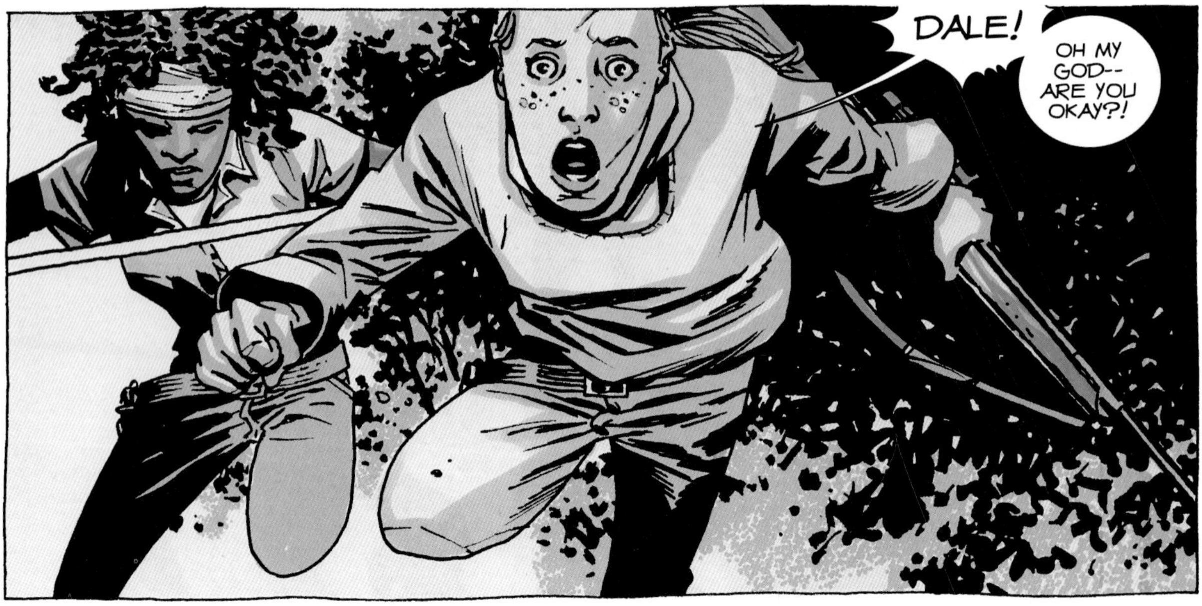
DALE!
OH MY GOD-- ARE YOU OKAY?!

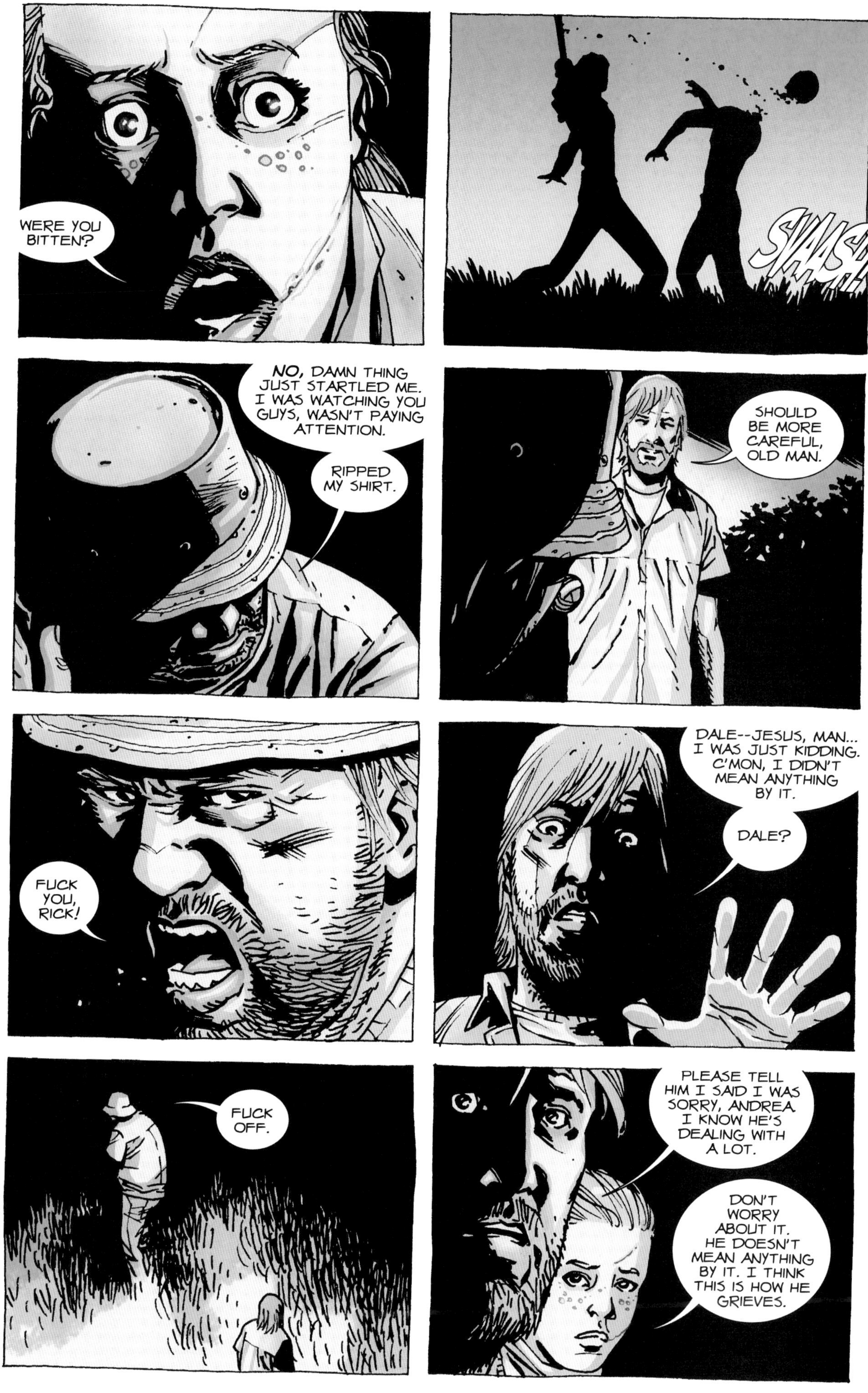
WERE YOU BITTEN?
SWASH!
NO, DAMN THING JUST STARTLED ME. I WAS WATCHING YOU GUYS, WASN'T PAYING ATTENTION.
RIPPED MY SHIRT.
SHOULD BE MORE CAREFUL, OLD MAN.
FUCK YOU, RICK!
DALE--JESUS, MAN... I WAS JUST KIDDING. C'MON, I DIDN'T MEAN ANYTHING BY IT.
DALE?
FUCK OFF.
PLEASE TELL HIM I SAID I WAS SORRY, ANDREA. I KNOW HE'S DEALING WITH A LOT.
DON'T WORRY ABOUT IT. HE DOESN'T MEAN ANYTHING BY IT. I THINK THIS IS HOW HE GRIEVES.

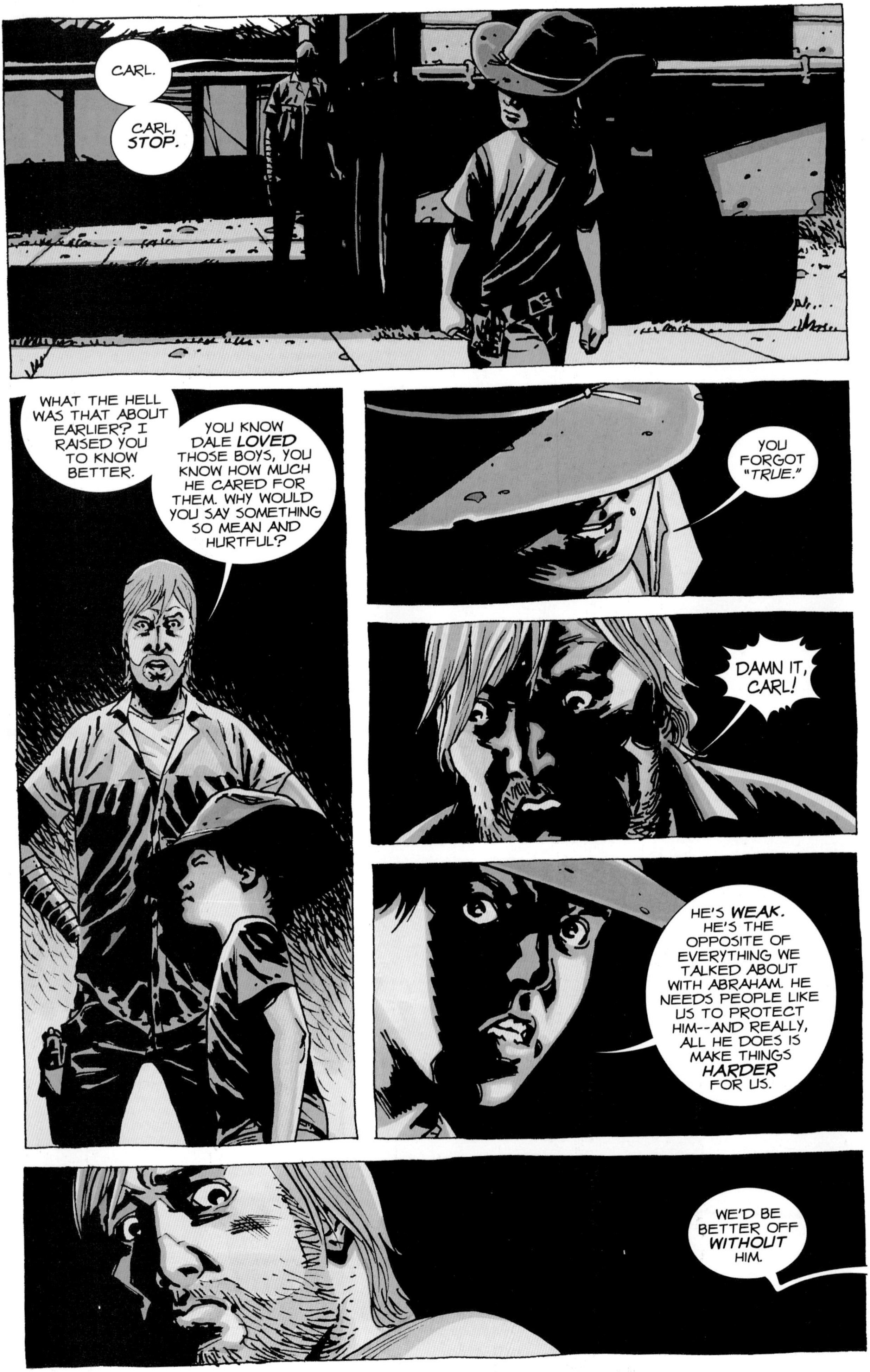
CARL.
CARL, STOP.
WHAT THE HELL WAS THAT ABOUT EARLIER? I RAISED YOU TO KNOW BETTER.
YOU KNOW DALE LOVED THOSE BOYS, YOU KNOW HOW MUCH HE CARED FOR THEM. WHY WOULD YOU SAY SOMETHING SO MEAN AND HURTFUL?
YOU FORGOT "TRUE."
DAMN IT, CARL!
HE'S WEAK. HE'S THE OPPOSITE OF EVERYTHING WE TALKED ABOUT WITH ABRAHAM. HE NEEDS PEOPLE LIKE US TO PROTECT HIM--AND REALLY, ALL HE DOES IS MAKE THINGS HARDER FOR US.
WE'D BE BETTER OFF WITHOUT HIM.

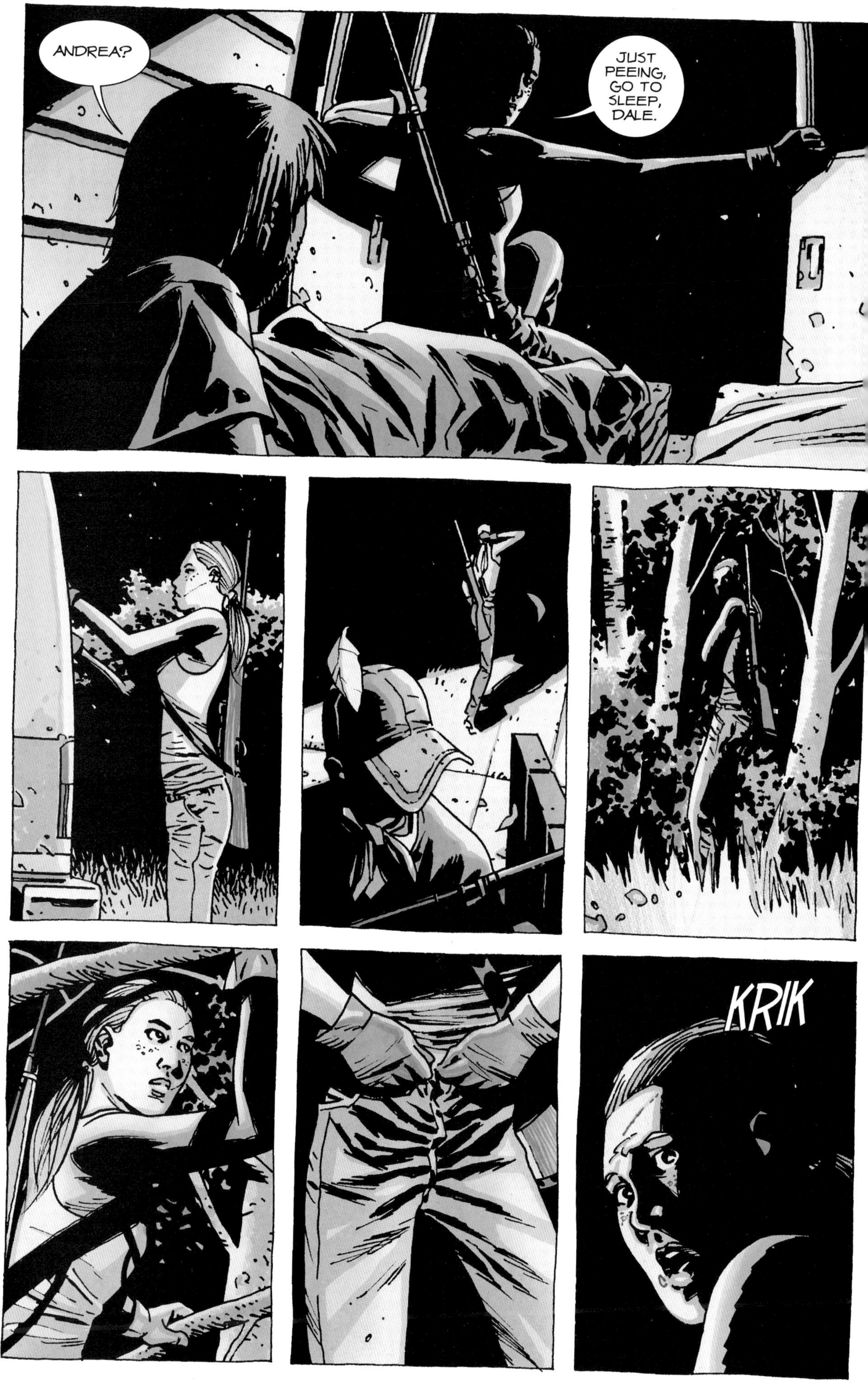
ANDREA?
JUST PEEING, GO TO SLEEP, DALE.
KRIK

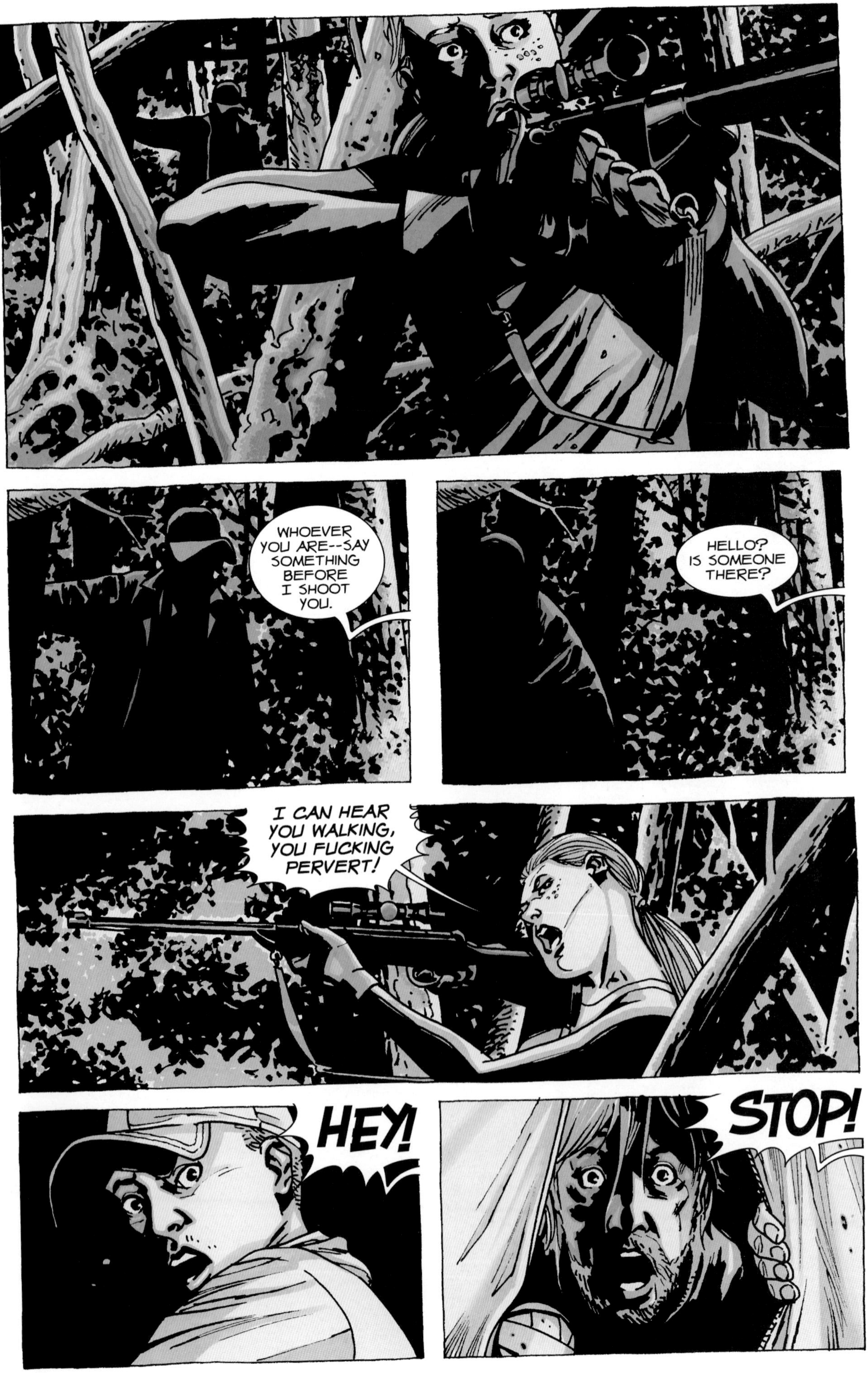
WHOEVER YOU ARE--SAY SOMETHING BEFORE I SHOOT YOU.
HELLO? IS SOMEONE THERE?
I CAN HEAR YOU WALKING, YOU FUCKING PERVERT!
HEY!
STOP!

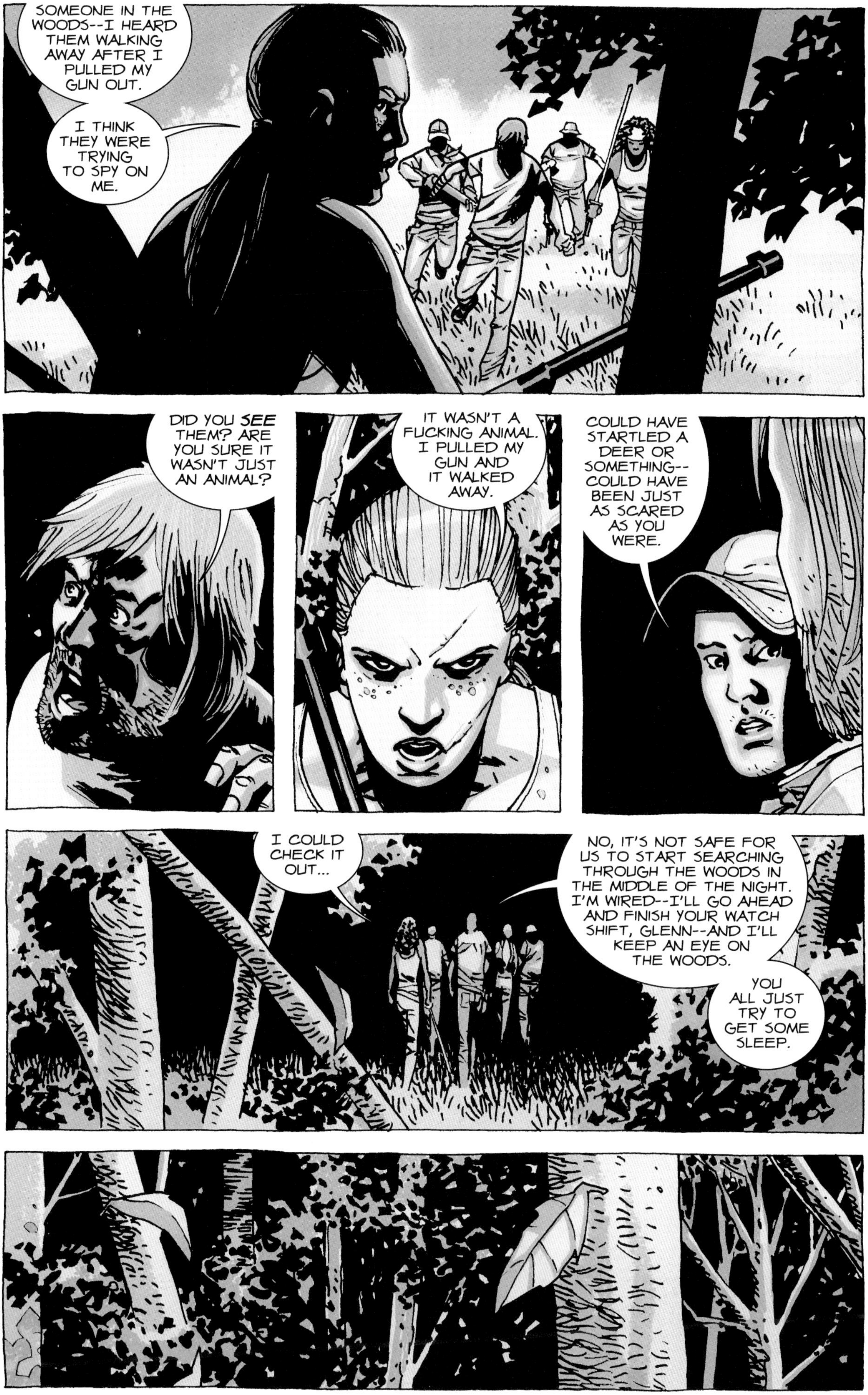
SOMEONE IN THE WOODS--I HEARD THEM WALKING AWAY AFTER I PULLED MY GUN OUT.
I THINK THEY WERE TRYING TO SPY ON ME.
DID YOU SEE THEM? ARE YOU SURE IT WASN'T JUST AN ANIMAL?
IT WASN'T A FUCKING ANIMAL. I PULLED MY GUN AND IT WALKED AWAY.
COULD HAVE STARTLED A DEER OR SOMETHING--COULD HAVE BEEN JUST AS SCARED AS YOU WERE.
I COULD CHECK IT OUT...
NO, IT'S NOT SAFE FOR US TO START SEARCHING THROUGH THE WOODS IN THE MIDDLE OF THE NIGHT. I'M WIRED--I'LL GO AHEAD AND FINISH YOUR WATCH SHIFT, GLENN--AND I'LL KEEP AN EYE ON THE WOODS.
YOU ALL JUST TRY TO GET SOME SLEEP.

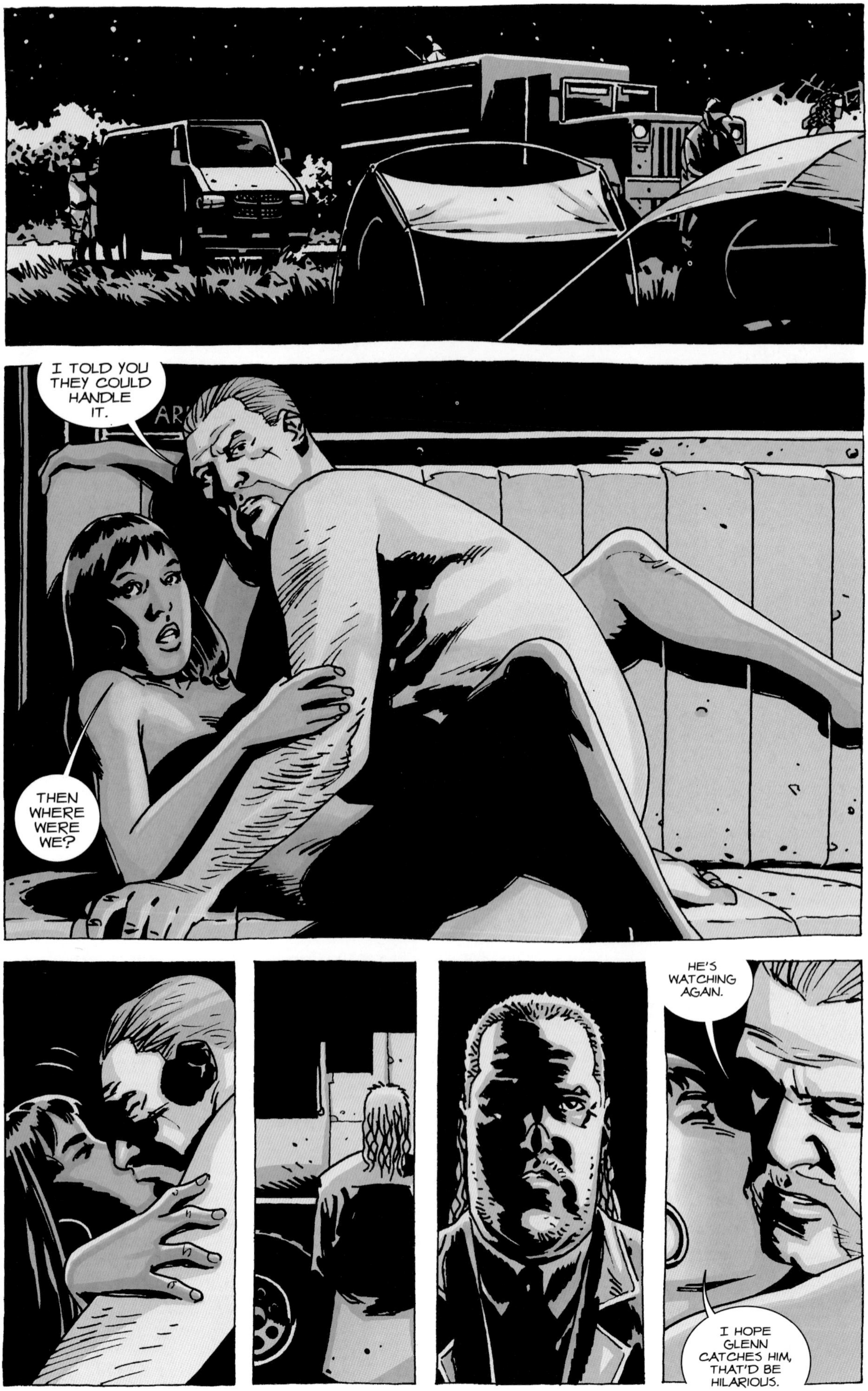
I TOLD YOU THEY COULD HANDLE IT.
THEN WHERE WERE WE?
HE'S WATCHING AGAIN.
I HOPE GLENN CATCHES HIM, THAT'D BE HILARIOUS.

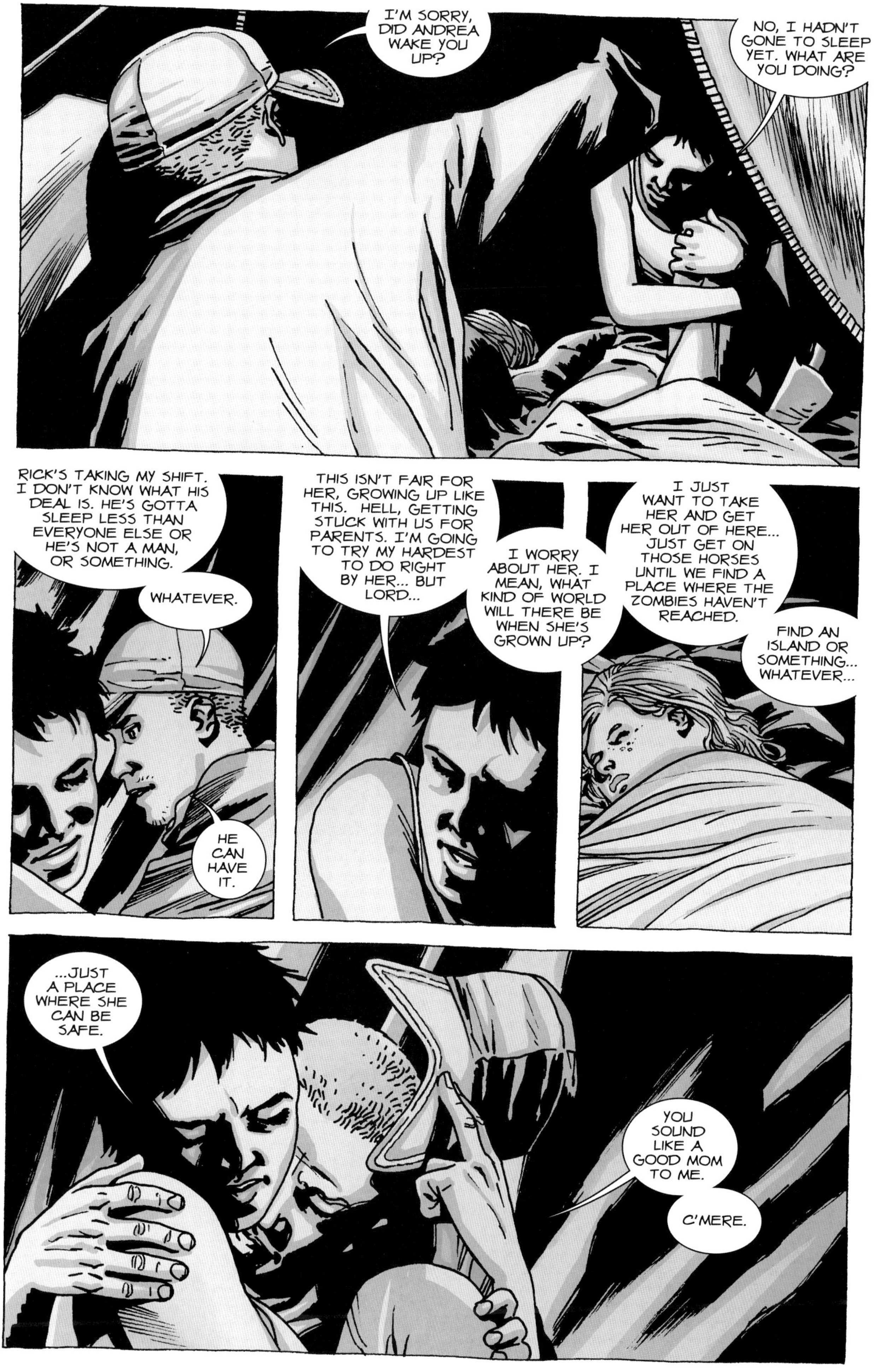
I'M SORRY, DID ANDREA WAKE YOU UP?
NO, I HADN'T GONE TO SLEEP YET. WHAT ARE YOU DOING?
RICK'S TAKING MY SHIFT. I DON'T KNOW WHAT HIS DEAL IS. HE'S GOTTA SLEEP LESS THAN EVERYONE ELSE OR HE'S NOT A MAN, OR SOMETHING.
WHATEVER.
HE CAN HAVE IT.
THIS ISN'T FAIR FOR HER, GROWING UP LIKE THIS. HELL, GETTING STUCK WITH US FOR PARENTS. I'M GOING TO TRY MY HARDEST TO DO RIGHT BY HER... BUT LORD...
I WORRY ABOUT HER. I MEAN, WHAT KIND OF WORLD WILL THERE BE WHEN SHE'S GROWN UP?
I JUST WANT TO TAKE HER AND GET HER OUT OF HERE... JUST GET ON THOSE HORSES UNTIL WE FIND A PLACE WHERE THE ZOMBIES HAVEN'T REACHED.
FIND AN ISLAND OR SOMETHING... WHATEVER...
...JUST A PLACE WHERE SHE CAN BE SAFE.
YOU SOUND LIKE A GOOD MOM TO ME.
C'MERE.

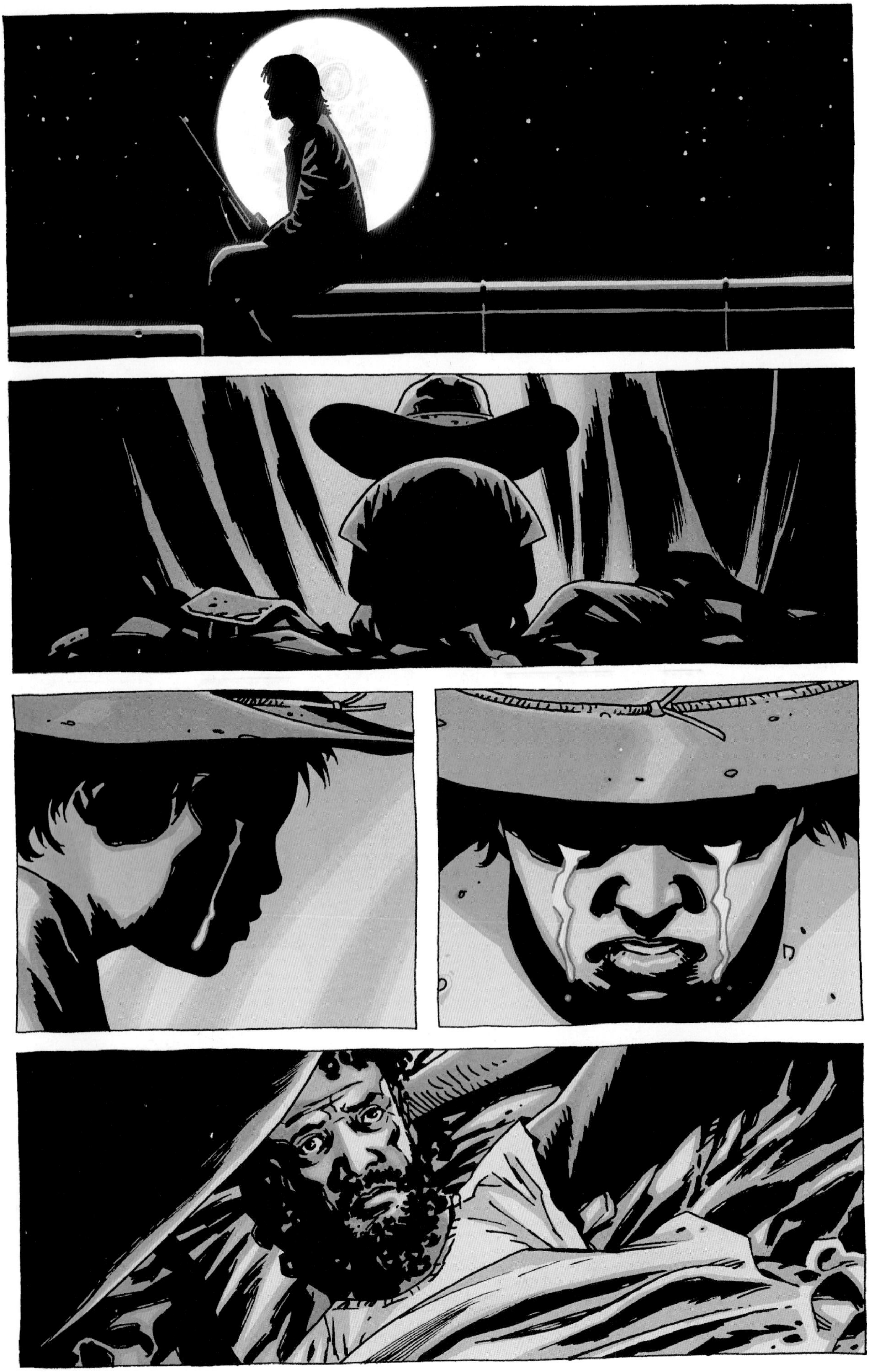

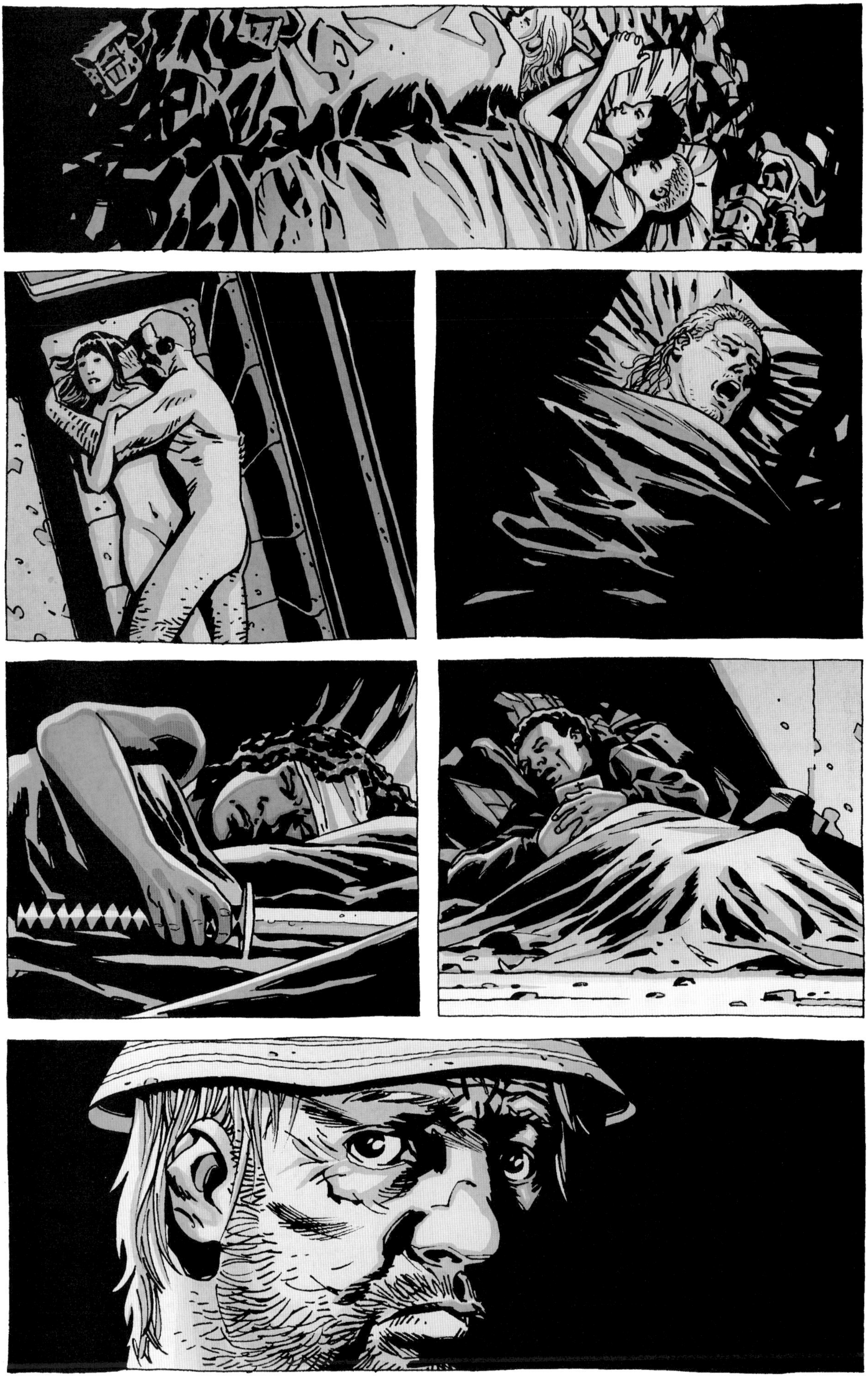

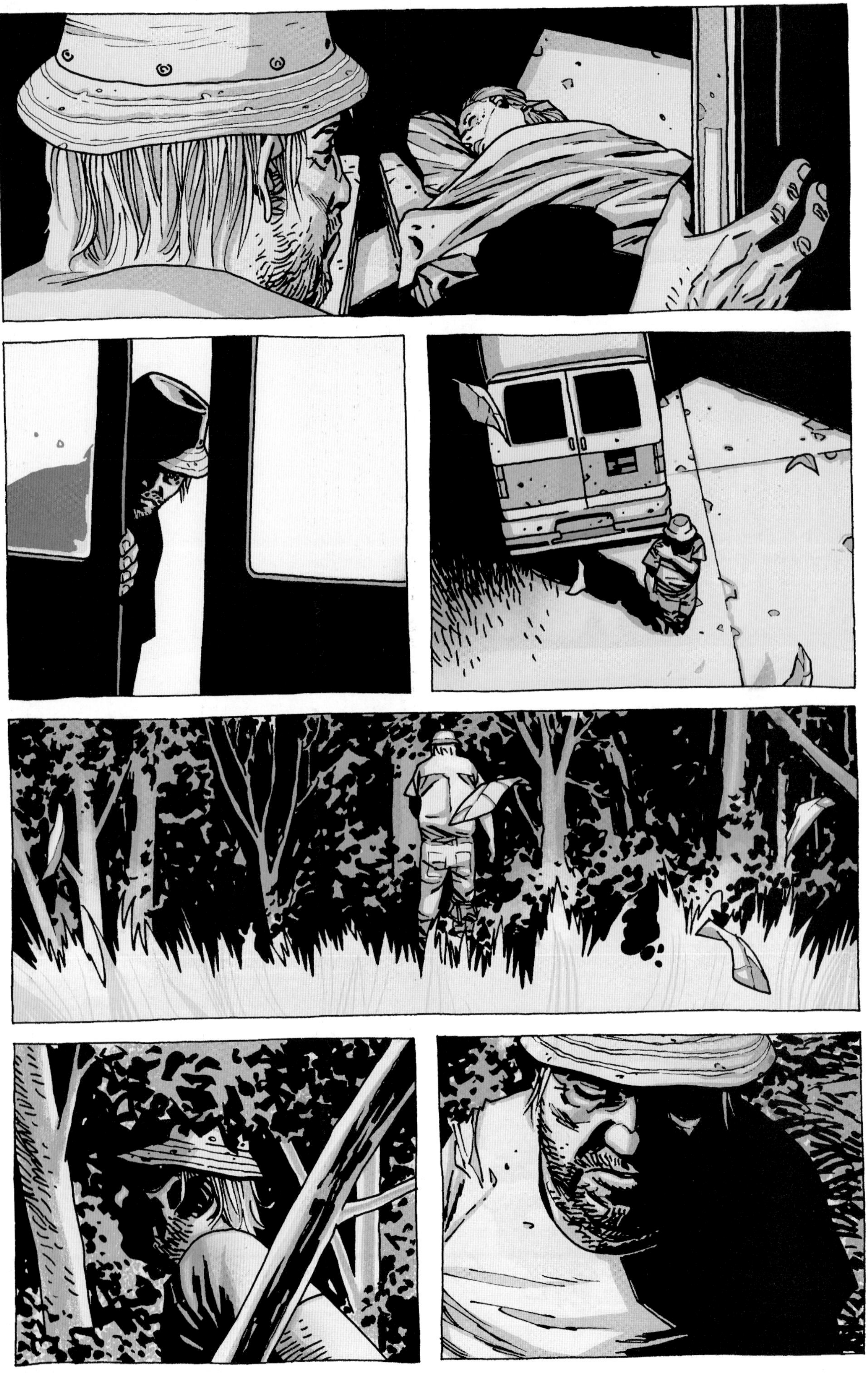

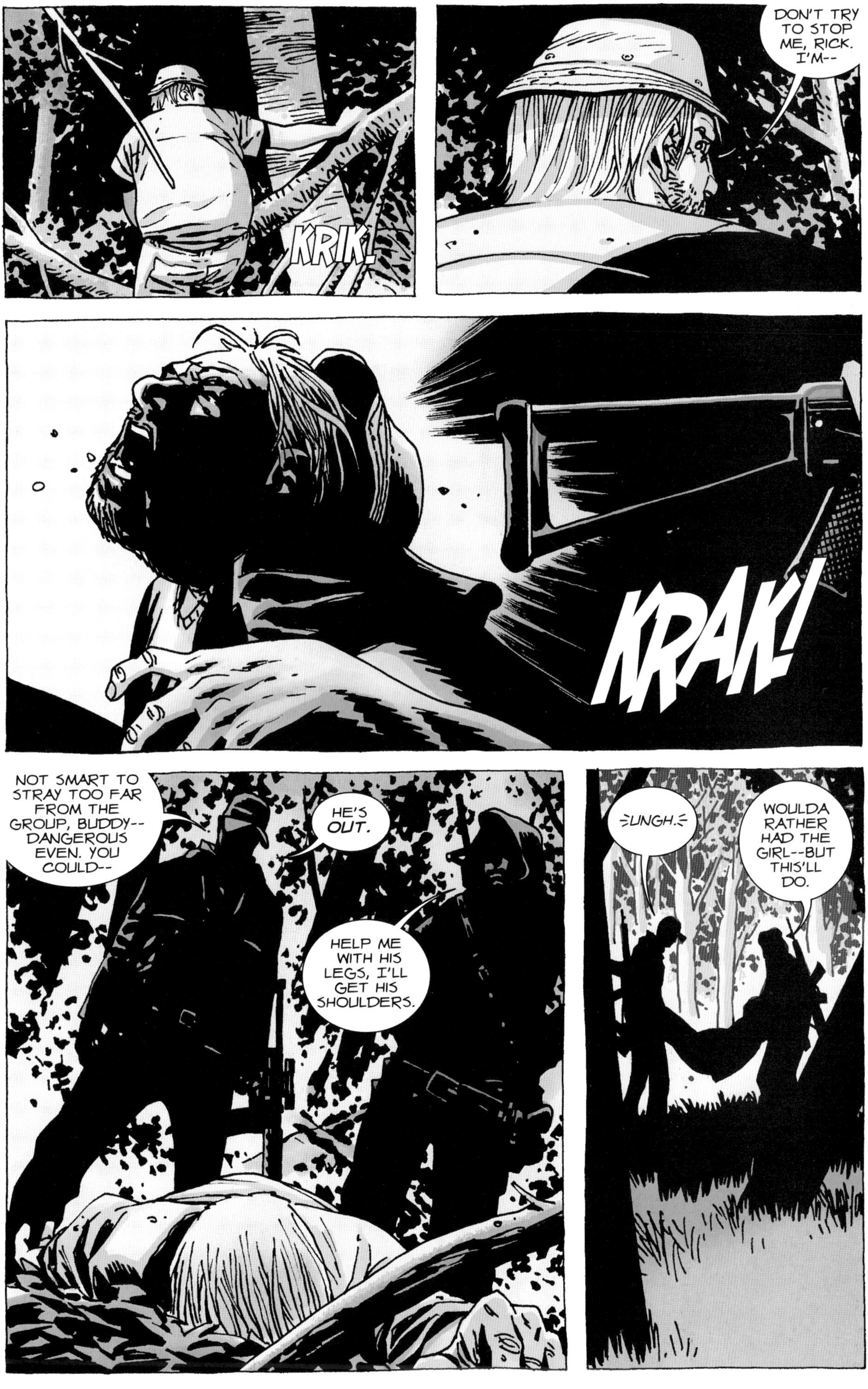
KRIK.
DON'T TRY TO STOP ME, RICK. I'M--
KRAK!
NOT SMART TO STRAY TOO FAR FROM THE GROUP, BUDDY--DANGEROUS EVEN. YOU COULD--
HE'S OUT.
HELP ME WITH HIS LEGS, I'LL GET HIS SHOULDERS.
UNGH.
WOULDA RATHER HAD THE GIRL--BUT THIS'LL DO.

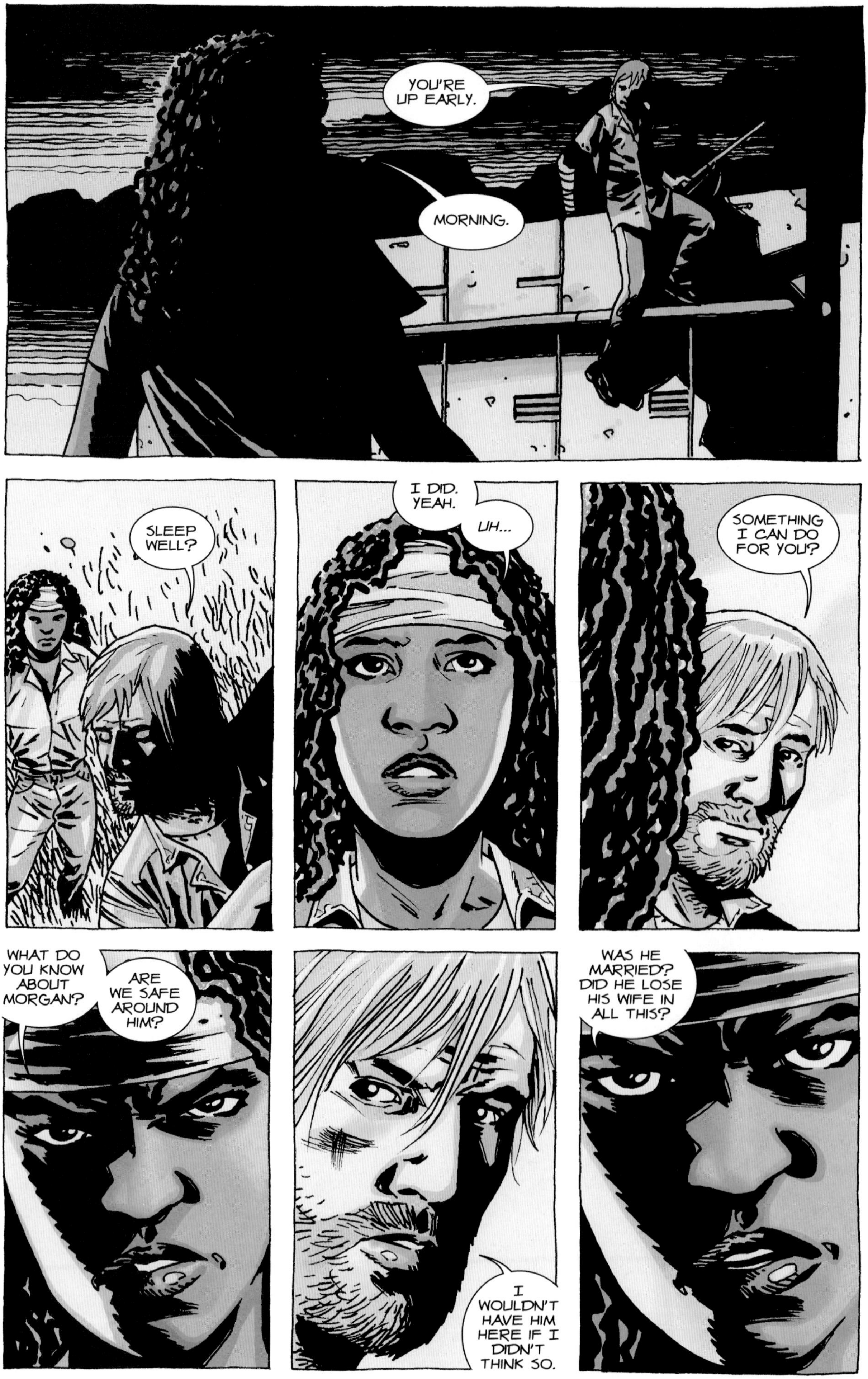
YOU'RE UP EARLY.
MORNING.
SLEEP WELL?
I DID. YEAH.
UH...
SOMETHING I CAN DO FOR YOU?
WHAT DO YOU KNOW ABOUT MORGAN?
ARE WE SAFE AROUND HIM?
I WOULDN'T HAVE HIM HERE IF I DIDN'T THINK SO.
WAS HE MARRIED? DID HE LOSE HIS WIFE IN ALL THIS?

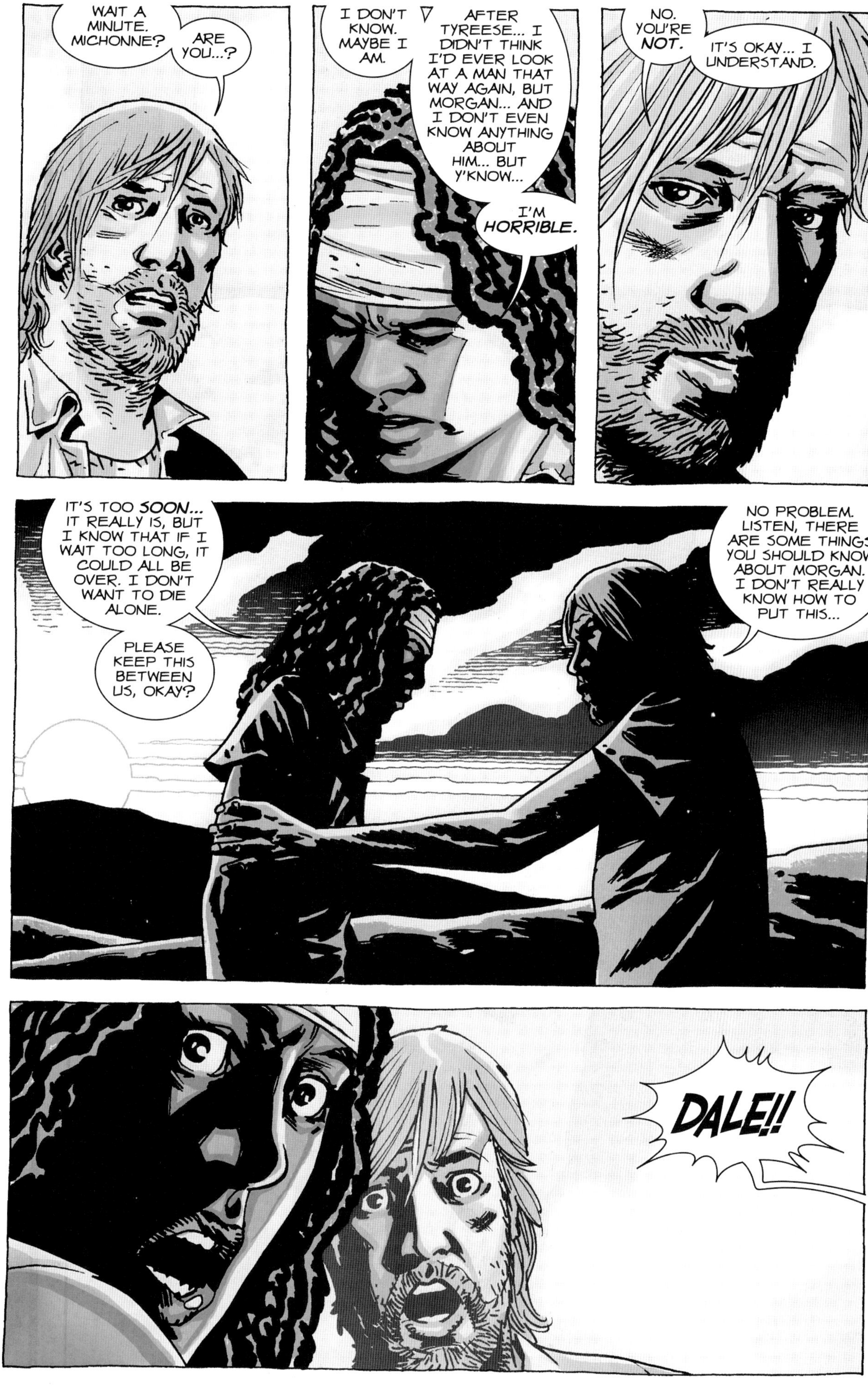
WAIT A MINUTE. MICHONNE?
ARE YOU...?
I DON'T KNOW. MAYBE I AM.
AFTER TYREESE... I DIDN'T THINK I'D EVER LOOK AT A MAN THAT WAY AGAIN, BUT MORGAN... AND I DON'T EVEN KNOW ANYTHING ABOUT HIM... BUT Y'KNOW...
I'M HORRIBLE.
NO. YOU'RE NOT.
IT'S OKAY... I UNDERSTAND.
IT'S TOO SOON... IT REALLY IS, BUT I KNOW THAT IF I WAIT TOO LONG, IT COULD ALL BE OVER. I DON'T WANT TO DIE ALONE.
PLEASE KEEP THIS BETWEEN US, OKAY?
NO PROBLEM. LISTEN, THERE ARE SOME THINGS YOU SHOULD KNOW ABOUT MORGAN. I DON'T REALLY KNOW HOW TO PUT THIS...
DALE!!

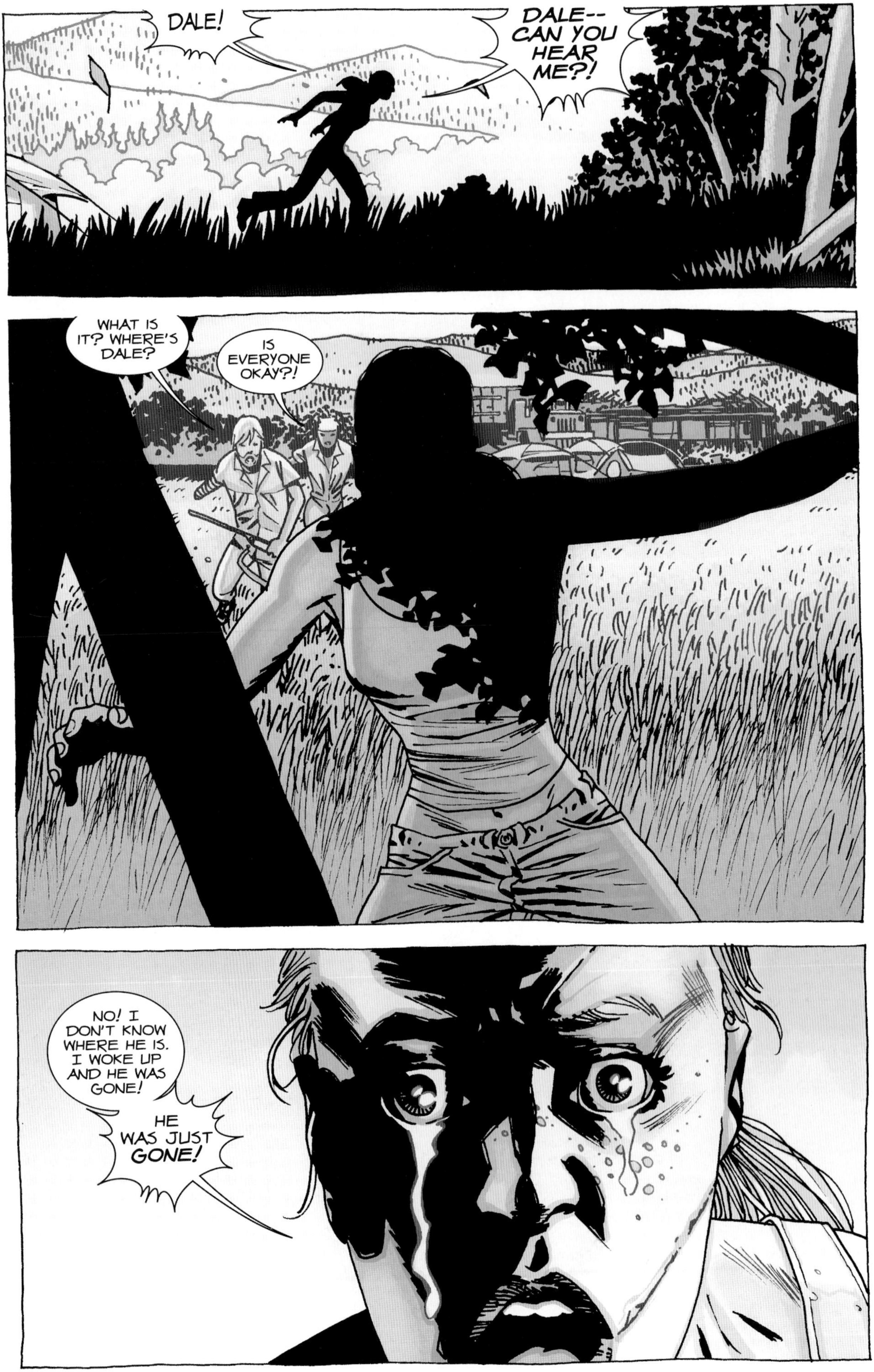
DALE!
DALE-- CAN YOU HEAR ME?!
WHAT IS IT? WHERE'S DALE?
IS EVERYONE OKAY?!
NO! I DON'T KNOW WHERE HE IS. I WOKE UP AND HE WAS GONE!
HE WAS JUST GONE!

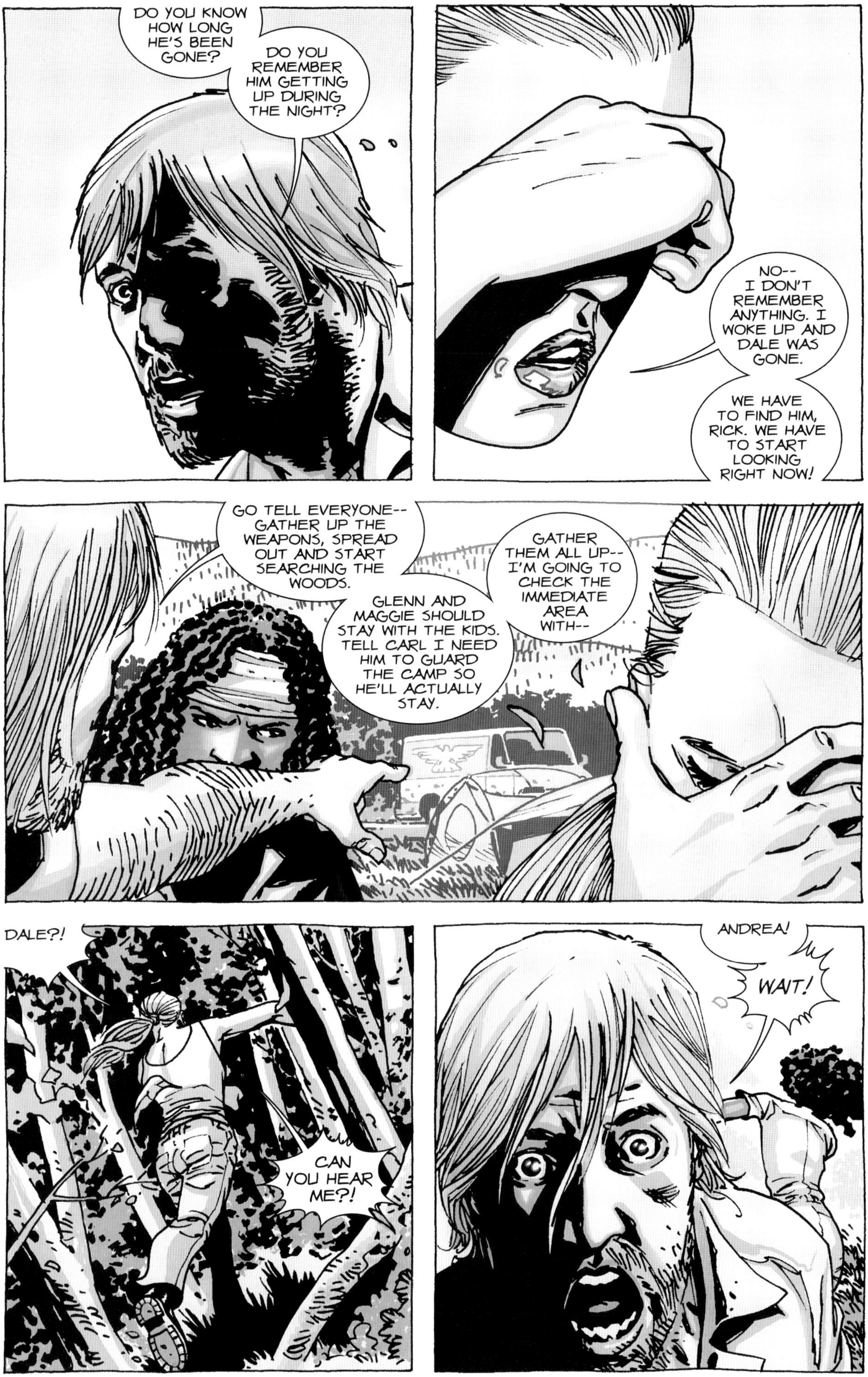
DO YOU KNOW HOW LONG HE'S BEEN GONE?
DO YOU REMEMBER HIM GETTING UP DURING THE NIGHT?
NO-- I DON'T REMEMBER ANYTHING. I WOKE UP AND DALE WAS GONE.
WE HAVE TO FIND HIM, RICK. WE HAVE TO START LOOKING RIGHT NOW!
GO TELL EVERYONE-- GATHER UP THE WEAPONS, SPREAD OUT AND START SEARCHING THE WOODS.
GLENN AND MAGGIE SHOULD STAY WITH THE KIDS. TELL CARL I NEED HIM TO GUARD THE CAMP SO HE'LL ACTUALLY STAY.
GATHER THEM ALL UP-- I'M GOING TO CHECK THE IMMEDIATE AREA WITH--
DALE?!
CAN YOU HEAR ME?!
ANDREA!
WAIT!

WE'RE NOT ALONE IN HERE, EVEN IF IT SEEMS LIKE WE ARE. I WANT TO FIND DALE AS MUCH AS THE NEXT GUY--BUT KEEP YOUR EARS OPEN FOR BITERS AS WELL.

NO YELLING OUT--THAT'LL JUST DRAW ATTENTION TO US.

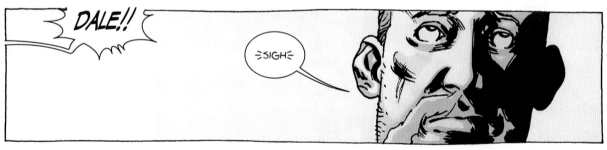

DALE!!

≥SIGH≤

WE'RE GOING TO FIND HIM, ANDREA I PROMISE.

BUT I DON'T THINK WE SHOULD BE YELLING, IT'S JUST GOING TO DRAW ATTENTION OUR WAY.

EVERYONE'S HERE--I'M GOING TO TALK TO THEM. PLEASE, NO MORE YELLING.

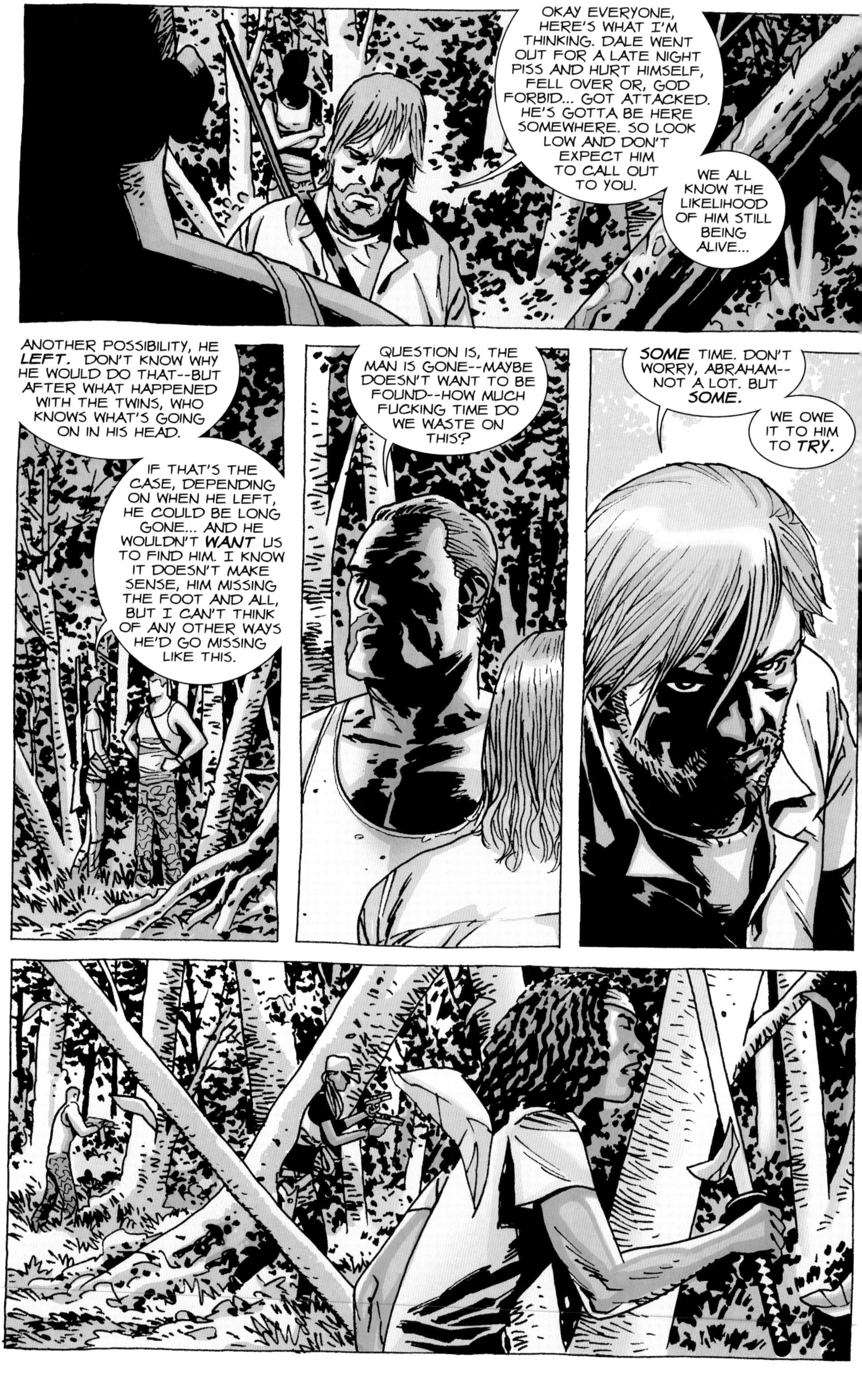
OKAY EVERYONE, HERE'S WHAT I'M THINKING. DALE WENT OUT FOR A LATE NIGHT PISS AND HURT HIMSELF, FELL OVER OR, GOD FORBID... GOT ATTACKED. HE'S GOTTA BE HERE SOMEWHERE. SO LOOK LOW AND DON'T EXPECT HIM TO CALL OUT TO YOU.
WE ALL KNOW THE LIKELIHOOD OF HIM STILL BEING ALIVE...
ANOTHER POSSIBILITY, HE LEFT. DON'T KNOW WHY HE WOULD DO THAT--BUT AFTER WHAT HAPPENED WITH THE TWINS, WHO KNOWS WHAT'S GOING ON IN HIS HEAD.
IF THAT'S THE CASE, DEPENDING ON WHEN HE LEFT, HE COULD BE LONG GONE... AND HE WOULDN'T WANT US TO FIND HIM. I KNOW IT DOESN'T MAKE SENSE, HIM MISSING THE FOOT AND ALL, BUT I CAN'T THINK OF ANY OTHER WAYS HE'D GO MISSING LIKE THIS.
QUESTION IS, THE MAN IS GONE--MAYBE DOESN'T WANT TO BE FOUND--HOW MUCH FUCKING TIME DO WE WASTE ON THIS?
SOME TIME. DON'T WORRY, ABRAHAM-- NOT A LOT. BUT SOME.
WE OWE IT TO HIM TO TRY.

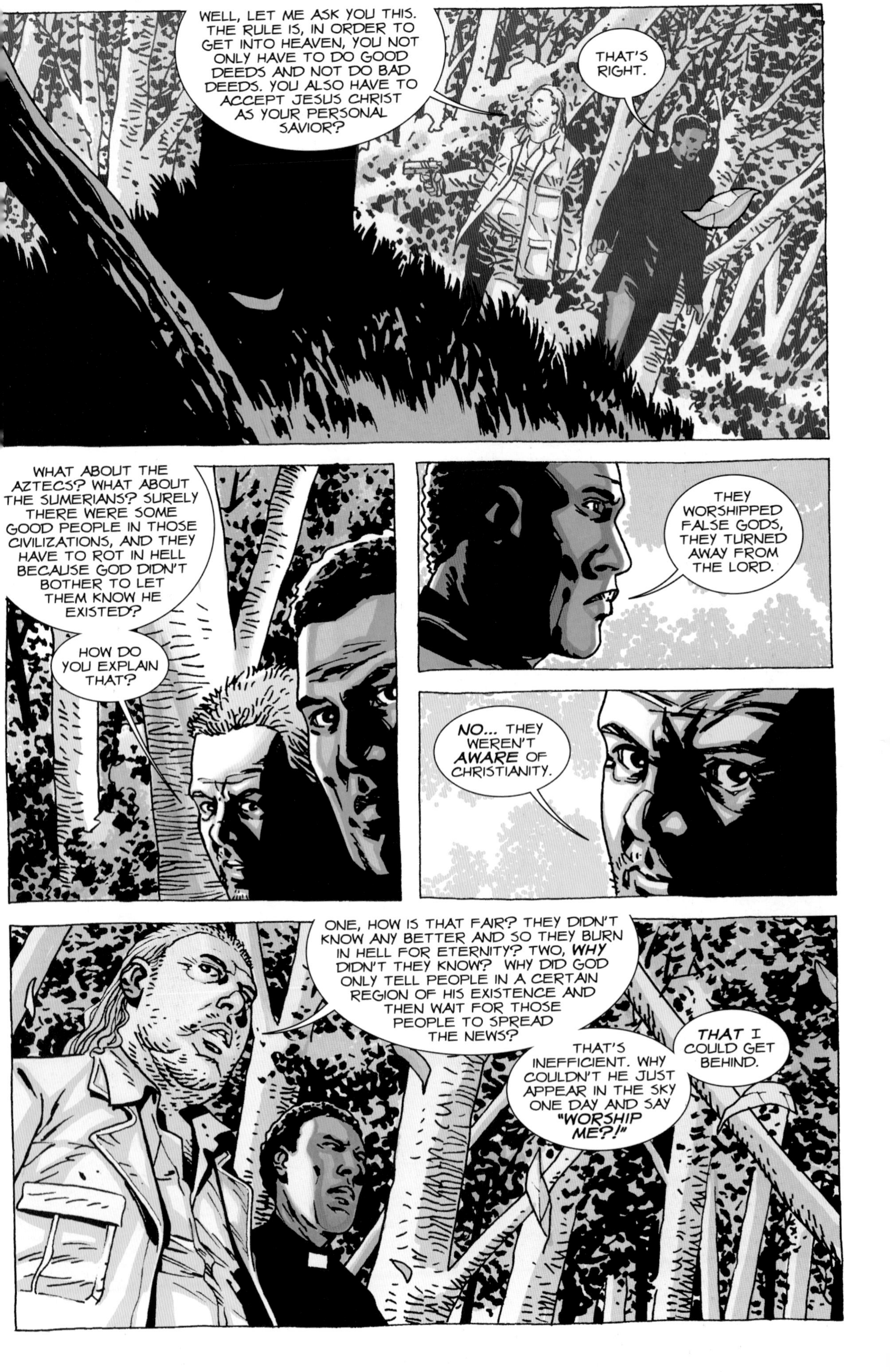

WELL, LET ME ASK YOU THIS. THE RULE IS, IN ORDER TO GET INTO HEAVEN, YOU NOT ONLY HAVE TO DO GOOD DEEDS AND NOT DO BAD DEEDS. YOU ALSO HAVE TO ACCEPT JESUS CHRIST AS YOUR PERSONAL SAVIOR?
THAT'S RIGHT.
WHAT ABOUT THE AZTECS? WHAT ABOUT THE SUMERIANS? SURELY THERE WERE SOME GOOD PEOPLE IN THOSE CIVILIZATIONS, AND THEY HAVE TO ROT IN HELL BECAUSE GOD DIDN'T BOTHER TO LET THEM KNOW HE EXISTED?
HOW DO YOU EXPLAIN THAT?
THEY WORSHIPPED FALSE GODS, THEY TURNED AWAY FROM THE LORD.
NO... THEY WEREN'T AWARE OF CHRISTIANITY.
ONE, HOW IS THAT FAIR? THEY DIDN'T KNOW ANY BETTER AND SO THEY BURN IN HELL FOR ETERNITY? TWO, WHY DIDN'T THEY KNOW? WHY DID GOD ONLY TELL PEOPLE IN A CERTAIN REGION OF HIS EXISTENCE AND THEN WAIT FOR THOSE PEOPLE TO SPREAD THE NEWS?
THAT'S INEFFICIENT. WHY COULDN'T HE JUST APPEAR IN THE SKY ONE DAY AND SAY "WORSHIP ME?!"
THAT I COULD GET BEHIND.

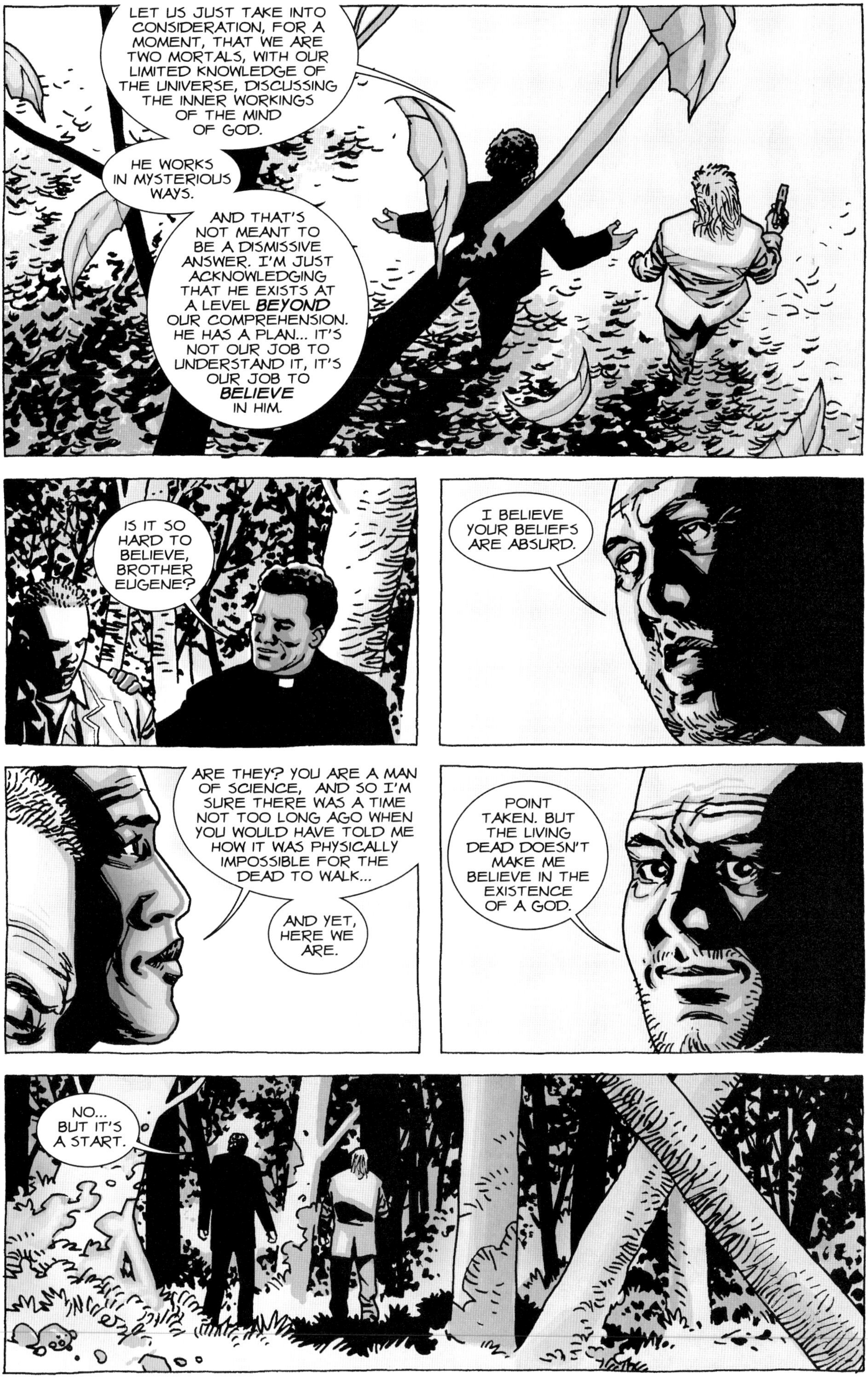
LET US JUST TAKE INTO CONSIDERATION, FOR A MOMENT, THAT WE ARE TWO MORTALS, WITH OUR LIMITED KNOWLEDGE OF THE UNIVERSE, DISCUSSING THE INNER WORKINGS OF THE MIND OF GOD.
HE WORKS IN MYSTERIOUS WAYS.
AND THAT'S NOT MEANT TO BE A DISMISSIVE ANSWER. I'M JUST ACKNOWLEDGING THAT HE EXISTS AT A LEVEL BEYOND OUR COMPREHENSION. HE HAS A PLAN... IT'S NOT OUR JOB TO UNDERSTAND IT, IT'S OUR JOB TO BELIEVE IN HIM.
IS IT SO HARD TO BELIEVE, BROTHER EUGENE?
I BELIEVE YOUR BELIEFS ARE ABSURD.
ARE THEY? YOU ARE A MAN OF SCIENCE, AND SO I'M SURE THERE WAS A TIME NOT TOO LONG AGO WHEN YOU WOULD HAVE TOLD ME HOW IT WAS PHYSICALLY IMPOSSIBLE FOR THE DEAD TO WALK...
AND YET, HERE WE ARE.
POINT TAKEN. BUT THE LIVING DEAD DOESN'T MAKE ME BELIEVE IN THE EXISTENCE OF A GOD.
NO... BUT IT'S A START.

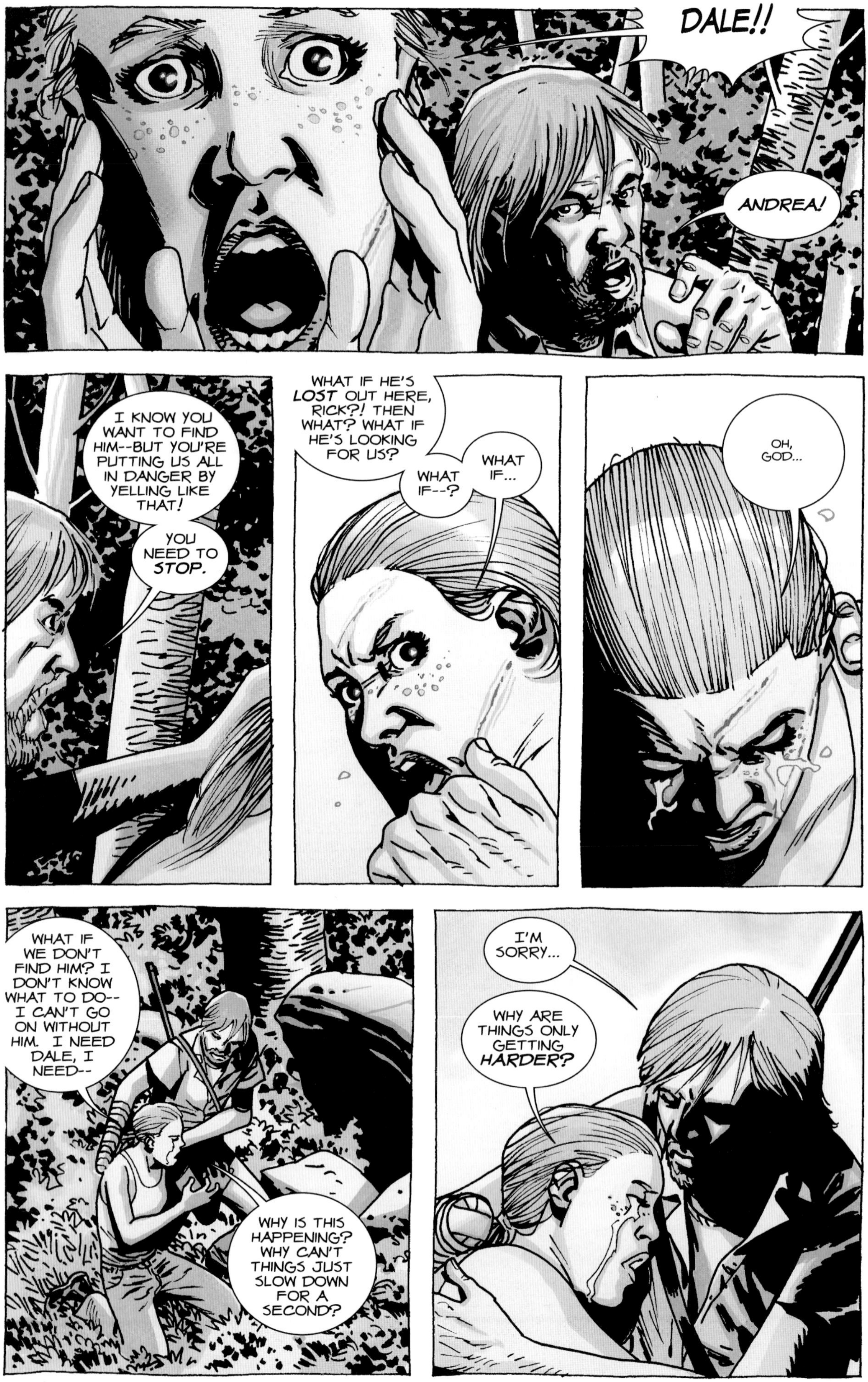
DALE!!
ANDREA!
I KNOW YOU WANT TO FIND HIM--BUT YOU'RE PUTTING US ALL IN DANGER BY YELLING LIKE THAT!
YOU NEED TO STOP.
WHAT IF HE'S LOST OUT HERE, RICK?! THEN WHAT? WHAT IF HE'S LOOKING FOR US?
WHAT IF--?
WHAT IF...
OH, GOD...
WHAT IF WE DON'T FIND HIM? I DON'T KNOW WHAT TO DO-- I CAN'T GO ON WITHOUT HIM. I NEED DALE, I NEED--
WHY IS THIS HAPPENING? WHY CAN'T THINGS JUST SLOW DOWN FOR A SECOND?
I'M SORRY...
WHY ARE THINGS ONLY GETTING HARDER?

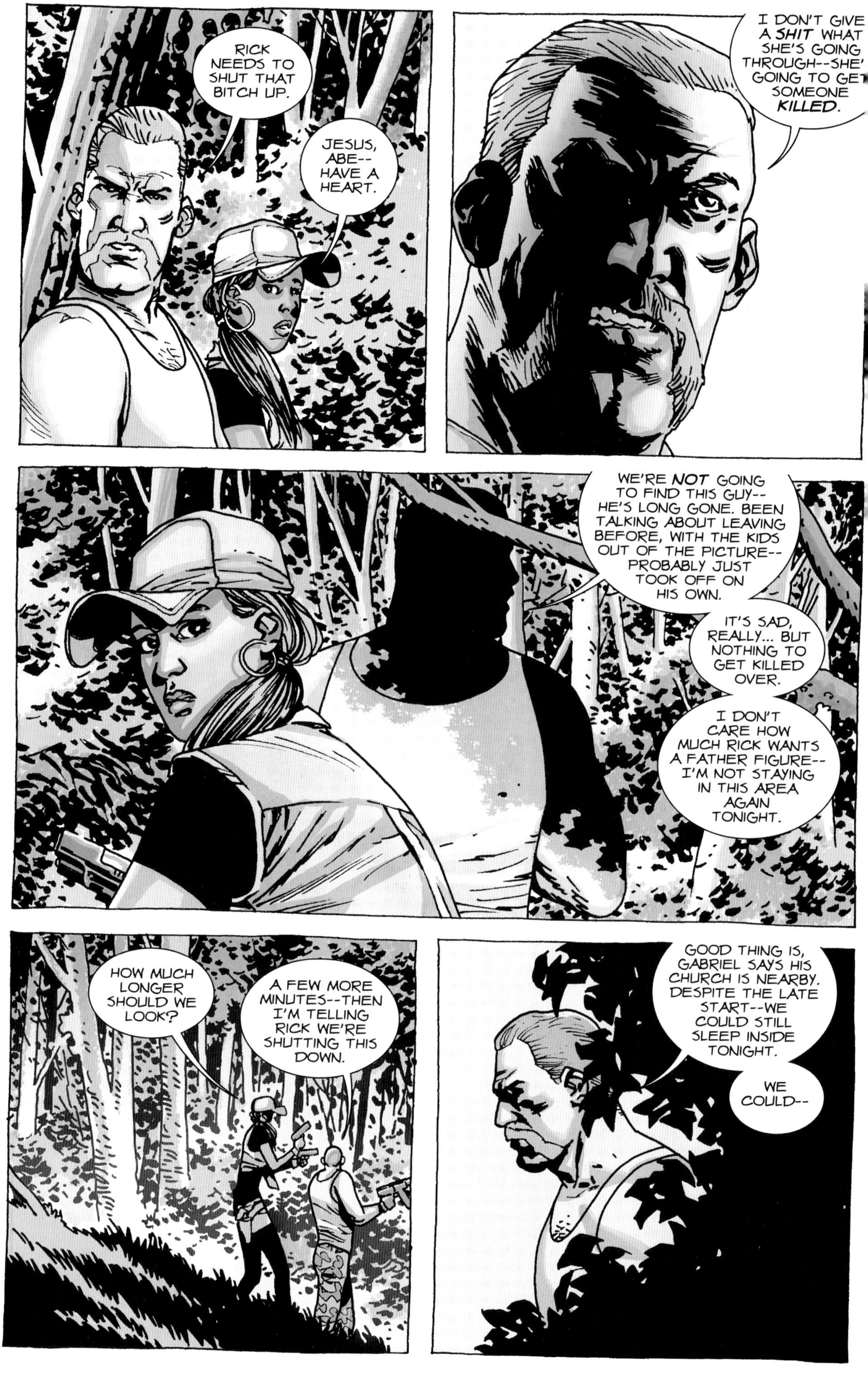
RICK NEEDS TO SHUT THAT BITCH UP.
JESUS, ABE-- HAVE A HEART.
I DON'T GIVE A *SHIT* WHAT SHE'S GOING THROUGH--SHE' GOING TO GET SOMEONE *KILLED*.
WE'RE *NOT* GOING TO FIND THIS GUY-- HE'S LONG GONE. BEEN TALKING ABOUT LEAVING BEFORE, WITH THE KIDS OUT OF THE PICTURE-- PROBABLY JUST TOOK OFF ON HIS OWN.
IT'S SAD, REALLY... BUT NOTHING TO GET KILLED OVER.
I DON'T CARE HOW MUCH RICK WANTS A FATHER FIGURE-- I'M NOT STAYING IN THIS AREA AGAIN TONIGHT.
HOW MUCH LONGER SHOULD WE LOOK?
A FEW MORE MINUTES--THEN I'M TELLING RICK WE'RE SHUTTING THIS DOWN.
GOOD THING IS, GABRIEL SAYS HIS CHURCH IS NEARBY. DESPITE THE LATE START--WE COULD STILL SLEEP INSIDE TONIGHT.
WE COULD--

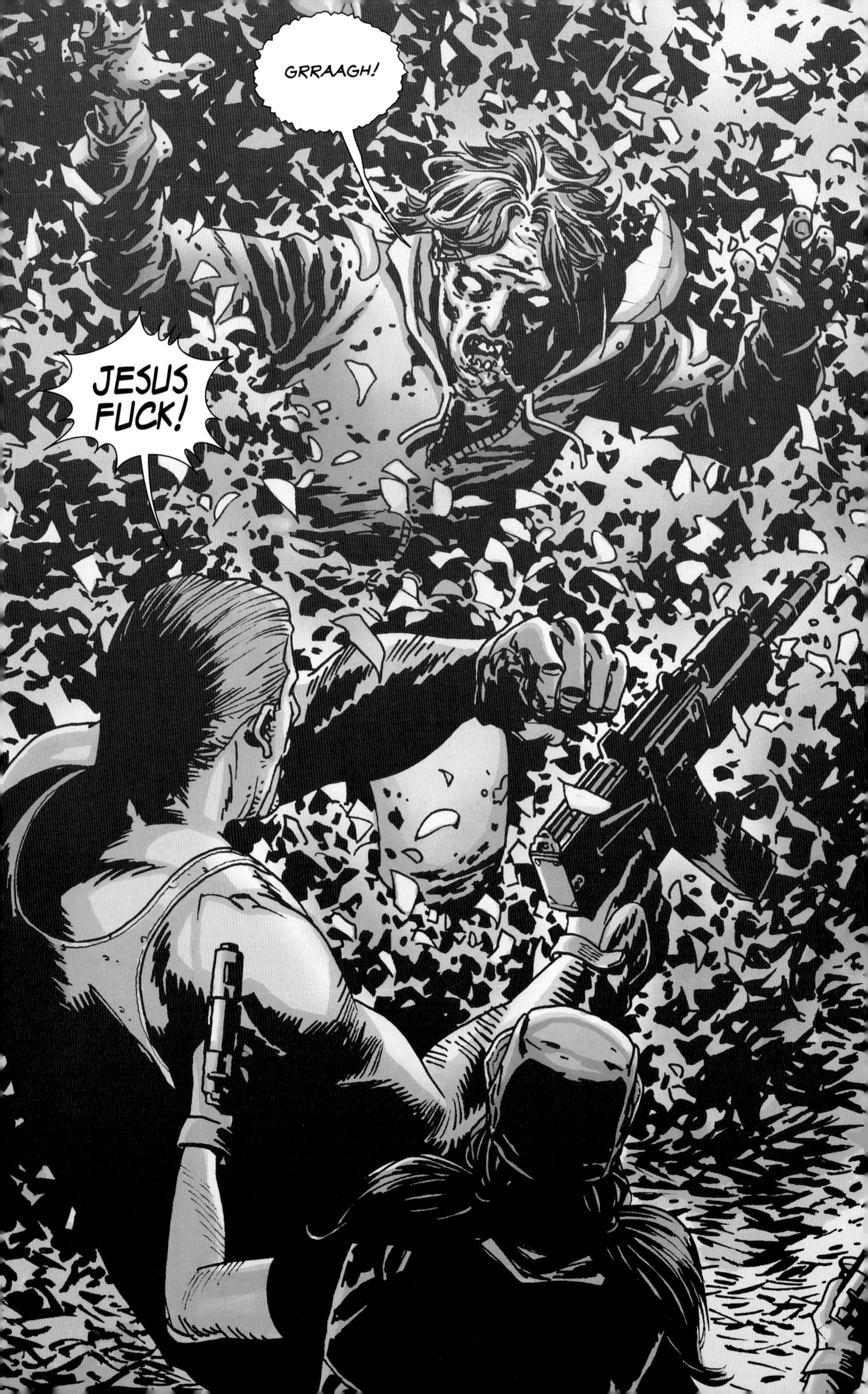
GRRAAGH!
JESUS FUCK!

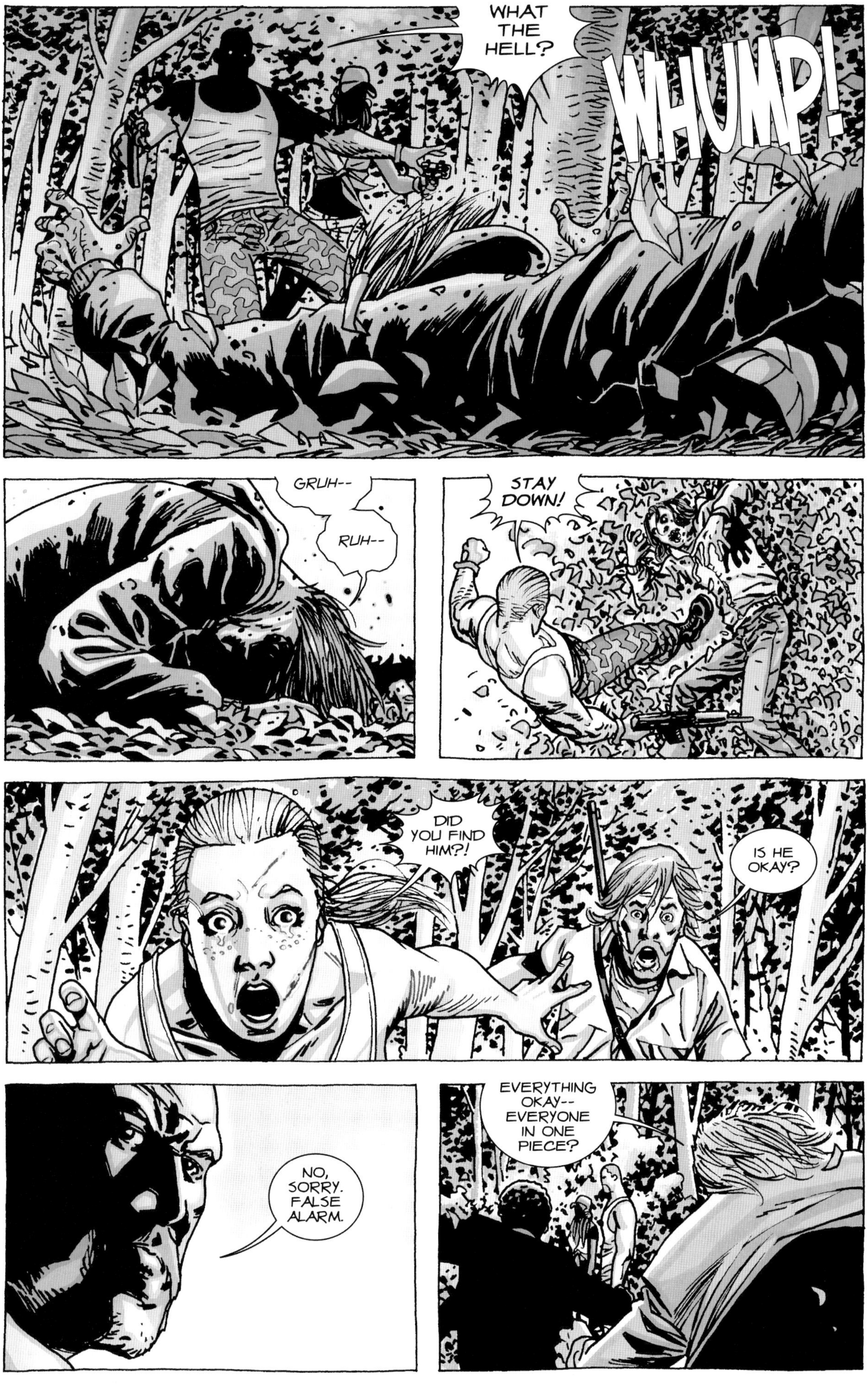
WHAT THE HELL?
WHUMP!
GRUH--
RUH--
STAY DOWN!
DID YOU FIND HIM?!
IS HE OKAY?
NO, SORRY. FALSE ALARM.
EVERYTHING OKAY-- EVERYONE IN ONE PIECE?

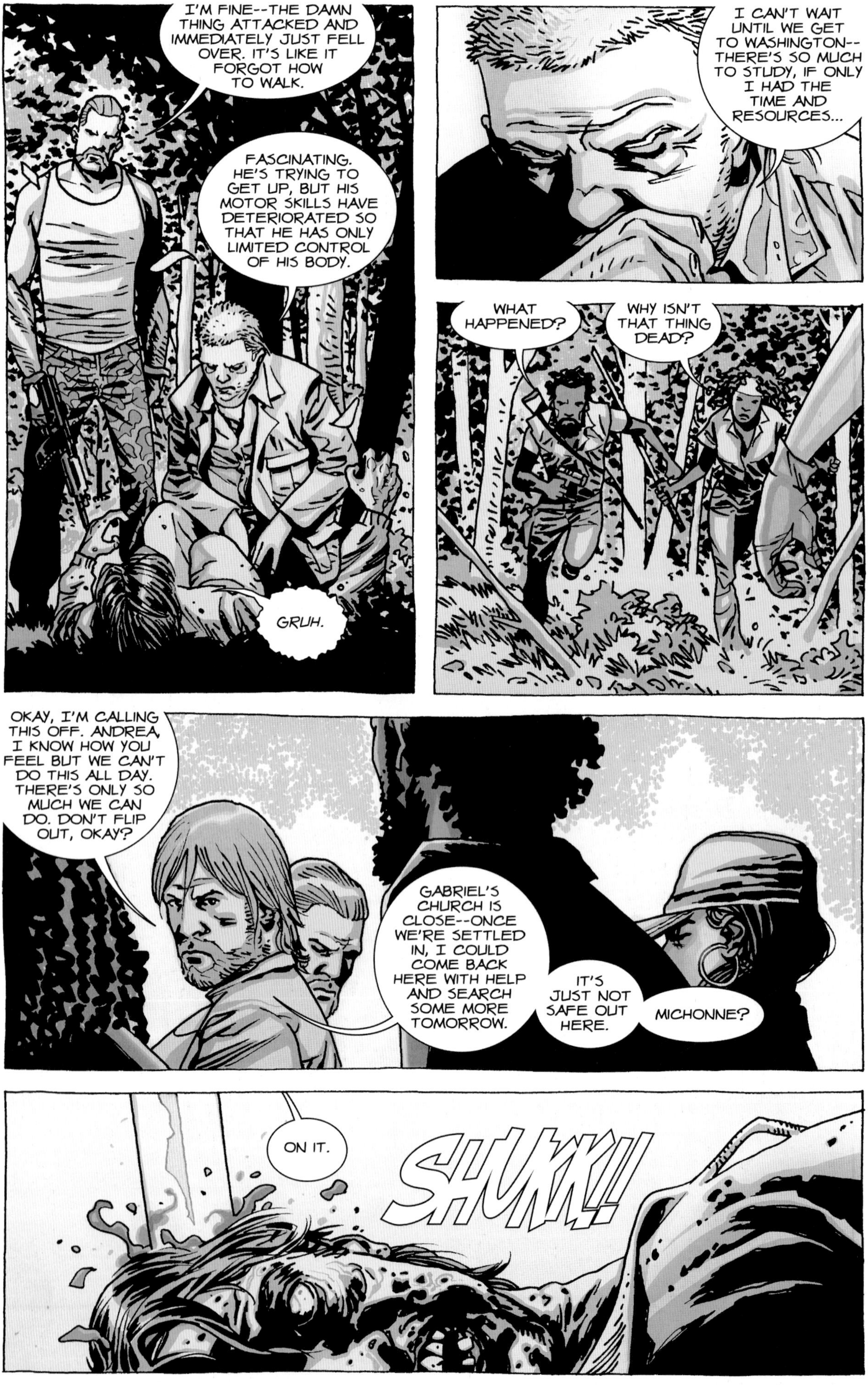
I'M FINE--THE DAMN THING ATTACKED AND IMMEDIATELY JUST FELL OVER. IT'S LIKE IT FORGOT HOW TO WALK.
FASCINATING. HE'S TRYING TO GET UP, BUT HIS MOTOR SKILLS HAVE DETERIORATED SO THAT HE HAS ONLY LIMITED CONTROL OF HIS BODY.
GRUH.
I CAN'T WAIT UNTIL WE GET TO WASHINGTON--THERE'S SO MUCH TO STUDY, IF ONLY I HAD THE TIME AND RESOURCES...
WHAT HAPPENED?
WHY ISN'T THAT THING DEAD?
OKAY, I'M CALLING THIS OFF. ANDREA, I KNOW HOW YOU FEEL BUT WE CAN'T DO THIS ALL DAY. THERE'S ONLY SO MUCH WE CAN DO. DON'T FLIP OUT, OKAY?
GABRIEL'S CHURCH IS CLOSE--ONCE WE'RE SETTLED IN, I COULD COME BACK HERE WITH HELP AND SEARCH SOME MORE TOMORROW.
IT'S JUST NOT SAFE OUT HERE.
MICHONNE?
ON IT.
SHUNK!!

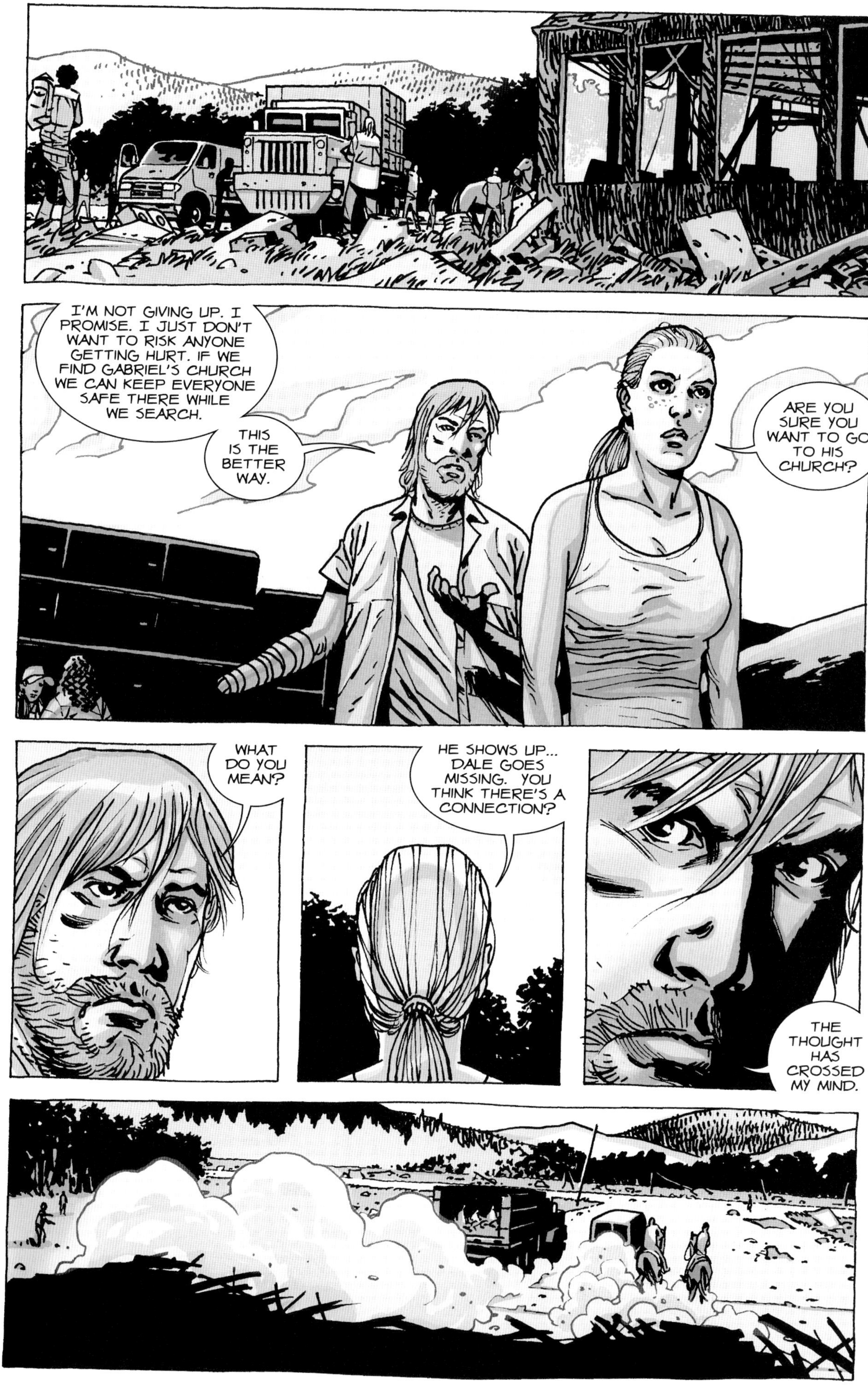
I'M NOT GIVING UP. I PROMISE. I JUST DON'T WANT TO RISK ANYONE GETTING HURT. IF WE FIND GABRIEL'S CHURCH WE CAN KEEP EVERYONE SAFE THERE WHILE WE SEARCH.
THIS IS THE BETTER WAY.
ARE YOU SURE YOU WANT TO GO TO HIS CHURCH?
WHAT DO YOU MEAN?
HE SHOWS UP... DALE GOES MISSING. YOU THINK THERE'S A CONNECTION?
THE THOUGHT HAS CROSSED MY MIND.

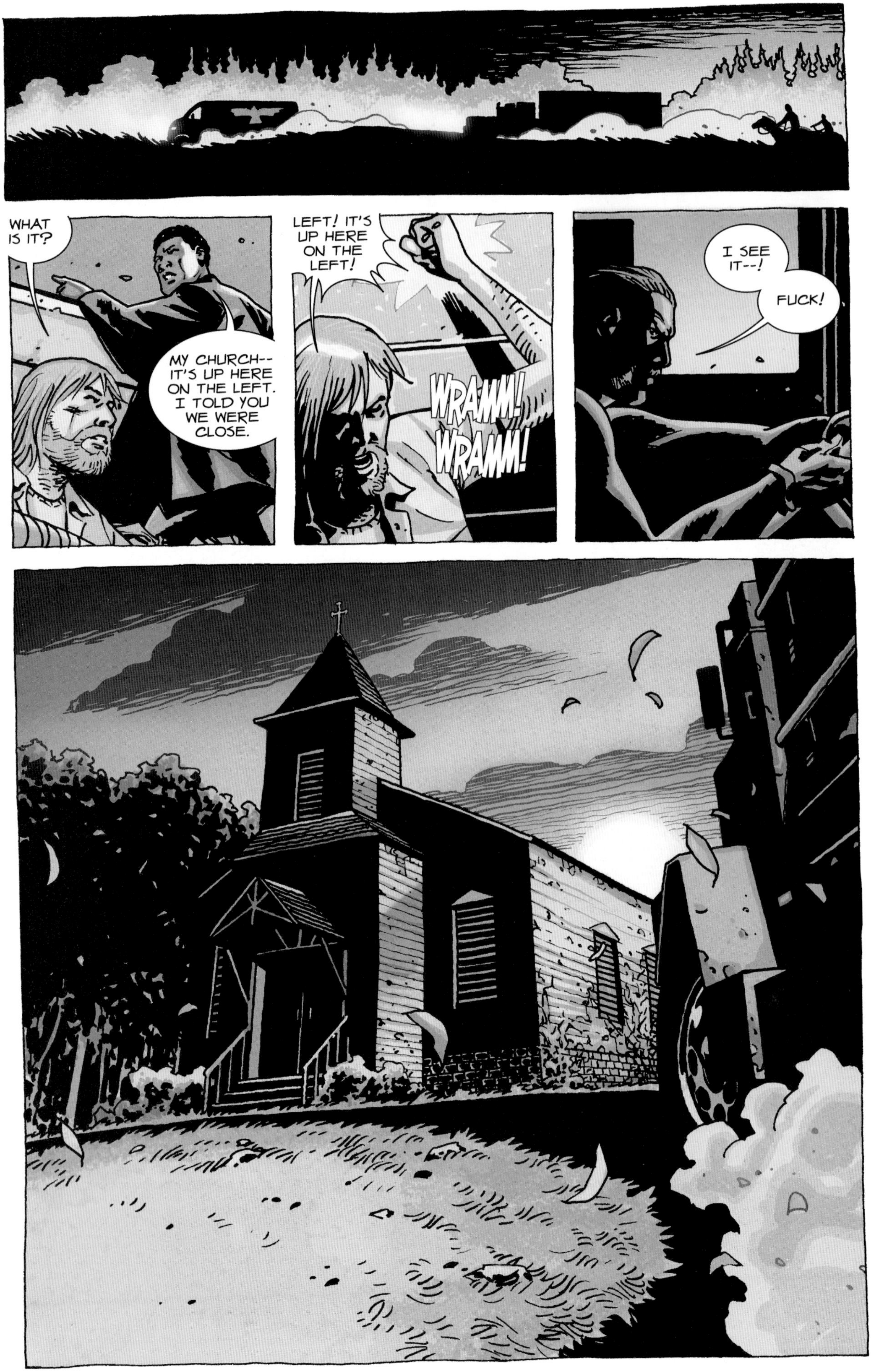
WHAT IS IT?
MY CHURCH-- IT'S UP HERE ON THE LEFT. I TOLD YOU WE WERE CLOSE.
LEFT! IT'S UP HERE ON THE LEFT!
WRAMM! WRAMM!
I SEE IT--!
FUCK!

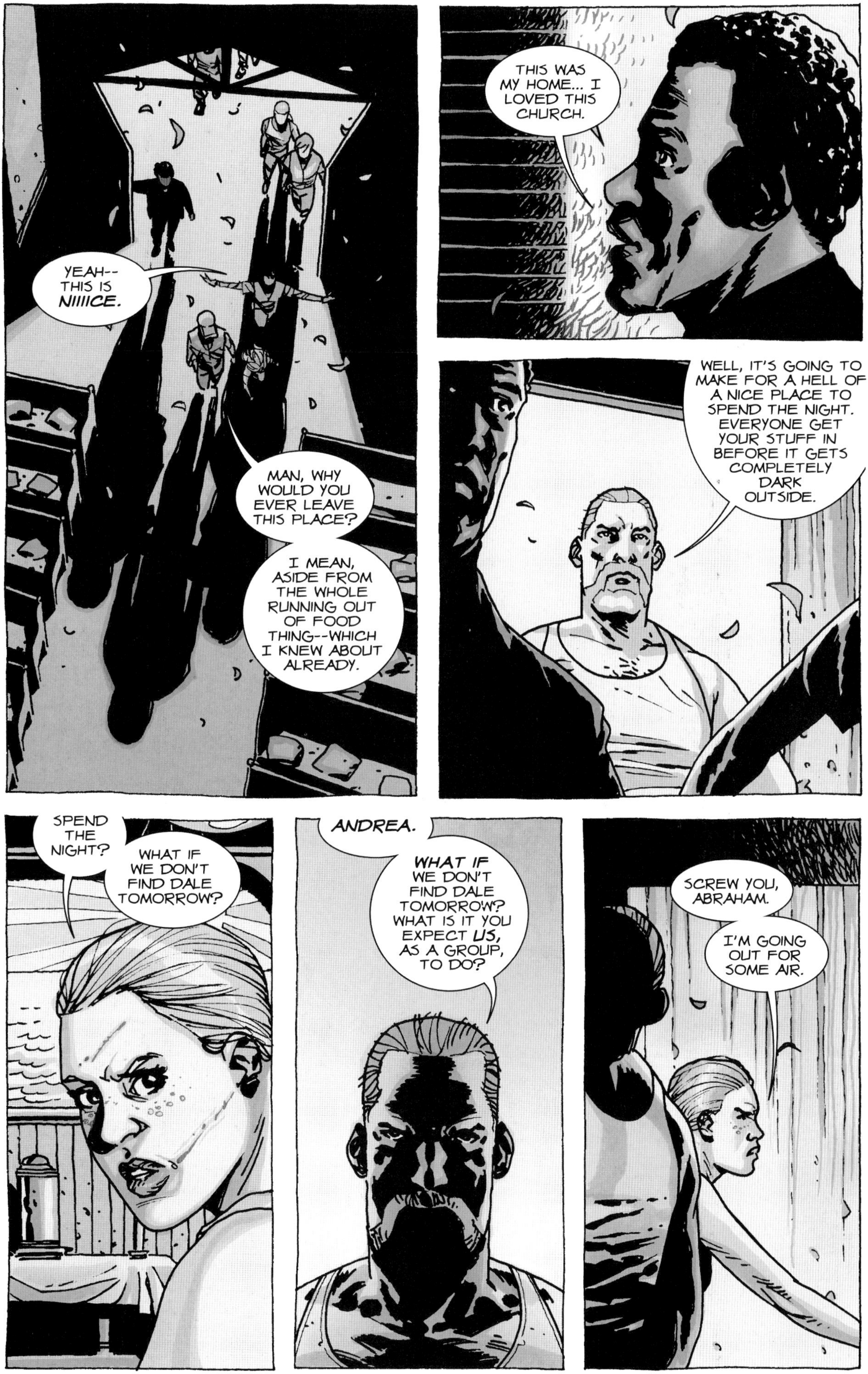
YEAH-- THIS IS NIIIICE.
MAN, WHY WOULD YOU EVER LEAVE THIS PLACE?
I MEAN, ASIDE FROM THE WHOLE RUNNING OUT OF FOOD THING--WHICH I KNEW ABOUT ALREADY.
THIS WAS MY HOME... I LOVED THIS CHURCH.
WELL, IT'S GOING TO MAKE FOR A HELL OF A NICE PLACE TO SPEND THE NIGHT. EVERYONE GET YOUR STUFF IN BEFORE IT GETS COMPLETELY DARK OUTSIDE.
SPEND THE NIGHT?
WHAT IF WE DON'T FIND DALE TOMORROW?
ANDREA.
WHAT IF WE DON'T FIND DALE TOMORROW? WHAT IS IT YOU EXPECT US, AS A GROUP, TO DO?
SCREW YOU, ABRAHAM.
I'M GOING OUT FOR SOME AIR.

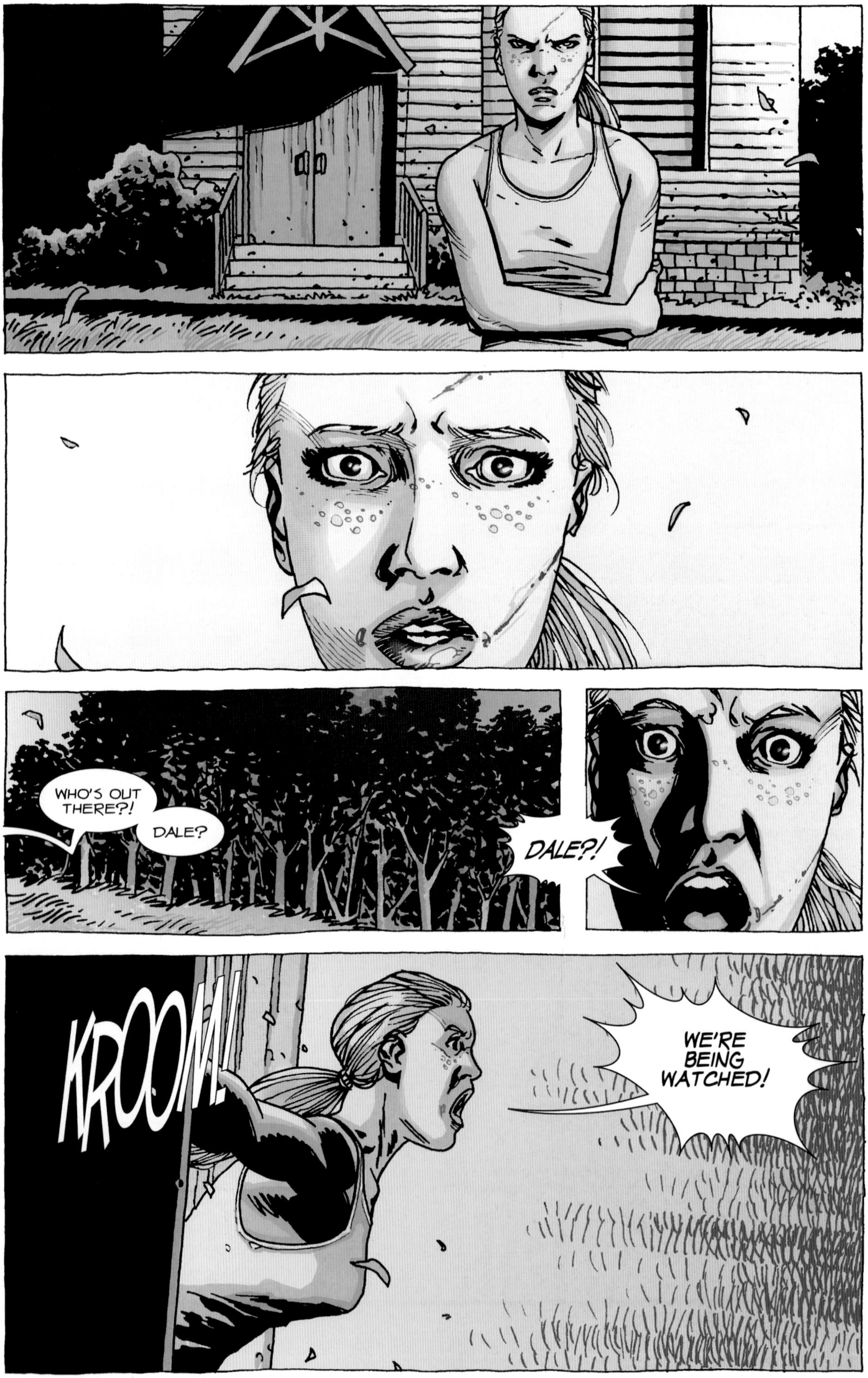
WHO'S OUT THERE?!
DALE?
DALE?!
KROOM!!
WE'RE BEING WATCHED!

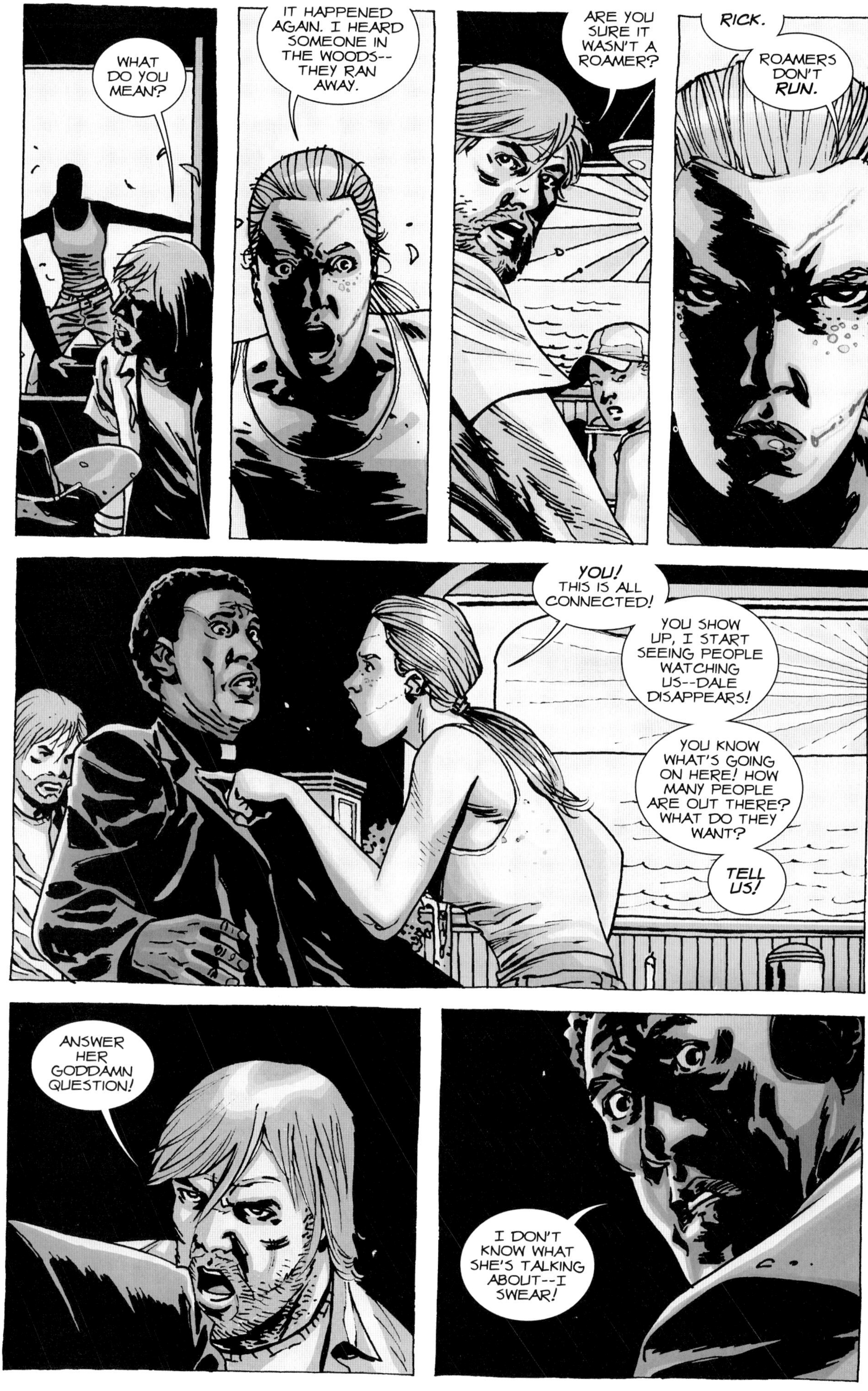

WHAT DO YOU MEAN?
IT HAPPENED AGAIN. I HEARD SOMEONE IN THE WOODS-- THEY RAN AWAY.
ARE YOU SURE IT WASN'T A ROAMER?
RICK.
ROAMERS DON'T RUN.
YOU! THIS IS ALL CONNECTED!
YOU SHOW UP, I START SEEING PEOPLE WATCHING US--DALE DISAPPEARS!
YOU KNOW WHAT'S GOING ON HERE! HOW MANY PEOPLE ARE OUT THERE? WHAT DO THEY WANT?
TELL US!
ANSWER HER GODDAMN QUESTION!
I DON'T KNOW WHAT SHE'S TALKING ABOUT--I SWEAR!

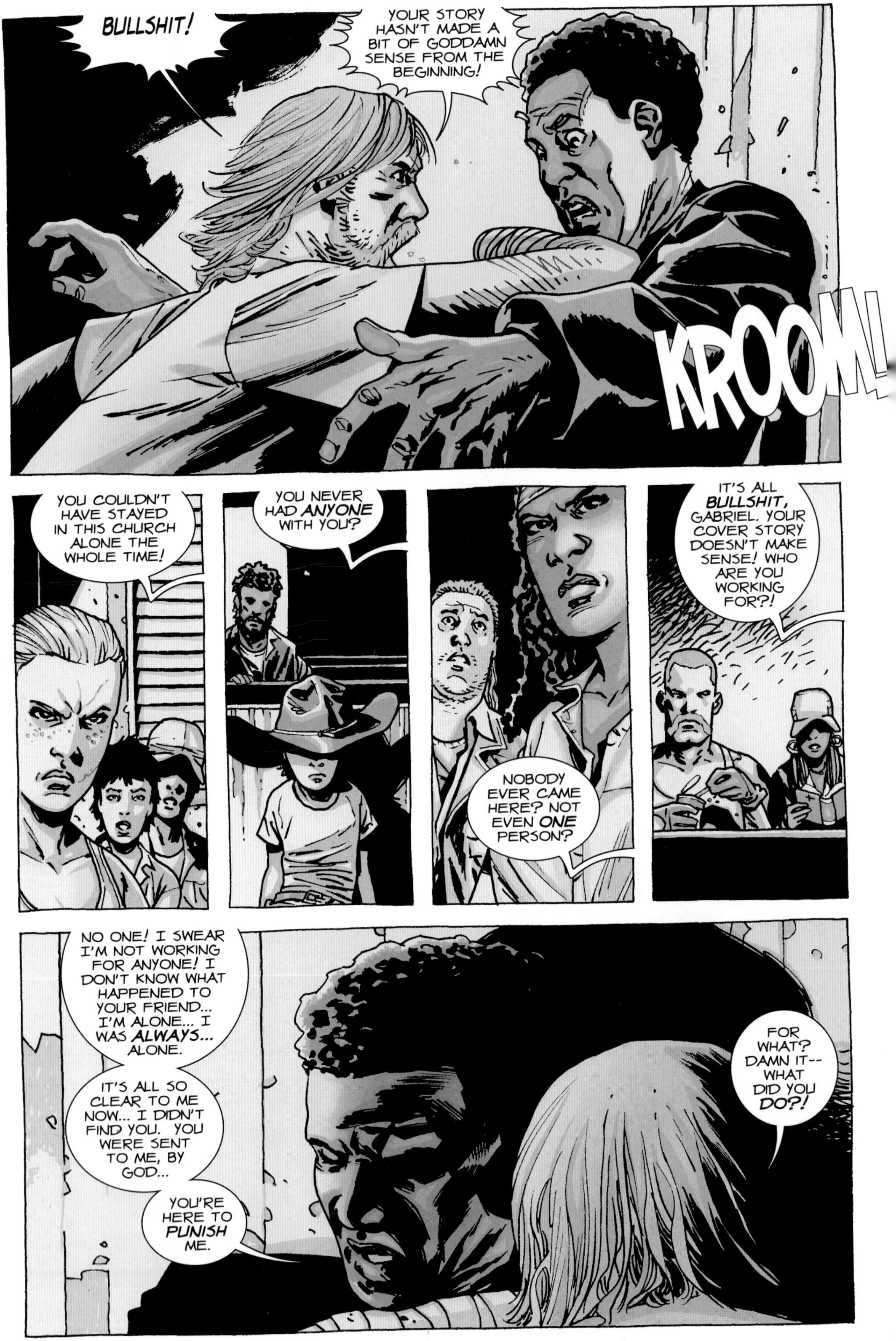
BULLSHIT!
YOUR STORY HASN'T MADE A BIT OF GODDAMN SENSE FROM THE BEGINNING!
KROOM!
YOU COULDN'T HAVE STAYED IN THIS CHURCH ALONE THE WHOLE TIME!
YOU NEVER HAD ANYONE WITH YOU?
NOBODY EVER CAME HERE? NOT EVEN ONE PERSON?
IT'S ALL BULLSHIT, GABRIEL. YOUR COVER STORY DOESN'T MAKE SENSE! WHO ARE YOU WORKING FOR?!
NO ONE! I SWEAR I'M NOT WORKING FOR ANYONE! I DON'T KNOW WHAT HAPPENED TO YOUR FRIEND... I'M ALONE... I WAS ALWAYS... ALONE.
FOR WHAT? DAMN IT-- WHAT DID YOU DO?!
IT'S ALL SO CLEAR TO ME NOW... I DIDN'T FIND YOU. YOU WERE SENT TO ME, BY GOD...
YOU'RE HERE TO PUNISH ME.

WHEN IT ALL STARTED, I WAS *HERE*--ALONE. IT WAS LATE AT NIGHT WHEN I FIRST HEARD ABOUT EVERYTHING. I GOT SCARED--I LOCKED UP--JUST TO BE SAFE.

THE NEXT MORNING... THEY STARTED COMING.

NEIGHBORS, FRIENDS... MEMBERS OF MY CONGREGATION... NOT MANY AT FIRST, THEN MORE AS THE DAYS WENT ON. THEY WANTED A SAFE PLACE TO STAY--A SANCTUARY.

I TURNED THEM ALL AWAY...

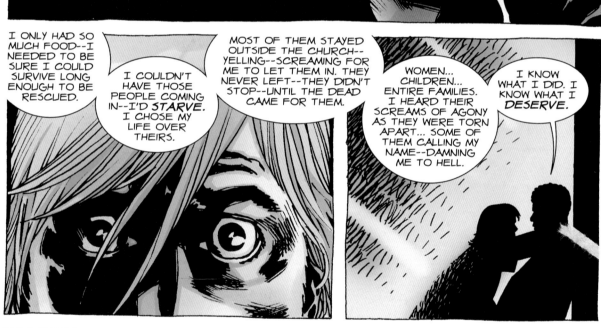

I ONLY HAD SO MUCH FOOD--I NEEDED TO BE SURE I COULD SURVIVE LONG ENOUGH TO BE RESCUED.

I COULDN'T HAVE THOSE PEOPLE COMING IN--I'D *STARVE*. I CHOSE MY LIFE OVER THEIRS.

MOST OF THEM STAYED OUTSIDE THE CHURCH-- YELLING--SCREAMING FOR ME TO LET THEM IN. THEY NEVER LEFT--THEY DIDN'T STOP--UNTIL THE DEAD CAME FOR THEM.

WOMEN... CHILDREN... ENTIRE FAMILIES. I HEARD THEIR SCREAMS OF AGONY AS THEY WERE TORN APART... SOME OF THEM CALLING MY NAME--DAMNING ME TO HELL.

I KNOW WHAT I DID. I KNOW WHAT I *DESERVE*.

KILL ME. PLEASE, I'VE SUFFERED ENOUGH--I *WANT* YOU TO DO IT.

I FORGIVE YOU. KILL ME AND I FORGIVE YOU. YOU ARE ONLY CARRYING OUT GOD'S WILL.

THEY DIED-- THEY *ALL* DIED BECAUSE OF ME.

YOU HAVE TO MAKE THIS RIGHT.

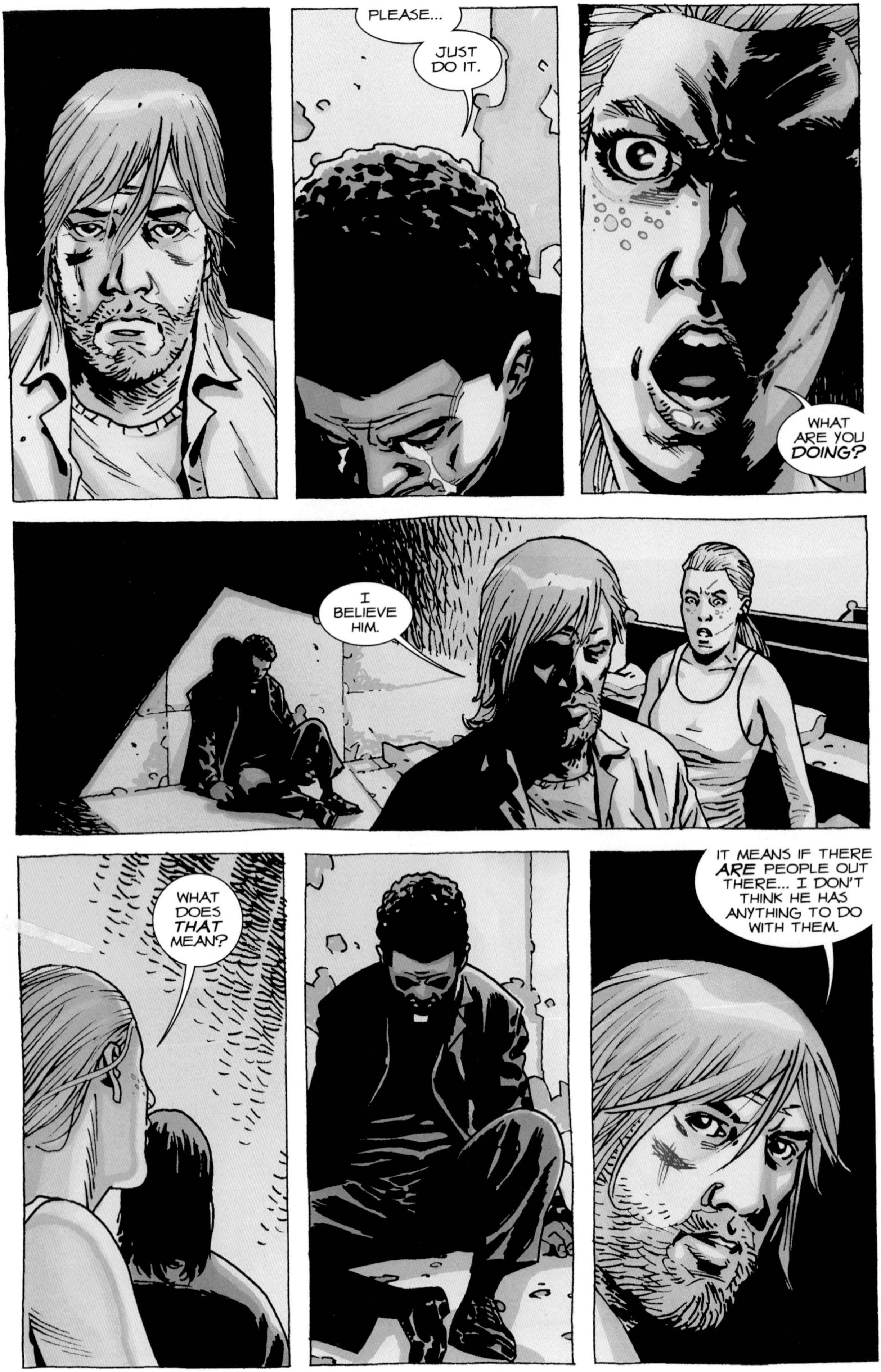
PLEASE...
JUST DO IT.
WHAT ARE YOU DOING?
I BELIEVE HIM.
WHAT DOES THAT MEAN?
IT MEANS IF THERE ARE PEOPLE OUT THERE... I DON'T THINK HE HAS ANYTHING TO DO WITH THEM.

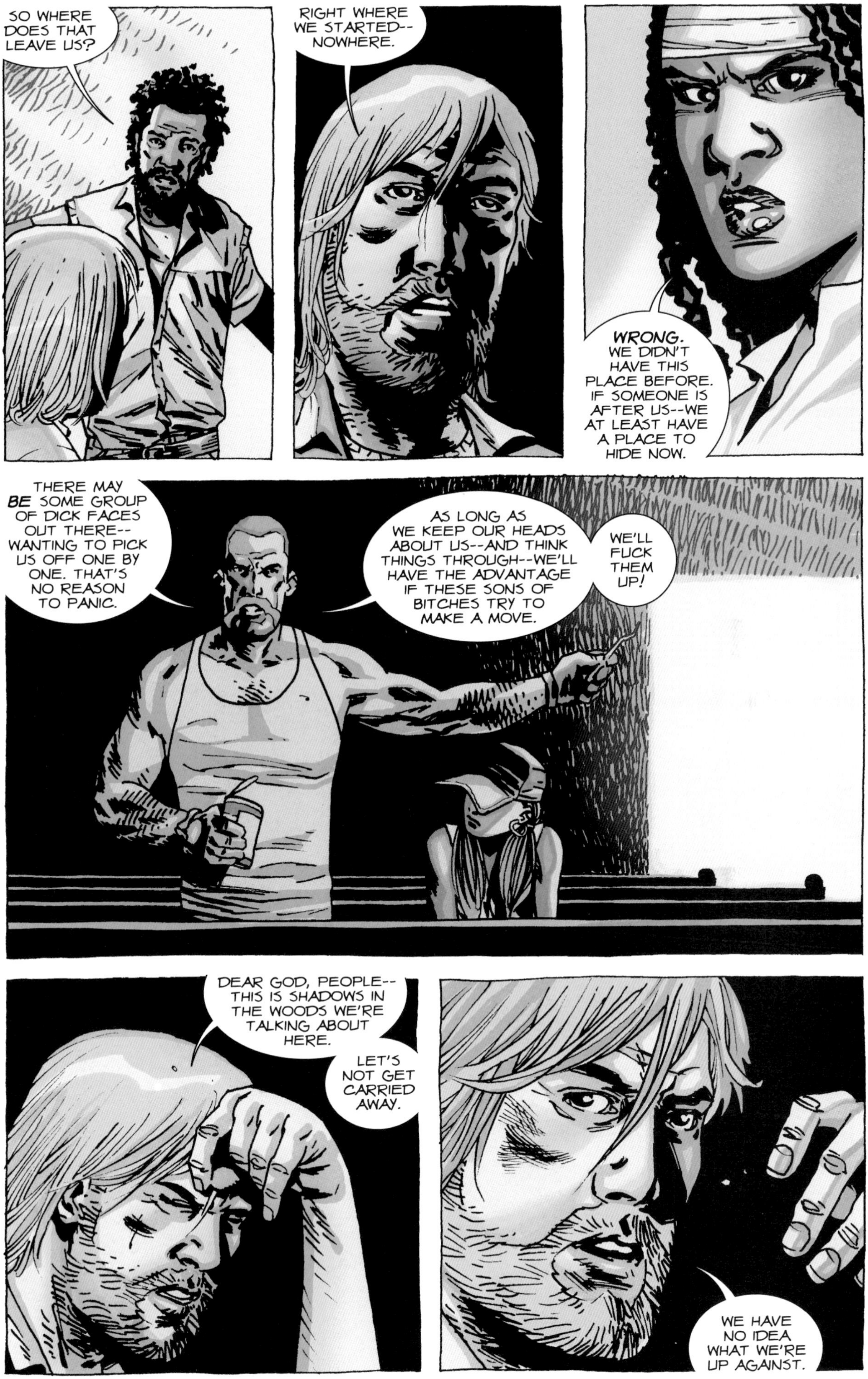
SO WHERE DOES THAT LEAVE US?
RIGHT WHERE WE STARTED-- NOWHERE.
WRONG. WE DIDN'T HAVE THIS PLACE BEFORE. IF SOMEONE IS AFTER US--WE AT LEAST HAVE A PLACE TO HIDE NOW.
THERE MAY BE SOME GROUP OF DICK FACES OUT THERE-- WANTING TO PICK US OFF ONE BY ONE. THAT'S NO REASON TO PANIC.
AS LONG AS WE KEEP OUR HEADS ABOUT US--AND THINK THINGS THROUGH--WE'LL HAVE THE ADVANTAGE IF THESE SONS OF BITCHES TRY TO MAKE A MOVE.
WE'LL FUCK THEM UP!
DEAR GOD, PEOPLE-- THIS IS SHADOWS IN THE WOODS WE'RE TALKING ABOUT HERE.
LET'S NOT GET CARRIED AWAY.
WE HAVE NO IDEA WHAT WE'RE UP AGAINST.

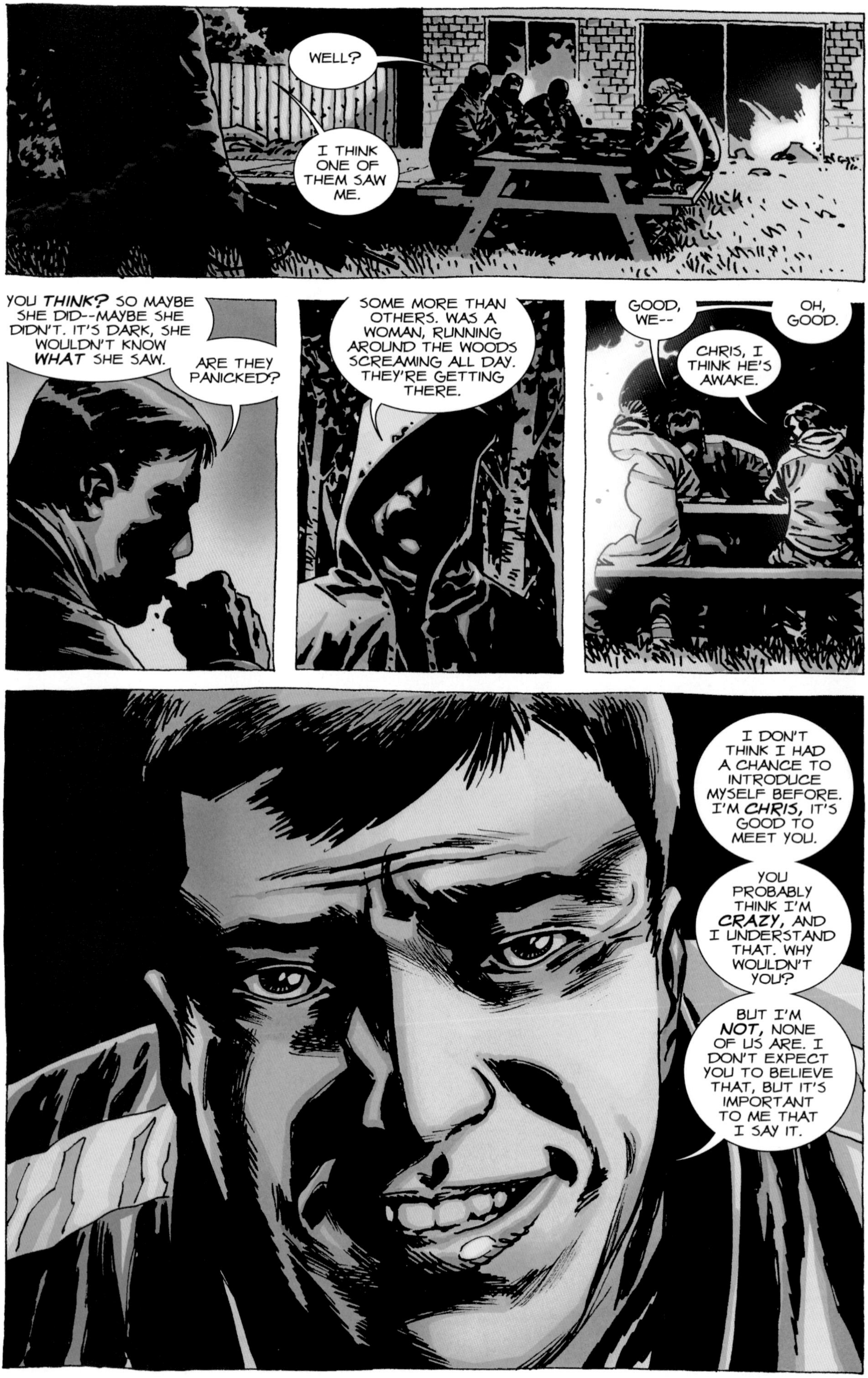
WELL?
I THINK ONE OF THEM SAW ME.
YOU THINK? SO MAYBE SHE DID--MAYBE SHE DIDN'T. IT'S DARK, SHE WOULDN'T KNOW WHAT SHE SAW.
ARE THEY PANICKED?
SOME MORE THAN OTHERS. WAS A WOMAN, RUNNING AROUND THE WOODS SCREAMING ALL DAY. THEY'RE GETTING THERE.
GOOD, WE--
OH, GOOD.
CHRIS, I THINK HE'S AWAKE.
I DON'T THINK I HAD A CHANCE TO INTRODUCE MYSELF BEFORE. I'M CHRIS, IT'S GOOD TO MEET YOU.
YOU PROBABLY THINK I'M CRAZY, AND I UNDERSTAND THAT. WHY WOULDN'T YOU?
BUT I'M NOT, NONE OF US ARE. I DON'T EXPECT YOU TO BELIEVE THAT, BUT IT'S IMPORTANT TO ME THAT I SAY IT.

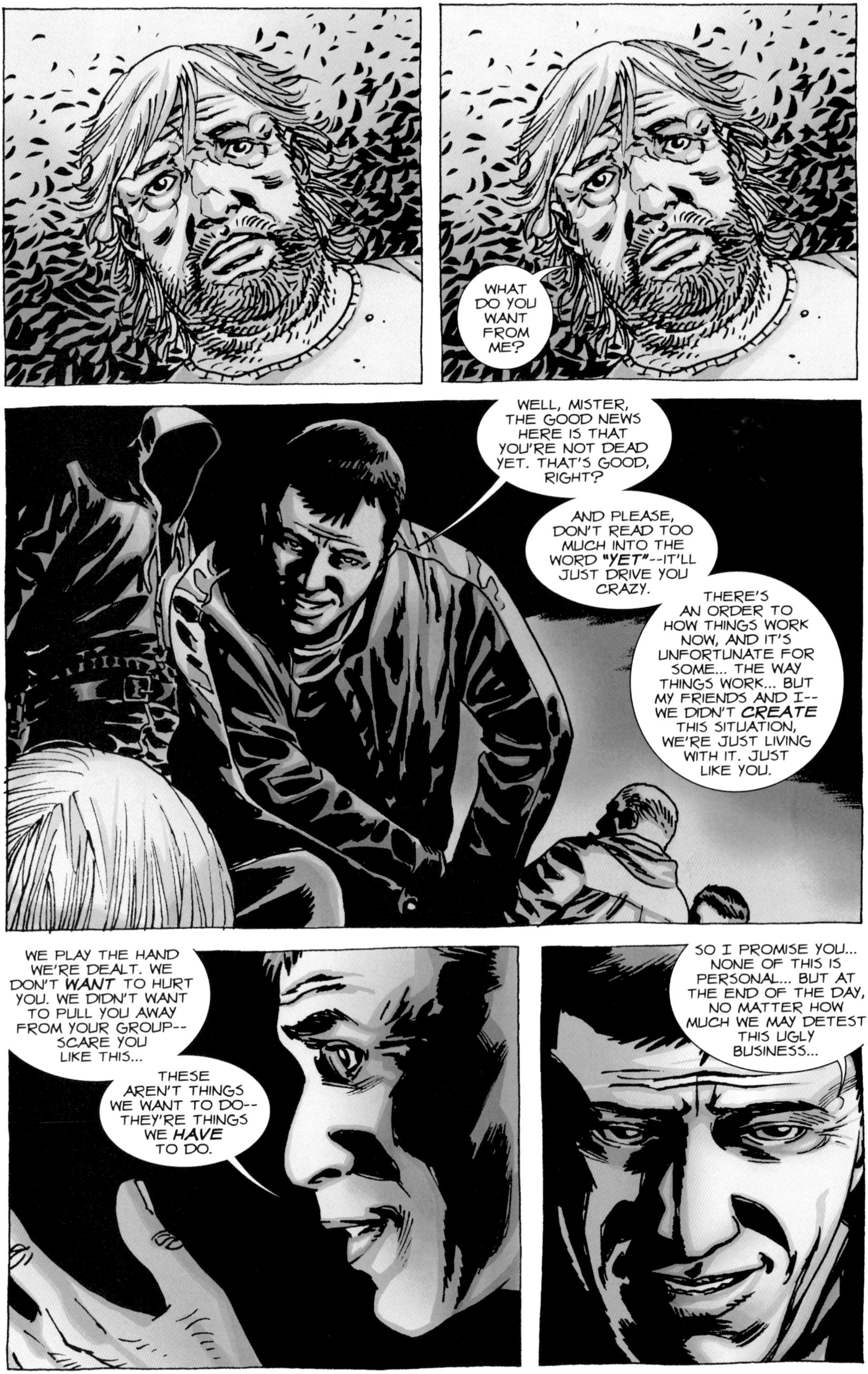
WHAT DO YOU WANT FROM ME?
WELL, MISTER, THE GOOD NEWS HERE IS THAT YOU'RE NOT DEAD YET. THAT'S GOOD, RIGHT?
AND PLEASE, DON'T READ TOO MUCH INTO THE WORD "YET"--IT'LL JUST DRIVE YOU CRAZY.
THERE'S AN ORDER TO HOW THINGS WORK NOW, AND IT'S UNFORTUNATE FOR SOME... THE WAY THINGS WORK... BUT MY FRIENDS AND I-- WE DIDN'T CREATE THIS SITUATION, WE'RE JUST LIVING WITH IT. JUST LIKE YOU.
WE PLAY THE HAND WE'RE DEALT. WE DON'T WANT TO HURT YOU. WE DIDN'T WANT TO PULL YOU AWAY FROM YOUR GROUP-- SCARE YOU LIKE THIS...
THESE AREN'T THINGS WE WANT TO DO-- THEY'RE THINGS WE HAVE TO DO.
SO I PROMISE YOU... NONE OF THIS IS PERSONAL... BUT AT THE END OF THE DAY, NO MATTER HOW MUCH WE MAY DETEST THIS UGLY BUSINESS...

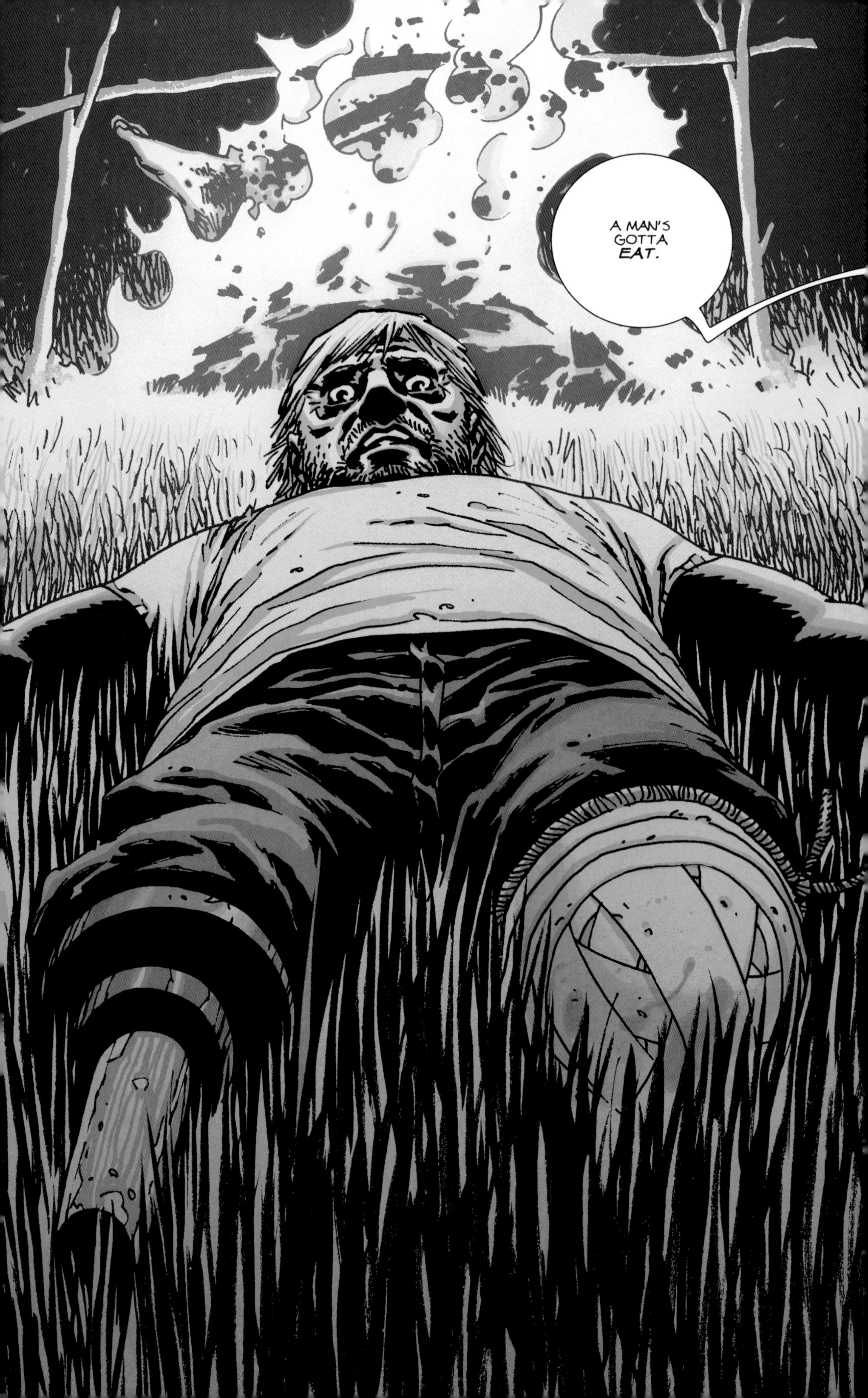
A MAN'S GOTTA EAT.

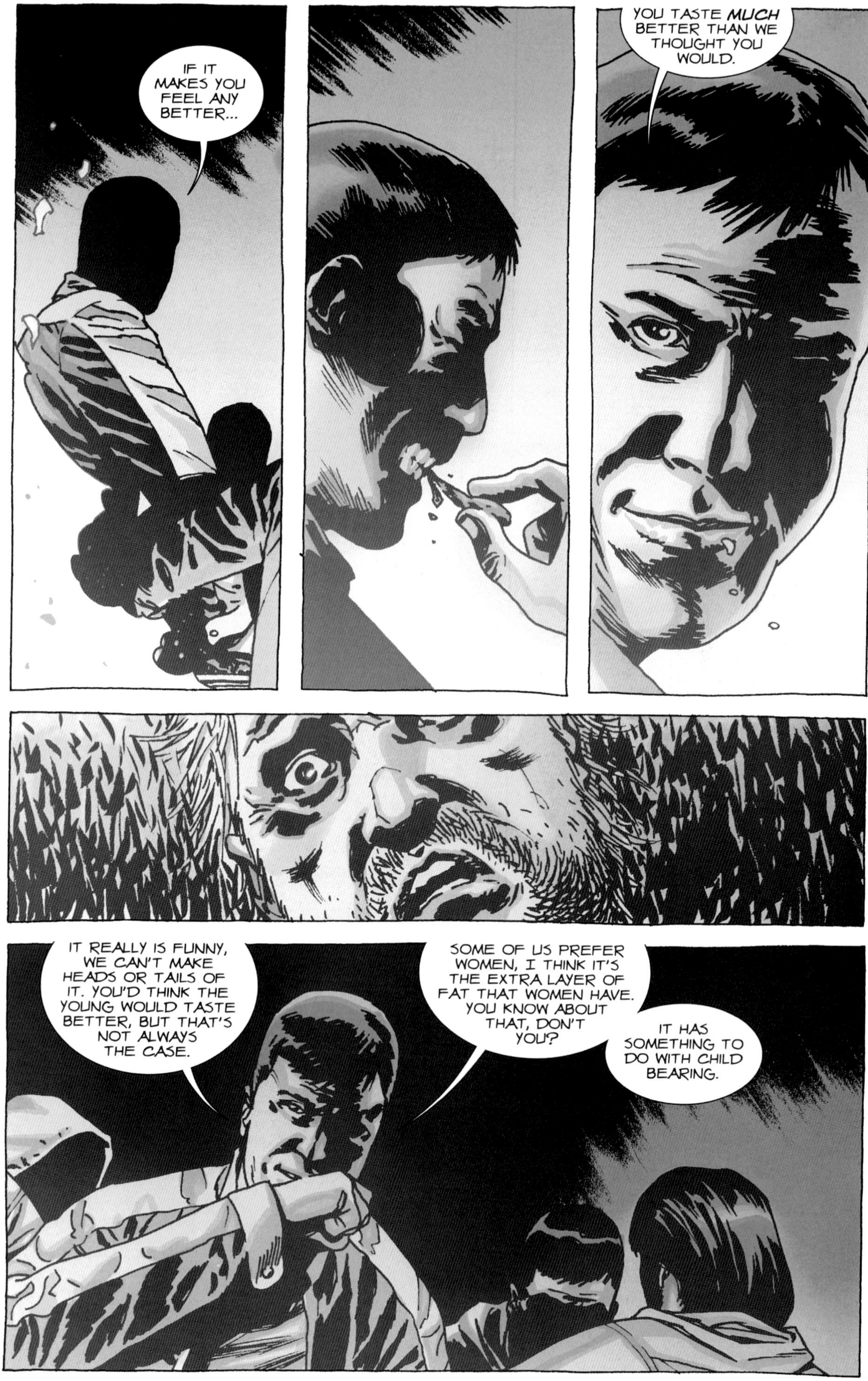
IF IT MAKES YOU FEEL ANY BETTER...
YOU TASTE MUCH BETTER THAN WE THOUGHT YOU WOULD.
IT REALLY IS FUNNY, WE CAN'T MAKE HEADS OR TAILS OF IT. YOU'D THINK THE YOUNG WOULD TASTE BETTER, BUT THAT'S NOT ALWAYS THE CASE.
SOME OF US PREFER WOMEN, I THINK IT'S THE EXTRA LAYER OF FAT THAT WOMEN HAVE. YOU KNOW ABOUT THAT, DON'T YOU?
IT HAS SOMETHING TO DO WITH CHILD BEARING.

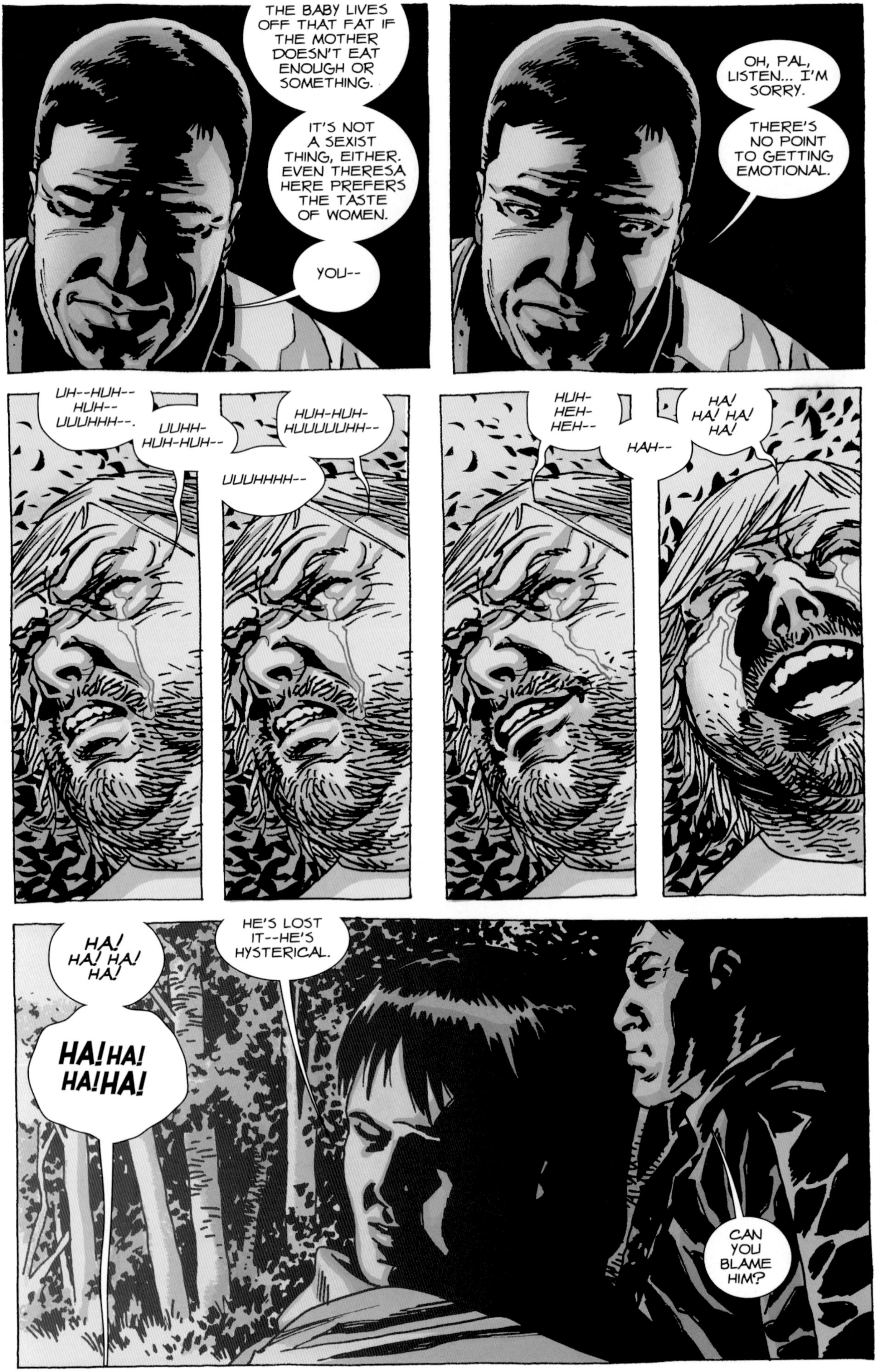

THE BABY LIVES OFF THAT FAT IF THE MOTHER DOESN'T EAT ENOUGH OR SOMETHING.
IT'S NOT A SEXIST THING, EITHER. EVEN THERESA HERE PREFERS THE TASTE OF WOMEN.
YOU--
OH, PAL, LISTEN... I'M SORRY.
THERE'S NO POINT TO GETTING EMOTIONAL.
UH--HUH-- HUH-- UUUHHH--.
UUHH-HUH-HUH--
HUH-HUH-HUUUUUHH--
UUUHHHH--
HUH-HEH-HEH--
HAH--
HA! HA! HA! HA!
HA! HA! HA! HA!
HA!HA! HA!HA!
HE'S LOST IT--HE'S HYSTERICAL.
CAN YOU BLAME HIM?

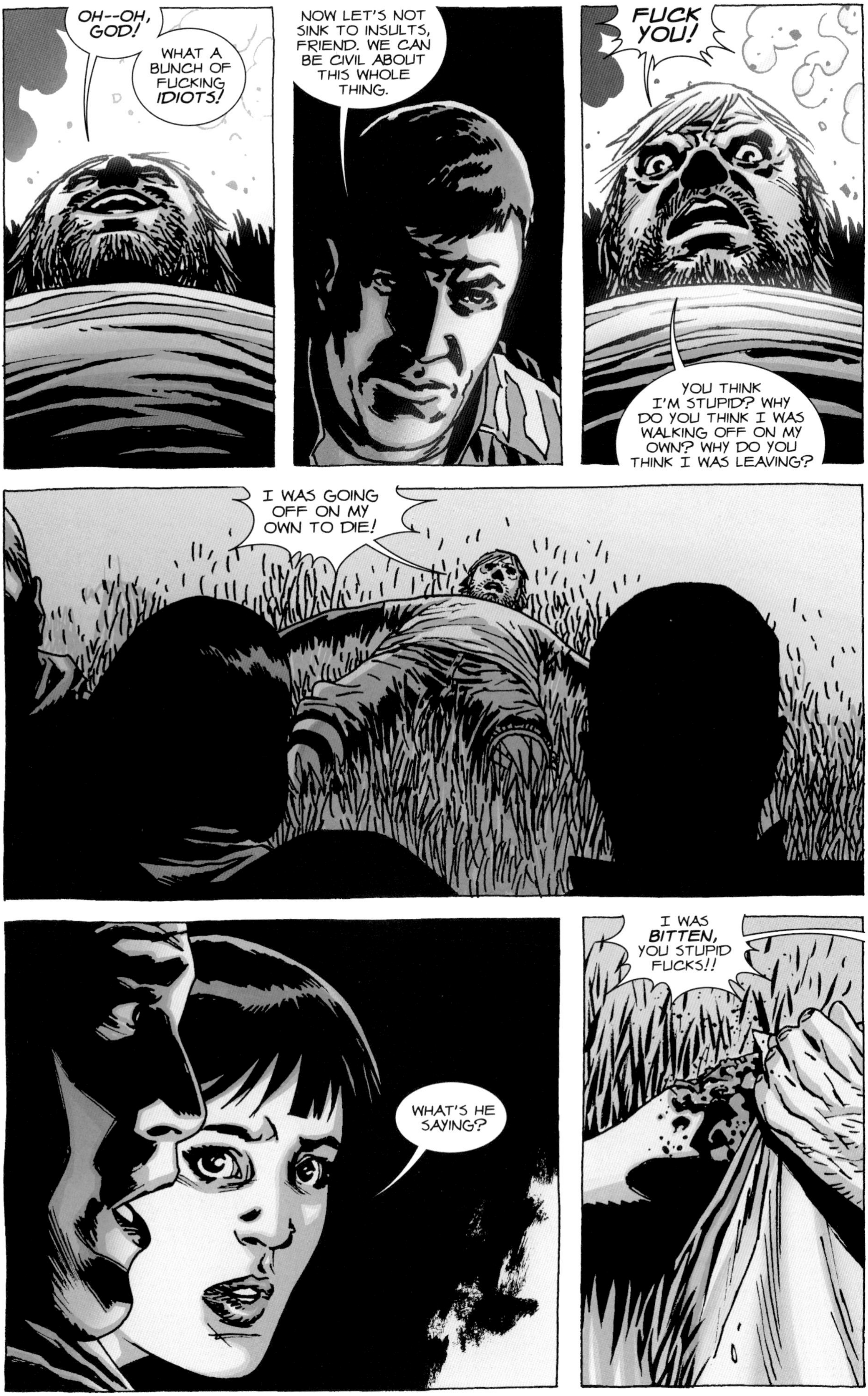
OH--OH, GOD!
WHAT A BUNCH OF FUCKING *IDIOTS!*
NOW LET'S NOT SINK TO INSULTS, FRIEND. WE CAN BE CIVIL ABOUT THIS WHOLE THING.
FUCK YOU!
YOU THINK I'M STUPID? WHY DO YOU THINK I WAS WALKING OFF ON MY OWN? WHY DO YOU THINK I WAS LEAVING?
I WAS GOING OFF ON MY OWN TO DIE!
WHAT'S HE SAYING?
I WAS *BITTEN,* YOU STUPID FUCKS!!

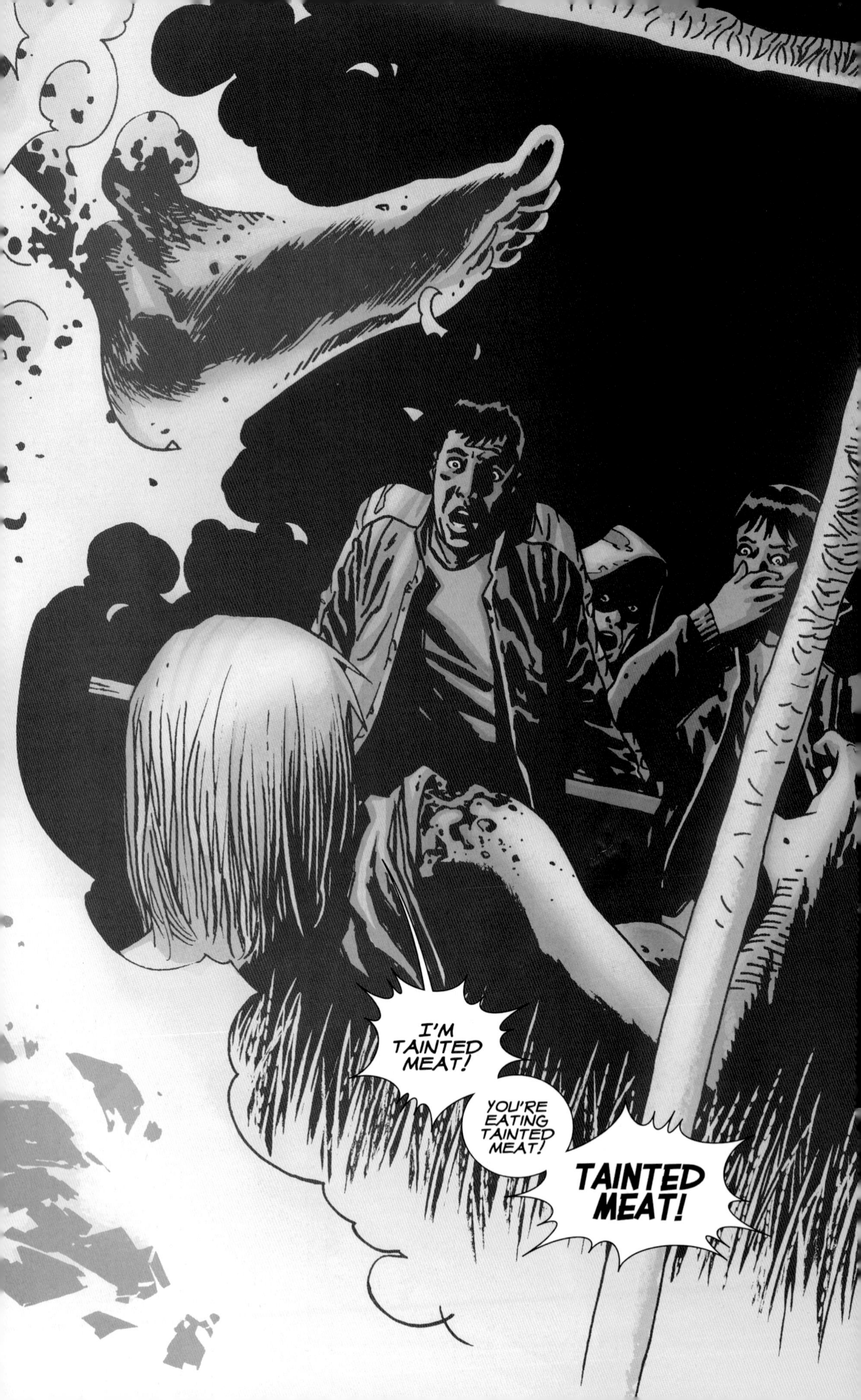
I'M TAINTED MEAT!
YOU'RE EATING TAINTED MEAT!
TAINTED MEAT!

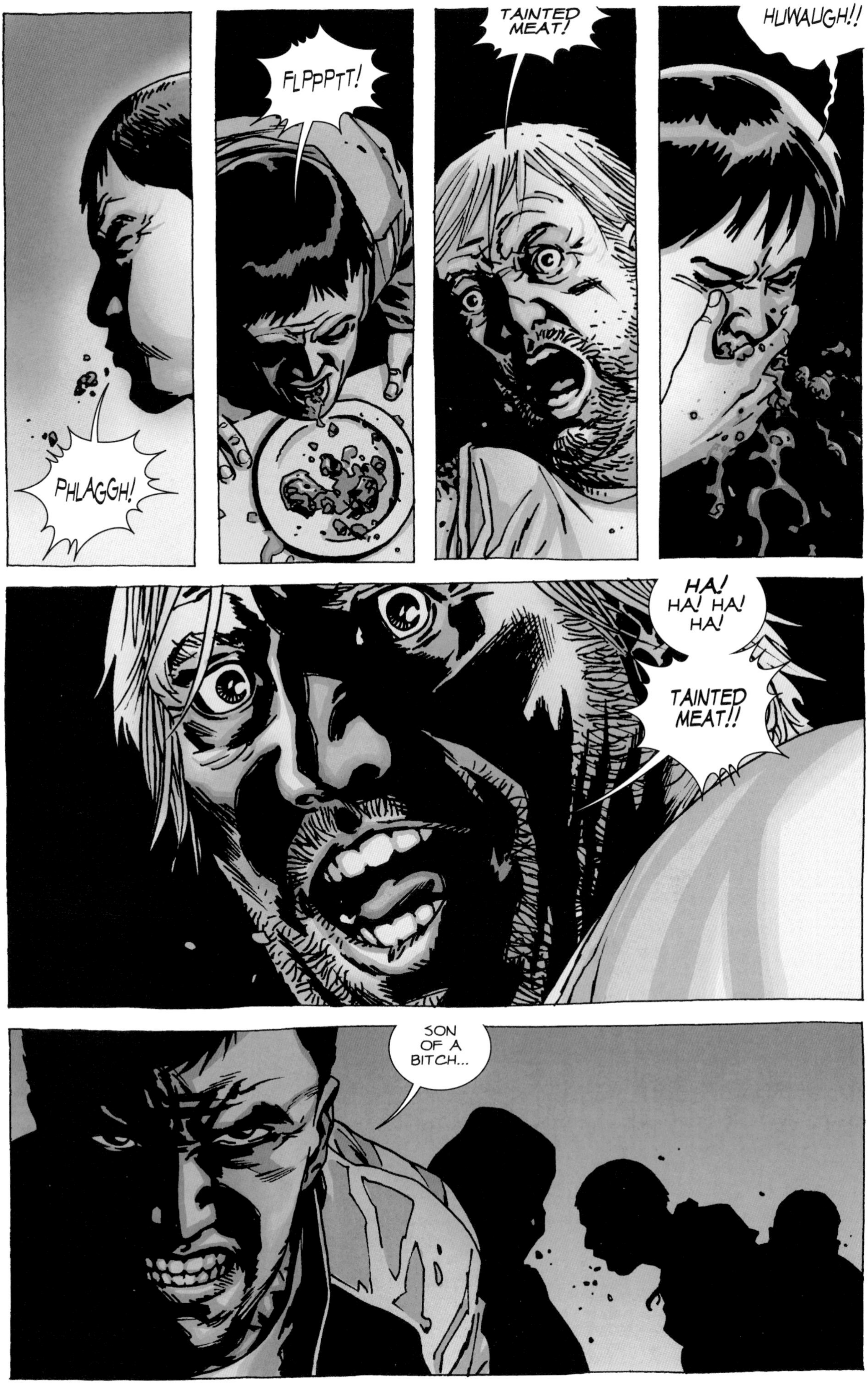
PHLAGGH!
FLPPPTT!
TAINTED MEAT!
HUWAUGH!!
HA! HA! HA! HA!
TAINTED MEAT!!
SON OF A BITCH...

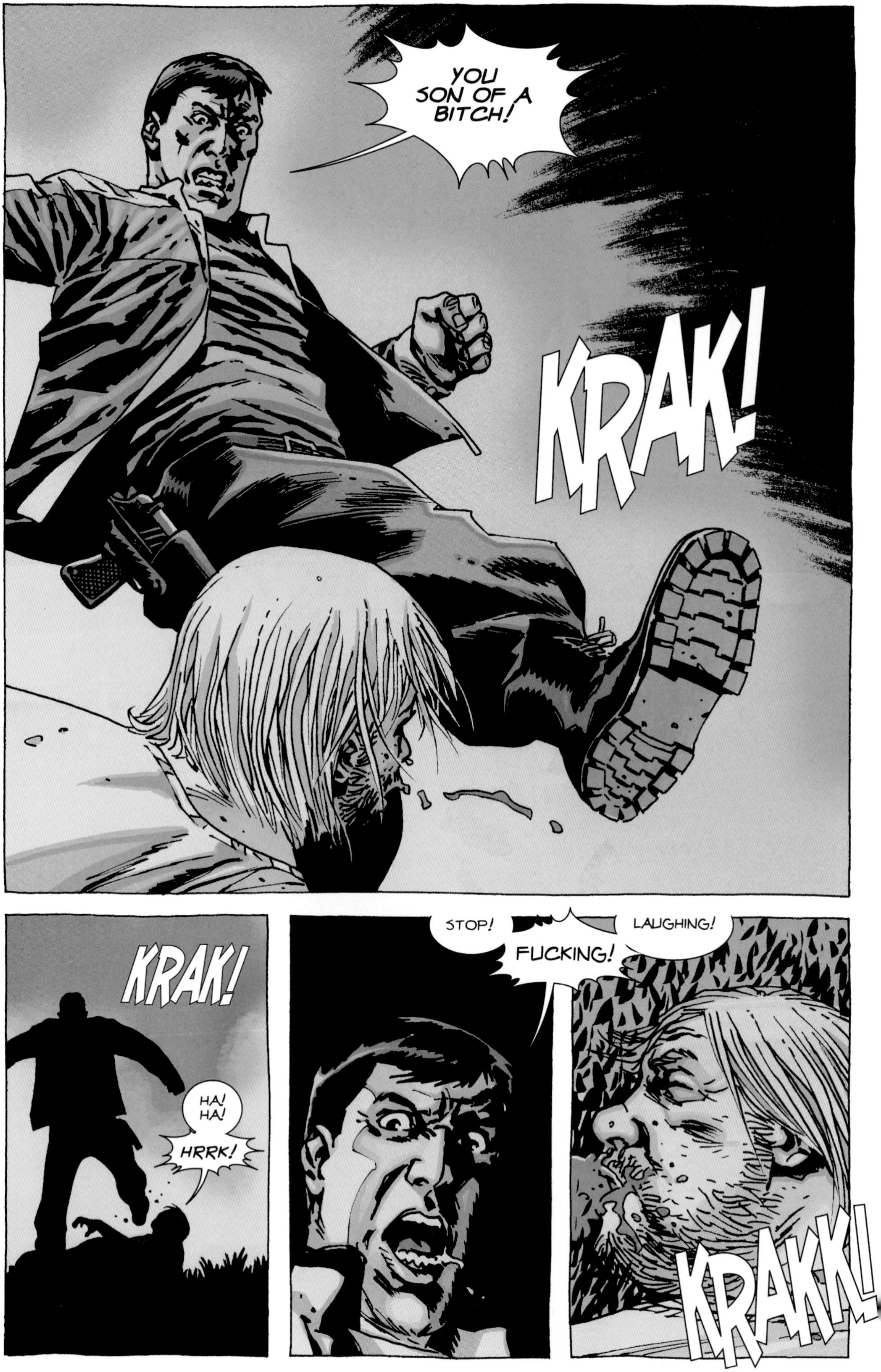
YOU SON OF A BITCH!
KRAK!
KRAK!
HA! HA!
HRRK!
STOP!
FUCKING!
LAUGHING!
KRAKK!

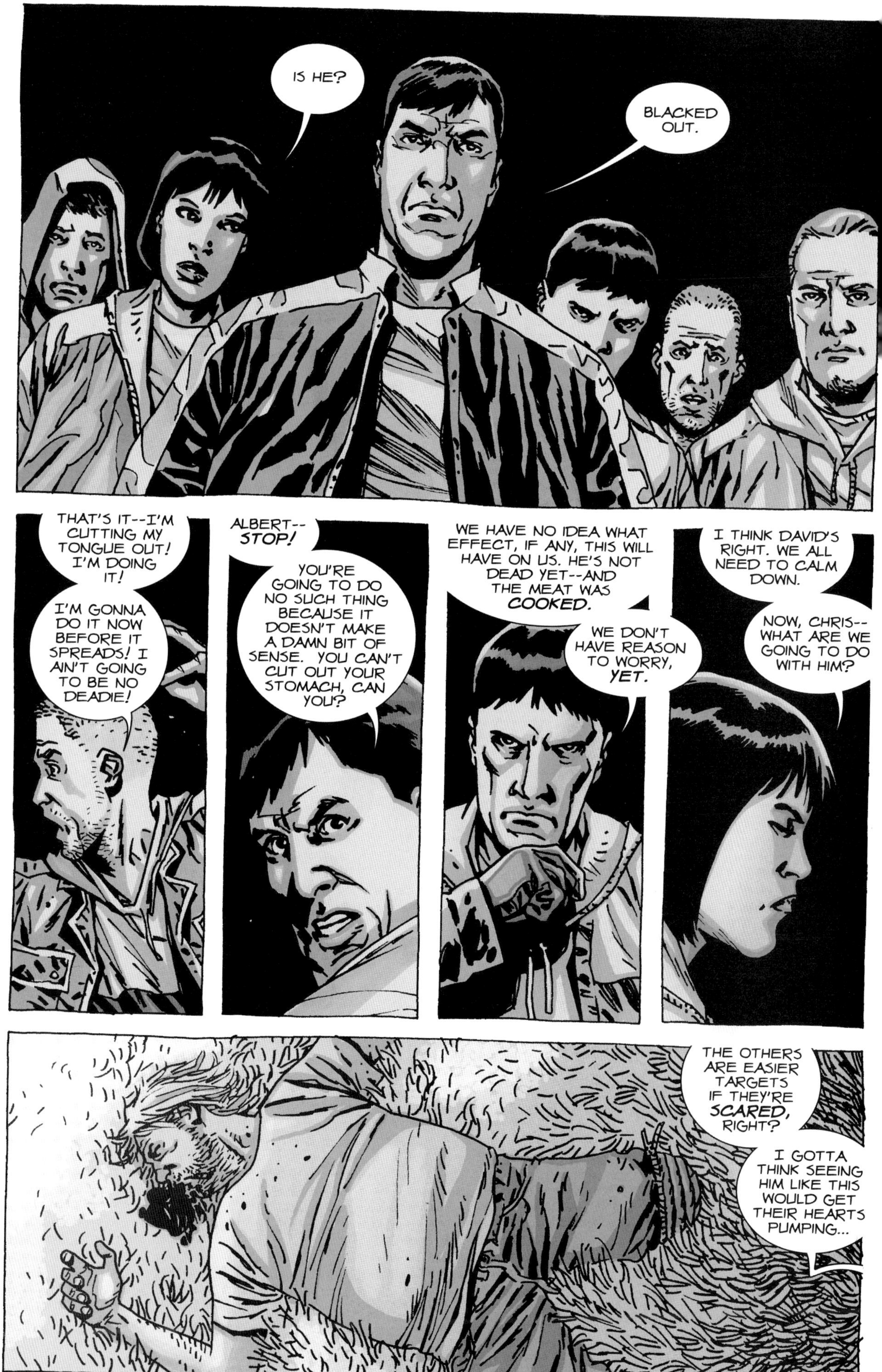
IS HE?
BLACKED OUT.
THAT'S IT--I'M CUTTING MY TONGUE OUT! I'M DOING IT!
I'M GONNA DO IT NOW BEFORE IT SPREADS! I AIN'T GOING TO BE NO DEADIE!
ALBERT-- STOP!
YOU'RE GOING TO DO NO SUCH THING BECAUSE IT DOESN'T MAKE A DAMN BIT OF SENSE. YOU CAN'T CUT OUT YOUR STOMACH, CAN YOU?
WE HAVE NO IDEA WHAT EFFECT, IF ANY, THIS WILL HAVE ON US. HE'S NOT DEAD YET--AND THE MEAT WAS COOKED.
WE DON'T HAVE REASON TO WORRY, YET.
I THINK DAVID'S RIGHT. WE ALL NEED TO CALM DOWN.
NOW, CHRIS-- WHAT ARE WE GOING TO DO WITH HIM?
THE OTHERS ARE EASIER TARGETS IF THEY'RE SCARED, RIGHT?
I GOTTA THINK SEEING HIM LIKE THIS WOULD GET THEIR HEARTS PUMPING...

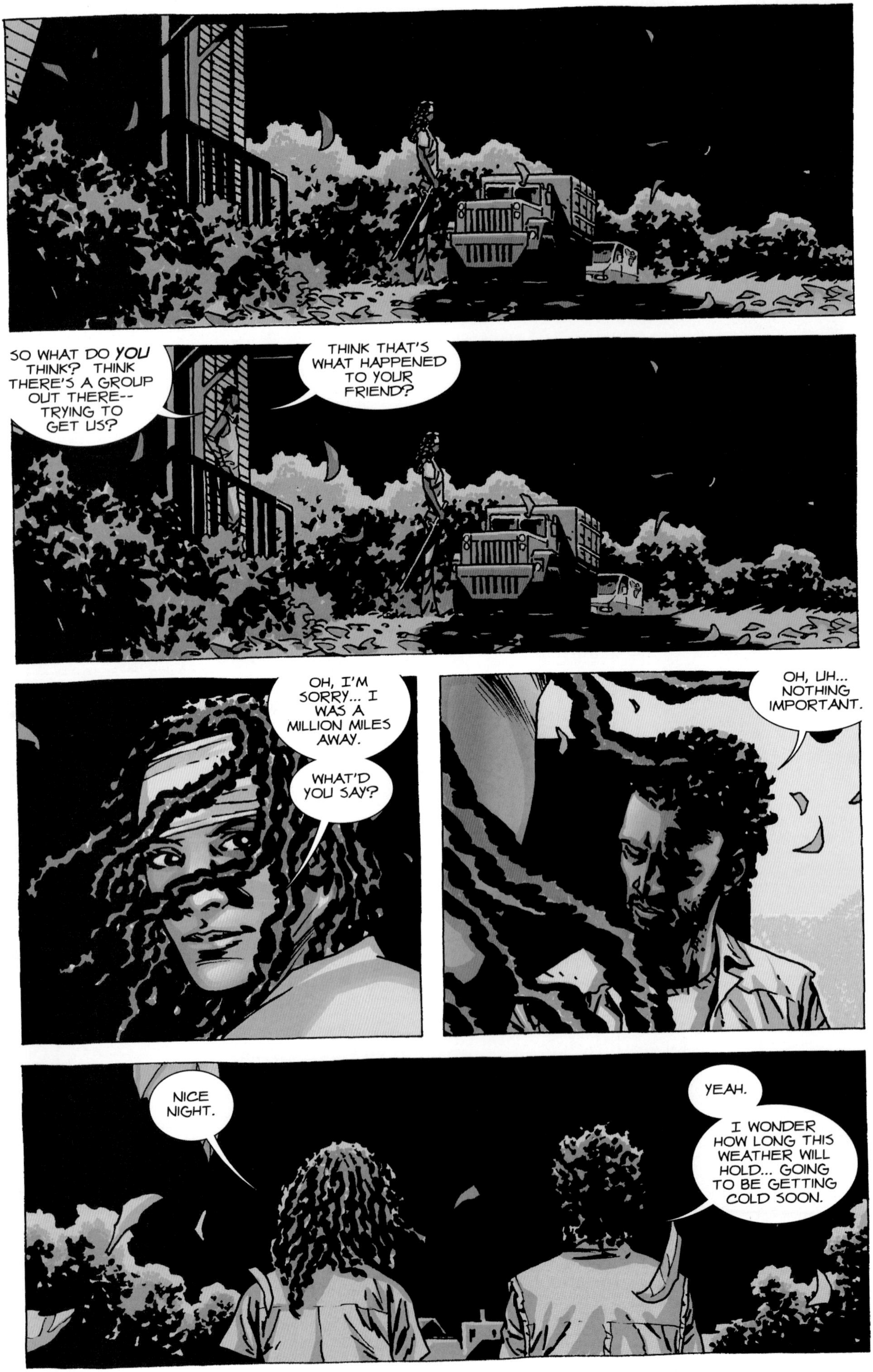
SO WHAT DO YOU THINK? THINK THERE'S A GROUP OUT THERE-- TRYING TO GET US?
THINK THAT'S WHAT HAPPENED TO YOUR FRIEND?
OH, I'M SORRY... I WAS A MILLION MILES AWAY.
WHAT'D YOU SAY?
OH, UH... NOTHING IMPORTANT.
NICE NIGHT.
YEAH.
I WONDER HOW LONG THIS WEATHER WILL HOLD... GOING TO BE GETTING COLD SOON.

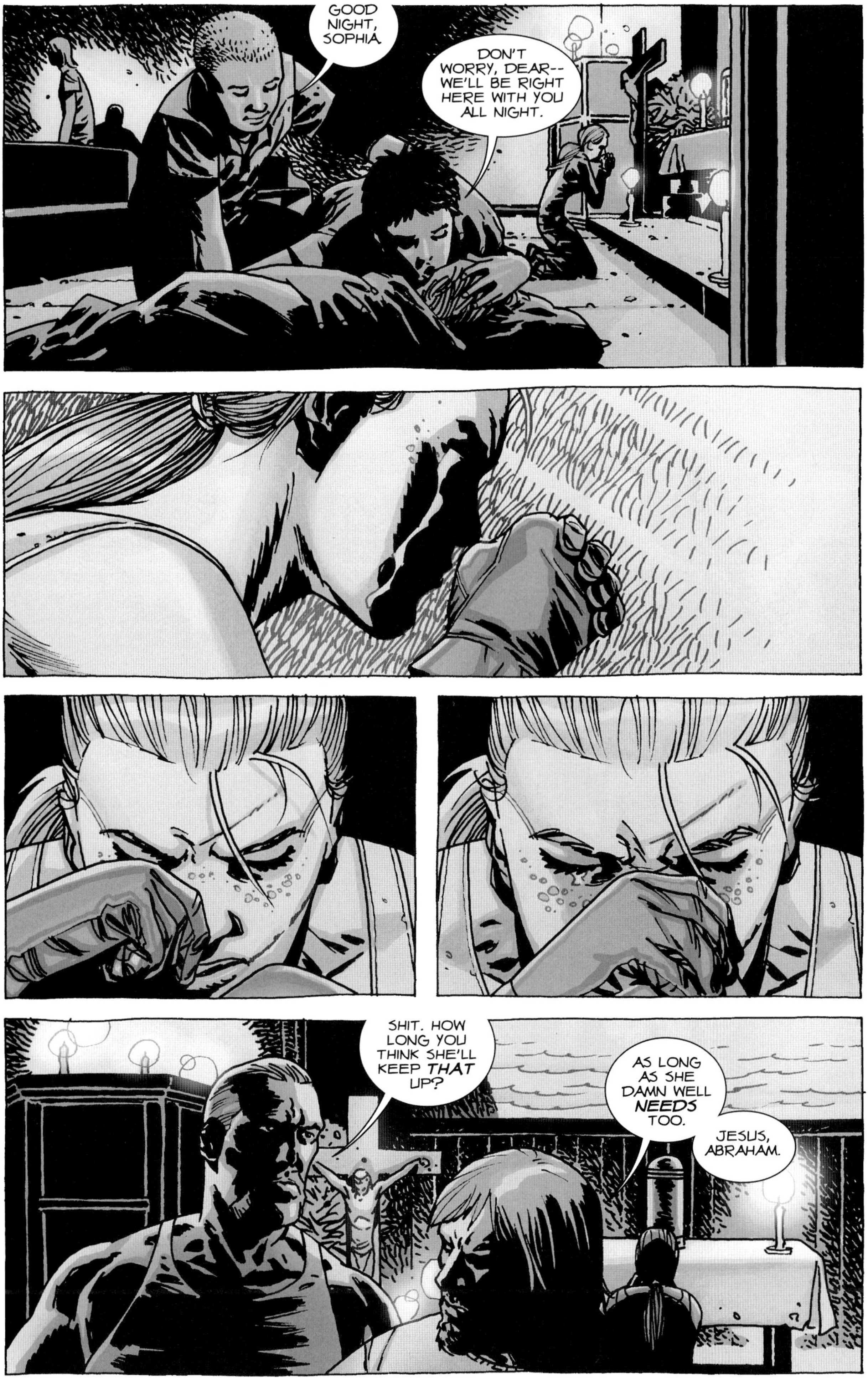
GOOD NIGHT, SOPHIA.
DON'T WORRY, DEAR-- WE'LL BE RIGHT HERE WITH YOU ALL NIGHT.
SHIT. HOW LONG YOU THINK SHE'LL KEEP THAT UP?
AS LONG AS SHE DAMN WELL NEEDS TOO.
JESUS, ABRAHAM.

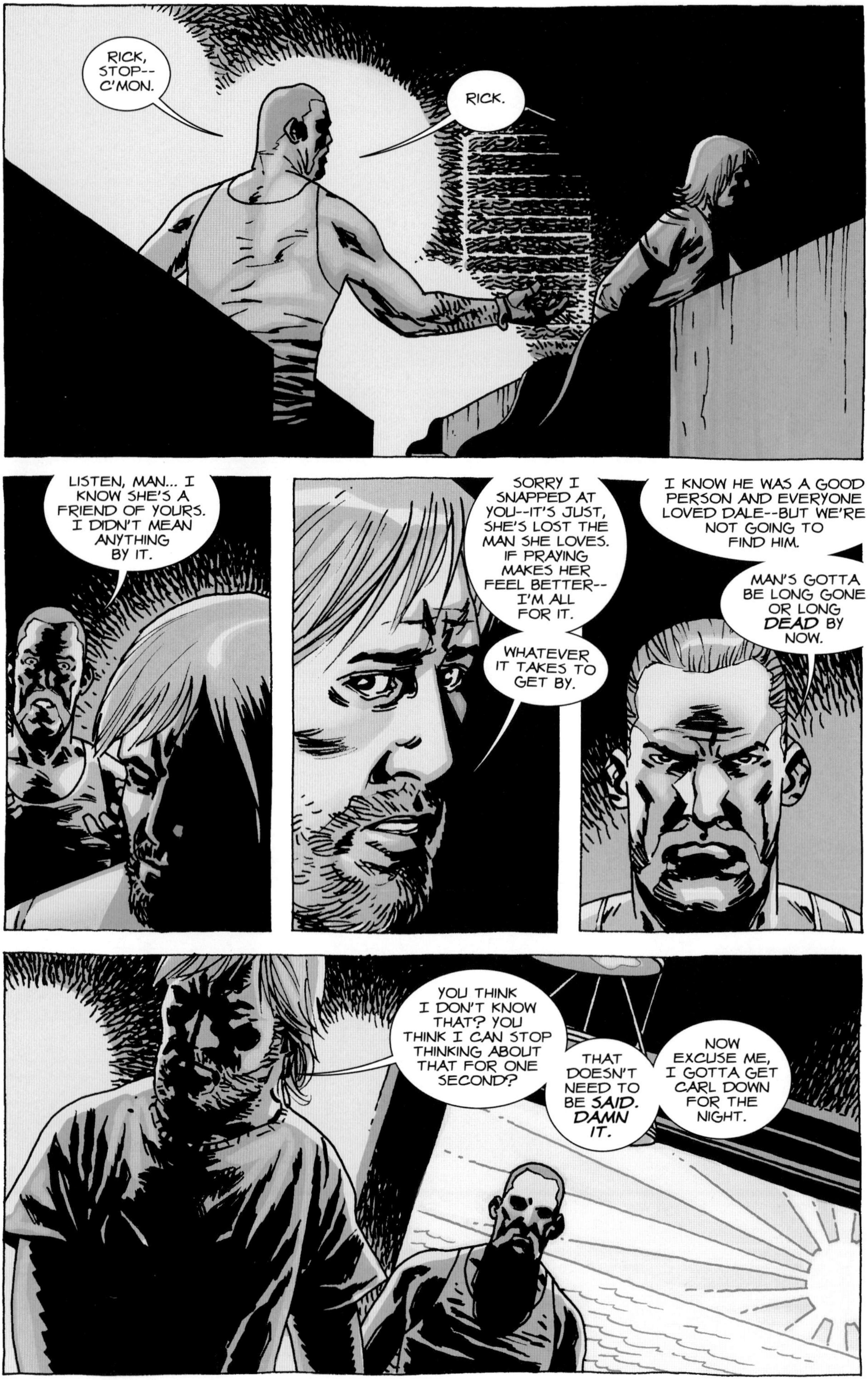
RICK, STOP-- C'MON.
RICK.
LISTEN, MAN... I KNOW SHE'S A FRIEND OF YOURS. I DIDN'T MEAN ANYTHING BY IT.
SORRY I SNAPPED AT YOU--IT'S JUST, SHE'S LOST THE MAN SHE LOVES. IF PRAYING MAKES HER FEEL BETTER-- I'M ALL FOR IT.
WHATEVER IT TAKES TO GET BY.
I KNOW HE WAS A GOOD PERSON AND EVERYONE LOVED DALE--BUT WE'RE NOT GOING TO FIND HIM.
MAN'S GOTTA BE LONG GONE OR LONG DEAD BY NOW.
YOU THINK I DON'T KNOW THAT? YOU THINK I CAN STOP THINKING ABOUT THAT FOR ONE SECOND?
THAT DOESN'T NEED TO BE SAID. DAMN IT.
NOW EXCUSE ME, I GOTTA GET CARL DOWN FOR THE NIGHT.

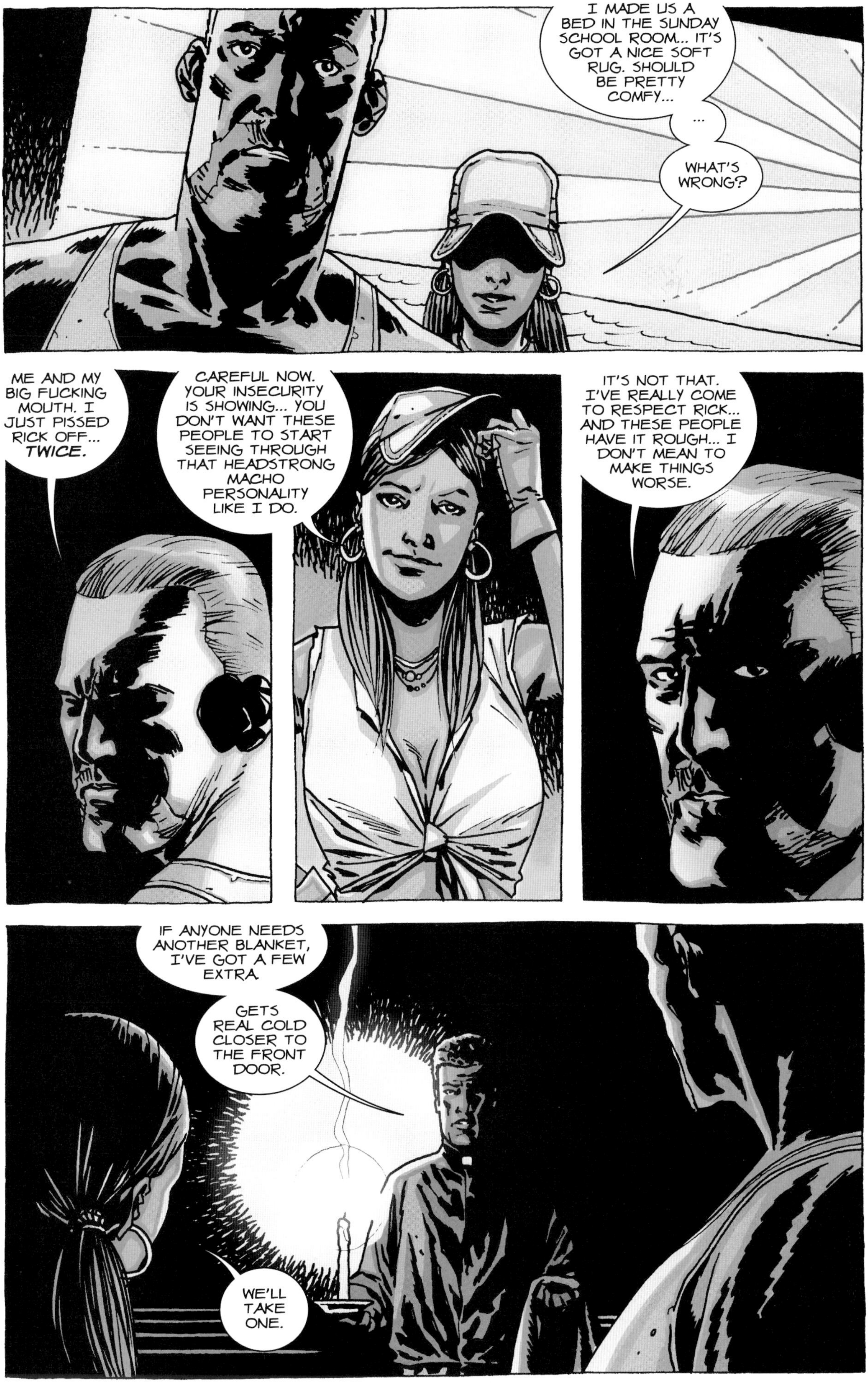
I MADE US A BED IN THE SUNDAY SCHOOL ROOM... IT'S GOT A NICE SOFT RUG. SHOULD BE PRETTY COMFY...
...
WHAT'S WRONG?
ME AND MY BIG FUCKING MOUTH. I JUST PISSED RICK OFF... TWICE.
CAREFUL NOW. YOUR INSECURITY IS SHOWING... YOU DON'T WANT THESE PEOPLE TO START SEEING THROUGH THAT HEADSTRONG MACHO PERSONALITY LIKE I DO.
IT'S NOT THAT. I'VE REALLY COME TO RESPECT RICK... AND THESE PEOPLE HAVE IT ROUGH... I DON'T MEAN TO MAKE THINGS WORSE.
IF ANYONE NEEDS ANOTHER BLANKET, I'VE GOT A FEW EXTRA.
GETS REAL COLD CLOSER TO THE FRONT DOOR.
WE'LL TAKE ONE.

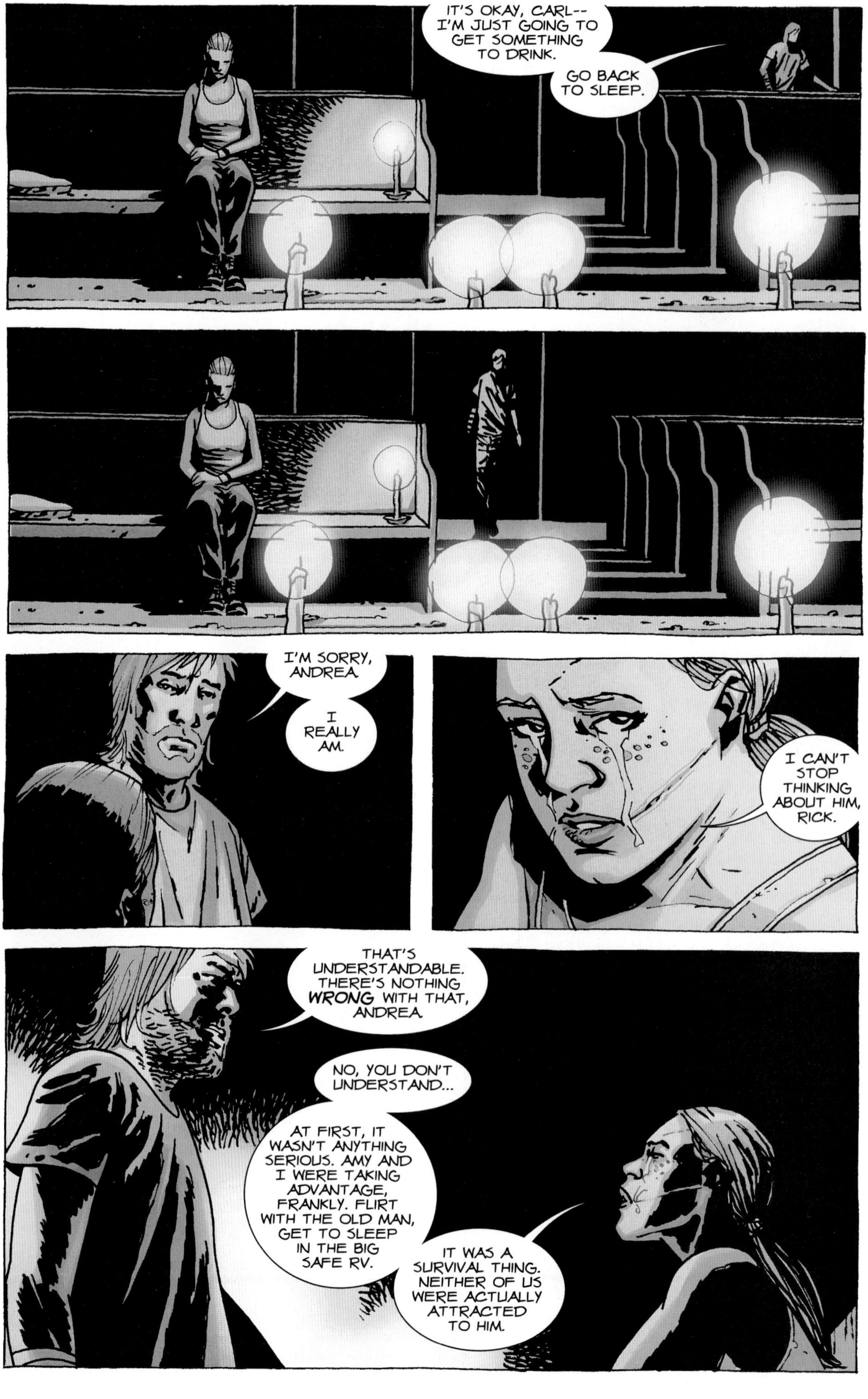
IT'S OKAY, CARL-- I'M JUST GOING TO GET SOMETHING TO DRINK.
GO BACK TO SLEEP.
I'M SORRY, ANDREA.
I REALLY AM.
I CAN'T STOP THINKING ABOUT HIM, RICK.
THAT'S UNDERSTANDABLE. THERE'S NOTHING WRONG WITH THAT, ANDREA.
NO, YOU DON'T UNDERSTAND...
AT FIRST, IT WASN'T ANYTHING SERIOUS. AMY AND I WERE TAKING ADVANTAGE, FRANKLY. FLIRT WITH THE OLD MAN, GET TO SLEEP IN THE BIG SAFE RV.
IT WAS A SURVIVAL THING. NEITHER OF US WERE ACTUALLY ATTRACTED TO HIM.

YOU DON'T HAVE TO DO THIS. THERE'S NO NEED--

NO, LET ME SAY THIS...

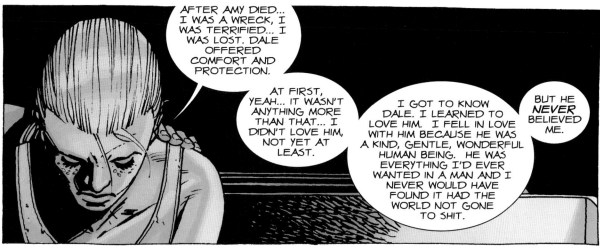

AFTER AMY DIED... I WAS A WRECK, I WAS TERRIFIED... I WAS LOST. DALE OFFERED COMFORT AND PROTECTION.

AT FIRST, YEAH... IT WASN'T ANYTHING MORE THAN THAT... I DIDN'T LOVE HIM, NOT YET AT LEAST.

I GOT TO KNOW DALE. I LEARNED TO LOVE HIM. I FELL IN LOVE WITH HIM BECAUSE HE WAS A KIND, GENTLE, WONDERFUL HUMAN BEING. HE WAS EVERYTHING I'D EVER WANTED IN A MAN AND I NEVER WOULD HAVE FOUND IT HAD THE WORLD NOT GONE TO SHIT.

BUT HE NEVER BELIEVED ME.

HE ALWAYS TALKED ABOUT HOW OLD HE WAS. HE APPRECIATED HAVING ME AROUND, BUT I DON'T THINK HE EVER THOUGHT IT WAS REAL.

AND I ALWAYS TREATED IT LIKE A JOKE.

THE HEARTACHE IN HIS EYES... EVERY TIME HE HAD TO SIT DOWN, EVERY TIME HE NEEDED HELP, EVERY TIME HE COULDN'T PERFORM.

AND I JUST LAUGHED IT OFF.

WHAT SCARES ME THE MOST RIGHT NOW--IS THAT I'LL NEVER GET TO TALK TO HIM AGAIN.

I'LL NEVER BE ABLE TO TELL HIM HOW DEEPLY I CARED FOR HIM.

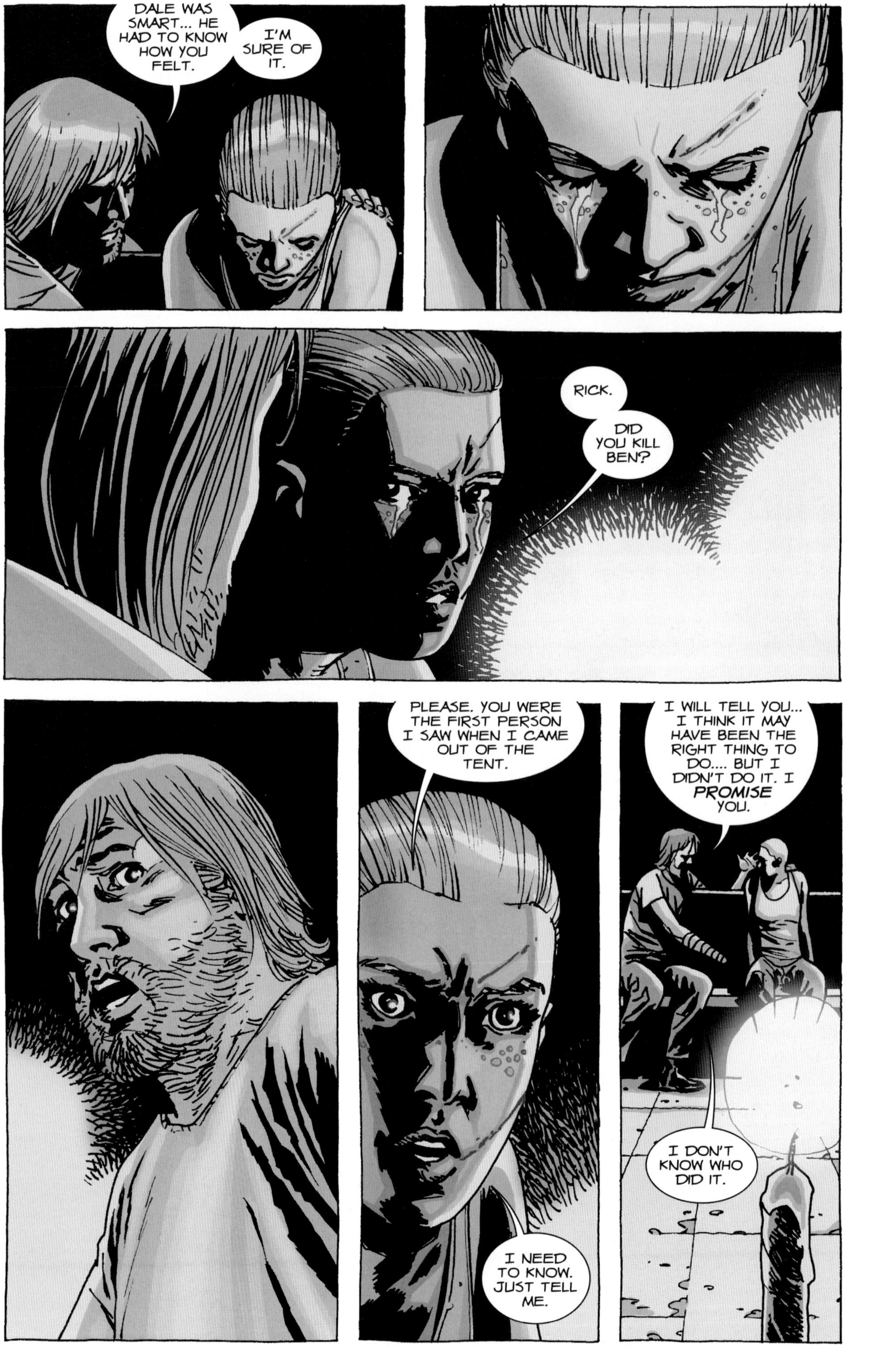
DALE WAS SMART... HE HAD TO KNOW HOW YOU FELT.
I'M SURE OF IT.
RICK.
DID YOU KILL BEN?
PLEASE. YOU WERE THE FIRST PERSON I SAW WHEN I CAME OUT OF THE TENT.
I NEED TO KNOW. JUST TELL ME.
I WILL TELL YOU... I THINK IT MAY HAVE BEEN THE RIGHT THING TO DO.... BUT I DIDN'T DO IT. I PROMISE YOU.
I DON'T KNOW WHO DID IT.

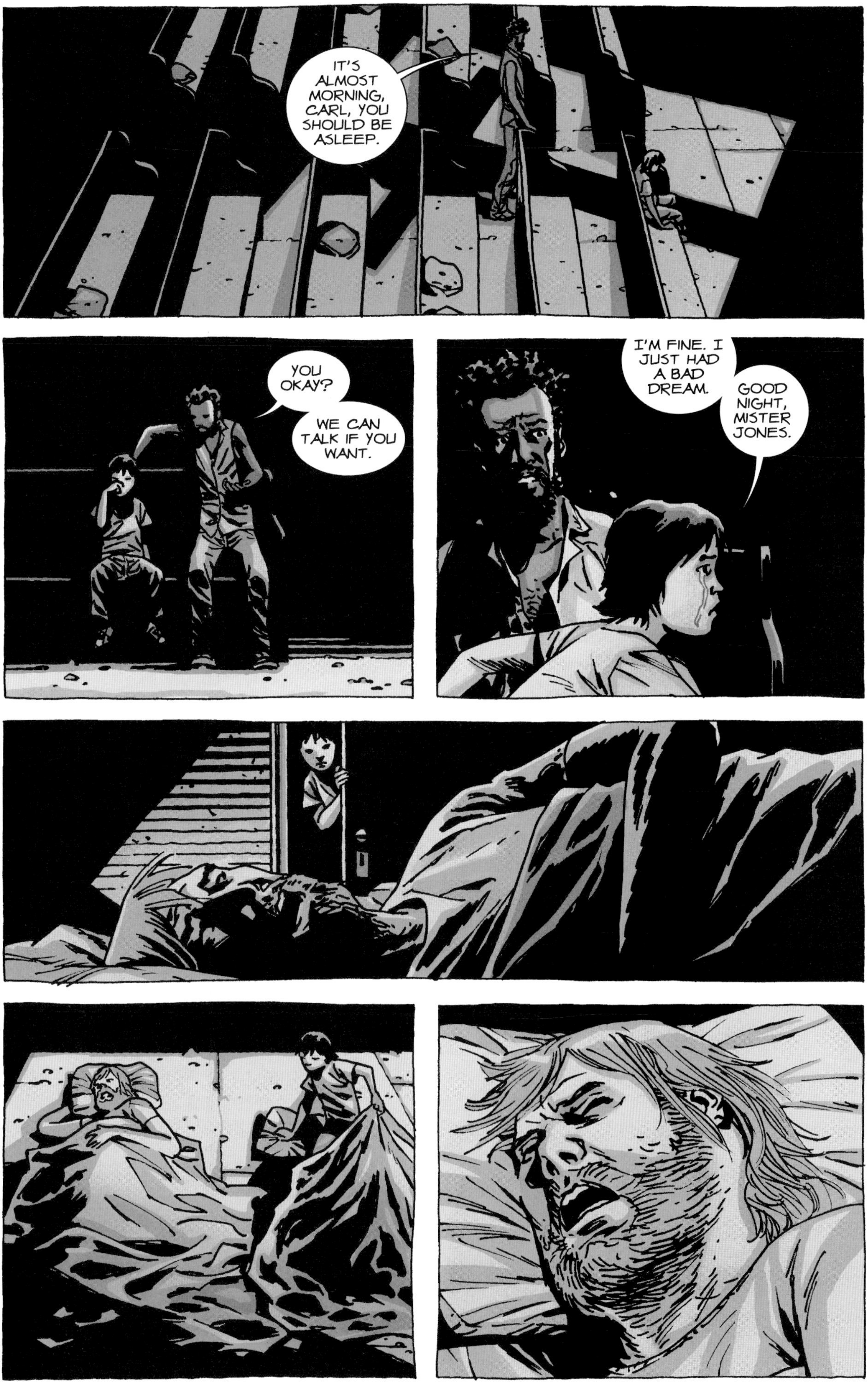
IT'S ALMOST MORNING, CARL, YOU SHOULD BE ASLEEP.
YOU OKAY?
WE CAN TALK IF YOU WANT.
I'M FINE. I JUST HAD A BAD DREAM.
GOOD NIGHT, MISTER JONES.

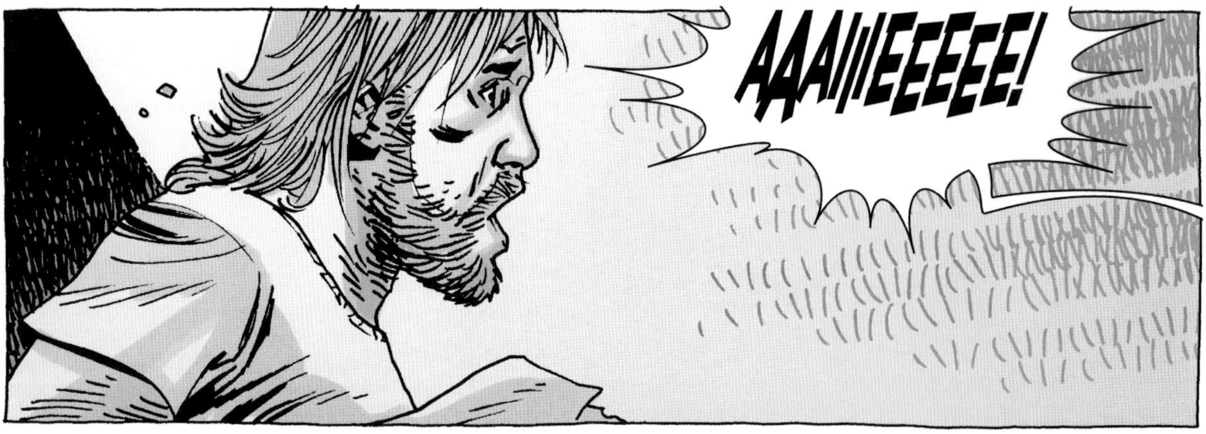
AAAIIIIEEEEEE!

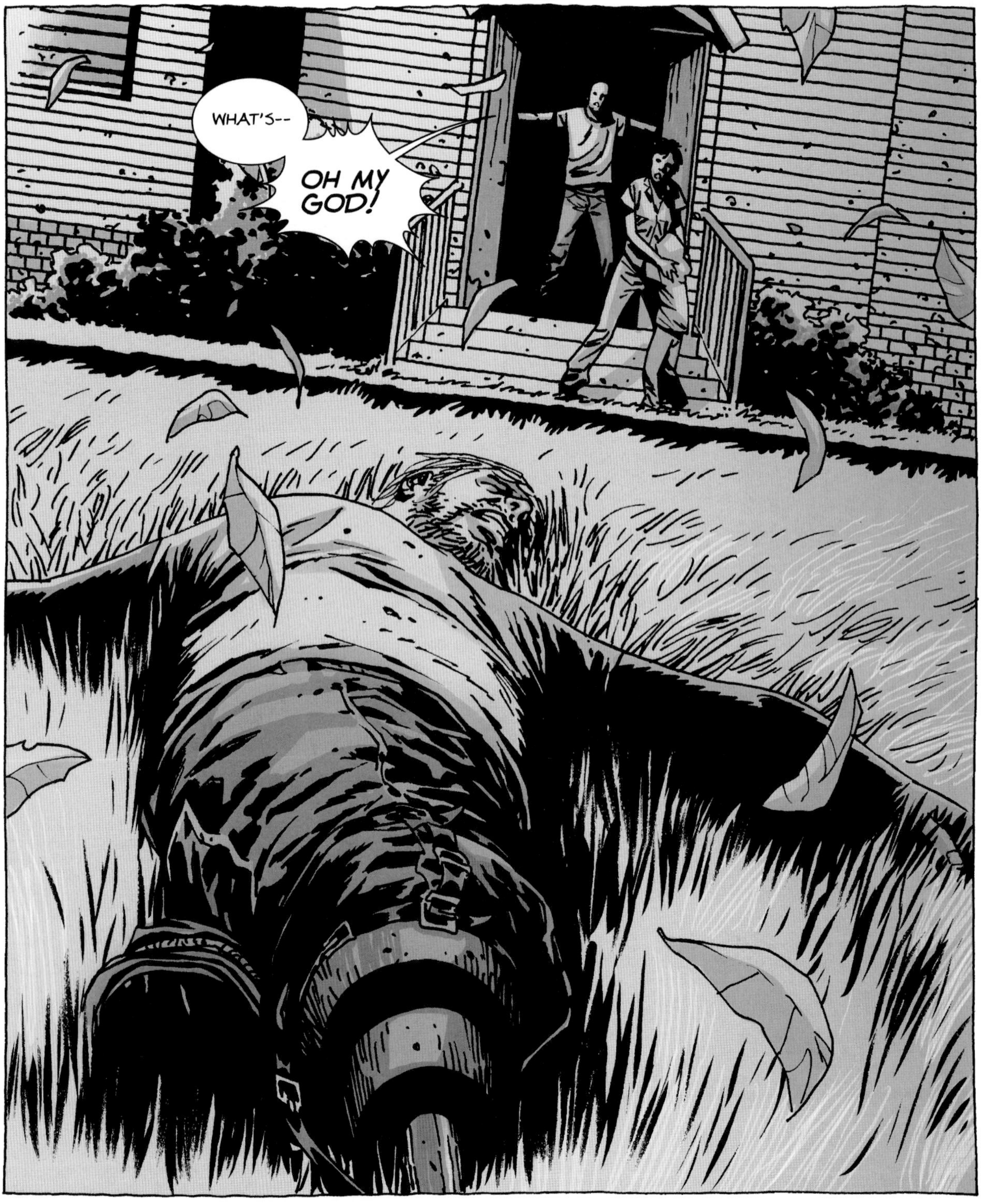
WHAT'S--
OH MY GOD!

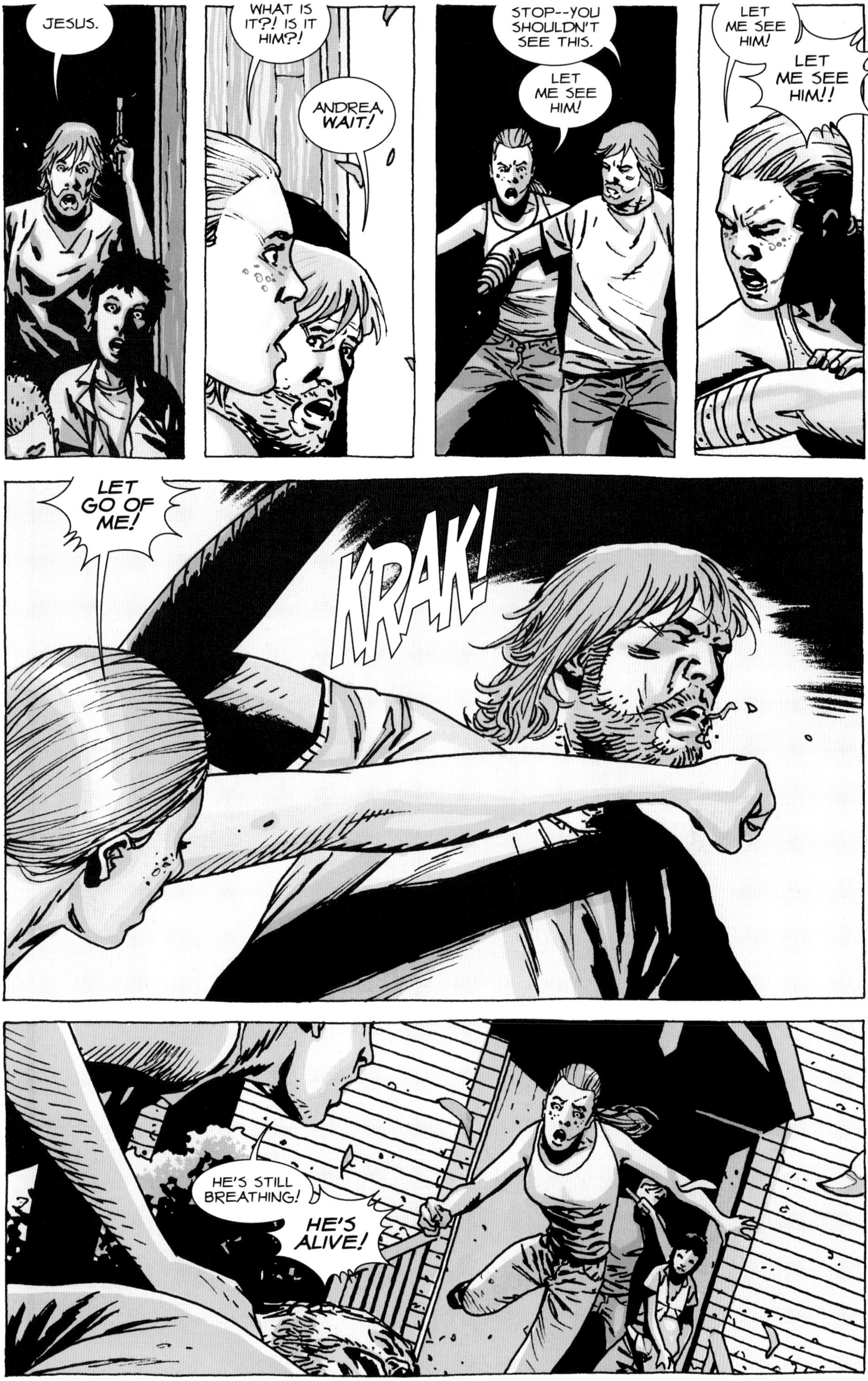

JESUS.
WHAT IS IT?! IS IT HIM?!
ANDREA, WAIT!
STOP--YOU SHOULDN'T SEE THIS.
LET ME SEE HIM!
LET ME SEE HIM!
LET ME SEE HIM!!
LET GO OF ME!
KRAK!
HE'S STILL BREATHING!
HE'S ALIVE!

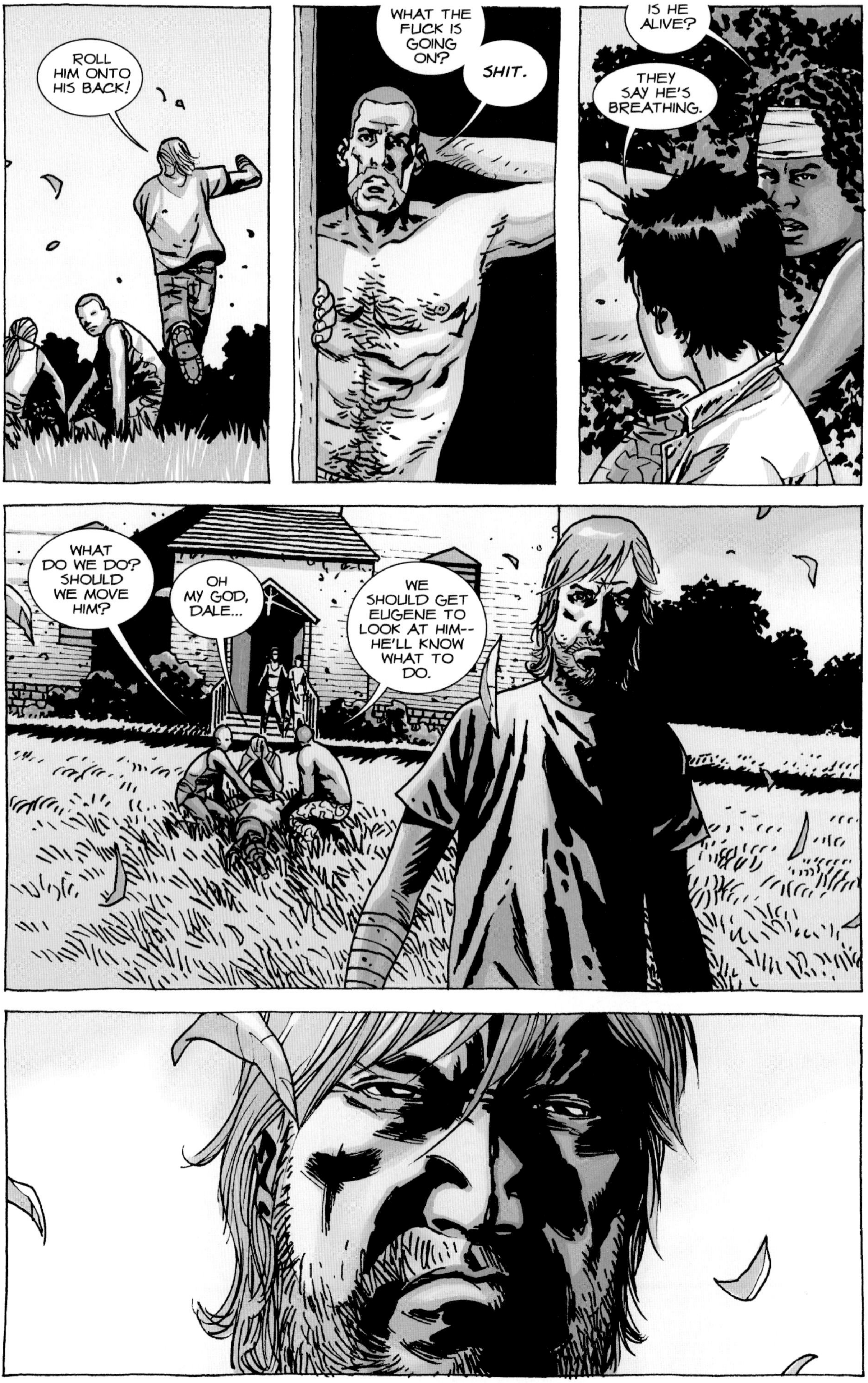
ROLL HIM ONTO HIS BACK!
WHAT THE FUCK IS GOING ON?
SHIT.
IS HE ALIVE?
THEY SAY HE'S BREATHING.
WHAT DO WE DO? SHOULD WE MOVE HIM?
OH MY GOD, DALE...
WE SHOULD GET EUGENE TO LOOK AT HIM-- HE'LL KNOW WHAT TO DO.

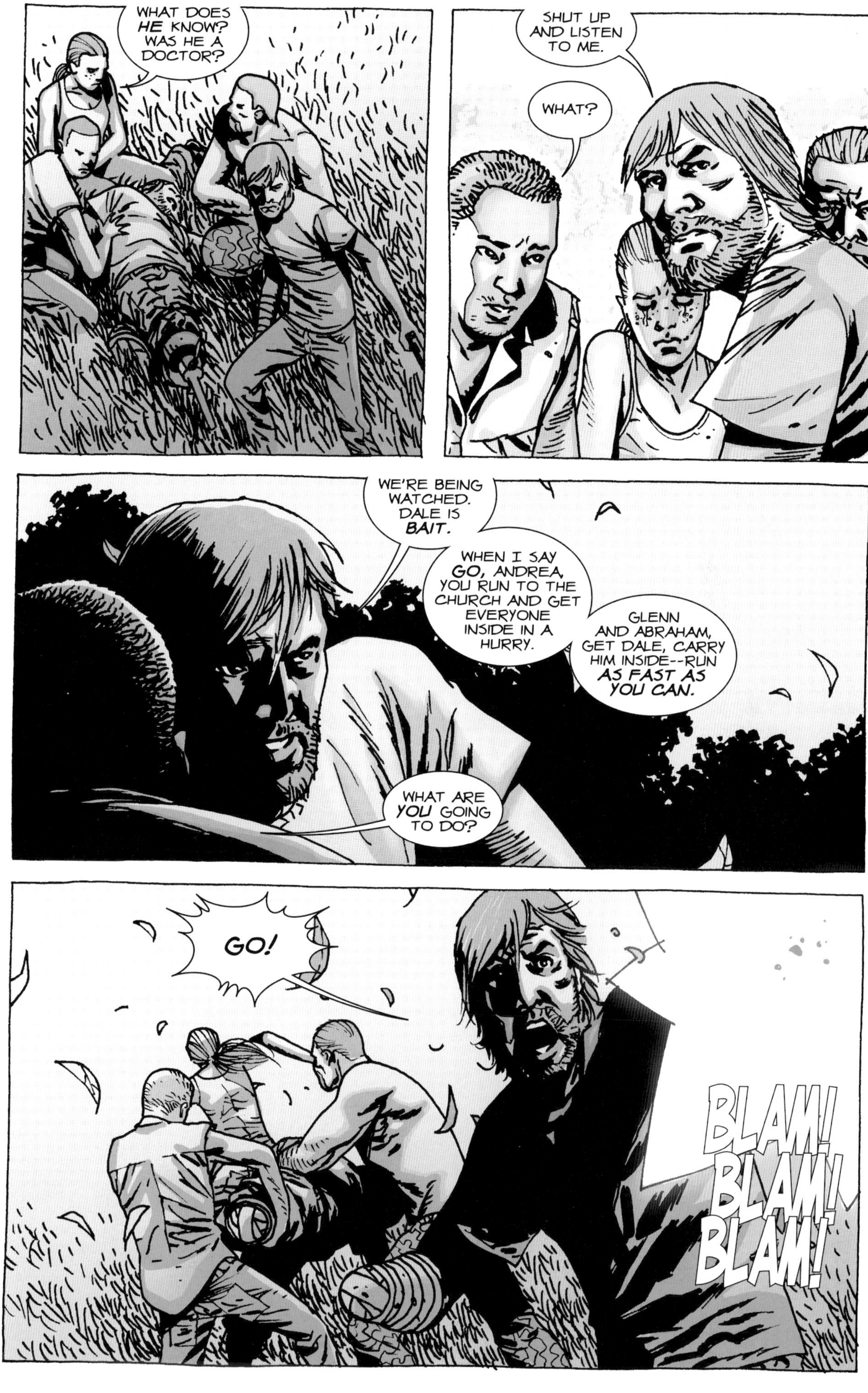

WHAT DOES *HE* KNOW? WAS HE A DOCTOR?
SHUT UP AND LISTEN TO ME.
WHAT?
WE'RE BEING WATCHED. DALE IS *BAIT.*
WHEN I SAY *GO,* ANDREA, YOU RUN TO THE CHURCH AND GET EVERYONE INSIDE IN A HURRY.
GLENN AND ABRAHAM, GET DALE, CARRY HIM INSIDE--RUN *AS FAST AS YOU CAN.*
WHAT ARE *YOU* GOING TO DO?
GO!
BLAM! BLAM! BLAM!

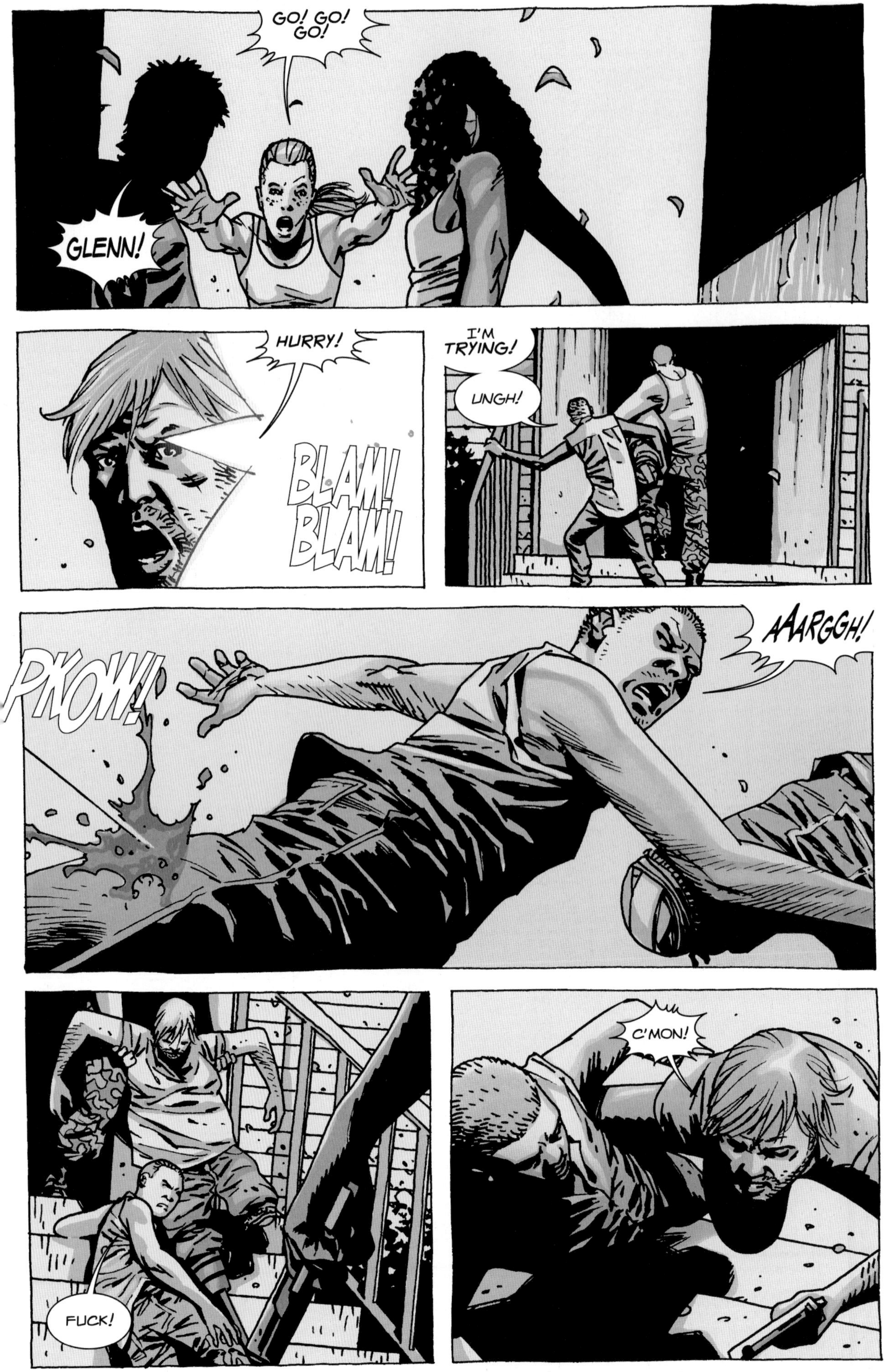
GO! GO! GO!
GLENN!
HURRY!
BLAM! BLAM!
I'M TRYING!
UNGH!
PKOW!
AAARGGH!
FUCK!
C'MON!

SHUT THE DOORS! LOCK THEM!

UNG.

EVERYONE GET DOWN. STAY AWAY FROM THE WINDOWS.

THEY'RE STILL OUT THERE!

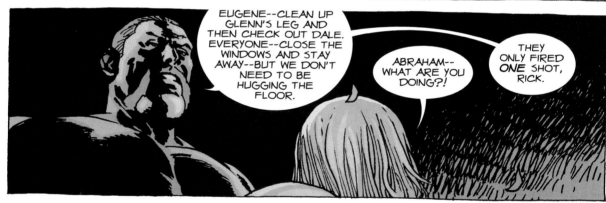

EUGENE--CLEAN UP GLENN'S LEG AND THEN CHECK OUT DALE. EVERYONE--CLOSE THE WINDOWS AND STAY AWAY--BUT WE DON'T NEED TO BE HUGGING THE FLOOR.

ABRAHAM-- WHAT ARE YOU DOING?!

THEY ONLY FIRED ONE SHOT, RICK.

WHAT DO YOU MEAN?

THEY ONLY FIRED ONE SHOT. HIT GLENN RIGHT IN THE LEG... THEY AREN'T TRYING TO KILL HIM OR ANY OF US.

THEY'RE TOYING WITH US.

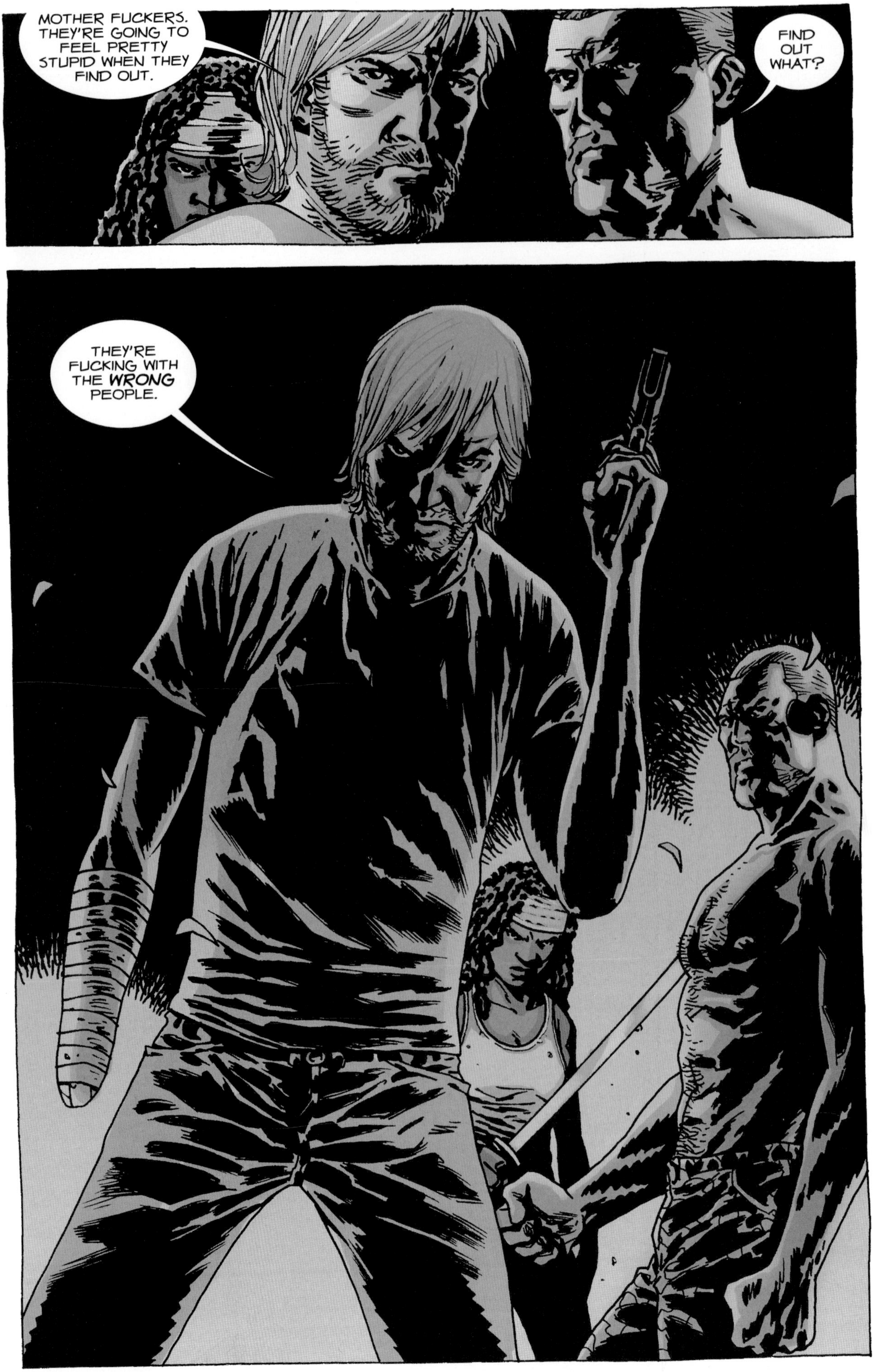
MOTHER FUCKERS. THEY'RE GOING TO FEEL PRETTY STUPID WHEN THEY FIND OUT.
FIND OUT WHAT?
THEY'RE FUCKING WITH THE WRONG PEOPLE.

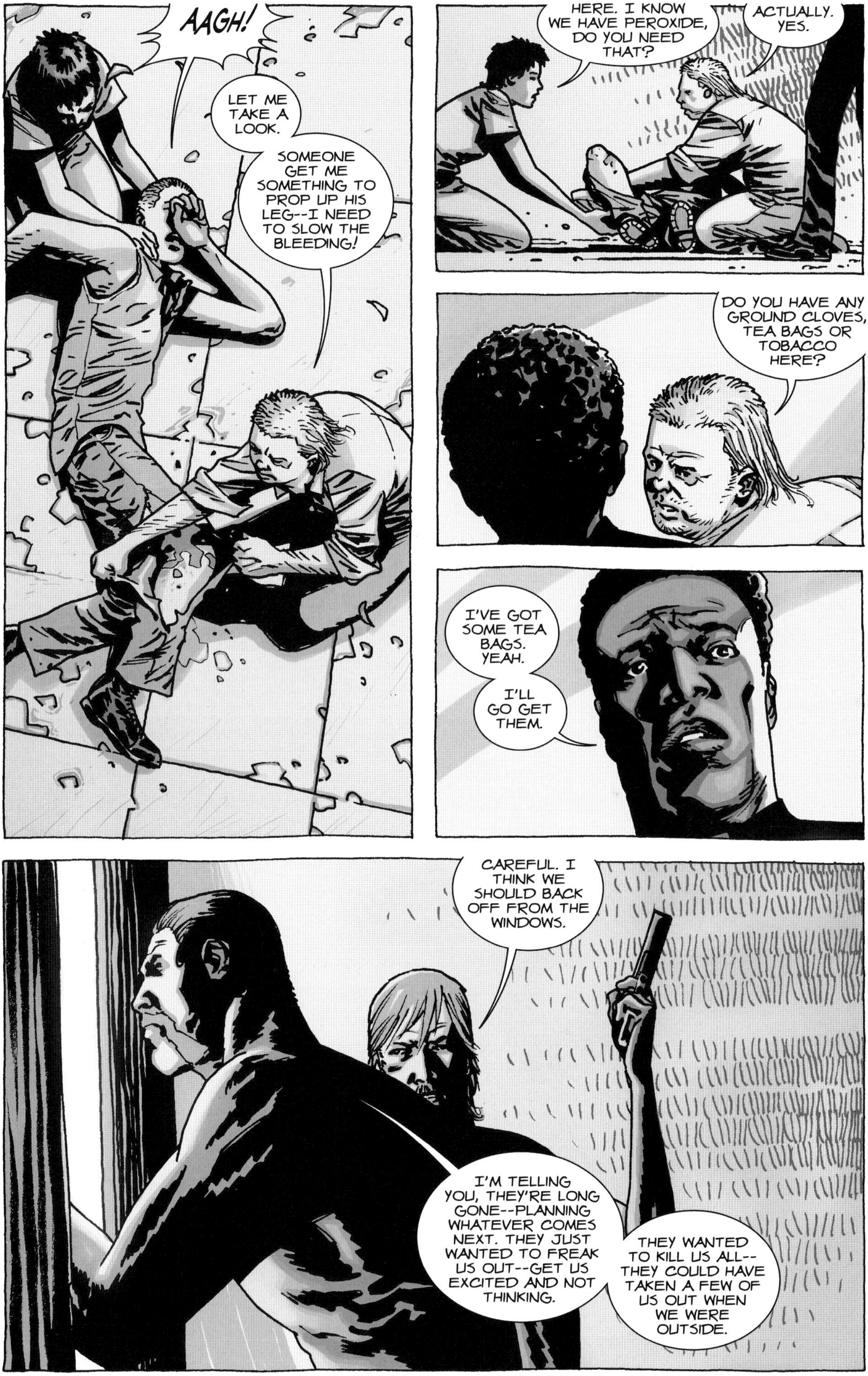
AAGH!
LET ME TAKE A LOOK.
SOMEONE GET ME SOMETHING TO PROP UP HIS LEG--I NEED TO SLOW THE BLEEDING!
HERE. I KNOW WE HAVE PEROXIDE, DO YOU NEED THAT?
ACTUALLY. YES.
DO YOU HAVE ANY GROUND CLOVES, TEA BAGS OR TOBACCO HERE?
I'VE GOT SOME TEA BAGS. YEAH.
I'LL GO GET THEM.
CAREFUL. I THINK WE SHOULD BACK OFF FROM THE WINDOWS.
I'M TELLING YOU, THEY'RE LONG GONE--PLANNING WHATEVER COMES NEXT. THEY JUST WANTED TO FREAK US OUT--GET US EXCITED AND NOT THINKING.
THEY WANTED TO KILL US ALL--THEY COULD HAVE TAKEN A FEW OF US OUT WHEN WE WERE OUTSIDE.

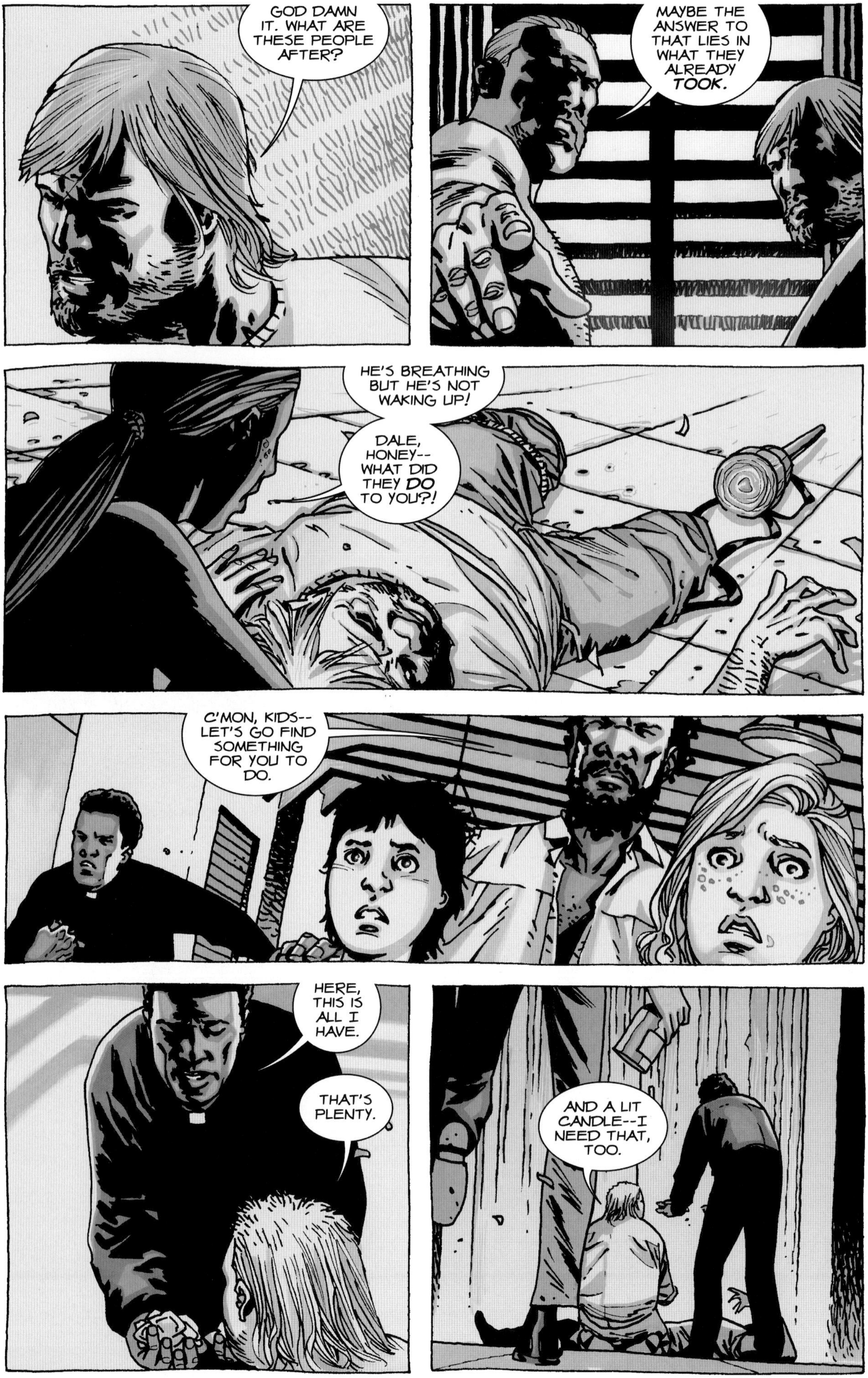
GOD DAMN IT. WHAT ARE THESE PEOPLE AFTER?
MAYBE THE ANSWER TO THAT LIES IN WHAT THEY ALREADY *TOOK.*
HE'S BREATHING BUT HE'S NOT WAKING UP!
DALE, HONEY-- WHAT DID THEY *DO* TO YOU?!
C'MON, KIDS-- LET'S GO FIND SOMETHING FOR YOU TO DO.
HERE, THIS IS ALL I HAVE.
THAT'S PLENTY.
AND A LIT CANDLE--I NEED THAT, TOO.

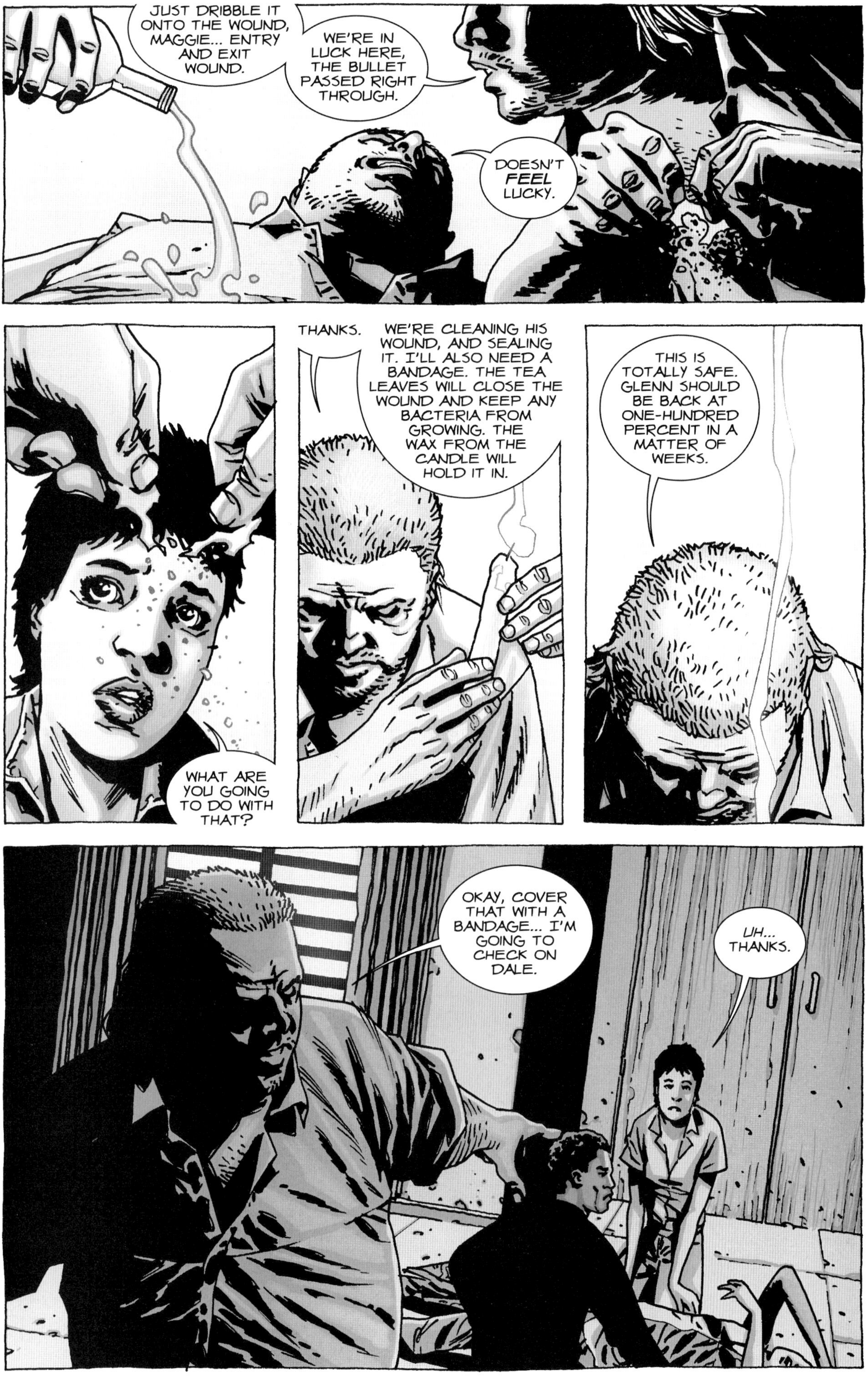
JUST DRIBBLE IT ONTO THE WOUND, MAGGIE... ENTRY AND EXIT WOUND.
WE'RE IN LUCK HERE, THE BULLET PASSED RIGHT THROUGH.
DOESN'T FEEL LUCKY.
WHAT ARE YOU GOING TO DO WITH THAT?
THANKS.
WE'RE CLEANING HIS WOUND, AND SEALING IT. I'LL ALSO NEED A BANDAGE. THE TEA LEAVES WILL CLOSE THE WOUND AND KEEP ANY BACTERIA FROM GROWING. THE WAX FROM THE CANDLE WILL HOLD IT IN.
THIS IS TOTALLY SAFE. GLENN SHOULD BE BACK AT ONE-HUNDRED PERCENT IN A MATTER OF WEEKS.
OKAY, COVER THAT WITH A BANDAGE... I'M GOING TO CHECK ON DALE.
UH... THANKS.

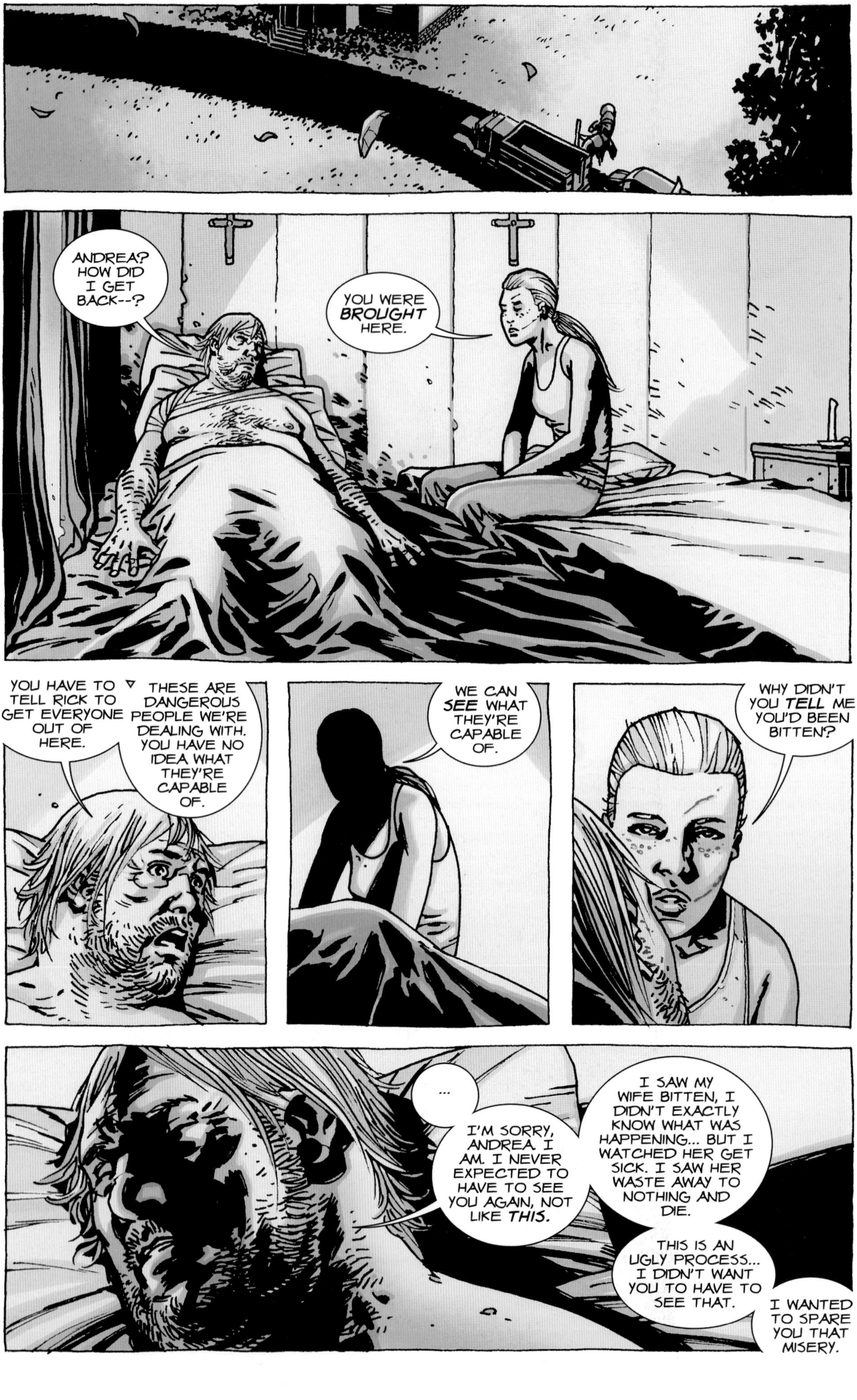
ANDREA? HOW DID I GET BACK--?
YOU WERE BROUGHT HERE.
YOU HAVE TO TELL RICK TO GET EVERYONE OUT OF HERE.
THESE ARE DANGEROUS PEOPLE WE'RE DEALING WITH. YOU HAVE NO IDEA WHAT THEY'RE CAPABLE OF.
WE CAN SEE WHAT THEY'RE CAPABLE OF.
WHY DIDN'T YOU TELL ME YOU'D BEEN BITTEN?
...
I'M SORRY, ANDREA. I AM. I NEVER EXPECTED TO HAVE TO SEE YOU AGAIN, NOT LIKE THIS.
I SAW MY WIFE BITTEN, I DIDN'T EXACTLY KNOW WHAT WAS HAPPENING... BUT I WATCHED HER GET SICK. I SAW HER WASTE AWAY TO NOTHING AND DIE.
THIS IS AN UGLY PROCESS... I DIDN'T WANT YOU TO HAVE TO SEE THAT.
I WANTED TO SPARE YOU THAT MISERY.

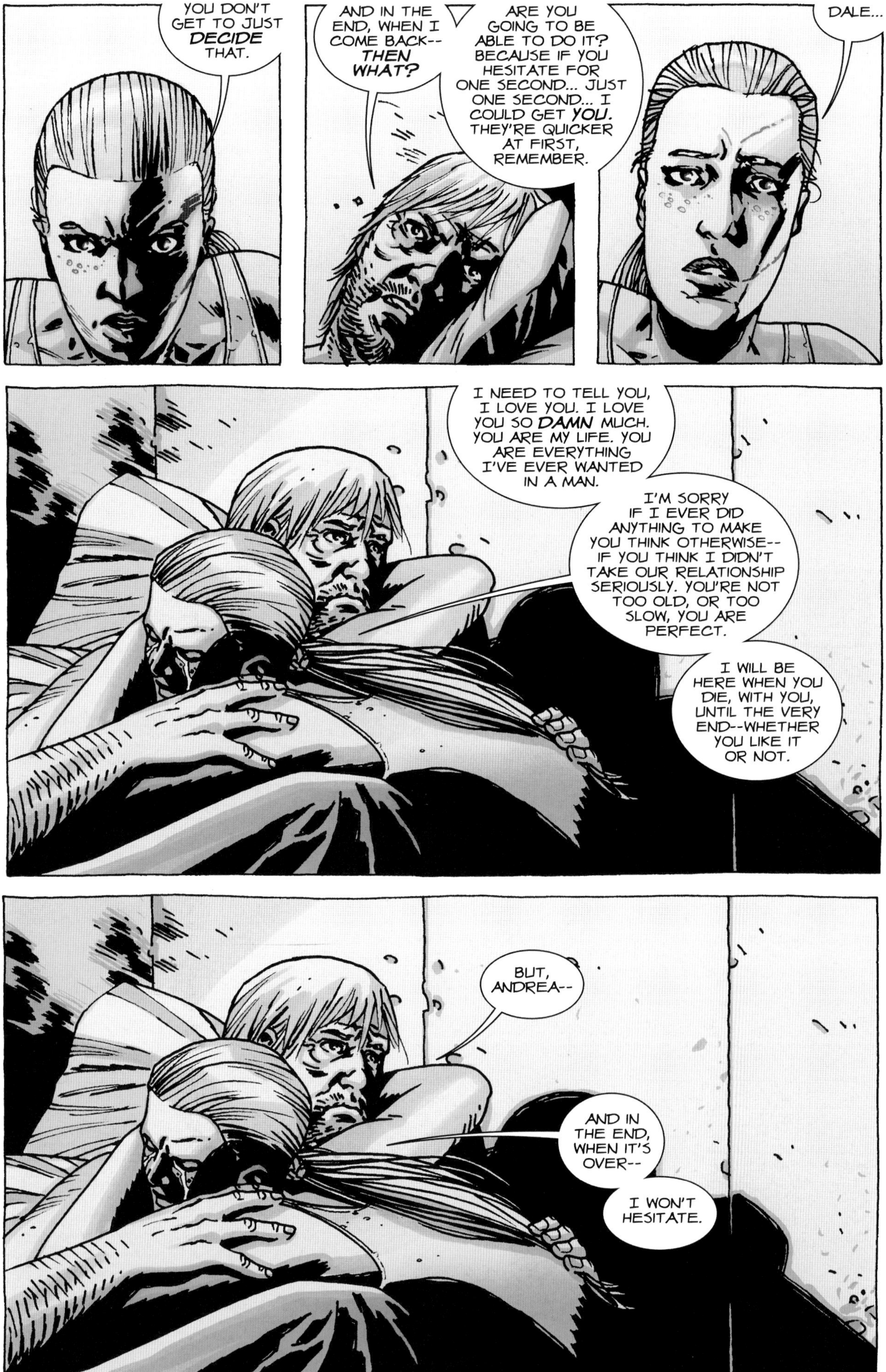

YOU DON'T GET TO JUST DECIDE THAT.
AND IN THE END, WHEN I COME BACK-- THEN WHAT?
ARE YOU GOING TO BE ABLE TO DO IT? BECAUSE IF YOU HESITATE FOR ONE SECOND... JUST ONE SECOND... I COULD GET YOU. THEY'RE QUICKER AT FIRST, REMEMBER.
DALE...
I NEED TO TELL YOU, I LOVE YOU. I LOVE YOU SO DAMN MUCH. YOU ARE MY LIFE. YOU ARE EVERYTHING I'VE EVER WANTED IN A MAN.
I'M SORRY IF I EVER DID ANYTHING TO MAKE YOU THINK OTHERWISE-- IF YOU THINK I DIDN'T TAKE OUR RELATIONSHIP SERIOUSLY. YOU'RE NOT TOO OLD, OR TOO SLOW, YOU ARE PERFECT.
I WILL BE HERE WHEN YOU DIE, WITH YOU, UNTIL THE VERY END--WHETHER YOU LIKE IT OR NOT.
BUT, ANDREA--
AND IN THE END, WHEN IT'S OVER--
I WON'T HESITATE.

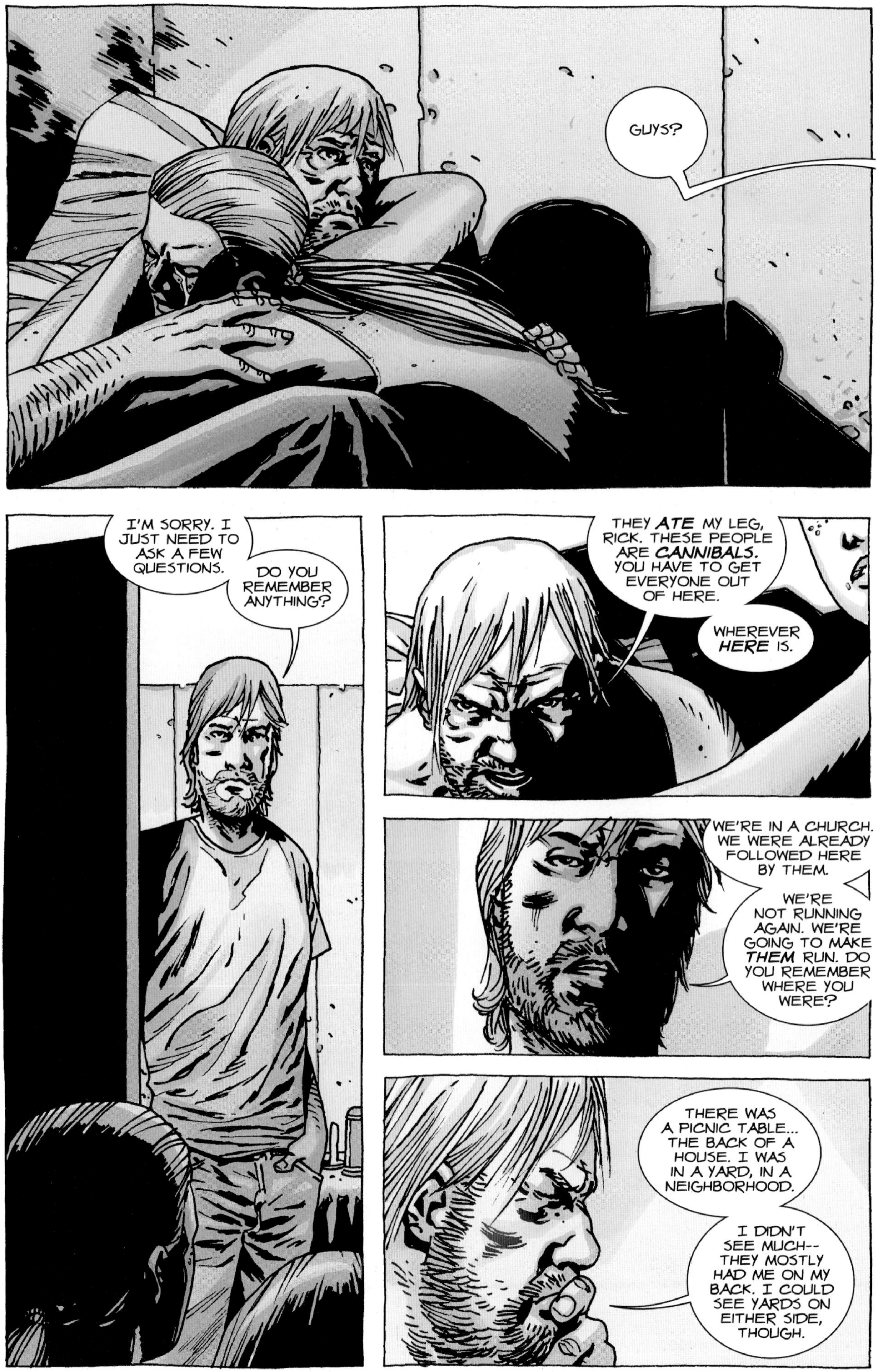
GUYS?
I'M SORRY. I JUST NEED TO ASK A FEW QUESTIONS.
DO YOU REMEMBER ANYTHING?
THEY ATE MY LEG, RICK. THESE PEOPLE ARE CANNIBALS. YOU HAVE TO GET EVERYONE OUT OF HERE.
WHEREVER HERE IS.
WE'RE IN A CHURCH. WE WERE ALREADY FOLLOWED HERE BY THEM.
WE'RE NOT RUNNING AGAIN. WE'RE GOING TO MAKE THEM RUN. DO YOU REMEMBER WHERE YOU WERE?
THERE WAS A PICNIC TABLE... THE BACK OF A HOUSE. I WAS IN A YARD, IN A NEIGHBORHOOD.
I DIDN'T SEE MUCH-- THEY MOSTLY HAD ME ON MY BACK. I COULD SEE YARDS ON EITHER SIDE, THOUGH.

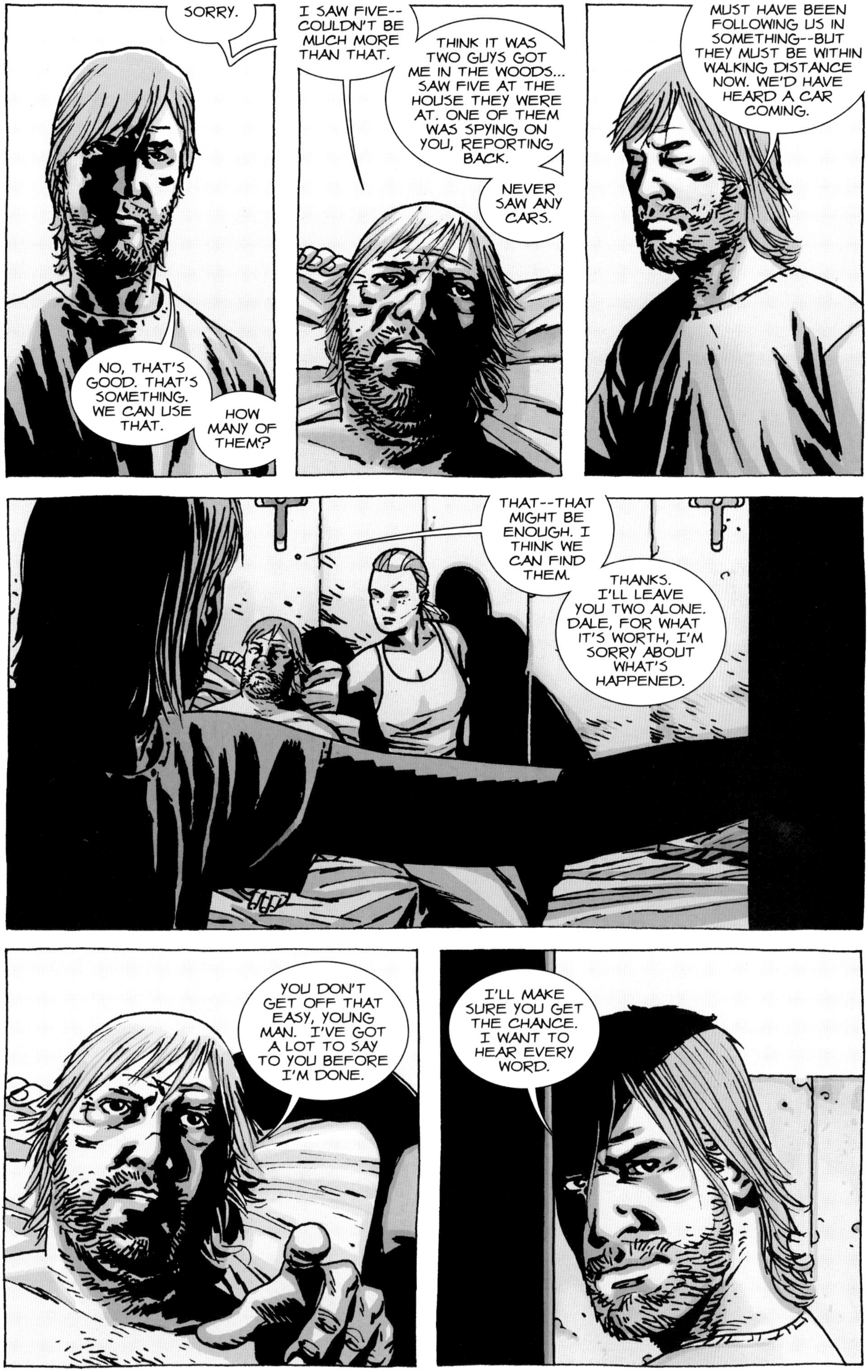
SORRY.
NO, THAT'S GOOD. THAT'S SOMETHING. WE CAN USE THAT.
HOW MANY OF THEM?
I SAW FIVE-- COULDN'T BE MUCH MORE THAN THAT.
THINK IT WAS TWO GUYS GOT ME IN THE WOODS... SAW FIVE AT THE HOUSE THEY WERE AT. ONE OF THEM WAS SPYING ON YOU, REPORTING BACK.
NEVER SAW ANY CARS.
MUST HAVE BEEN FOLLOWING US IN SOMETHING--BUT THEY MUST BE WITHIN WALKING DISTANCE NOW. WE'D HAVE HEARD A CAR COMING.
THAT--THAT MIGHT BE ENOUGH. I THINK WE CAN FIND THEM.
THANKS. I'LL LEAVE YOU TWO ALONE. DALE, FOR WHAT IT'S WORTH, I'M SORRY ABOUT WHAT'S HAPPENED.
YOU DON'T GET OFF THAT EASY, YOUNG MAN. I'VE GOT A LOT TO SAY TO YOU BEFORE I'M DONE.
I'LL MAKE SURE YOU GET THE CHANCE. I WANT TO HEAR EVERY WORD.

WE'VE GOT A PROBLEM.

REALLY, YOU DON'T SAY.

NOT THAT-- WE'RE RUNNING OUT OF FOOD.

WE'RE ADDING PEOPLE--AND WE'RE FINDING LESS AND LESS TO FEED THEM. WE'VE GOT MAYBE THREE DAYS' WORTH OF FOOD BEFORE WE'RE OUT.

I THINK WE SHOULD START RATIONING.

FINE. *DO IT.* YOU DON'T NEED MY PERMISSION. FIGURE OUT HOW TO STRETCH THAT FOOD OUT AS LONG AS POSSIBLE.

IN THE MEANTIME-- ABRAHAM, HELP ME FIND GABRIEL.

WHAT IS IT YOU WANT?

DALE WAS KEPT IN A NEIGHBORHOOD WITHIN WALKING DISTANCE FROM HERE. HOW MANY DO YOU KNOW OF?

WITHIN WALKING DISTANCE? ONLY... FIVE, MAYBE. YEAH, THREE ARE CLOSE... BUT THERE'S FIVE WITHIN WALKING DISTANCE.

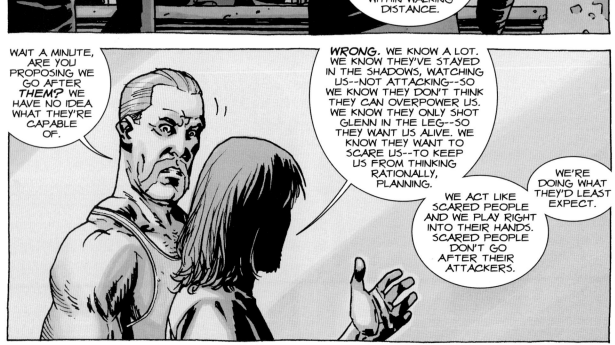

WAIT A MINUTE, ARE YOU PROPOSING WE GO AFTER *THEM?* WE HAVE NO IDEA WHAT THEY'RE CAPABLE OF.

WRONG. WE KNOW A LOT. WE KNOW THEY'VE STAYED IN THE SHADOWS, WATCHING US--NOT ATTACKING--SO WE KNOW THEY DON'T THINK THEY CAN OVERPOWER US. WE KNOW THEY ONLY SHOT GLENN IN THE LEG--SO THEY WANT US ALIVE. WE KNOW THEY WANT TO SCARE US--TO KEEP US FROM THINKING RATIONALLY, PLANNING.

WE ACT LIKE SCARED PEOPLE AND WE PLAY RIGHT INTO THEIR HANDS. SCARED PEOPLE DON'T GO AFTER THEIR ATTACKERS.

WE'RE DOING WHAT THEY'D LEAST EXPECT.

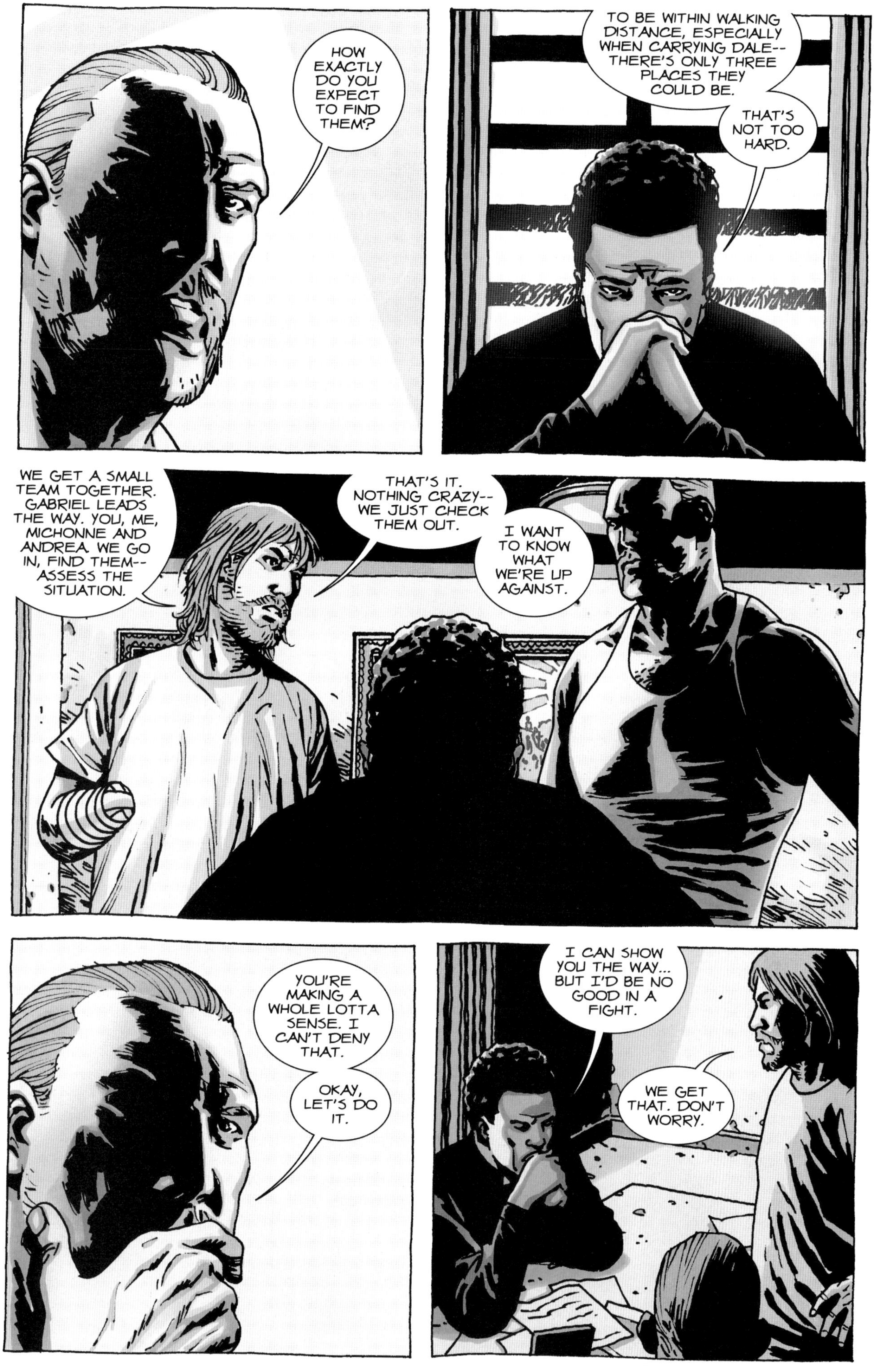
HOW EXACTLY DO YOU EXPECT TO FIND THEM?
TO BE WITHIN WALKING DISTANCE, ESPECIALLY WHEN CARRYING DALE-- THERE'S ONLY THREE PLACES THEY COULD BE.
THAT'S NOT TOO HARD.
WE GET A SMALL TEAM TOGETHER. GABRIEL LEADS THE WAY. YOU, ME, MICHONNE AND ANDREA. WE GO IN, FIND THEM-- ASSESS THE SITUATION.
THAT'S IT. NOTHING CRAZY-- WE JUST CHECK THEM OUT.
I WANT TO KNOW WHAT WE'RE UP AGAINST.
YOU'RE MAKING A WHOLE LOTTA SENSE. I CAN'T DENY THAT.
OKAY, LET'S DO IT.
I CAN SHOW YOU THE WAY... BUT I'D BE NO GOOD IN A FIGHT.
WE GET THAT. DON'T WORRY.

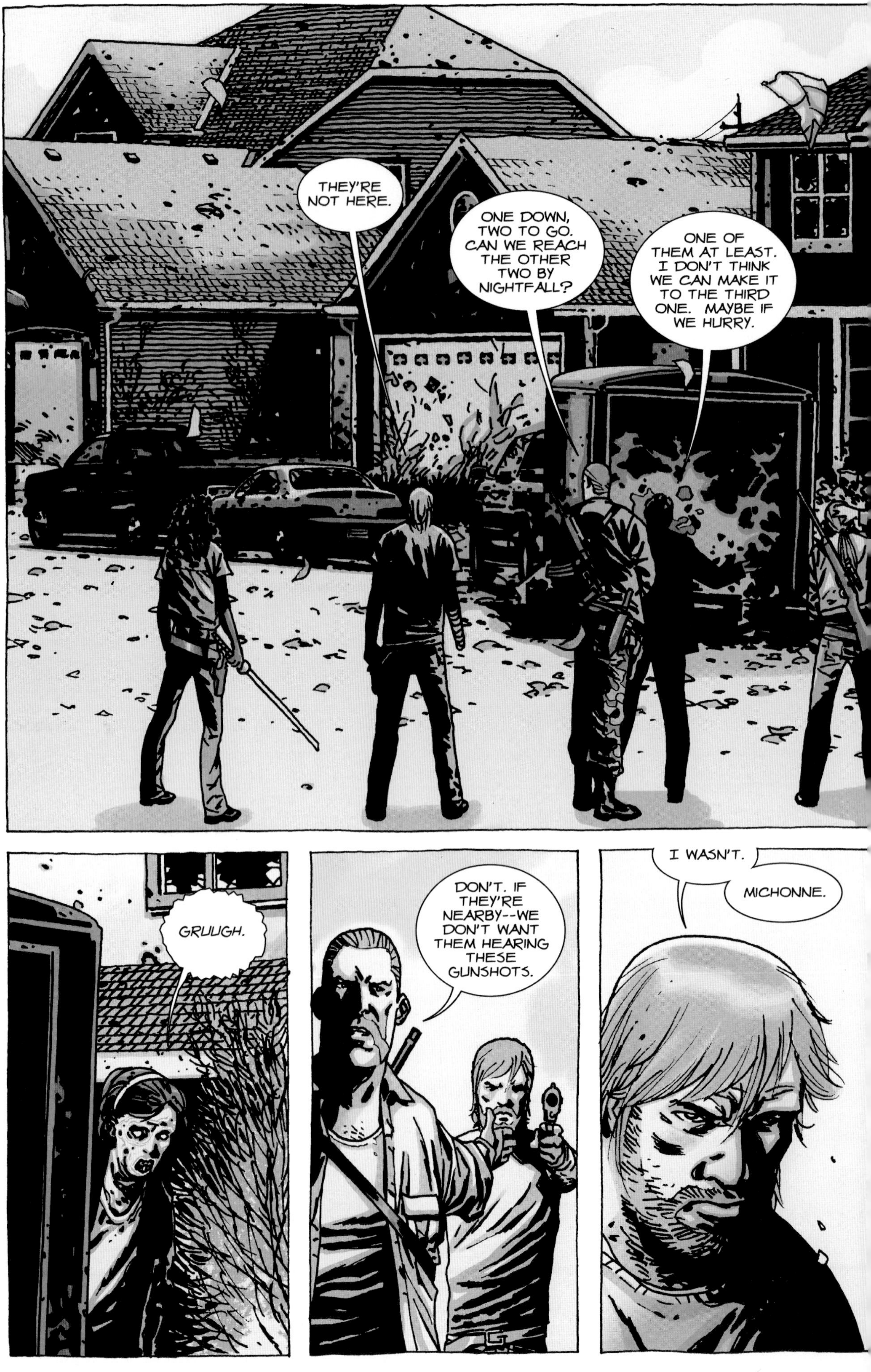
THEY'RE NOT HERE.
ONE DOWN, TWO TO GO. CAN WE REACH THE OTHER TWO BY NIGHTFALL?
ONE OF THEM AT LEAST. I DON'T THINK WE CAN MAKE IT TO THE THIRD ONE. MAYBE IF WE HURRY.
GRUUGH.
DON'T. IF THEY'RE NEARBY--WE DON'T WANT THEM HEARING THESE GUNSHOTS.
I WASN'T.
MICHONNE.

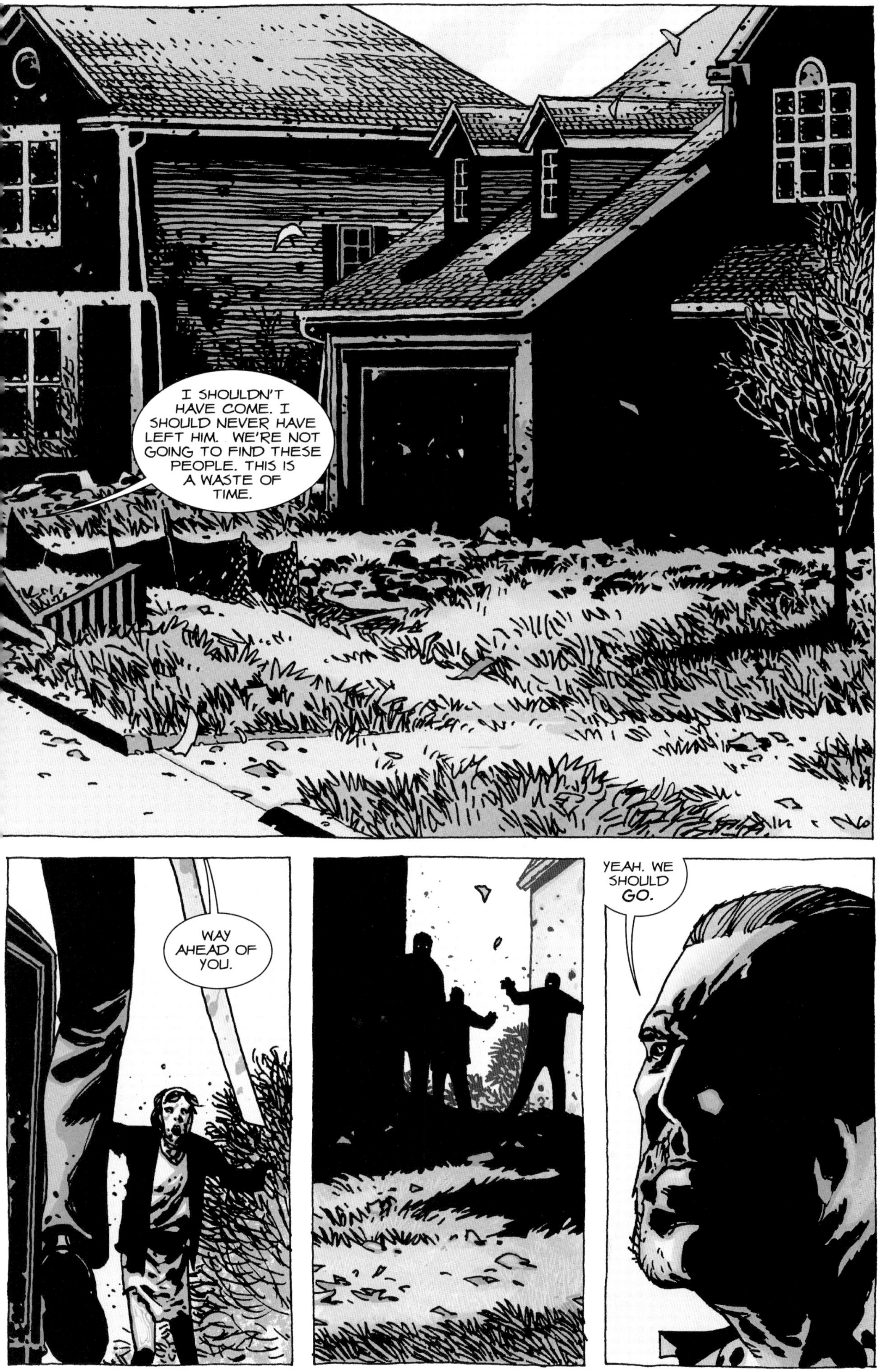
I SHOULDN'T HAVE COME. I SHOULD NEVER HAVE LEFT HIM. WE'RE NOT GOING TO FIND THESE PEOPLE. THIS IS A WASTE OF TIME.
WAY AHEAD OF YOU.
YEAH. WE SHOULD GO.

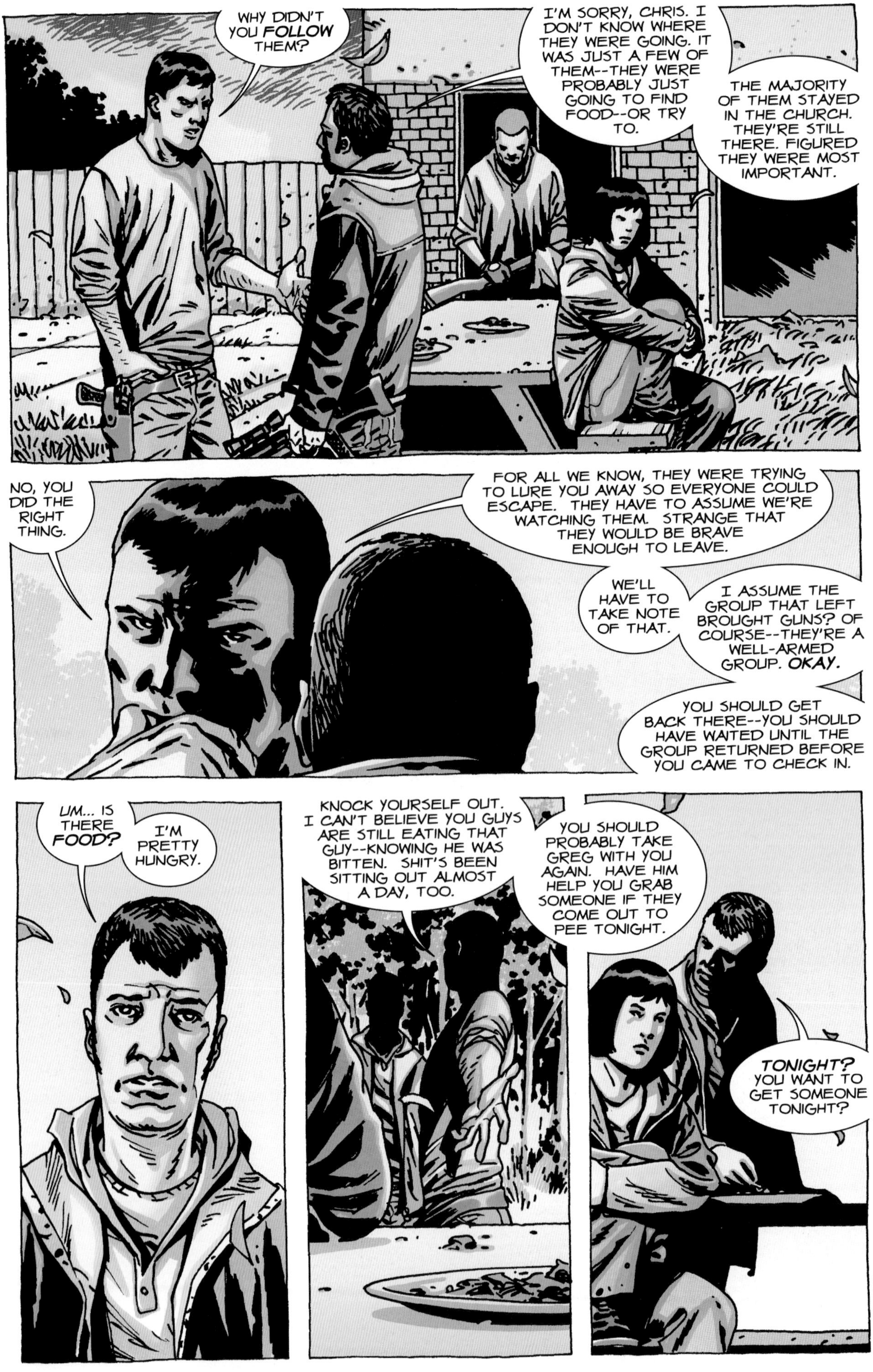
WHY DIDN'T YOU FOLLOW THEM?
I'M SORRY, CHRIS. I DON'T KNOW WHERE THEY WERE GOING. IT WAS JUST A FEW OF THEM--THEY WERE PROBABLY JUST GOING TO FIND FOOD--OR TRY TO.
THE MAJORITY OF THEM STAYED IN THE CHURCH. THEY'RE STILL THERE. FIGURED THEY WERE MOST IMPORTANT.
NO, YOU DID THE RIGHT THING.
FOR ALL WE KNOW, THEY WERE TRYING TO LURE YOU AWAY SO EVERYONE COULD ESCAPE. THEY HAVE TO ASSUME WE'RE WATCHING THEM. STRANGE THAT THEY WOULD BE BRAVE ENOUGH TO LEAVE.
WE'LL HAVE TO TAKE NOTE OF THAT.
I ASSUME THE GROUP THAT LEFT BROUGHT GUNS? OF COURSE--THEY'RE A WELL-ARMED GROUP. OKAY.
YOU SHOULD GET BACK THERE--YOU SHOULD HAVE WAITED UNTIL THE GROUP RETURNED BEFORE YOU CAME TO CHECK IN.
UM... IS THERE FOOD?
I'M PRETTY HUNGRY.
KNOCK YOURSELF OUT. I CAN'T BELIEVE YOU GUYS ARE STILL EATING THAT GUY--KNOWING HE WAS BITTEN. SHIT'S BEEN SITTING OUT ALMOST A DAY, TOO.
YOU SHOULD PROBABLY TAKE GREG WITH YOU AGAIN. HAVE HIM HELP YOU GRAB SOMEONE IF THEY COME OUT TO PEE TONIGHT.
TONIGHT? YOU WANT TO GET SOMEONE TONIGHT?

YOU KNOW THE DRILL--WE'VE GOT TO KEEP THESE PEOPLE SCARED SHITLESS. I KNOW WE'VE NEVER DONE A GROUP THIS LARGE BEFORE, BUT IT'S THE SAME DEAL.

WE SHOULD ACTUALLY PICK THEM OFF SOONER, THIN THEIR NUMBERS OUT AND MAKE THEM FEAR FOR THEIR LIVES.

WISH THEY HADN'T FOUND THAT CHURCH. IT'D BE EASIER IF THEY WERE ON THE MOVE. WE'D HAVE MORE OPPORTUNITIES TO SNAG SOMEONE.

WHAT IF THEY STAY IN THAT CHURCH ALL NIGHT? MIGHT NOT HAVE TO GO OUTSIDE TO USE THE JOHN. WHAT DO I DO THEN?

JUST WAIT. SOMEONE WILL GET STUPID SOONER OR LATER. THEY ALWAYS DO.

WE'VE BOUGHT OURSELVES A LITTLE TIME BY DROPPING OFF THE OLD MAN. HE'LL BE A CONSTANT REMINDER OF THE DEEP SHIT THEY'RE IN.

SEEING THEIR MAN LIKE THAT... THAT SHOULD DRIVE THEM CRAZY.

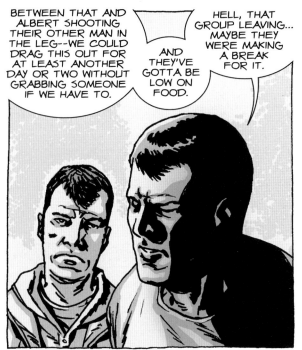

BETWEEN THAT AND ALBERT SHOOTING THEIR OTHER MAN IN THE LEG--WE COULD DRAG THIS OUT FOR AT LEAST ANOTHER DAY OR TWO WITHOUT GRABBING SOMEONE IF WE HAVE TO.

AND THEY'VE GOTTA BE LOW ON FOOD.

HELL, THAT GROUP LEAVING... MAYBE THEY WERE MAKING A BREAK FOR IT.

THEY'RE ALL PROBABLY SHITTING THEMSELVES RIGHT NOW.

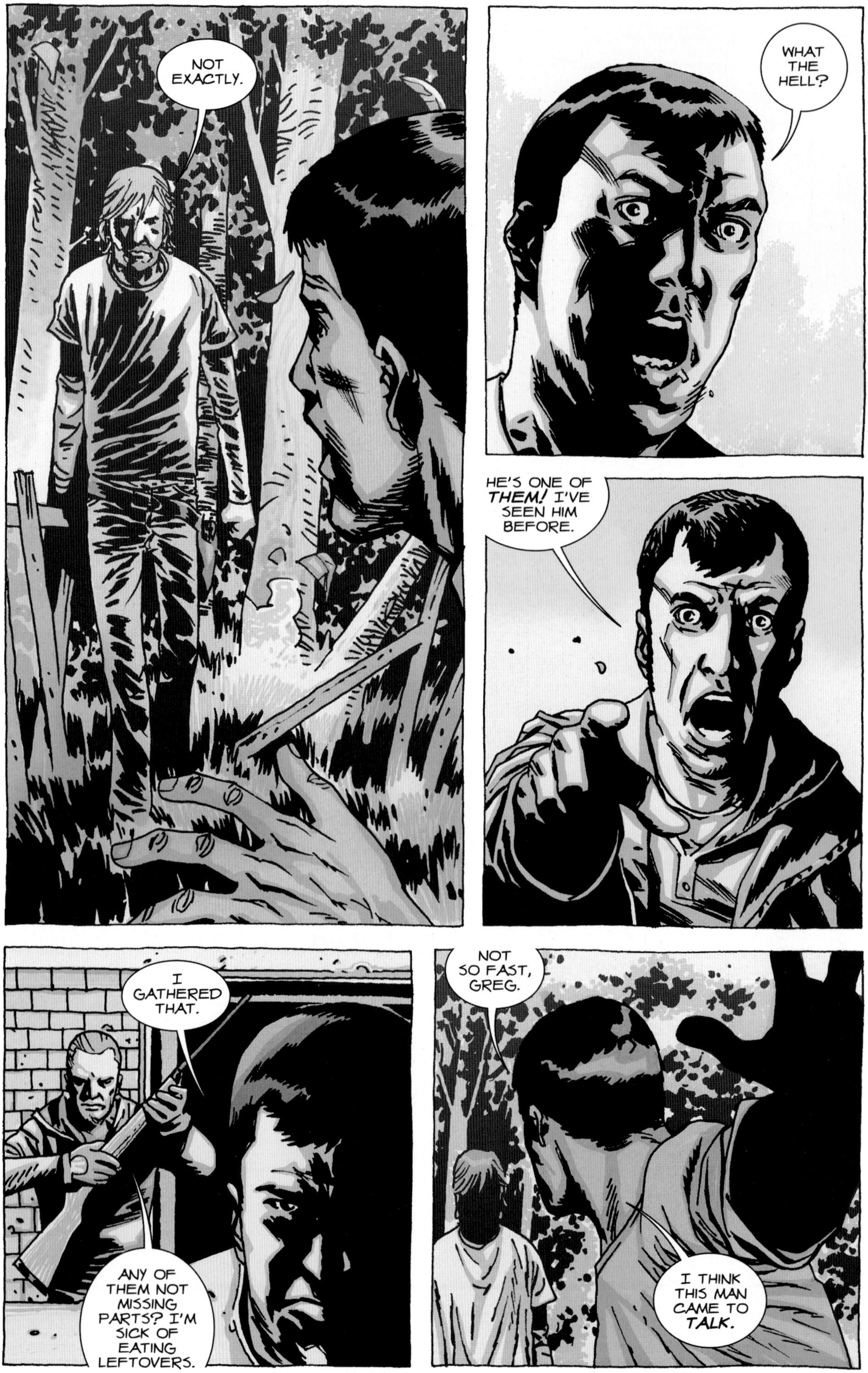
NOT EXACTLY.
WHAT THE HELL?
HE'S ONE OF *THEM!* I'VE SEEN HIM BEFORE.
I GATHERED THAT.
ANY OF THEM NOT MISSING PARTS? I'M SICK OF EATING LEFTOVERS.
NOT SO FAST, GREG.
I THINK THIS MAN CAME TO *TALK.*

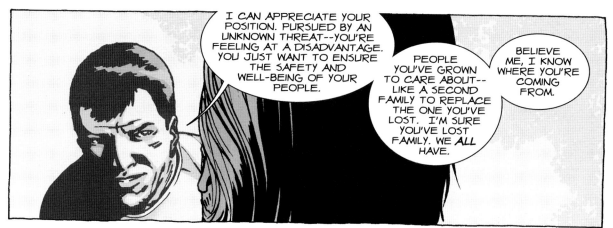

I CAN APPRECIATE YOUR POSITION. PURSUED BY AN UNKNOWN THREAT--YOU'RE FEELING AT A DISADVANTAGE. YOU JUST WANT TO ENSURE THE SAFETY AND WELL-BEING OF YOUR PEOPLE.

PEOPLE YOU'VE GROWN TO CARE ABOUT--LIKE A SECOND FAMILY TO REPLACE THE ONE YOU'VE LOST. I'M SURE YOU'VE LOST FAMILY. WE *ALL* HAVE.

BELIEVE ME, I KNOW WHERE YOU'RE COMING FROM.

IS THAT SO?

YES, YES IT IS.

YOU CAME HERE ALONE, TO TRY AND NEGOTIATE WITH US. THAT'S VERY *VERY* BRAVE OF YOU BY THE WAY.

THAT'S ADMIRABLE.

JUST CAME TO ASK YOU THIS.

ANY AMOUNT OF TALKING GOING TO GET YOU TO BACK OFF? WILL YOU STOP COMING AFTER MY PEOPLE?

IN ALL HONESTY?

PROBABLY NOT.

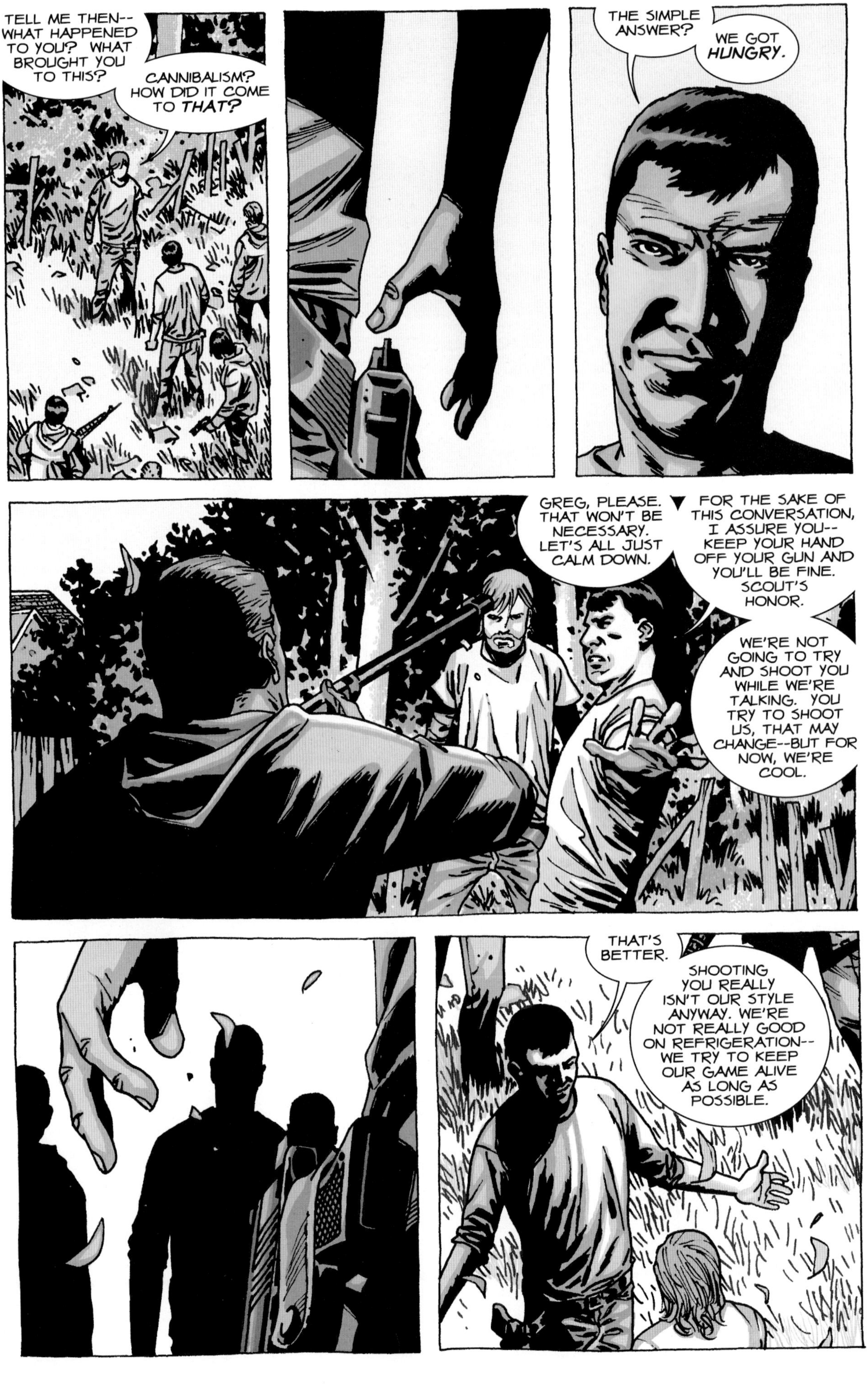
TELL ME THEN-- WHAT HAPPENED TO YOU? WHAT BROUGHT YOU TO THIS?
CANNIBALISM? HOW DID IT COME TO THAT?
THE SIMPLE ANSWER?
WE GOT HUNGRY.
GREG, PLEASE. THAT WON'T BE NECESSARY. LET'S ALL JUST CALM DOWN.
FOR THE SAKE OF THIS CONVERSATION, I ASSURE YOU-- KEEP YOUR HAND OFF YOUR GUN AND YOU'LL BE FINE. SCOUT'S HONOR.
WE'RE NOT GOING TO TRY AND SHOOT YOU WHILE WE'RE TALKING. YOU TRY TO SHOOT US, THAT MAY CHANGE--BUT FOR NOW, WE'RE COOL.
THAT'S BETTER.
SHOOTING YOU REALLY ISN'T OUR STYLE ANYWAY. WE'RE NOT REALLY GOOD ON REFRIGERATION-- WE TRY TO KEEP OUR GAME ALIVE AS LONG AS POSSIBLE.

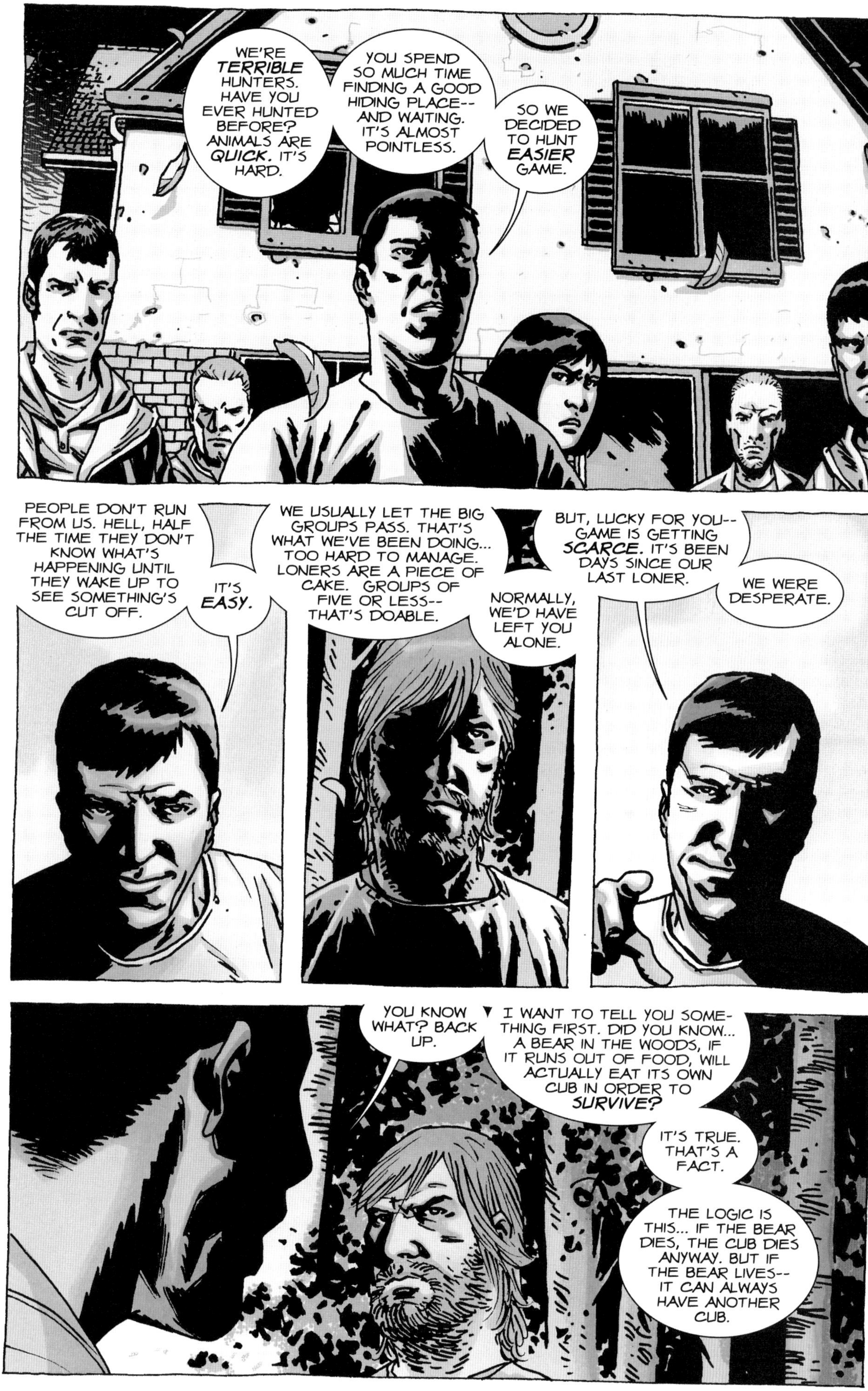
WE'RE TERRIBLE HUNTERS. HAVE YOU EVER HUNTED BEFORE? ANIMALS ARE QUICK. IT'S HARD.
YOU SPEND SO MUCH TIME FINDING A GOOD HIDING PLACE-- AND WAITING. IT'S ALMOST POINTLESS.
SO WE DECIDED TO HUNT EASIER GAME.
PEOPLE DON'T RUN FROM US. HELL, HALF THE TIME THEY DON'T KNOW WHAT'S HAPPENING UNTIL THEY WAKE UP TO SEE SOMETHING'S CUT OFF.
IT'S EASY.
WE USUALLY LET THE BIG GROUPS PASS. THAT'S WHAT WE'VE BEEN DOING... TOO HARD TO MANAGE. LONERS ARE A PIECE OF CAKE. GROUPS OF FIVE OR LESS-- THAT'S DOABLE.
NORMALLY, WE'D HAVE LEFT YOU ALONE.
BUT, LUCKY FOR YOU-- GAME IS GETTING SCARCE. IT'S BEEN DAYS SINCE OUR LAST LONER.
WE WERE DESPERATE.
YOU KNOW WHAT? BACK UP.
I WANT TO TELL YOU SOMETHING FIRST. DID YOU KNOW... A BEAR IN THE WOODS, IF IT RUNS OUT OF FOOD, WILL ACTUALLY EAT ITS OWN CUB IN ORDER TO SURVIVE?
IT'S TRUE. THAT'S A FACT.
THE LOGIC IS THIS... IF THE BEAR DIES, THE CUB DIES ANYWAY. BUT IF THE BEAR LIVES-- IT CAN ALWAYS HAVE ANOTHER CUB.

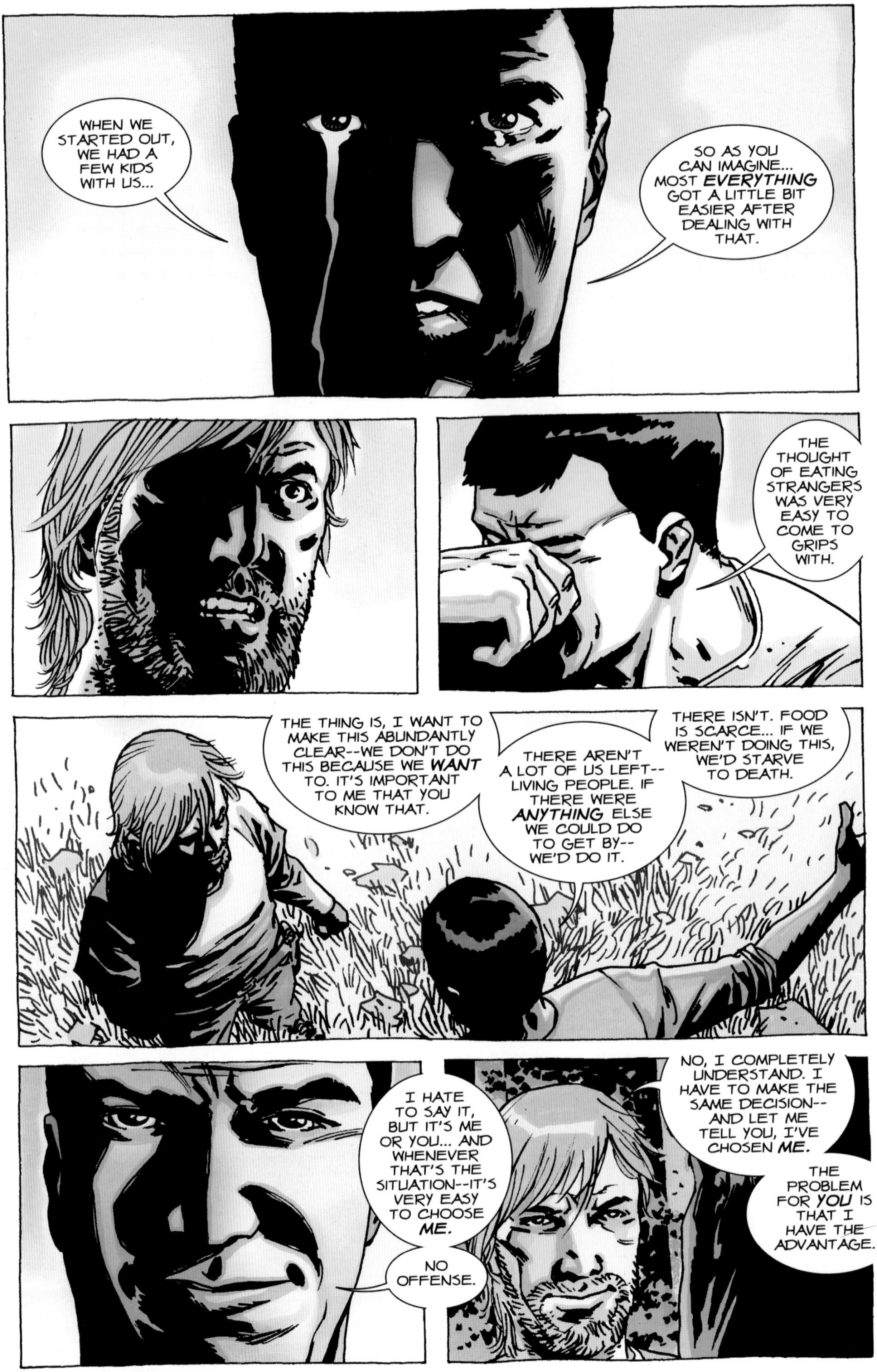
WHEN WE STARTED OUT, WE HAD A FEW KIDS WITH US...
SO AS YOU CAN IMAGINE... MOST EVERYTHING GOT A LITTLE BIT EASIER AFTER DEALING WITH THAT.
THE THOUGHT OF EATING STRANGERS WAS VERY EASY TO COME TO GRIPS WITH.
THE THING IS, I WANT TO MAKE THIS ABUNDANTLY CLEAR--WE DON'T DO THIS BECAUSE WE WANT TO. IT'S IMPORTANT TO ME THAT YOU KNOW THAT.
THERE AREN'T A LOT OF US LEFT--LIVING PEOPLE. IF THERE WERE ANYTHING ELSE WE COULD DO TO GET BY--WE'D DO IT.
THERE ISN'T. FOOD IS SCARCE... IF WE WEREN'T DOING THIS, WE'D STARVE TO DEATH.
I HATE TO SAY IT, BUT IT'S ME OR YOU... AND WHENEVER THAT'S THE SITUATION--IT'S VERY EASY TO CHOOSE ME.
NO OFFENSE.
NO, I COMPLETELY UNDERSTAND. I HAVE TO MAKE THE SAME DECISION--AND LET ME TELL YOU, I'VE CHOSEN ME.
THE PROBLEM FOR YOU IS THAT I HAVE THE ADVANTAGE.

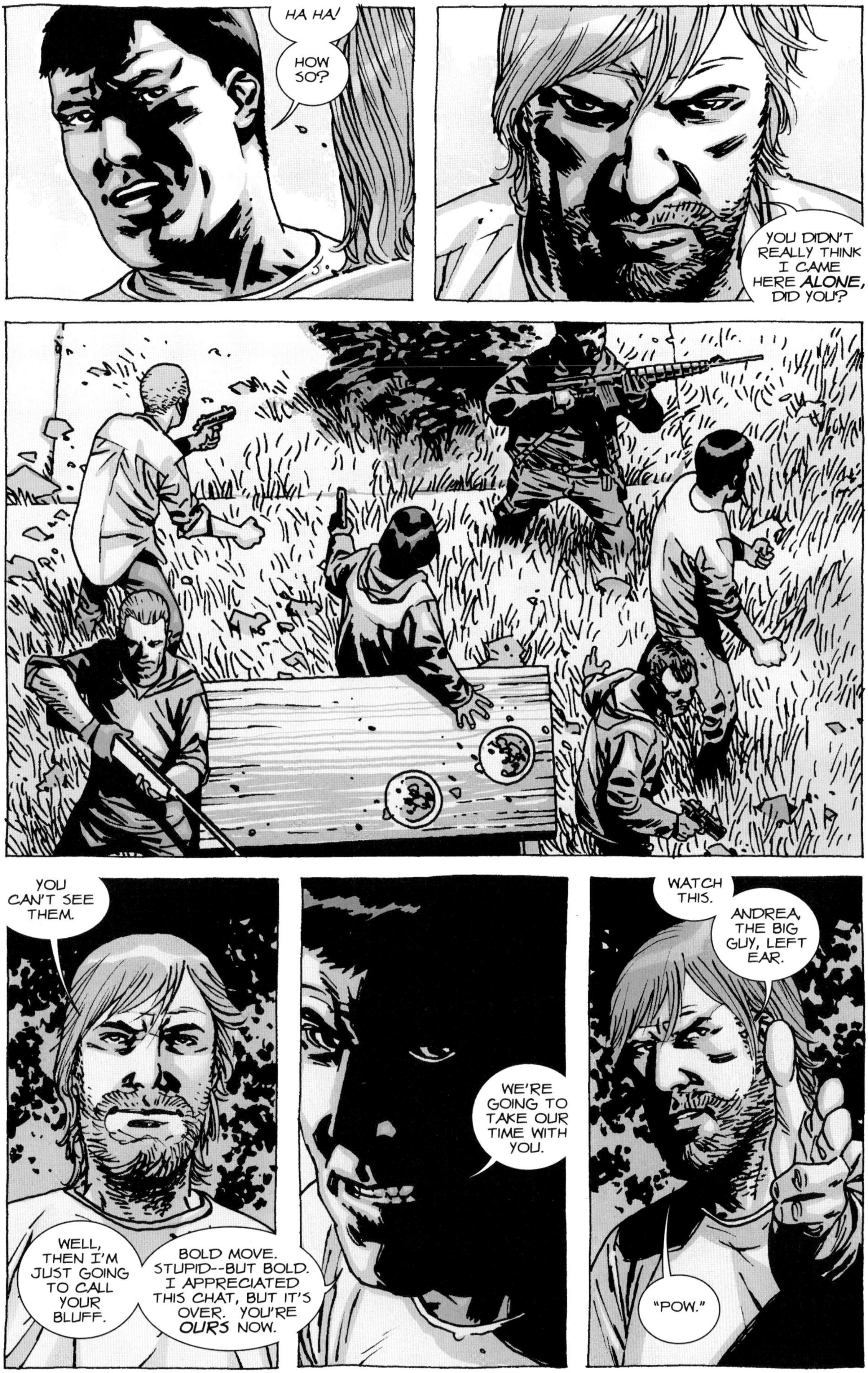
HA HA!
HOW SO?
YOU DIDN'T REALLY THINK I CAME HERE ALONE, DID YOU?
YOU CAN'T SEE THEM.
WELL, THEN I'M JUST GOING TO CALL YOUR BLUFF.
BOLD MOVE. STUPID--BUT BOLD. I APPRECIATED THIS CHAT, BUT IT'S OVER. YOU'RE OURS NOW.
WE'RE GOING TO TAKE OUR TIME WITH YOU.
WATCH THIS.
ANDREA, THE BIG GUY, LEFT EAR.
"POW."

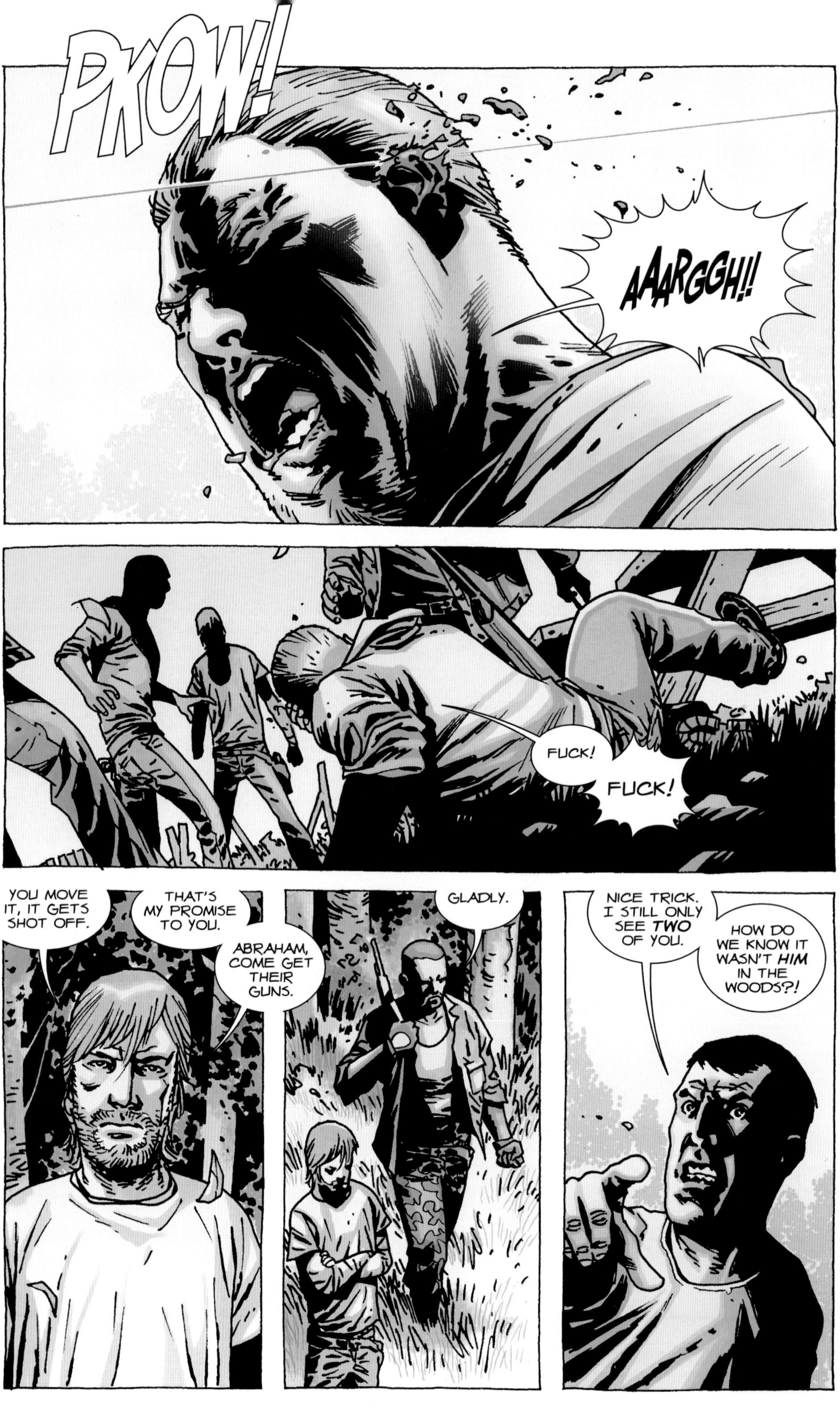
PKOW!
AAARGGH!!
FUCK!
FUCK!
YOU MOVE IT, IT GETS SHOT OFF.
THAT'S MY PROMISE TO YOU.
ABRAHAM, COME GET THEIR GUNS.
GLADLY.
NICE TRICK. I STILL ONLY SEE TWO OF YOU.
HOW DO WE KNOW IT WASN'T HIM IN THE WOODS?!

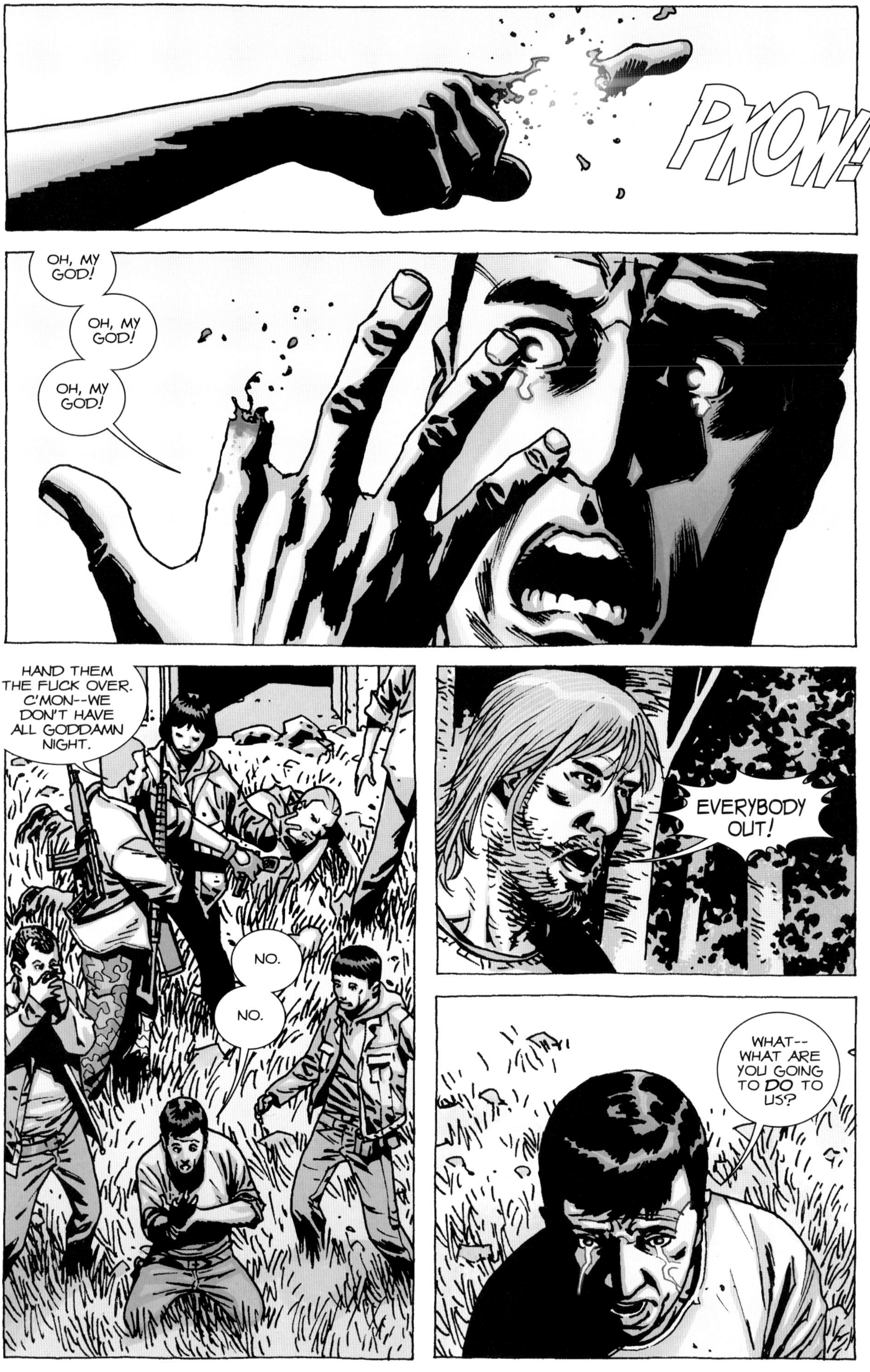
PKOW!
OH, MY GOD!
OH, MY GOD!
OH, MY GOD!
HAND THEM THE FUCK OVER. C'MON--WE DON'T HAVE ALL GODDAMN NIGHT.
NO.
NO.
EVERYBODY OUT!
WHAT-- WHAT ARE YOU GOING TO DO TO US?

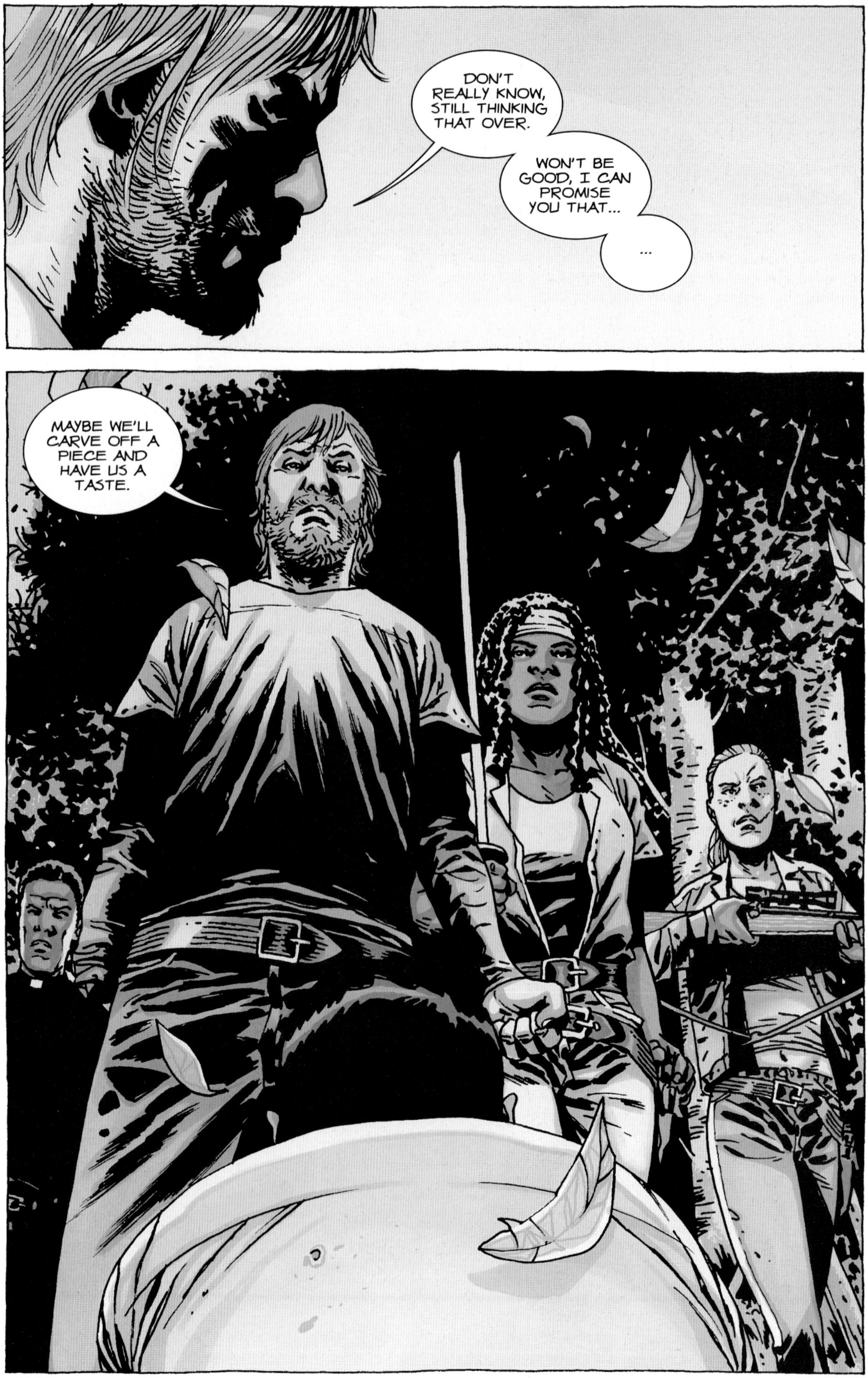
DON'T REALLY KNOW, STILL THINKING THAT OVER.
WON'T BE GOOD, I CAN PROMISE YOU THAT...
...
MAYBE WE'LL CARVE OFF A PIECE AND HAVE US A TASTE.

PLEASE, I'M BEGGING YOU HERE-- JUST MOVE ON. LEAVE US BE AND MOVE ON.

WE WON'T COME AFTER YOU--I *PROMISE*. JUST LEAVE US HERE. YOU HAVE MY WORD.

NOT WHAT YOU WERE SAYING A FEW MINUTES AGO. AS I RECALL, YOU MADE IT PRETTY CLEAR THAT YOU PLANNED ON HUNTING ALL OF MY PEOPLE DOWN AND *EATING* THEM.

YOU OR US... REMEMBER?

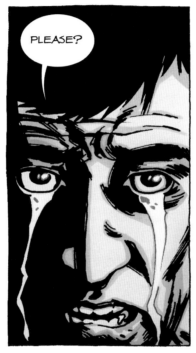

PLEASE?

NOT GOING TO WORK... BUT LOOK ON THE BRIGHT SIDE, WE'RE PROBABLY NOT REALLY GOING TO EAT YOU.

RICK, I DON'T--

YOU MAY NOT WANT TO BE HERE FOR THIS, GABRIEL.

PUT HIM ON THE PICNIC TABLE.

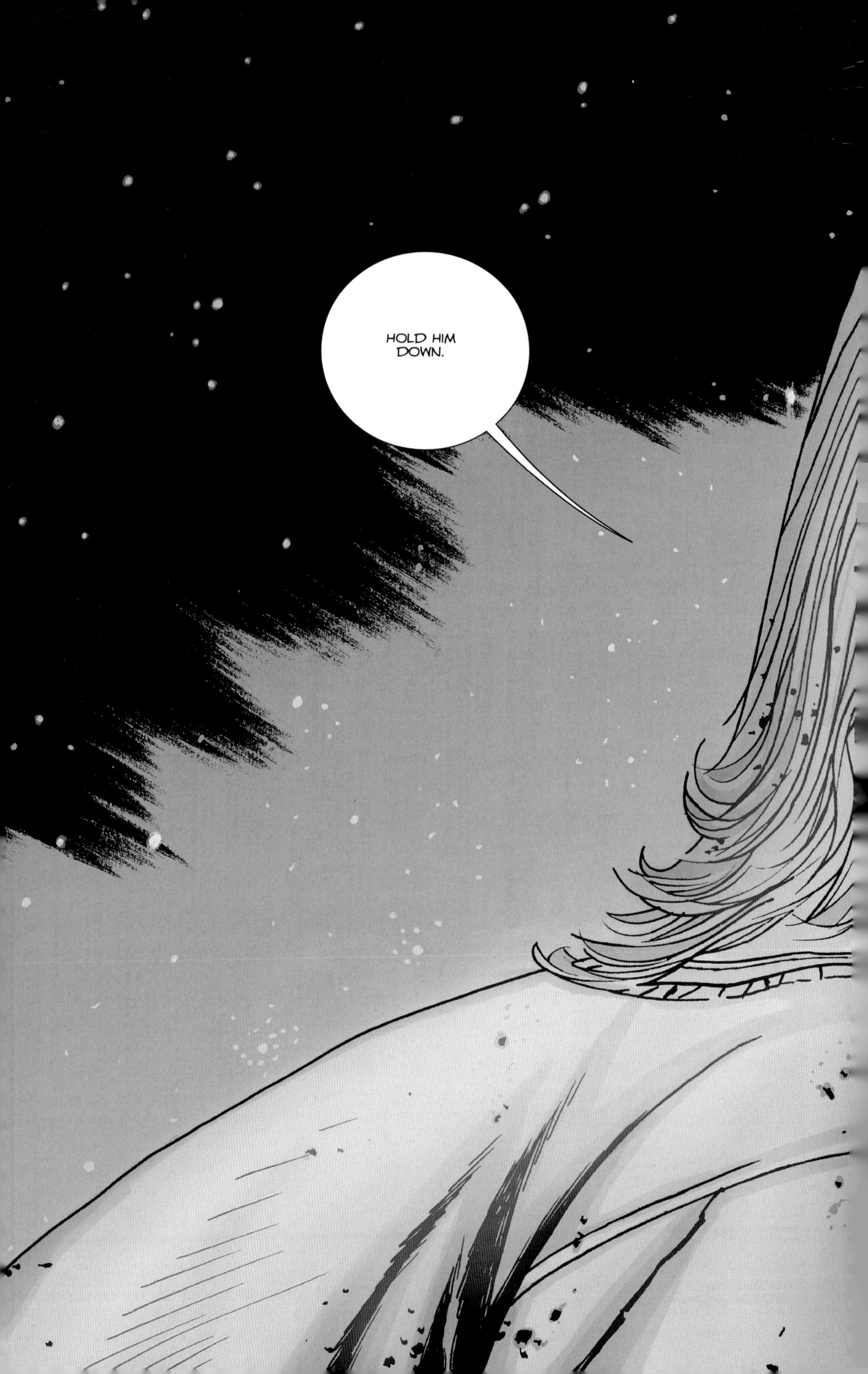
HOLD HIM DOWN.

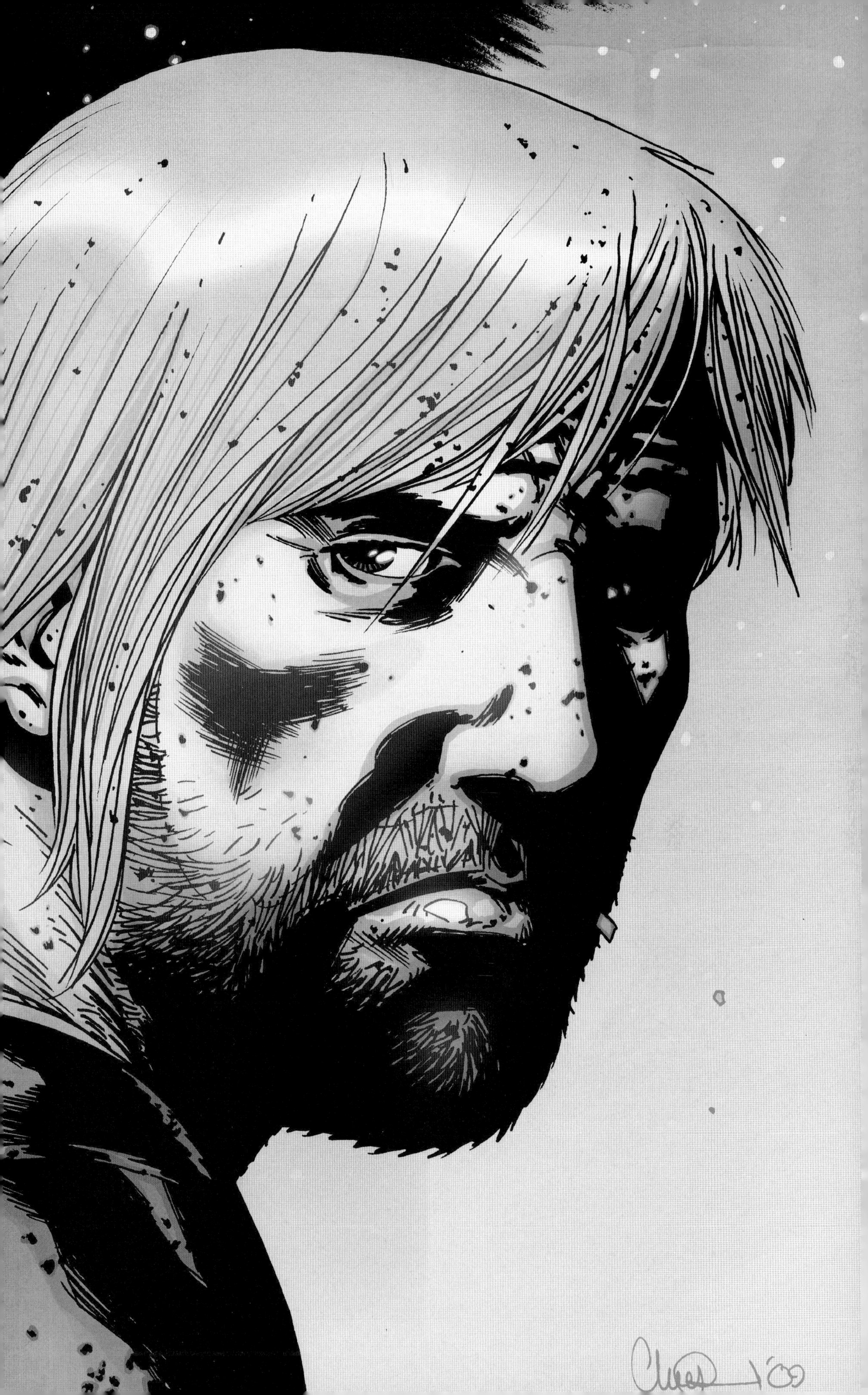

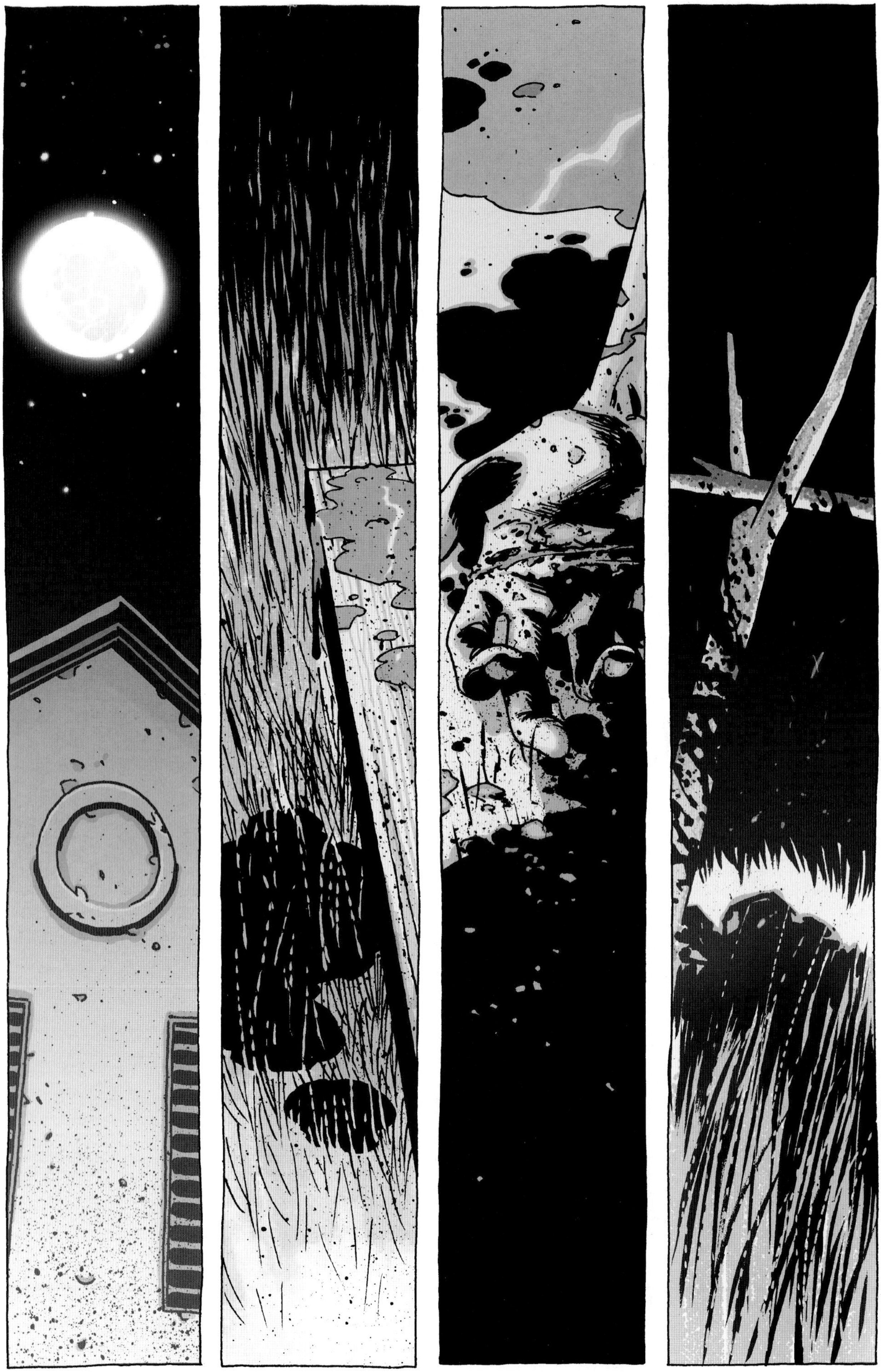

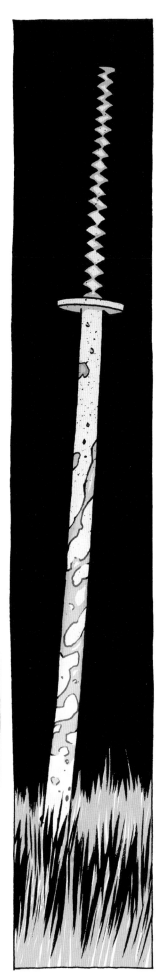
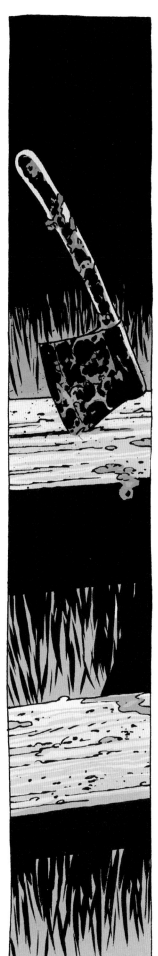

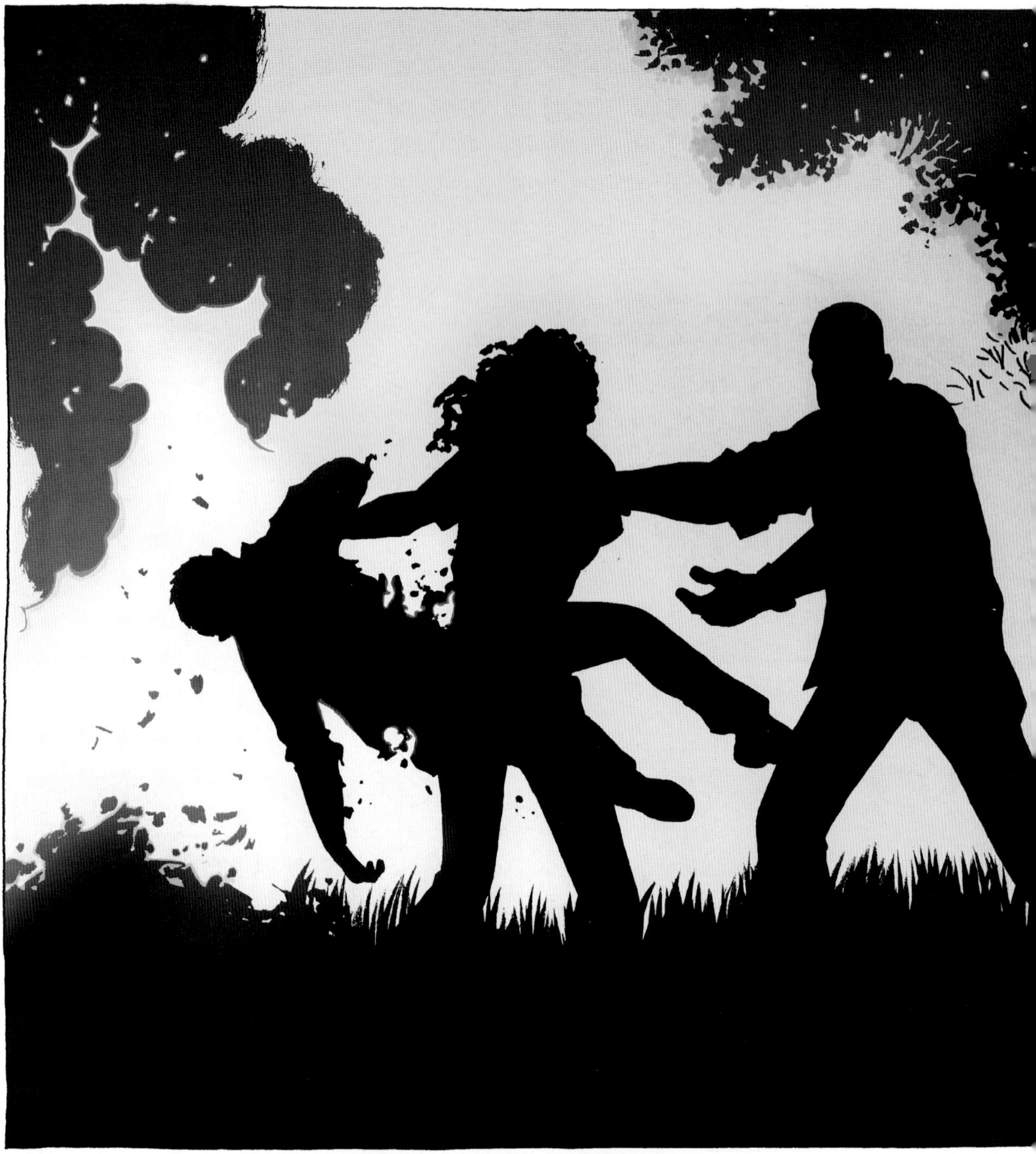
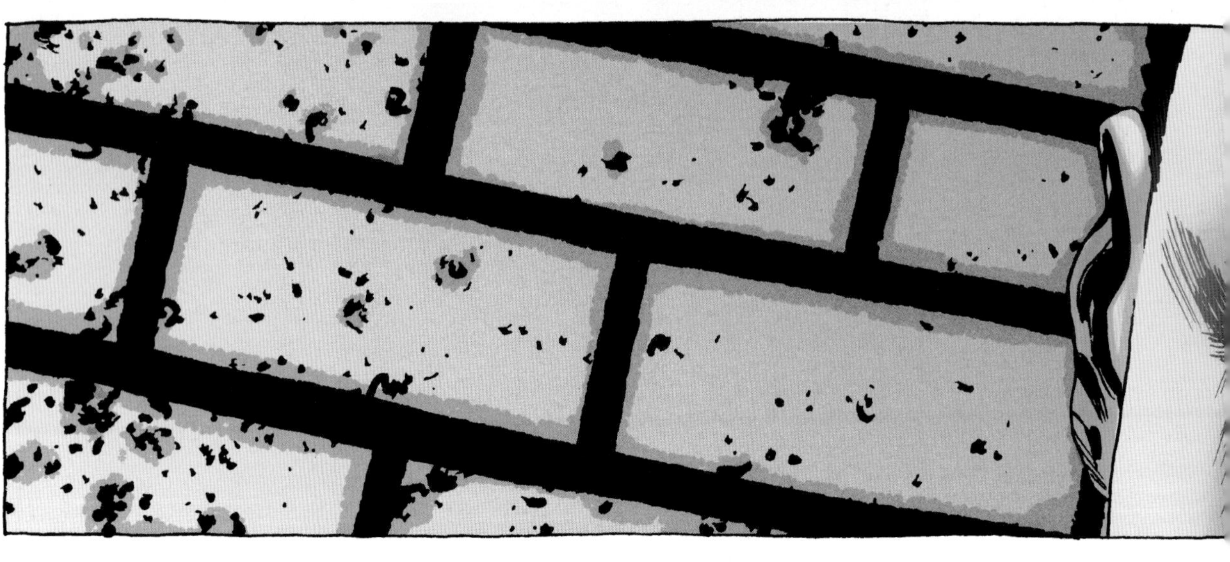

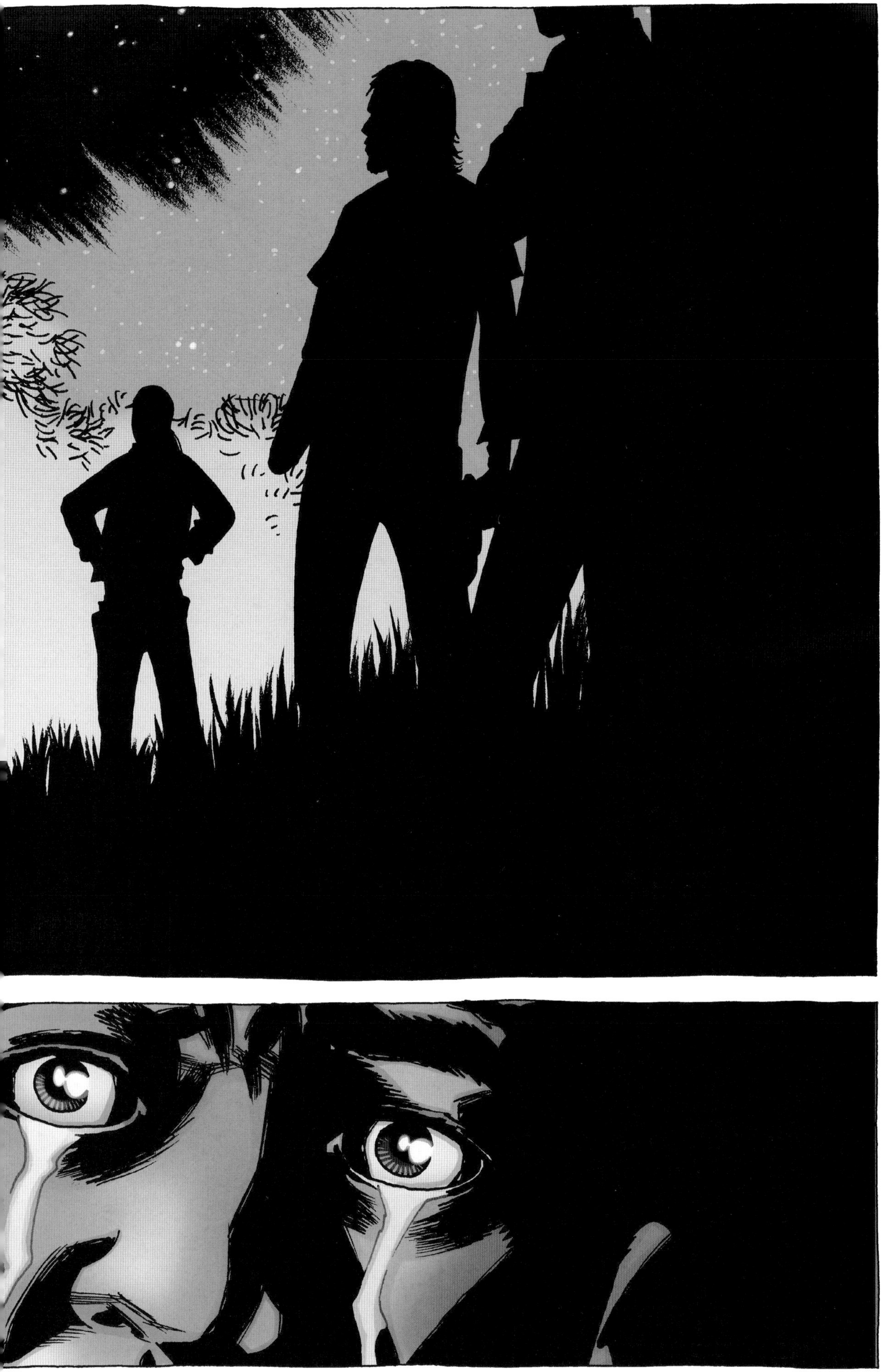

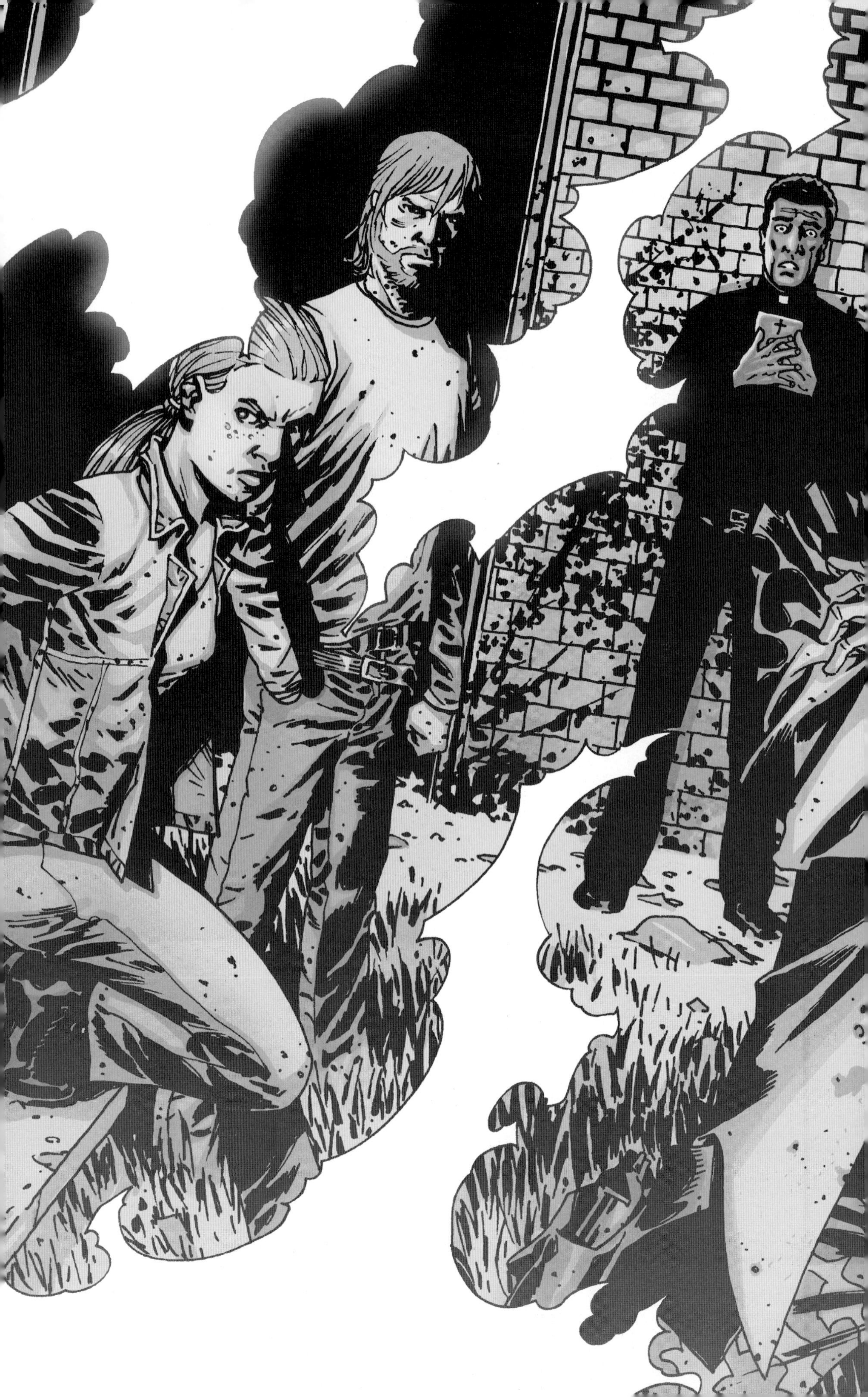

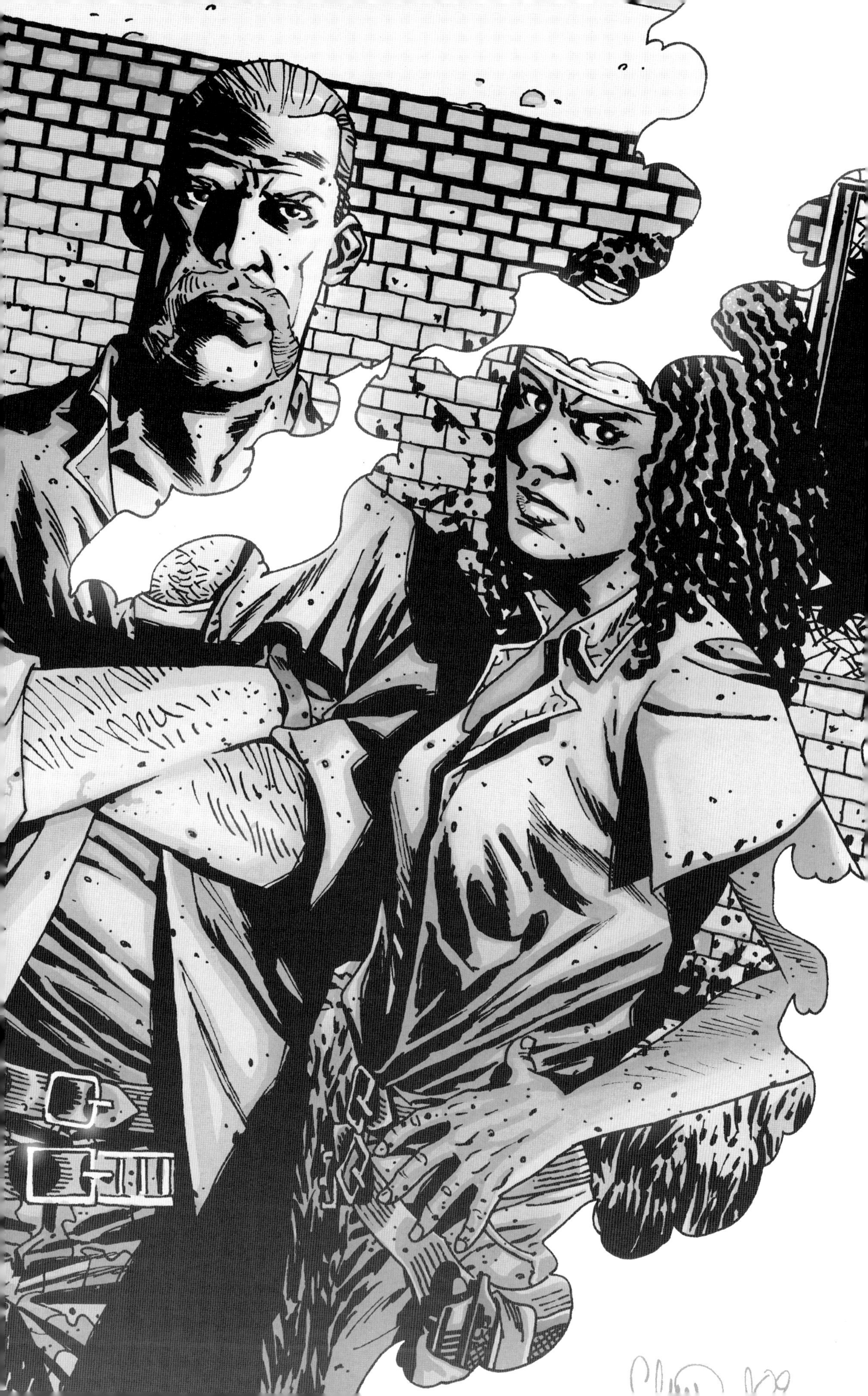

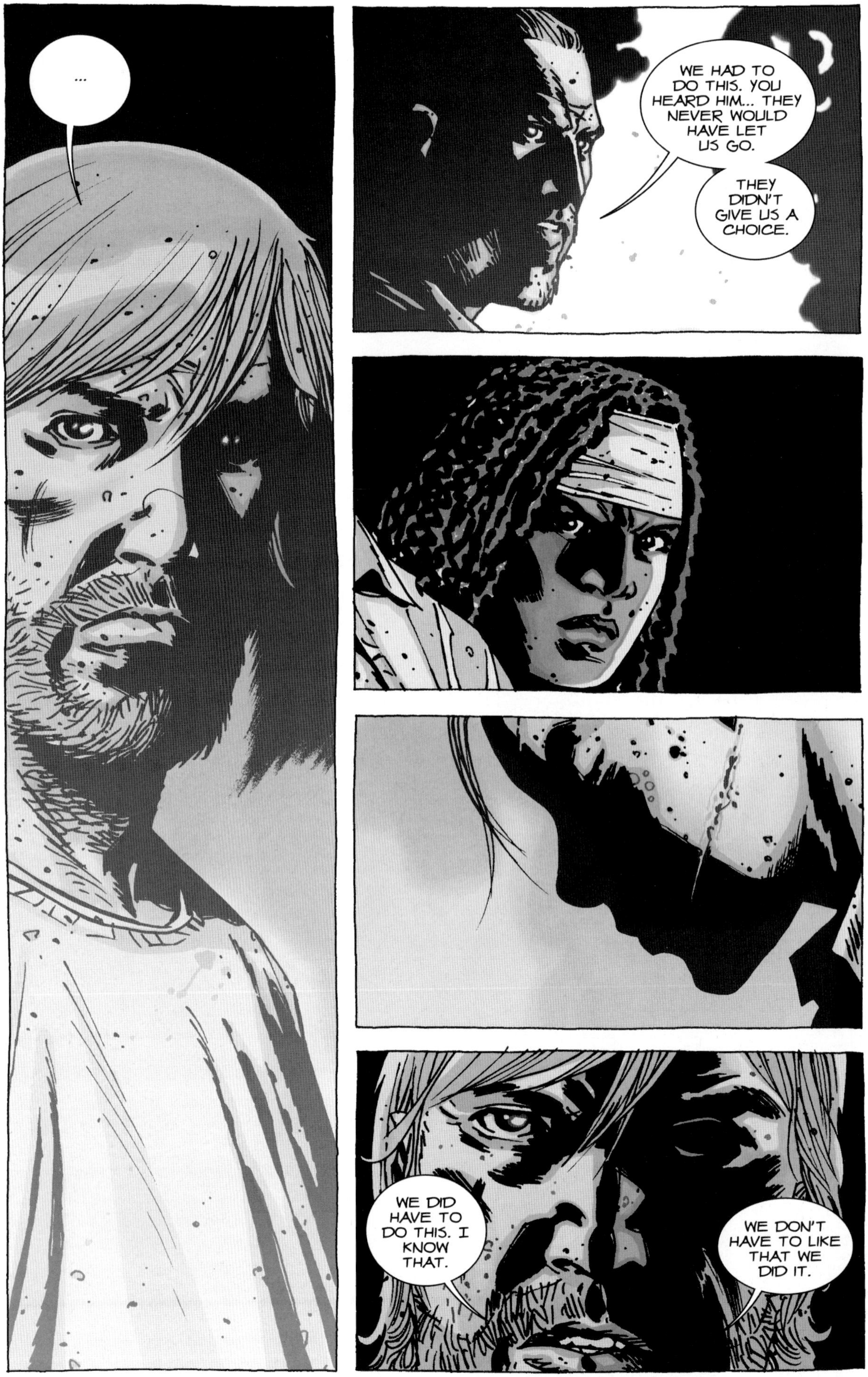
...
WE HAD TO DO THIS. YOU HEARD HIM... THEY NEVER WOULD HAVE LET US GO.
THEY DIDN'T GIVE US A CHOICE.
WE DID HAVE TO DO THIS. I KNOW THAT.
WE DON'T HAVE TO LIKE THAT WE DID IT.

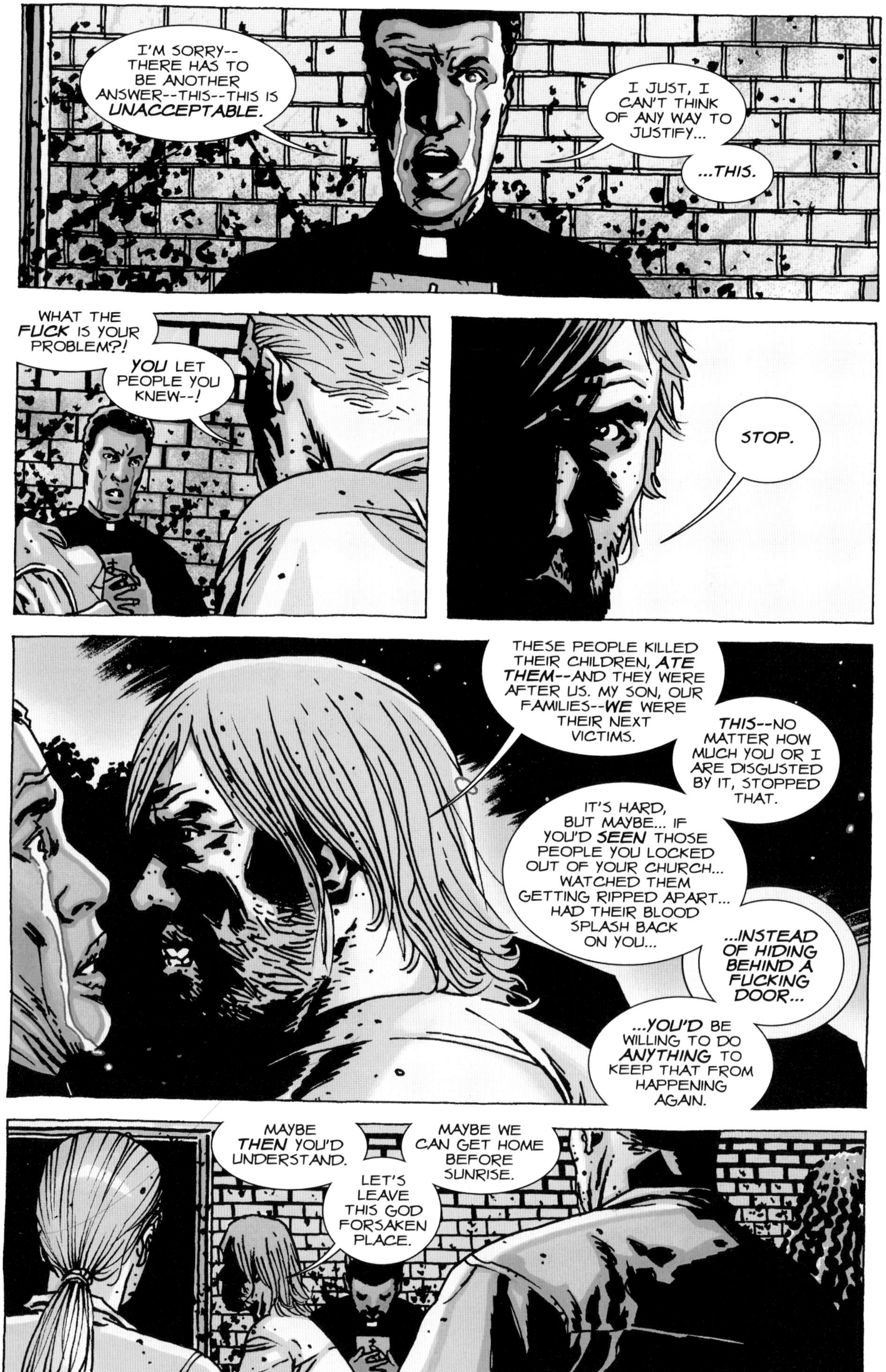
I'M SORRY-- THERE HAS TO BE ANOTHER ANSWER--THIS--THIS IS UNACCEPTABLE.
I JUST, I CAN'T THINK OF ANY WAY TO JUSTIFY...
...THIS.
WHAT THE FUCK IS YOUR PROBLEM?!
YOU LET PEOPLE YOU KNEW--!
STOP.
THESE PEOPLE KILLED THEIR CHILDREN, ATE THEM--AND THEY WERE AFTER US. MY SON, OUR FAMILIES--WE WERE THEIR NEXT VICTIMS.
THIS--NO MATTER HOW MUCH YOU OR I ARE DISGUSTED BY IT, STOPPED THAT.
IT'S HARD, BUT MAYBE... IF YOU'D SEEN THOSE PEOPLE YOU LOCKED OUT OF YOUR CHURCH... WATCHED THEM GETTING RIPPED APART... HAD THEIR BLOOD SPLASH BACK ON YOU...
...INSTEAD OF HIDING BEHIND A FUCKING DOOR...
...YOU'D BE WILLING TO DO ANYTHING TO KEEP THAT FROM HAPPENING AGAIN.
MAYBE THEN YOU'D UNDERSTAND.
LET'S LEAVE THIS GOD FORSAKEN PLACE.
MAYBE WE CAN GET HOME BEFORE SUNRISE.

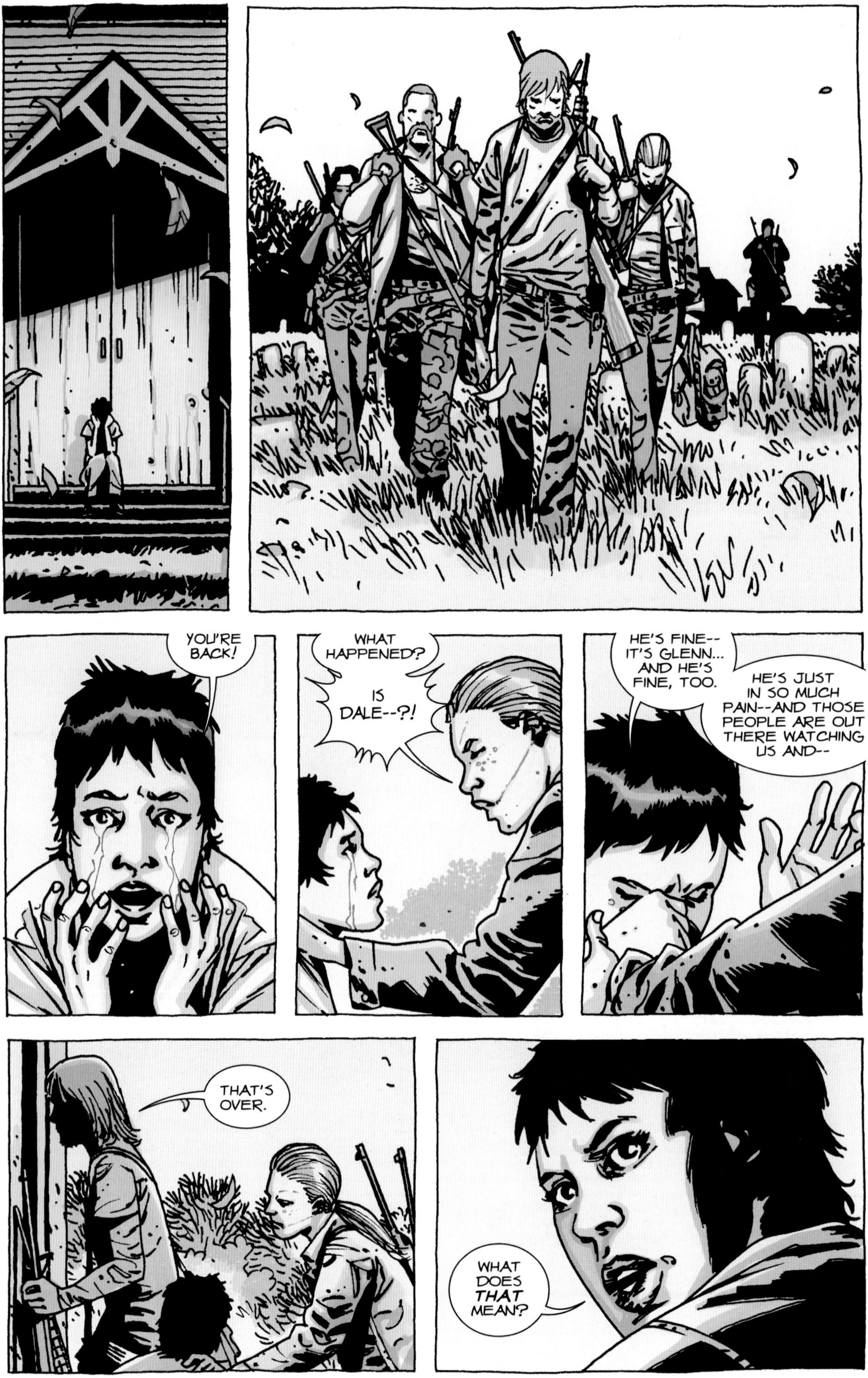
YOU'RE BACK!
WHAT HAPPENED?
IS DALE--?!
HE'S FINE-- IT'S GLENN... AND HE'S FINE, TOO.
HE'S JUST IN SO MUCH PAIN--AND THOSE PEOPLE ARE OUT THERE WATCHING US AND--
THAT'S OVER.
WHAT DOES *THAT* MEAN?

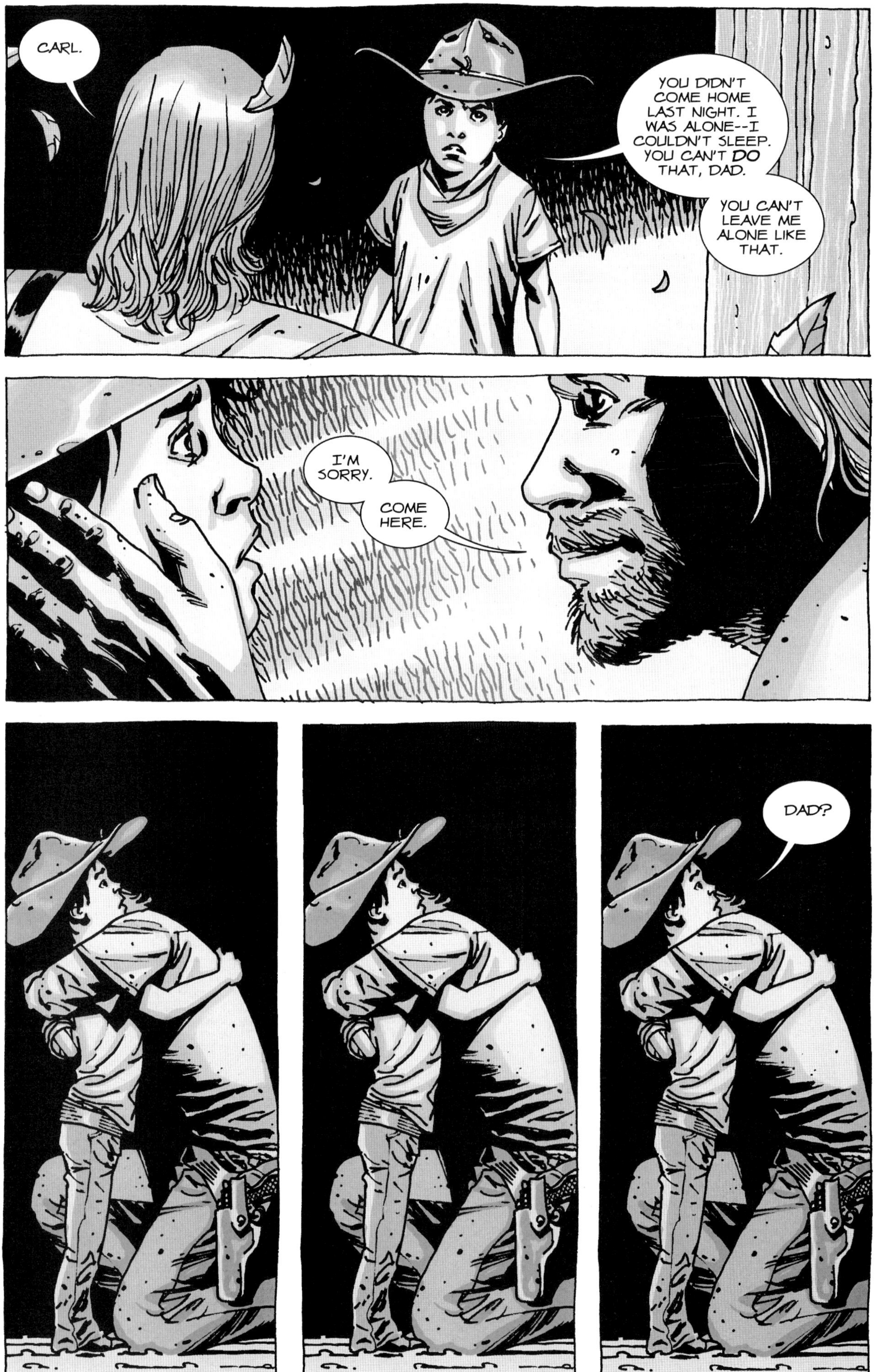
CARL.
YOU DIDN'T COME HOME LAST NIGHT. I WAS ALONE--I COULDN'T SLEEP. YOU CAN'T **DO** THAT, DAD.
YOU CAN'T LEAVE ME ALONE LIKE THAT.
I'M SORRY.
COME HERE.
DAD?

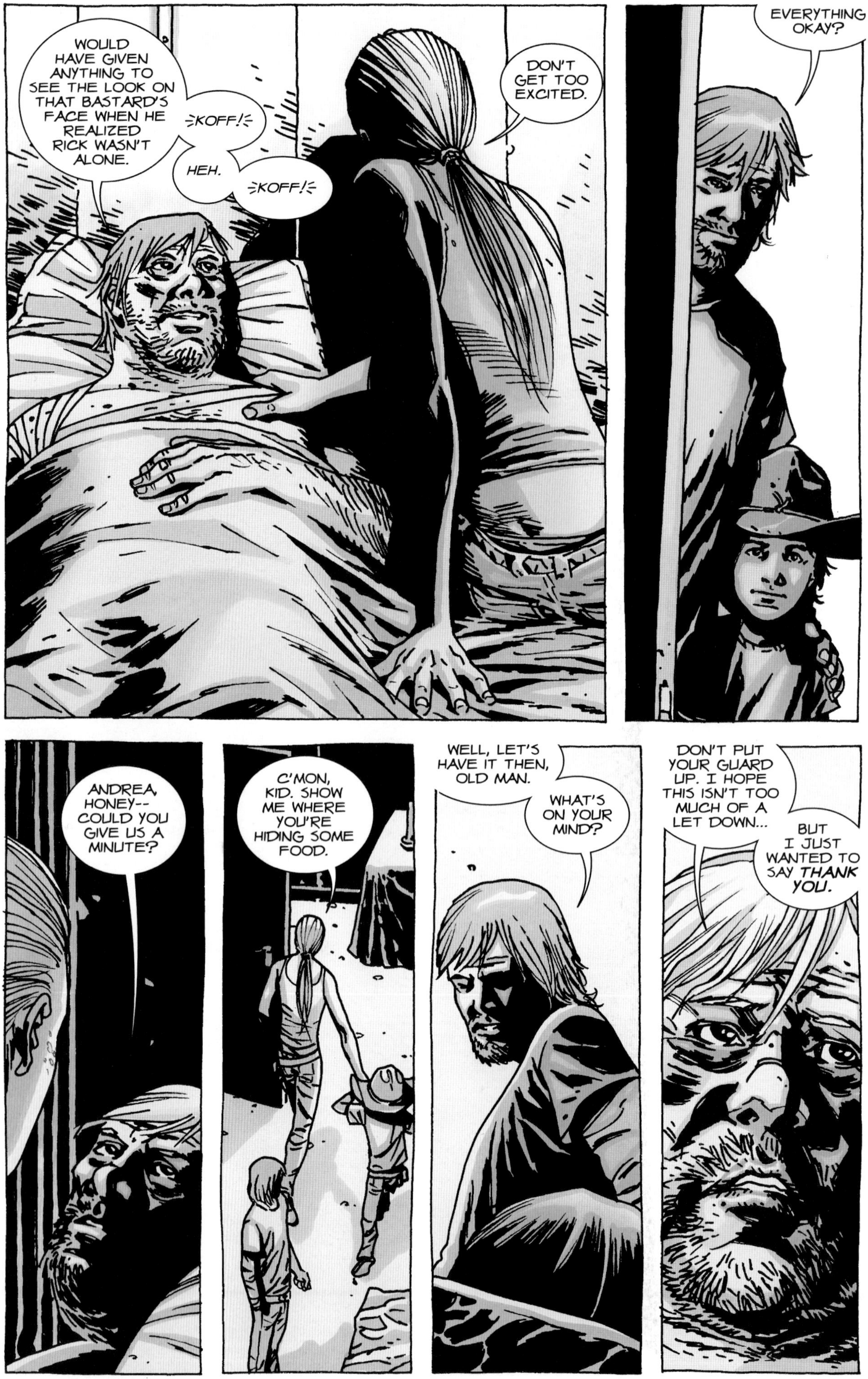
WOULD HAVE GIVEN ANYTHING TO SEE THE LOOK ON THAT BASTARD'S FACE WHEN HE REALIZED RICK WASN'T ALONE.
KOFF!
HEH.
KOFF!
DON'T GET TOO EXCITED.
EVERYTHING OKAY?
ANDREA, HONEY-- COULD YOU GIVE US A MINUTE?
C'MON, KID. SHOW ME WHERE YOU'RE HIDING SOME FOOD.
WELL, LET'S HAVE IT THEN, OLD MAN.
WHAT'S ON YOUR MIND?
DON'T PUT YOUR GUARD UP. I HOPE THIS ISN'T TOO MUCH OF A LET DOWN...
BUT I JUST WANTED TO SAY *THANK YOU.*

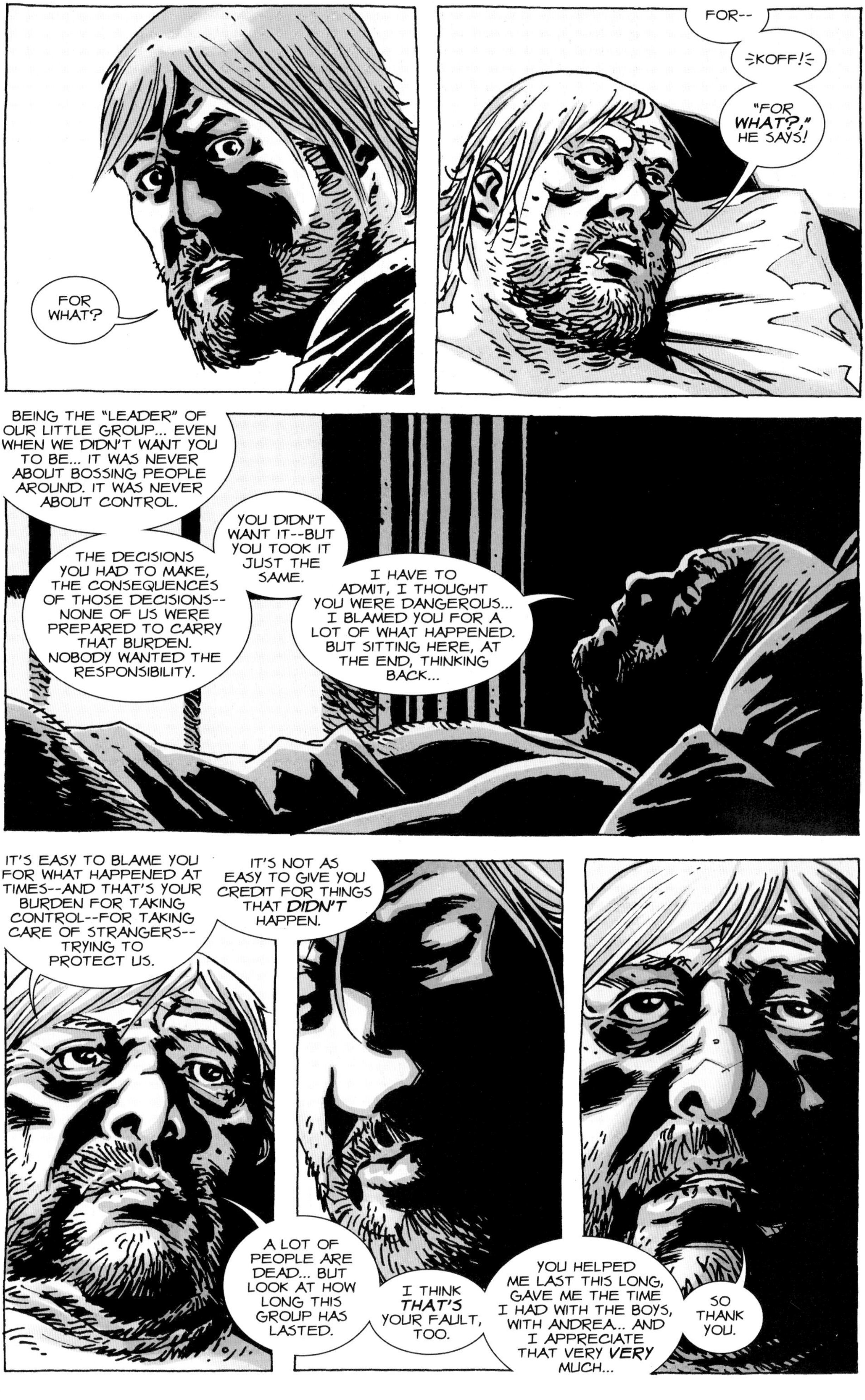
FOR WHAT?
FOR--
KOFF!
"FOR WHAT?," HE SAYS!
BEING THE "LEADER" OF OUR LITTLE GROUP... EVEN WHEN WE DIDN'T WANT YOU TO BE... IT WAS NEVER ABOUT BOSSING PEOPLE AROUND. IT WAS NEVER ABOUT CONTROL.
THE DECISIONS YOU HAD TO MAKE, THE CONSEQUENCES OF THOSE DECISIONS-- NONE OF US WERE PREPARED TO CARRY THAT BURDEN. NOBODY WANTED THE RESPONSIBILITY.
YOU DIDN'T WANT IT--BUT YOU TOOK IT JUST THE SAME.
I HAVE TO ADMIT, I THOUGHT YOU WERE DANGEROUS... I BLAMED YOU FOR A LOT OF WHAT HAPPENED. BUT SITTING HERE, AT THE END, THINKING BACK...
IT'S EASY TO BLAME YOU FOR WHAT HAPPENED AT TIMES--AND THAT'S YOUR BURDEN FOR TAKING CONTROL--FOR TAKING CARE OF STRANGERS-- TRYING TO PROTECT US.
IT'S NOT AS EASY TO GIVE YOU CREDIT FOR THINGS THAT DIDN'T HAPPEN.
A LOT OF PEOPLE ARE DEAD... BUT LOOK AT HOW LONG THIS GROUP HAS LASTED.
I THINK THAT'S YOUR FAULT, TOO.
YOU HELPED ME LAST THIS LONG, GAVE ME THE TIME I HAD WITH THE BOYS, WITH ANDREA... AND I APPRECIATE THAT VERY VERY MUCH...
SO THANK YOU.

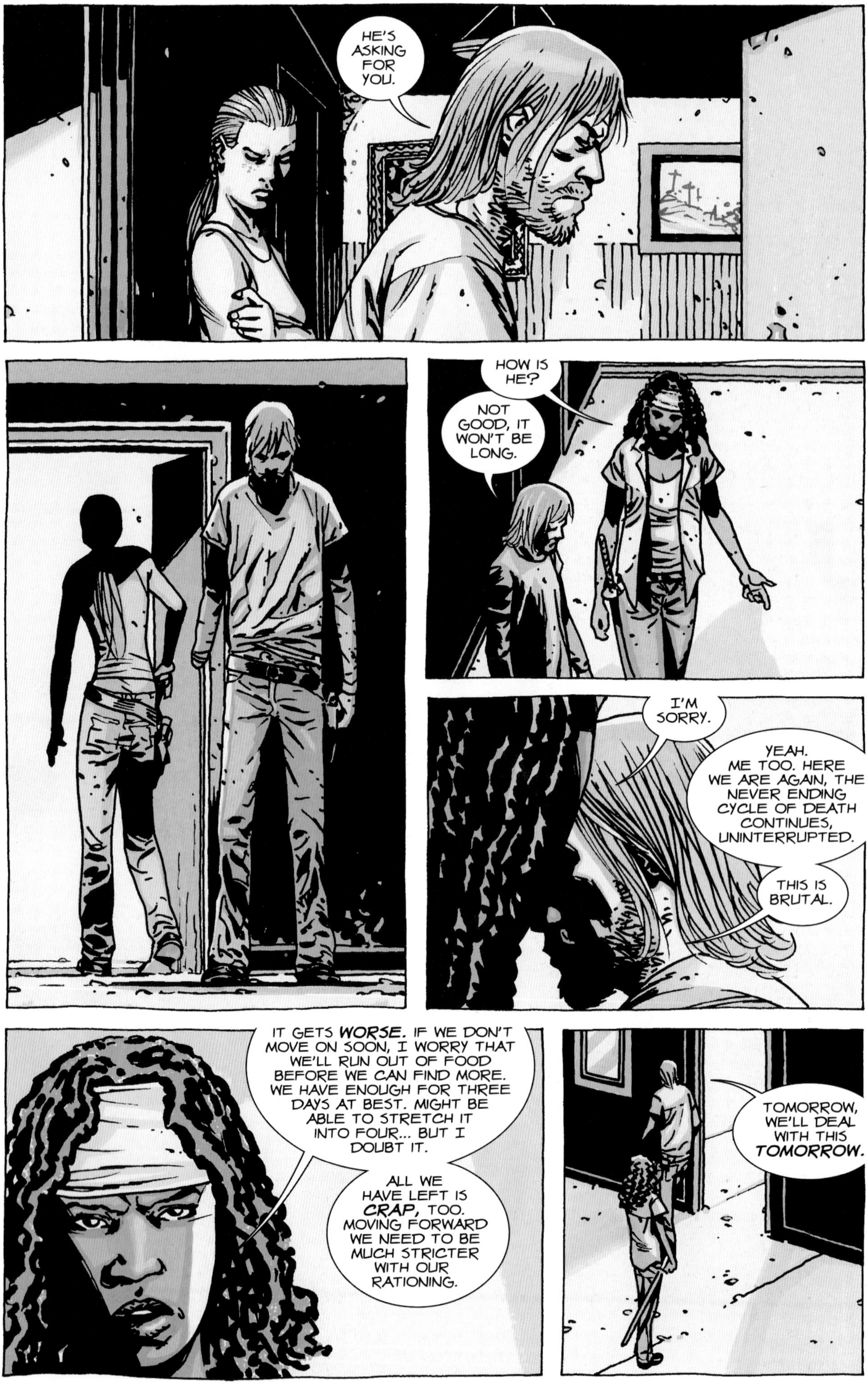
HE'S ASKING FOR YOU.
HOW IS HE?
NOT GOOD, IT WON'T BE LONG.
I'M SORRY.
YEAH. ME TOO. HERE WE ARE AGAIN, THE NEVER ENDING CYCLE OF DEATH CONTINUES, UNINTERRUPTED.
THIS IS BRUTAL.
IT GETS *WORSE.* IF WE DON'T MOVE ON SOON, I WORRY THAT WE'LL RUN OUT OF FOOD BEFORE WE CAN FIND MORE. WE HAVE ENOUGH FOR THREE DAYS AT BEST. MIGHT BE ABLE TO STRETCH IT INTO FOUR... BUT I DOUBT IT.
ALL WE HAVE LEFT IS *CRAP,* TOO. MOVING FORWARD WE NEED TO BE MUCH STRICTER WITH OUR RATIONING.
TOMORROW, WE'LL DEAL WITH THIS *TOMORROW.*

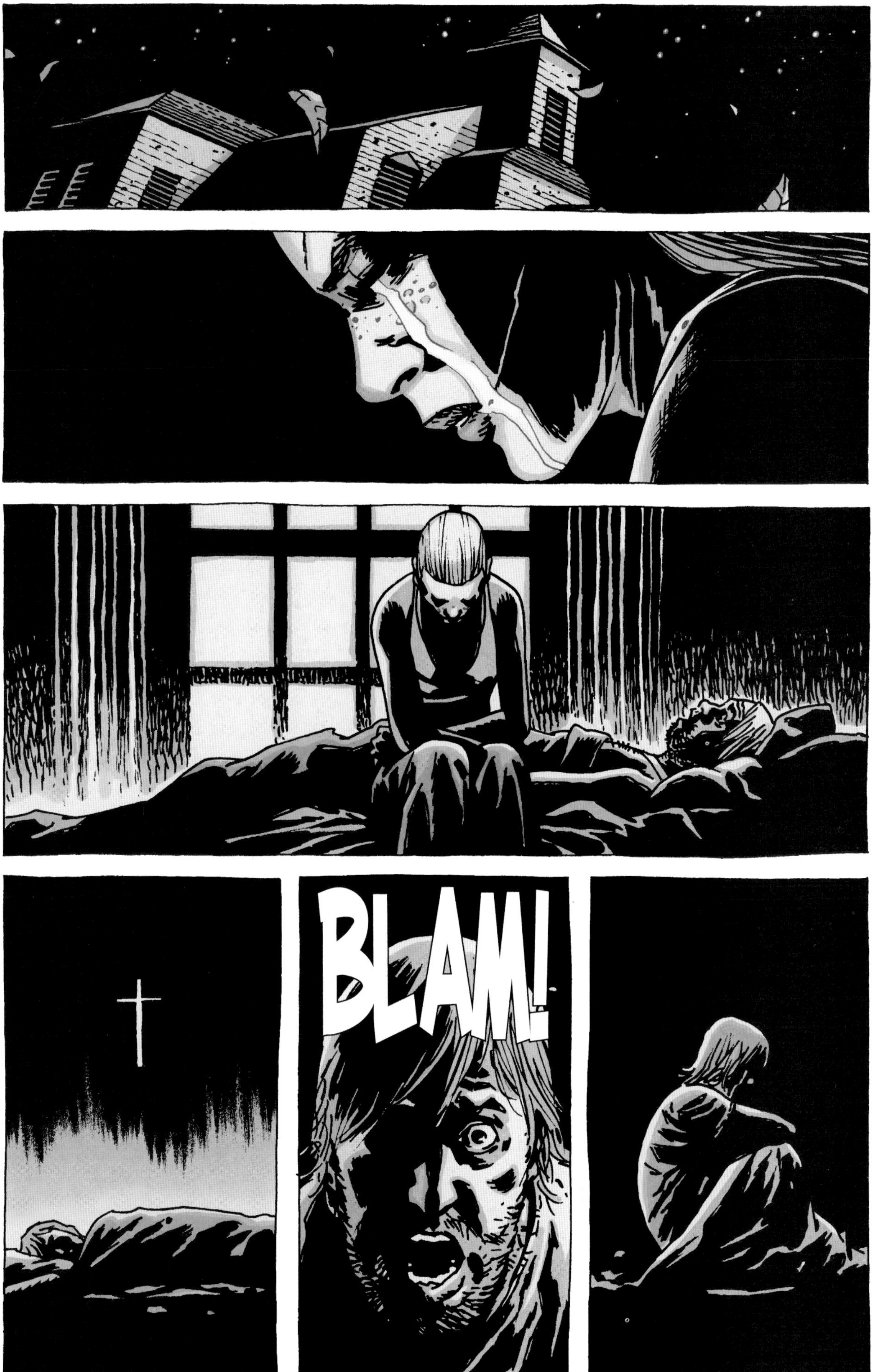
BLAM!

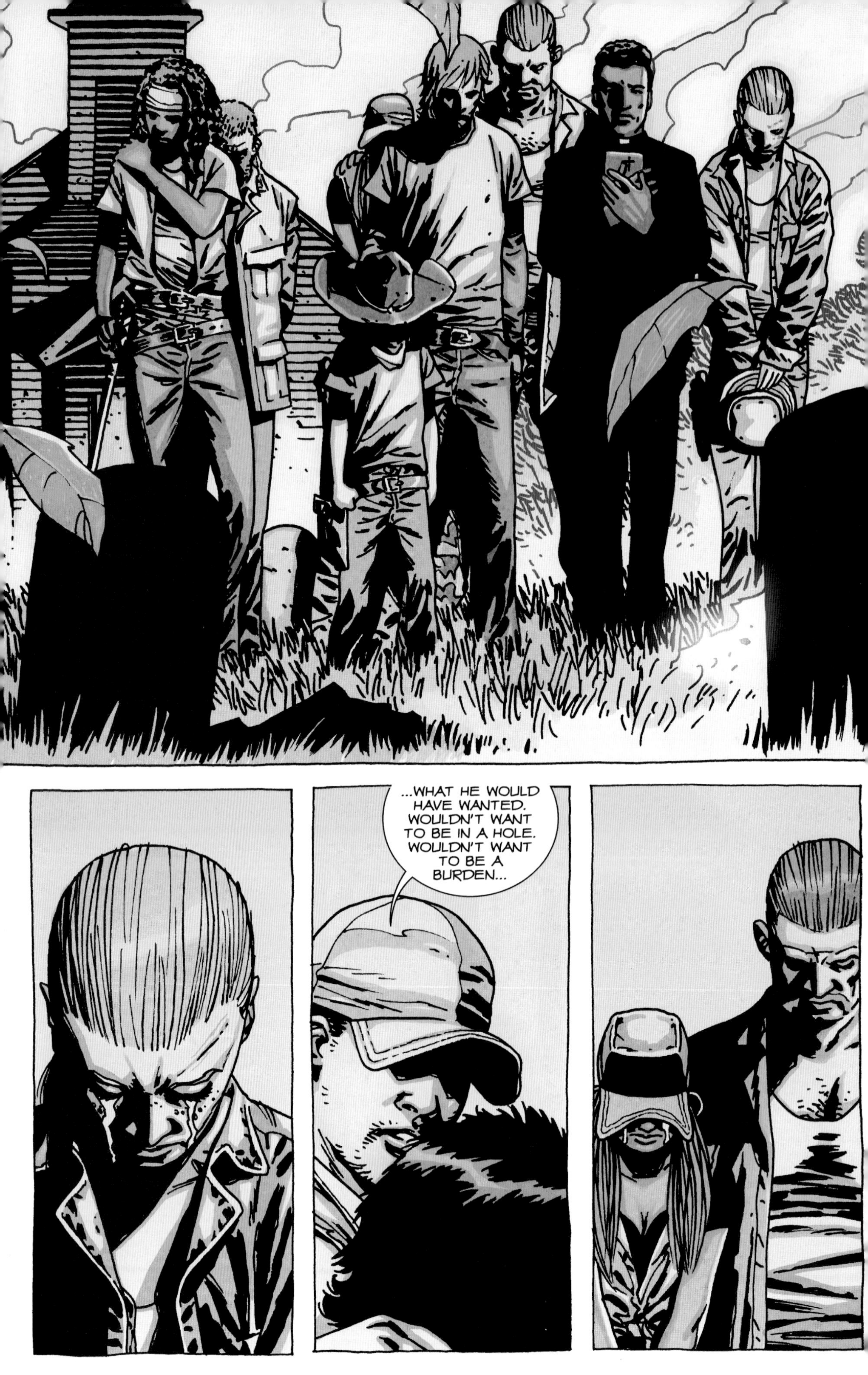
...WHAT HE WOULD HAVE WANTED. WOULDN'T WANT TO BE IN A HOLE. WOULDN'T WANT TO BE A BURDEN...

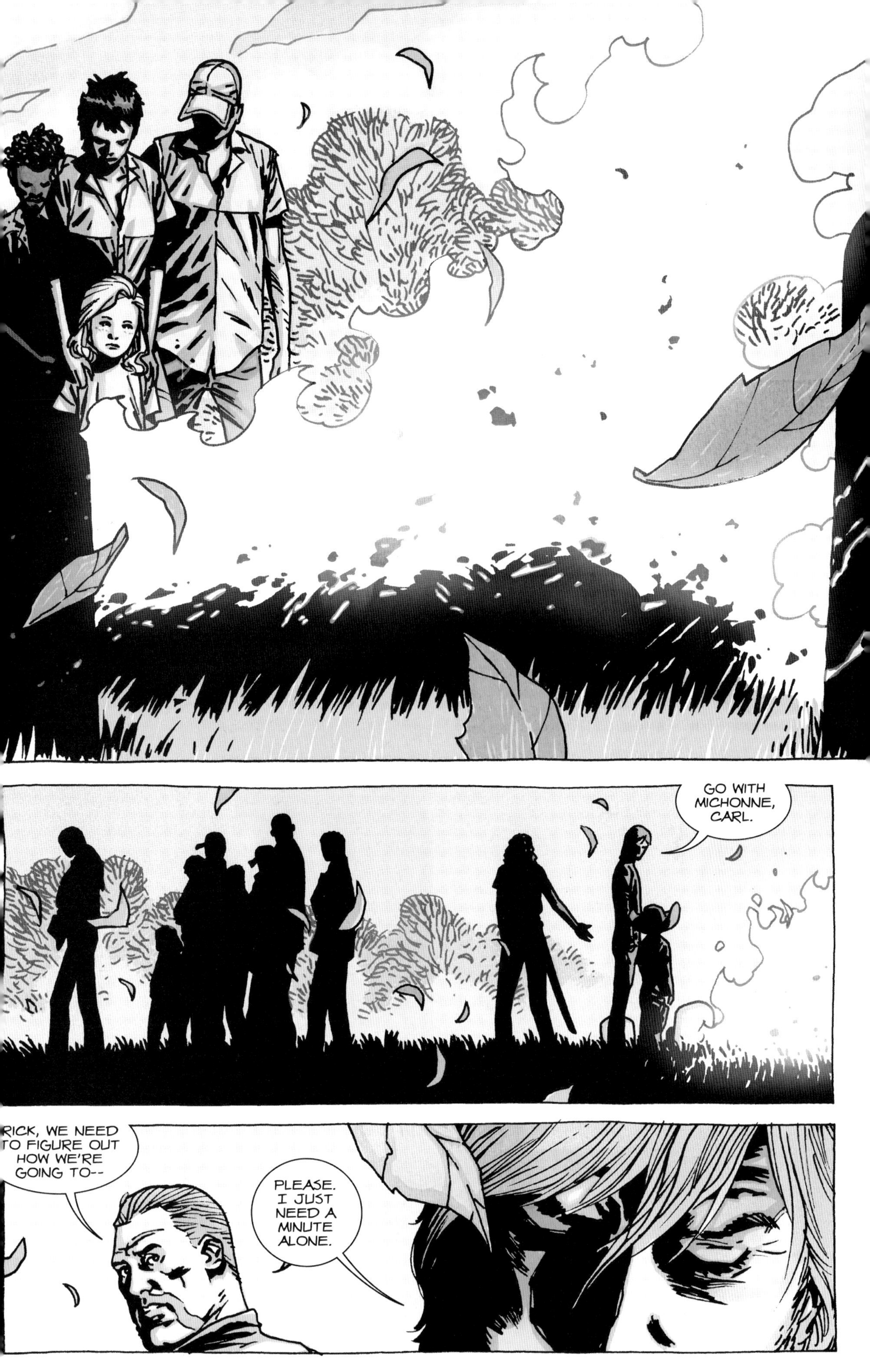
GO WITH MICHONNE, CARL.
RICK, WE NEED TO FIGURE OUT HOW WE'RE GOING TO--
PLEASE. I JUST NEED A MINUTE ALONE.

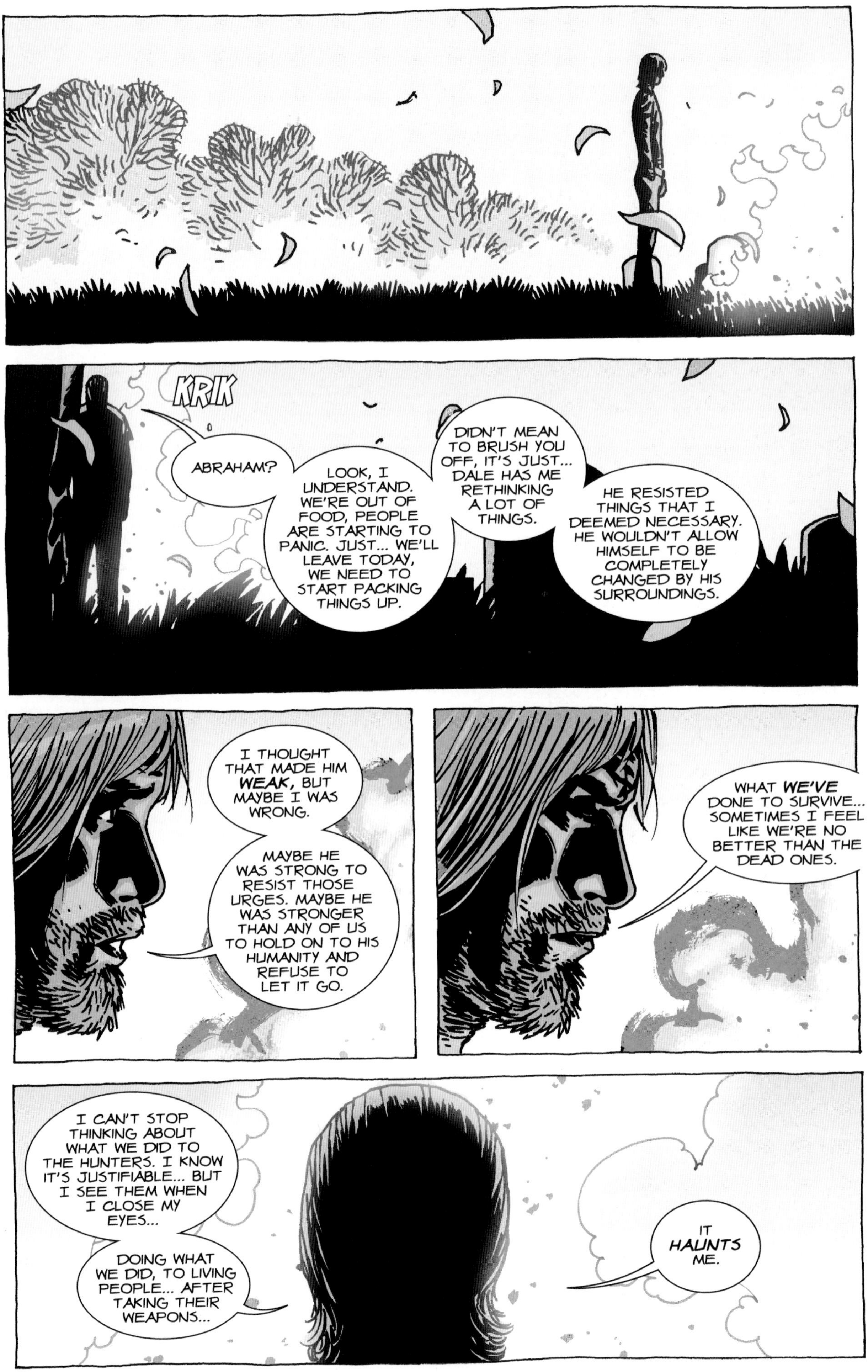
KRIK
ABRAHAM?
LOOK, I UNDERSTAND. WE'RE OUT OF FOOD, PEOPLE ARE STARTING TO PANIC. JUST... WE'LL LEAVE TODAY, WE NEED TO START PACKING THINGS UP.
DIDN'T MEAN TO BRUSH YOU OFF, IT'S JUST... DALE HAS ME RETHINKING A LOT OF THINGS.
HE RESISTED THINGS THAT I DEEMED NECESSARY. HE WOULDN'T ALLOW HIMSELF TO BE COMPLETELY CHANGED BY HIS SURROUNDINGS.
I THOUGHT THAT MADE HIM **WEAK,** BUT MAYBE I WAS WRONG.
MAYBE HE WAS STRONG TO RESIST THOSE URGES. MAYBE HE WAS STRONGER THAN ANY OF US TO HOLD ON TO HIS HUMANITY AND REFUSE TO LET IT GO.
WHAT **WE'VE** DONE TO SURVIVE... SOMETIMES I FEEL LIKE WE'RE NO BETTER THAN THE DEAD ONES.
I CAN'T STOP THINKING ABOUT WHAT WE DID TO THE HUNTERS. I KNOW IT'S JUSTIFIABLE... BUT I SEE THEM WHEN I CLOSE MY EYES...
DOING WHAT WE DID, TO LIVING PEOPLE... AFTER TAKING THEIR WEAPONS...
IT **HAUNTS** ME.

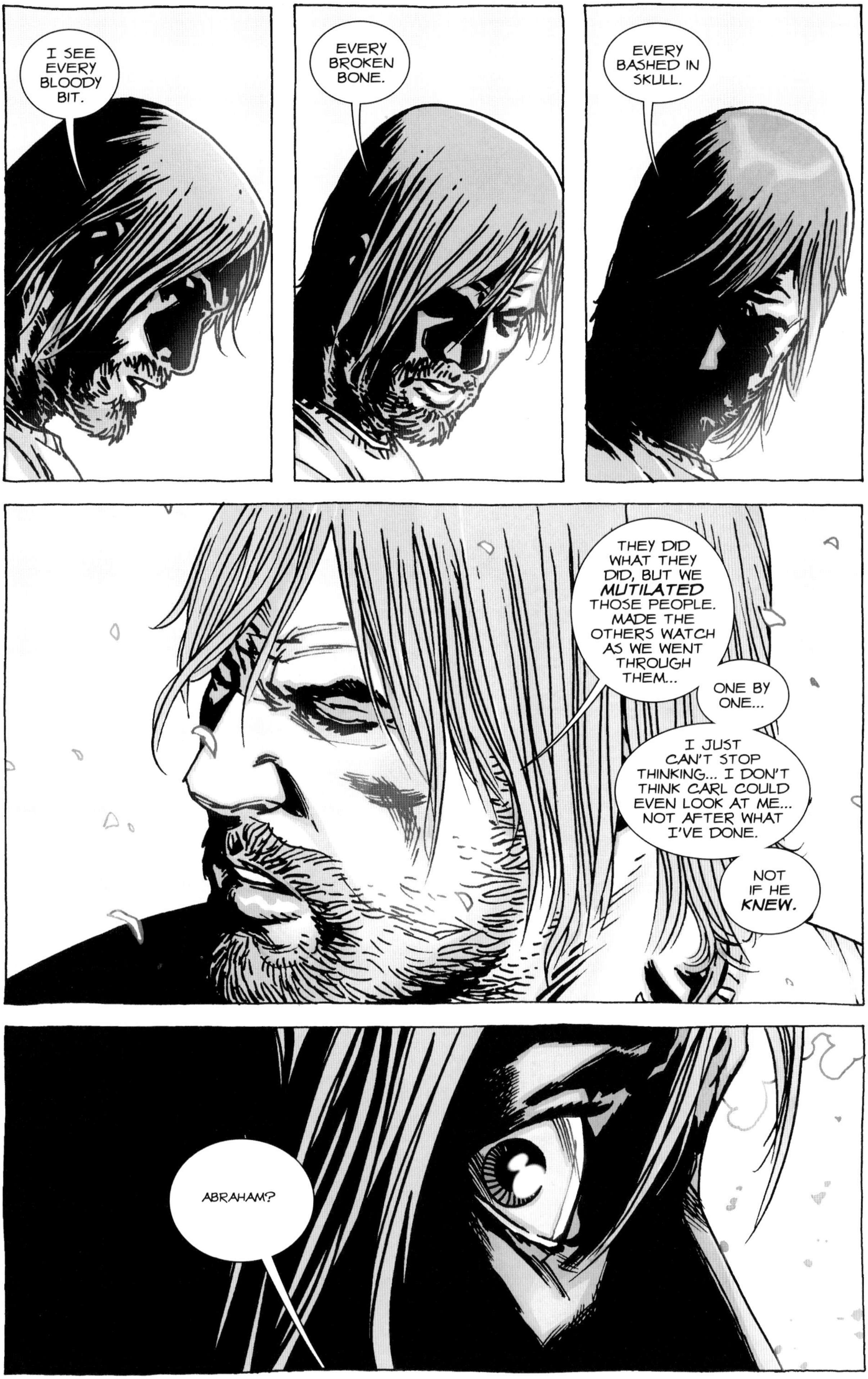
I SEE EVERY BLOODY BIT.
EVERY BROKEN BONE.
EVERY BASHED IN SKULL.
THEY DID WHAT THEY DID, BUT WE MUTILATED THOSE PEOPLE. MADE THE OTHERS WATCH AS WE WENT THROUGH THEM...
ONE BY ONE...
I JUST CAN'T STOP THINKING... I DON'T THINK CARL COULD EVEN LOOK AT ME... NOT AFTER WHAT I'VE DONE.
NOT IF HE KNEW.
ABRAHAM?

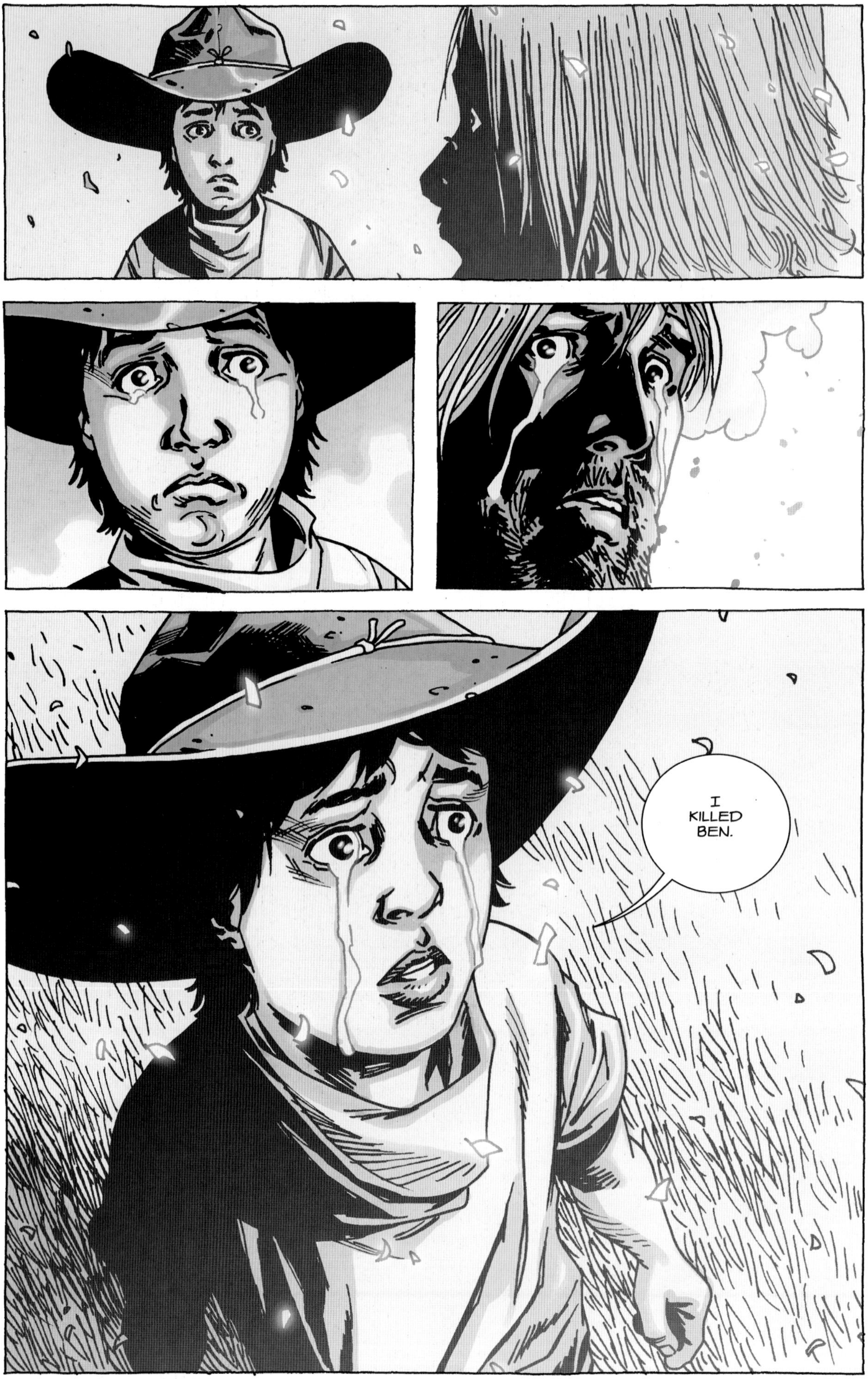
I KILLED BEN.

Chapter Twelve:
Life Among Them

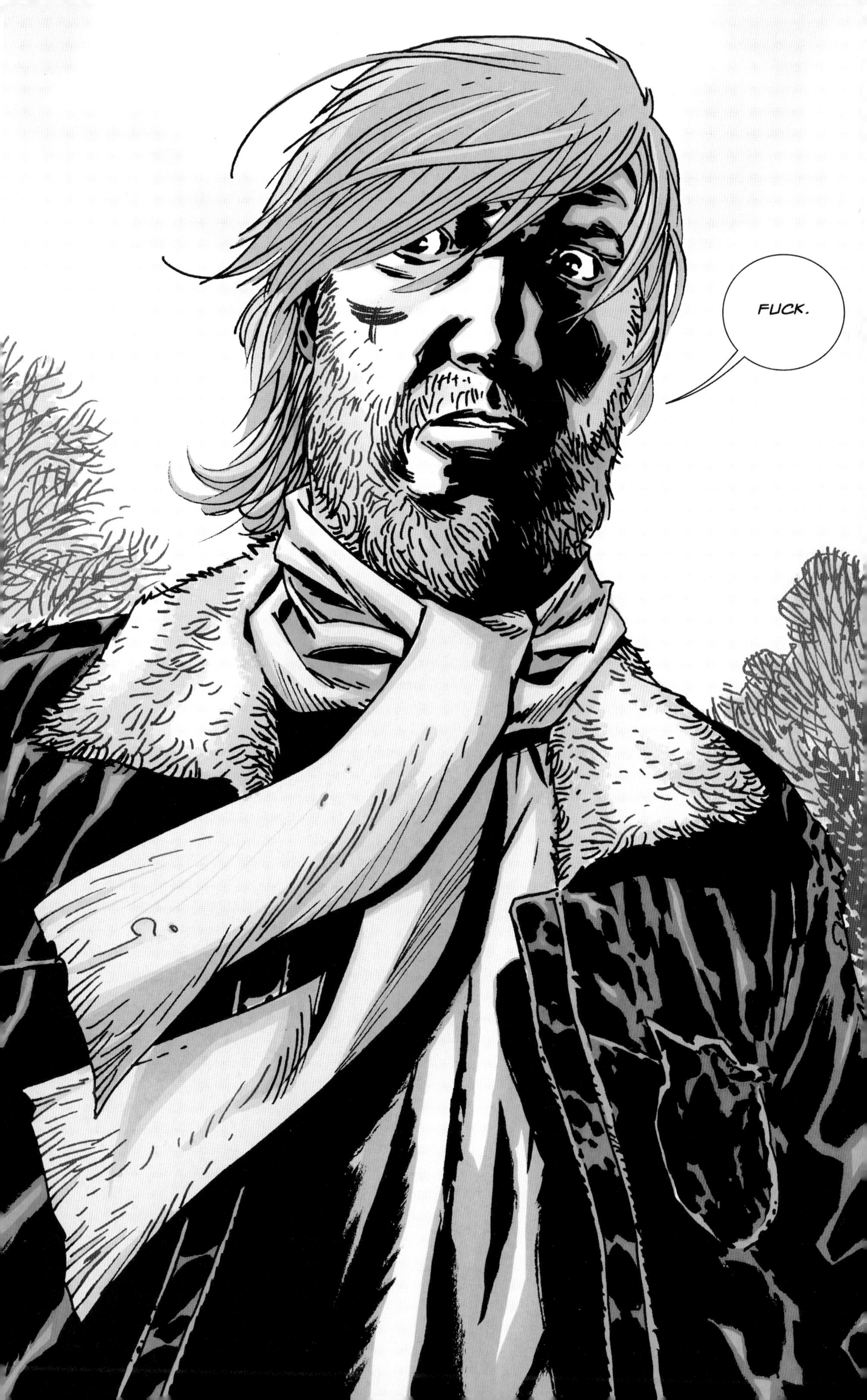
FUCK.

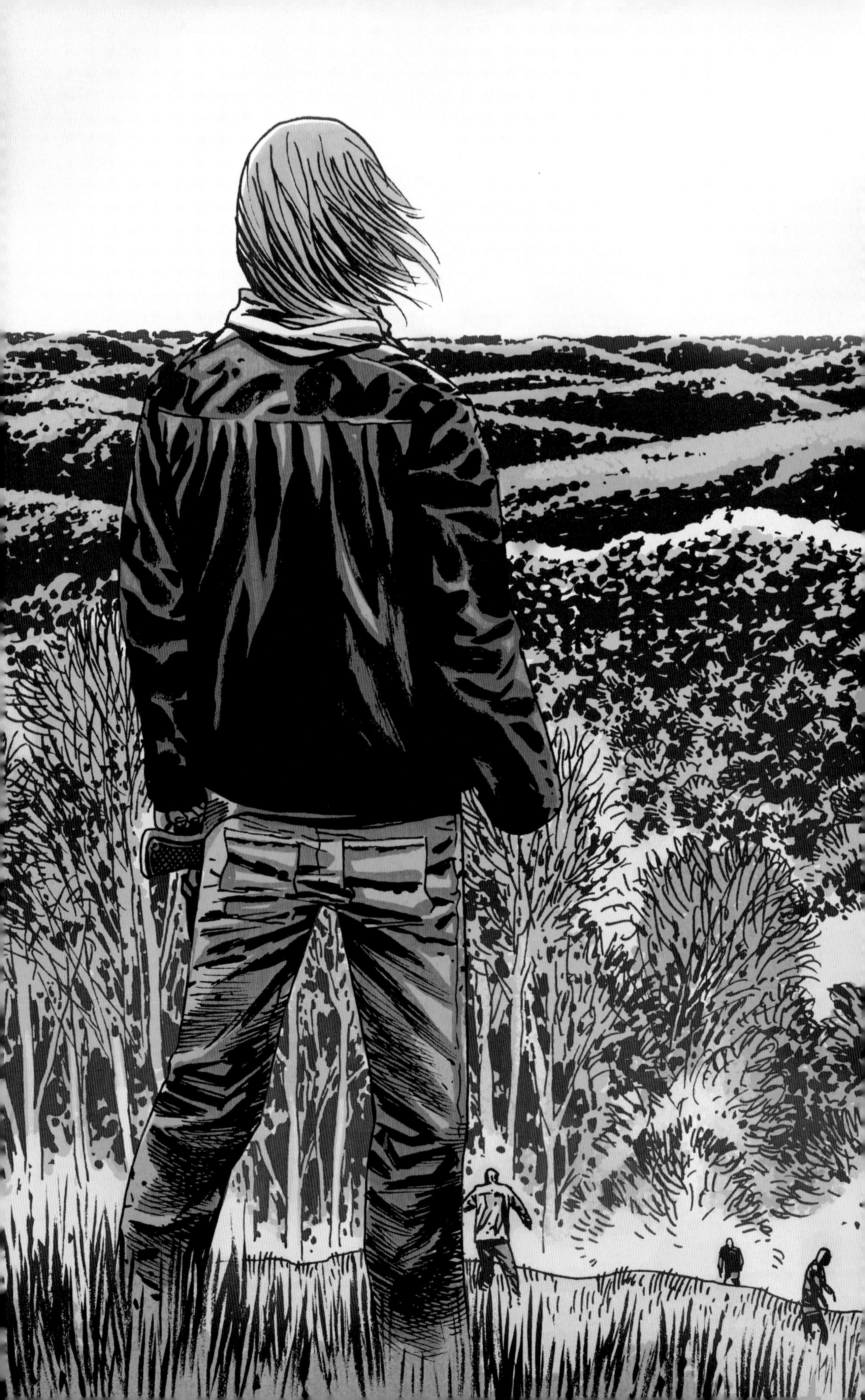

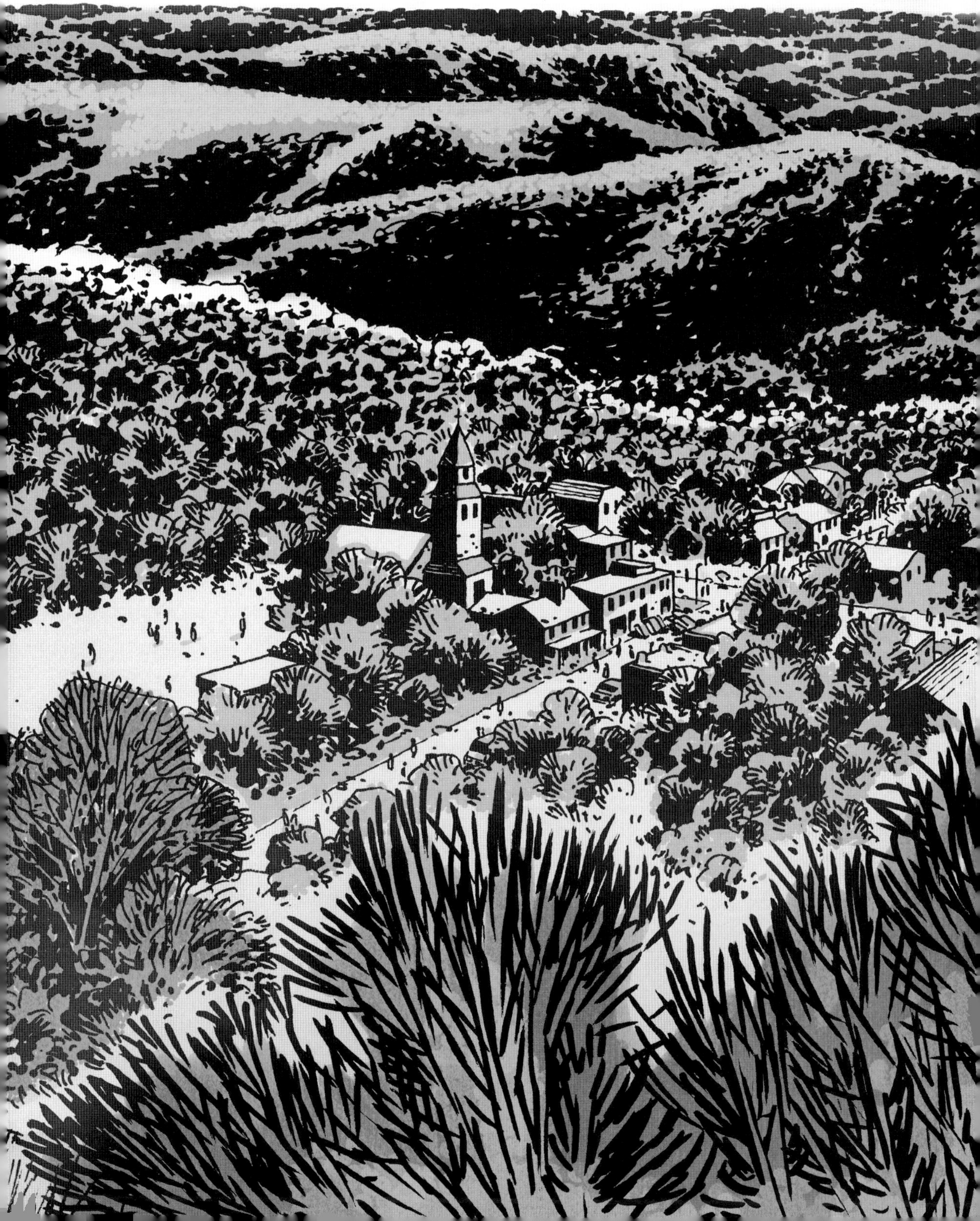

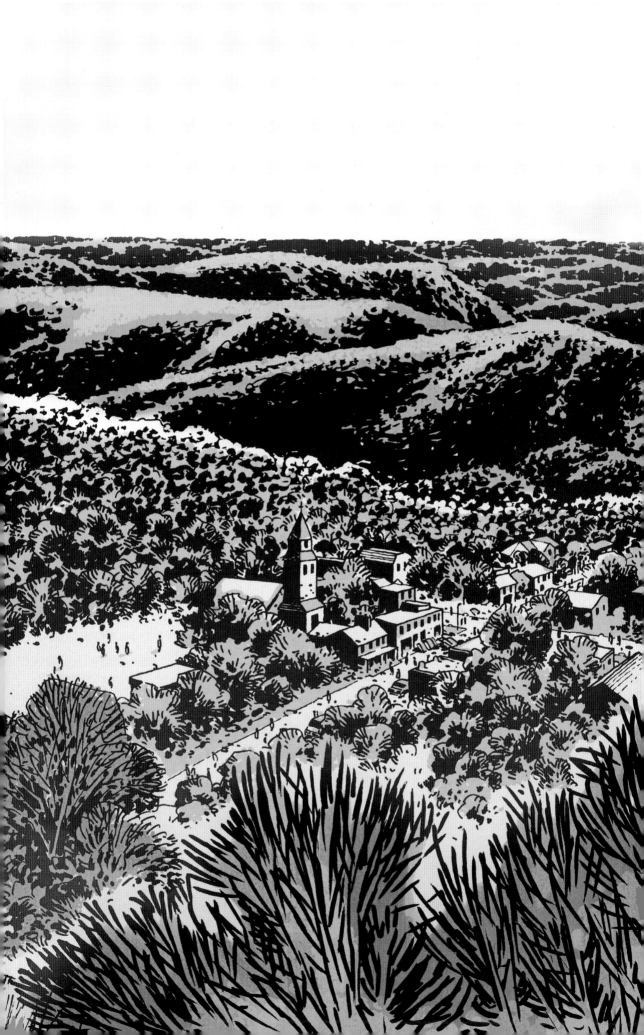

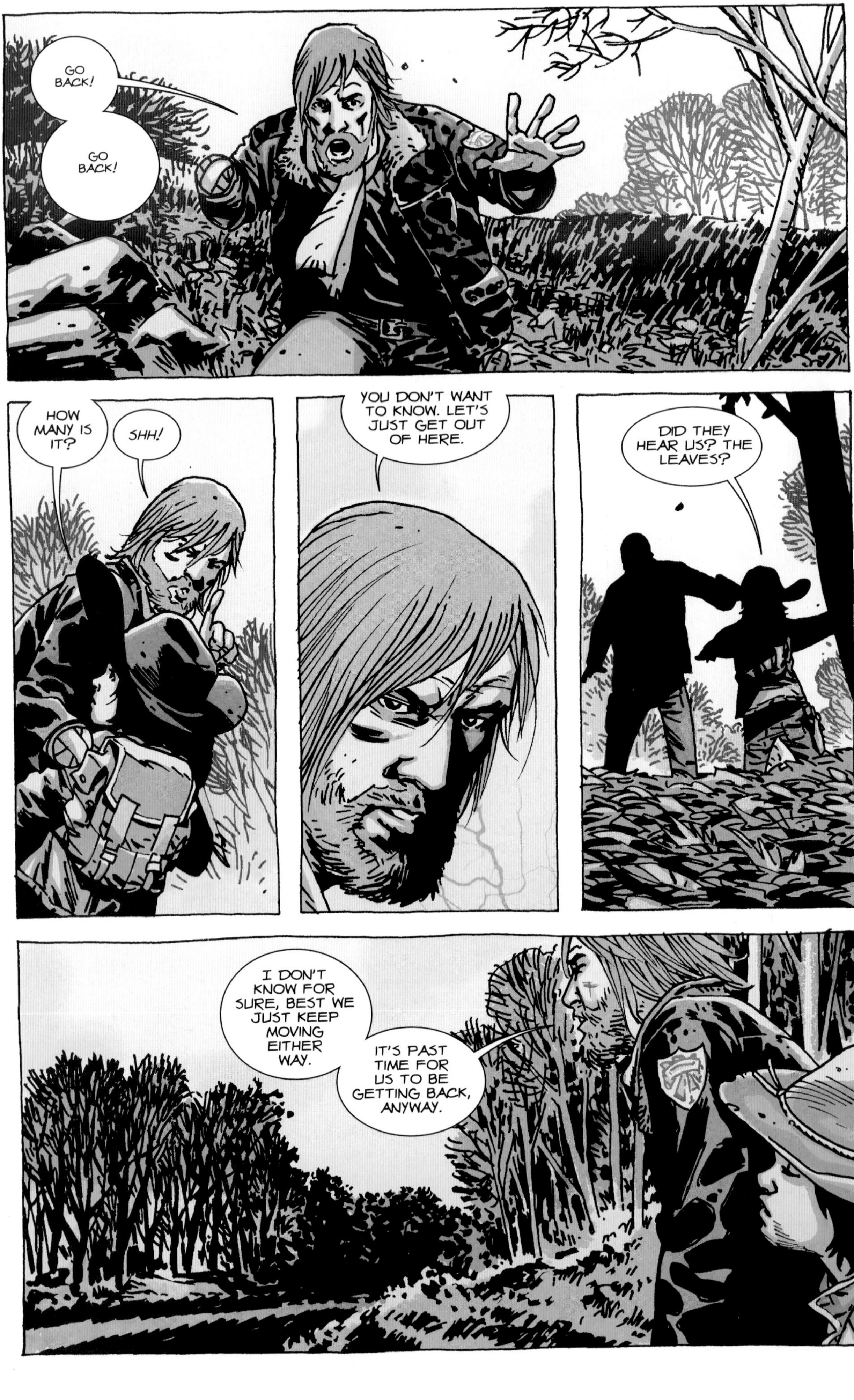
GO BACK!
GO BACK!
HOW MANY IS IT?
SHH!
YOU DON'T WANT TO KNOW. LET'S JUST GET OUT OF HERE.
DID THEY HEAR US? THE LEAVES?
I DON'T KNOW FOR SURE, BEST WE JUST KEEP MOVING EITHER WAY.
IT'S PAST TIME FOR US TO BE GETTING BACK, ANYWAY.

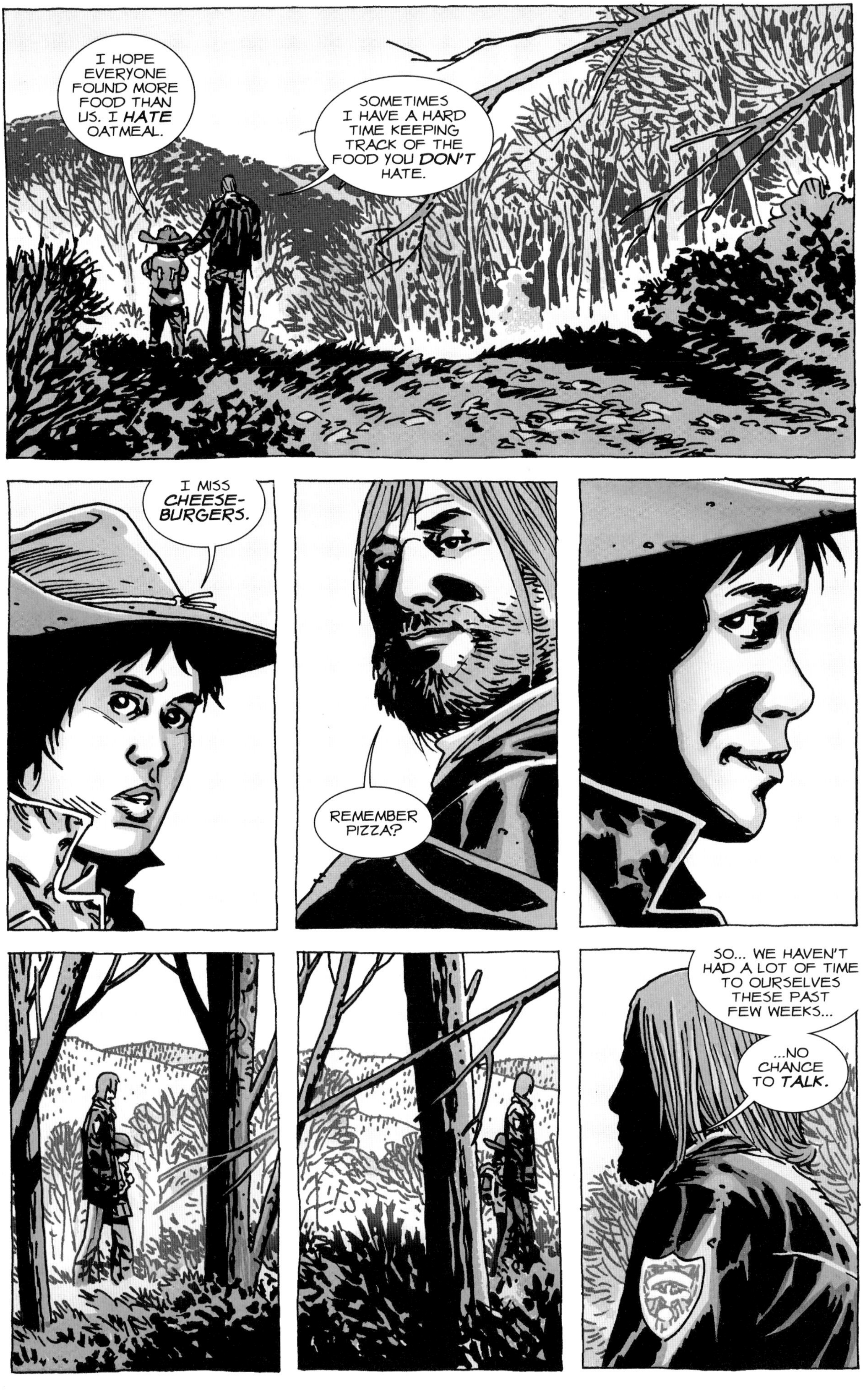
I HOPE EVERYONE FOUND MORE FOOD THAN US. I HATE OATMEAL.
SOMETIMES I HAVE A HARD TIME KEEPING TRACK OF THE FOOD YOU DON'T HATE.
I MISS CHEESE-BURGERS.
REMEMBER PIZZA?
SO... WE HAVEN'T HAD A LOT OF TIME TO OURSELVES THESE PAST FEW WEEKS...
...NO CHANCE TO TALK.

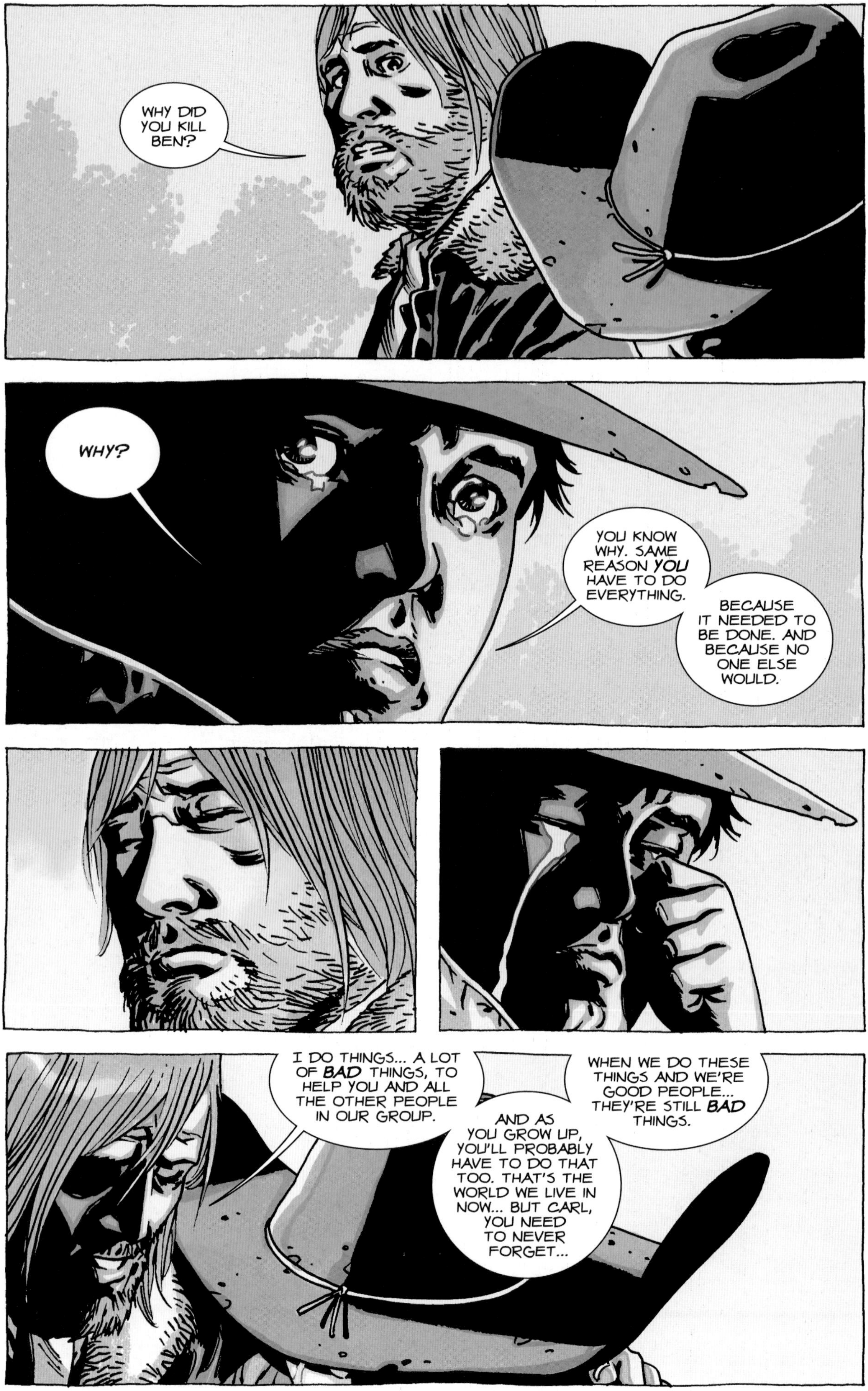
WHY DID YOU KILL BEN?
WHY?
YOU KNOW WHY. SAME REASON YOU HAVE TO DO EVERYTHING.
BECAUSE IT NEEDED TO BE DONE. AND BECAUSE NO ONE ELSE WOULD.
I DO THINGS... A LOT OF BAD THINGS, TO HELP YOU AND ALL THE OTHER PEOPLE IN OUR GROUP.
WHEN WE DO THESE THINGS AND WE'RE GOOD PEOPLE... THEY'RE STILL BAD THINGS.
AND AS YOU GROW UP, YOU'LL PROBABLY HAVE TO DO THAT TOO. THAT'S THE WORLD WE LIVE IN NOW... BUT CARL, YOU NEED TO NEVER FORGET...

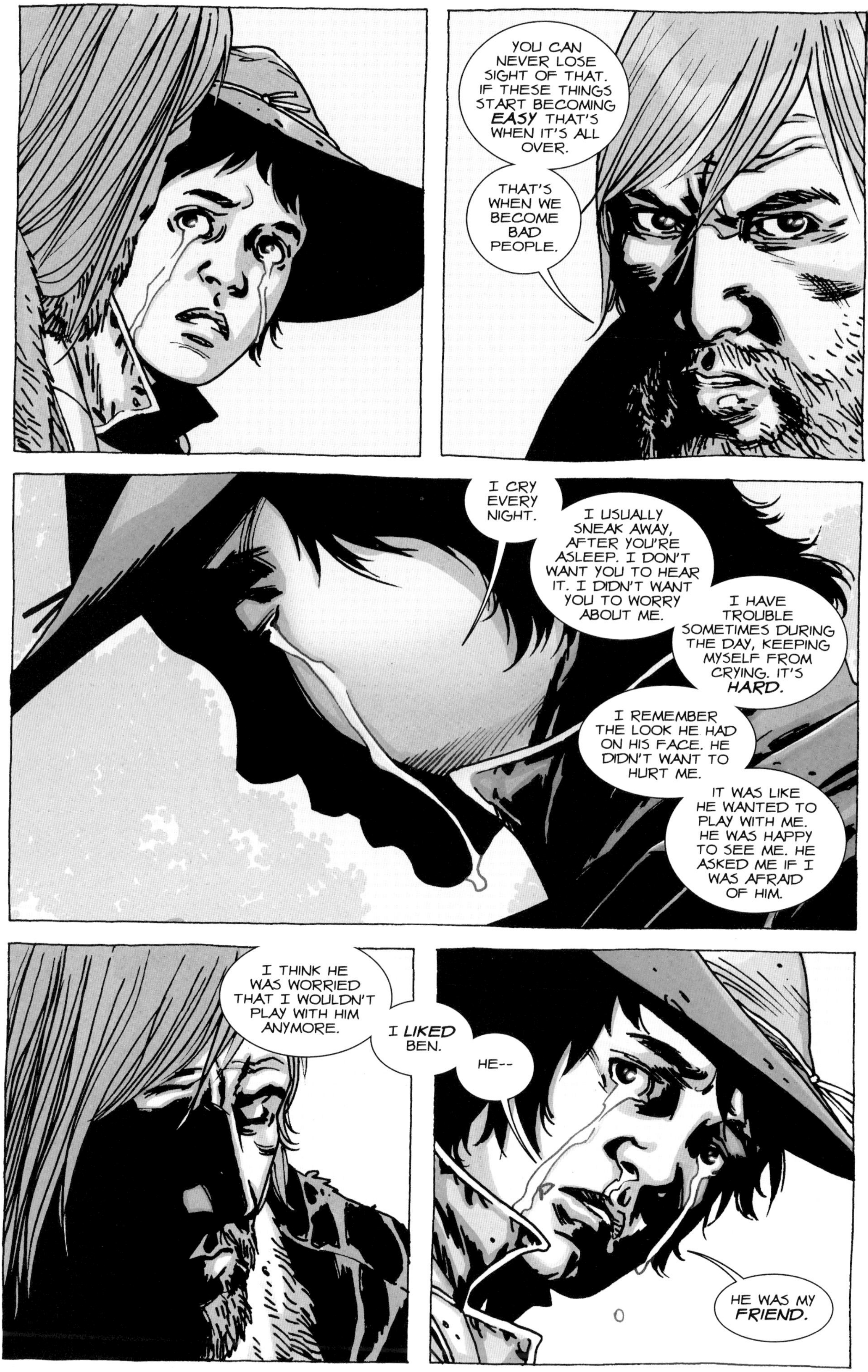

YOU CAN NEVER LOSE SIGHT OF THAT. IF THESE THINGS START BECOMING *EASY* THAT'S WHEN IT'S ALL OVER.
THAT'S WHEN WE BECOME BAD PEOPLE.
I CRY EVERY NIGHT.
I USUALLY SNEAK AWAY, AFTER YOU'RE ASLEEP. I DON'T WANT YOU TO HEAR IT. I DIDN'T WANT YOU TO WORRY ABOUT ME.
I HAVE TROUBLE SOMETIMES DURING THE DAY, KEEPING MYSELF FROM CRYING. IT'S *HARD.*
I REMEMBER THE LOOK HE HAD ON HIS FACE. HE DIDN'T WANT TO HURT ME.
IT WAS LIKE HE WANTED TO PLAY WITH ME. HE WAS HAPPY TO SEE ME. HE ASKED ME IF I WAS AFRAID OF HIM.
I THINK HE WAS WORRIED THAT I WOULDN'T PLAY WITH HIM ANYMORE.
I *LIKED* BEN.
HE--
HE WAS MY *FRIEND.*

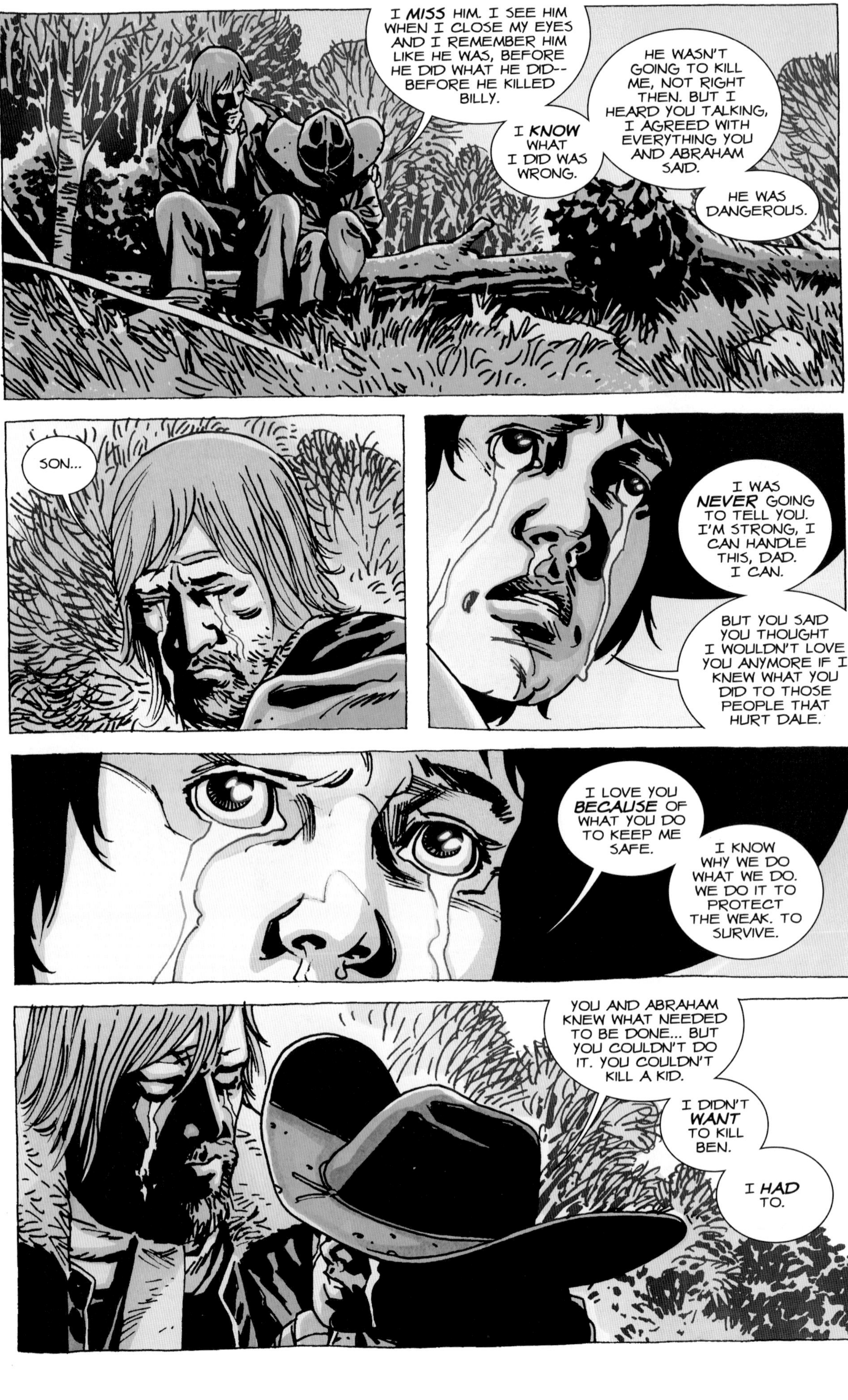
I MISS HIM. I SEE HIM WHEN I CLOSE MY EYES AND I REMEMBER HIM LIKE HE WAS, BEFORE HE DID WHAT HE DID-- BEFORE HE KILLED BILLY.
I KNOW WHAT I DID WAS WRONG.
HE WASN'T GOING TO KILL ME, NOT RIGHT THEN. BUT I HEARD YOU TALKING, I AGREED WITH EVERYTHING YOU AND ABRAHAM SAID.
HE WAS DANGEROUS.
SON...
I WAS NEVER GOING TO TELL YOU. I'M STRONG, I CAN HANDLE THIS, DAD. I CAN.
BUT YOU SAID YOU THOUGHT I WOULDN'T LOVE YOU ANYMORE IF I KNEW WHAT YOU DID TO THOSE PEOPLE THAT HURT DALE.
I LOVE YOU BECAUSE OF WHAT YOU DO TO KEEP ME SAFE.
I KNOW WHY WE DO WHAT WE DO. WE DO IT TO PROTECT THE WEAK. TO SURVIVE.
YOU AND ABRAHAM KNEW WHAT NEEDED TO BE DONE... BUT YOU COULDN'T DO IT. YOU COULDN'T KILL A KID.
I DIDN'T WANT TO KILL BEN.
I HAD TO.

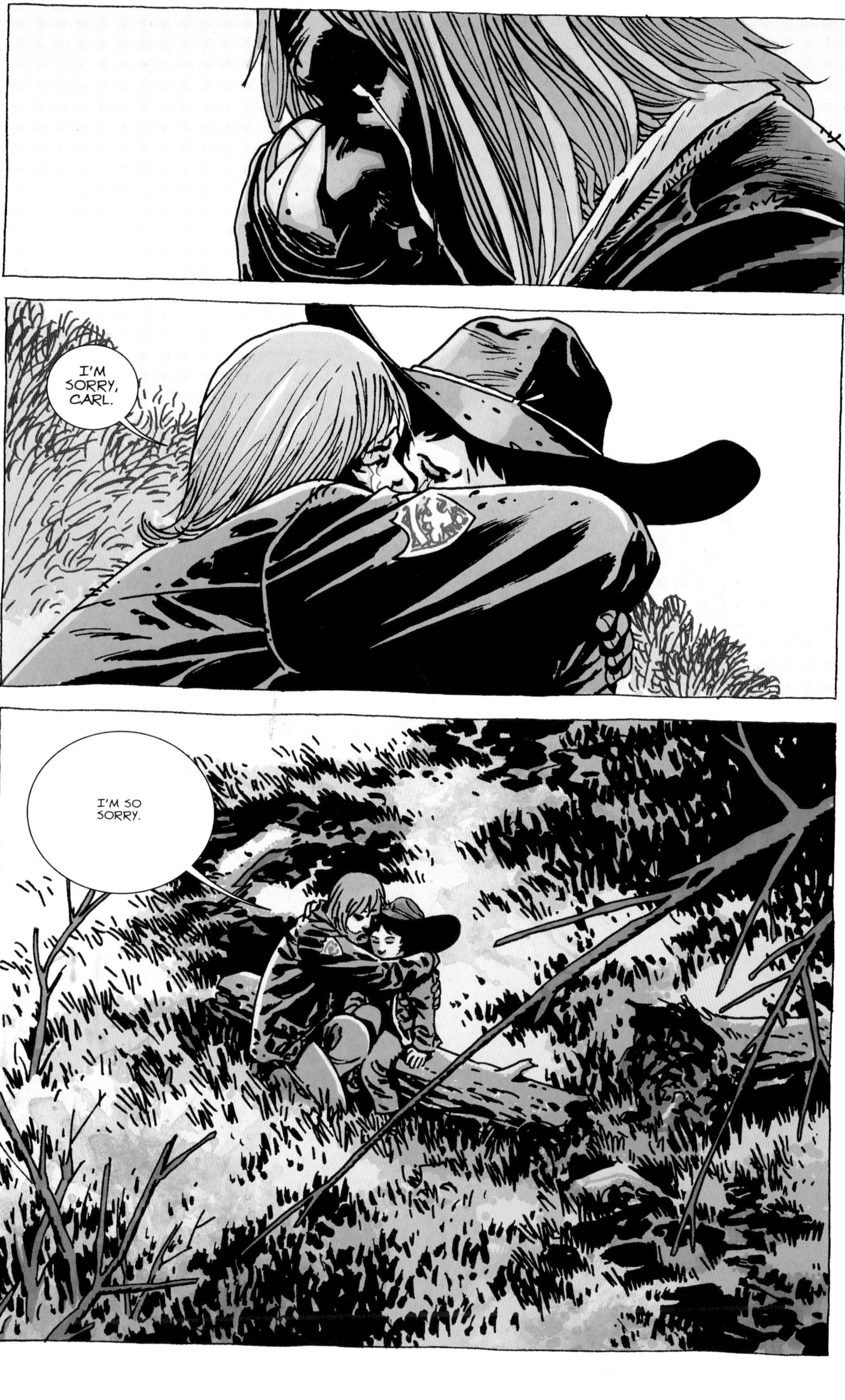
I'M SORRY, CARL.
I'M SO SORRY.

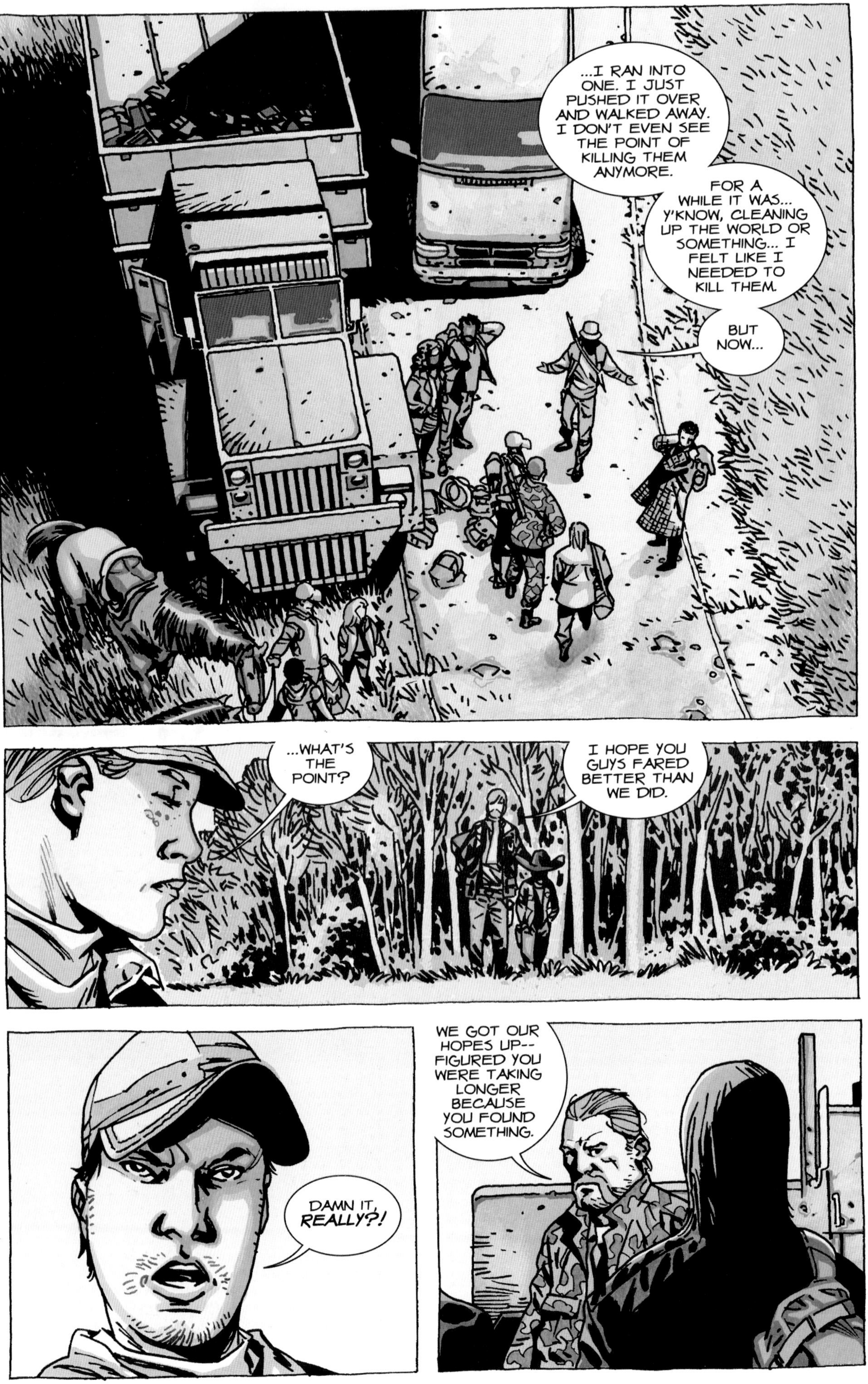
...I RAN INTO ONE. I JUST PUSHED IT OVER AND WALKED AWAY. I DON'T EVEN SEE THE POINT OF KILLING THEM ANYMORE.
FOR A WHILE IT WAS... Y'KNOW, CLEANING UP THE WORLD OR SOMETHING... I FELT LIKE I NEEDED TO KILL THEM.
BUT NOW...
...WHAT'S THE POINT?
I HOPE YOU GUYS FARED BETTER THAN WE DID.
DAMN IT, REALLY?!
WE GOT OUR HOPES UP-- FIGURED YOU WERE TAKING LONGER BECAUSE YOU FOUND SOMETHING.

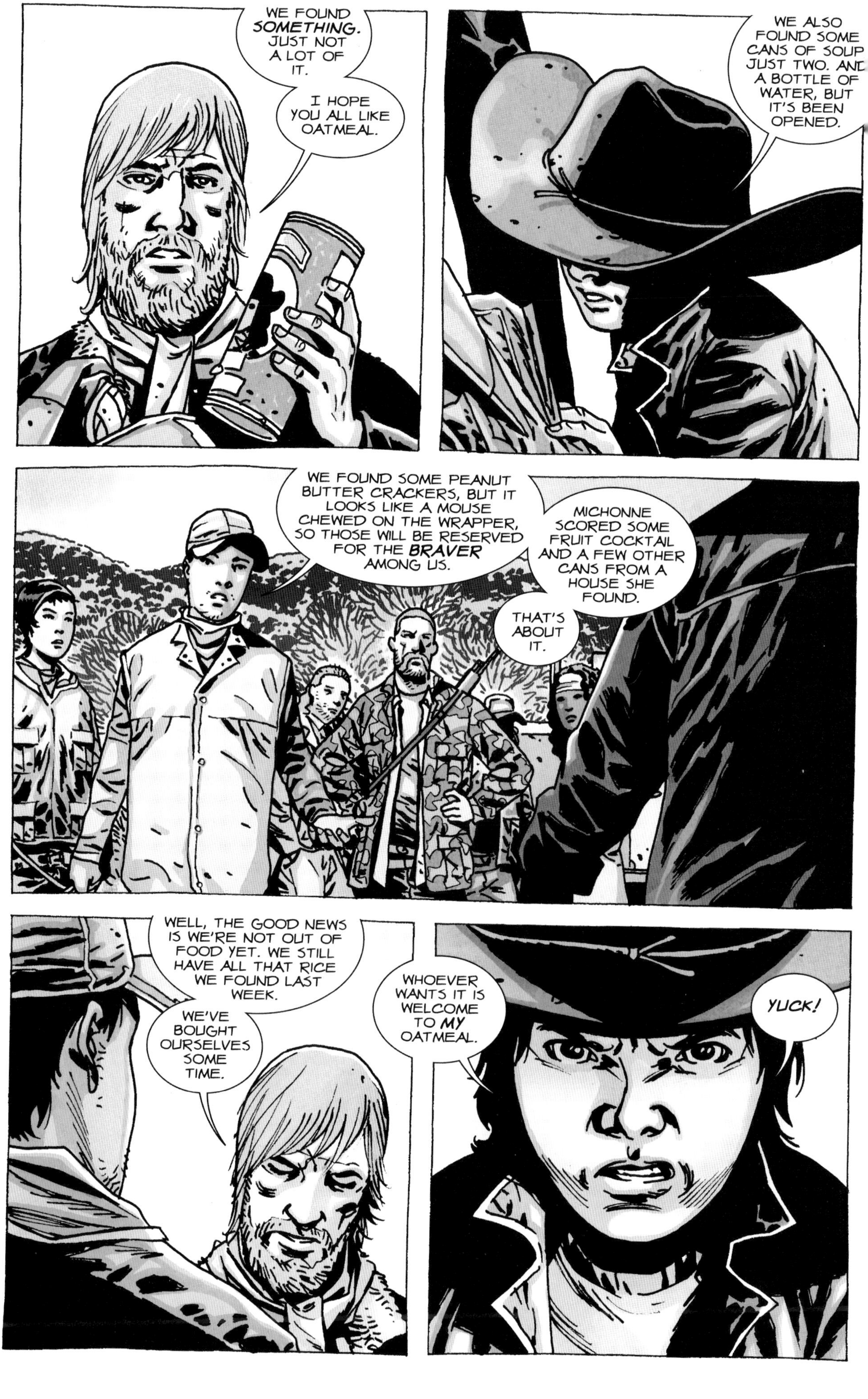
WE FOUND SOMETHING. JUST NOT A LOT OF IT.
I HOPE YOU ALL LIKE OATMEAL.
WE ALSO FOUND SOME CANS OF SOUP JUST TWO. AND A BOTTLE OF WATER, BUT IT'S BEEN OPENED.
WE FOUND SOME PEANUT BUTTER CRACKERS, BUT IT LOOKS LIKE A MOUSE CHEWED ON THE WRAPPER, SO THOSE WILL BE RESERVED FOR THE BRAVER AMONG US.
MICHONNE SCORED SOME FRUIT COCKTAIL AND A FEW OTHER CANS FROM A HOUSE SHE FOUND.
THAT'S ABOUT IT.
WELL, THE GOOD NEWS IS WE'RE NOT OUT OF FOOD YET. WE STILL HAVE ALL THAT RICE WE FOUND LAST WEEK.
WE'VE BOUGHT OURSELVES SOME TIME.
WHOEVER WANTS IT IS WELCOME TO MY OATMEAL.
YUCK!

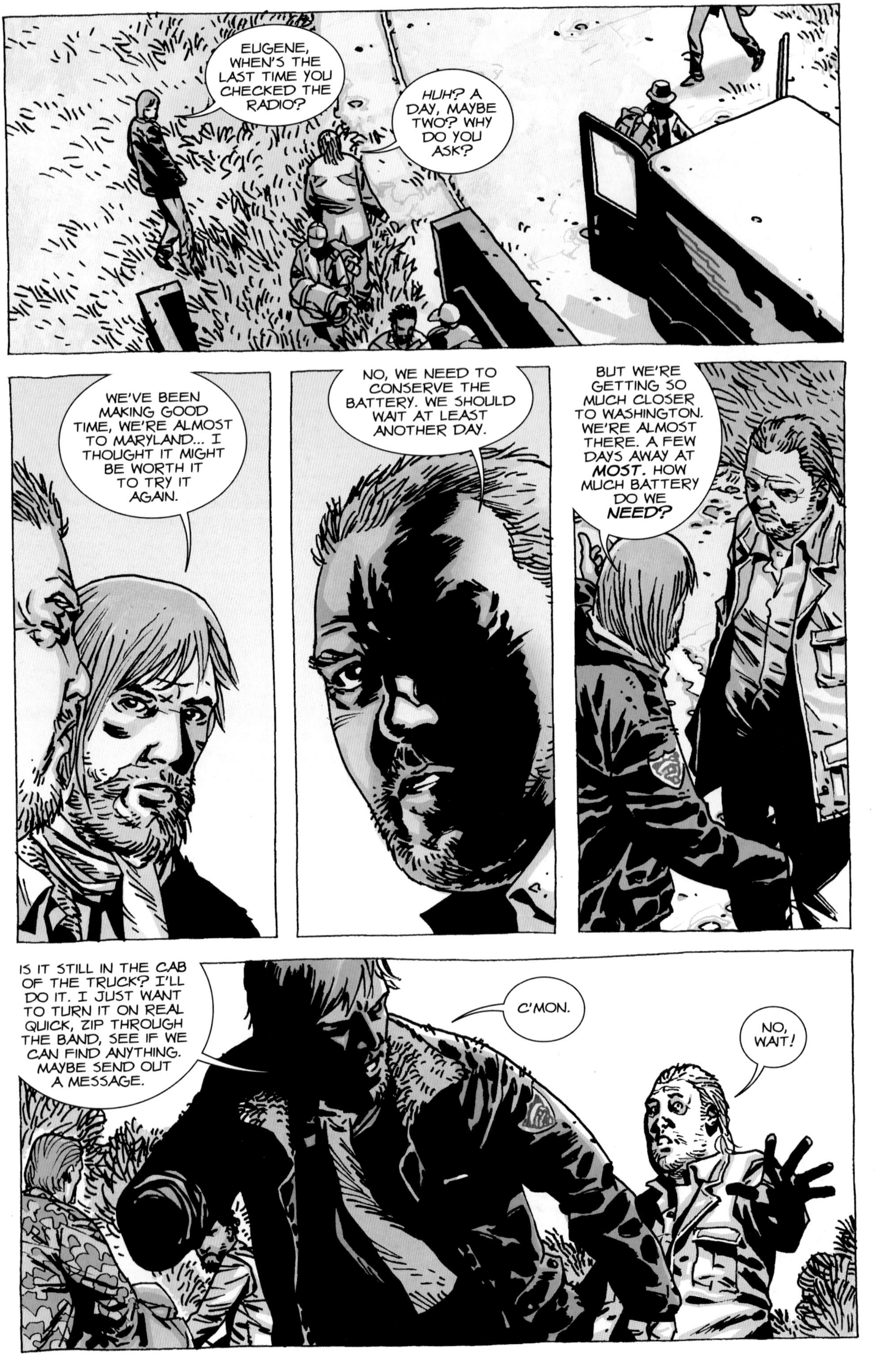
EUGENE, WHEN'S THE LAST TIME YOU CHECKED THE RADIO?
HUH? A DAY, MAYBE TWO? WHY DO YOU ASK?
WE'VE BEEN MAKING GOOD TIME, WE'RE ALMOST TO MARYLAND... I THOUGHT IT MIGHT BE WORTH IT TO TRY IT AGAIN.
NO, WE NEED TO CONSERVE THE BATTERY. WE SHOULD WAIT AT LEAST ANOTHER DAY.
BUT WE'RE GETTING SO MUCH CLOSER TO WASHINGTON. WE'RE ALMOST THERE. A FEW DAYS AWAY AT MOST. HOW MUCH BATTERY DO WE NEED?
IS IT STILL IN THE CAB OF THE TRUCK? I'LL DO IT. I JUST WANT TO TURN IT ON REAL QUICK, ZIP THROUGH THE BAND, SEE IF WE CAN FIND ANYTHING. MAYBE SEND OUT A MESSAGE.
C'MON.
NO, WAIT!

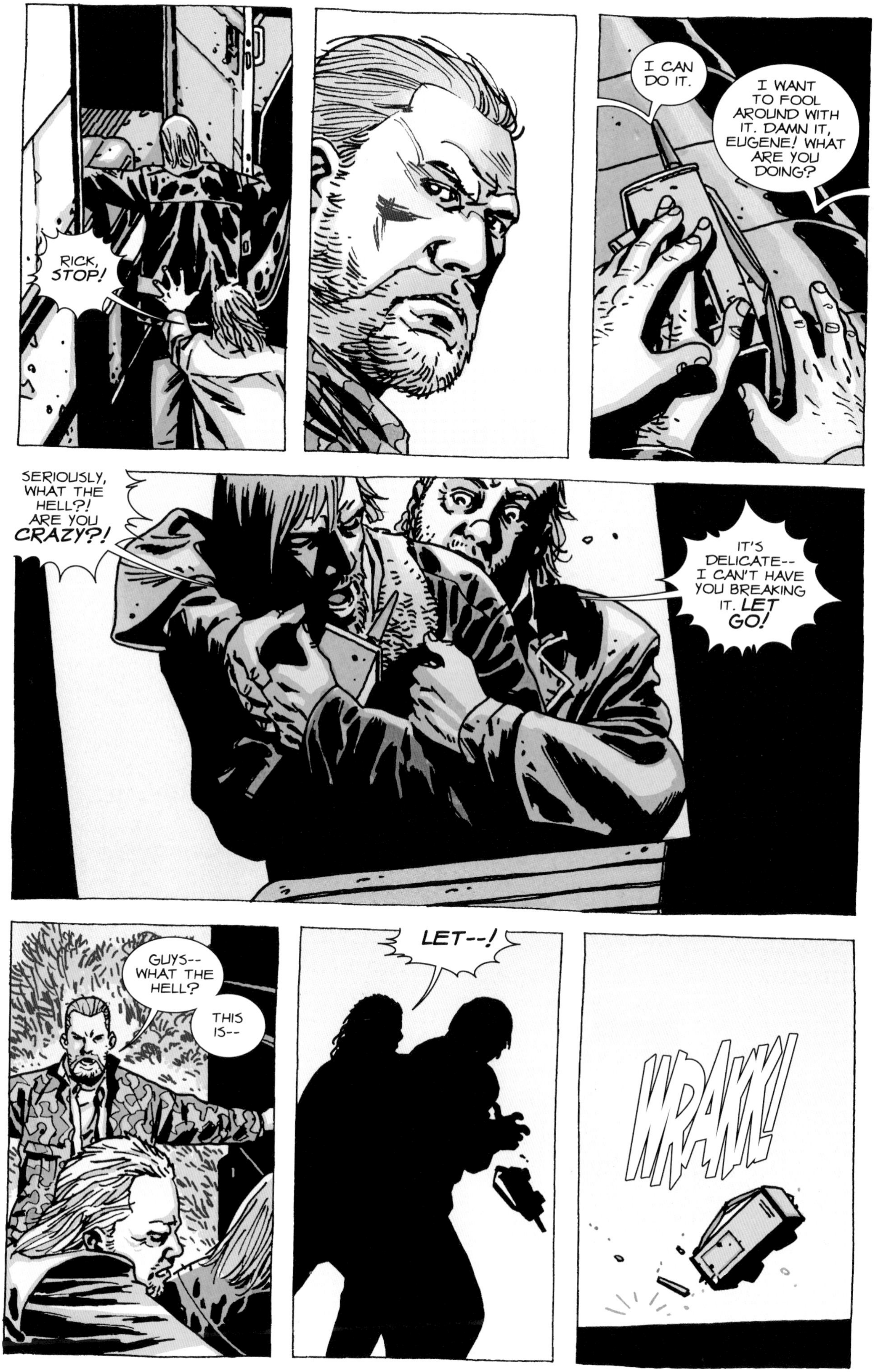
RICK, STOP!
I CAN DO IT.
I WANT TO FOOL AROUND WITH IT. DAMN IT, EUGENE! WHAT ARE YOU DOING?
SERIOUSLY, WHAT THE HELL?! ARE YOU CRAZY?!
IT'S DELICATE-- I CAN'T HAVE YOU BREAKING IT. LET GO!
GUYS-- WHAT THE HELL?
THIS IS--
LET--!
WRAKK!

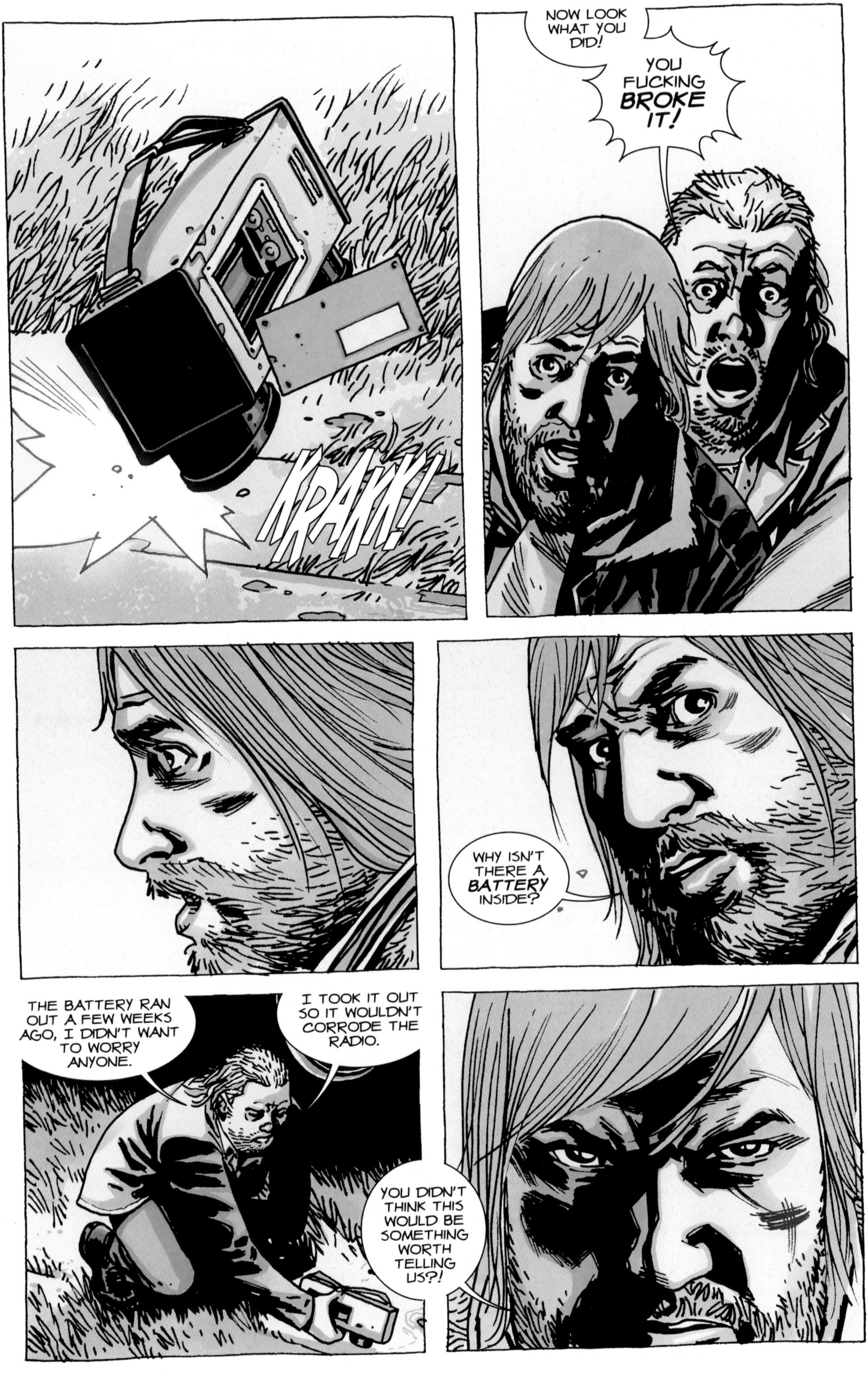
KRAKK!
NOW LOOK WHAT YOU DID!
YOU FUCKING BROKE IT!
WHY ISN'T THERE A BATTERY INSIDE?
THE BATTERY RAN OUT A FEW WEEKS AGO, I DIDN'T WANT TO WORRY ANYONE.
I TOOK IT OUT SO IT WOULDN'T CORRODE THE RADIO.
YOU DIDN'T THINK THIS WOULD BE SOMETHING WORTH TELLING US?!

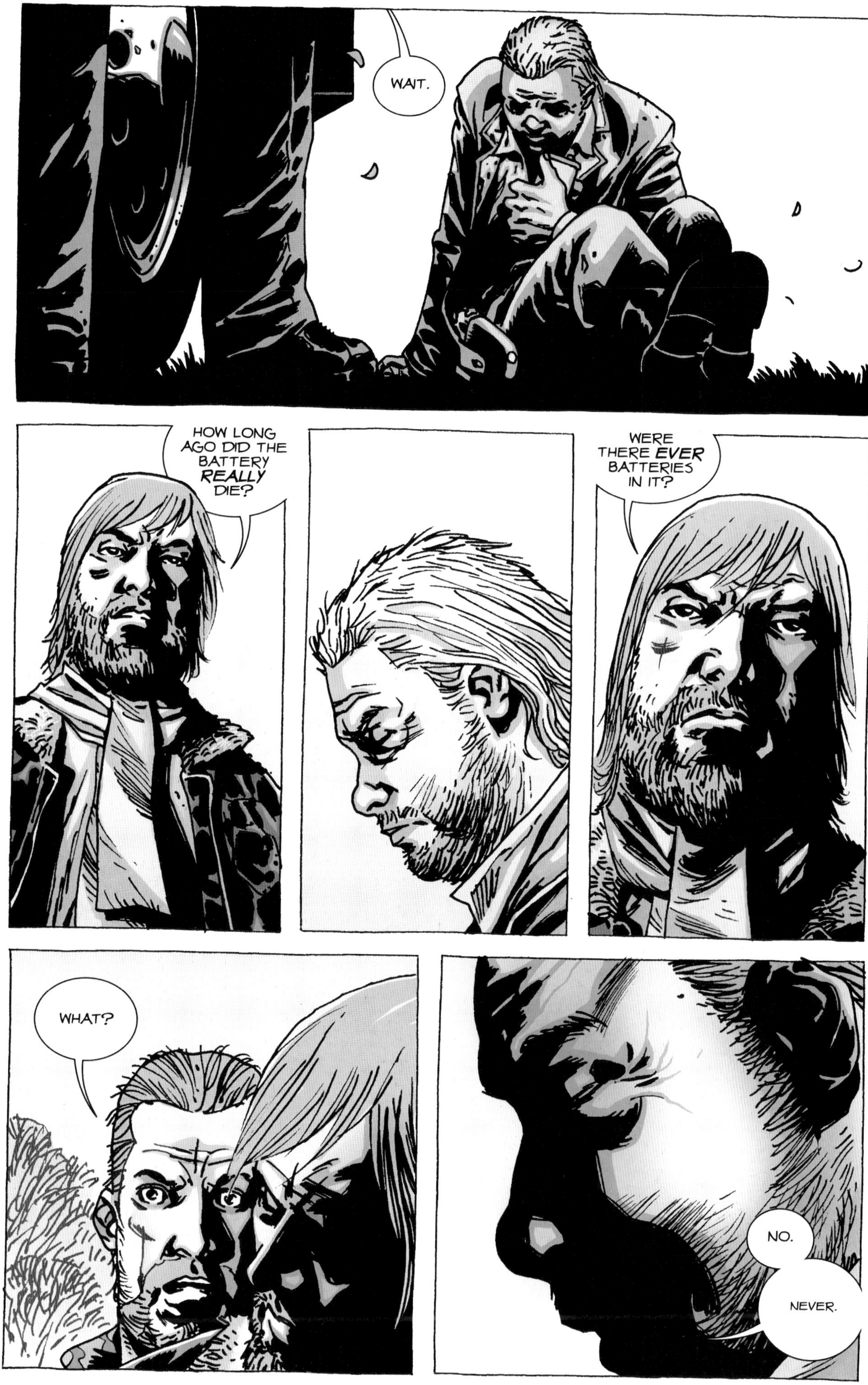
WAIT.
HOW LONG AGO DID THE BATTERY *REALLY* DIE?
WERE THERE *EVER* BATTERIES IN IT?
WHAT?
NO.
NEVER.

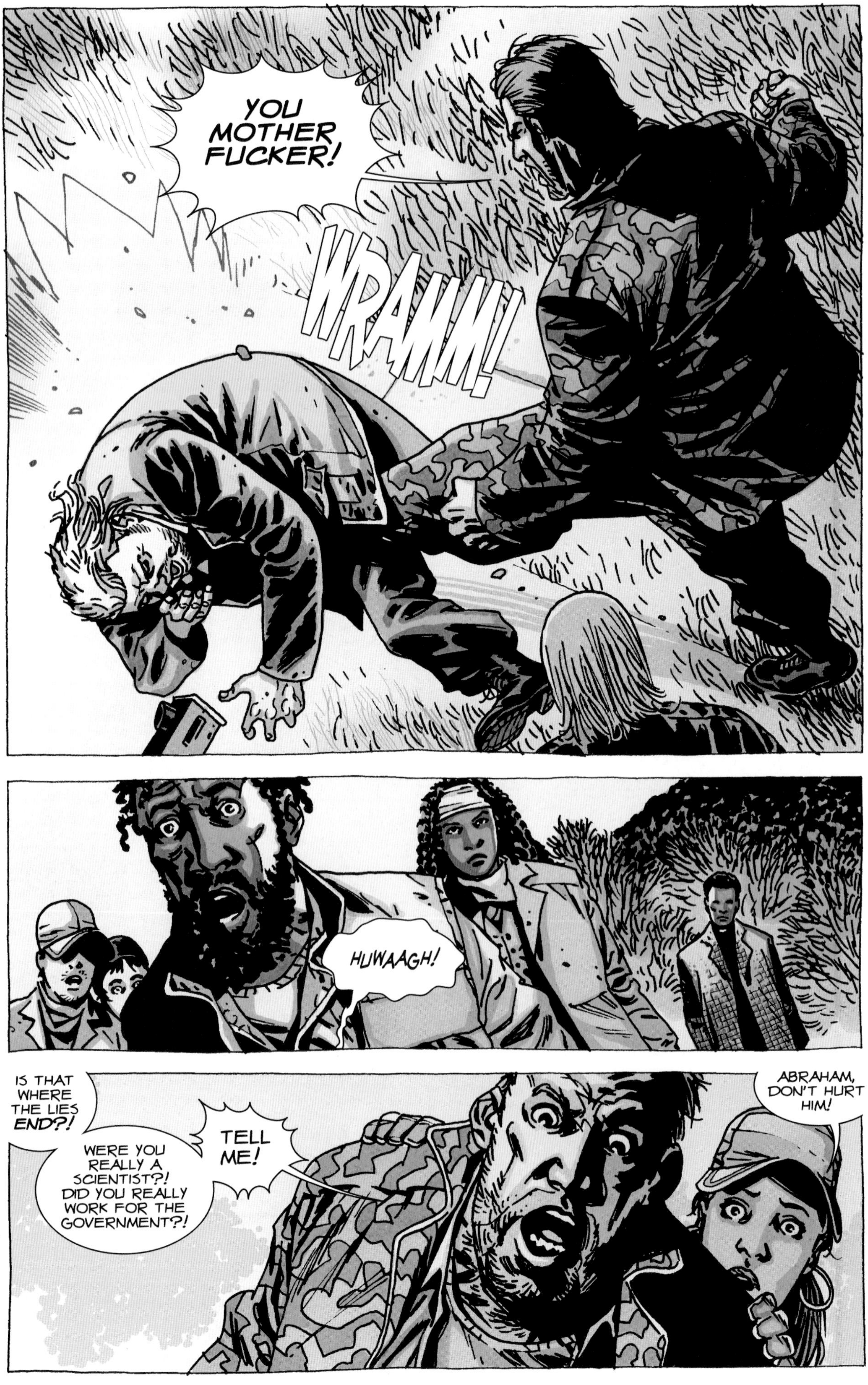
YOU MOTHER FUCKER!
WRAMMM!
HUWAAGH!
IS THAT WHERE THE LIES END?!
WERE YOU REALLY A SCIENTIST?! DID YOU REALLY WORK FOR THE GOVERNMENT?!
TELL ME!
ABRAHAM, DON'T HURT HIM!

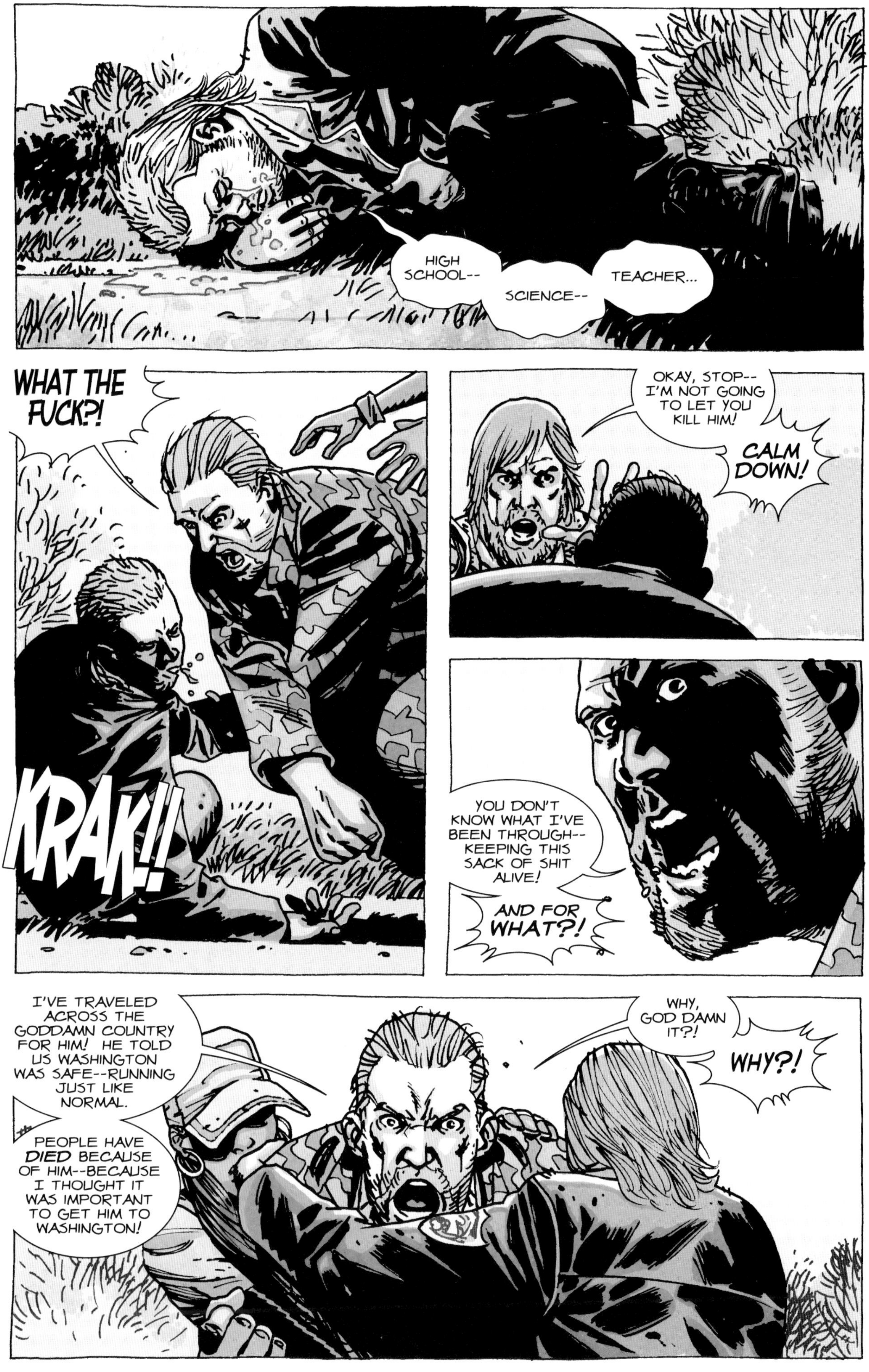

HIGH SCHOOL--
SCIENCE--
TEACHER...
WHAT THE FUCK?!
KRAK!!
OKAY, STOP-- I'M NOT GOING TO LET YOU KILL HIM!
CALM DOWN!
YOU DON'T KNOW WHAT I'VE BEEN THROUGH-- KEEPING THIS SACK OF SHIT ALIVE!
AND FOR WHAT?!
I'VE TRAVELED ACROSS THE GODDAMN COUNTRY FOR HIM! HE TOLD US WASHINGTON WAS SAFE--RUNNING JUST LIKE NORMAL.
PEOPLE HAVE DIED BECAUSE OF HIM--BECAUSE I THOUGHT IT WAS IMPORTANT TO GET HIM TO WASHINGTON!
WHY, GOD DAMN IT?!
WHY?!

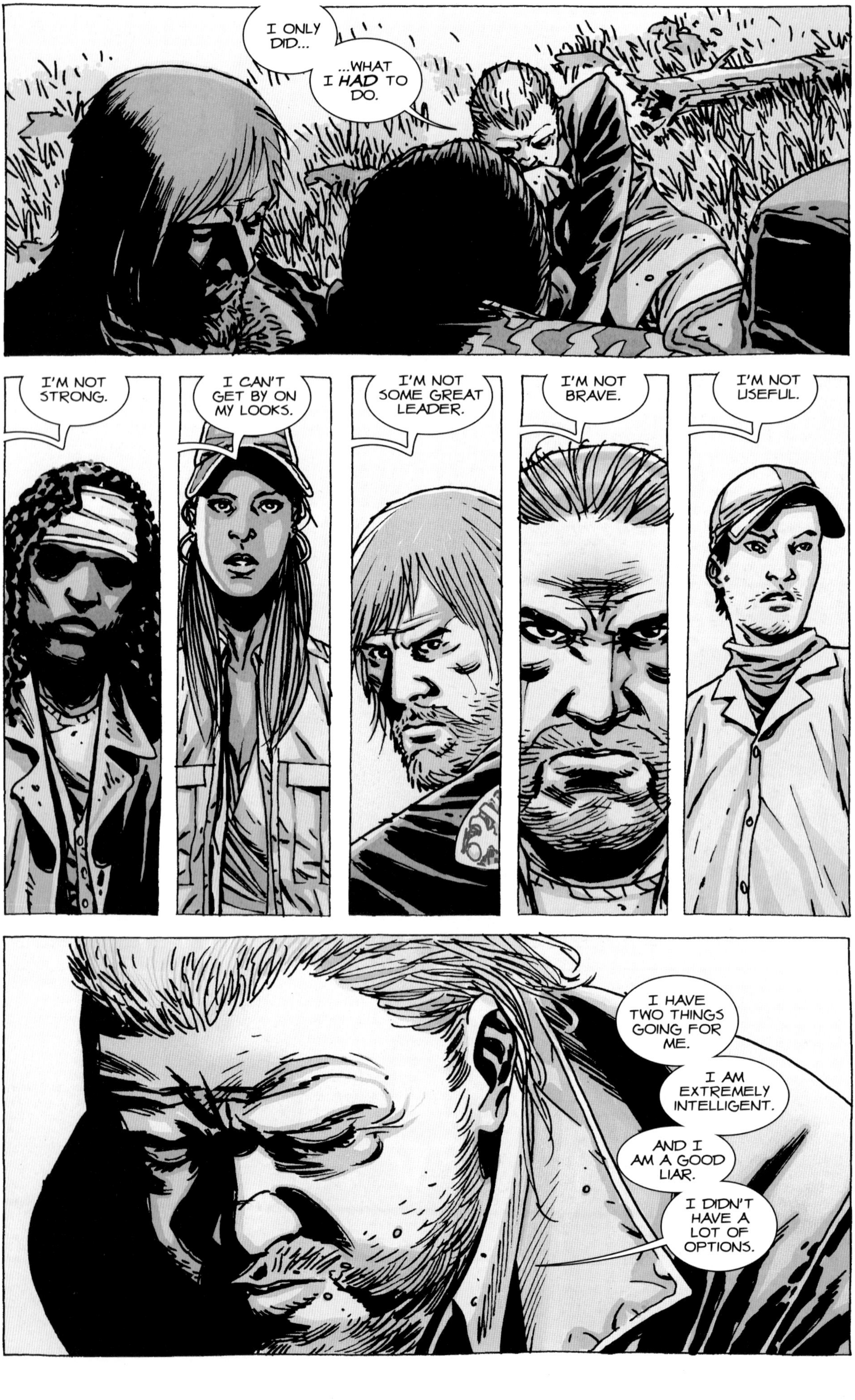
I ONLY DID...
...WHAT I HAD TO DO.
I'M NOT STRONG.
I CAN'T GET BY ON MY LOOKS.
I'M NOT SOME GREAT LEADER.
I'M NOT BRAVE.
I'M NOT USEFUL.
I HAVE TWO THINGS GOING FOR ME.
I AM EXTREMELY INTELLIGENT.
AND I AM A GOOD LIAR.
I DIDN'T HAVE A LOT OF OPTIONS.

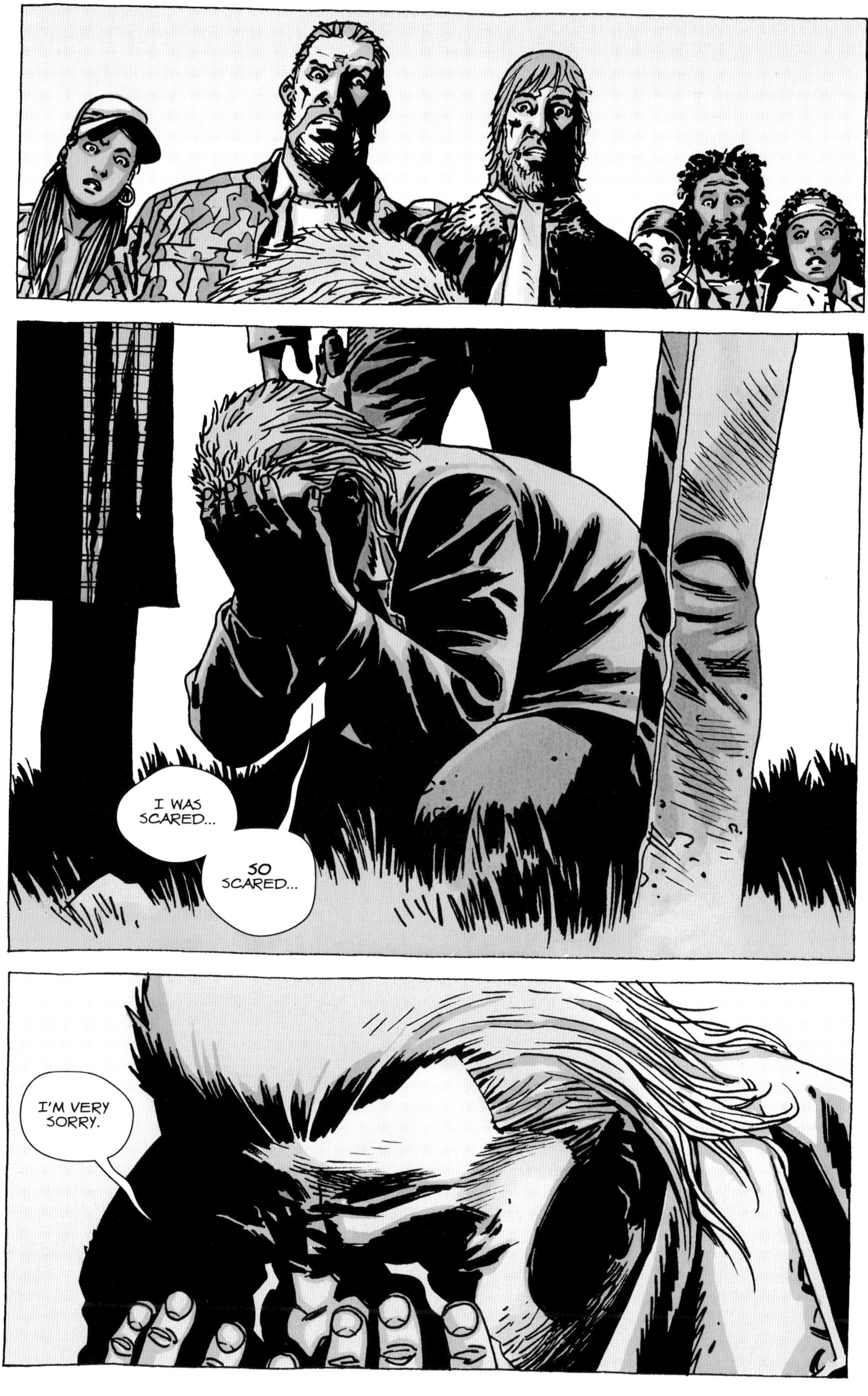
I WAS SCARED...
SO SCARED...
I'M VERY SORRY.

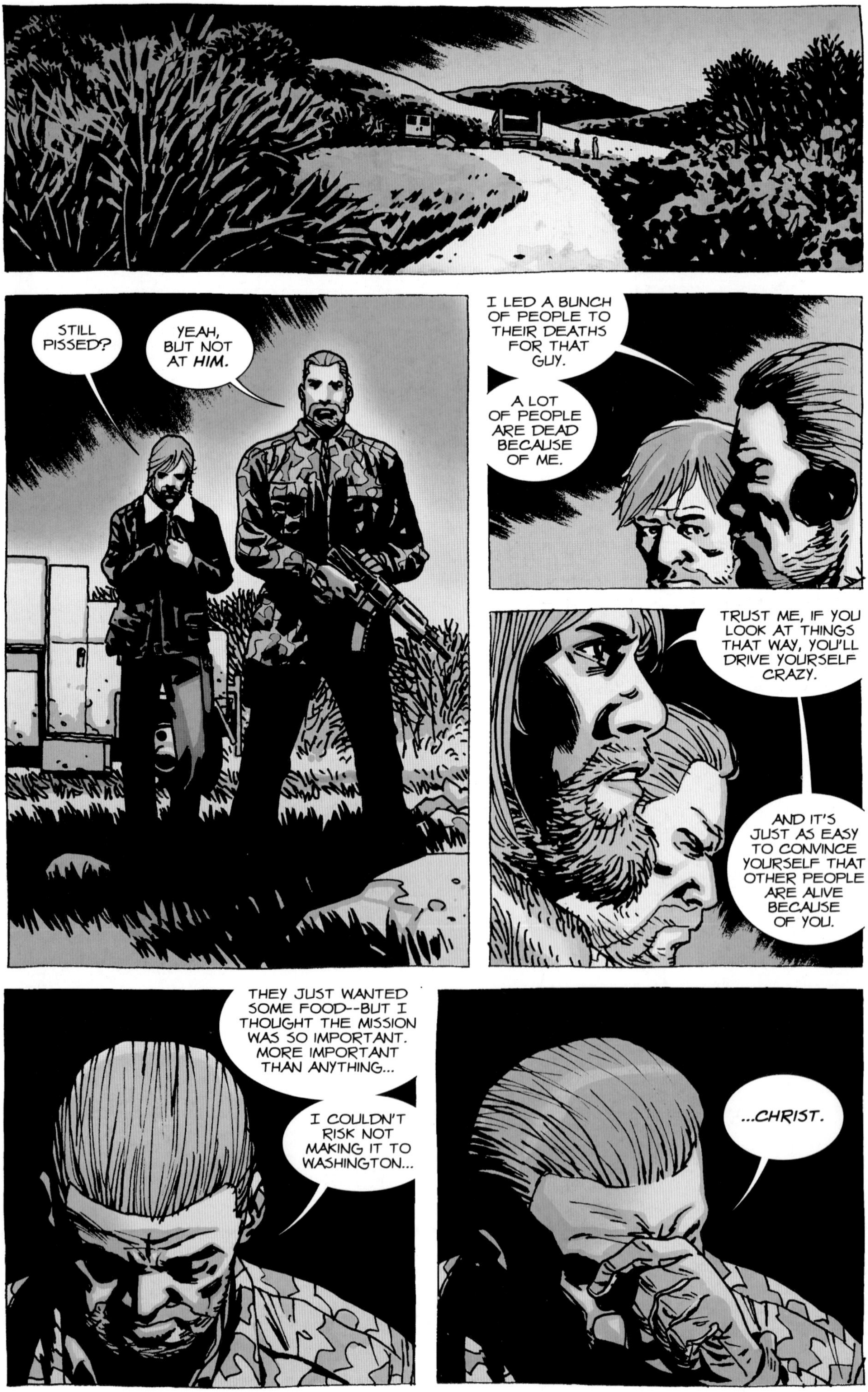
STILL PISSED?
YEAH, BUT NOT AT *HIM*.
I LED A BUNCH OF PEOPLE TO THEIR DEATHS FOR THAT GUY.
A LOT OF PEOPLE ARE DEAD BECAUSE OF ME.
TRUST ME, IF YOU LOOK AT THINGS THAT WAY, YOU'LL DRIVE YOURSELF CRAZY.
AND IT'S JUST AS EASY TO CONVINCE YOURSELF THAT OTHER PEOPLE ARE ALIVE BECAUSE OF YOU.
THEY JUST WANTED SOME FOOD--BUT I THOUGHT THE MISSION WAS SO IMPORTANT. MORE IMPORTANT THAN ANYTHING...
I COULDN'T RISK NOT MAKING IT TO WASHINGTON...
...*CHRIST*.

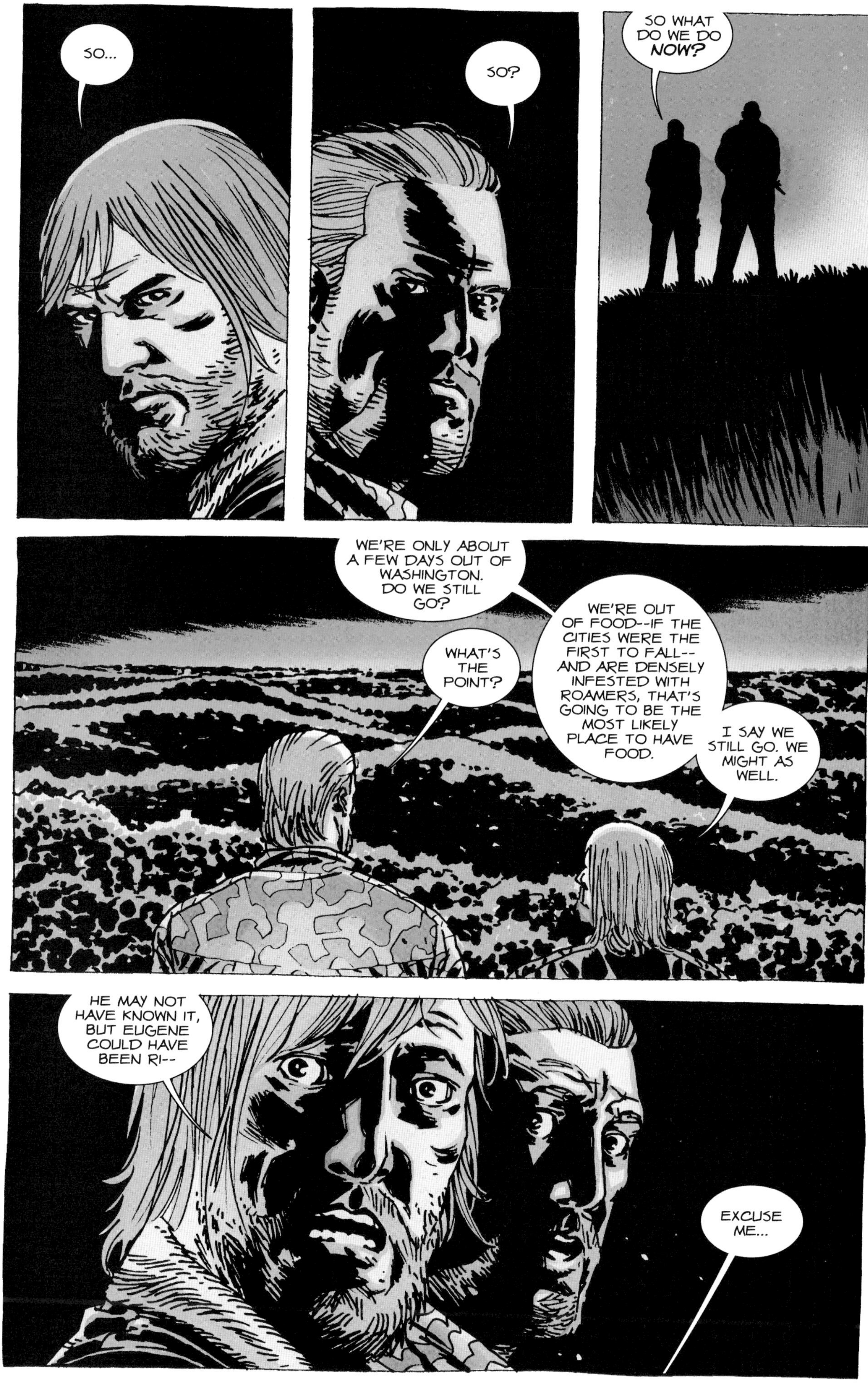
SO...
SO?
SO WHAT DO WE DO NOW?
WE'RE ONLY ABOUT A FEW DAYS OUT OF WASHINGTON. DO WE STILL GO?
WHAT'S THE POINT?
WE'RE OUT OF FOOD--IF THE CITIES WERE THE FIRST TO FALL-- AND ARE DENSELY INFESTED WITH ROAMERS, THAT'S GOING TO BE THE MOST LIKELY PLACE TO HAVE FOOD.
I SAY WE STILL GO. WE MIGHT AS WELL.
HE MAY NOT HAVE KNOWN IT, BUT EUGENE COULD HAVE BEEN RI--
EXCUSE ME...

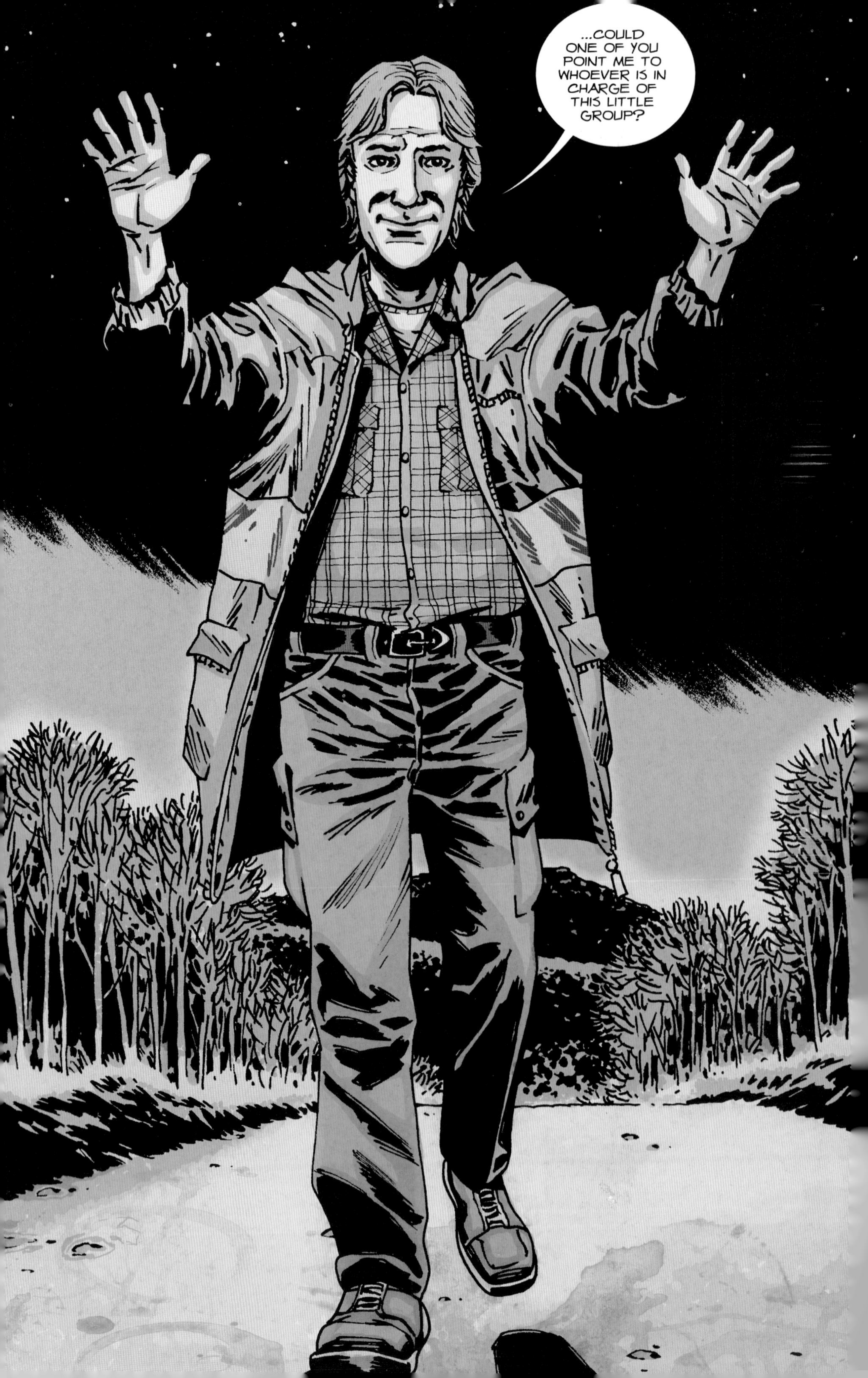
...COULD ONE OF YOU POINT ME TO WHOEVER IS IN CHARGE OF THIS LITTLE GROUP?

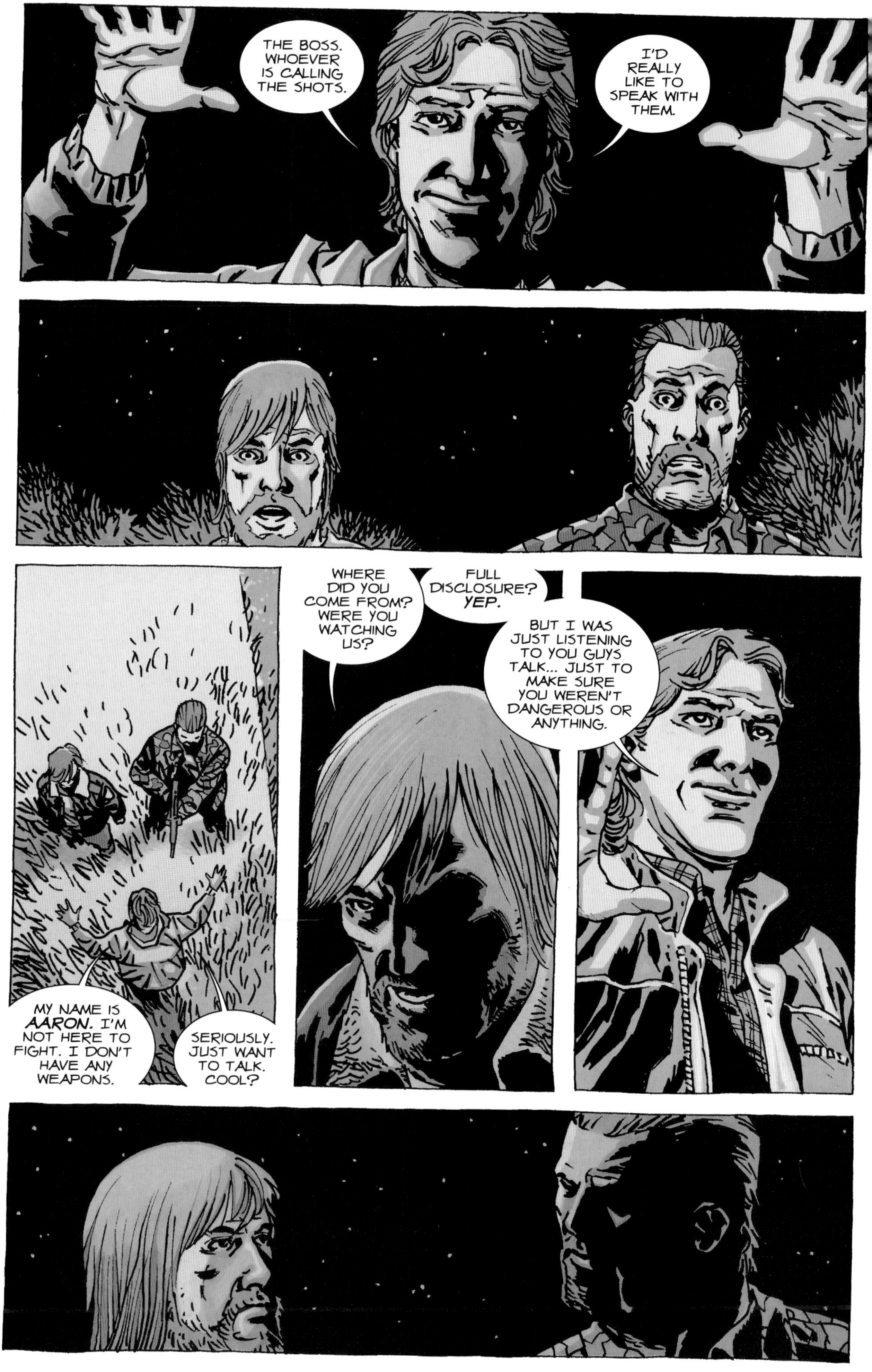
THE BOSS. WHOEVER IS CALLING THE SHOTS.
I'D REALLY LIKE TO SPEAK WITH THEM.
MY NAME IS AARON. I'M NOT HERE TO FIGHT. I DON'T HAVE ANY WEAPONS.
SERIOUSLY. JUST WANT TO TALK. COOL?
WHERE DID YOU COME FROM? WERE YOU WATCHING US?
FULL DISCLOSURE? YEP.
BUT I WAS JUST LISTENING TO YOU GUYS TALK... JUST TO MAKE SURE YOU WEREN'T DANGEROUS OR ANYTHING.

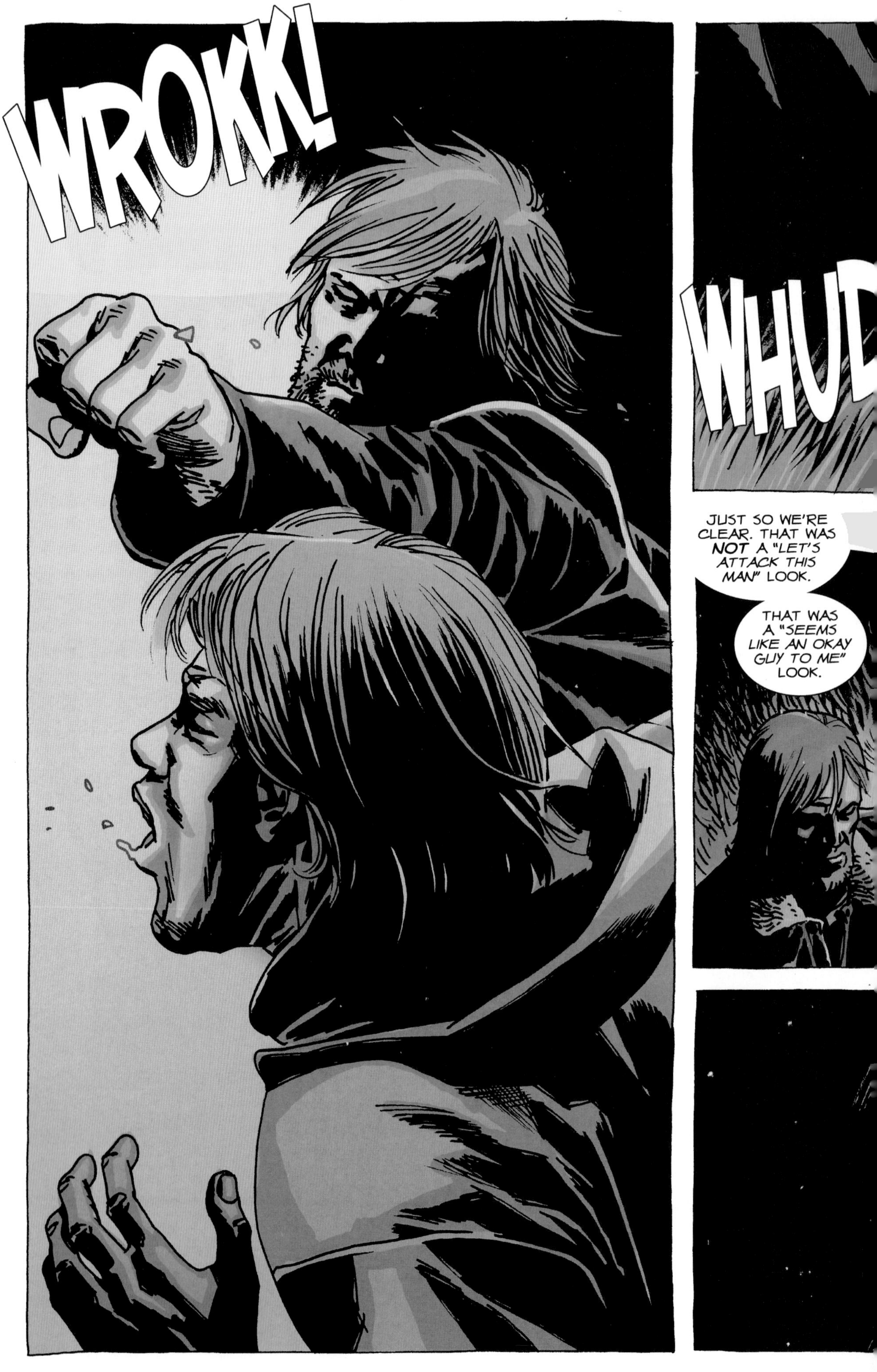
WROKK!
WHUD
JUST SO WE'RE CLEAR. THAT WAS NOT A "LET'S ATTACK THIS MAN" LOOK.
THAT WAS A "SEEMS LIKE AN OKAY GUY TO ME" LOOK.

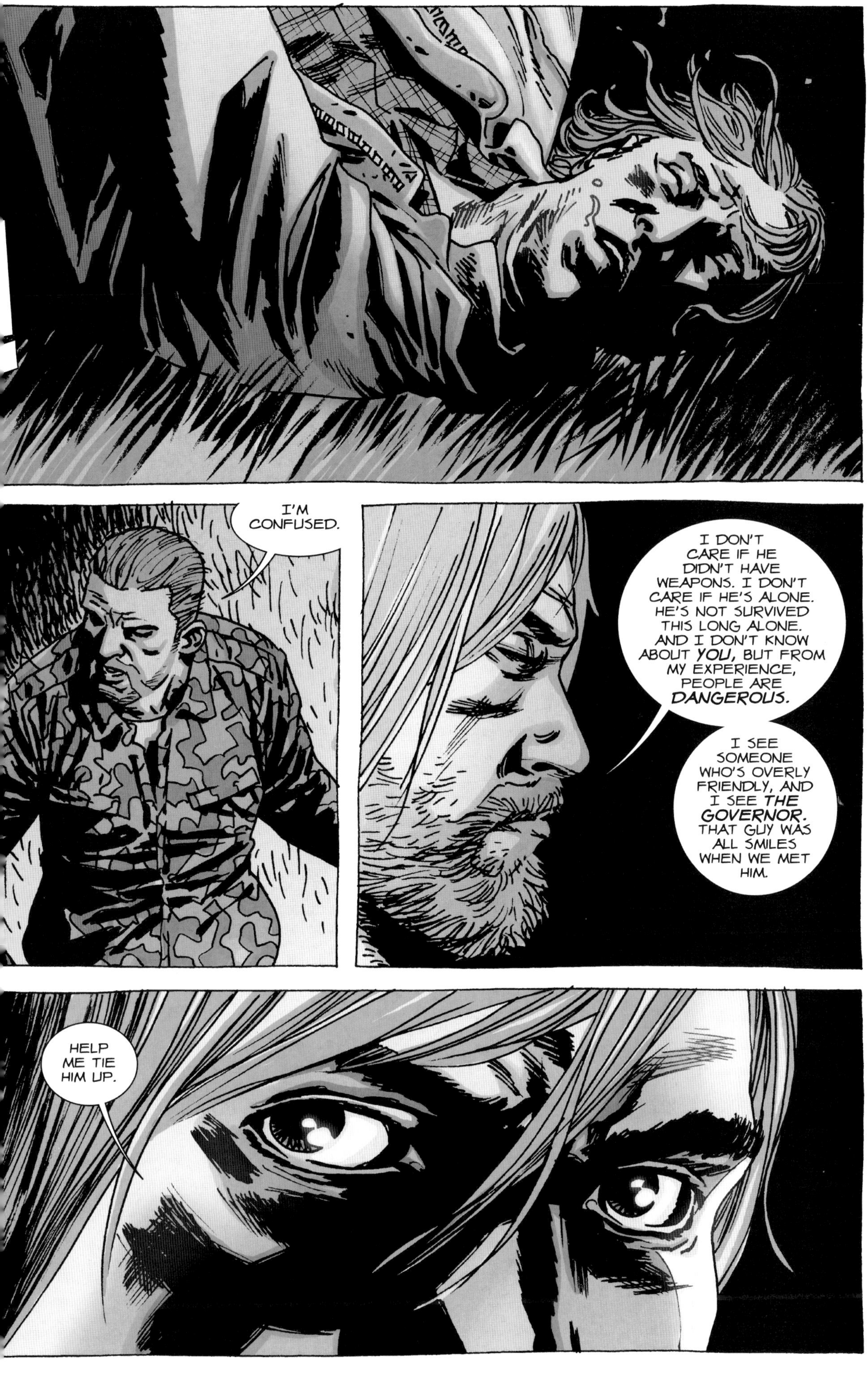
I'M CONFUSED.
I DON'T CARE IF HE DIDN'T HAVE WEAPONS. I DON'T CARE IF HE'S ALONE. HE'S NOT SURVIVED THIS LONG ALONE. AND I DON'T KNOW ABOUT YOU, BUT FROM MY EXPERIENCE, PEOPLE ARE DANGEROUS.
I SEE SOMEONE WHO'S OVERLY FRIENDLY, AND I SEE THE GOVERNOR. THAT GUY WAS ALL SMILES WHEN WE MET HIM.
HELP ME TIE HIM UP.

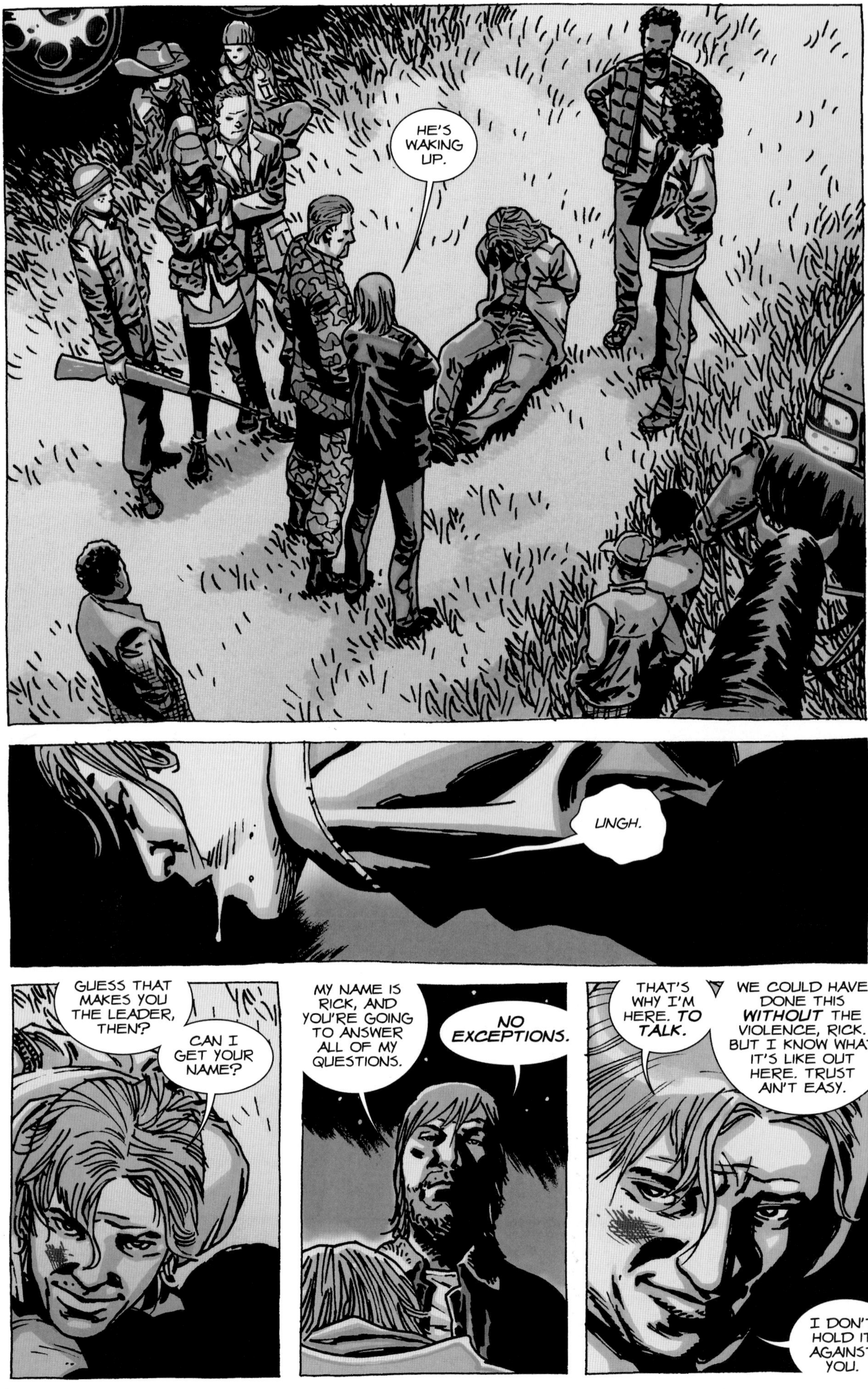
HE'S WAKING UP.
UNGH.
GUESS THAT MAKES YOU THE LEADER, THEN?
CAN I GET YOUR NAME?
MY NAME IS RICK, AND YOU'RE GOING TO ANSWER ALL OF MY QUESTIONS.
NO EXCEPTIONS.
THAT'S WHY I'M HERE. TO TALK.
WE COULD HAVE DONE THIS WITHOUT THE VIOLENCE, RICK. BUT I KNOW WHAT IT'S LIKE OUT HERE. TRUST AIN'T EASY.
I DON'T HOLD IT AGAINST YOU.

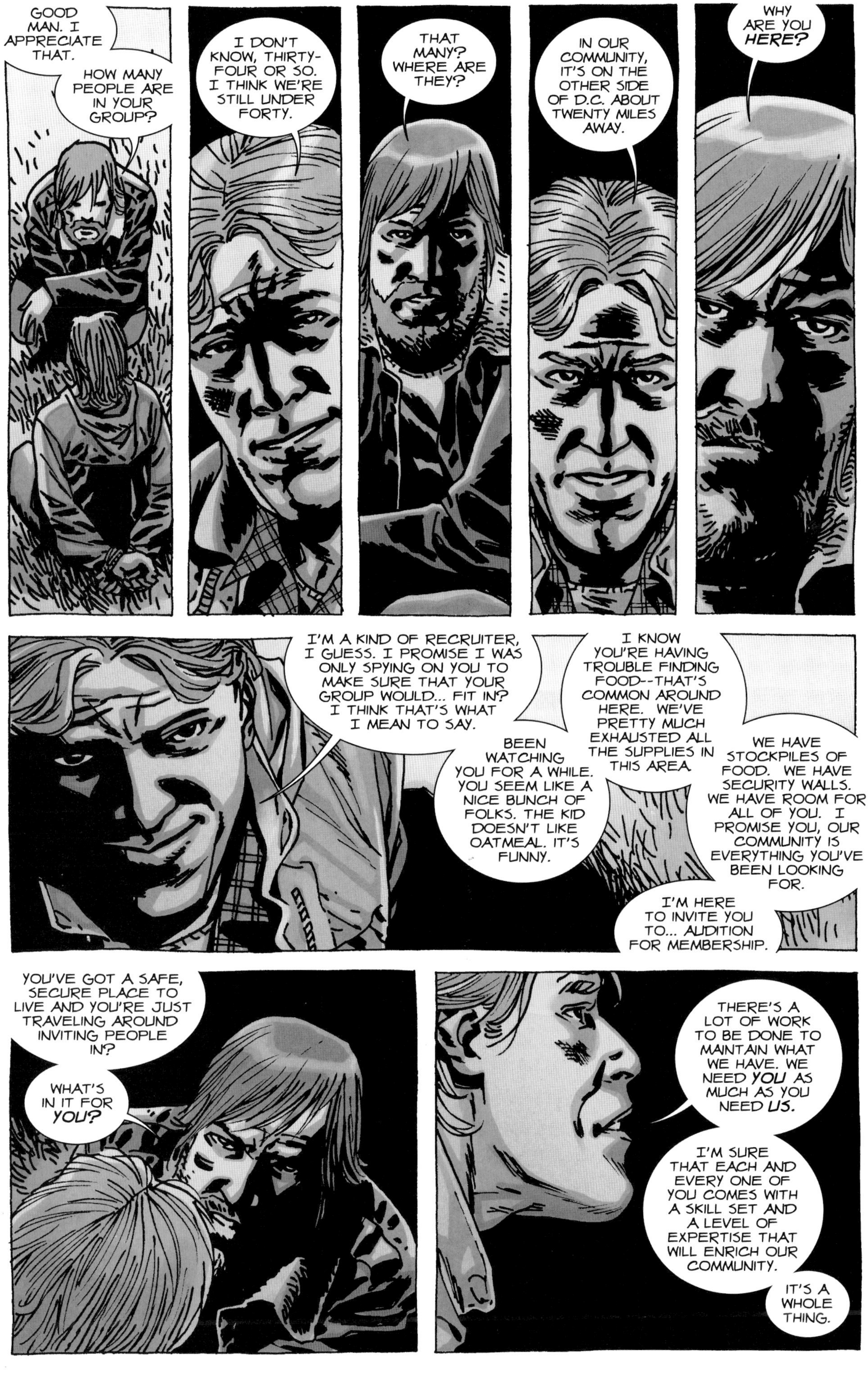
GOOD MAN. I APPRECIATE THAT.
HOW MANY PEOPLE ARE IN YOUR GROUP?
I DON'T KNOW, THIRTY-FOUR OR SO. I THINK WE'RE STILL UNDER FORTY.
THAT MANY? WHERE ARE THEY?
IN OUR COMMUNITY, IT'S ON THE OTHER SIDE OF D.C. ABOUT TWENTY MILES AWAY.
WHY ARE YOU HERE?
I'M A KIND OF RECRUITER, I GUESS. I PROMISE I WAS ONLY SPYING ON YOU TO MAKE SURE THAT YOUR GROUP WOULD... FIT IN? I THINK THAT'S WHAT I MEAN TO SAY.
BEEN WATCHING YOU FOR A WHILE. YOU SEEM LIKE A NICE BUNCH OF FOLKS. THE KID DOESN'T LIKE OATMEAL. IT'S FUNNY.
I KNOW YOU'RE HAVING TROUBLE FINDING FOOD--THAT'S COMMON AROUND HERE. WE'VE PRETTY MUCH EXHAUSTED ALL THE SUPPLIES IN THIS AREA.
WE HAVE STOCKPILES OF FOOD. WE HAVE SECURITY WALLS. WE HAVE ROOM FOR ALL OF YOU. I PROMISE YOU, OUR COMMUNITY IS EVERYTHING YOU'VE BEEN LOOKING FOR.
I'M HERE TO INVITE YOU TO... AUDITION FOR MEMBERSHIP.
YOU'VE GOT A SAFE, SECURE PLACE TO LIVE AND YOU'RE JUST TRAVELING AROUND INVITING PEOPLE IN?
WHAT'S IN IT FOR YOU?
THERE'S A LOT OF WORK TO BE DONE TO MAINTAIN WHAT WE HAVE. WE NEED YOU AS MUCH AS YOU NEED US.
I'M SURE THAT EACH AND EVERY ONE OF YOU COMES WITH A SKILL SET AND A LEVEL OF EXPERTISE THAT WILL ENRICH OUR COMMUNITY.
IT'S A WHOLE THING.

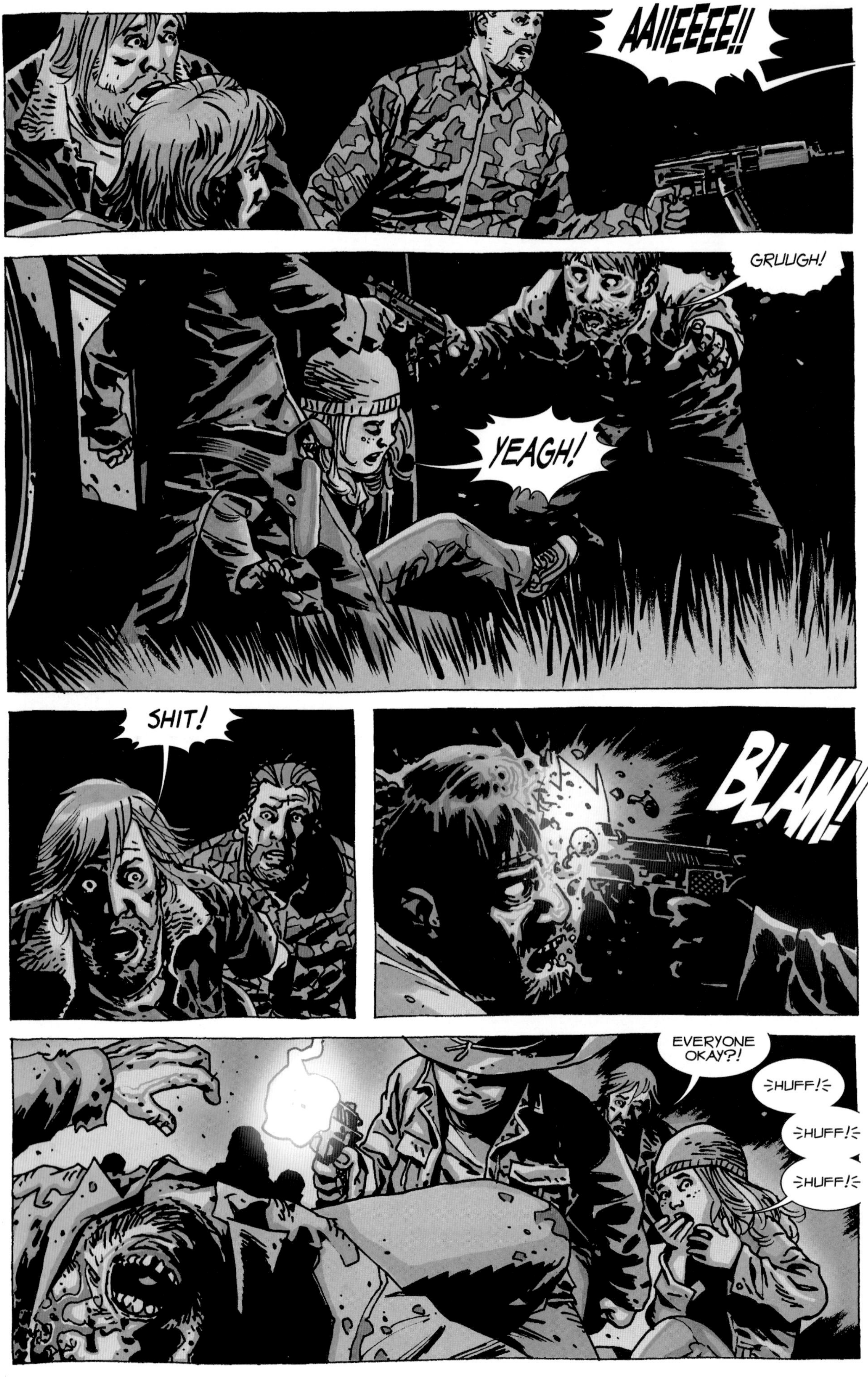
AAIIEEEE!!
GRUUGH!
YEAGH!
SHIT!
BLAM!
EVERYONE OKAY?!
HUFF!
HUFF!
HUFF!

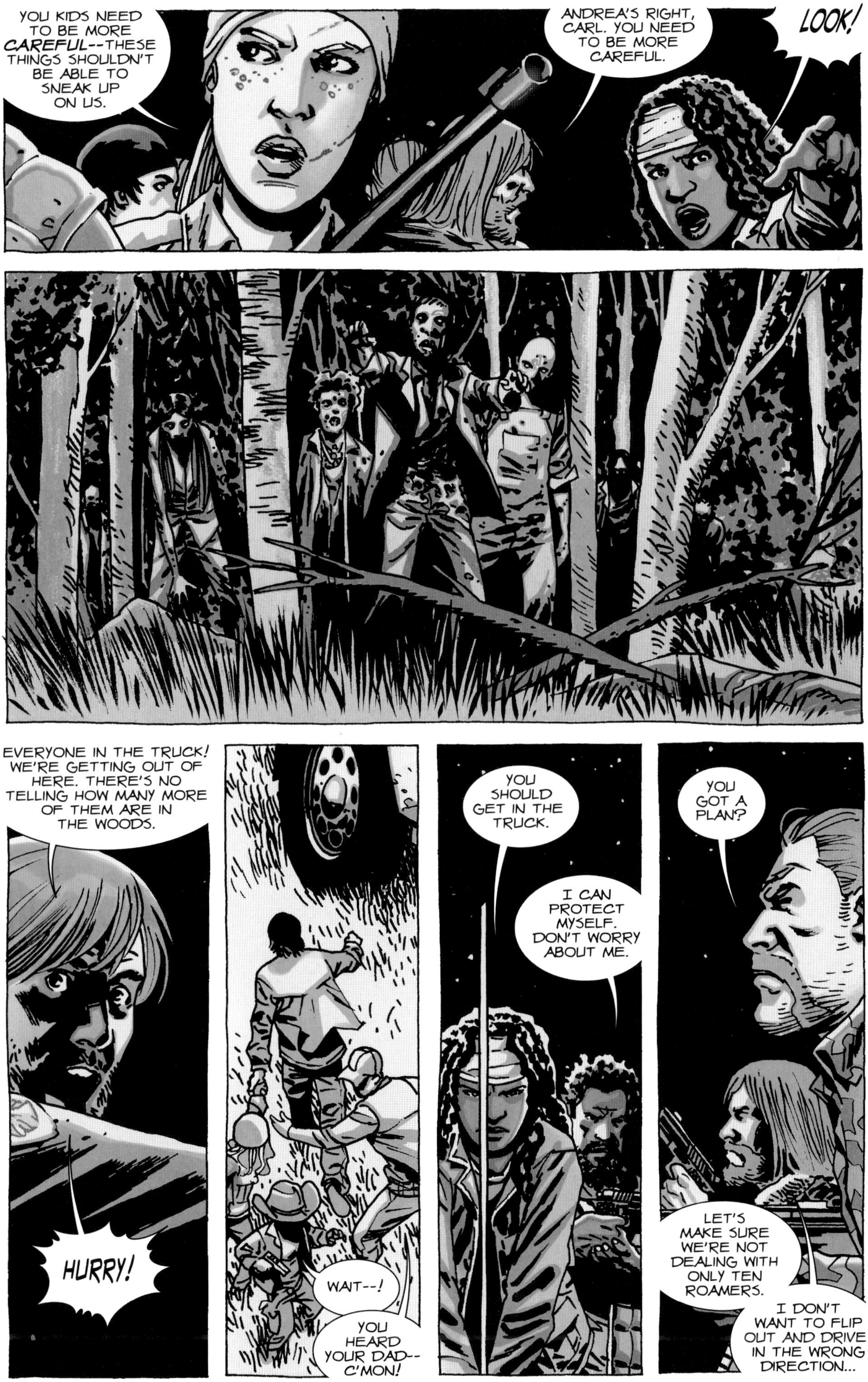
YOU KIDS NEED TO BE MORE CAREFUL--THESE THINGS SHOULDN'T BE ABLE TO SNEAK UP ON US.
ANDREA'S RIGHT, CARL. YOU NEED TO BE MORE CAREFUL.
LOOK!
EVERYONE IN THE TRUCK! WE'RE GETTING OUT OF HERE. THERE'S NO TELLING HOW MANY MORE OF THEM ARE IN THE WOODS.
HURRY!
WAIT--!
YOU HEARD YOUR DAD--C'MON!
YOU SHOULD GET IN THE TRUCK.
I CAN PROTECT MYSELF. DON'T WORRY ABOUT ME.
YOU GOT A PLAN?
LET'S MAKE SURE WE'RE NOT DEALING WITH ONLY TEN ROAMERS.
I DON'T WANT TO FLIP OUT AND DRIVE IN THE WRONG DIRECTION...

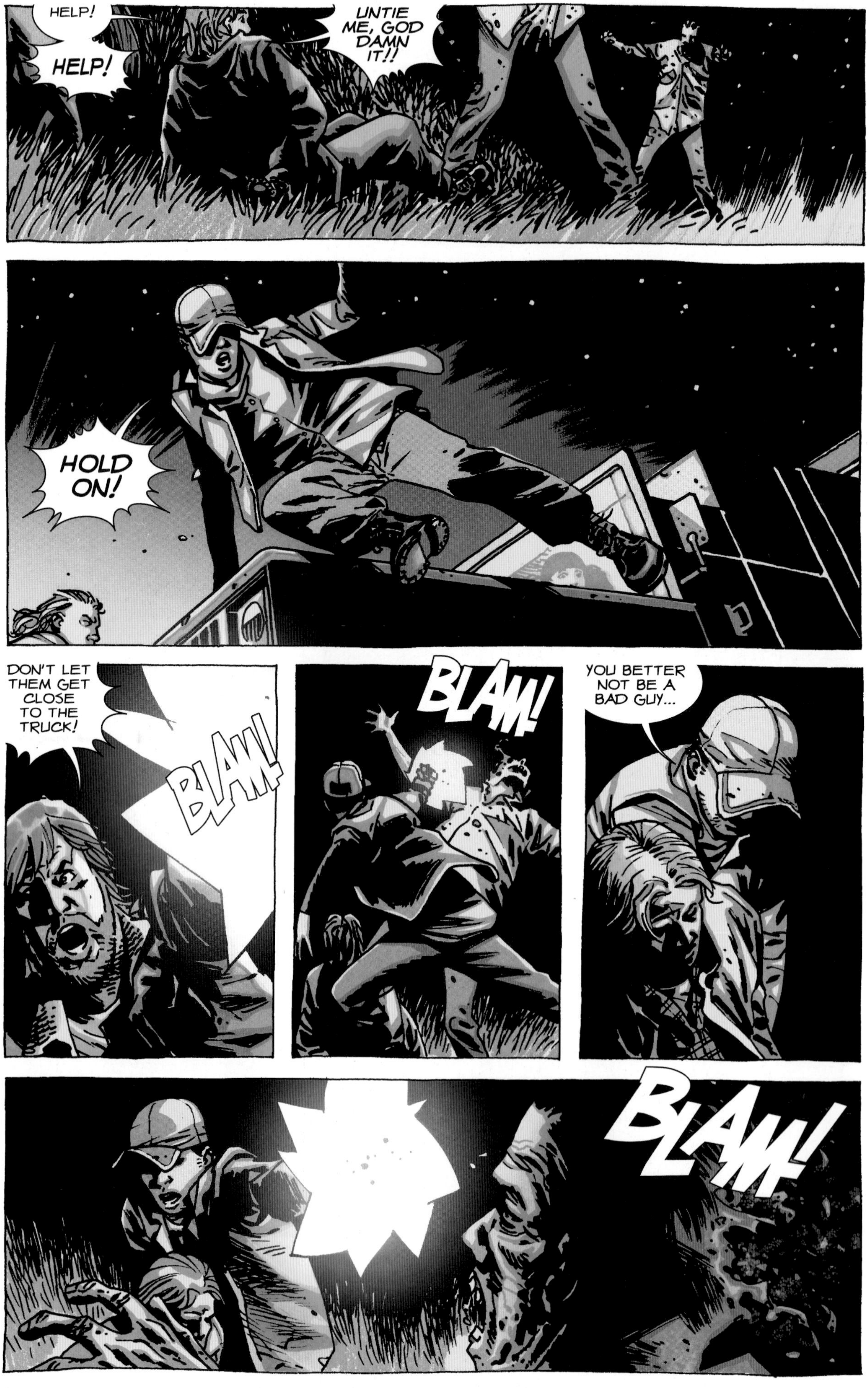
HELP!
HELP!
UNTIE ME, GOD DAMN IT!!
HOLD ON!
DON'T LET THEM GET CLOSE TO THE TRUCK!
BLAM!
BLAM!
YOU BETTER NOT BE A BAD GUY...
BLAM!

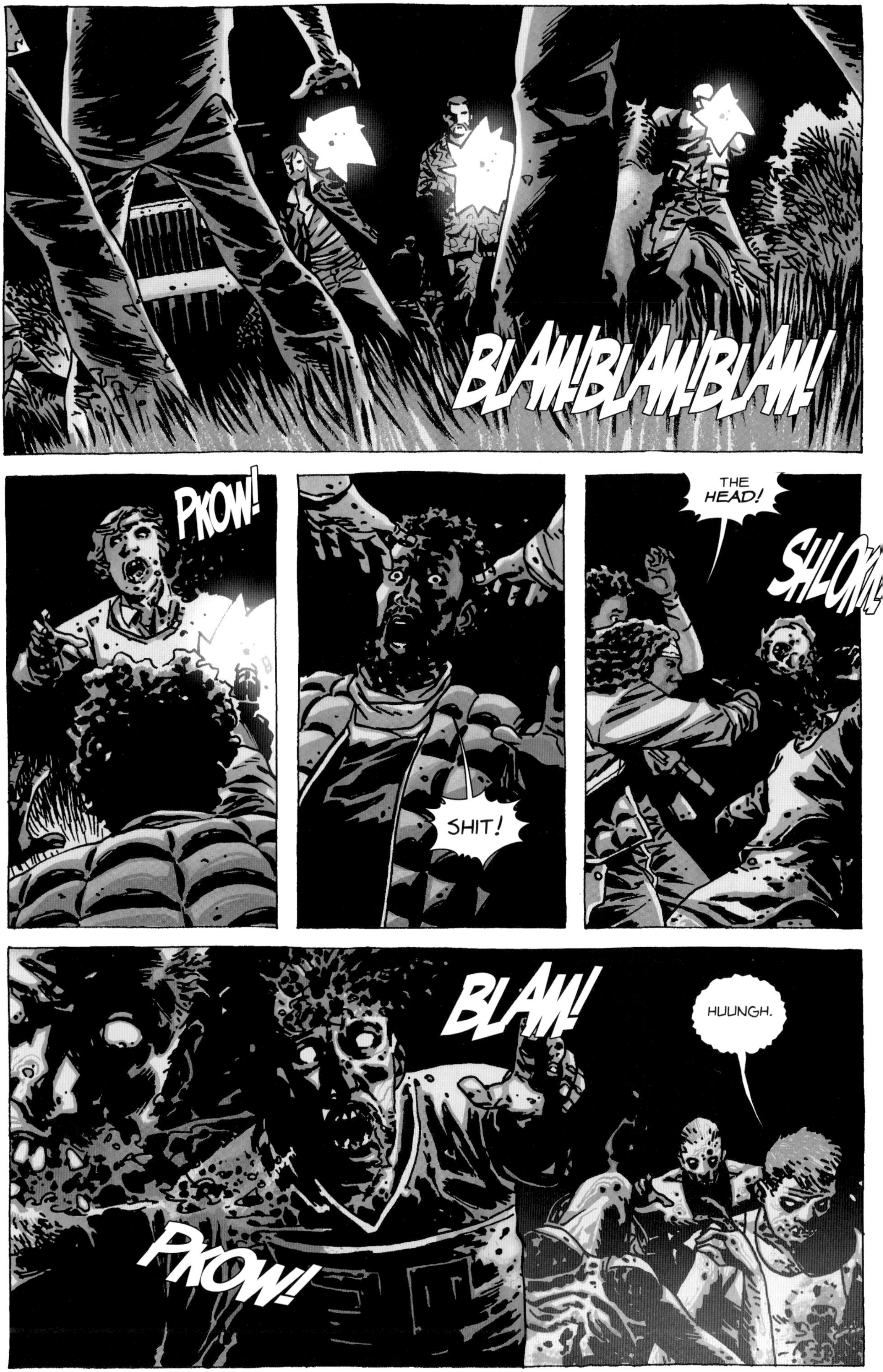
BLAM-BLAM-BLAM!
PKOW!
SHIT!
THE HEAD!
SHLOK
BLAM!
PKOW!
HUUNGH.

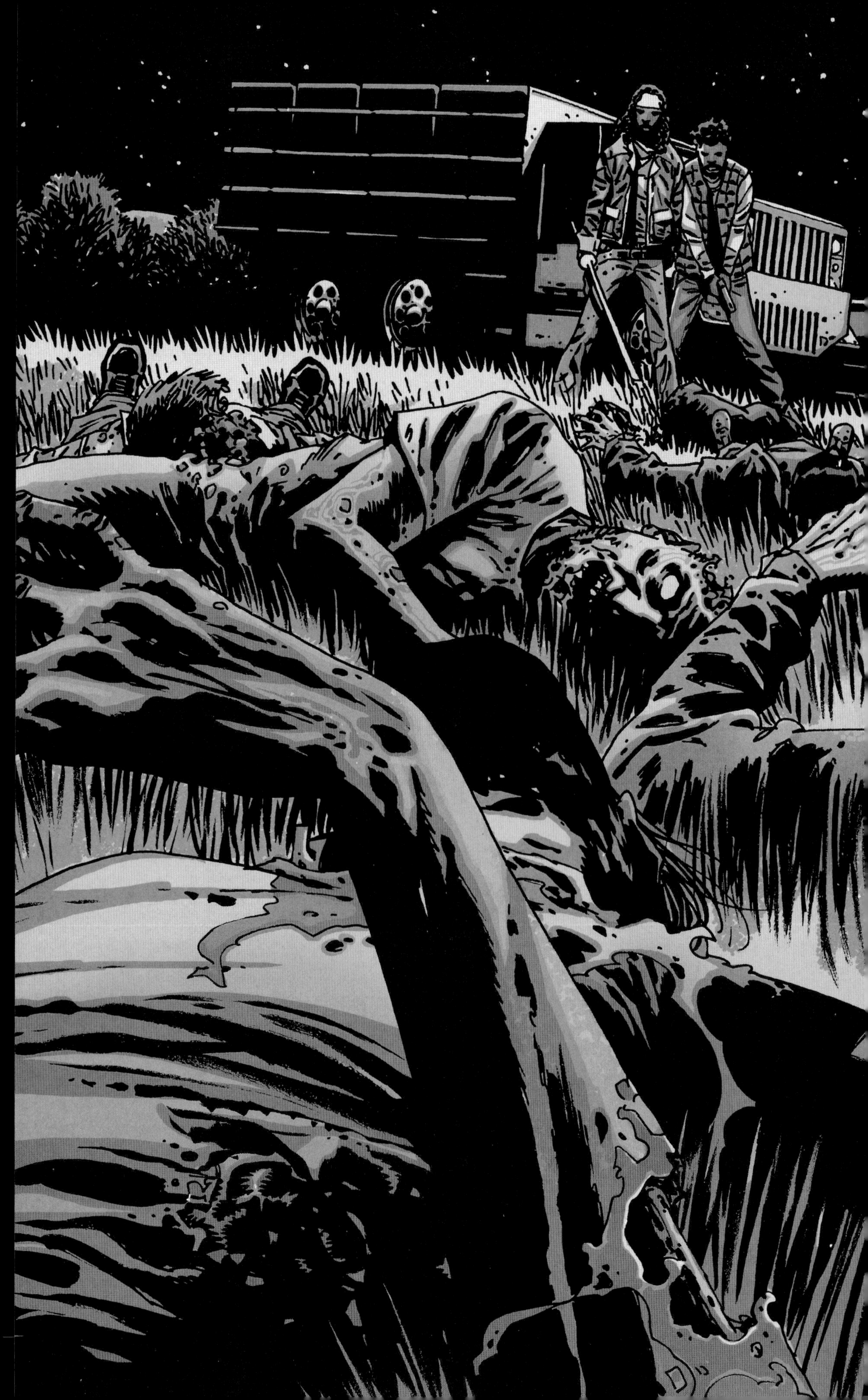

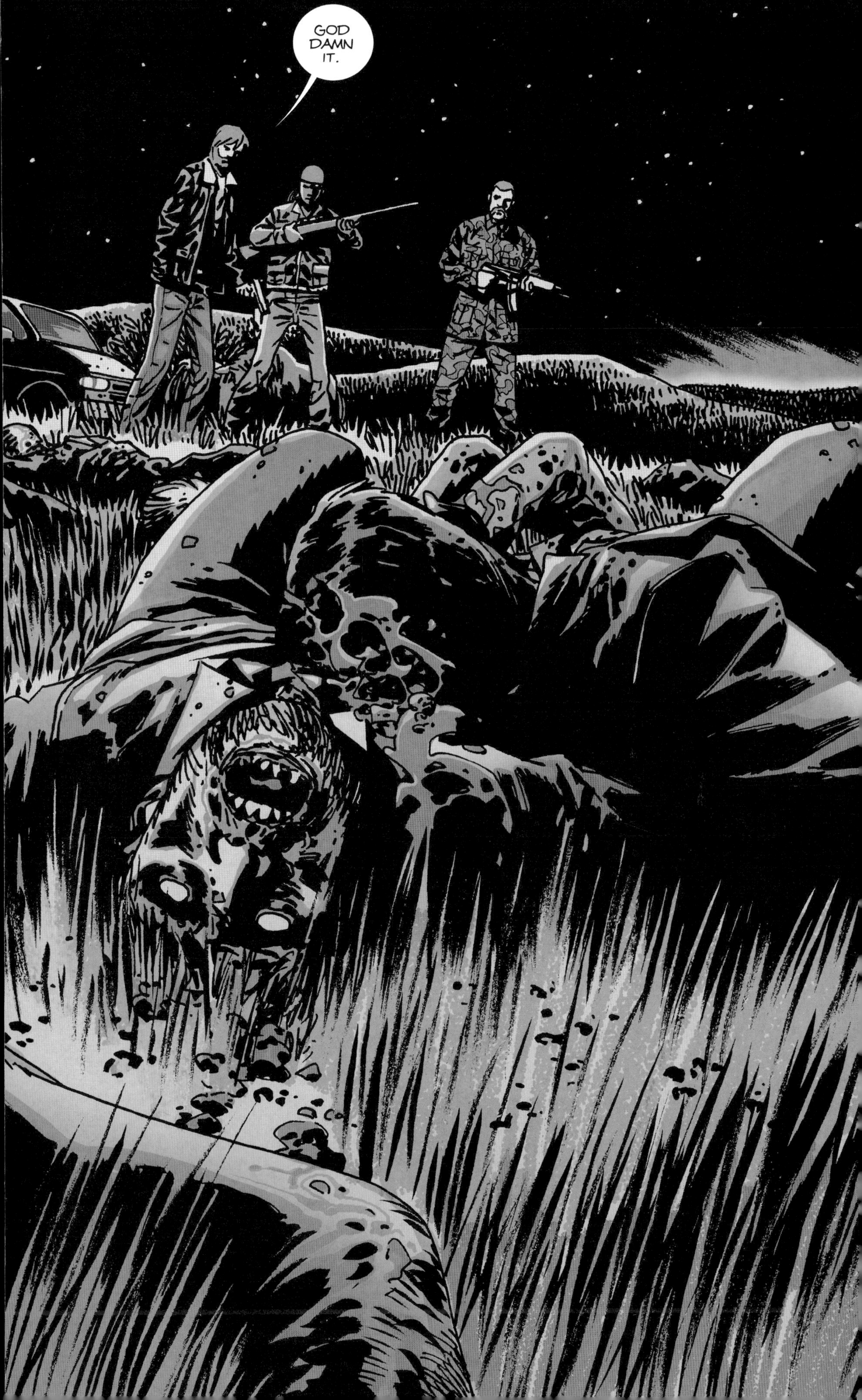
GOD DAMN IT.

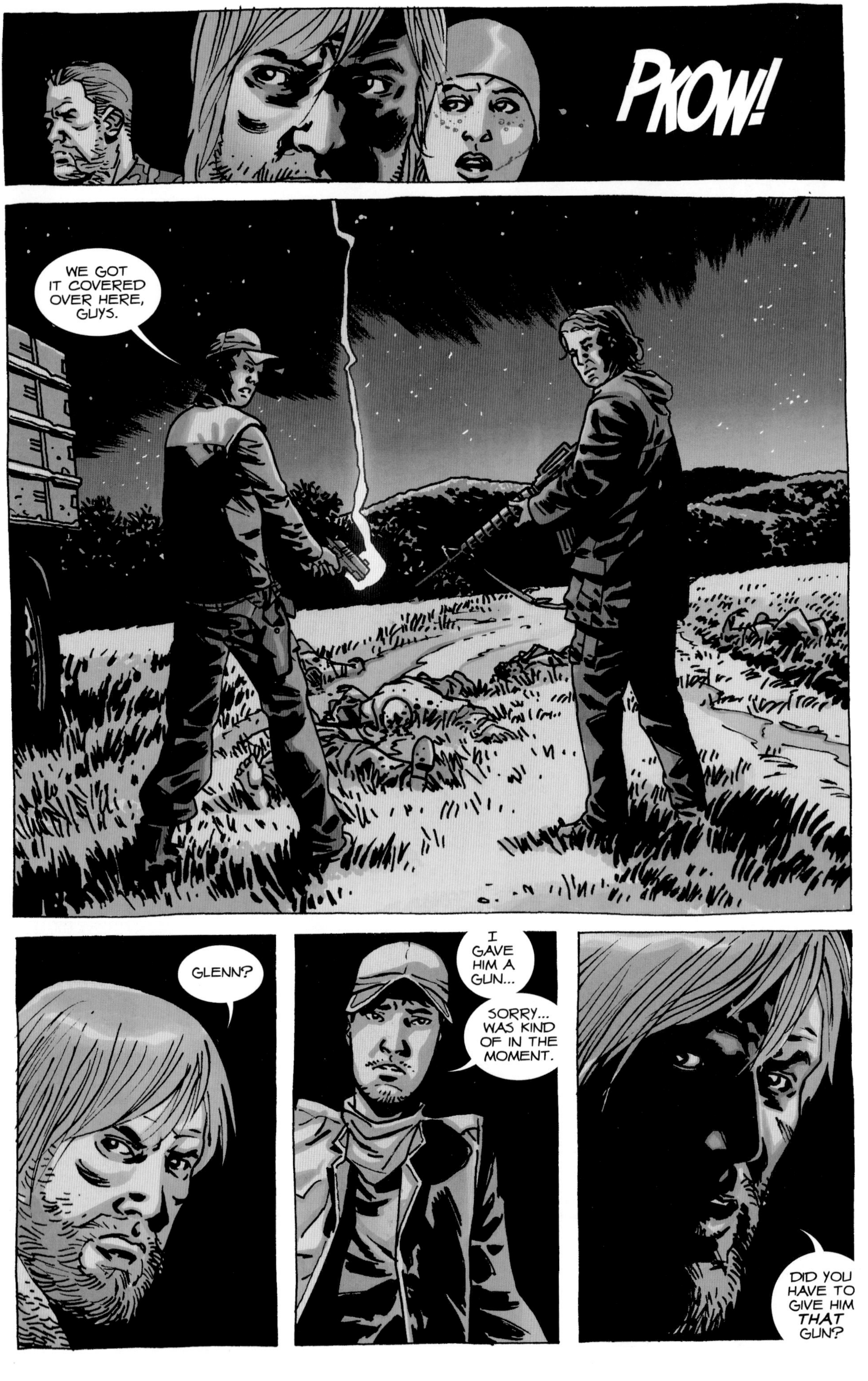

PKOW!
WE GOT IT COVERED OVER HERE, GUYS.
GLENN?
I GAVE HIM A GUN...
SORRY... WAS KIND OF IN THE MOMENT.
DID YOU HAVE TO GIVE HIM *THAT* GUN?

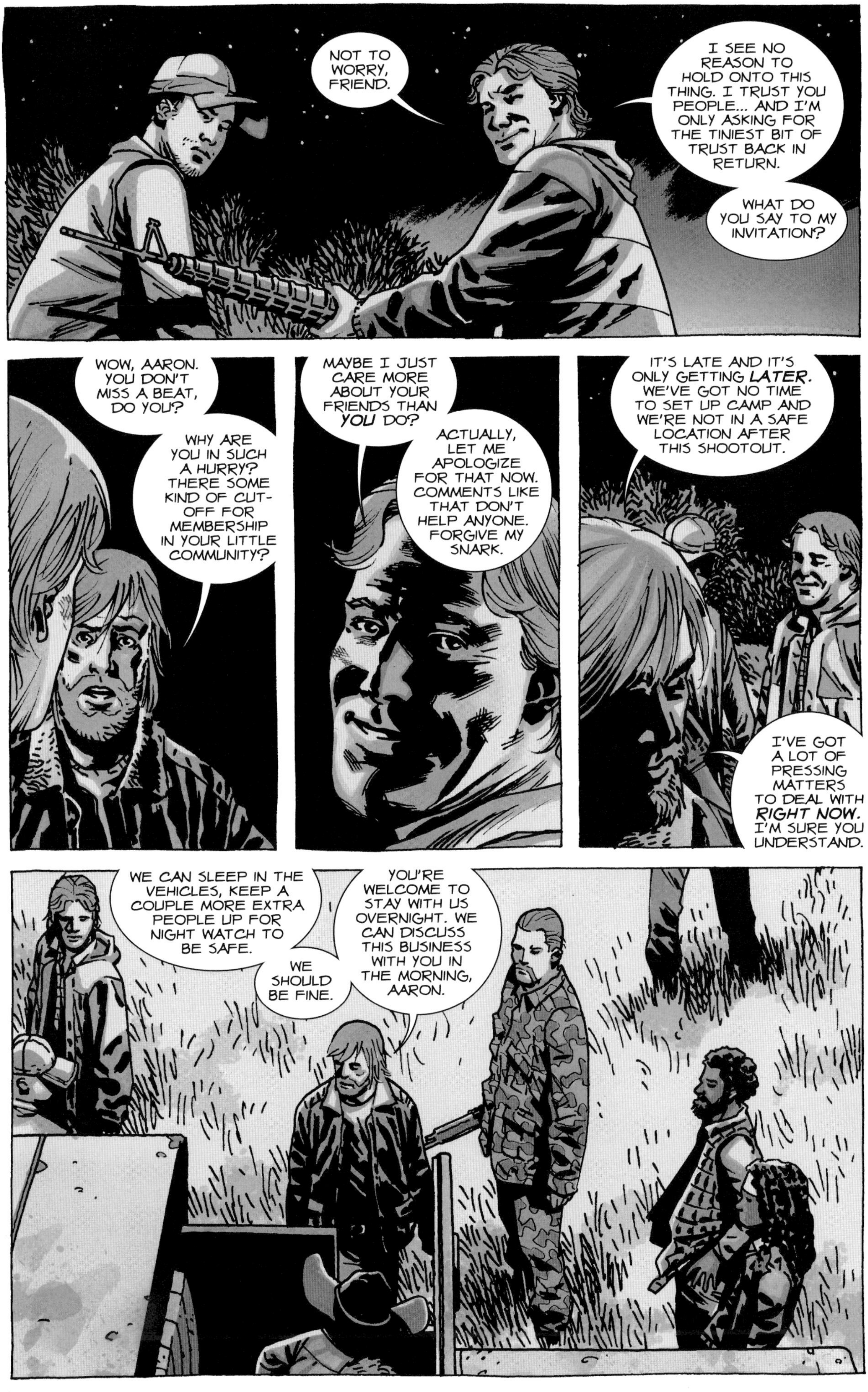
NOT TO WORRY, FRIEND.
I SEE NO REASON TO HOLD ONTO THIS THING. I TRUST YOU PEOPLE... AND I'M ONLY ASKING FOR THE TINIEST BIT OF TRUST BACK IN RETURN.
WHAT DO YOU SAY TO MY INVITATION?
WOW, AARON. YOU DON'T MISS A BEAT, DO YOU?
WHY ARE YOU IN SUCH A HURRY? THERE SOME KIND OF CUT-OFF FOR MEMBERSHIP IN YOUR LITTLE COMMUNITY?
MAYBE I JUST CARE MORE ABOUT YOUR FRIENDS THAN *YOU* DO?
ACTUALLY, LET ME APOLOGIZE FOR THAT NOW. COMMENTS LIKE THAT DON'T HELP ANYONE. FORGIVE MY SNARK.
IT'S LATE AND IT'S ONLY GETTING **LATER.** WE'VE GOT NO TIME TO SET UP CAMP AND WE'RE NOT IN A SAFE LOCATION AFTER THIS SHOOTOUT.
I'VE GOT A LOT OF PRESSING MATTERS TO DEAL WITH **RIGHT NOW.** I'M SURE YOU UNDERSTAND.
WE CAN SLEEP IN THE VEHICLES, KEEP A COUPLE MORE EXTRA PEOPLE UP FOR NIGHT WATCH TO BE SAFE.
WE SHOULD BE FINE.
YOU'RE WELCOME TO STAY WITH US OVERNIGHT. WE CAN DISCUSS THIS BUSINESS WITH YOU IN THE MORNING, AARON.

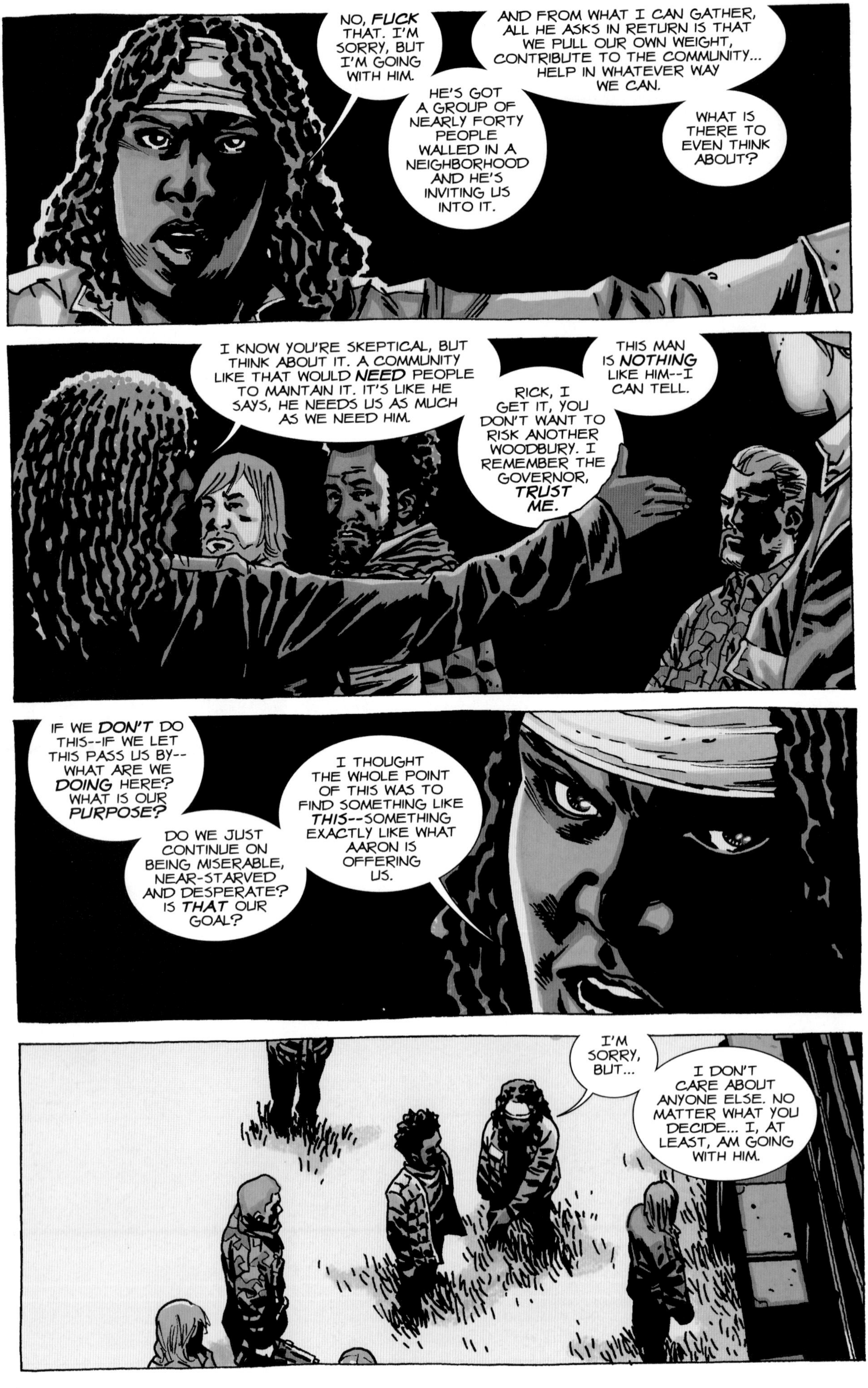
NO, FUCK THAT. I'M SORRY, BUT I'M GOING WITH HIM.
HE'S GOT A GROUP OF NEARLY FORTY PEOPLE WALLED IN A NEIGHBORHOOD AND HE'S INVITING US INTO IT.
AND FROM WHAT I CAN GATHER, ALL HE ASKS IN RETURN IS THAT WE PULL OUR OWN WEIGHT, CONTRIBUTE TO THE COMMUNITY... HELP IN WHATEVER WAY WE CAN.
WHAT IS THERE TO EVEN THINK ABOUT?
I KNOW YOU'RE SKEPTICAL, BUT THINK ABOUT IT. A COMMUNITY LIKE THAT WOULD NEED PEOPLE TO MAINTAIN IT. IT'S LIKE HE SAYS, HE NEEDS US AS MUCH AS WE NEED HIM.
RICK, I GET IT, YOU DON'T WANT TO RISK ANOTHER WOODBURY. I REMEMBER THE GOVERNOR, TRUST ME.
THIS MAN IS NOTHING LIKE HIM--I CAN TELL.
IF WE DON'T DO THIS--IF WE LET THIS PASS US BY--WHAT ARE WE DOING HERE? WHAT IS OUR PURPOSE?
DO WE JUST CONTINUE ON BEING MISERABLE, NEAR-STARVED AND DESPERATE? IS THAT OUR GOAL?
I THOUGHT THE WHOLE POINT OF THIS WAS TO FIND SOMETHING LIKE THIS--SOMETHING EXACTLY LIKE WHAT AARON IS OFFERING US.
I'M SORRY, BUT...
I DON'T CARE ABOUT ANYONE ELSE. NO MATTER WHAT YOU DECIDE... I, AT LEAST, AM GOING WITH HIM.

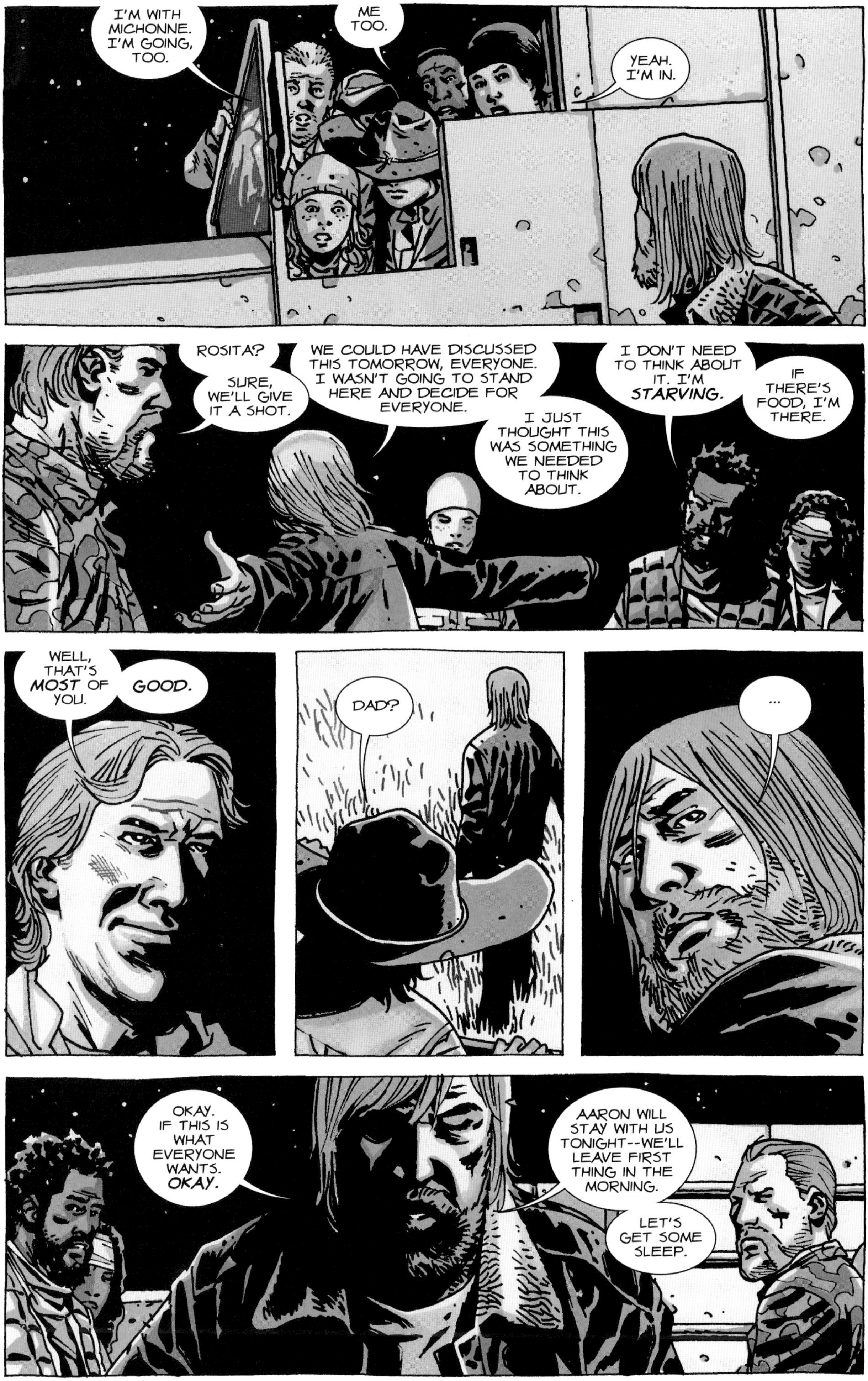
I'M WITH MICHONNE. I'M GOING, TOO.
ME TOO.
YEAH. I'M IN.
ROSITA?
SURE, WE'LL GIVE IT A SHOT.
WE COULD HAVE DISCUSSED THIS TOMORROW, EVERYONE. I WASN'T GOING TO STAND HERE AND DECIDE FOR EVERYONE.
I JUST THOUGHT THIS WAS SOMETHING WE NEEDED TO THINK ABOUT.
I DON'T NEED TO THINK ABOUT IT. I'M STARVING.
IF THERE'S FOOD, I'M THERE.
WELL, THAT'S MOST OF YOU.
GOOD.
DAD?
...
OKAY. IF THIS IS WHAT EVERYONE WANTS. OKAY.
AARON WILL STAY WITH US TONIGHT--WE'LL LEAVE FIRST THING IN THE MORNING.
LET'S GET SOME SLEEP.

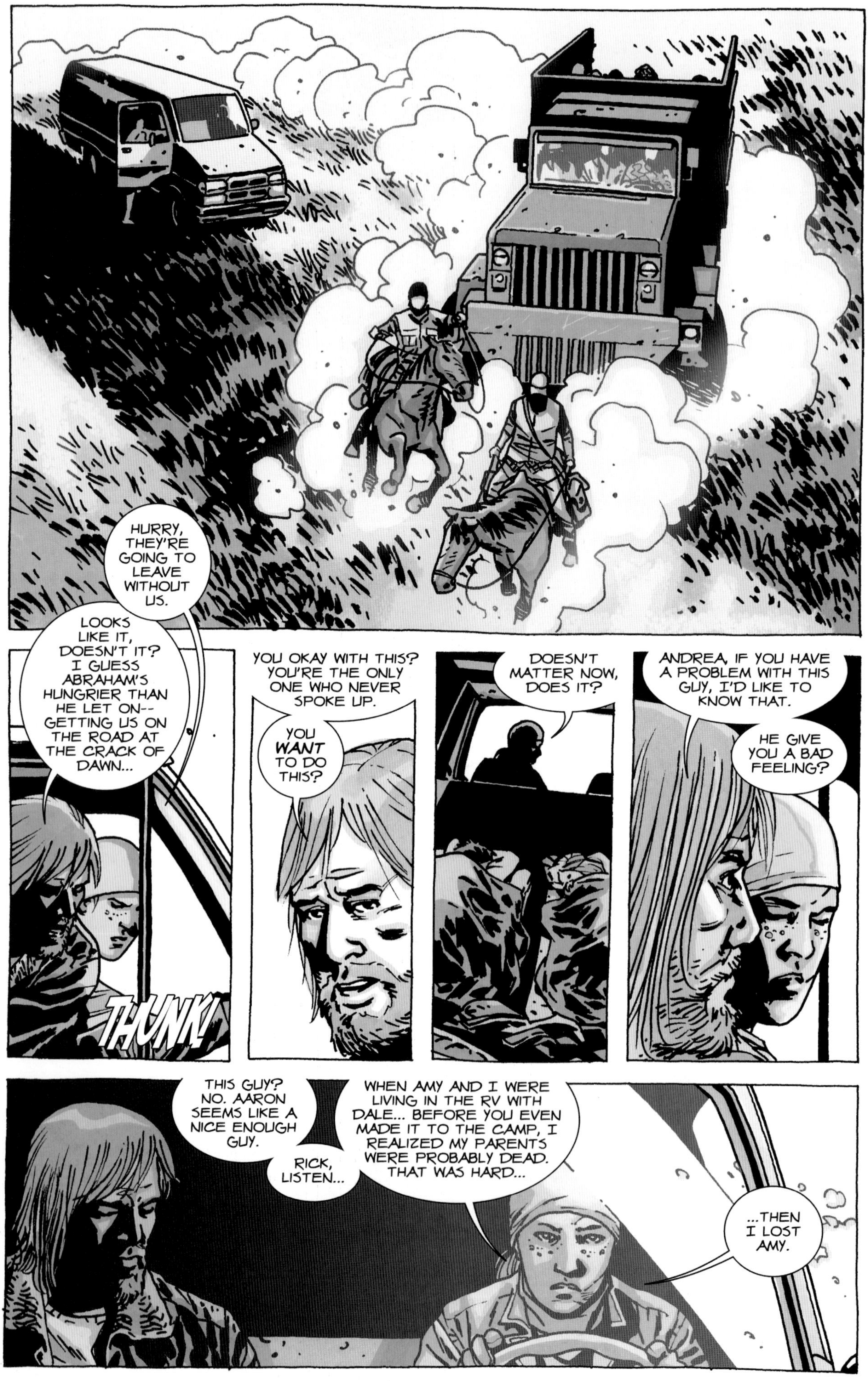
HURRY, THEY'RE GOING TO LEAVE WITHOUT US.
LOOKS LIKE IT, DOESN'T IT? I GUESS ABRAHAM'S HUNGRIER THAN HE LET ON-- GETTING US ON THE ROAD AT THE CRACK OF DAWN...
THUNK!
YOU OKAY WITH THIS? YOU'RE THE ONLY ONE WHO NEVER SPOKE UP.
YOU *WANT* TO DO THIS?
DOESN'T MATTER NOW, DOES IT?
ANDREA, IF YOU HAVE A PROBLEM WITH THIS GUY, I'D LIKE TO KNOW THAT.
HE GIVE YOU A BAD FEELING?
THIS GUY? NO. AARON SEEMS LIKE A NICE ENOUGH GUY.
RICK, LISTEN...
WHEN AMY AND I WERE LIVING IN THE RV WITH DALE... BEFORE YOU EVEN MADE IT TO THE CAMP, I REALIZED MY PARENTS WERE PROBABLY DEAD. THAT WAS HARD...
...THEN I LOST AMY.

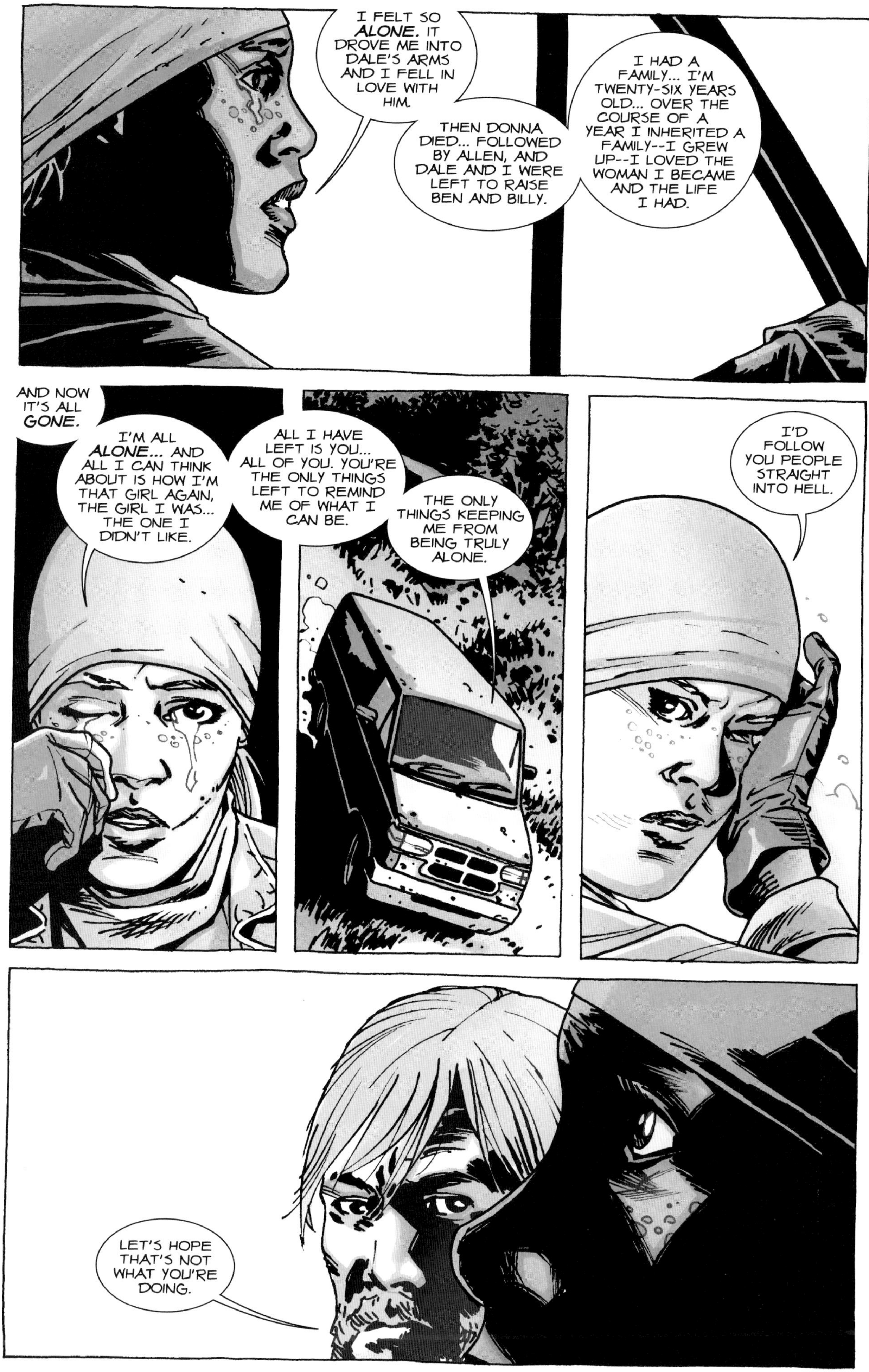
I FELT SO ALONE. IT DROVE ME INTO DALE'S ARMS AND I FELL IN LOVE WITH HIM.
THEN DONNA DIED... FOLLOWED BY ALLEN, AND DALE AND I WERE LEFT TO RAISE BEN AND BILLY.
I HAD A FAMILY... I'M TWENTY-SIX YEARS OLD... OVER THE COURSE OF A YEAR I INHERITED A FAMILY--I GREW UP--I LOVED THE WOMAN I BECAME AND THE LIFE I HAD.
AND NOW IT'S ALL GONE.
I'M ALL ALONE... AND ALL I CAN THINK ABOUT IS HOW I'M THAT GIRL AGAIN, THE GIRL I WAS... THE ONE I DIDN'T LIKE.
ALL I HAVE LEFT IS YOU... ALL OF YOU. YOU'RE THE ONLY THINGS LEFT TO REMIND ME OF WHAT I CAN BE.
THE ONLY THINGS KEEPING ME FROM BEING TRULY ALONE.
I'D FOLLOW YOU PEOPLE STRAIGHT INTO HELL.
LET'S HOPE THAT'S NOT WHAT YOU'RE DOING.

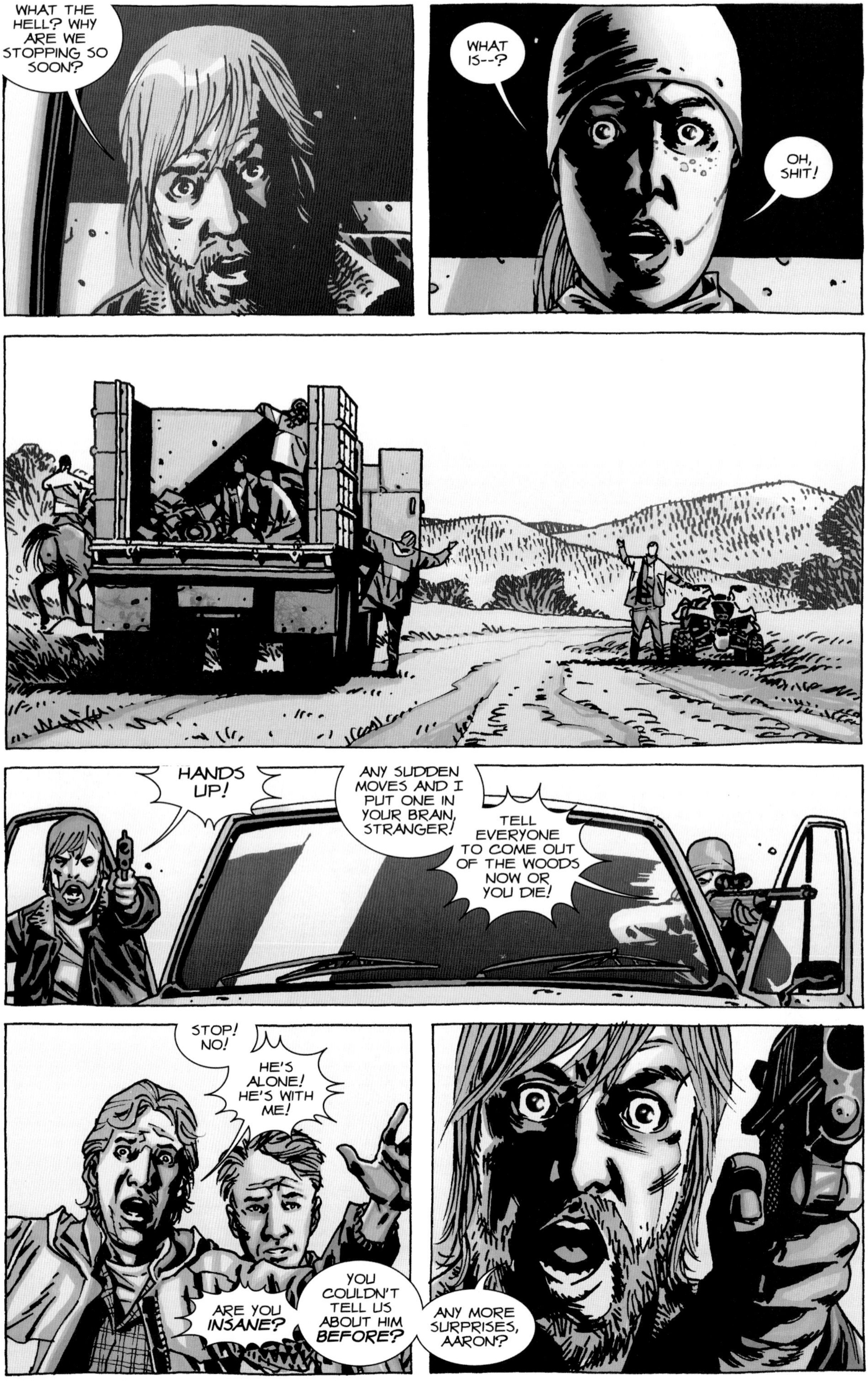
WHAT THE HELL? WHY ARE WE STOPPING SO SOON?
WHAT IS--?
OH, SHIT!
HANDS UP!
ANY SUDDEN MOVES AND I PUT ONE IN YOUR BRAIN, STRANGER!
TELL EVERYONE TO COME OUT OF THE WOODS NOW OR YOU DIE!
STOP! NO!
HE'S ALONE! HE'S WITH ME!
ARE YOU *INSANE?*
YOU COULDN'T TELL US ABOUT HIM *BEFORE?*
ANY MORE SURPRISES, AARON?

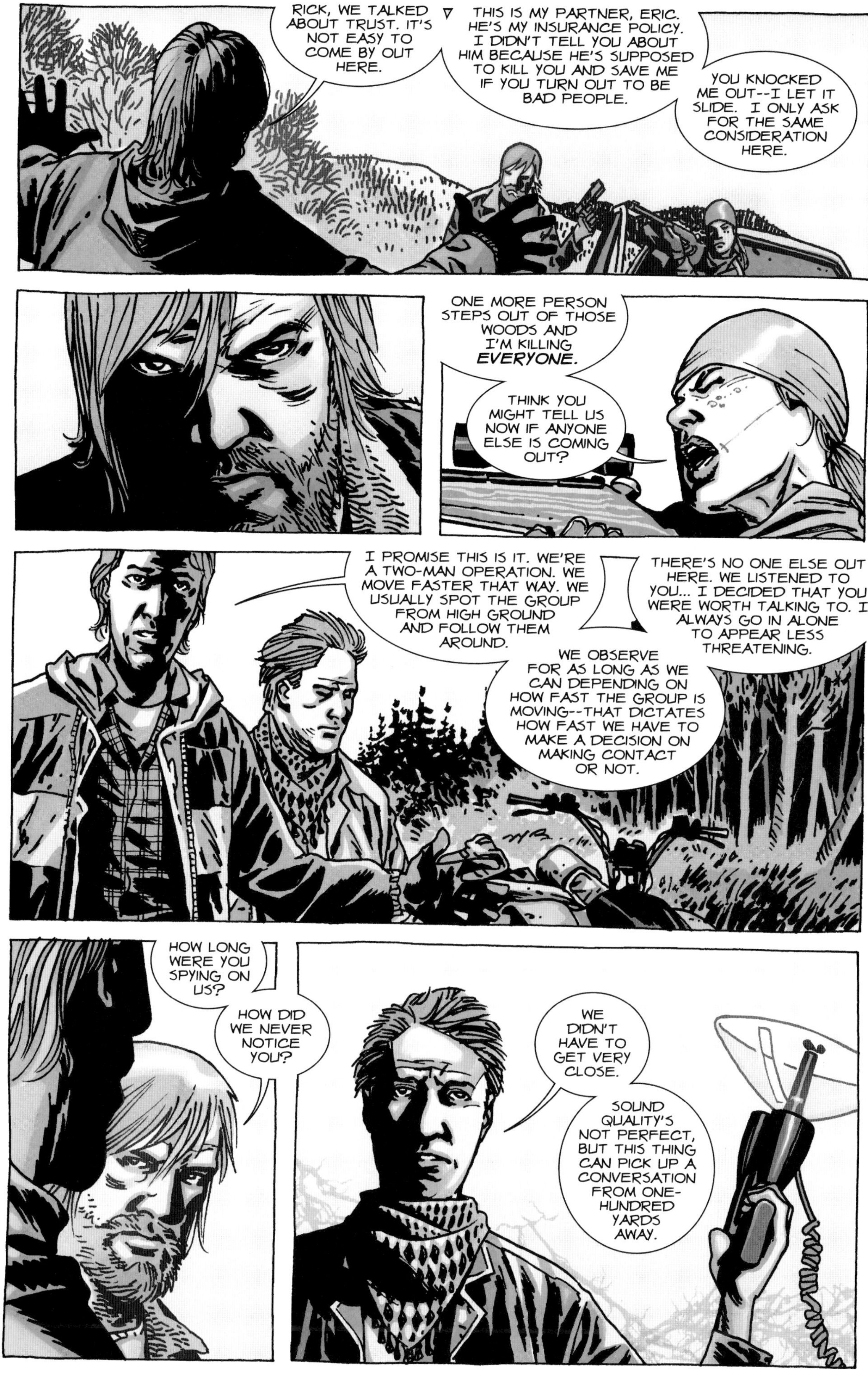
RICK, WE TALKED ABOUT TRUST. IT'S NOT EASY TO COME BY OUT HERE.
THIS IS MY PARTNER, ERIC. HE'S MY INSURANCE POLICY. I DIDN'T TELL YOU ABOUT HIM BECAUSE HE'S SUPPOSED TO KILL YOU AND SAVE ME IF YOU TURN OUT TO BE BAD PEOPLE.
YOU KNOCKED ME OUT--I LET IT SLIDE. I ONLY ASK FOR THE SAME CONSIDERATION HERE.
ONE MORE PERSON STEPS OUT OF THOSE WOODS AND I'M KILLING EVERYONE.
THINK YOU MIGHT TELL US NOW IF ANYONE ELSE IS COMING OUT?
I PROMISE THIS IS IT. WE'RE A TWO-MAN OPERATION. WE MOVE FASTER THAT WAY. WE USUALLY SPOT THE GROUP FROM HIGH GROUND AND FOLLOW THEM AROUND.
WE OBSERVE FOR AS LONG AS WE CAN DEPENDING ON HOW FAST THE GROUP IS MOVING--THAT DICTATES HOW FAST WE HAVE TO MAKE A DECISION ON MAKING CONTACT OR NOT.
THERE'S NO ONE ELSE OUT HERE. WE LISTENED TO YOU... I DECIDED THAT YOU WERE WORTH TALKING TO. I ALWAYS GO IN ALONE TO APPEAR LESS THREATENING.
HOW LONG WERE YOU SPYING ON US?
HOW DID WE NEVER NOTICE YOU?
WE DIDN'T HAVE TO GET VERY CLOSE.
SOUND QUALITY'S NOT PERFECT, BUT THIS THING CAN PICK UP A CONVERSATION FROM ONE-HUNDRED YARDS AWAY.

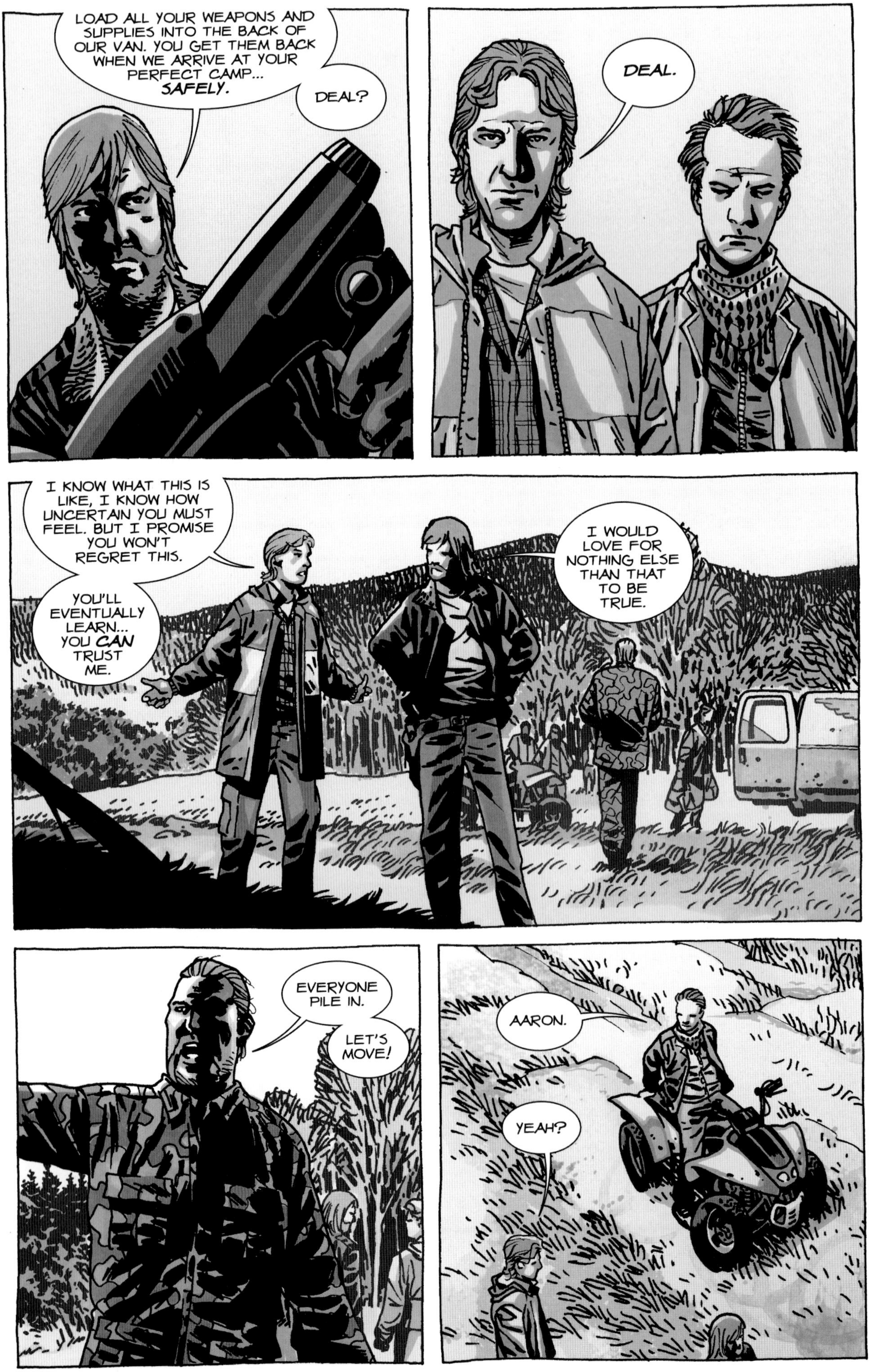
LOAD ALL YOUR WEAPONS AND SUPPLIES INTO THE BACK OF OUR VAN. YOU GET THEM BACK WHEN WE ARRIVE AT YOUR PERFECT CAMP... SAFELY.
DEAL?
DEAL.
I KNOW WHAT THIS IS LIKE, I KNOW HOW UNCERTAIN YOU MUST FEEL. BUT I PROMISE YOU WON'T REGRET THIS.
YOU'LL EVENTUALLY LEARN... YOU CAN TRUST ME.
I WOULD LOVE FOR NOTHING ELSE THAN THAT TO BE TRUE.
EVERYONE PILE IN.
LET'S MOVE!
AARON.
YEAH?

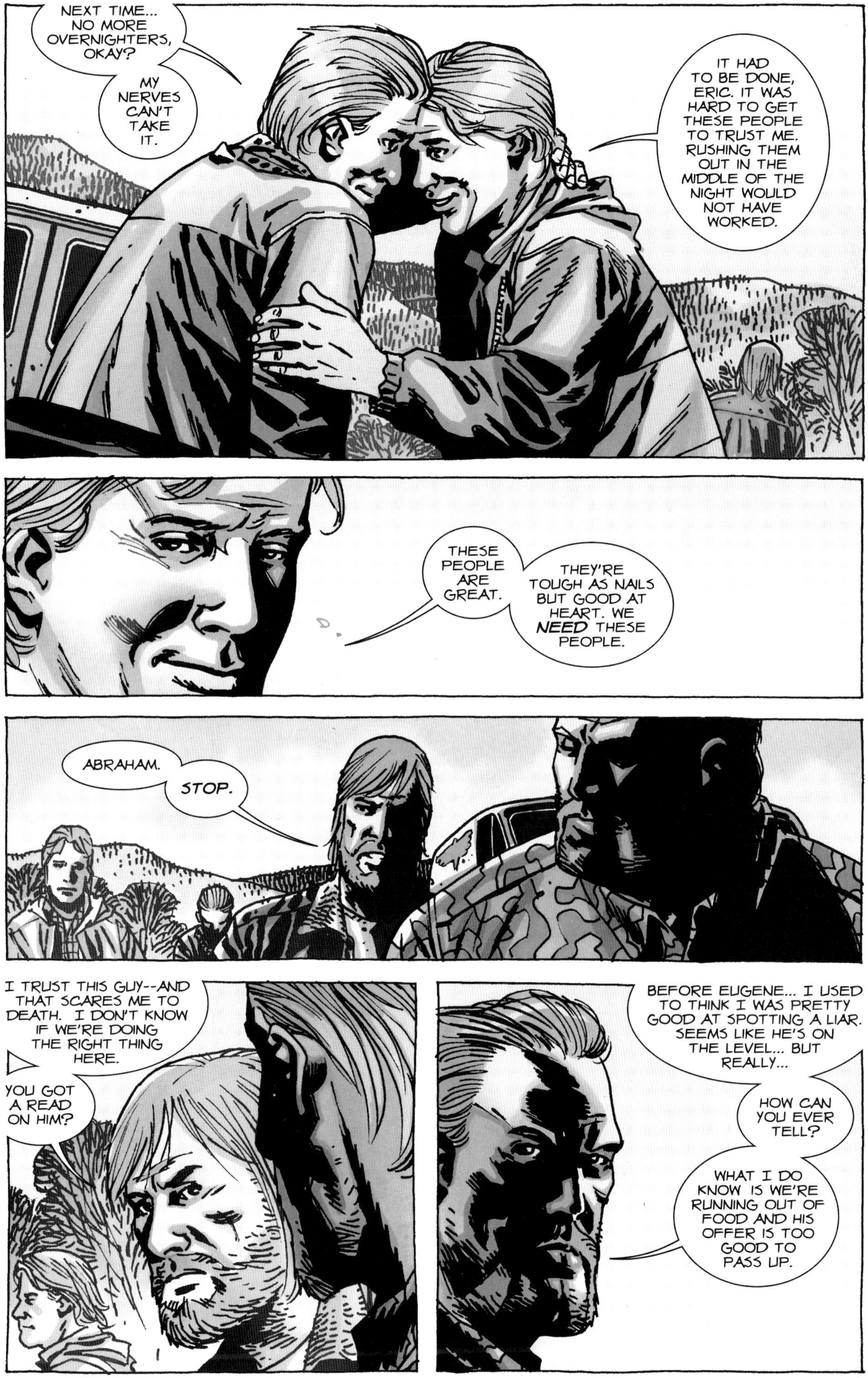
NEXT TIME... NO MORE OVERNIGHTERS, OKAY?
MY NERVES CAN'T TAKE IT.
IT HAD TO BE DONE, ERIC. IT WAS HARD TO GET THESE PEOPLE TO TRUST ME. RUSHING THEM OUT IN THE MIDDLE OF THE NIGHT WOULD NOT HAVE WORKED.
THESE PEOPLE ARE GREAT.
THEY'RE TOUGH AS NAILS BUT GOOD AT HEART. WE *NEED* THESE PEOPLE.
ABRAHAM.
STOP.
I TRUST THIS GUY--AND THAT SCARES ME TO DEATH. I DON'T KNOW IF WE'RE DOING THE RIGHT THING HERE.
YOU GOT A READ ON HIM?
BEFORE EUGENE... I USED TO THINK I WAS PRETTY GOOD AT SPOTTING A LIAR. SEEMS LIKE HE'S ON THE LEVEL... BUT REALLY...
HOW CAN YOU EVER TELL?
WHAT I DO KNOW IS WE'RE RUNNING OUT OF FOOD AND HIS OFFER IS TOO GOOD TO PASS UP.

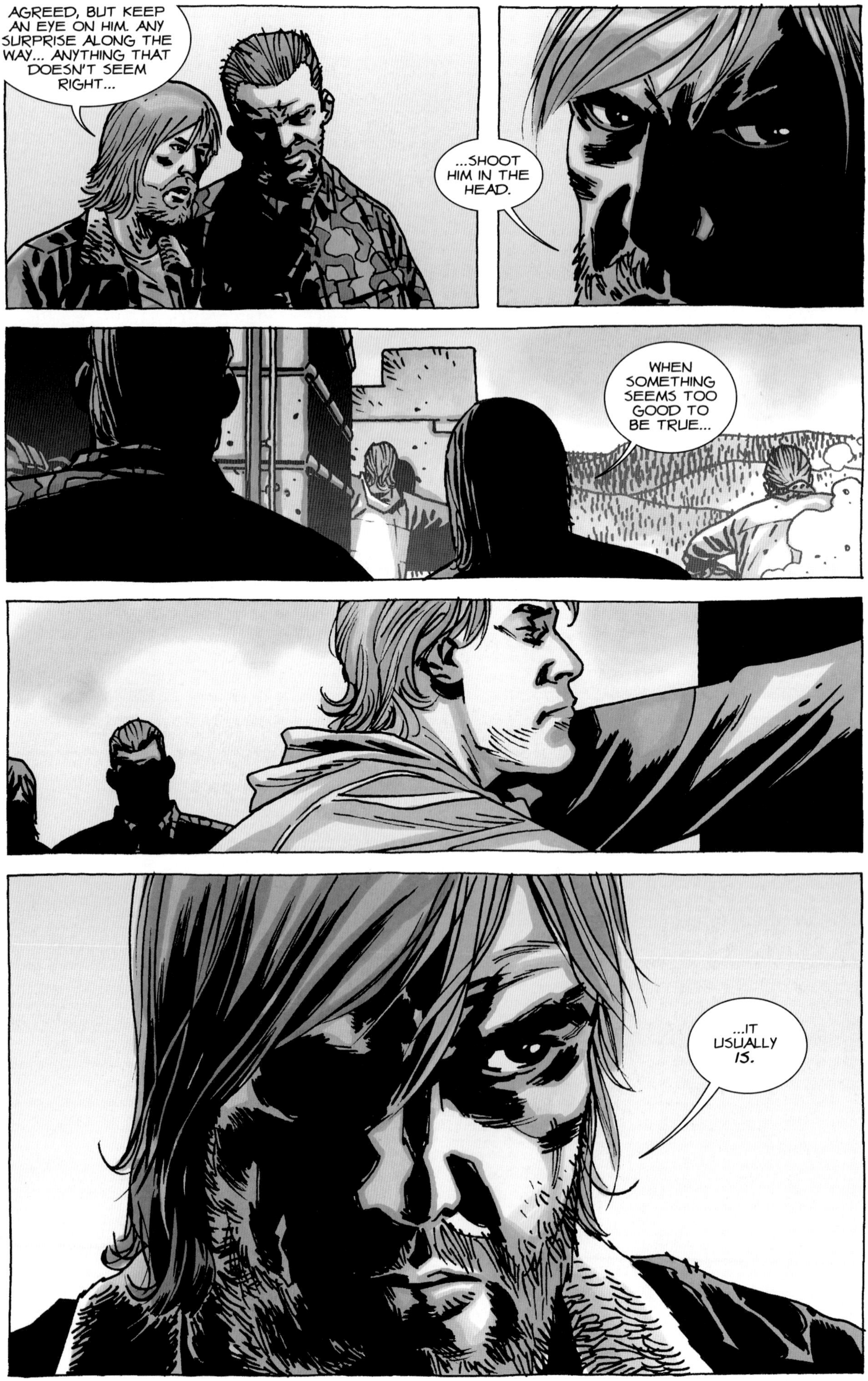
AGREED, BUT KEEP AN EYE ON HIM. ANY SURPRISE ALONG THE WAY... ANYTHING THAT DOESN'T SEEM RIGHT...
...SHOOT HIM IN THE HEAD.
WHEN SOMETHING SEEMS TOO GOOD TO BE TRUE...
...IT USUALLY IS.

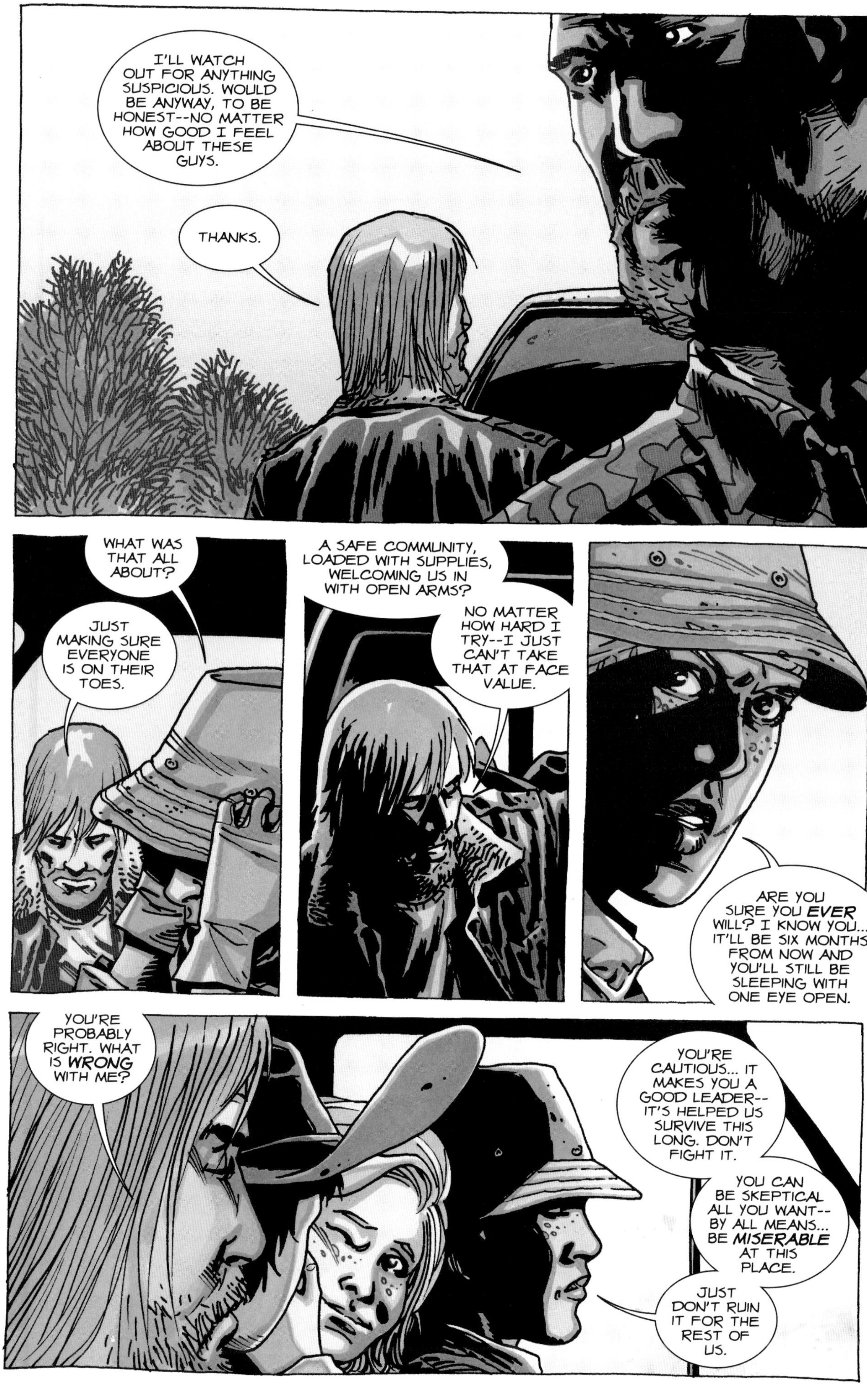

I'LL WATCH OUT FOR ANYTHING SUSPICIOUS. WOULD BE ANYWAY, TO BE HONEST--NO MATTER HOW GOOD I FEEL ABOUT THESE GUYS.
THANKS.
WHAT WAS THAT ALL ABOUT?
JUST MAKING SURE EVERYONE IS ON THEIR TOES.
A SAFE COMMUNITY, LOADED WITH SUPPLIES, WELCOMING US IN WITH OPEN ARMS?
NO MATTER HOW HARD I TRY--I JUST CAN'T TAKE THAT AT FACE VALUE.
ARE YOU SURE YOU EVER WILL? I KNOW YOU... IT'LL BE SIX MONTHS FROM NOW AND YOU'LL STILL BE SLEEPING WITH ONE EYE OPEN.
YOU'RE PROBABLY RIGHT. WHAT IS WRONG WITH ME?
YOU'RE CAUTIOUS... IT MAKES YOU A GOOD LEADER-- IT'S HELPED US SURVIVE THIS LONG. DON'T FIGHT IT.
YOU CAN BE SKEPTICAL ALL YOU WANT-- BY ALL MEANS... BE MISERABLE AT THIS PLACE.
JUST DON'T RUIN IT FOR THE REST OF US.

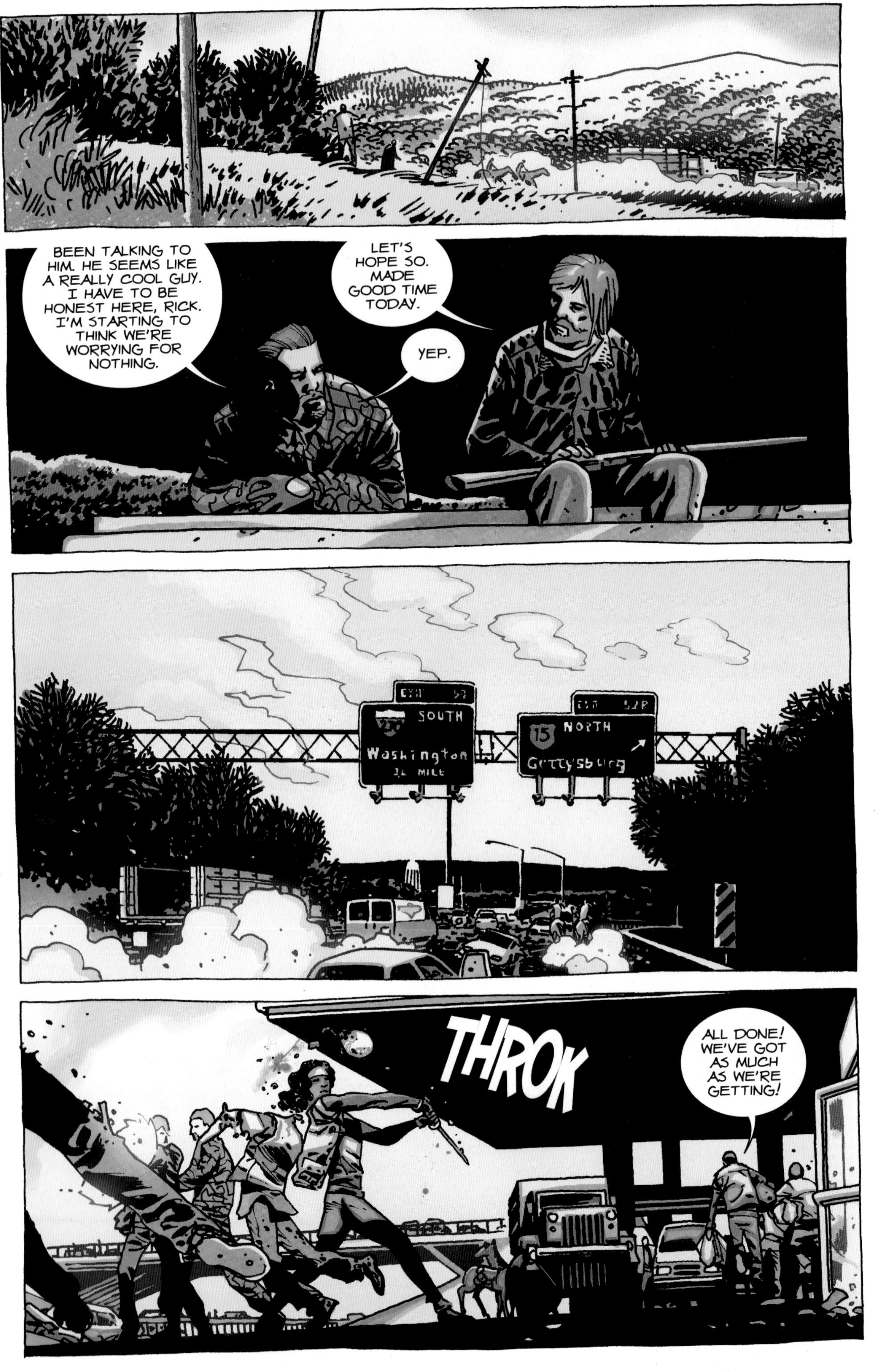
BEEN TALKING TO HIM. HE SEEMS LIKE A REALLY COOL GUY. I HAVE TO BE HONEST HERE, RICK. I'M STARTING TO THINK WE'RE WORRYING FOR NOTHING.
YEP.
LET'S HOPE SO. MADE GOOD TIME TODAY.
SOUTH
Washington
NORTH
15
Gettysburg
THROK
ALL DONE! WE'VE GOT AS MUCH AS WE'RE GETTING!

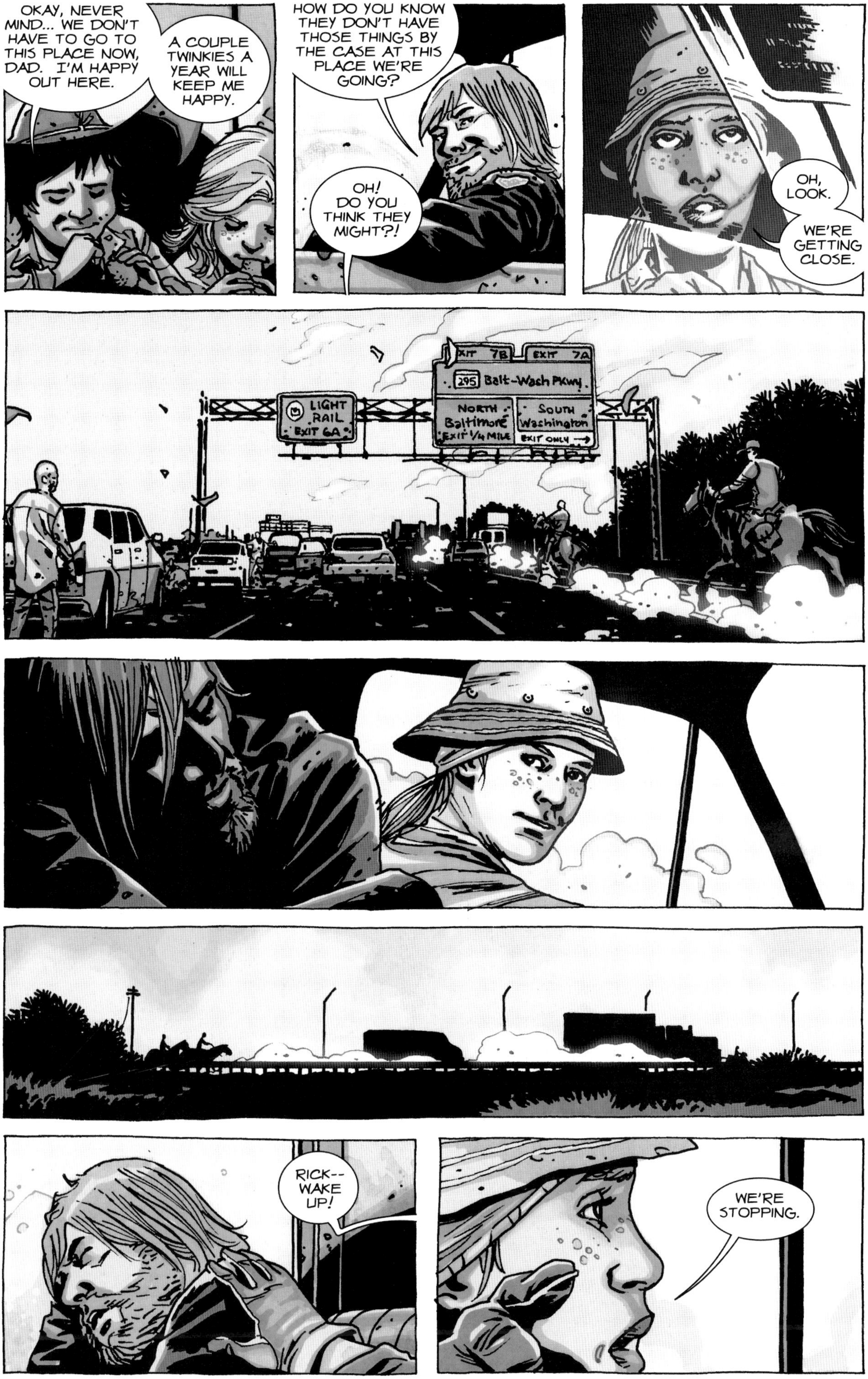
OKAY, NEVER MIND... WE DON'T HAVE TO GO TO THIS PLACE NOW, DAD. I'M HAPPY OUT HERE.
A COUPLE TWINKIES A YEAR WILL KEEP ME HAPPY.
HOW DO YOU KNOW THEY DON'T HAVE THOSE THINGS BY THE CASE AT THIS PLACE WE'RE GOING?
OH! DO YOU THINK THEY MIGHT?!
OH, LOOK.
WE'RE GETTING CLOSE.
LIGHT RAIL EXIT 6A
EXIT 7B
EXIT 7A
295 Balt-Wash PKwy
NORTH Baltimore EXIT 1/4 MILE
South Washington EXIT ONLY
RICK-- WAKE UP!
WE'RE STOPPING.

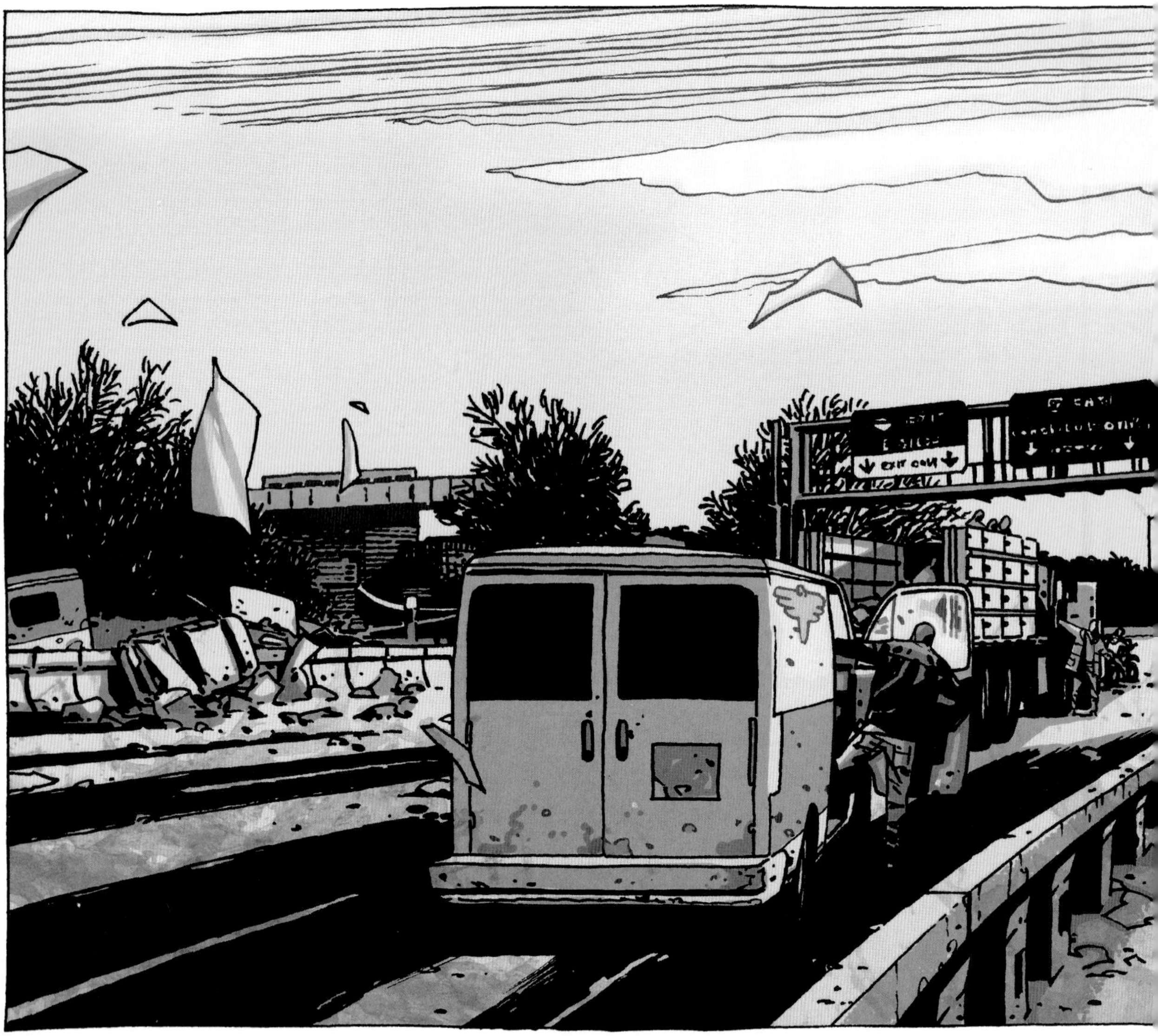

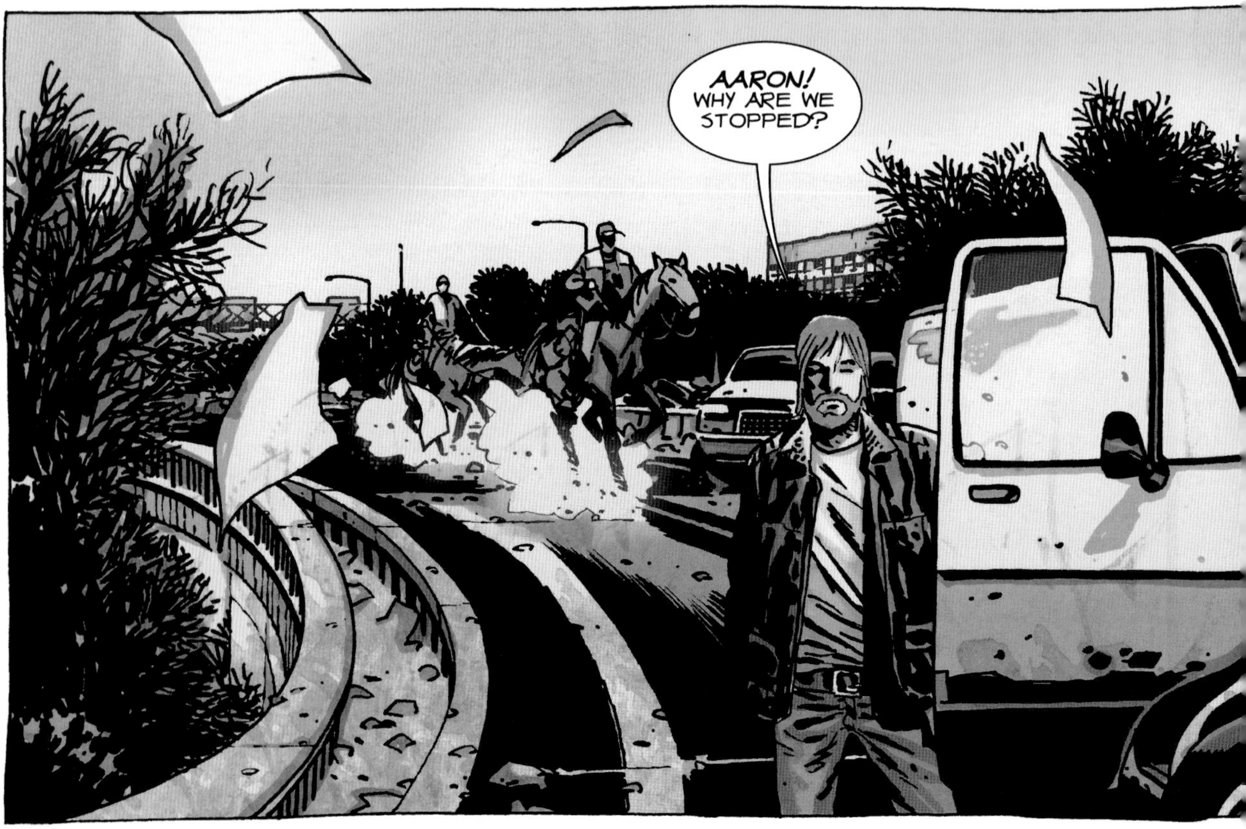
AARON! WHY ARE WE STOPPED?

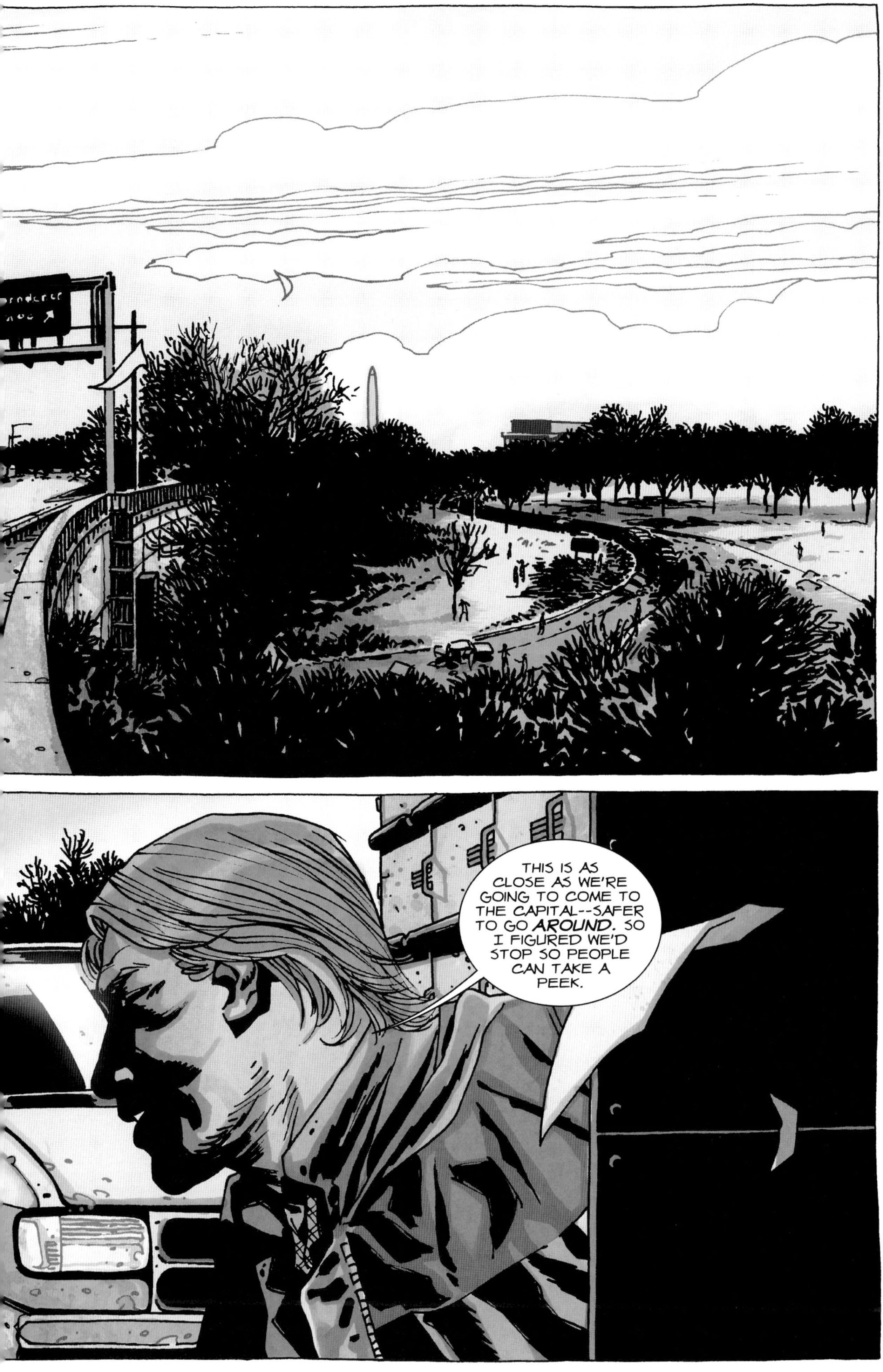
THIS IS AS CLOSE AS WE'RE GOING TO COME TO THE CAPITAL--SAFER TO GO *AROUND.* SO I FIGURED WE'D STOP SO PEOPLE CAN TAKE A PEEK.

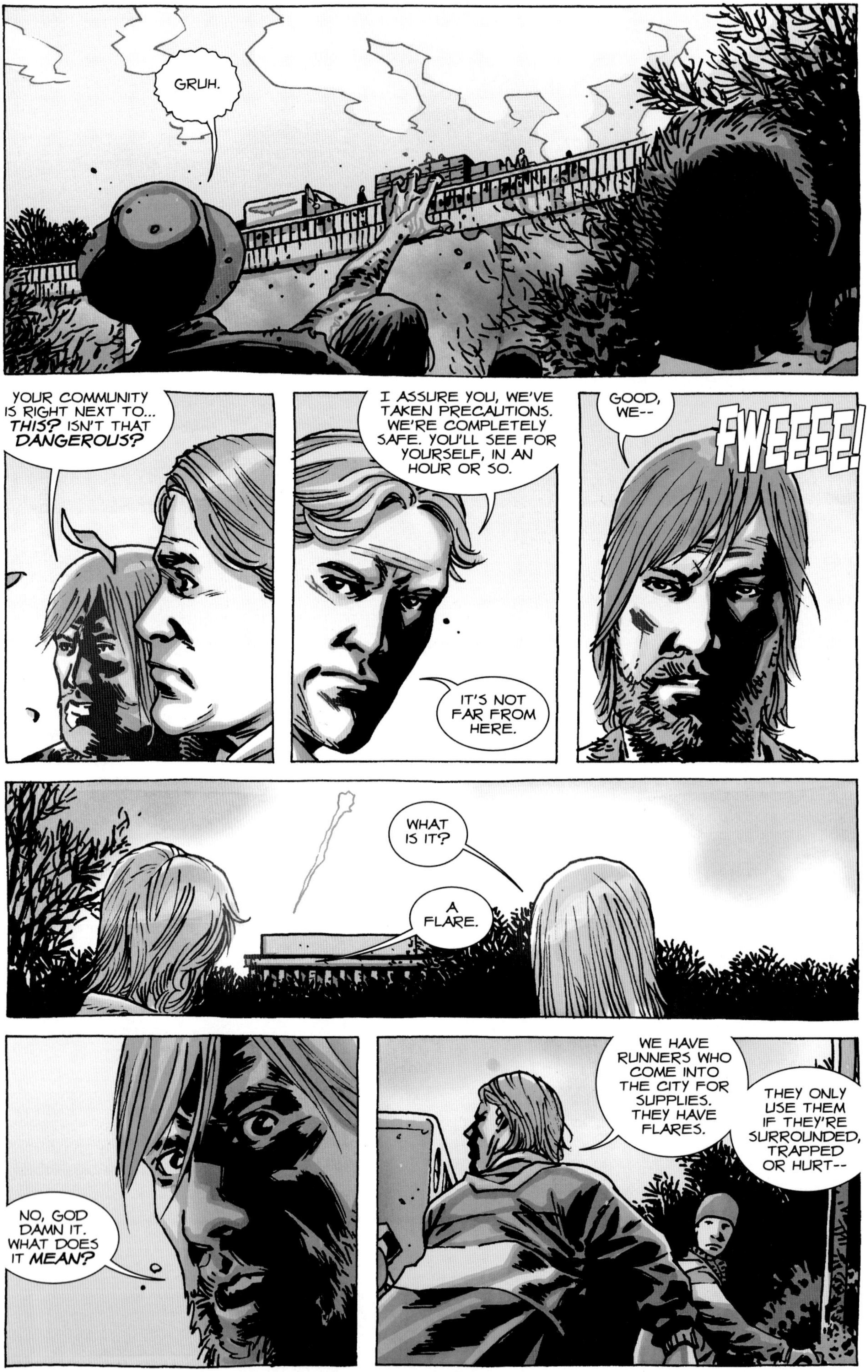
GRUH.
YOUR COMMUNITY IS RIGHT NEXT TO... THIS? ISN'T THAT DANGEROUS?
I ASSURE YOU, WE'VE TAKEN PRECAUTIONS. WE'RE COMPLETELY SAFE. YOU'LL SEE FOR YOURSELF, IN AN HOUR OR SO.
IT'S NOT FAR FROM HERE.
GOOD, WE--
FWEEEE!
WHAT IS IT?
A FLARE.
NO, GOD DAMN IT. WHAT DOES IT MEAN?
WE HAVE RUNNERS WHO COME INTO THE CITY FOR SUPPLIES. THEY HAVE FLARES.
THEY ONLY USE THEM IF THEY'RE SURROUNDED, TRAPPED OR HURT--

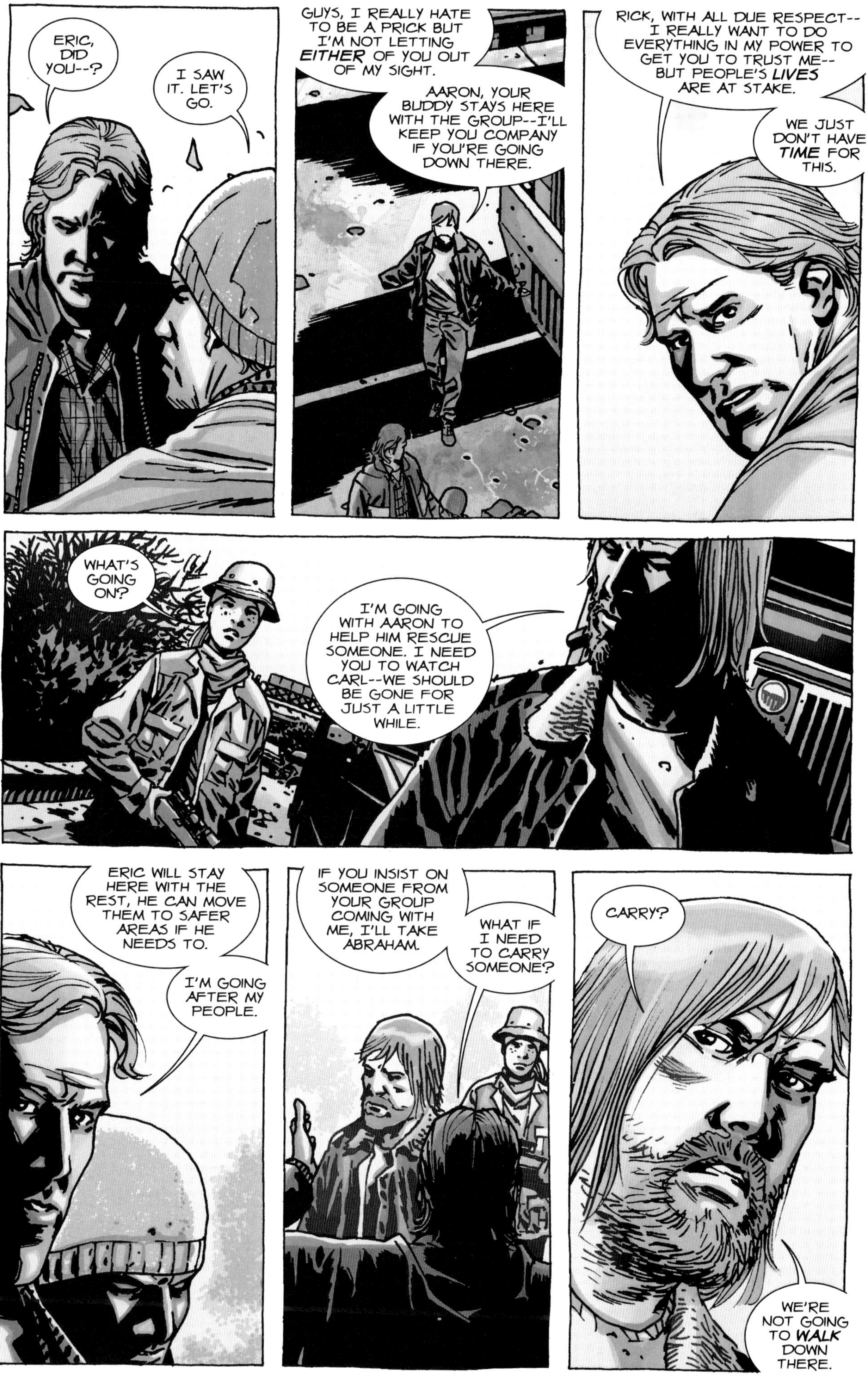
ERIC, DID YOU--?
I SAW IT. LET'S GO.
GUYS, I REALLY HATE TO BE A PRICK BUT I'M NOT LETTING EITHER OF YOU OUT OF MY SIGHT.
AARON, YOUR BUDDY STAYS HERE WITH THE GROUP--I'LL KEEP YOU COMPANY IF YOU'RE GOING DOWN THERE.
RICK, WITH ALL DUE RESPECT-- I REALLY WANT TO DO EVERYTHING IN MY POWER TO GET YOU TO TRUST ME-- BUT PEOPLE'S LIVES ARE AT STAKE.
WE JUST DON'T HAVE TIME FOR THIS.
WHAT'S GOING ON?
I'M GOING WITH AARON TO HELP HIM RESCUE SOMEONE. I NEED YOU TO WATCH CARL--WE SHOULD BE GONE FOR JUST A LITTLE WHILE.
ERIC WILL STAY HERE WITH THE REST, HE CAN MOVE THEM TO SAFER AREAS IF HE NEEDS TO.
I'M GOING AFTER MY PEOPLE.
IF YOU INSIST ON SOMEONE FROM YOUR GROUP COMING WITH ME, I'LL TAKE ABRAHAM.
WHAT IF I NEED TO CARRY SOMEONE?
CARRY?
WE'RE NOT GOING TO WALK DOWN THERE.

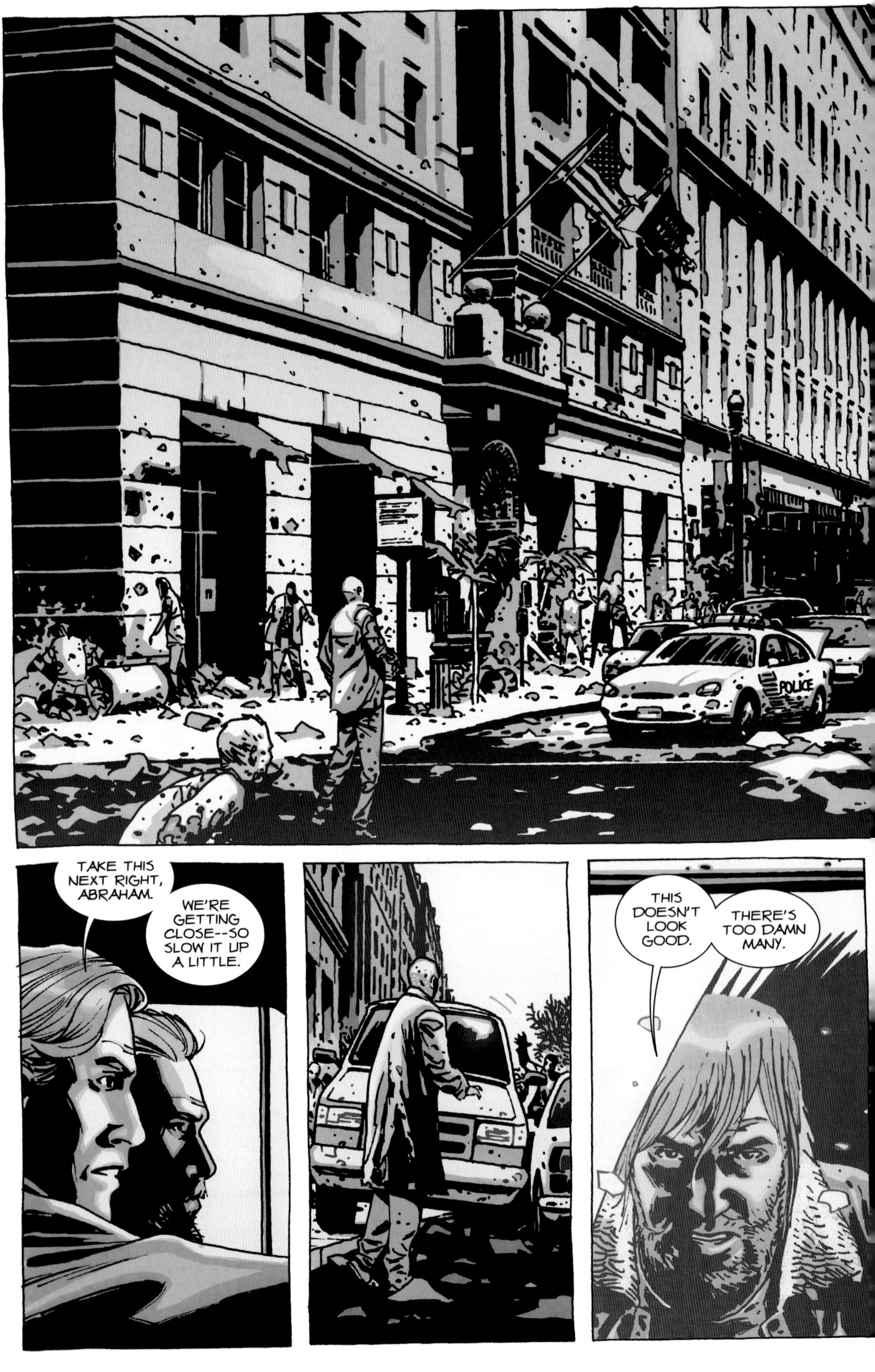
POLICE
TAKE THIS NEXT RIGHT, ABRAHAM.
WE'RE GETTING CLOSE--SO SLOW IT UP A LITTLE.
THIS DOESN'T LOOK GOOD.
THERE'S TOO DAMN MANY.

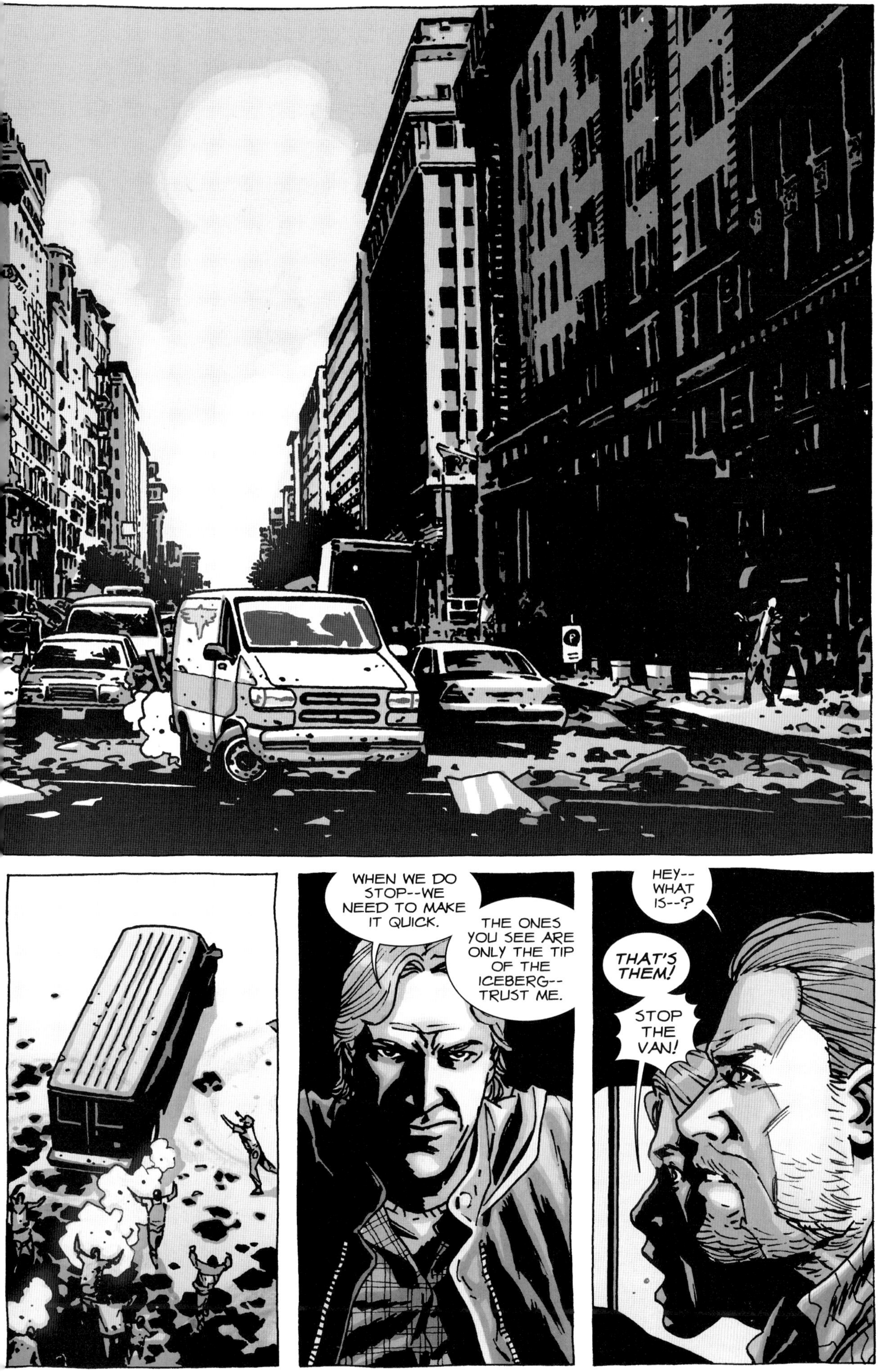
WHEN WE DO STOP--WE NEED TO MAKE IT QUICK.
THE ONES YOU SEE ARE ONLY THE TIP OF THE ICEBERG-- TRUST ME.
HEY-- WHAT IS--?
THAT'S THEM!
STOP THE VAN!

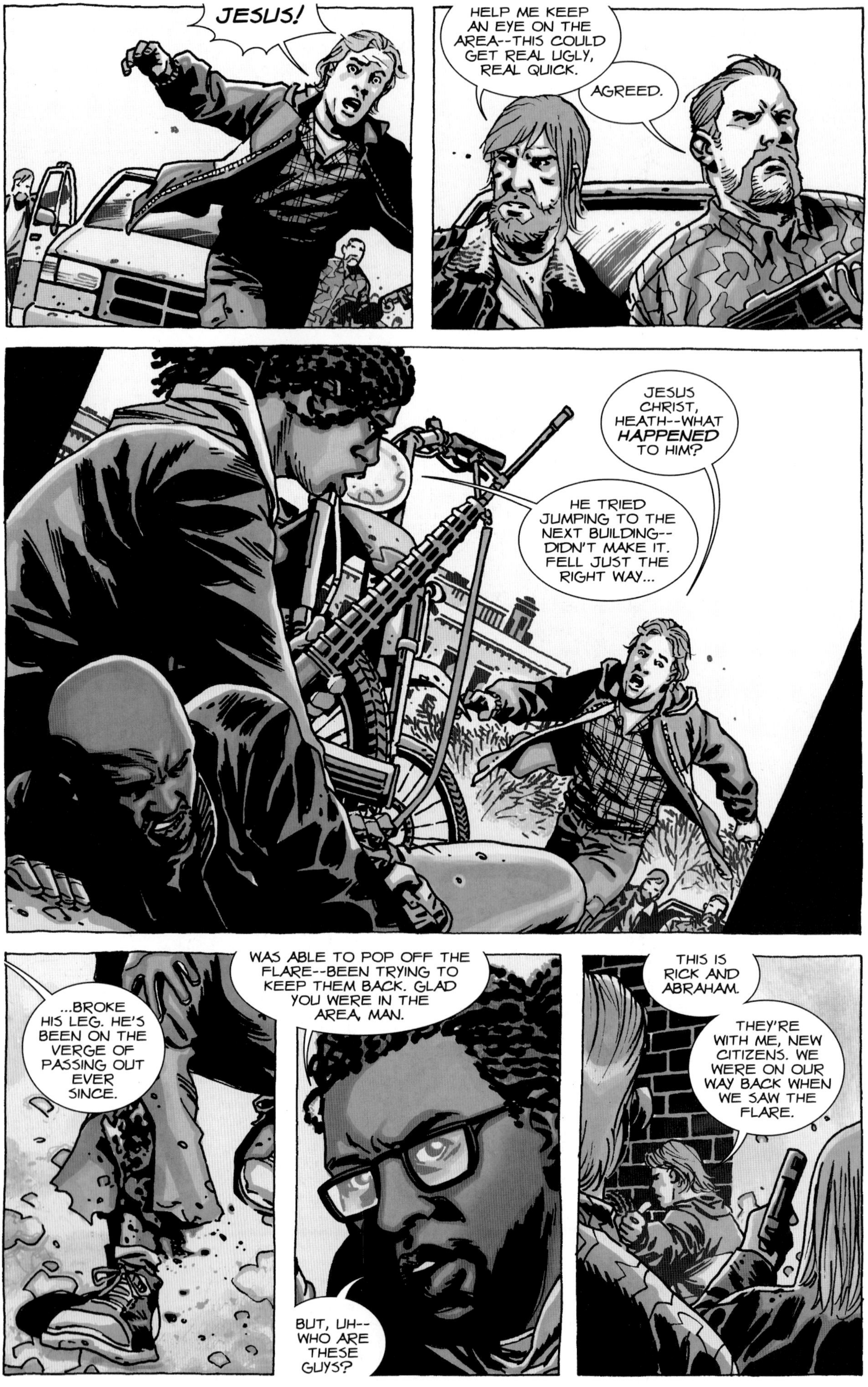
JESUS!
HELP ME KEEP AN EYE ON THE AREA--THIS COULD GET REAL UGLY, REAL QUICK.
AGREED.
JESUS CHRIST, HEATH--WHAT HAPPENED TO HIM?
HE TRIED JUMPING TO THE NEXT BUILDING--DIDN'T MAKE IT. FELL JUST THE RIGHT WAY...
...BROKE HIS LEG. HE'S BEEN ON THE VERGE OF PASSING OUT EVER SINCE.
WAS ABLE TO POP OFF THE FLARE--BEEN TRYING TO KEEP THEM BACK. GLAD YOU WERE IN THE AREA, MAN.
BUT, UH--WHO ARE THESE GUYS?
THIS IS RICK AND ABRAHAM.
THEY'RE WITH ME, NEW CITIZENS. WE WERE ON OUR WAY BACK WHEN WE SAW THE FLARE.

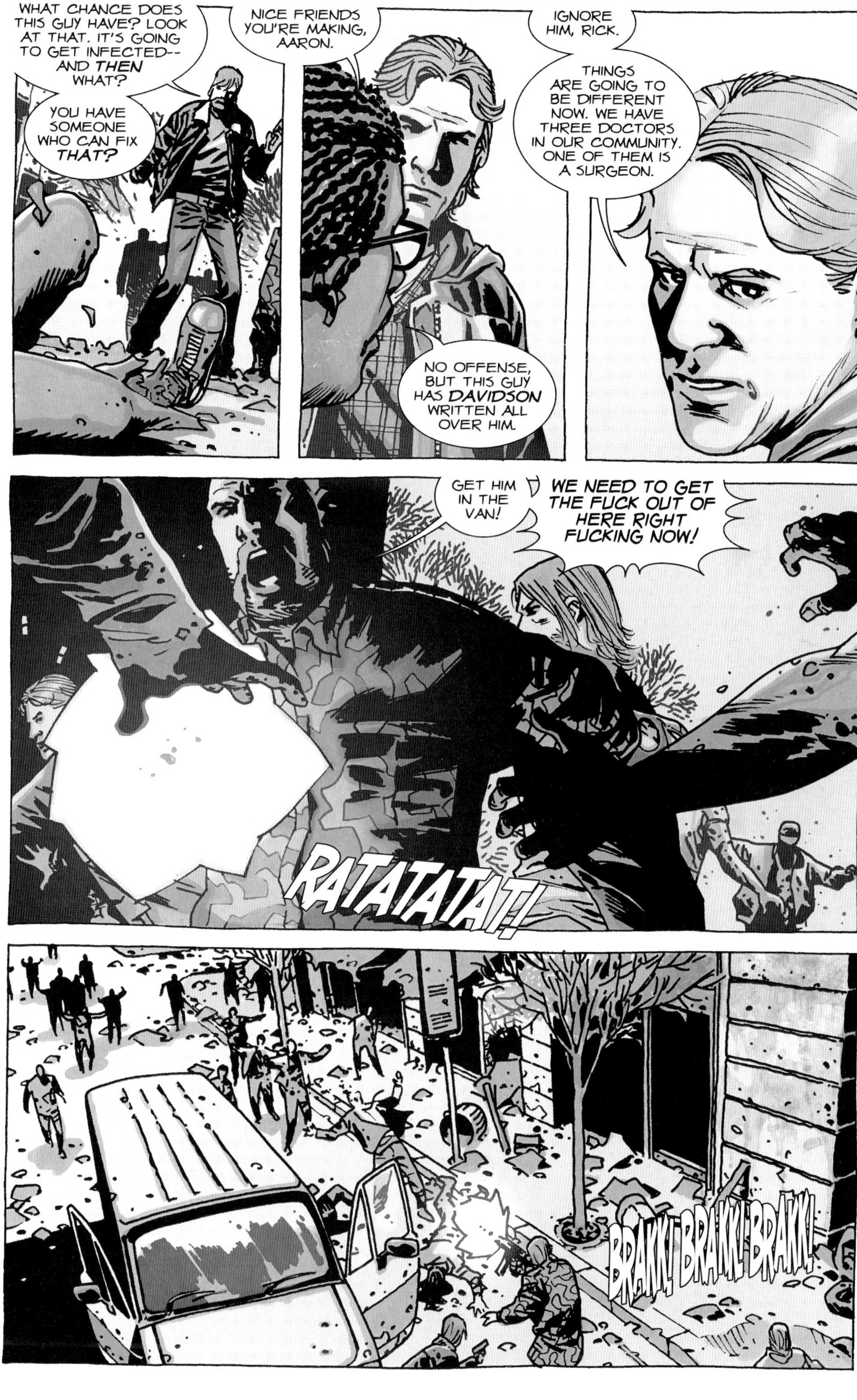
WHAT CHANCE DOES THIS GUY HAVE? LOOK AT THAT. IT'S GOING TO GET INFECTED-- AND THEN WHAT?
YOU HAVE SOMEONE WHO CAN FIX THAT?
NICE FRIENDS YOU'RE MAKING, AARON.
NO OFFENSE, BUT THIS GUY HAS DAVIDSON WRITTEN ALL OVER HIM.
IGNORE HIM, RICK.
THINGS ARE GOING TO BE DIFFERENT NOW. WE HAVE THREE DOCTORS IN OUR COMMUNITY. ONE OF THEM IS A SURGEON.
GET HIM IN THE VAN!
WE NEED TO GET THE FUCK OUT OF HERE RIGHT FUCKING NOW!
RATATATAT!
BRAKK! BRAKK! BRAKK!

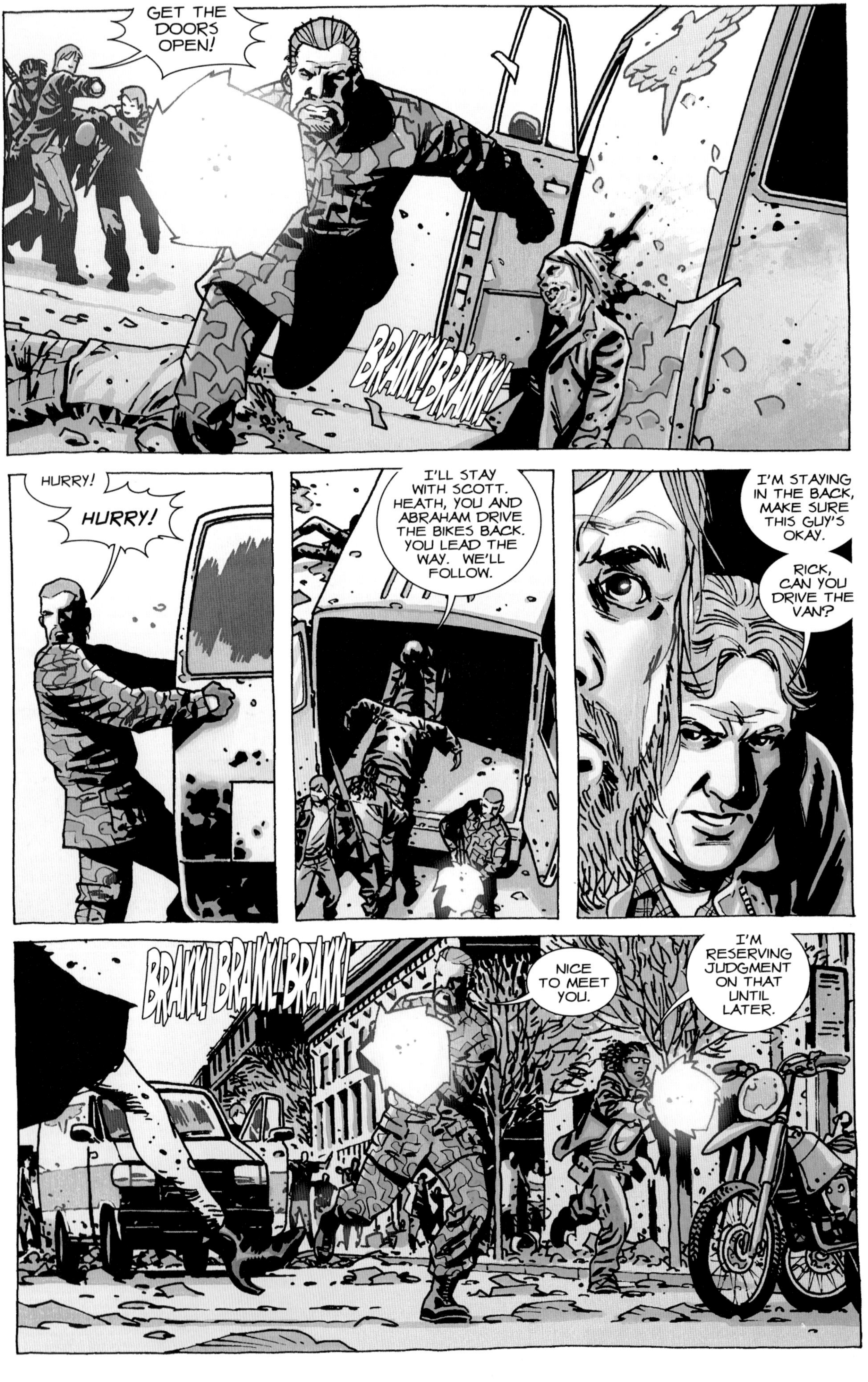
GET THE DOORS OPEN!
BRAKK! BRAKK!
HURRY!
HURRY!
I'LL STAY WITH SCOTT. HEATH, YOU AND ABRAHAM DRIVE THE BIKES BACK. YOU LEAD THE WAY. WE'LL FOLLOW.
I'M STAYING IN THE BACK, MAKE SURE THIS GUY'S OKAY.
RICK, CAN YOU DRIVE THE VAN?
BRAKK! BRAKK! BRAKK!
NICE TO MEET YOU.
I'M RESERVING JUDGMENT ON THAT UNTIL LATER.

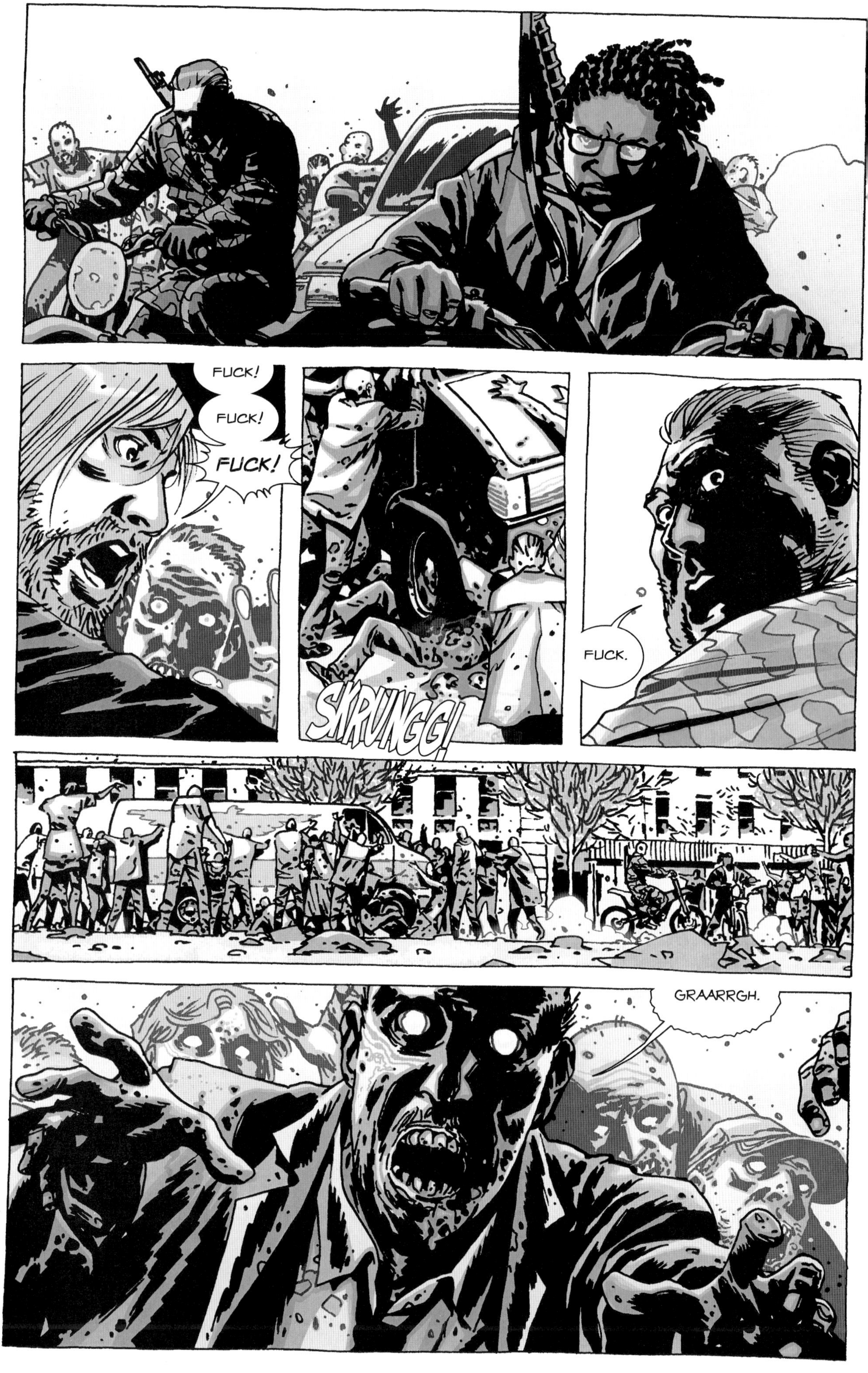
FUCK!
FUCK!
FUCK!
SKRUNGG!
FUCK.
GRAARRGH.

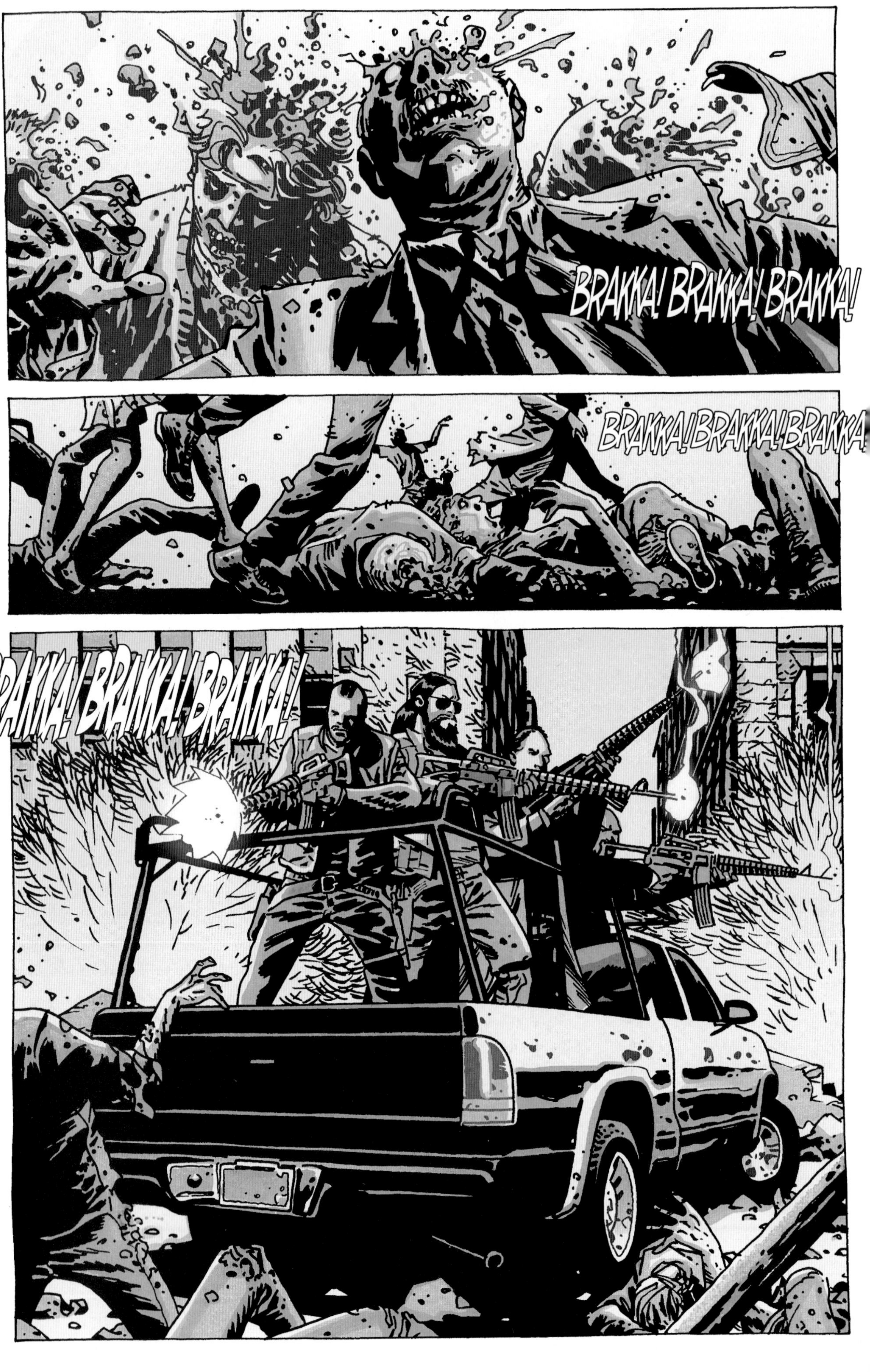
BRAKKA! BRAKKA! BRAKKA!
BRAKKA! BRAKKA! BRAKKA!
BRAKKA! BRAKKA! BRAKKA!

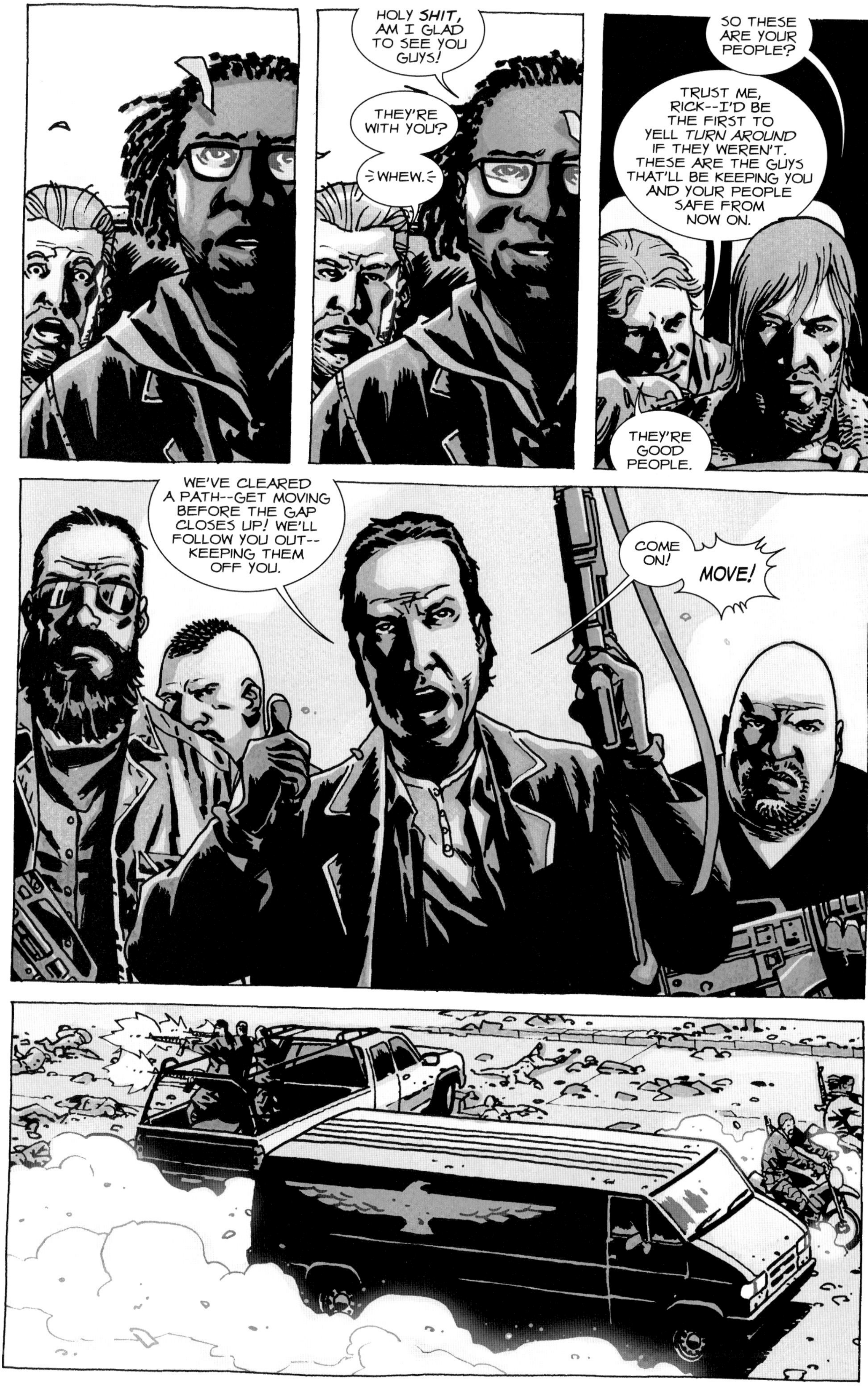

HOLY SHIT, AM I GLAD TO SEE YOU GUYS!
THEY'RE WITH YOU?
WHEW.
SO THESE ARE YOUR PEOPLE?
TRUST ME, RICK--I'D BE THE FIRST TO YELL TURN AROUND IF THEY WEREN'T. THESE ARE THE GUYS THAT'LL BE KEEPING YOU AND YOUR PEOPLE SAFE FROM NOW ON.
THEY'RE GOOD PEOPLE.
WE'VE CLEARED A PATH--GET MOVING BEFORE THE GAP CLOSES UP! WE'LL FOLLOW YOU OUT--KEEPING THEM OFF YOU.
COME ON!
MOVE!

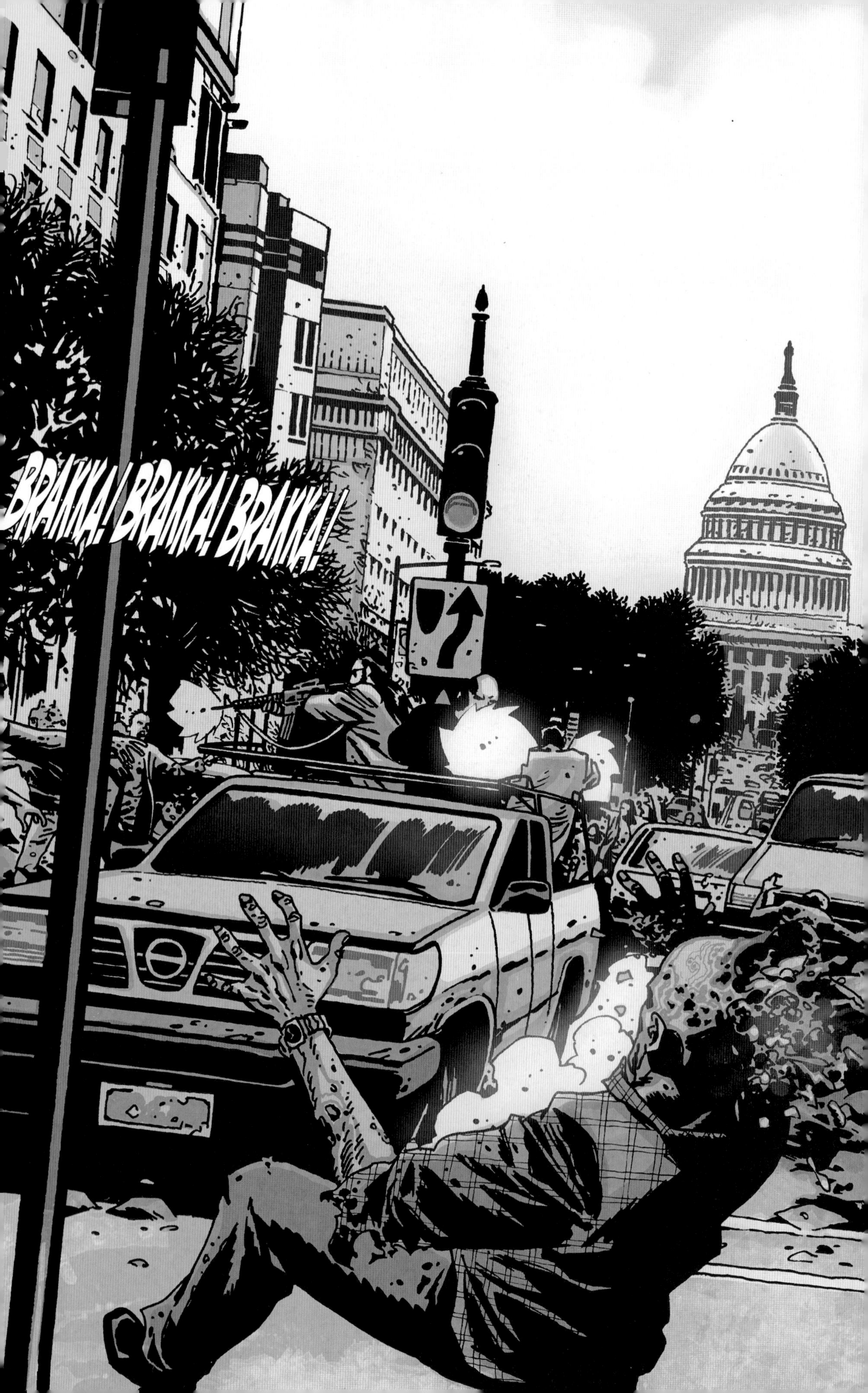
BRAKKA! BRAKKA! BRAKKA!

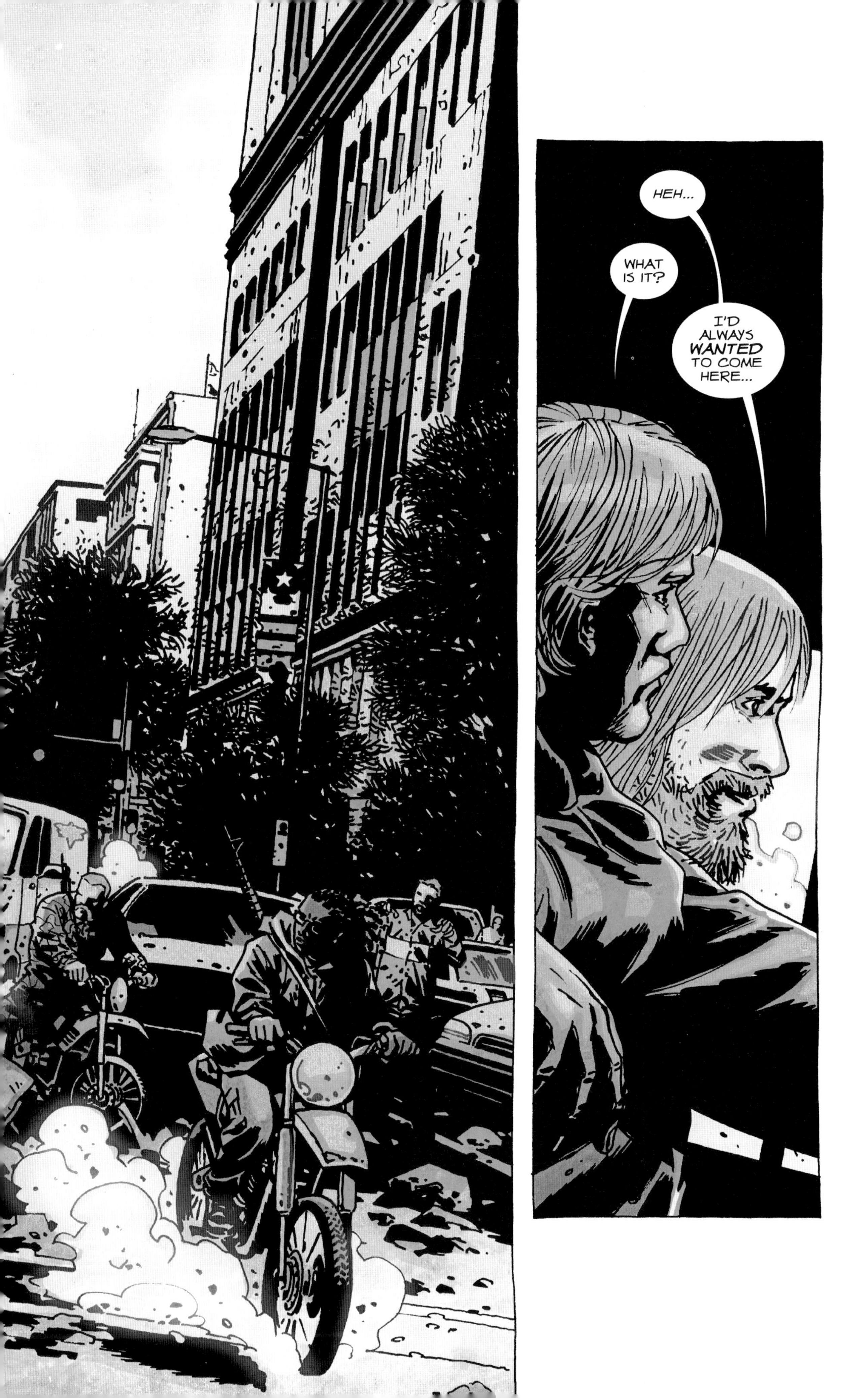

HEH...
WHAT IS IT?
I'D ALWAYS WANTED TO COME HERE...

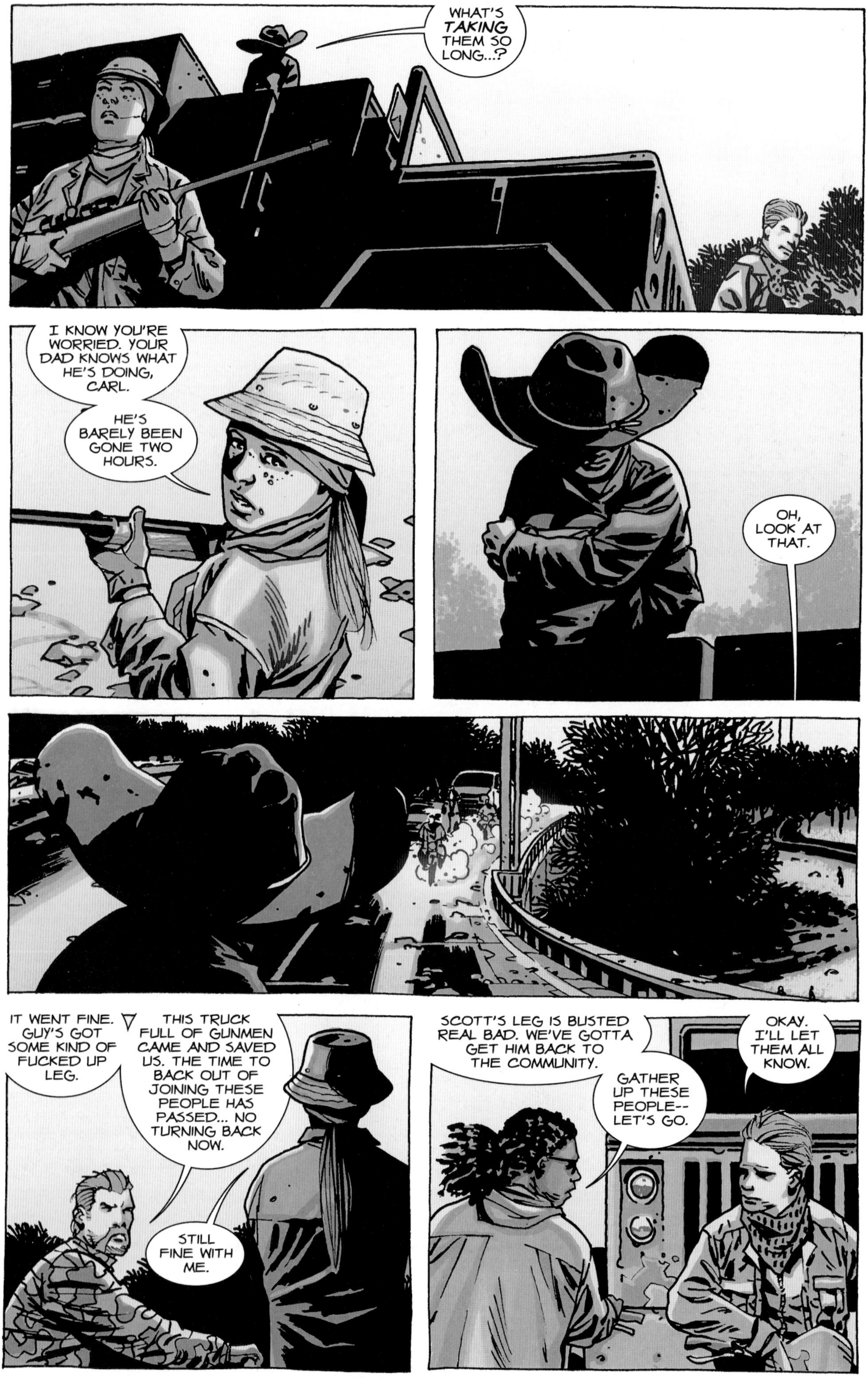
WHAT'S TAKING THEM SO LONG...?
I KNOW YOU'RE WORRIED. YOUR DAD KNOWS WHAT HE'S DOING, CARL.
HE'S BARELY BEEN GONE TWO HOURS.
OH, LOOK AT THAT.
IT WENT FINE. GUY'S GOT SOME KIND OF FUCKED UP LEG.
THIS TRUCK FULL OF GUNMEN CAME AND SAVED US. THE TIME TO BACK OUT OF JOINING THESE PEOPLE HAS PASSED... NO TURNING BACK NOW.
STILL FINE WITH ME.
SCOTT'S LEG IS BUSTED REAL BAD. WE'VE GOTTA GET HIM BACK TO THE COMMUNITY.
GATHER UP THESE PEOPLE-- LET'S GO.
OKAY. I'LL LET THEM ALL KNOW.

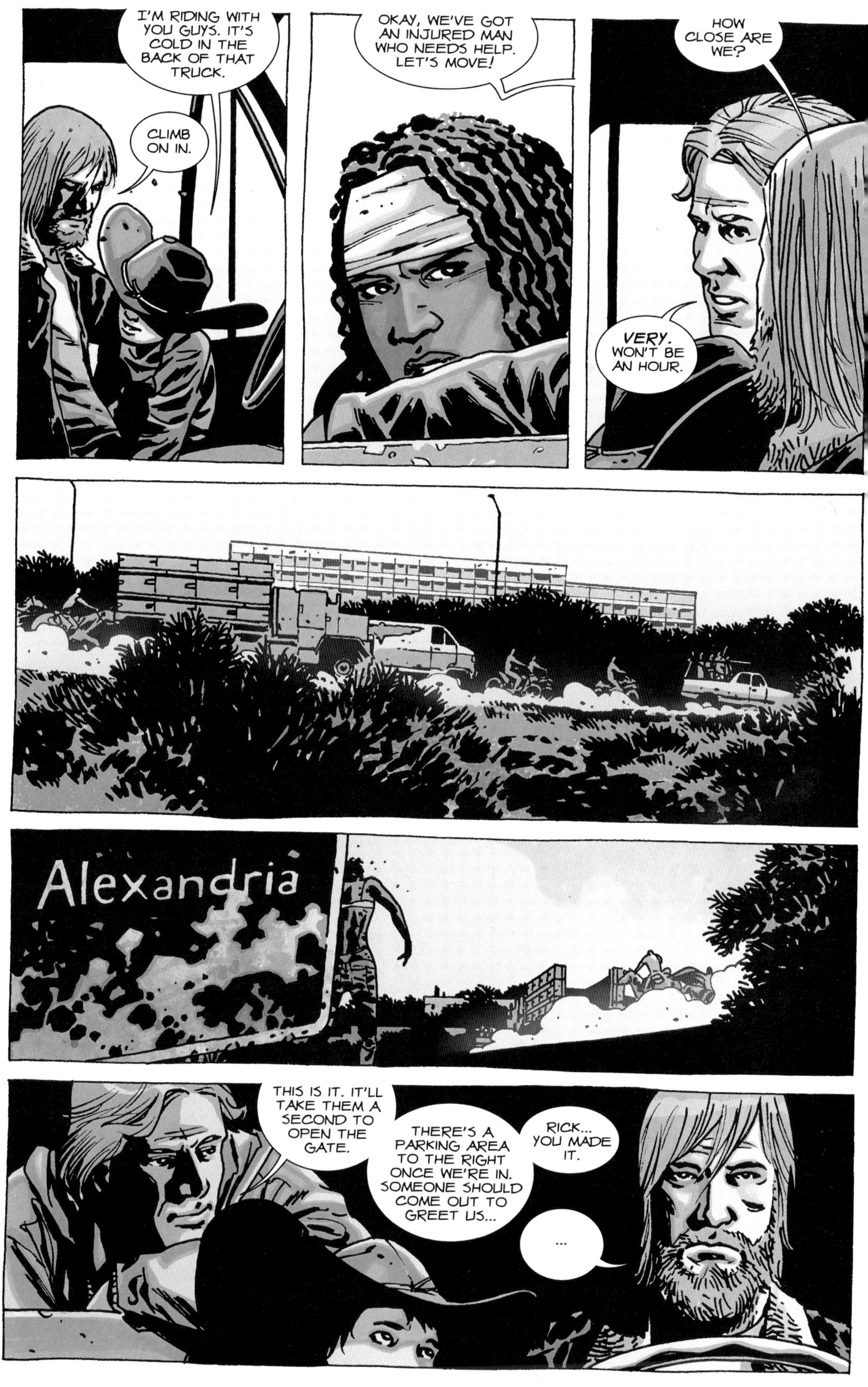
I'M RIDING WITH YOU GUYS. IT'S COLD IN THE BACK OF THAT TRUCK.
CLIMB ON IN.
OKAY, WE'VE GOT AN INJURED MAN WHO NEEDS HELP. LET'S MOVE!
HOW CLOSE ARE WE?
VERY. WON'T BE AN HOUR.
Alexandria
THIS IS IT. IT'LL TAKE THEM A SECOND TO OPEN THE GATE.
THERE'S A PARKING AREA TO THE RIGHT ONCE WE'RE IN. SOMEONE SHOULD COME OUT TO GREET US...
RICK... YOU MADE IT.
...

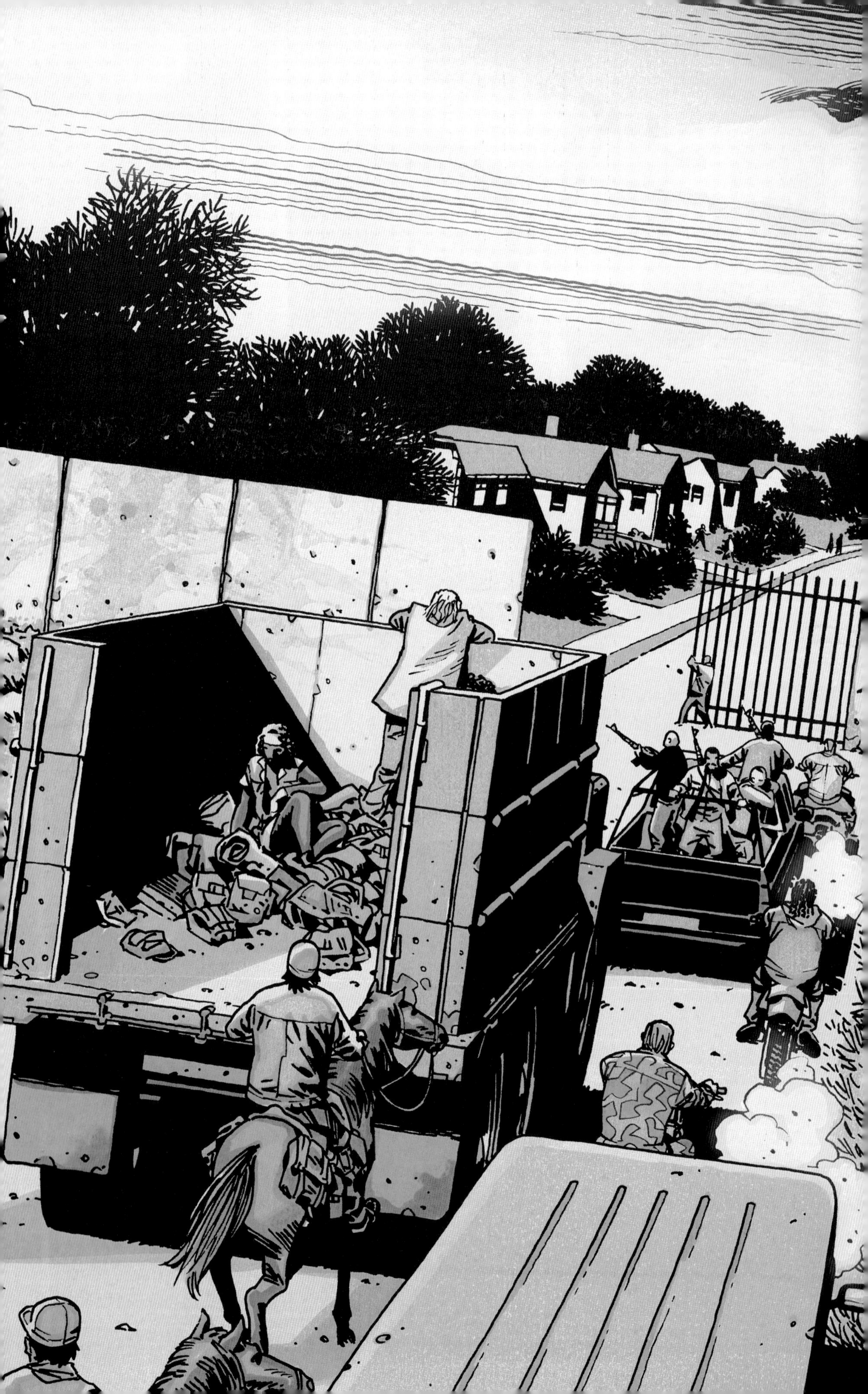

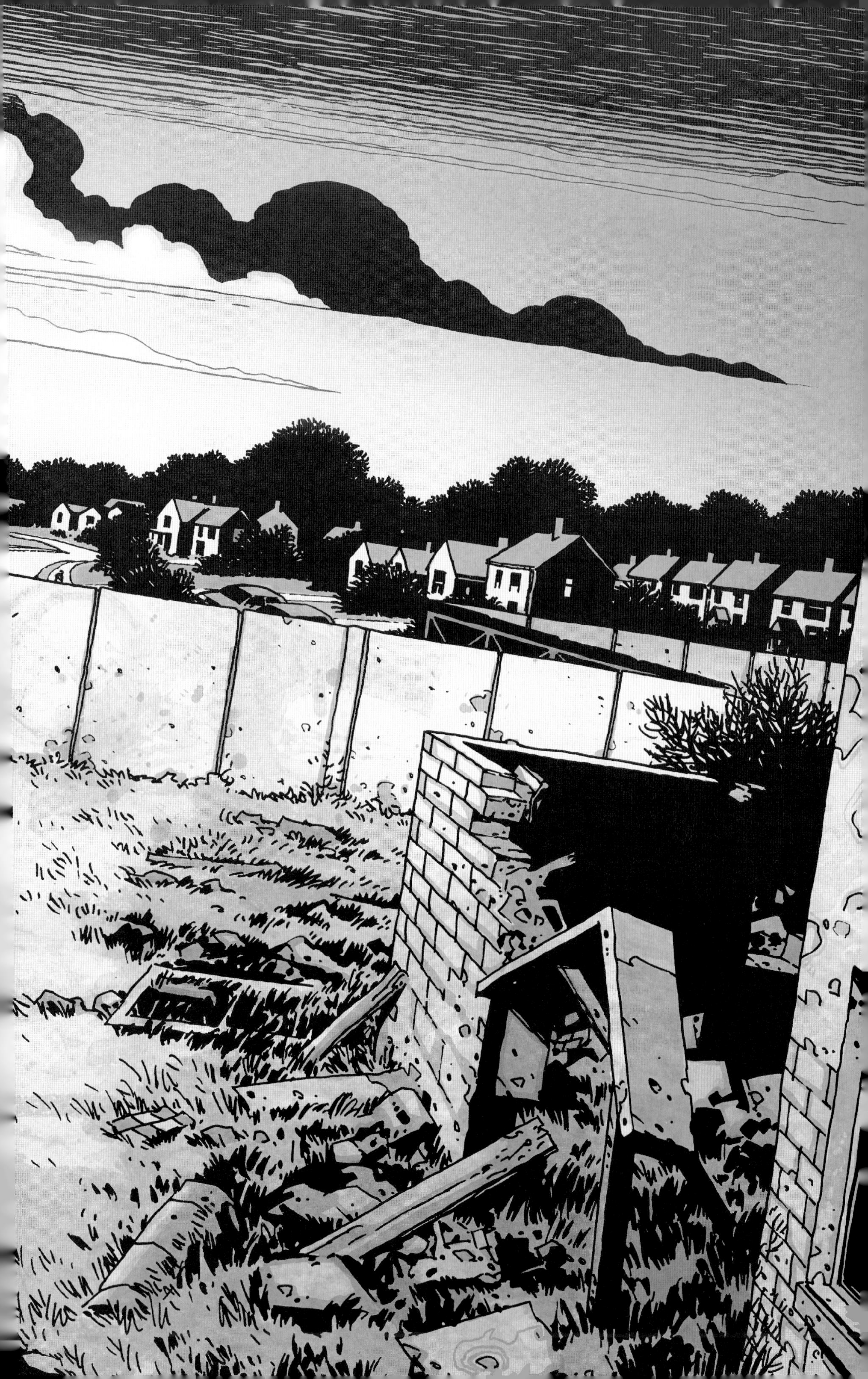

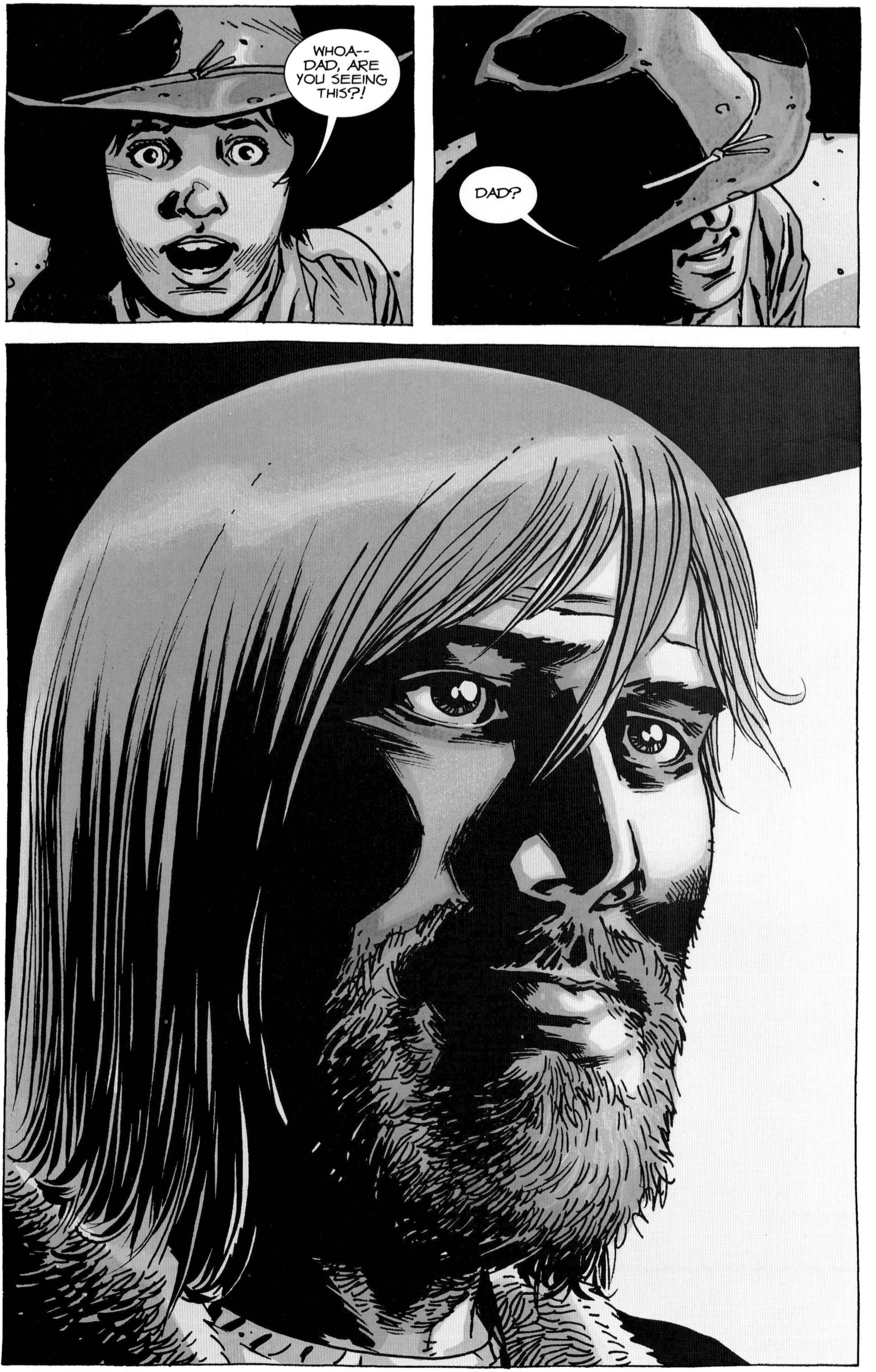
WHOA--
DAD, ARE
YOU SEEING
THIS?!
DAD?

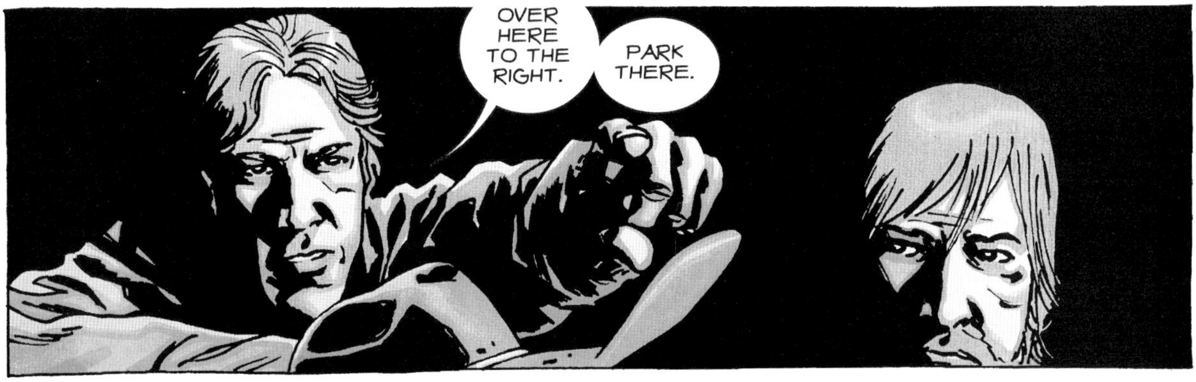
OVER HERE TO THE RIGHT.
PARK THERE.

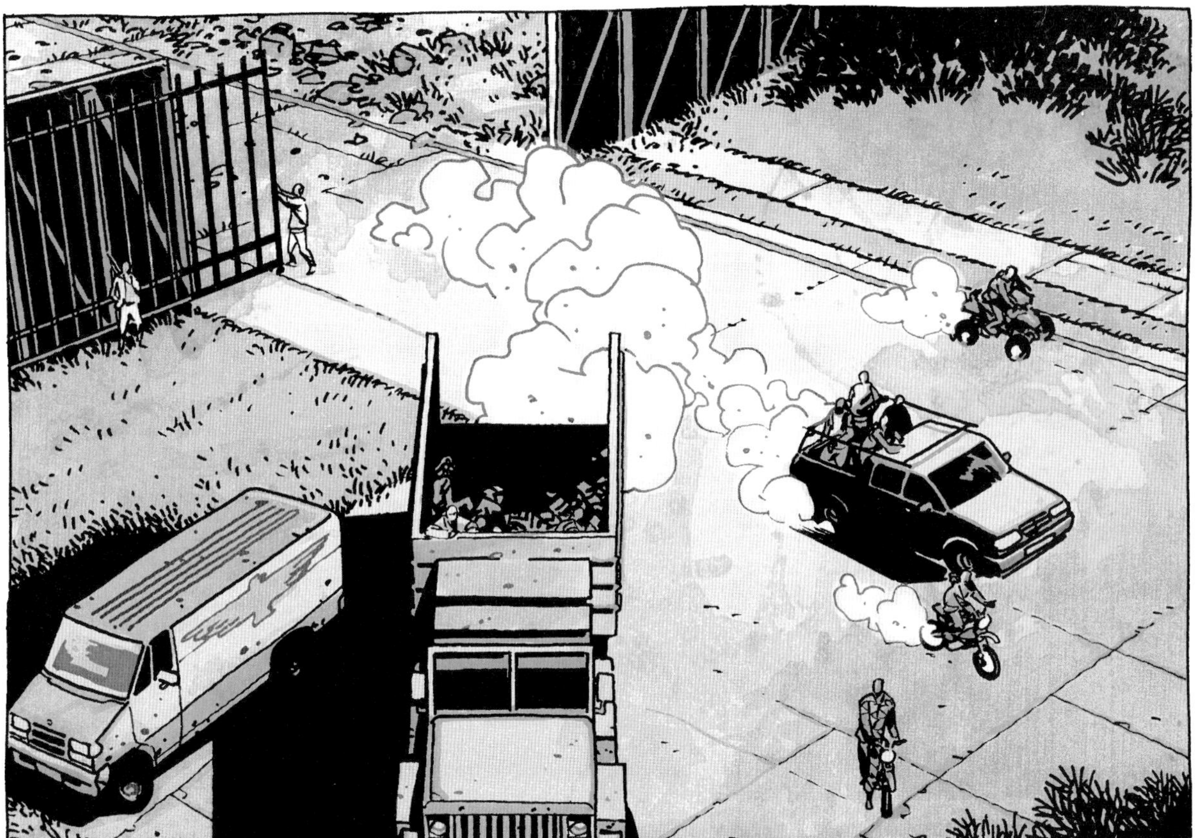

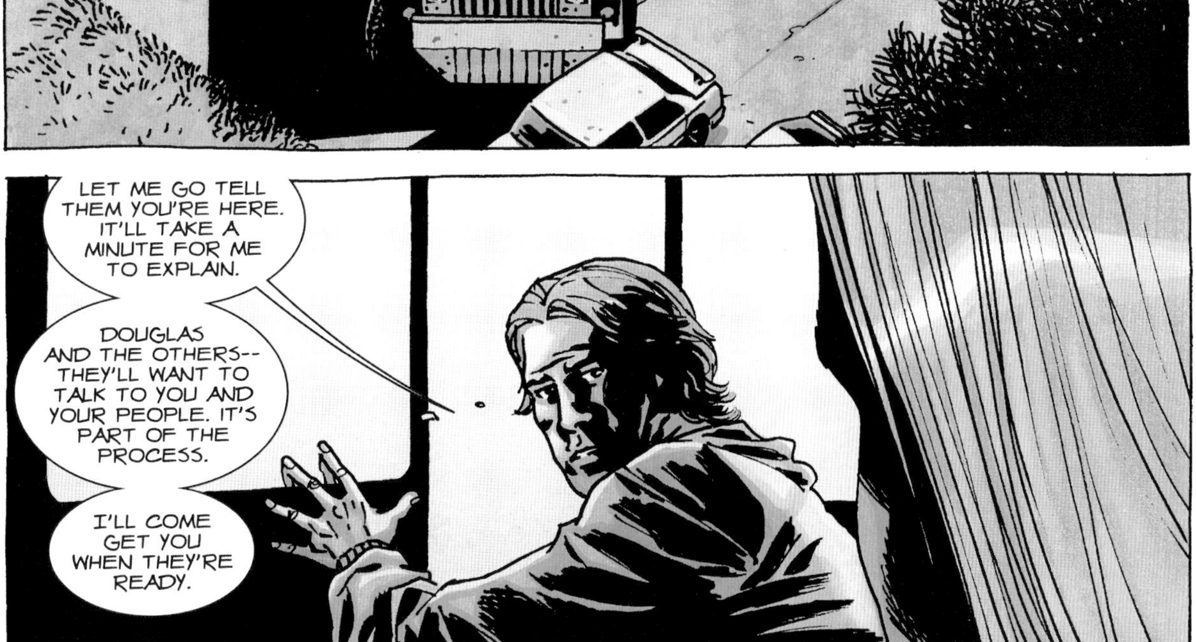
LET ME GO TELL THEM YOU'RE HERE. IT'LL TAKE A MINUTE FOR ME TO EXPLAIN.
DOUGLAS AND THE OTHERS-- THEY'LL WANT TO TALK TO YOU AND YOUR PEOPLE. IT'S PART OF THE PROCESS.
I'LL COME GET YOU WHEN THEY'RE READY.

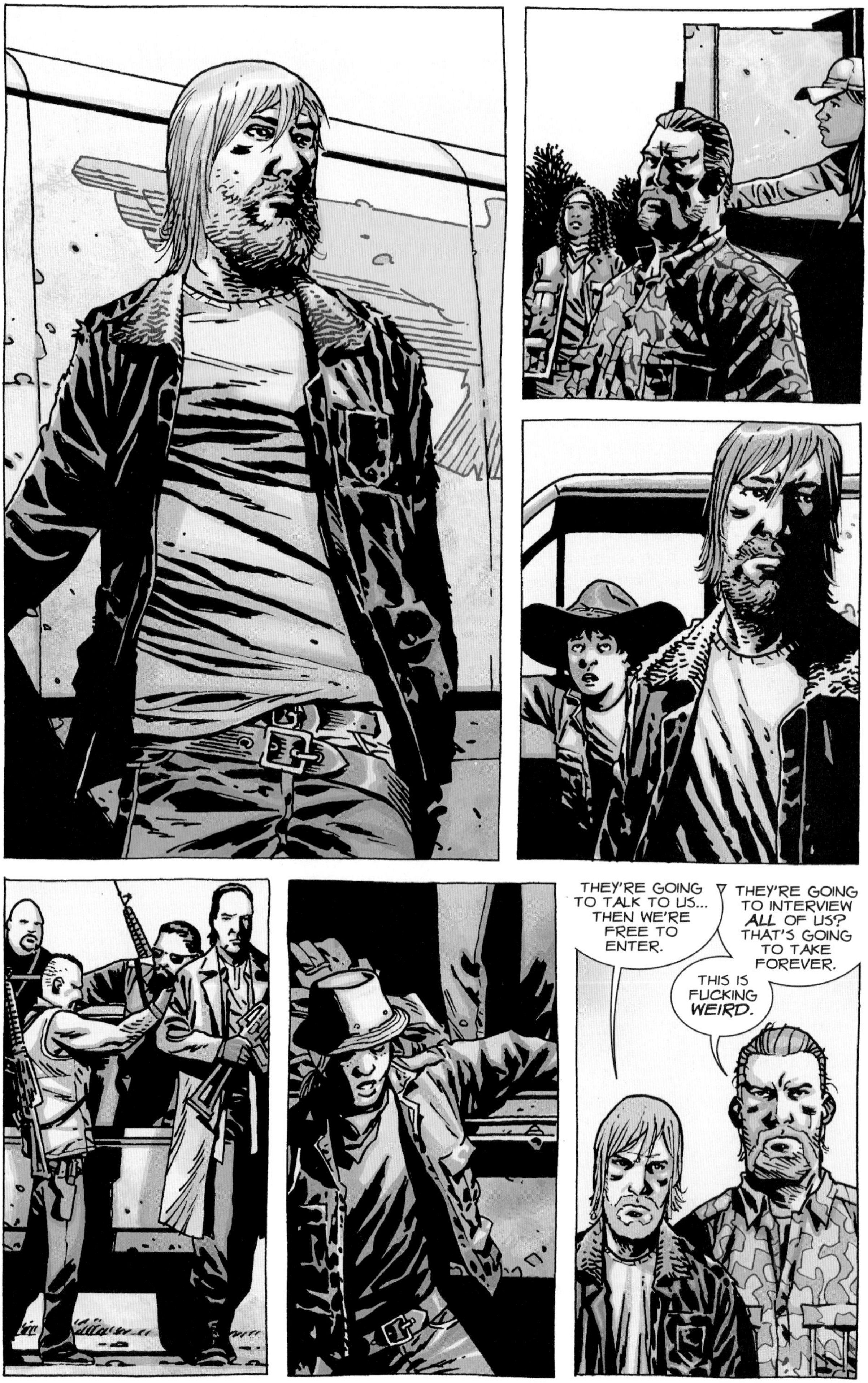
THEY'RE GOING TO TALK TO US... THEN WE'RE FREE TO ENTER.
THEY'RE GOING TO INTERVIEW ALL OF US? THAT'S GOING TO TAKE FOREVER.
THIS IS FUCKING WEIRD.

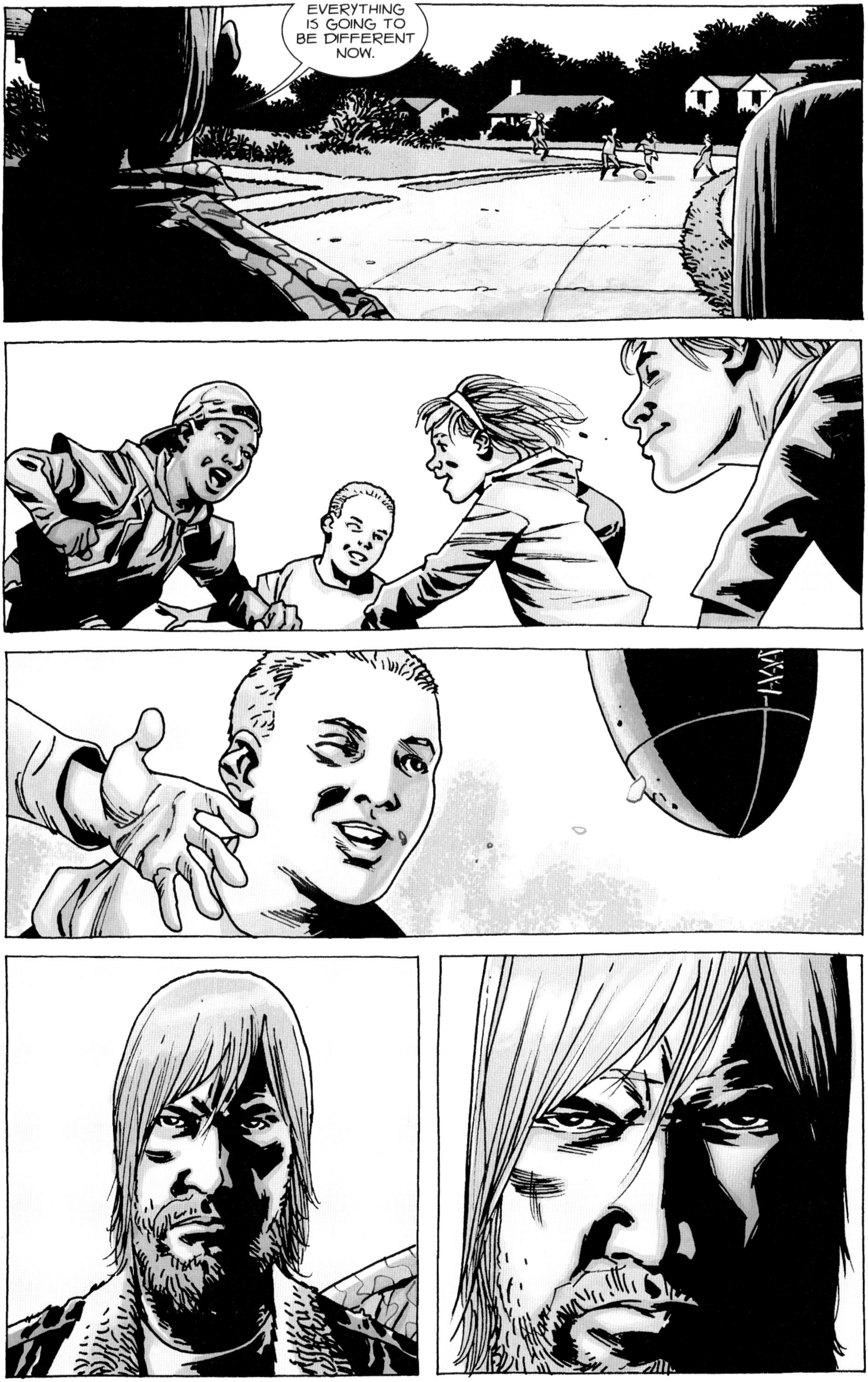
EVERYTHING IS GOING TO BE DIFFERENT NOW.

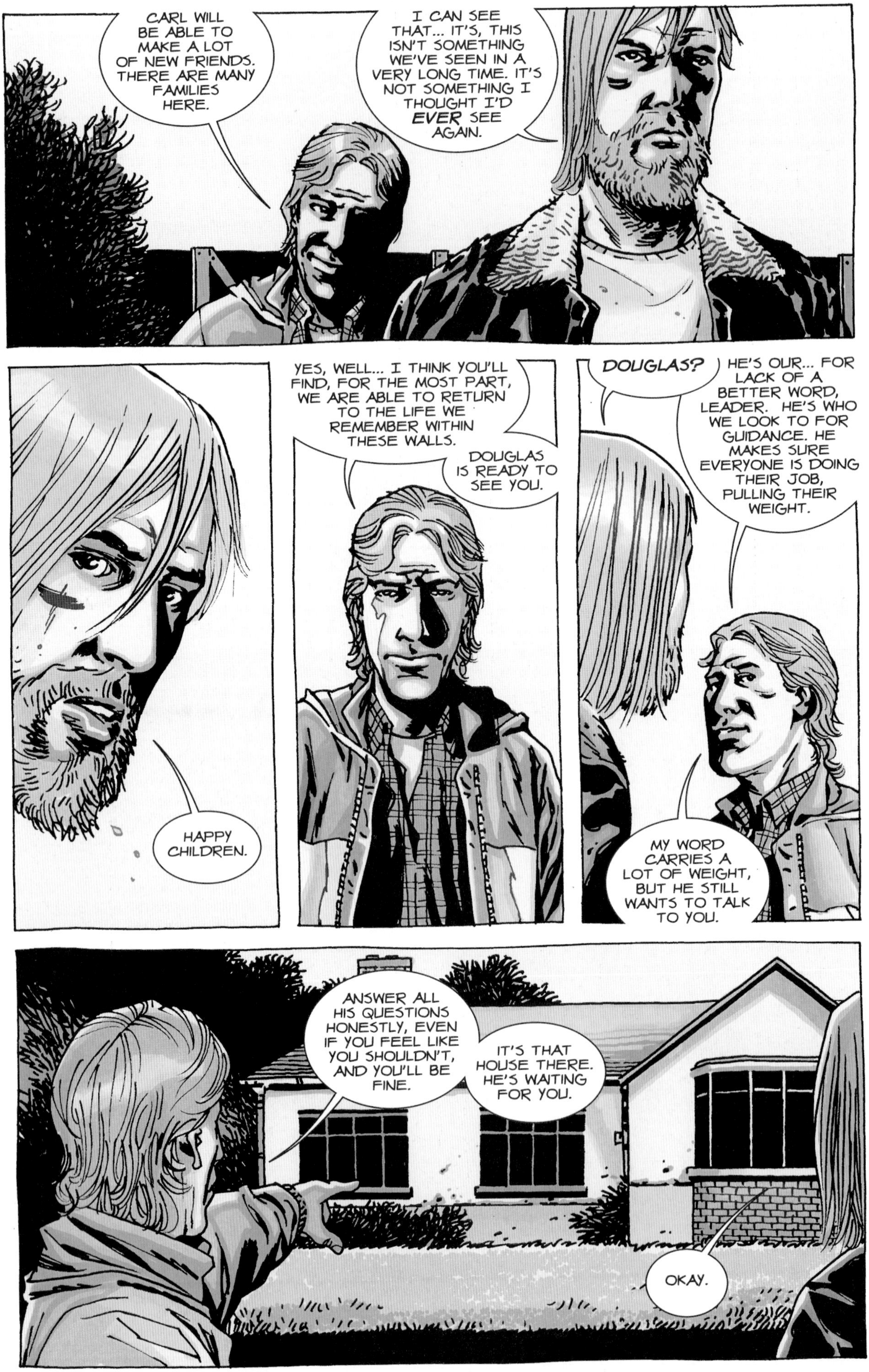
CARL WILL BE ABLE TO MAKE A LOT OF NEW FRIENDS. THERE ARE MANY FAMILIES HERE.
I CAN SEE THAT... IT'S, THIS ISN'T SOMETHING WE'VE SEEN IN A VERY LONG TIME. IT'S NOT SOMETHING I THOUGHT I'D EVER SEE AGAIN.
HAPPY CHILDREN.
YES, WELL... I THINK YOU'LL FIND, FOR THE MOST PART, WE ARE ABLE TO RETURN TO THE LIFE WE REMEMBER WITHIN THESE WALLS.
DOUGLAS IS READY TO SEE YOU.
DOUGLAS?
HE'S OUR... FOR LACK OF A BETTER WORD, LEADER. HE'S WHO WE LOOK TO FOR GUIDANCE. HE MAKES SURE EVERYONE IS DOING THEIR JOB, PULLING THEIR WEIGHT.
MY WORD CARRIES A LOT OF WEIGHT, BUT HE STILL WANTS TO TALK TO YOU.
ANSWER ALL HIS QUESTIONS HONESTLY, EVEN IF YOU FEEL LIKE YOU SHOULDN'T, AND YOU'LL BE FINE.
IT'S THAT HOUSE THERE. HE'S WAITING FOR YOU.
OKAY.

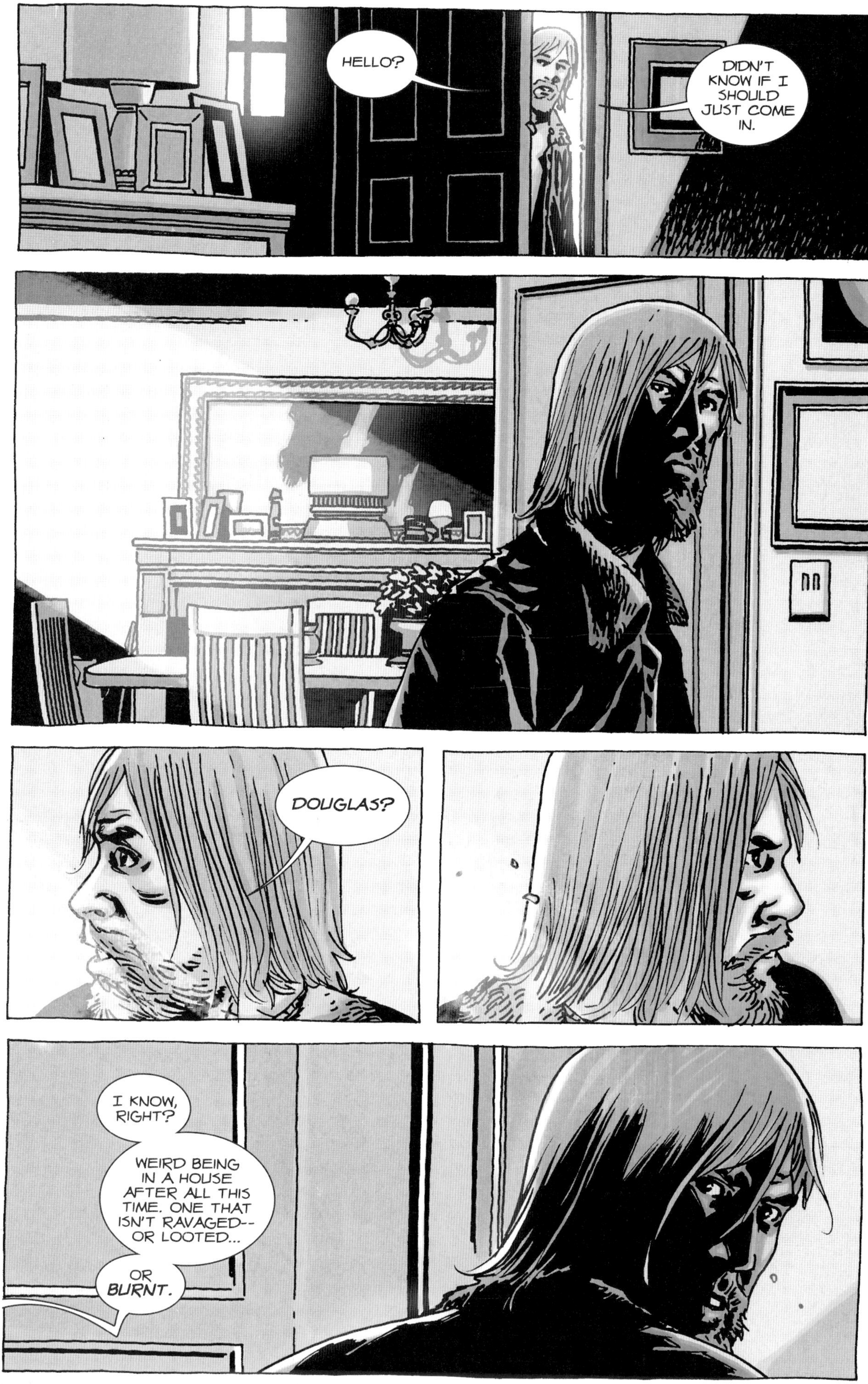
HELLO?
DIDN'T KNOW IF I SHOULD JUST COME IN.
DOUGLAS?
I KNOW, RIGHT?
WEIRD BEING IN A HOUSE AFTER ALL THIS TIME. ONE THAT ISN'T RAVAGED-- OR LOOTED...
OR BURNT.

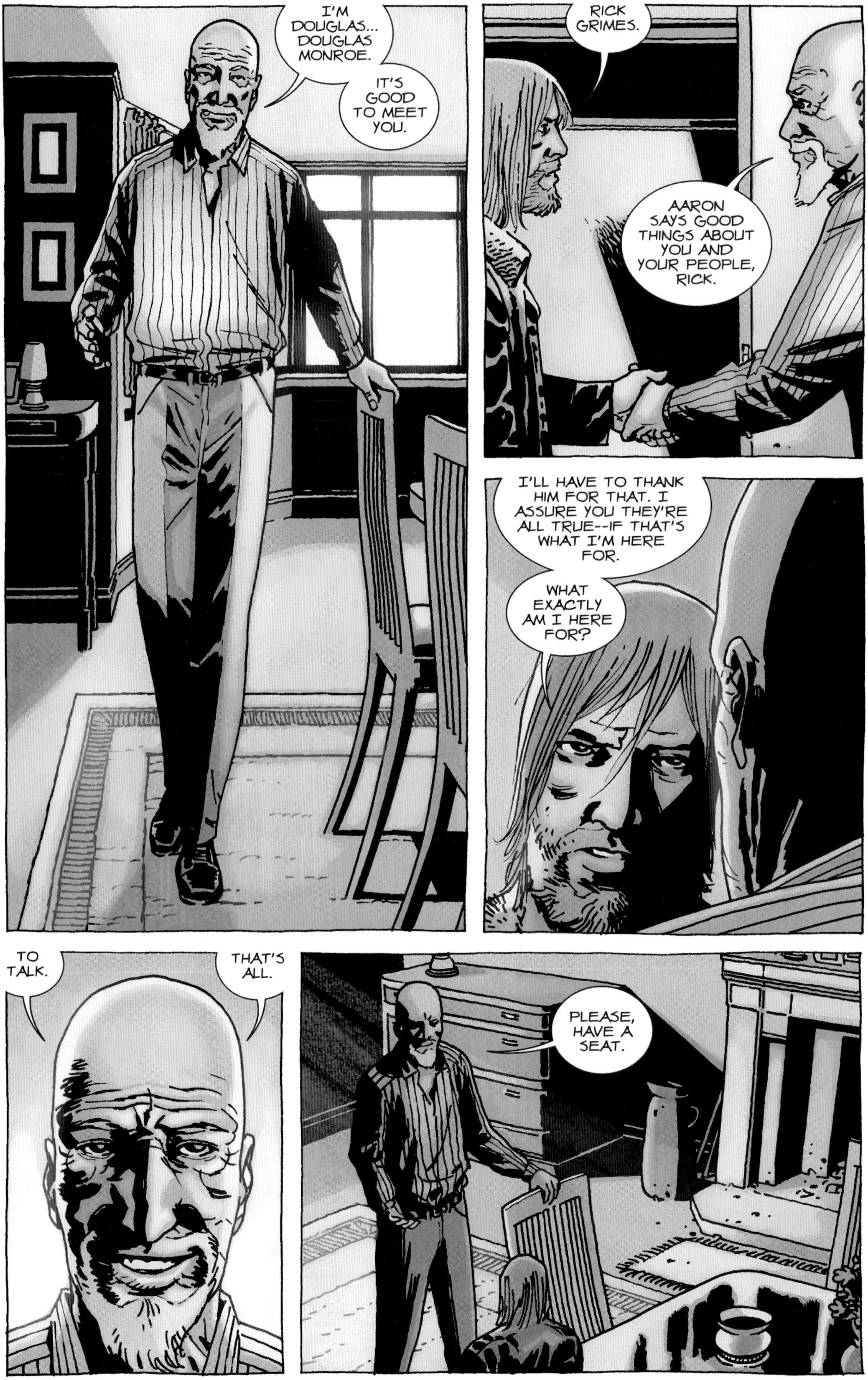
I'M DOUGLAS... DOUGLAS MONROE.
IT'S GOOD TO MEET YOU.
RICK GRIMES.
AARON SAYS GOOD THINGS ABOUT YOU AND YOUR PEOPLE, RICK.
I'LL HAVE TO THANK HIM FOR THAT. I ASSURE YOU THEY'RE ALL TRUE--IF THAT'S WHAT I'M HERE FOR.
WHAT EXACTLY AM I HERE FOR?
TO TALK.
THAT'S ALL.
PLEASE, HAVE A SEAT.

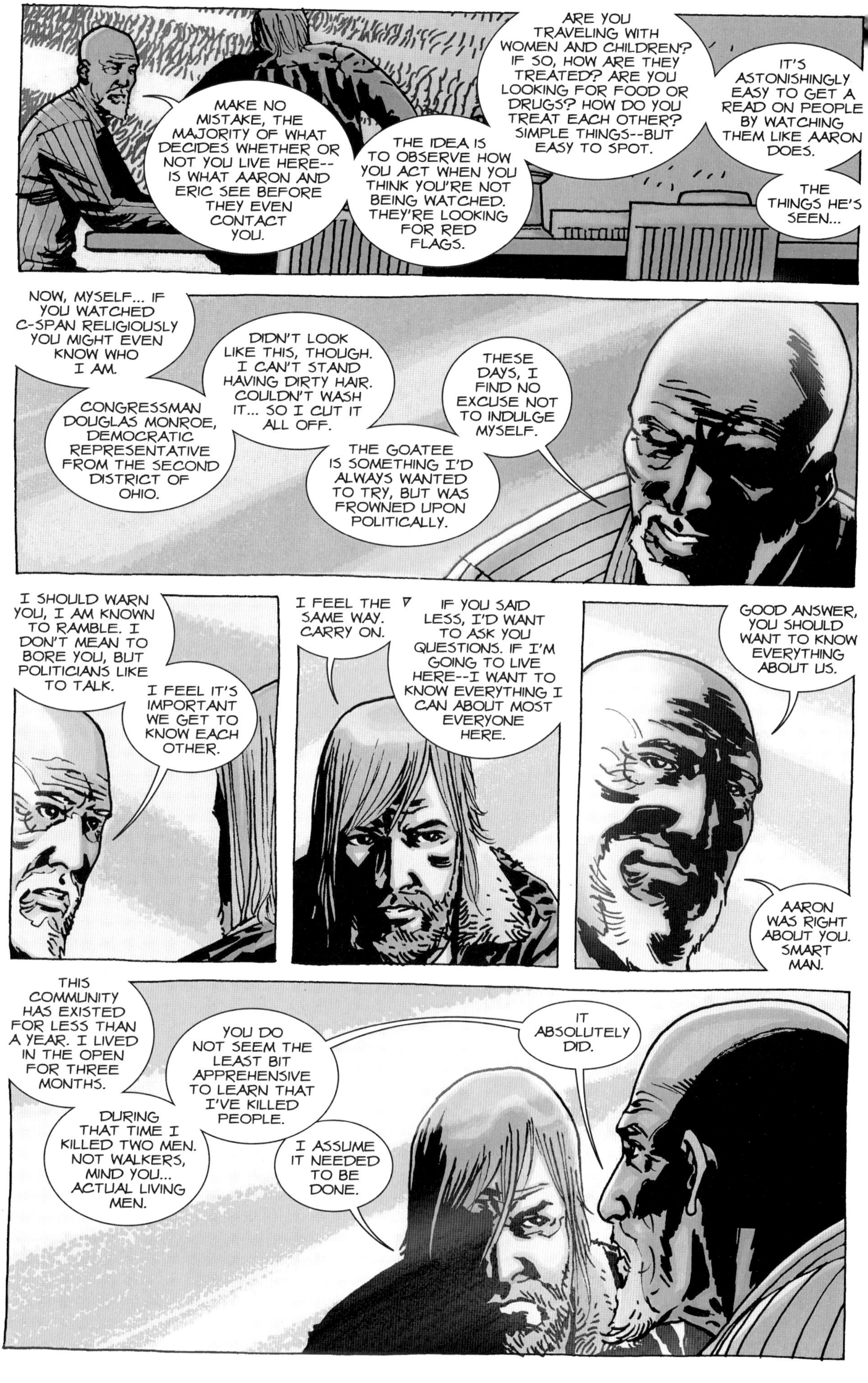
MAKE NO MISTAKE, THE MAJORITY OF WHAT DECIDES WHETHER OR NOT YOU LIVE HERE-- IS WHAT AARON AND ERIC SEE BEFORE THEY EVEN CONTACT YOU.
THE IDEA IS TO OBSERVE HOW YOU ACT WHEN YOU THINK YOU'RE NOT BEING WATCHED. THEY'RE LOOKING FOR RED FLAGS.
ARE YOU TRAVELING WITH WOMEN AND CHILDREN? IF SO, HOW ARE THEY TREATED? ARE YOU LOOKING FOR FOOD OR DRUGS? HOW DO YOU TREAT EACH OTHER? SIMPLE THINGS--BUT EASY TO SPOT.
IT'S ASTONISHINGLY EASY TO GET A READ ON PEOPLE BY WATCHING THEM LIKE AARON DOES.
THE THINGS HE'S SEEN...
NOW, MYSELF... IF YOU WATCHED C-SPAN RELIGIOUSLY YOU MIGHT EVEN KNOW WHO I AM.
CONGRESSMAN DOUGLAS MONROE, DEMOCRATIC REPRESENTATIVE FROM THE SECOND DISTRICT OF OHIO.
DIDN'T LOOK LIKE THIS, THOUGH. I CAN'T STAND HAVING DIRTY HAIR. COULDN'T WASH IT... SO I CUT IT ALL OFF.
THE GOATEE IS SOMETHING I'D ALWAYS WANTED TO TRY, BUT WAS FROWNED UPON POLITICALLY.
THESE DAYS, I FIND NO EXCUSE NOT TO INDULGE MYSELF.
I SHOULD WARN YOU, I AM KNOWN TO RAMBLE. I DON'T MEAN TO BORE YOU, BUT POLITICIANS LIKE TO TALK.
I FEEL IT'S IMPORTANT WE GET TO KNOW EACH OTHER.
I FEEL THE SAME WAY. CARRY ON.
IF YOU SAID LESS, I'D WANT TO ASK YOU QUESTIONS. IF I'M GOING TO LIVE HERE--I WANT TO KNOW EVERYTHING I CAN ABOUT MOST EVERYONE HERE.
GOOD ANSWER. YOU SHOULD WANT TO KNOW EVERYTHING ABOUT US.
AARON WAS RIGHT ABOUT YOU. SMART MAN.
THIS COMMUNITY HAS EXISTED FOR LESS THAN A YEAR. I LIVED IN THE OPEN FOR THREE MONTHS.
DURING THAT TIME I KILLED TWO MEN. NOT WALKERS, MIND YOU... ACTUAL LIVING MEN.
YOU DO NOT SEEM THE LEAST BIT APPREHENSIVE TO LEARN THAT I'VE KILLED PEOPLE.
I ASSUME IT NEEDED TO BE DONE.
IT ABSOLUTELY DID.

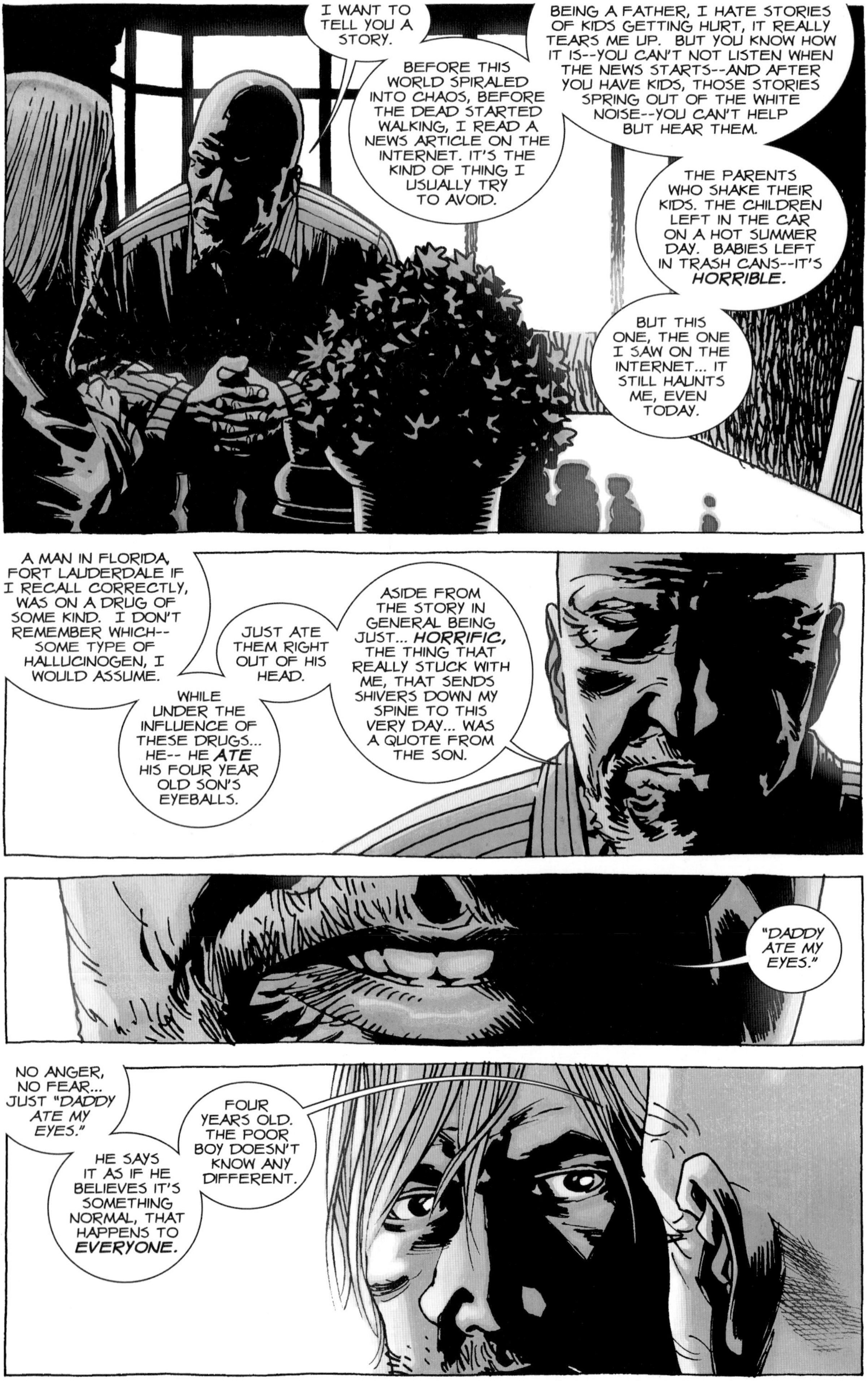
I WANT TO TELL YOU A STORY.
BEFORE THIS WORLD SPIRALED INTO CHAOS, BEFORE THE DEAD STARTED WALKING, I READ A NEWS ARTICLE ON THE INTERNET. IT'S THE KIND OF THING I USUALLY TRY TO AVOID.
BEING A FATHER, I HATE STORIES OF KIDS GETTING HURT, IT REALLY TEARS ME UP. BUT YOU KNOW HOW IT IS--YOU CAN'T NOT LISTEN WHEN THE NEWS STARTS--AND AFTER YOU HAVE KIDS, THOSE STORIES SPRING OUT OF THE WHITE NOISE--YOU CAN'T HELP BUT HEAR THEM.
THE PARENTS WHO SHAKE THEIR KIDS. THE CHILDREN LEFT IN THE CAR ON A HOT SUMMER DAY. BABIES LEFT IN TRASH CANS--IT'S ***HORRIBLE.***
BUT THIS ONE, THE ONE I SAW ON THE INTERNET... IT STILL HAUNTS ME, EVEN TODAY.
A MAN IN FLORIDA, FORT LAUDERDALE IF I RECALL CORRECTLY, WAS ON A DRUG OF SOME KIND. I DON'T REMEMBER WHICH-- SOME TYPE OF HALLUCINOGEN, I WOULD ASSUME.
WHILE UNDER THE INFLUENCE OF THESE DRUGS... HE-- HE ***ATE*** HIS FOUR YEAR OLD SON'S EYEBALLS.
JUST ATE THEM RIGHT OUT OF HIS HEAD.
ASIDE FROM THE STORY IN GENERAL BEING JUST... ***HORRIFIC,*** THE THING THAT REALLY STUCK WITH ME, THAT SENDS SHIVERS DOWN MY SPINE TO THIS VERY DAY... WAS A QUOTE FROM THE SON.
"DADDY ATE MY EYES."
NO ANGER, NO FEAR... JUST *"DADDY ATE MY EYES."*
HE SAYS IT AS IF HE BELIEVES IT'S SOMETHING NORMAL, THAT HAPPENS TO ***EVERYONE.***
FOUR YEARS OLD. THE POOR BOY DOESN'T KNOW ANY DIFFERENT.

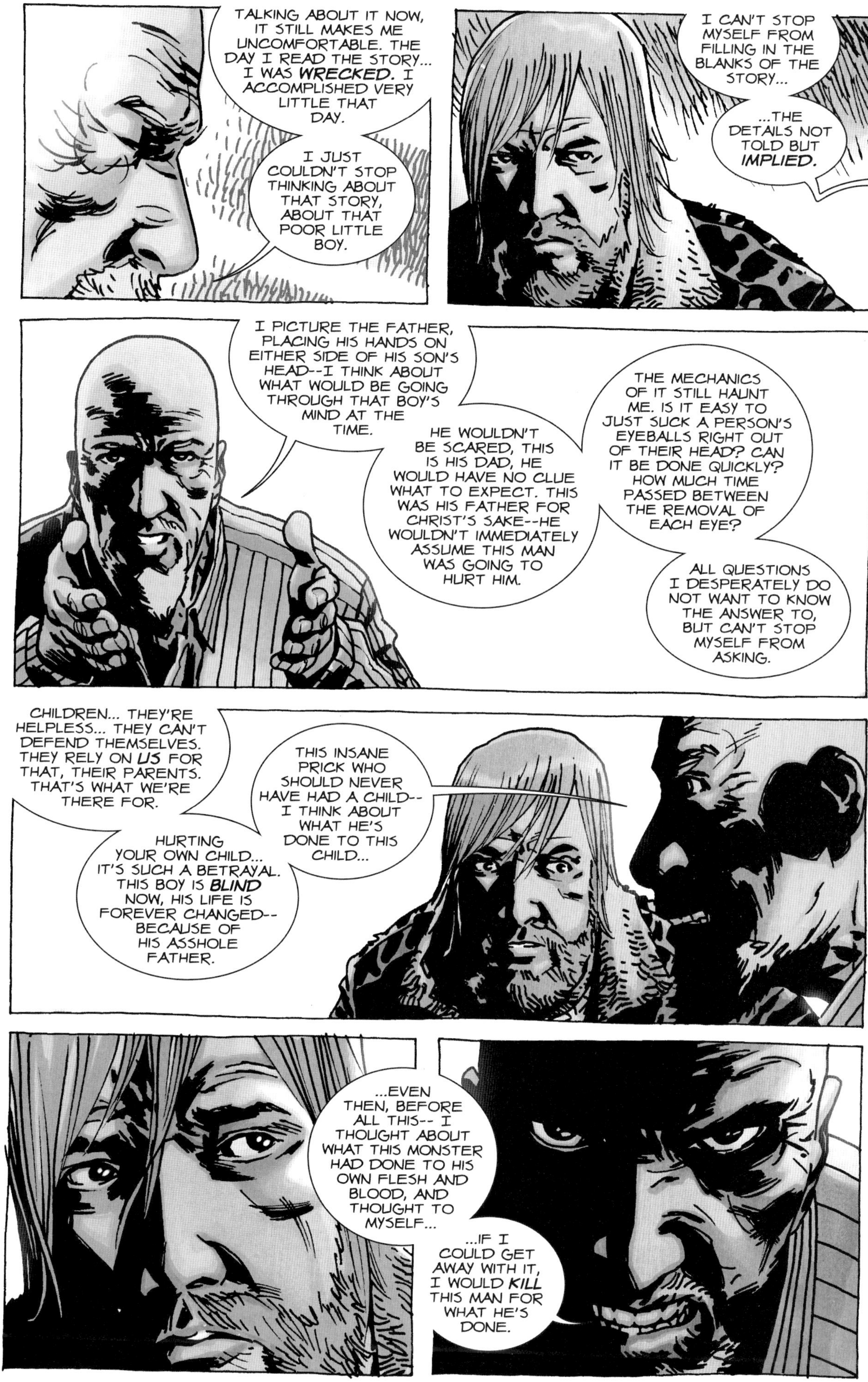

TALKING ABOUT IT NOW, IT STILL MAKES ME UNCOMFORTABLE. THE DAY I READ THE STORY... I WAS WRECKED. I ACCOMPLISHED VERY LITTLE THAT DAY.
I JUST COULDN'T STOP THINKING ABOUT THAT STORY, ABOUT THAT POOR LITTLE BOY.
I CAN'T STOP MYSELF FROM FILLING IN THE BLANKS OF THE STORY...
...THE DETAILS NOT TOLD BUT IMPLIED.
I PICTURE THE FATHER, PLACING HIS HANDS ON EITHER SIDE OF HIS SON'S HEAD--I THINK ABOUT WHAT WOULD BE GOING THROUGH THAT BOY'S MIND AT THE TIME.
HE WOULDN'T BE SCARED, THIS IS HIS DAD, HE WOULD HAVE NO CLUE WHAT TO EXPECT. THIS WAS HIS FATHER FOR CHRIST'S SAKE--HE WOULDN'T IMMEDIATELY ASSUME THIS MAN WAS GOING TO HURT HIM.
THE MECHANICS OF IT STILL HAUNT ME. IS IT EASY TO JUST SUCK A PERSON'S EYEBALLS RIGHT OUT OF THEIR HEAD? CAN IT BE DONE QUICKLY? HOW MUCH TIME PASSED BETWEEN THE REMOVAL OF EACH EYE?
ALL QUESTIONS I DESPERATELY DO NOT WANT TO KNOW THE ANSWER TO, BUT CAN'T STOP MYSELF FROM ASKING.
CHILDREN... THEY'RE HELPLESS... THEY CAN'T DEFEND THEMSELVES. THEY RELY ON US FOR THAT, THEIR PARENTS. THAT'S WHAT WE'RE THERE FOR.
HURTING YOUR OWN CHILD... IT'S SUCH A BETRAYAL. THIS BOY IS BLIND NOW, HIS LIFE IS FOREVER CHANGED-- BECAUSE OF HIS ASSHOLE FATHER.
THIS INSANE PRICK WHO SHOULD NEVER HAVE HAD A CHILD-- I THINK ABOUT WHAT HE'S DONE TO THIS CHILD...
...EVEN THEN, BEFORE ALL THIS-- I THOUGHT ABOUT WHAT THIS MONSTER HAD DONE TO HIS OWN FLESH AND BLOOD, AND THOUGHT TO MYSELF...
...IF I COULD GET AWAY WITH IT, I WOULD KILL THIS MAN FOR WHAT HE'S DONE.

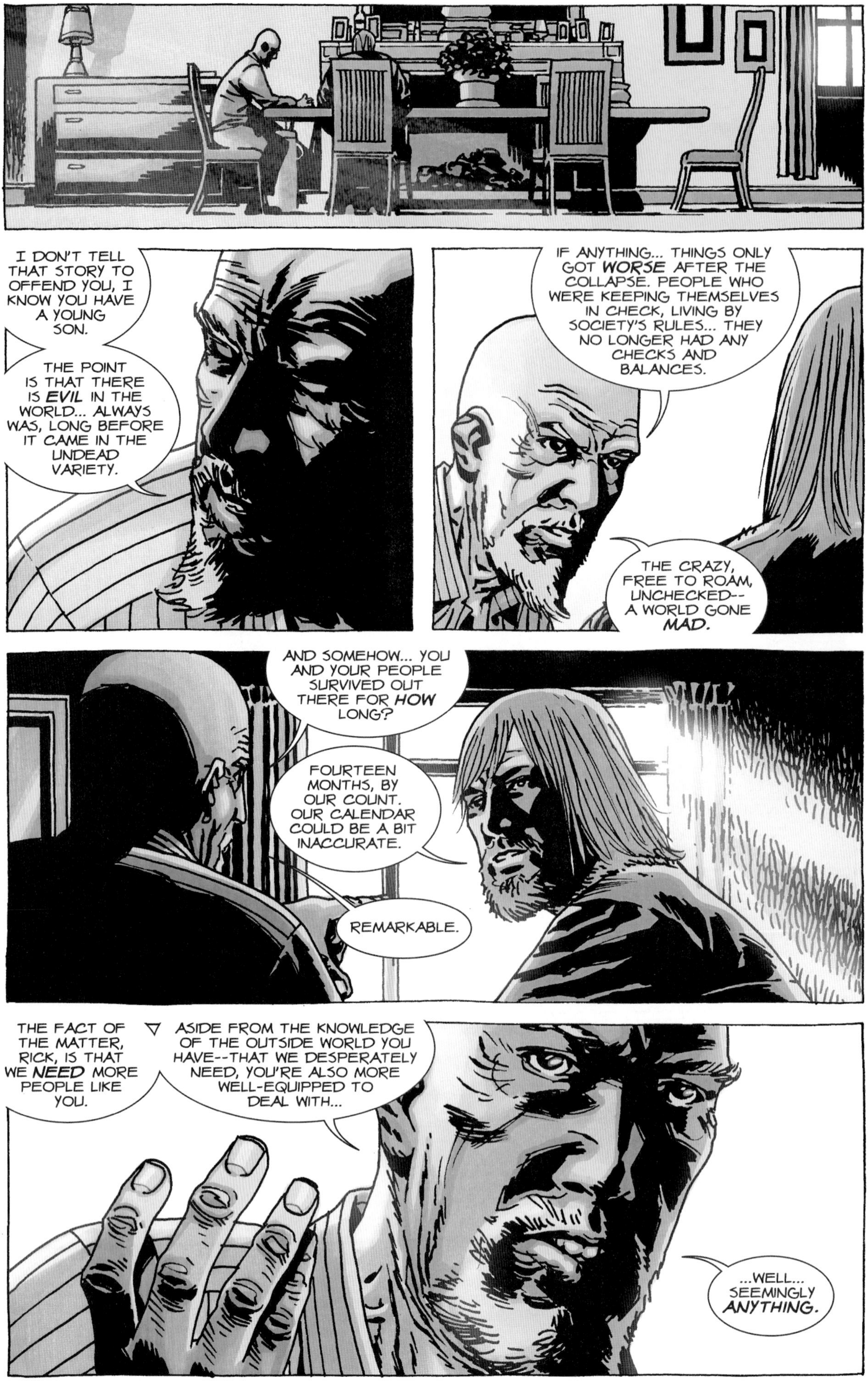
I DON'T TELL THAT STORY TO OFFEND YOU, I KNOW YOU HAVE A YOUNG SON.
THE POINT IS THAT THERE IS EVIL IN THE WORLD... ALWAYS WAS, LONG BEFORE IT CAME IN THE UNDEAD VARIETY.
IF ANYTHING... THINGS ONLY GOT WORSE AFTER THE COLLAPSE. PEOPLE WHO WERE KEEPING THEMSELVES IN CHECK, LIVING BY SOCIETY'S RULES... THEY NO LONGER HAD ANY CHECKS AND BALANCES.
THE CRAZY, FREE TO ROAM, UNCHECKED-- A WORLD GONE MAD.
AND SOMEHOW... YOU AND YOUR PEOPLE SURVIVED OUT THERE FOR HOW LONG?
FOURTEEN MONTHS, BY OUR COUNT. OUR CALENDAR COULD BE A BIT INACCURATE.
REMARKABLE.
THE FACT OF THE MATTER, RICK, IS THAT WE NEED MORE PEOPLE LIKE YOU.
ASIDE FROM THE KNOWLEDGE OF THE OUTSIDE WORLD YOU HAVE--THAT WE DESPERATELY NEED, YOU'RE ALSO MORE WELL-EQUIPPED TO DEAL WITH...
...WELL... SEEMINGLY ANYTHING.

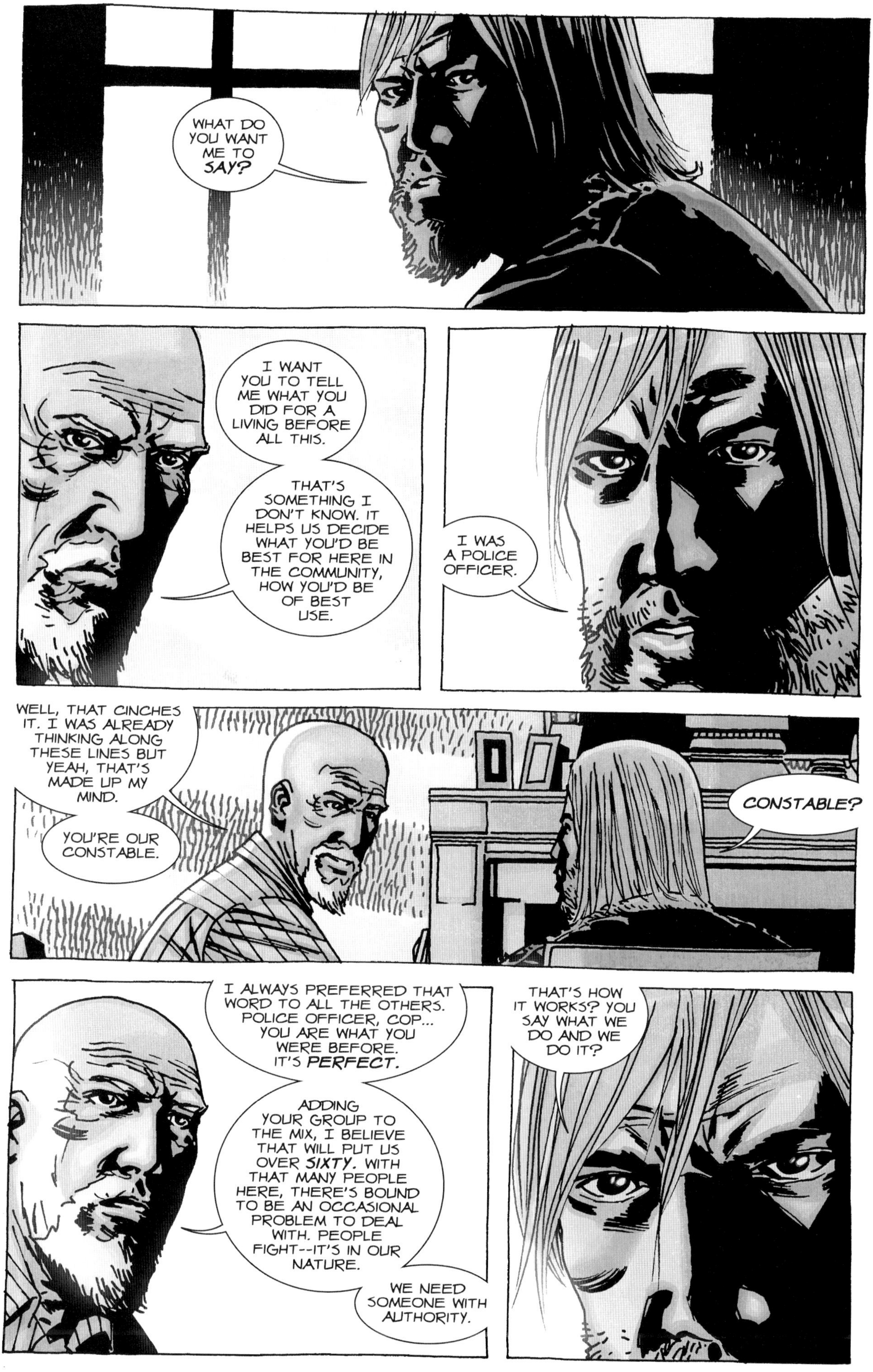
WHAT DO YOU WANT ME TO *SAY?*
I WANT YOU TO TELL ME WHAT YOU DID FOR A LIVING BEFORE ALL THIS.
THAT'S SOMETHING I DON'T KNOW. IT HELPS US DECIDE WHAT YOU'D BE BEST FOR HERE IN THE COMMUNITY, HOW YOU'D BE OF BEST USE.
I WAS A POLICE OFFICER.
WELL, THAT CINCHES IT. I WAS ALREADY THINKING ALONG THESE LINES BUT YEAH, THAT'S MADE UP MY MIND.
YOU'RE OUR CONSTABLE.
CONSTABLE?
I ALWAYS PREFERRED THAT WORD TO ALL THE OTHERS. POLICE OFFICER, COP... YOU ARE WHAT YOU WERE BEFORE. IT'S *PERFECT.*
ADDING YOUR GROUP TO THE MIX, I BELIEVE THAT WILL PUT US OVER *SIXTY.* WITH THAT MANY PEOPLE HERE, THERE'S BOUND TO BE AN OCCASIONAL PROBLEM TO DEAL WITH. PEOPLE FIGHT--IT'S IN OUR NATURE.
WE NEED SOMEONE WITH AUTHORITY.
THAT'S HOW IT WORKS? YOU SAY WHAT WE DO AND WE DO IT?

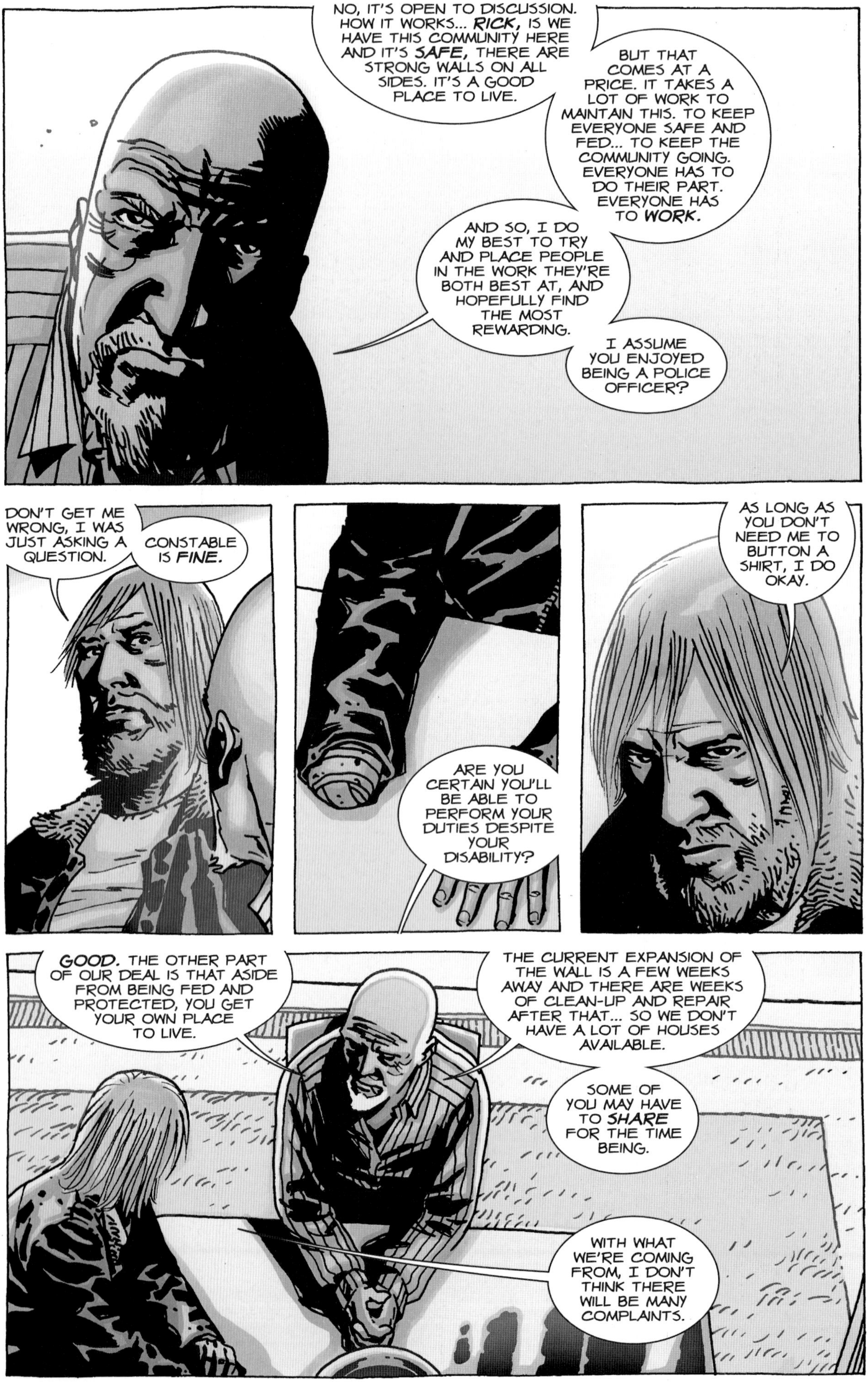
NO, IT'S OPEN TO DISCUSSION. HOW IT WORKS... RICK, IS WE HAVE THIS COMMUNITY HERE AND IT'S SAFE, THERE ARE STRONG WALLS ON ALL SIDES. IT'S A GOOD PLACE TO LIVE.
BUT THAT COMES AT A PRICE. IT TAKES A LOT OF WORK TO MAINTAIN THIS. TO KEEP EVERYONE SAFE AND FED... TO KEEP THE COMMUNITY GOING. EVERYONE HAS TO DO THEIR PART. EVERYONE HAS TO WORK.
AND SO, I DO MY BEST TO TRY AND PLACE PEOPLE IN THE WORK THEY'RE BOTH BEST AT, AND HOPEFULLY FIND THE MOST REWARDING.
I ASSUME YOU ENJOYED BEING A POLICE OFFICER?
DON'T GET ME WRONG, I WAS JUST ASKING A QUESTION.
CONSTABLE IS FINE.
ARE YOU CERTAIN YOU'LL BE ABLE TO PERFORM YOUR DUTIES DESPITE YOUR DISABILITY?
AS LONG AS YOU DON'T NEED ME TO BUTTON A SHIRT, I DO OKAY.
GOOD. THE OTHER PART OF OUR DEAL IS THAT ASIDE FROM BEING FED AND PROTECTED, YOU GET YOUR OWN PLACE TO LIVE.
THE CURRENT EXPANSION OF THE WALL IS A FEW WEEKS AWAY AND THERE ARE WEEKS OF CLEAN-UP AND REPAIR AFTER THAT... SO WE DON'T HAVE A LOT OF HOUSES AVAILABLE.
SOME OF YOU MAY HAVE TO SHARE FOR THE TIME BEING.
WITH WHAT WE'RE COMING FROM, I DON'T THINK THERE WILL BE MANY COMPLAINTS.

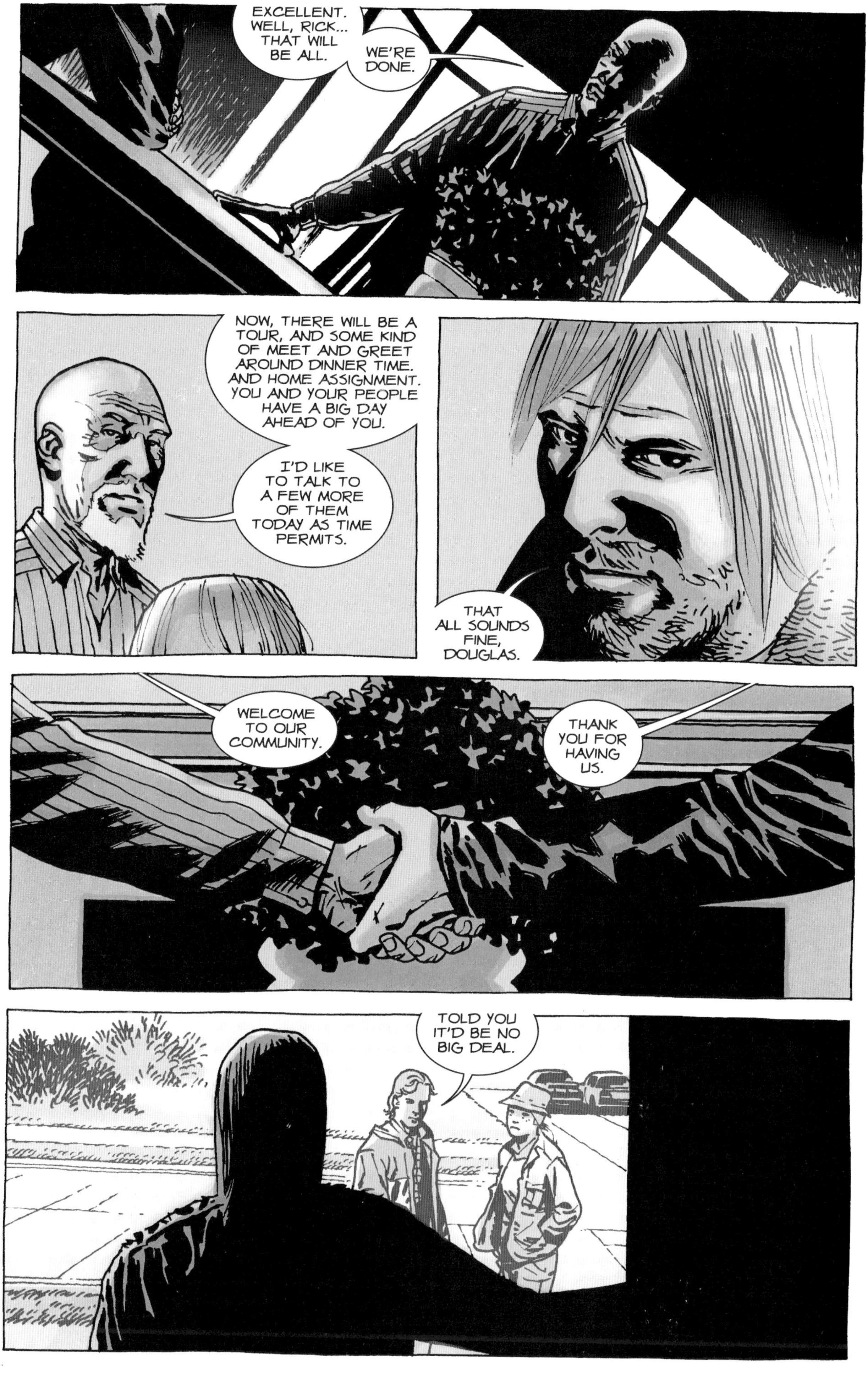
EXCELLENT. WELL, RICK... THAT WILL BE ALL.
WE'RE DONE.
NOW, THERE WILL BE A TOUR, AND SOME KIND OF MEET AND GREET AROUND DINNER TIME. AND HOME ASSIGNMENT. YOU AND YOUR PEOPLE HAVE A BIG DAY AHEAD OF YOU.
I'D LIKE TO TALK TO A FEW MORE OF THEM TODAY AS TIME PERMITS.
THAT ALL SOUNDS FINE, DOUGLAS.
WELCOME TO OUR COMMUNITY.
THANK YOU FOR HAVING US.
TOLD YOU IT'D BE NO BIG DEAL.

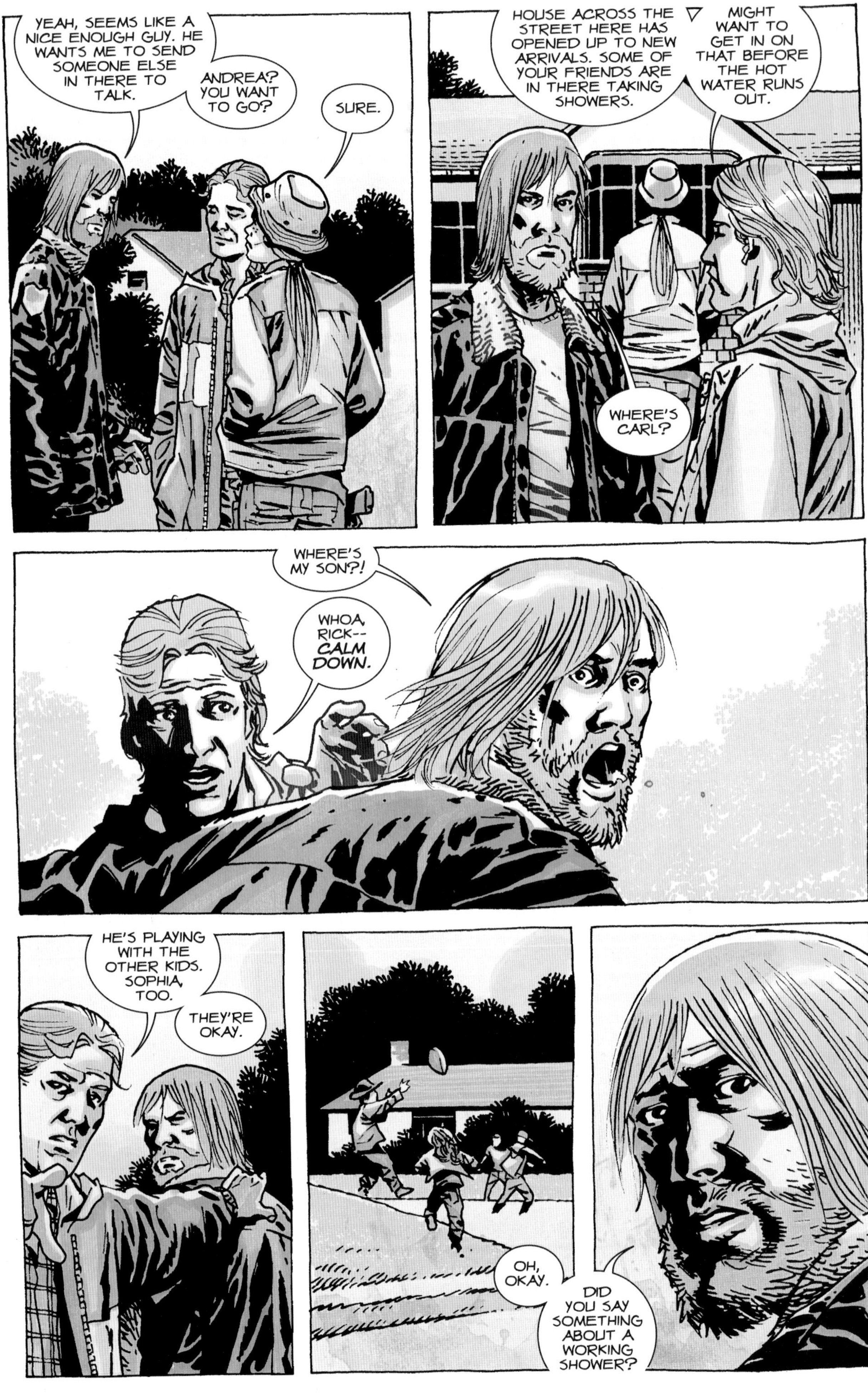
YEAH, SEEMS LIKE A NICE ENOUGH GUY. HE WANTS ME TO SEND SOMEONE ELSE IN THERE TO TALK.
ANDREA? YOU WANT TO GO?
SURE.
HOUSE ACROSS THE STREET HERE HAS OPENED UP TO NEW ARRIVALS. SOME OF YOUR FRIENDS ARE IN THERE TAKING SHOWERS.
MIGHT WANT TO GET IN ON THAT BEFORE THE HOT WATER RUNS OUT.
WHERE'S CARL?
WHERE'S MY SON?!
WHOA, RICK-- CALM DOWN.
HE'S PLAYING WITH THE OTHER KIDS. SOPHIA, TOO.
THEY'RE OKAY.
OH, OKAY.
DID YOU SAY SOMETHING ABOUT A WORKING SHOWER?

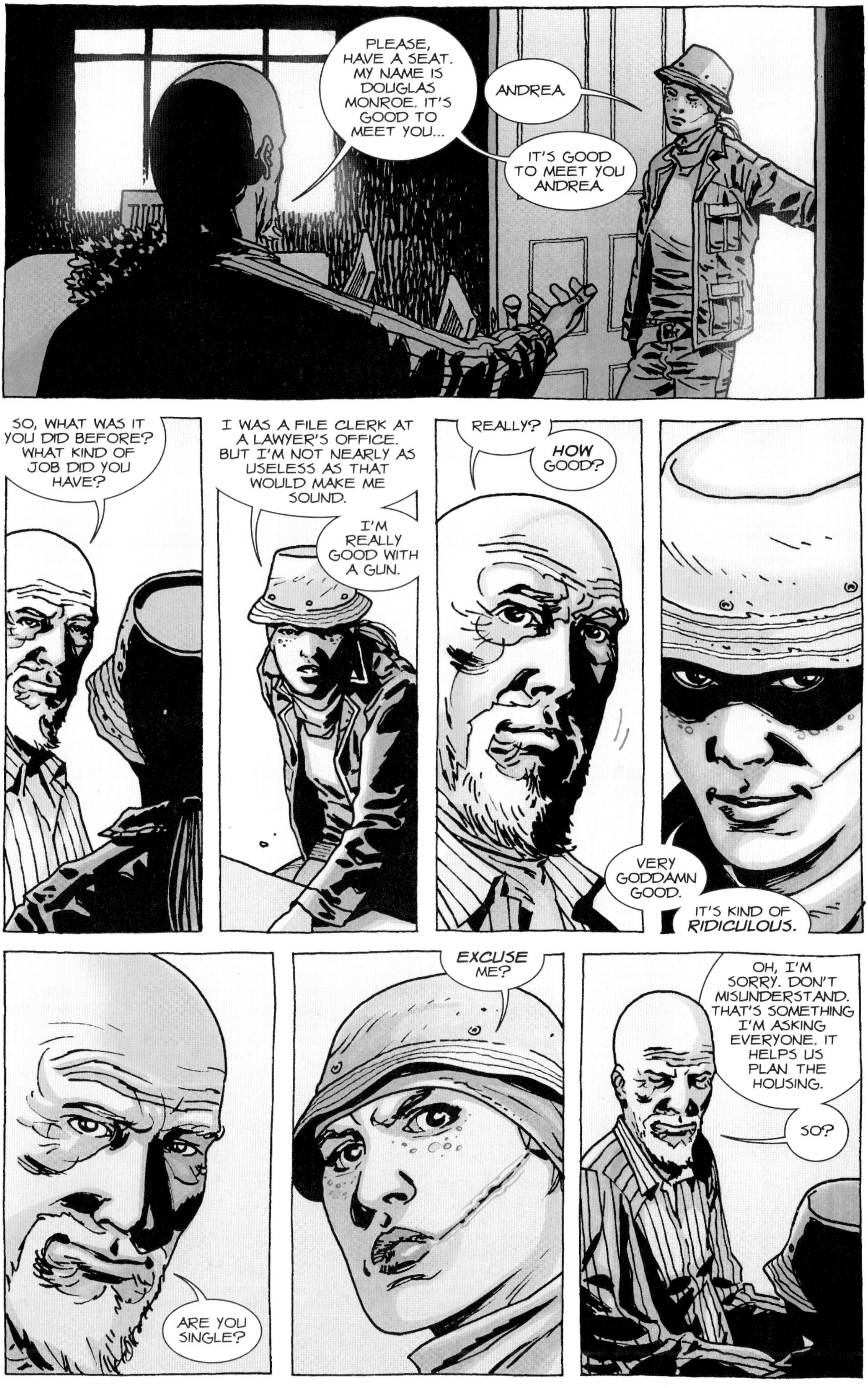
PLEASE, HAVE A SEAT. MY NAME IS DOUGLAS MONROE. IT'S GOOD TO MEET YOU...
ANDREA
IT'S GOOD TO MEET YOU ANDREA
SO, WHAT WAS IT YOU DID BEFORE? WHAT KIND OF JOB DID YOU HAVE?
I WAS A FILE CLERK AT A LAWYER'S OFFICE. BUT I'M NOT NEARLY AS USELESS AS THAT WOULD MAKE ME SOUND.
I'M REALLY GOOD WITH A GUN.
REALLY?
HOW GOOD?
VERY GODDAMN GOOD.
IT'S KIND OF RIDICULOUS.
ARE YOU SINGLE?
EXCUSE ME?
OH, I'M SORRY. DON'T MISUNDERSTAND. THAT'S SOMETHING I'M ASKING EVERYONE. IT HELPS US PLAN THE HOUSING.
SO?

WOW.

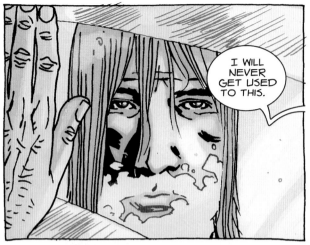

I WILL NEVER GET USED TO THIS.

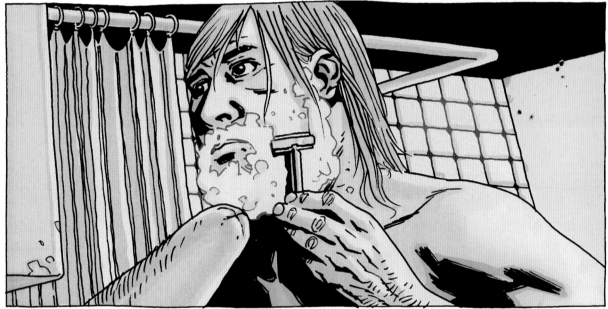

KNOCK! KNOCK!

JUST A MINUTE.

I'M SORRY TO BOTHER YOU, BUT DOUGLAS WANTED ME TO SEE IF THIS FITS.

WOW, HE DOESN'T WASTE ANY TIME.

YOU KNOW, I CAN CUT HAIR.

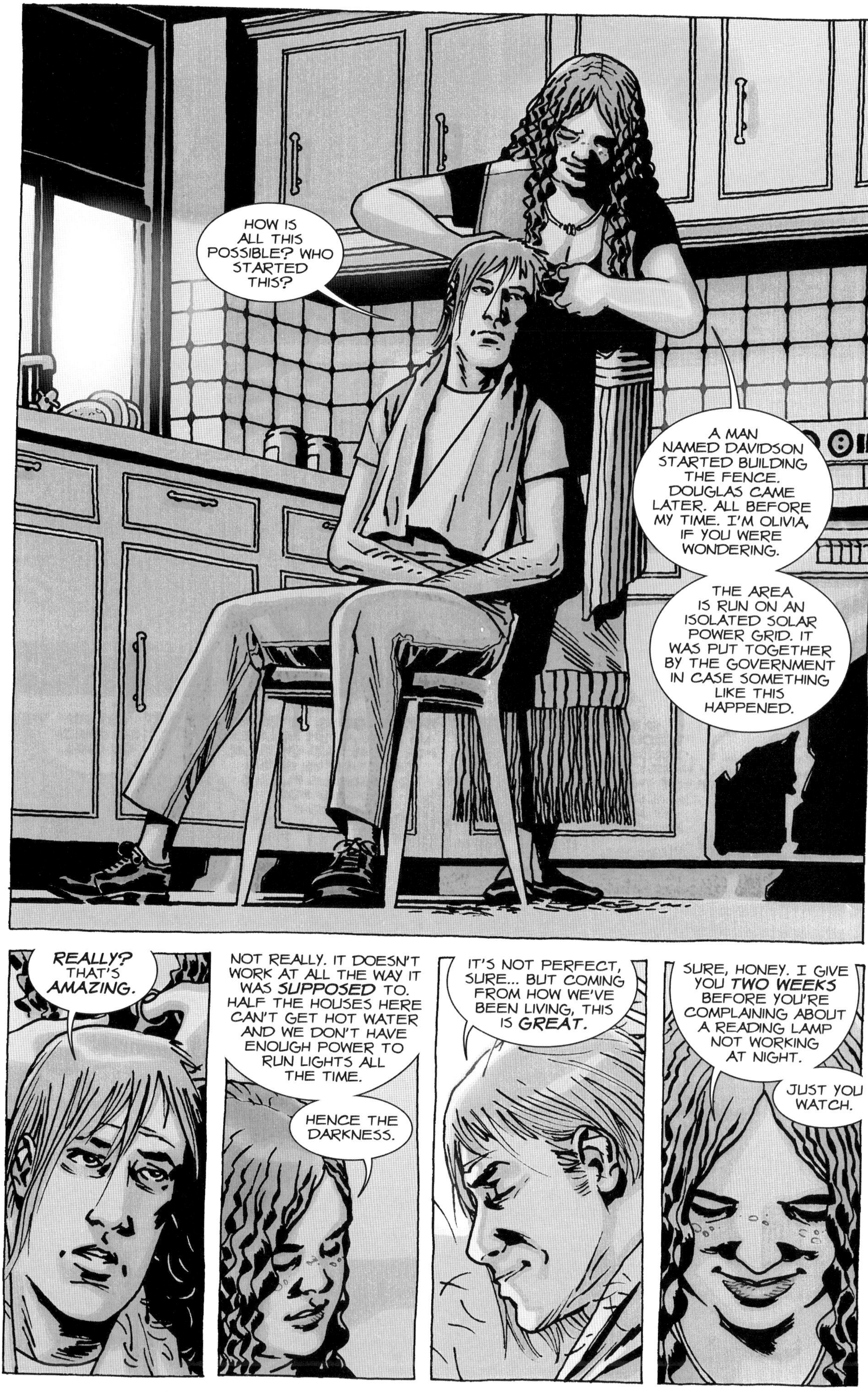
HOW IS ALL THIS POSSIBLE? WHO STARTED THIS?
A MAN NAMED DAVIDSON STARTED BUILDING THE FENCE. DOUGLAS CAME LATER. ALL BEFORE MY TIME. I'M OLIVIA, IF YOU WERE WONDERING.
THE AREA IS RUN ON AN ISOLATED SOLAR POWER GRID. IT WAS PUT TOGETHER BY THE GOVERNMENT IN CASE SOMETHING LIKE THIS HAPPENED.
REALLY? THAT'S AMAZING.
NOT REALLY. IT DOESN'T WORK AT ALL THE WAY IT WAS SUPPOSED TO. HALF THE HOUSES HERE CAN'T GET HOT WATER AND WE DON'T HAVE ENOUGH POWER TO RUN LIGHTS ALL THE TIME.
HENCE THE DARKNESS.
IT'S NOT PERFECT, SURE... BUT COMING FROM HOW WE'VE BEEN LIVING, THIS IS GREAT.
SURE, HONEY. I GIVE YOU TWO WEEKS BEFORE YOU'RE COMPLAINING ABOUT A READING LAMP NOT WORKING AT NIGHT.
JUST YOU WATCH.

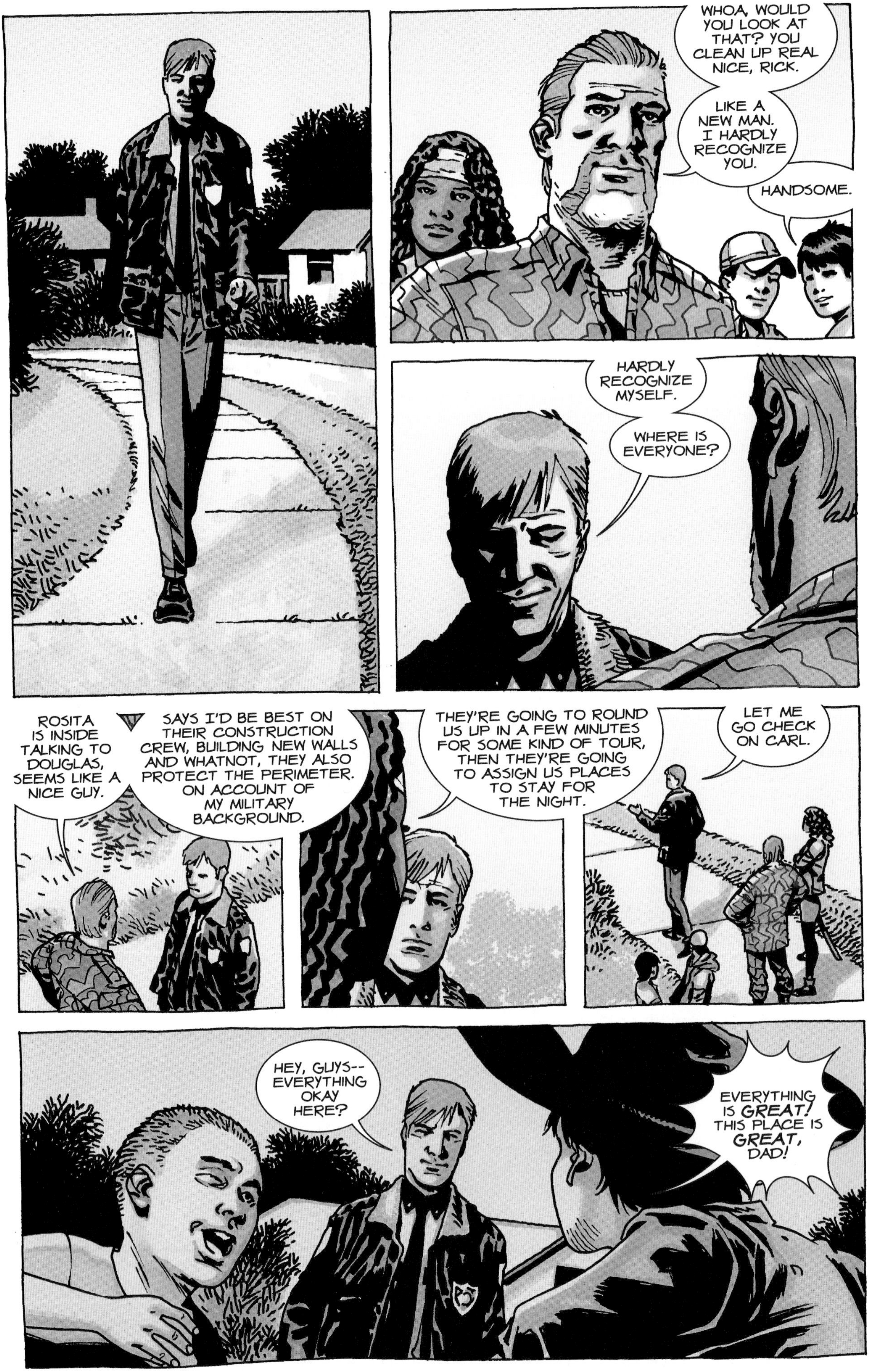

WHOA, WOULD YOU LOOK AT THAT? YOU CLEAN UP REAL NICE, RICK.
LIKE A NEW MAN. I HARDLY RECOGNIZE YOU.
HANDSOME.
HARDLY RECOGNIZE MYSELF.
WHERE IS EVERYONE?
ROSITA IS INSIDE TALKING TO DOUGLAS, SEEMS LIKE A NICE GUY.
SAYS I'D BE BEST ON THEIR CONSTRUCTION CREW, BUILDING NEW WALLS AND WHATNOT, THEY ALSO PROTECT THE PERIMETER. ON ACCOUNT OF MY MILITARY BACKGROUND.
THEY'RE GOING TO ROUND US UP IN A FEW MINUTES FOR SOME KIND OF TOUR, THEN THEY'RE GOING TO ASSIGN US PLACES TO STAY FOR THE NIGHT.
LET ME GO CHECK ON CARL.
HEY, GUYS-- EVERYTHING OKAY HERE?
EVERYTHING IS GREAT! THIS PLACE IS GREAT, DAD!

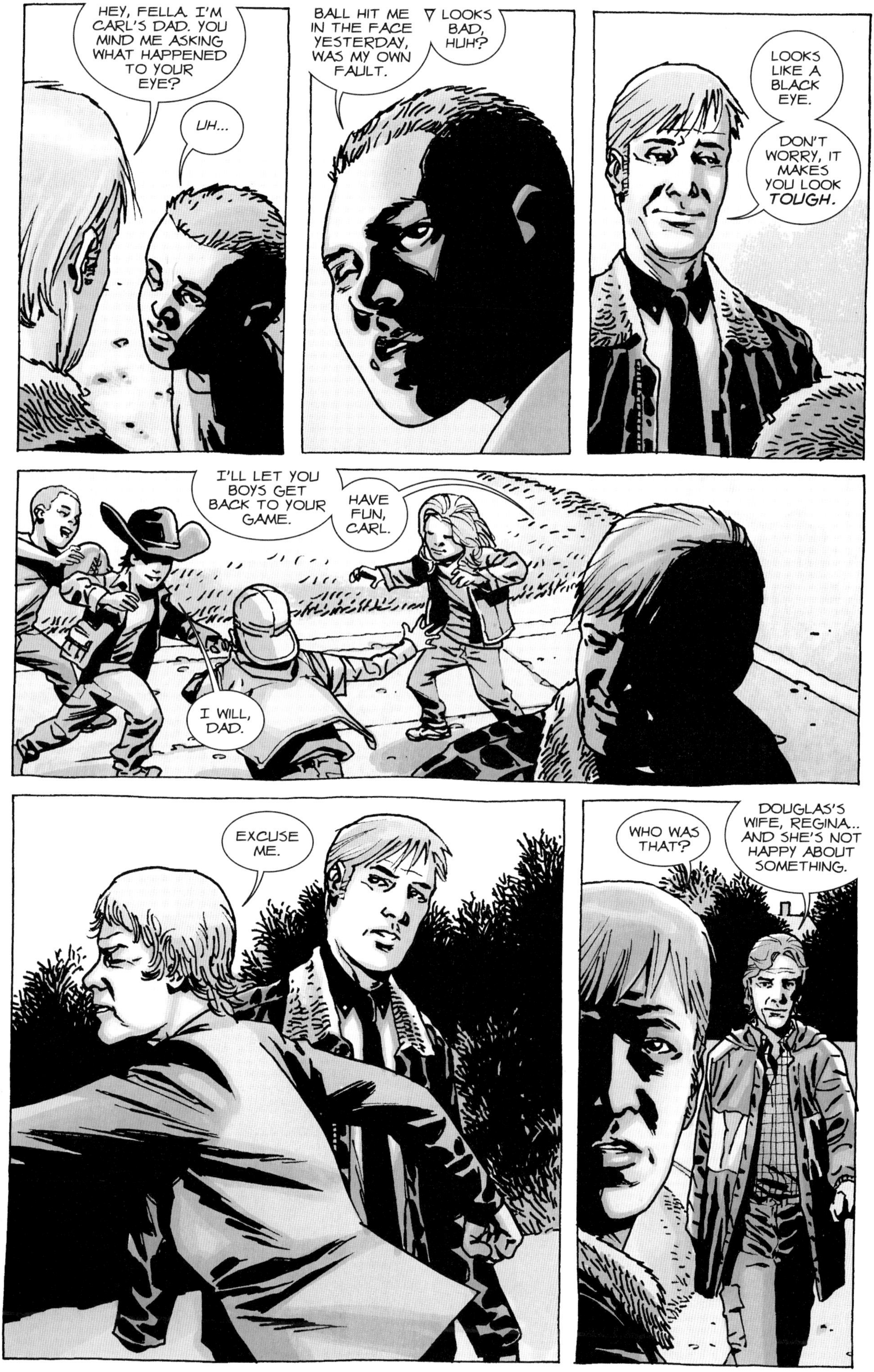
HEY, FELLA. I'M CARL'S DAD. YOU MIND ME ASKING WHAT HAPPENED TO YOUR EYE?
UH...
BALL HIT ME IN THE FACE YESTERDAY, WAS MY OWN FAULT.
LOOKS BAD, HUH?
LOOKS LIKE A BLACK EYE.
DON'T WORRY, IT MAKES YOU LOOK TOUGH.
I'LL LET YOU BOYS GET BACK TO YOUR GAME.
HAVE FUN, CARL.
I WILL, DAD.
EXCUSE ME.
WHO WAS THAT?
DOUGLAS'S WIFE, REGINA... AND SHE'S NOT HAPPY ABOUT SOMETHING.

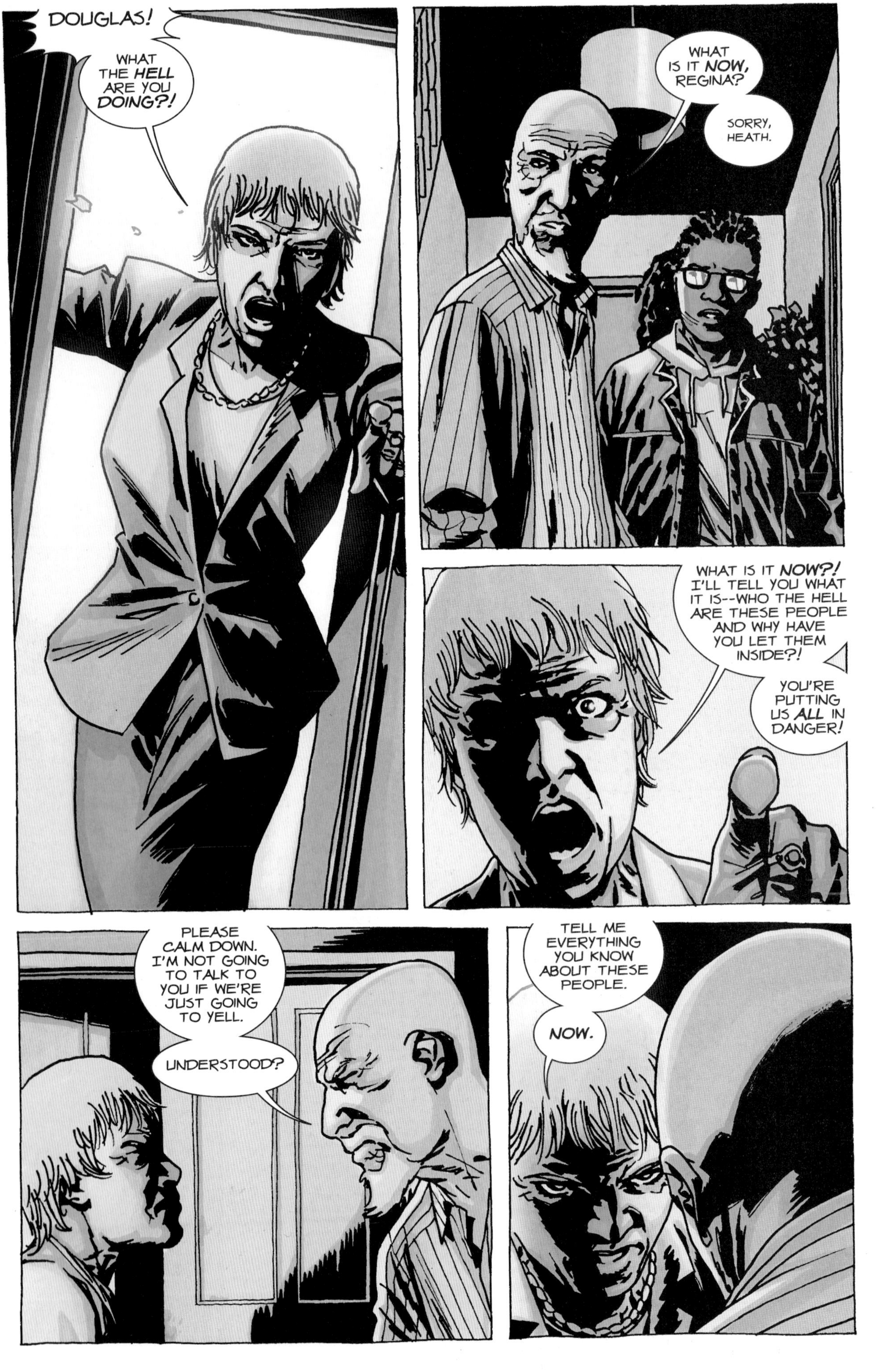
DOUGLAS!
WHAT THE HELL ARE YOU DOING?!
WHAT IS IT NOW, REGINA?
SORRY, HEATH.
WHAT IS IT NOW?! I'LL TELL YOU WHAT IT IS--WHO THE HELL ARE THESE PEOPLE AND WHY HAVE YOU LET THEM INSIDE?!
YOU'RE PUTTING US ALL IN DANGER!
PLEASE CALM DOWN. I'M NOT GOING TO TALK TO YOU IF WE'RE JUST GOING TO YELL.
UNDERSTOOD?
TELL ME EVERYTHING YOU KNOW ABOUT THESE PEOPLE.
NOW.

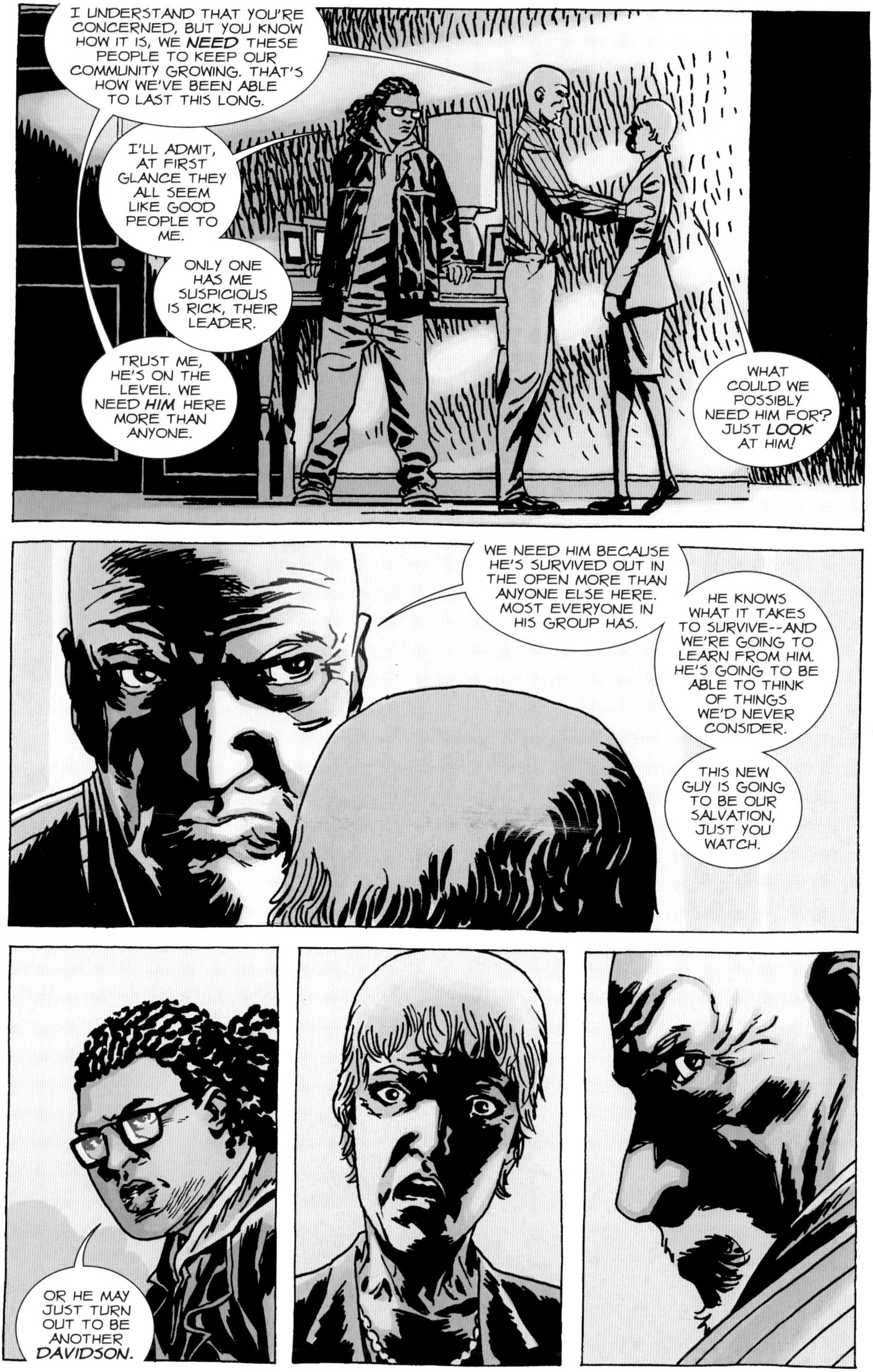
I UNDERSTAND THAT YOU'RE CONCERNED, BUT YOU KNOW HOW IT IS, WE *NEED* THESE PEOPLE TO KEEP OUR COMMUNITY GROWING. THAT'S HOW WE'VE BEEN ABLE TO LAST THIS LONG.
I'LL ADMIT, AT FIRST GLANCE THEY ALL SEEM LIKE GOOD PEOPLE TO ME.
ONLY ONE HAS ME SUSPICIOUS IS RICK, THEIR LEADER.
TRUST ME, HE'S ON THE LEVEL. WE NEED *HIM* HERE MORE THAN ANYONE.
WHAT COULD WE POSSIBLY NEED HIM FOR? JUST *LOOK* AT HIM!
WE NEED HIM BECAUSE HE'S SURVIVED OUT IN THE OPEN MORE THAN ANYONE ELSE HERE. MOST EVERYONE IN HIS GROUP HAS.
HE KNOWS WHAT IT TAKES TO SURVIVE--AND WE'RE GOING TO LEARN FROM HIM. HE'S GOING TO BE ABLE TO THINK OF THINGS WE'D NEVER CONSIDER.
THIS NEW GUY IS GOING TO BE OUR SALVATION, JUST YOU WATCH.
OR HE MAY JUST TURN OUT TO BE ANOTHER *DAVIDSON*.

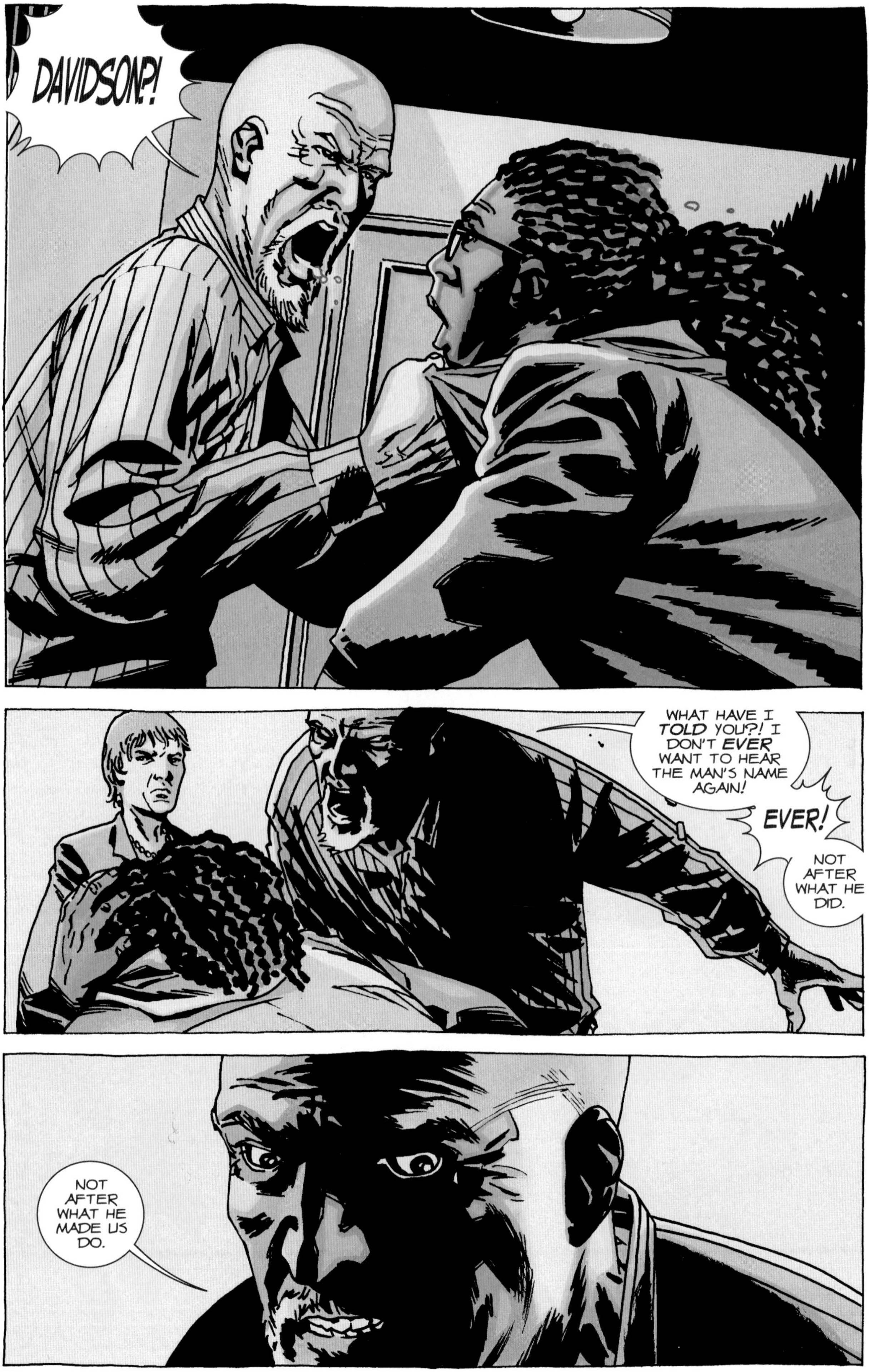
DAVIDSON?!
WHAT HAVE I TOLD YOU?! I DON'T EVER WANT TO HEAR THE MAN'S NAME AGAIN!
EVER!
NOT AFTER WHAT HE DID.
NOT AFTER WHAT HE MADE US DO.

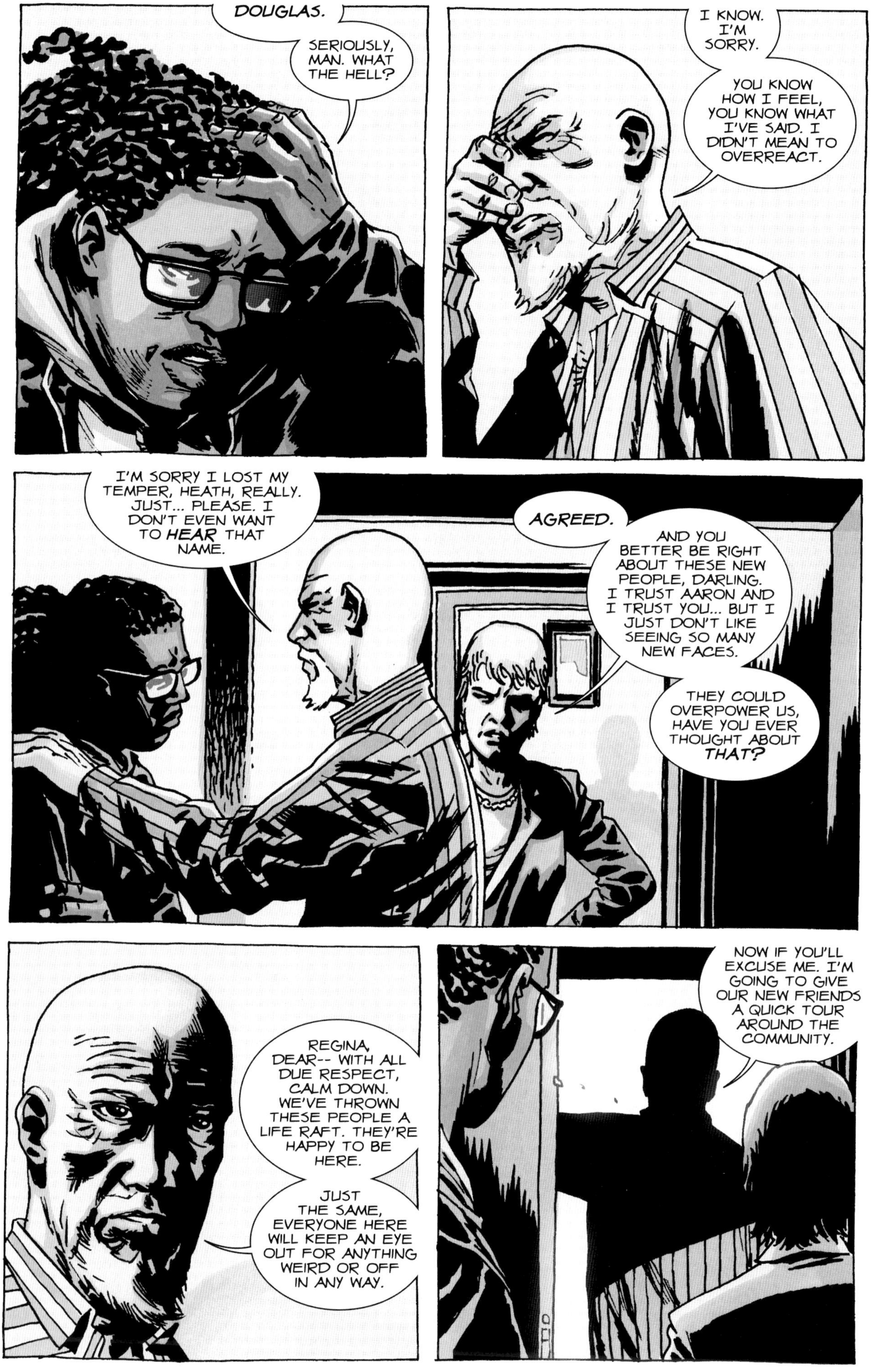
DOUGLAS.
SERIOUSLY, MAN. WHAT THE HELL?
I KNOW. I'M SORRY.
YOU KNOW HOW I FEEL, YOU KNOW WHAT I'VE SAID. I DIDN'T MEAN TO OVERREACT.
I'M SORRY I LOST MY TEMPER, HEATH, REALLY. JUST... PLEASE. I DON'T EVEN WANT TO HEAR THAT NAME.
AGREED.
AND YOU BETTER BE RIGHT ABOUT THESE NEW PEOPLE, DARLING. I TRUST AARON AND I TRUST YOU... BUT I JUST DON'T LIKE SEEING SO MANY NEW FACES.
THEY COULD OVERPOWER US, HAVE YOU EVER THOUGHT ABOUT THAT?
REGINA, DEAR-- WITH ALL DUE RESPECT, CALM DOWN. WE'VE THROWN THESE PEOPLE A LIFE RAFT. THEY'RE HAPPY TO BE HERE.
JUST THE SAME, EVERYONE HERE WILL KEEP AN EYE OUT FOR ANYTHING WEIRD OR OFF IN ANY WAY.
NOW IF YOU'LL EXCUSE ME. I'M GOING TO GIVE OUR NEW FRIENDS A QUICK TOUR AROUND THE COMMUNITY.

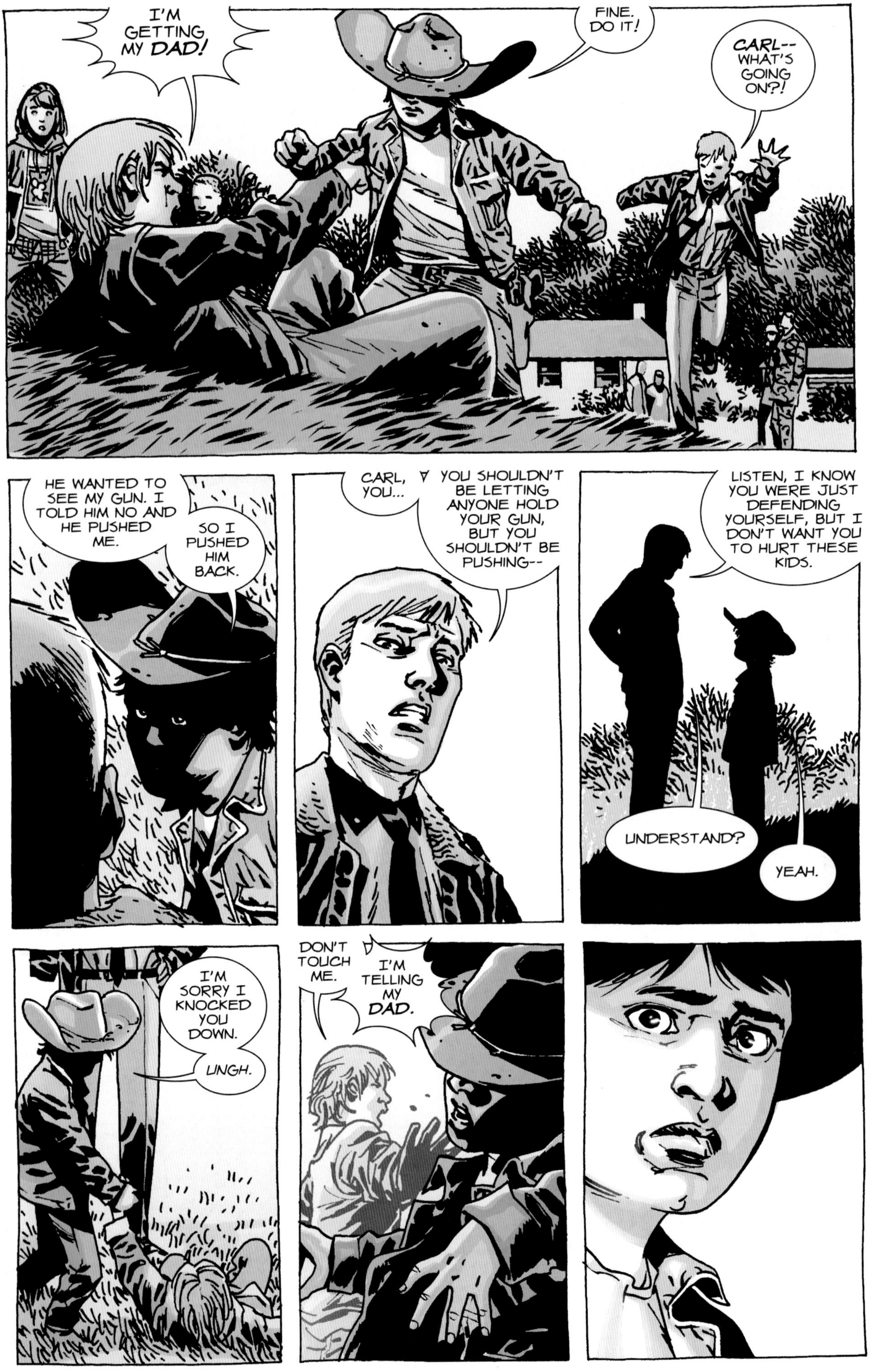
I'M GETTING MY DAD!
FINE. DO IT!
CARL-- WHAT'S GOING ON?!
HE WANTED TO SEE MY GUN. I TOLD HIM NO AND HE PUSHED ME.
SO I PUSHED HIM BACK.
CARL, YOU...
YOU SHOULDN'T BE LETTING ANYONE HOLD YOUR GUN, BUT YOU SHOULDN'T BE PUSHING--
LISTEN, I KNOW YOU WERE JUST DEFENDING YOURSELF, BUT I DON'T WANT YOU TO HURT THESE KIDS.
UNDERSTAND?
YEAH.
I'M SORRY I KNOCKED YOU DOWN.
UNGH.
DON'T TOUCH ME.
I'M TELLING MY DAD.

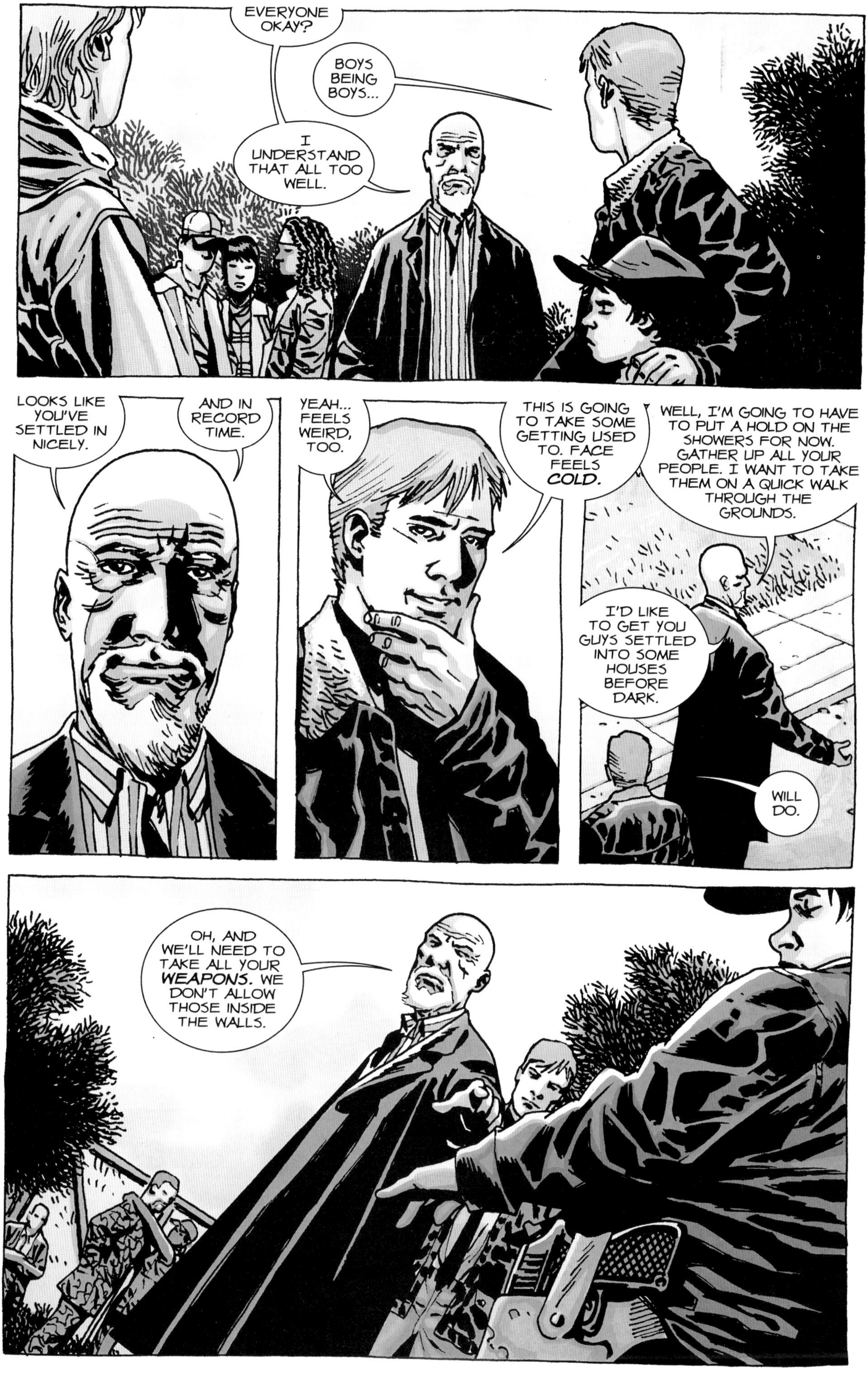
EVERYONE OKAY?
BOYS BEING BOYS...
I UNDERSTAND THAT ALL TOO WELL.
LOOKS LIKE YOU'VE SETTLED IN NICELY.
AND IN RECORD TIME.
YEAH... FEELS WEIRD, TOO.
THIS IS GOING TO TAKE SOME GETTING USED TO. FACE FEELS COLD.
WELL, I'M GOING TO HAVE TO PUT A HOLD ON THE SHOWERS FOR NOW. GATHER UP ALL YOUR PEOPLE. I WANT TO TAKE THEM ON A QUICK WALK THROUGH THE GROUNDS.
I'D LIKE TO GET YOU GUYS SETTLED INTO SOME HOUSES BEFORE DARK.
WILL DO.
OH, AND WE'LL NEED TO TAKE ALL YOUR WEAPONS. WE DON'T ALLOW THOSE INSIDE THE WALLS.

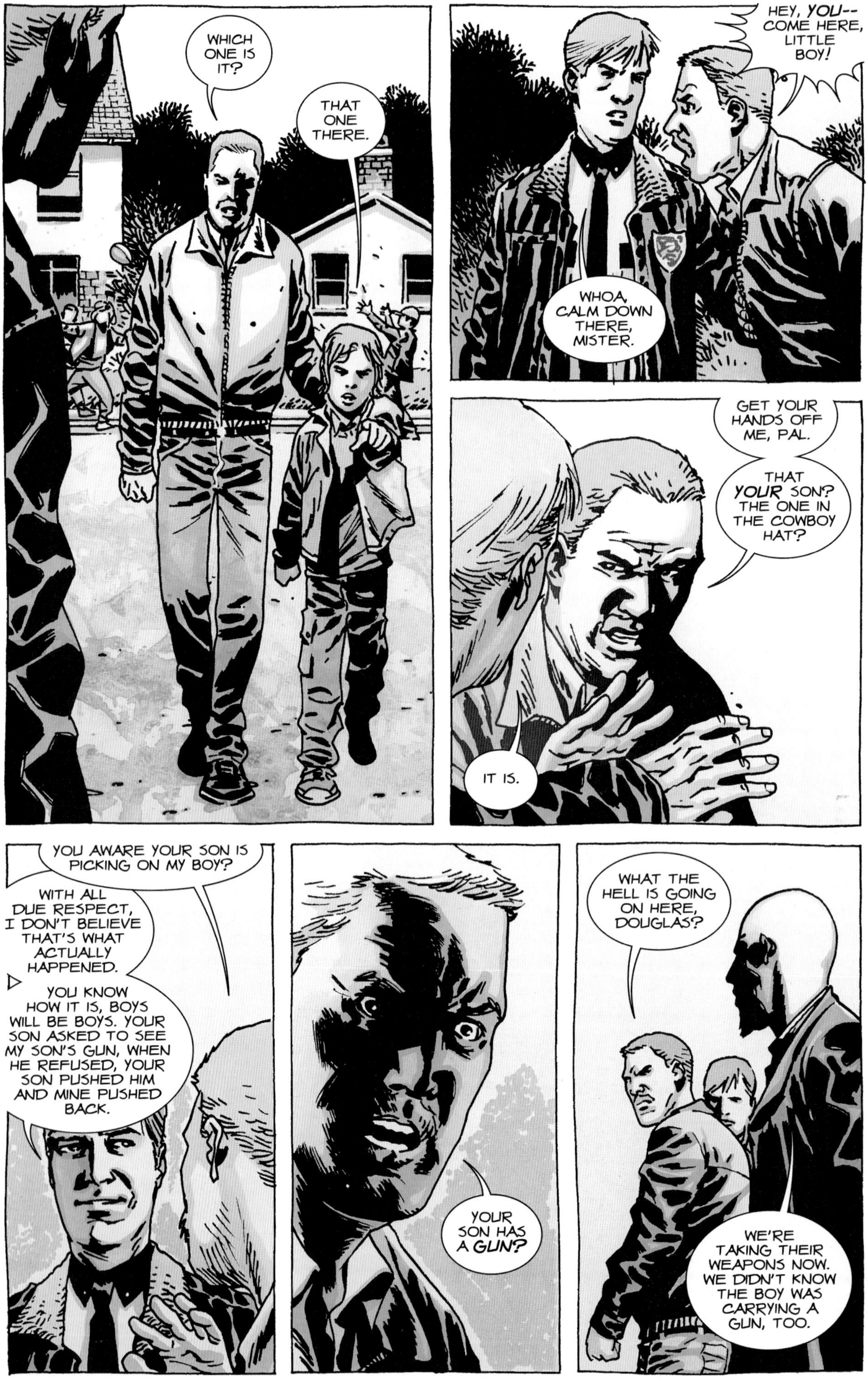

WHICH ONE IS IT?
THAT ONE THERE.
HEY, YOU-- COME HERE, LITTLE BOY!
WHOA, CALM DOWN THERE, MISTER.
GET YOUR HANDS OFF ME, PAL.
THAT YOUR SON? THE ONE IN THE COWBOY HAT?
IT IS.
YOU AWARE YOUR SON IS PICKING ON MY BOY?
WITH ALL DUE RESPECT, I DON'T BELIEVE THAT'S WHAT ACTUALLY HAPPENED.
YOU KNOW HOW IT IS, BOYS WILL BE BOYS. YOUR SON ASKED TO SEE MY SON'S GUN, WHEN HE REFUSED, YOUR SON PUSHED HIM AND MINE PUSHED BACK.
YOUR SON HAS A GUN?
WHAT THE HELL IS GOING ON HERE, DOUGLAS?
WE'RE TAKING THEIR WEAPONS NOW. WE DIDN'T KNOW THE BOY WAS CARRYING A GUN, TOO.

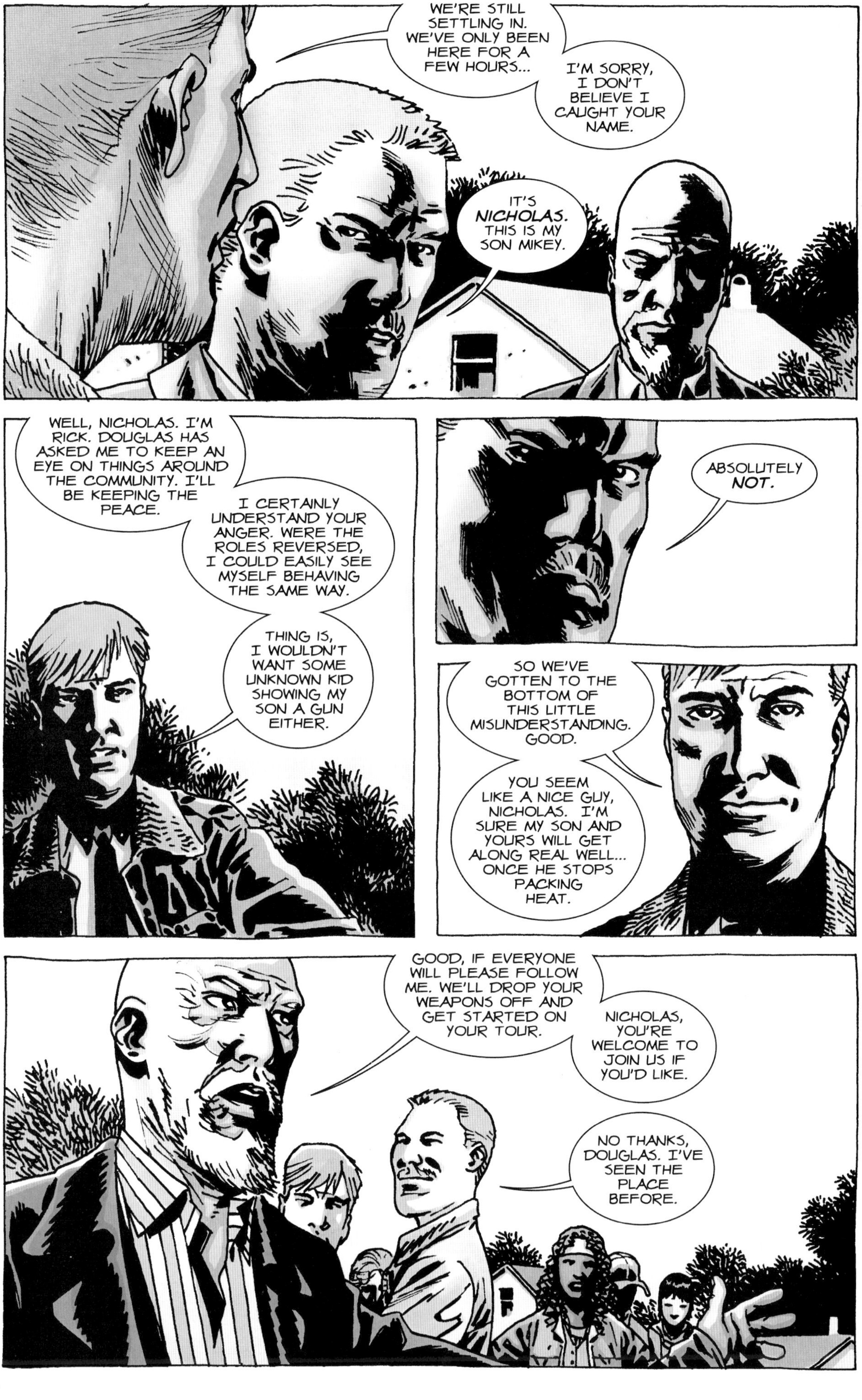
WE'RE STILL SETTLING IN. WE'VE ONLY BEEN HERE FOR A FEW HOURS...
I'M SORRY, I DON'T BELIEVE I CAUGHT YOUR NAME.
IT'S NICHOLAS. THIS IS MY SON MIKEY.
WELL, NICHOLAS. I'M RICK. DOUGLAS HAS ASKED ME TO KEEP AN EYE ON THINGS AROUND THE COMMUNITY. I'LL BE KEEPING THE PEACE.
I CERTAINLY UNDERSTAND YOUR ANGER. WERE THE ROLES REVERSED, I COULD EASILY SEE MYSELF BEHAVING THE SAME WAY.
THING IS, I WOULDN'T WANT SOME UNKNOWN KID SHOWING MY SON A GUN EITHER.
ABSOLUTELY NOT.
SO WE'VE GOTTEN TO THE BOTTOM OF THIS LITTLE MISUNDERSTANDING. GOOD.
YOU SEEM LIKE A NICE GUY, NICHOLAS. I'M SURE MY SON AND YOURS WILL GET ALONG REAL WELL... ONCE HE STOPS PACKING HEAT.
GOOD, IF EVERYONE WILL PLEASE FOLLOW ME. WE'LL DROP YOUR WEAPONS OFF AND GET STARTED ON YOUR TOUR.
NICHOLAS, YOU'RE WELCOME TO JOIN US IF YOU'D LIKE.
NO THANKS, DOUGLAS. I'VE SEEN THE PLACE BEFORE.

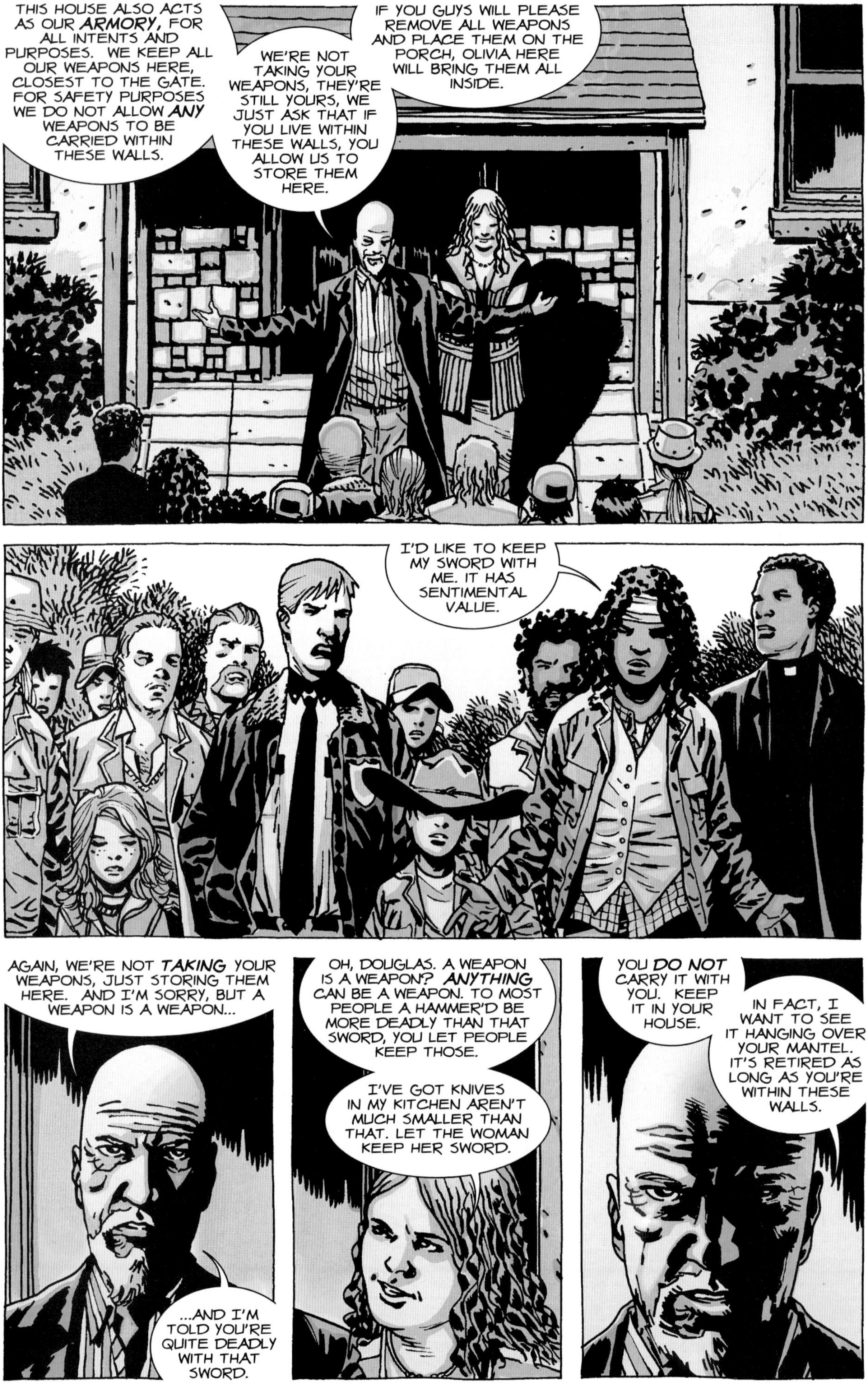
THIS HOUSE ALSO ACTS AS OUR ARMORY, FOR ALL INTENTS AND PURPOSES. WE KEEP ALL OUR WEAPONS HERE, CLOSEST TO THE GATE. FOR SAFETY PURPOSES WE DO NOT ALLOW ANY WEAPONS TO BE CARRIED WITHIN THESE WALLS.
WE'RE NOT TAKING YOUR WEAPONS, THEY'RE STILL YOURS, WE JUST ASK THAT IF YOU LIVE WITHIN THESE WALLS, YOU ALLOW US TO STORE THEM HERE.
IF YOU GUYS WILL PLEASE REMOVE ALL WEAPONS AND PLACE THEM ON THE PORCH, OLIVIA HERE WILL BRING THEM ALL INSIDE.
I'D LIKE TO KEEP MY SWORD WITH ME. IT HAS SENTIMENTAL VALUE.
AGAIN, WE'RE NOT TAKING YOUR WEAPONS, JUST STORING THEM HERE. AND I'M SORRY, BUT A WEAPON IS A WEAPON...
...AND I'M TOLD YOU'RE QUITE DEADLY WITH THAT SWORD.
OH, DOUGLAS. A WEAPON IS A WEAPON? ANYTHING CAN BE A WEAPON. TO MOST PEOPLE A HAMMER'D BE MORE DEADLY THAN THAT SWORD, YOU LET PEOPLE KEEP THOSE.
I'VE GOT KNIVES IN MY KITCHEN AREN'T MUCH SMALLER THAN THAT. LET THE WOMAN KEEP HER SWORD.
YOU DO NOT CARRY IT WITH YOU. KEEP IT IN YOUR HOUSE.
IN FACT, I WANT TO SEE IT HANGING OVER YOUR MANTEL. IT'S RETIRED AS LONG AS YOU'RE WITHIN THESE WALLS.

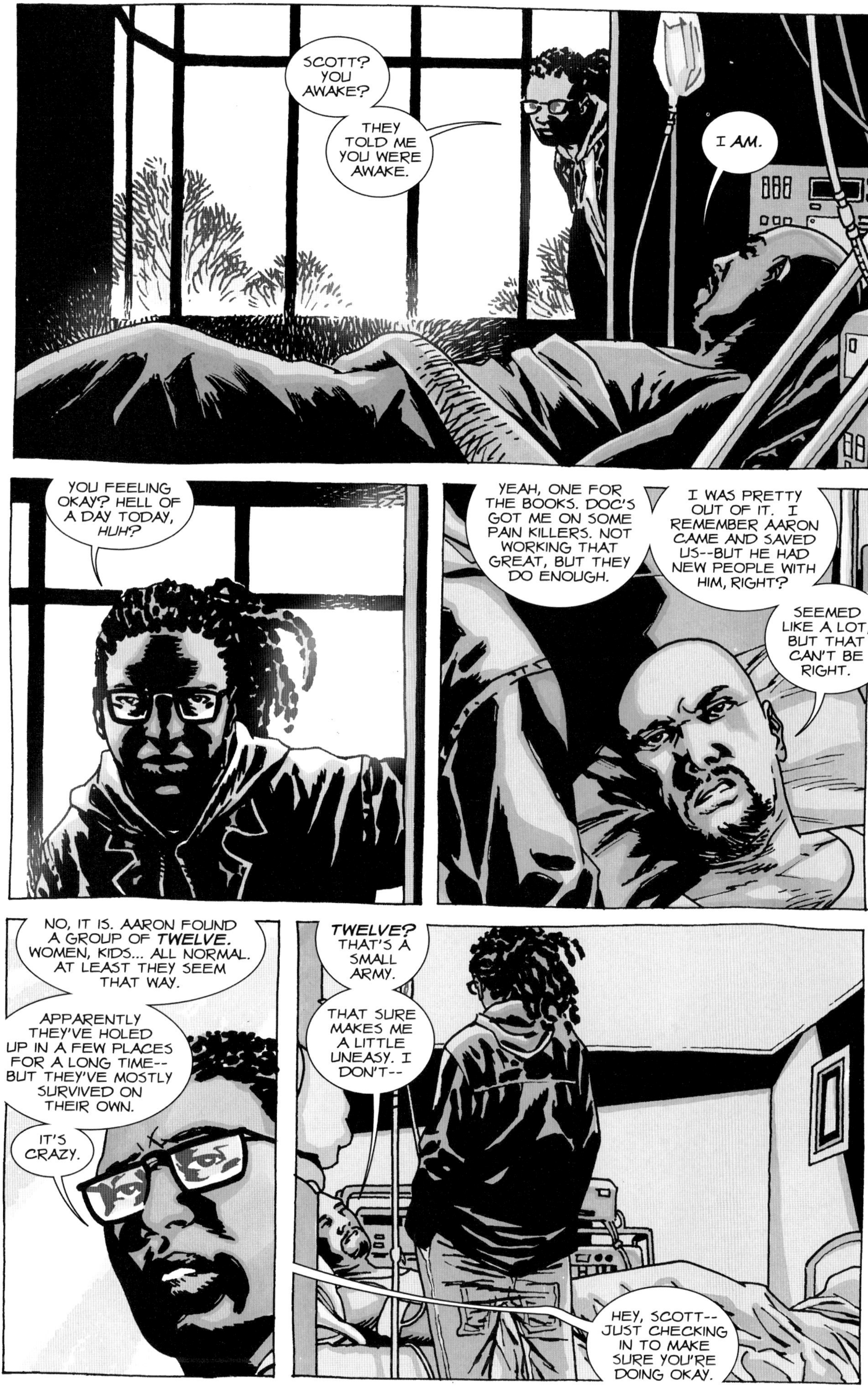
SCOTT? YOU AWAKE?
THEY TOLD ME YOU WERE AWAKE.
I *AM.*
YOU FEELING OKAY? HELL OF A DAY TODAY, *HUH?*
YEAH, ONE FOR THE BOOKS. DOC'S GOT ME ON SOME PAIN KILLERS. NOT WORKING THAT GREAT, BUT THEY DO ENOUGH.
I WAS PRETTY OUT OF IT. I REMEMBER AARON CAME AND SAVED US--BUT HE HAD NEW PEOPLE WITH HIM, RIGHT?
SEEMED LIKE A LOT, BUT THAT CAN'T BE RIGHT.
NO, IT IS. AARON FOUND A GROUP OF ***TWELVE.*** WOMEN, KIDS... ALL NORMAL. AT LEAST THEY SEEM THAT WAY.
APPARENTLY THEY'VE HOLED UP IN A FEW PLACES FOR A LONG TIME-- BUT THEY'VE MOSTLY SURVIVED ON THEIR OWN.
IT'S CRAZY.
TWELVE? THAT'S A SMALL ARMY.
THAT SURE MAKES ME A LITTLE UNEASY. I DON'T--
HEY, SCOTT-- JUST CHECKING IN TO MAKE SURE YOU'RE DOING OKAY.

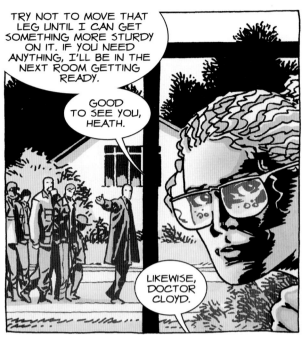

TRY NOT TO MOVE THAT LEG UNTIL I CAN GET SOMETHING MORE STURDY ON IT. IF YOU NEED ANYTHING, I'LL BE IN THE NEXT ROOM GETTING READY.

GOOD TO SEE YOU, HEATH.

LIKEWISE, DOCTOR CLOYD.

THIS HOUSE IS THE INFIRMARY. WE ACTUALLY HAVE THREE DOCTORS HERE IN THE COMMUNITY, ONE A SURGEON.

THANKS TO HEATH AND THE OTHER RUNNERS, WE HAVE SOME STATE OF THE ART EQUIPMENT. IT'S QUITE NICE.

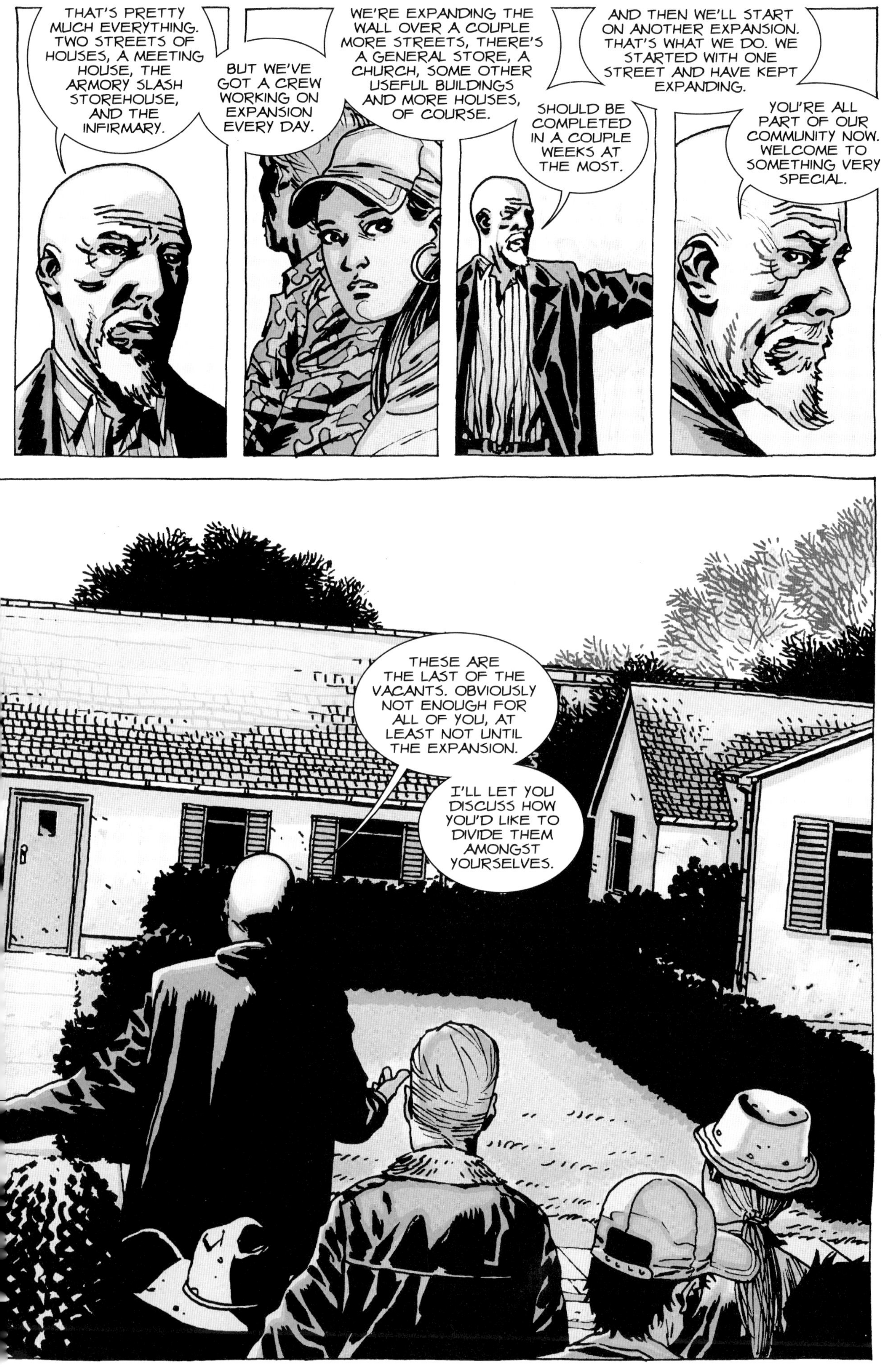
THAT'S PRETTY MUCH EVERYTHING. TWO STREETS OF HOUSES, A MEETING HOUSE, THE ARMORY SLASH STOREHOUSE, AND THE INFIRMARY.
BUT WE'VE GOT A CREW WORKING ON EXPANSION EVERY DAY.
WE'RE EXPANDING THE WALL OVER A COUPLE MORE STREETS, THERE'S A GENERAL STORE, A CHURCH, SOME OTHER USEFUL BUILDINGS AND MORE HOUSES, OF COURSE.
SHOULD BE COMPLETED IN A COUPLE WEEKS AT THE MOST.
AND THEN WE'LL START ON ANOTHER EXPANSION. THAT'S WHAT WE DO. WE STARTED WITH ONE STREET AND HAVE KEPT EXPANDING.
YOU'RE ALL PART OF OUR COMMUNITY NOW. WELCOME TO SOMETHING VERY SPECIAL.
THESE ARE THE LAST OF THE VACANTS. OBVIOUSLY NOT ENOUGH FOR ALL OF YOU, AT LEAST NOT UNTIL THE EXPANSION.
I'LL LET YOU DISCUSS HOW YOU'D LIKE TO DIVIDE THEM AMONGST YOURSELVES.

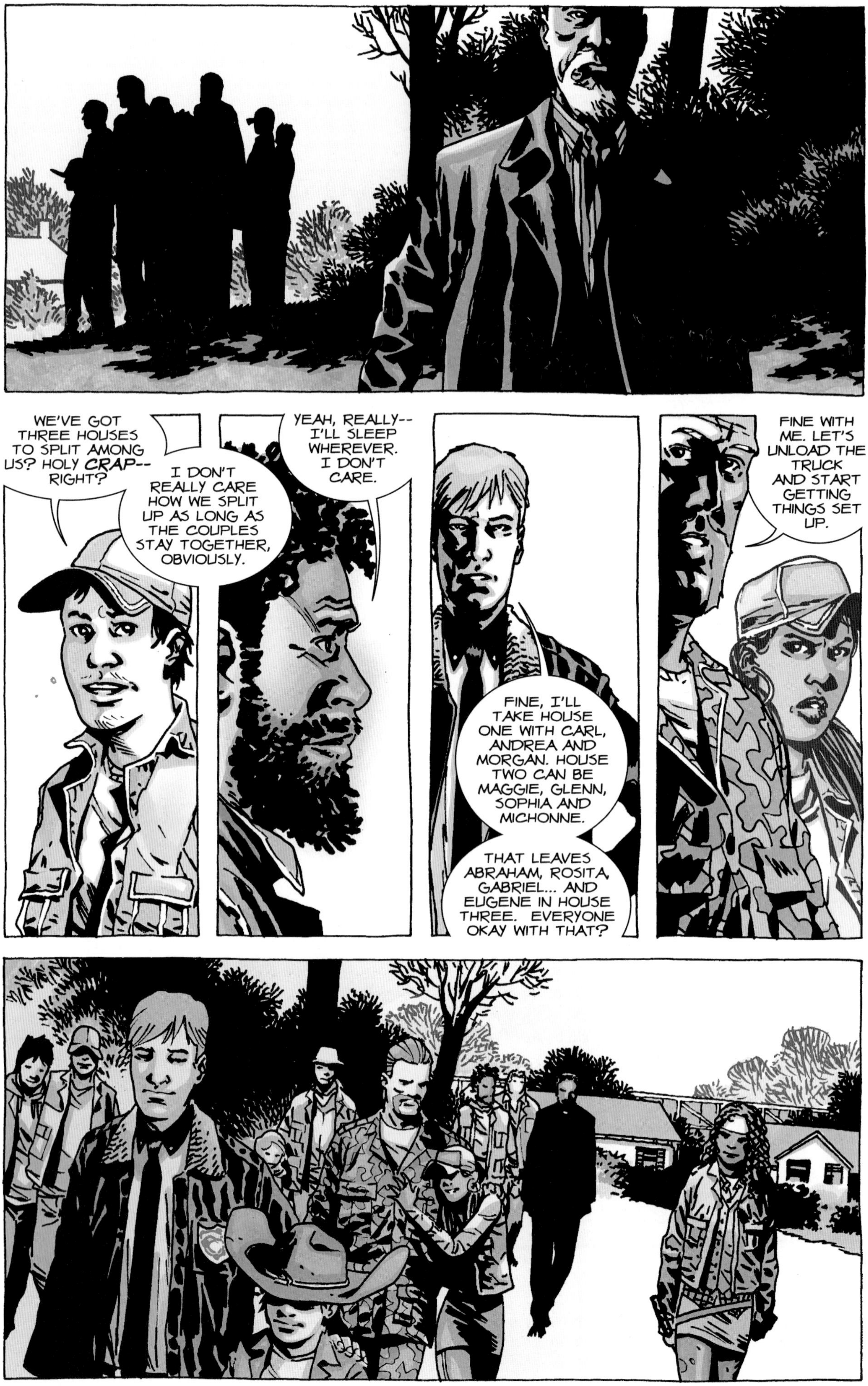

WE'VE GOT THREE HOUSES TO SPLIT AMONG US? HOLY CRAP-- RIGHT?
I DON'T REALLY CARE HOW WE SPLIT UP AS LONG AS THE COUPLES STAY TOGETHER, OBVIOUSLY.
YEAH, REALLY-- I'LL SLEEP WHEREVER. I DON'T CARE.
FINE, I'LL TAKE HOUSE ONE WITH CARL, ANDREA AND MORGAN. HOUSE TWO CAN BE MAGGIE, GLENN, SOPHIA AND MICHONNE.
THAT LEAVES ABRAHAM, ROSITA, GABRIEL... AND EUGENE IN HOUSE THREE. EVERYONE OKAY WITH THAT?
FINE WITH ME. LET'S UNLOAD THE TRUCK AND START GETTING THINGS SET UP.

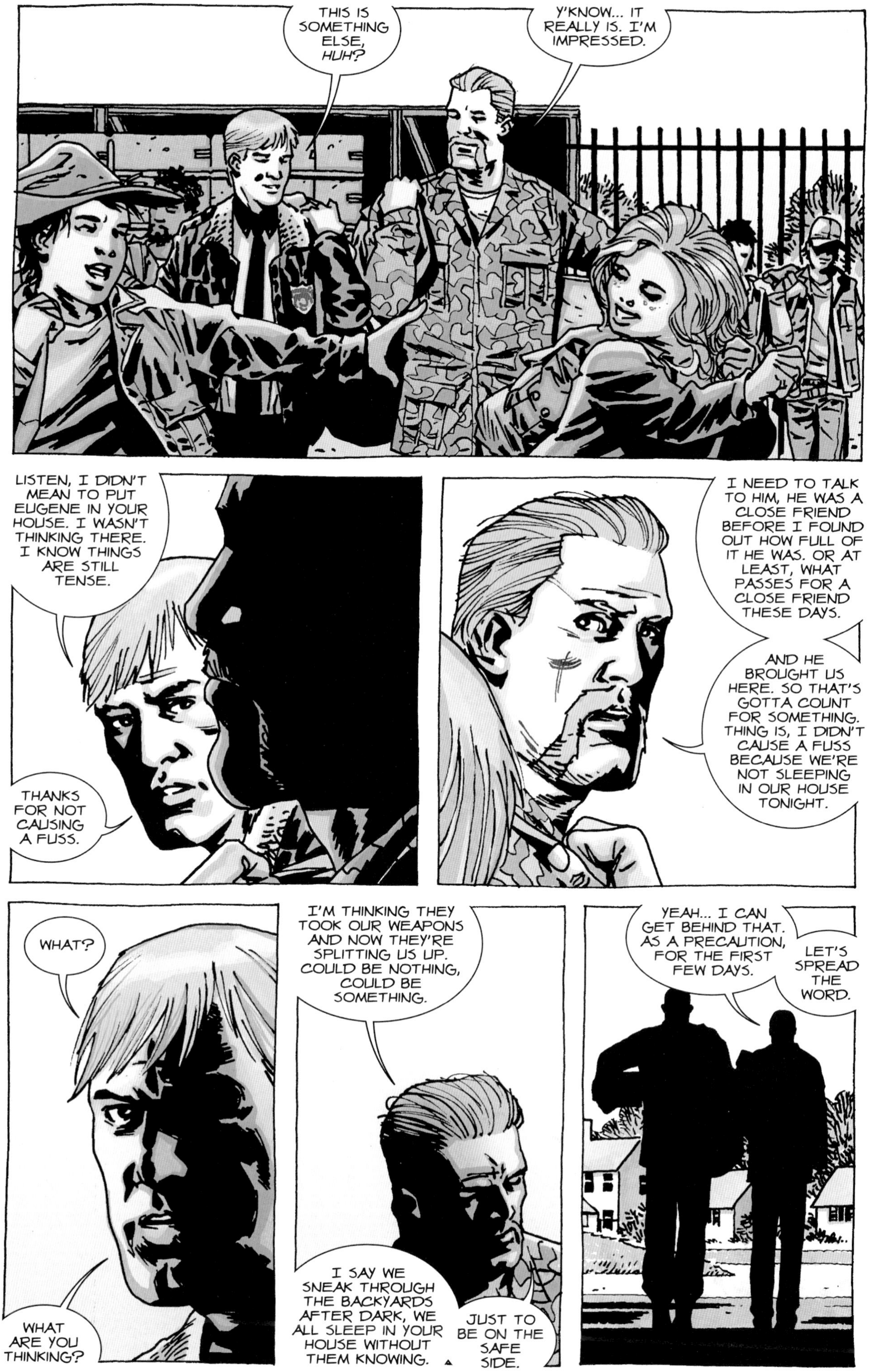
THIS IS SOMETHING ELSE, HUH?
Y'KNOW... IT REALLY IS. I'M IMPRESSED.
LISTEN, I DIDN'T MEAN TO PUT EUGENE IN YOUR HOUSE. I WASN'T THINKING THERE. I KNOW THINGS ARE STILL TENSE.
THANKS FOR NOT CAUSING A FUSS.
I NEED TO TALK TO HIM, HE WAS A CLOSE FRIEND BEFORE I FOUND OUT HOW FULL OF IT HE WAS. OR AT LEAST, WHAT PASSES FOR A CLOSE FRIEND THESE DAYS.
AND HE BROUGHT US HERE. SO THAT'S GOTTA COUNT FOR SOMETHING. THING IS, I DIDN'T CAUSE A FUSS BECAUSE WE'RE NOT SLEEPING IN OUR HOUSE TONIGHT.
WHAT?
WHAT ARE YOU THINKING?
I'M THINKING THEY TOOK OUR WEAPONS AND NOW THEY'RE SPLITTING US UP. COULD BE NOTHING, COULD BE SOMETHING.
I SAY WE SNEAK THROUGH THE BACKYARDS AFTER DARK, WE ALL SLEEP IN YOUR HOUSE WITHOUT THEM KNOWING.
JUST TO BE ON THE SAFE SIDE.
YEAH... I CAN GET BEHIND THAT. AS A PRECAUTION, FOR THE FIRST FEW DAYS.
LET'S SPREAD THE WORD.

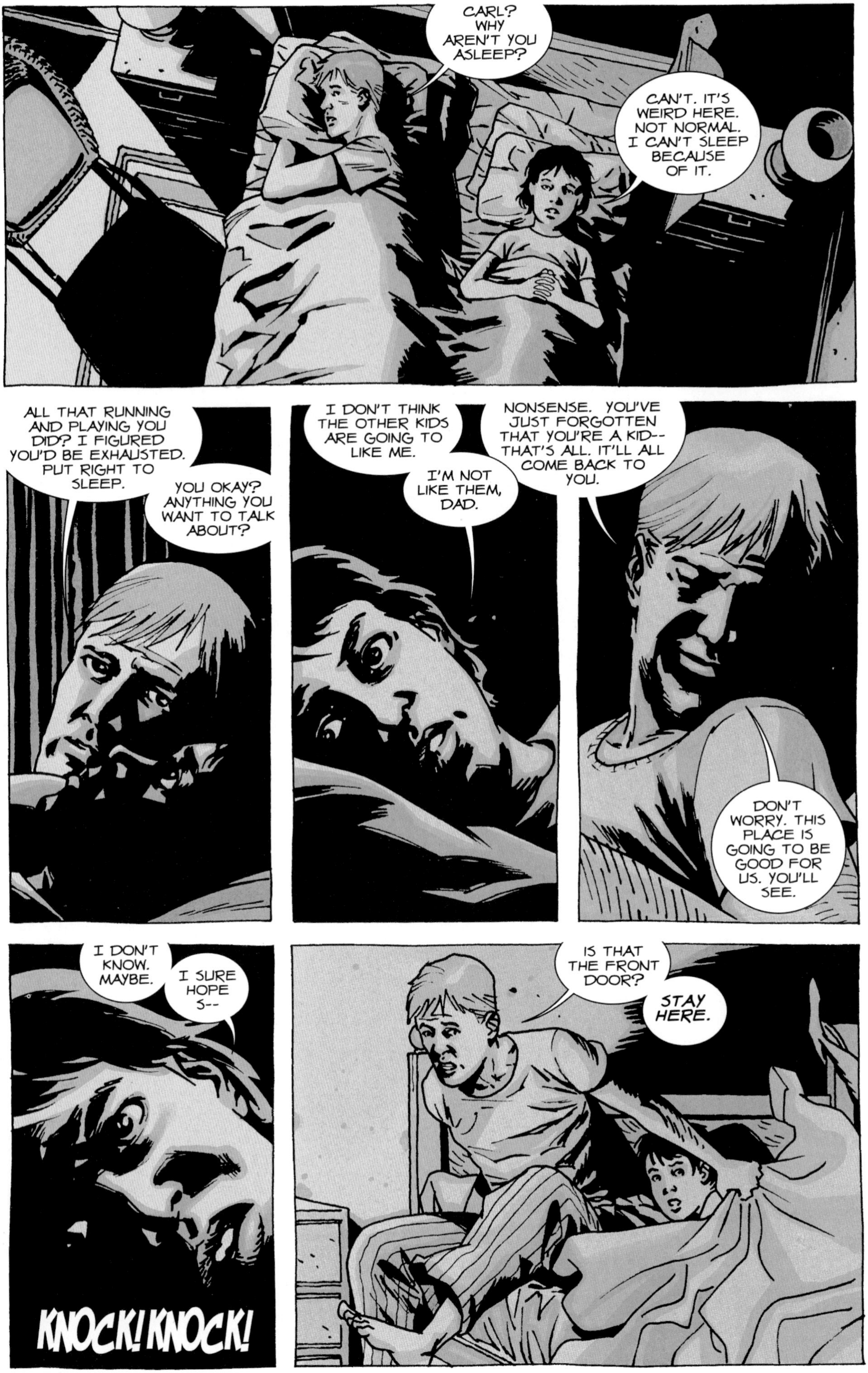
CARL? WHY AREN'T YOU ASLEEP?
CAN'T. IT'S WEIRD HERE. NOT NORMAL. I CAN'T SLEEP BECAUSE OF IT.
ALL THAT RUNNING AND PLAYING YOU DID? I FIGURED YOU'D BE EXHAUSTED. PUT RIGHT TO SLEEP.
YOU OKAY? ANYTHING YOU WANT TO TALK ABOUT?
I DON'T THINK THE OTHER KIDS ARE GOING TO LIKE ME.
I'M NOT LIKE THEM, DAD.
NONSENSE. YOU'VE JUST FORGOTTEN THAT YOU'RE A KID-- THAT'S ALL. IT'LL ALL COME BACK TO YOU.
DON'T WORRY. THIS PLACE IS GOING TO BE GOOD FOR US. YOU'LL SEE.
I DON'T KNOW. MAYBE.
I SURE HOPE S--
KNOCK! KNOCK!
IS THAT THE FRONT DOOR?
STAY HERE.

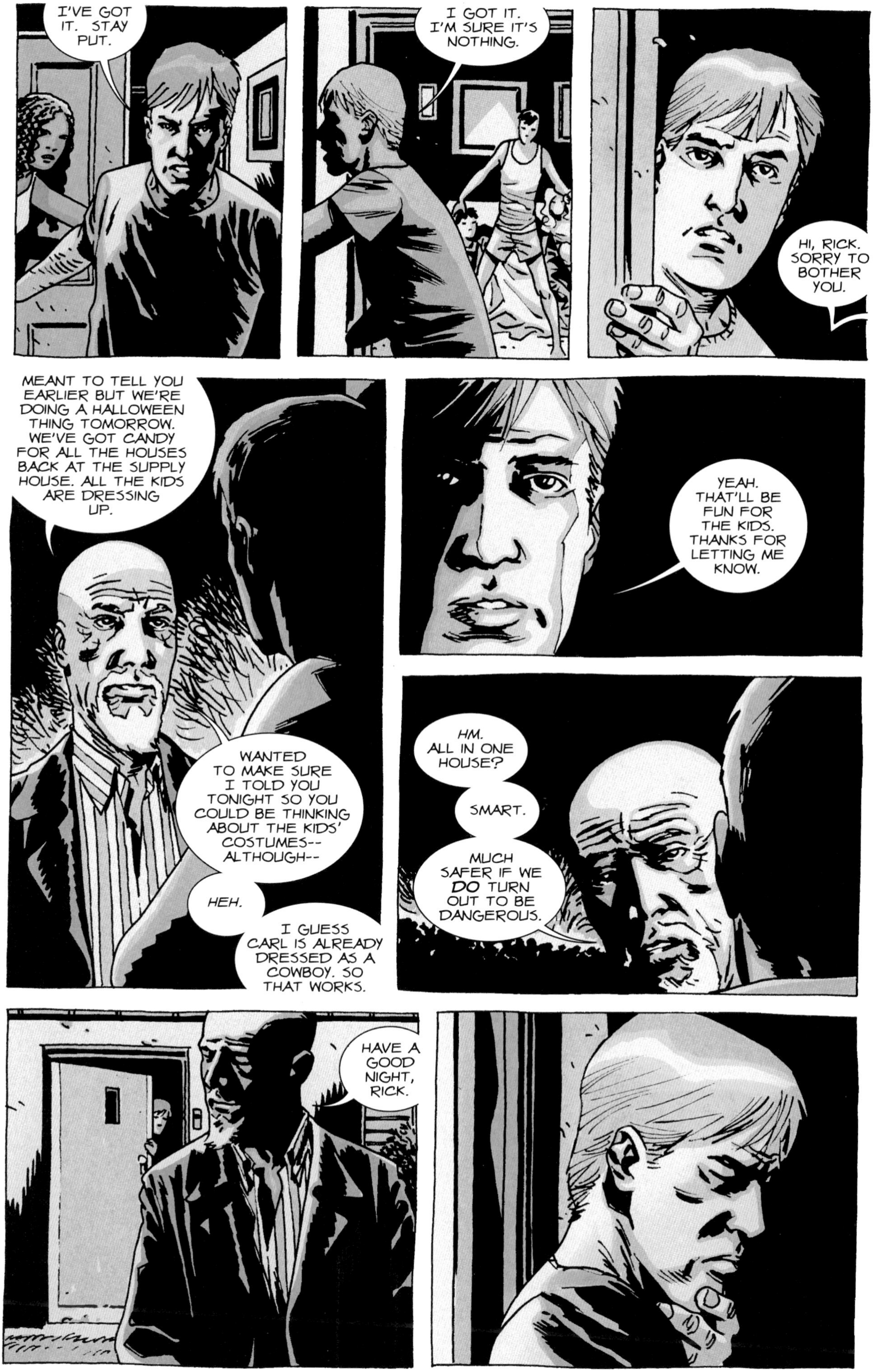
I'VE GOT IT. STAY PUT.
I GOT IT. I'M SURE IT'S NOTHING.
HI, RICK. SORRY TO BOTHER YOU.
MEANT TO TELL YOU EARLIER BUT WE'RE DOING A HALLOWEEN THING TOMORROW. WE'VE GOT CANDY FOR ALL THE HOUSES BACK AT THE SUPPLY HOUSE. ALL THE KIDS ARE DRESSING UP.
WANTED TO MAKE SURE I TOLD YOU TONIGHT SO YOU COULD BE THINKING ABOUT THE KIDS' COSTUMES-- ALTHOUGH--
HEH.
I GUESS CARL IS ALREADY DRESSED AS A COWBOY. SO THAT WORKS.
YEAH. THAT'LL BE FUN FOR THE KIDS. THANKS FOR LETTING ME KNOW.
HM. ALL IN ONE HOUSE?
SMART.
MUCH SAFER IF WE DO TURN OUT TO BE DANGEROUS.
HAVE A GOOD NIGHT, RICK.

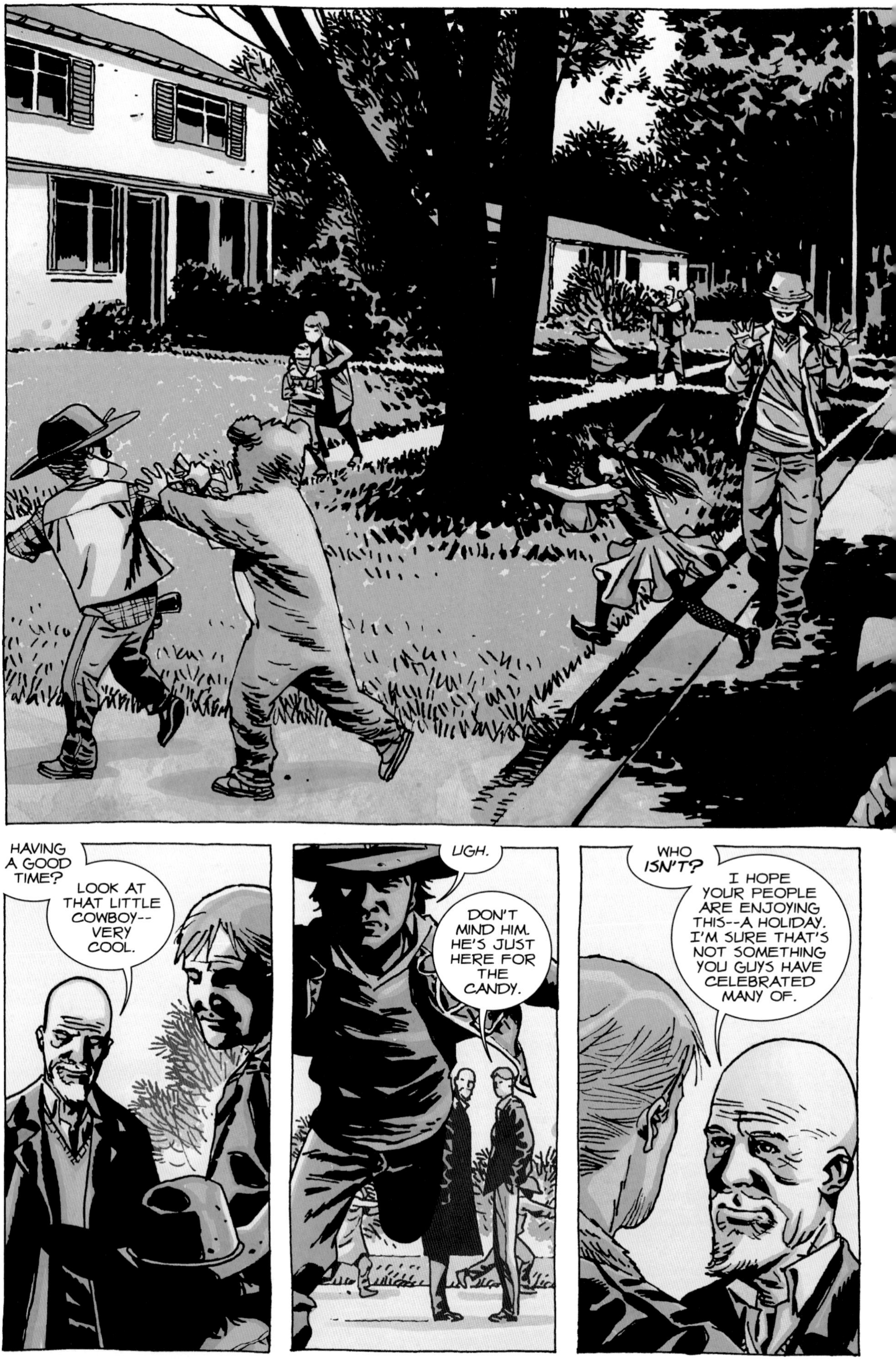
HAVING A GOOD TIME?
LOOK AT THAT LITTLE COWBOY-- VERY COOL.
UGH.
DON'T MIND HIM. HE'S JUST HERE FOR THE CANDY.
WHO *ISN'T?*
I HOPE YOUR PEOPLE ARE ENJOYING THIS--A HOLIDAY. I'M SURE THAT'S NOT SOMETHING YOU GUYS HAVE CELEBRATED MANY OF.

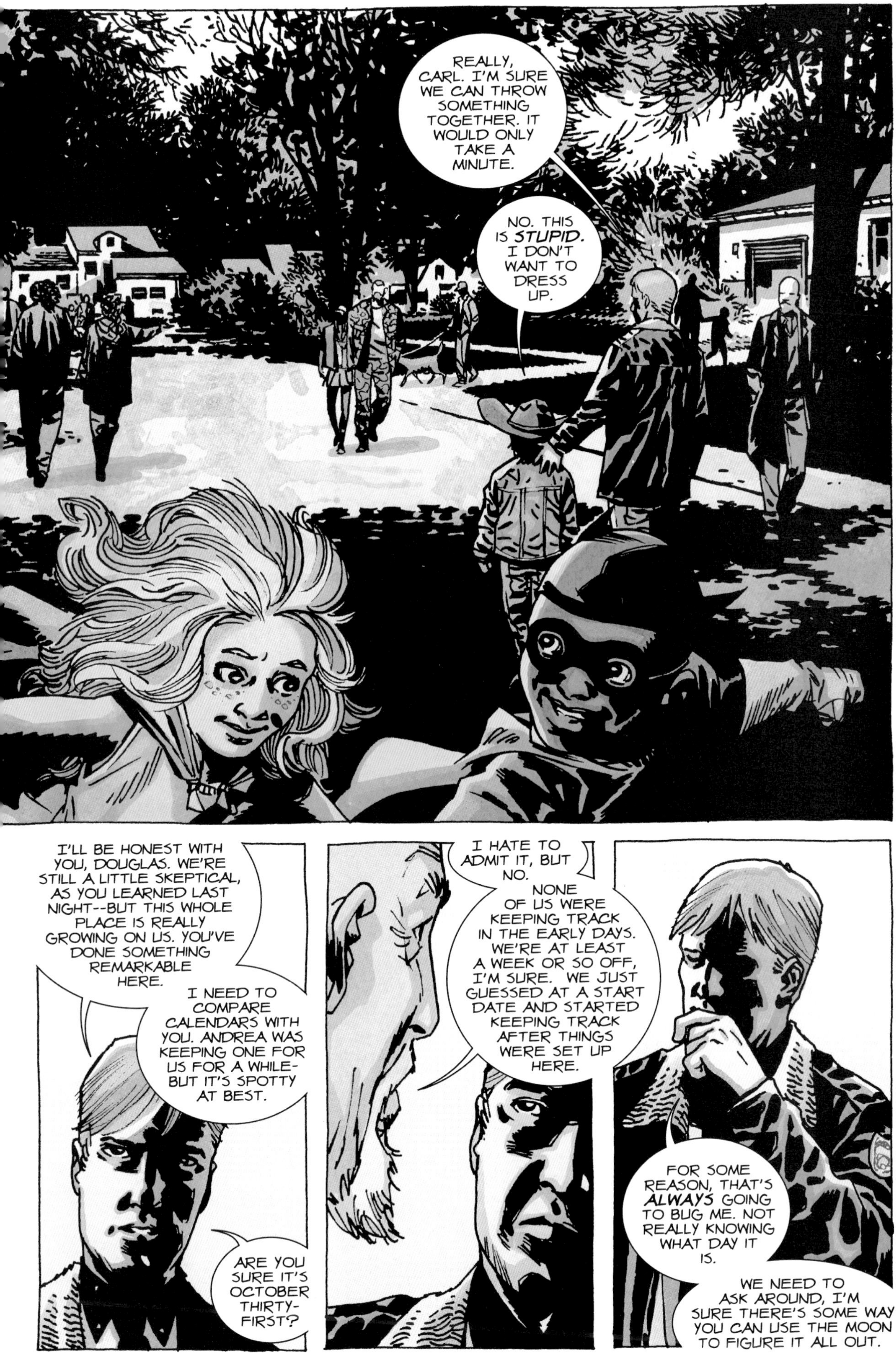
REALLY, CARL. I'M SURE WE CAN THROW SOMETHING TOGETHER. IT WOULD ONLY TAKE A MINUTE.
NO. THIS IS *STUPID.* I DON'T WANT TO DRESS UP.
I'LL BE HONEST WITH YOU, DOUGLAS. WE'RE STILL A LITTLE SKEPTICAL, AS YOU LEARNED LAST NIGHT--BUT THIS WHOLE PLACE IS REALLY GROWING ON US. YOU'VE DONE SOMETHING REMARKABLE HERE.
I NEED TO COMPARE CALENDARS WITH YOU. ANDREA WAS KEEPING ONE FOR US FOR A WHILE-BUT IT'S SPOTTY AT BEST.
ARE YOU SURE IT'S OCTOBER THIRTY-FIRST?
I HATE TO ADMIT IT, BUT NO.
NONE OF US WERE KEEPING TRACK IN THE EARLY DAYS. WE'RE AT LEAST A WEEK OR SO OFF, I'M SURE. WE JUST GUESSED AT A START DATE AND STARTED KEEPING TRACK AFTER THINGS WERE SET UP HERE.
FOR SOME REASON, THAT'S *ALWAYS* GOING TO BUG ME. NOT REALLY KNOWING WHAT DAY IT IS.
WE NEED TO ASK AROUND, I'M SURE THERE'S SOME WAY YOU CAN USE THE MOON TO FIGURE IT ALL OUT.

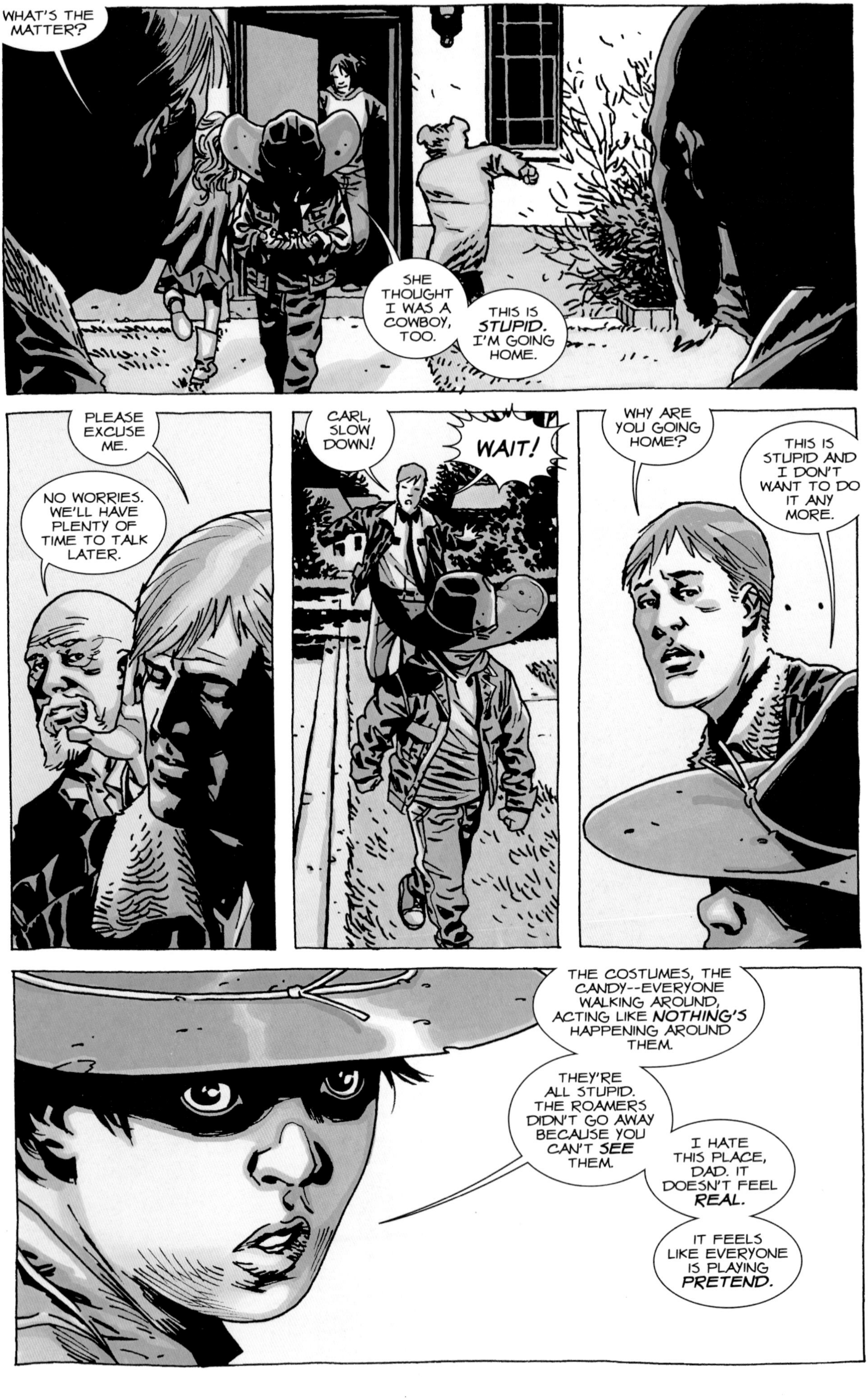
WHAT'S THE MATTER?
SHE THOUGHT I WAS A COWBOY, TOO.
THIS IS STUPID. I'M GOING HOME.
PLEASE EXCUSE ME.
NO WORRIES. WE'LL HAVE PLENTY OF TIME TO TALK LATER.
CARL, SLOW DOWN!
WAIT!
WHY ARE YOU GOING HOME?
THIS IS STUPID AND I DON'T WANT TO DO IT ANY MORE.
THE COSTUMES, THE CANDY--EVERYONE WALKING AROUND, ACTING LIKE NOTHING'S HAPPENING AROUND THEM.
THEY'RE ALL STUPID. THE ROAMERS DIDN'T GO AWAY BECAUSE YOU CAN'T SEE THEM.
I HATE THIS PLACE, DAD. IT DOESN'T FEEL REAL.
IT FEELS LIKE EVERYONE IS PLAYING PRETEND.

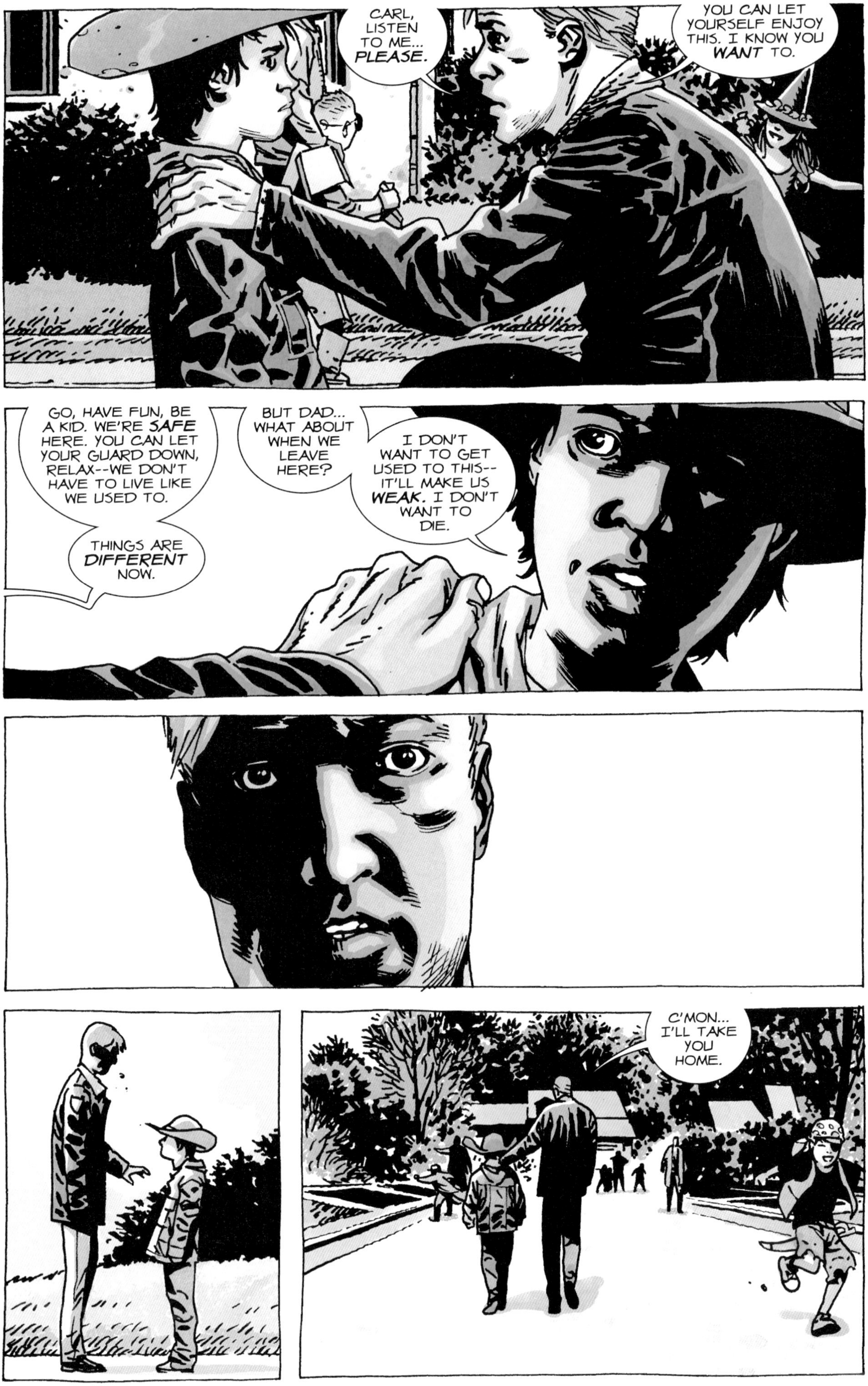
CARL, LISTEN TO ME... PLEASE.
YOU CAN LET YOURSELF ENJOY THIS. I KNOW YOU WANT TO.
GO, HAVE FUN, BE A KID. WE'RE SAFE HERE. YOU CAN LET YOUR GUARD DOWN, RELAX--WE DON'T HAVE TO LIVE LIKE WE USED TO.
THINGS ARE DIFFERENT NOW.
BUT DAD... WHAT ABOUT WHEN WE LEAVE HERE?
I DON'T WANT TO GET USED TO THIS-- IT'LL MAKE US WEAK. I DON'T WANT TO DIE.
C'MON... I'LL TAKE YOU HOME.

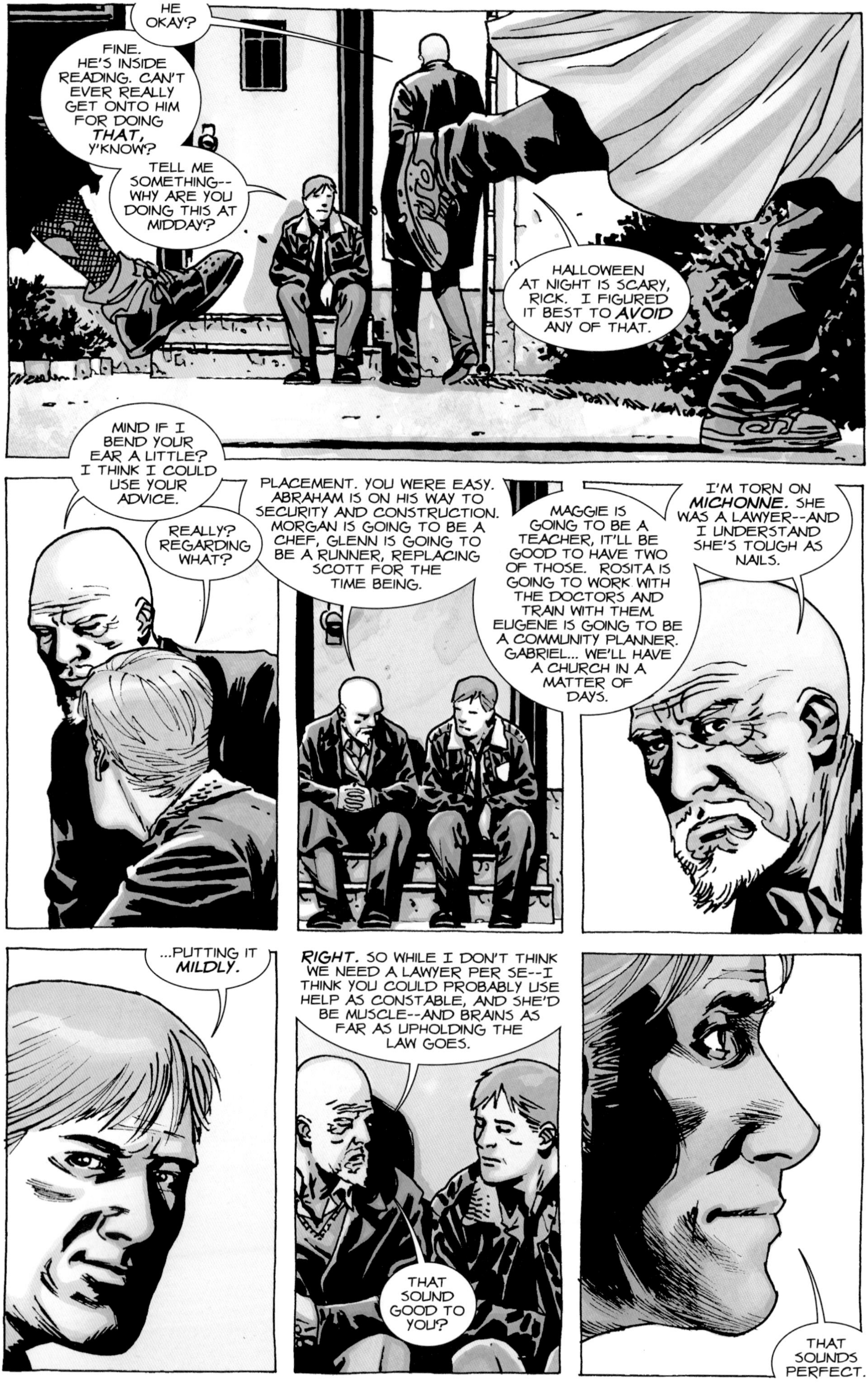

HE OKAY?
FINE. HE'S INSIDE READING. CAN'T EVER REALLY GET ONTO HIM FOR DOING *THAT,* Y'KNOW?
TELL ME SOMETHING-- WHY ARE YOU DOING THIS AT MIDDAY?
HALLOWEEN AT NIGHT IS SCARY, RICK. I FIGURED IT BEST TO *AVOID* ANY OF THAT.
MIND IF I BEND YOUR EAR A LITTLE? I THINK I COULD USE YOUR ADVICE.
REALLY? REGARDING WHAT?
PLACEMENT. YOU WERE EASY. ABRAHAM IS ON HIS WAY TO SECURITY AND CONSTRUCTION. MORGAN IS GOING TO BE A CHEF, GLENN IS GOING TO BE A RUNNER, REPLACING SCOTT FOR THE TIME BEING.
MAGGIE IS GOING TO BE A TEACHER, IT'LL BE GOOD TO HAVE TWO OF THOSE. ROSITA IS GOING TO WORK WITH THE DOCTORS AND TRAIN WITH THEM. EUGENE IS GOING TO BE A COMMUNITY PLANNER. GABRIEL... WE'LL HAVE A CHURCH IN A MATTER OF DAYS.
I'M TORN ON *MICHONNE.* SHE WAS A LAWYER--AND I UNDERSTAND SHE'S TOUGH AS NAILS.
...PUTTING IT *MILDLY.*
RIGHT. SO WHILE I DON'T THINK WE NEED A LAWYER PER SE--I THINK YOU COULD PROBABLY USE HELP AS CONSTABLE, AND SHE'D BE MUSCLE--AND BRAINS AS FAR AS UPHOLDING THE LAW GOES.
THAT SOUND GOOD TO YOU?
THAT SOUNDS PERFECT.

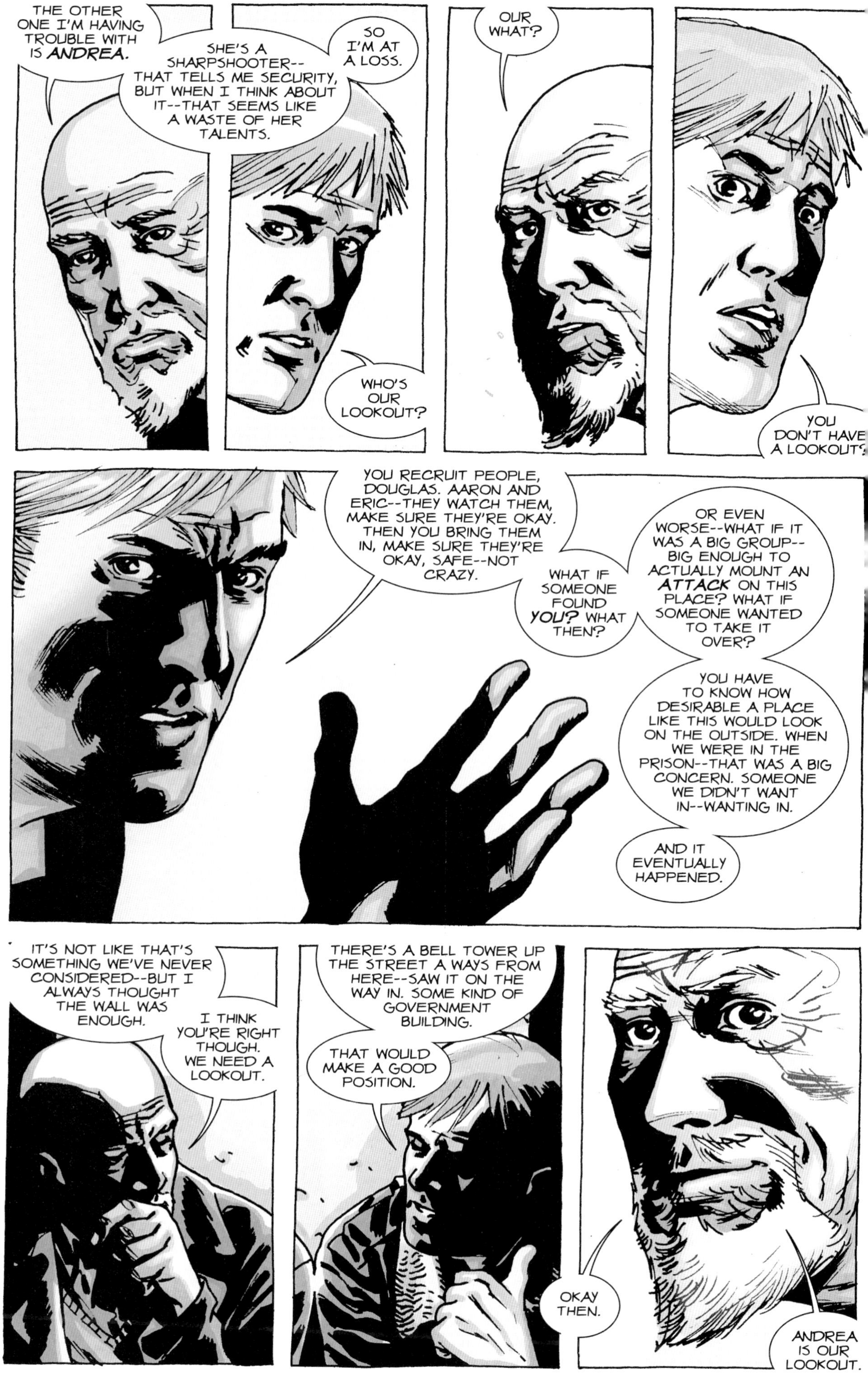
THE OTHER ONE I'M HAVING TROUBLE WITH IS ANDREA.
SHE'S A SHARPSHOOTER-- THAT TELLS ME SECURITY, BUT WHEN I THINK ABOUT IT--THAT SEEMS LIKE A WASTE OF HER TALENTS.
SO I'M AT A LOSS.
WHO'S OUR LOOKOUT?
OUR WHAT?
YOU DON'T HAVE A LOOKOUT?
YOU RECRUIT PEOPLE, DOUGLAS. AARON AND ERIC--THEY WATCH THEM, MAKE SURE THEY'RE OKAY. THEN YOU BRING THEM IN, MAKE SURE THEY'RE OKAY, SAFE--NOT CRAZY.
WHAT IF SOMEONE FOUND YOU? WHAT THEN?
OR EVEN WORSE--WHAT IF IT WAS A BIG GROUP-- BIG ENOUGH TO ACTUALLY MOUNT AN ATTACK ON THIS PLACE? WHAT IF SOMEONE WANTED TO TAKE IT OVER?
YOU HAVE TO KNOW HOW DESIRABLE A PLACE LIKE THIS WOULD LOOK ON THE OUTSIDE. WHEN WE WERE IN THE PRISON--THAT WAS A BIG CONCERN. SOMEONE WE DIDN'T WANT IN--WANTING IN.
AND IT EVENTUALLY HAPPENED.
IT'S NOT LIKE THAT'S SOMETHING WE'VE NEVER CONSIDERED--BUT I ALWAYS THOUGHT THE WALL WAS ENOUGH.
I THINK YOU'RE RIGHT THOUGH. WE NEED A LOOKOUT.
THERE'S A BELL TOWER UP THE STREET A WAYS FROM HERE--SAW IT ON THE WAY IN. SOME KIND OF GOVERNMENT BUILDING.
THAT WOULD MAKE A GOOD POSITION.
OKAY THEN.
ANDREA IS OUR LOOKOUT.

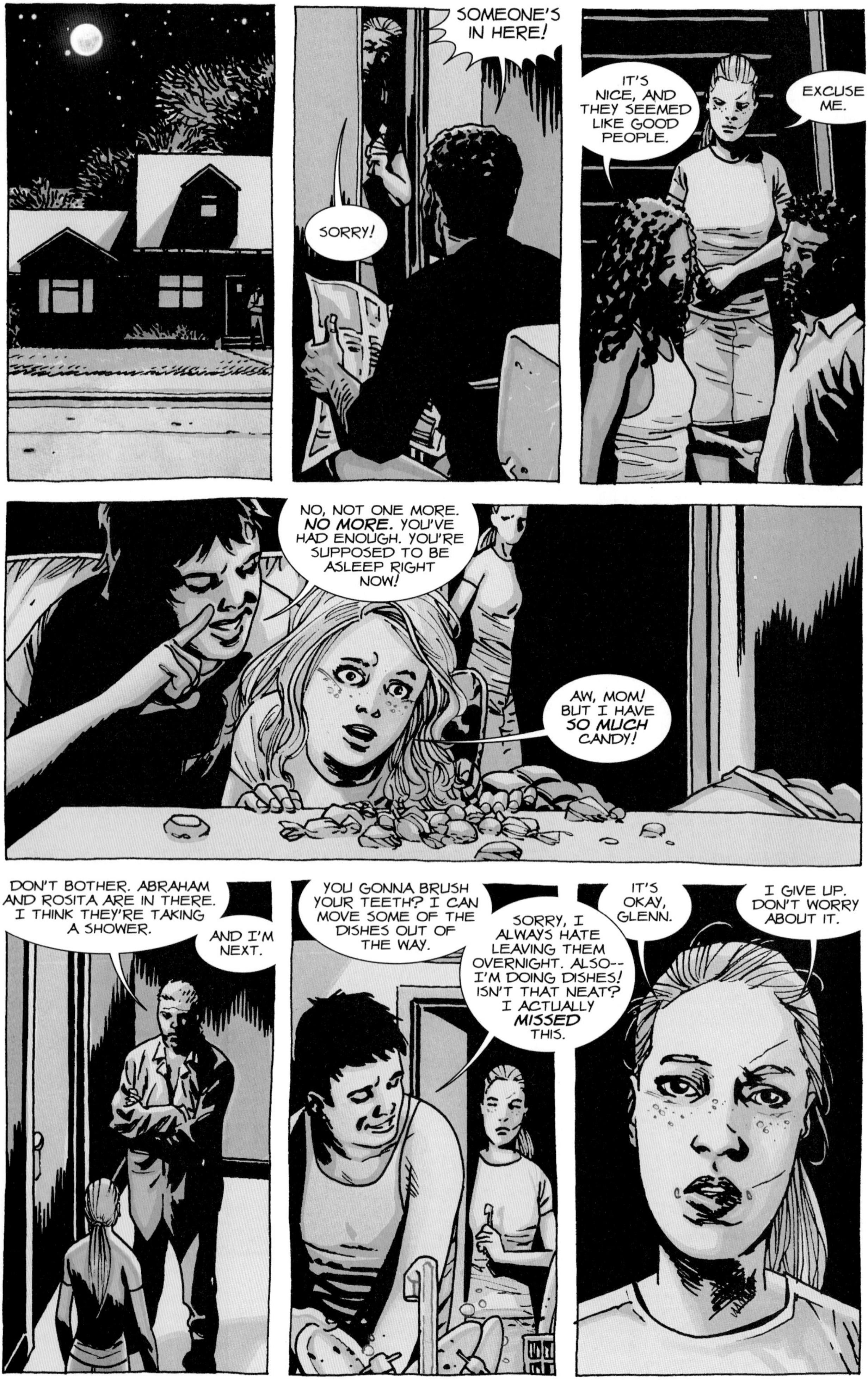
SOMEONE'S IN HERE!
SORRY!
IT'S NICE, AND THEY SEEMED LIKE GOOD PEOPLE.
EXCUSE ME.
NO, NOT ONE MORE. NO MORE. YOU'VE HAD ENOUGH. YOU'RE SUPPOSED TO BE ASLEEP RIGHT NOW!
AW, MOM! BUT I HAVE SO MUCH CANDY!
DON'T BOTHER. ABRAHAM AND ROSITA ARE IN THERE. I THINK THEY'RE TAKING A SHOWER.
AND I'M NEXT.
YOU GONNA BRUSH YOUR TEETH? I CAN MOVE SOME OF THE DISHES OUT OF THE WAY.
SORRY, I ALWAYS HATE LEAVING THEM OVERNIGHT. ALSO-- I'M DOING DISHES! ISN'T THAT NEAT? I ACTUALLY MISSED THIS.
IT'S OKAY, GLENN.
I GIVE UP. DON'T WORRY ABOUT IT.

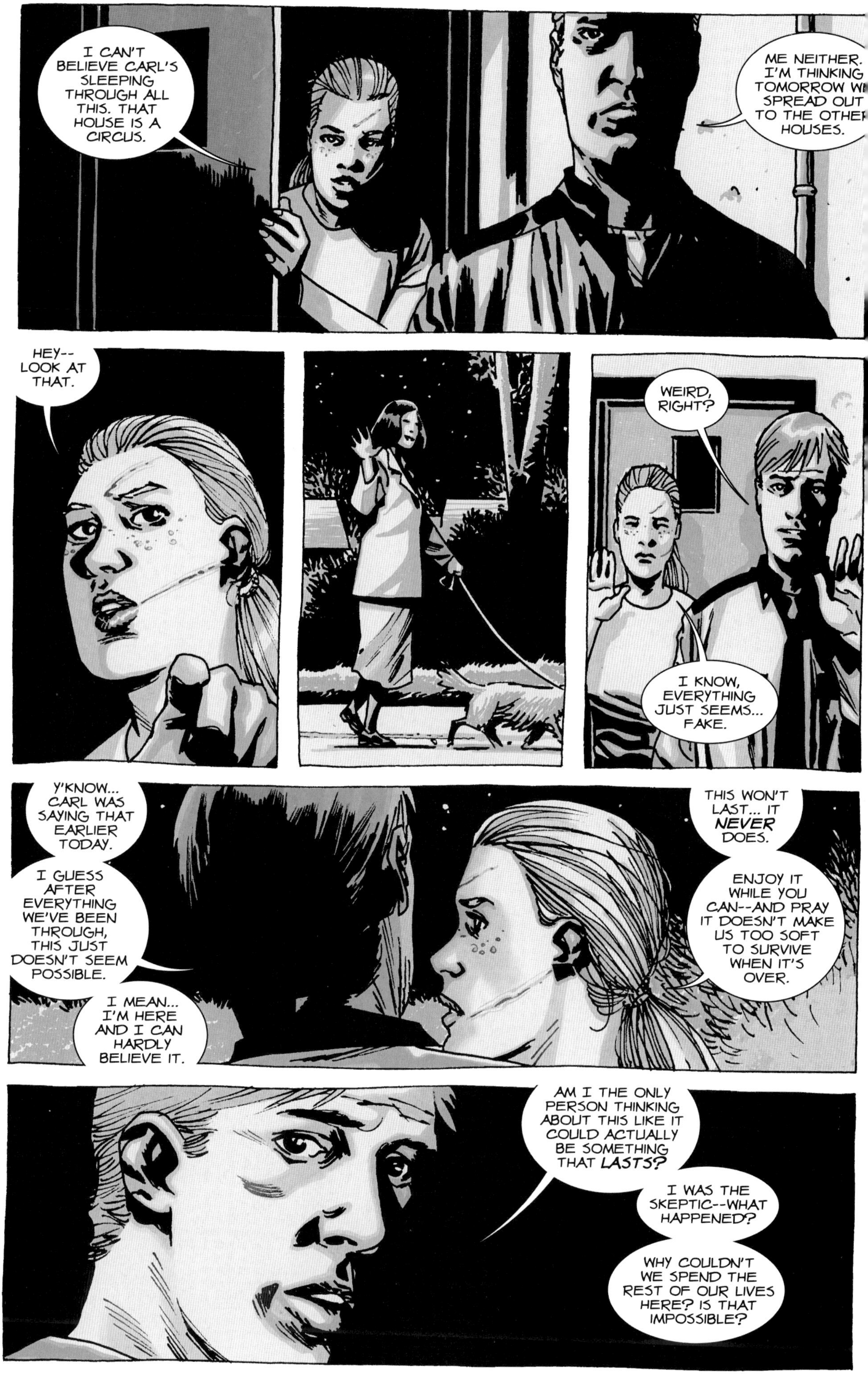
I CAN'T BELIEVE CARL'S SLEEPING THROUGH ALL THIS. THAT HOUSE IS A CIRCUS.
ME NEITHER. I'M THINKING TOMORROW WE SPREAD OUT TO THE OTHER HOUSES.
HEY-- LOOK AT THAT.
WEIRD, RIGHT?
I KNOW, EVERYTHING JUST SEEMS... FAKE.
Y'KNOW... CARL WAS SAYING THAT EARLIER TODAY.
I GUESS AFTER EVERYTHING WE'VE BEEN THROUGH, THIS JUST DOESN'T SEEM POSSIBLE.
I MEAN... I'M HERE AND I CAN HARDLY BELIEVE IT.
THIS WON'T LAST... IT *NEVER* DOES.
ENJOY IT WHILE YOU CAN--AND PRAY IT DOESN'T MAKE US TOO SOFT TO SURVIVE WHEN IT'S OVER.
AM I THE ONLY PERSON THINKING ABOUT THIS LIKE IT COULD ACTUALLY BE SOMETHING THAT *LASTS?*
I WAS THE SKEPTIC--WHAT HAPPENED?
WHY COULDN'T WE SPEND THE REST OF OUR LIVES HERE? IS THAT IMPOSSIBLE?

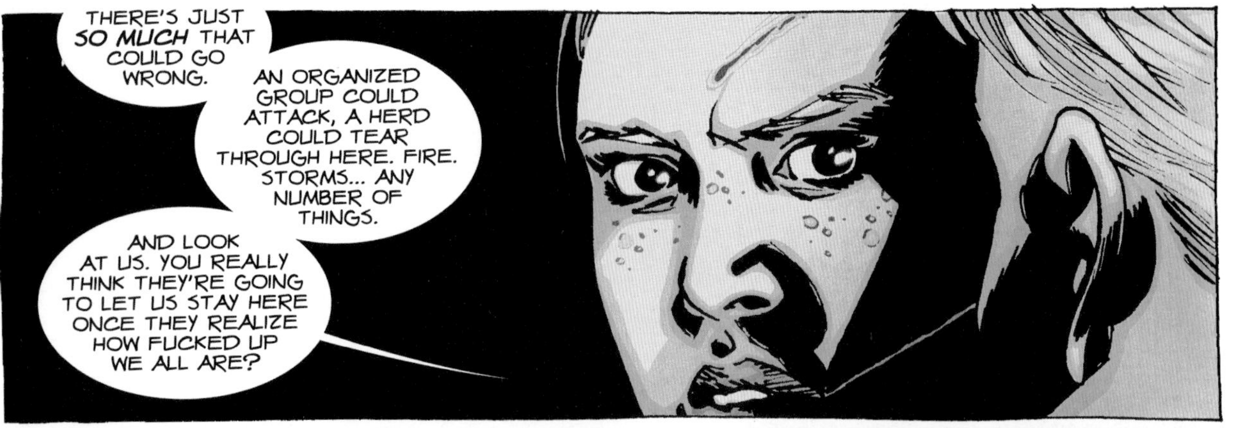
THERE'S JUST SO MUCH THAT COULD GO WRONG.
AN ORGANIZED GROUP COULD ATTACK, A HERD COULD TEAR THROUGH HERE. FIRE. STORMS... ANY NUMBER OF THINGS.
AND LOOK AT US. YOU REALLY THINK THEY'RE GOING TO LET US STAY HERE ONCE THEY REALIZE HOW FUCKED UP WE ALL ARE?

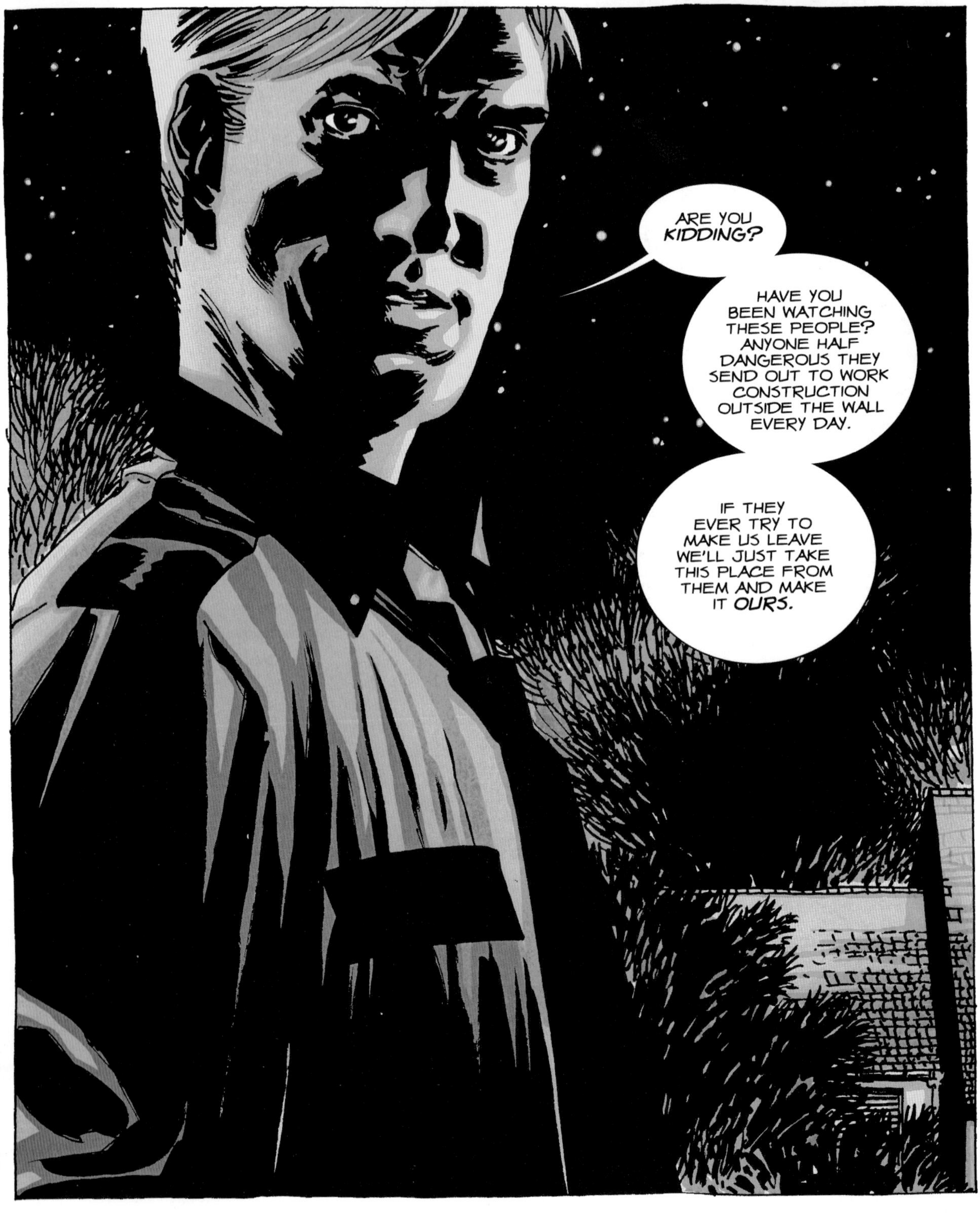
ARE YOU KIDDING?
HAVE YOU BEEN WATCHING THESE PEOPLE? ANYONE HALF DANGEROUS THEY SEND OUT TO WORK CONSTRUCTION OUTSIDE THE WALL EVERY DAY.
IF THEY EVER TRY TO MAKE US LEAVE WE'LL JUST TAKE THIS PLACE FROM THEM AND MAKE IT OURS.

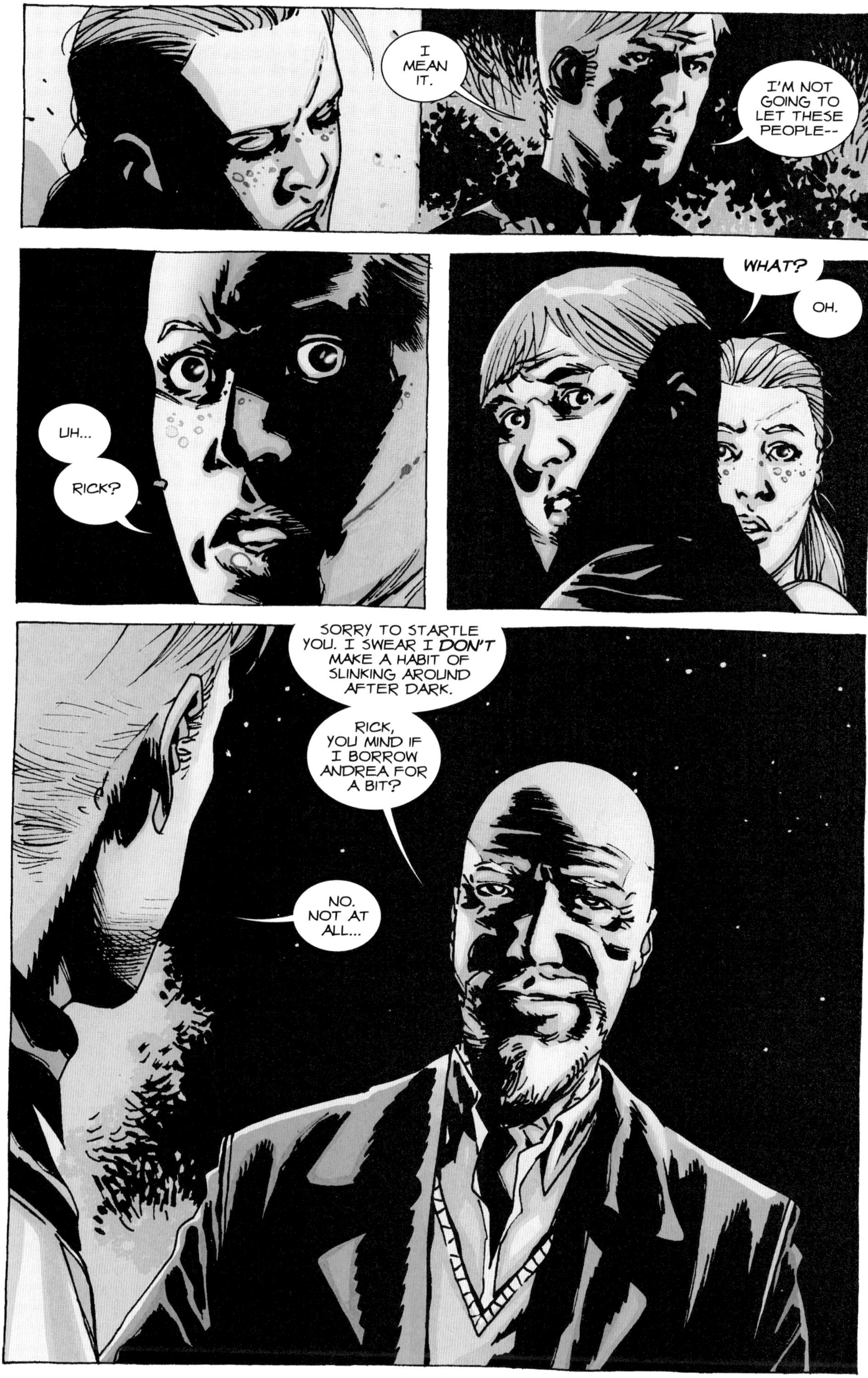
I MEAN IT.
I'M NOT GOING TO LET THESE PEOPLE--
UH...
RICK?
WHAT?
OH.
SORRY TO STARTLE YOU. I SWEAR I DON'T MAKE A HABIT OF SLINKING AROUND AFTER DARK.
RICK, YOU MIND IF I BORROW ANDREA FOR A BIT?
NO. NOT AT ALL...

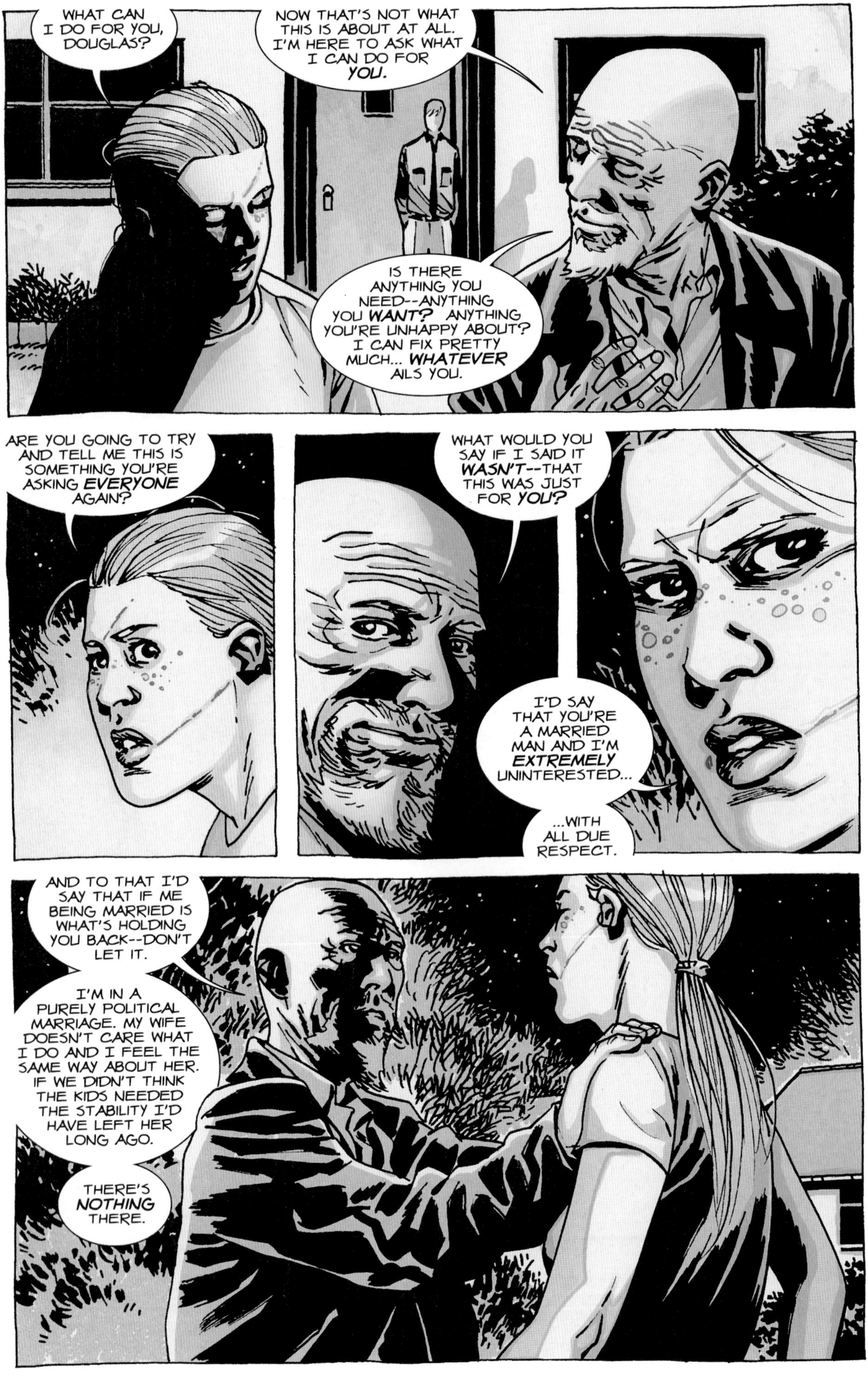
WHAT CAN I DO FOR YOU, DOUGLAS?
NOW THAT'S NOT WHAT THIS IS ABOUT AT ALL. I'M HERE TO ASK WHAT I CAN DO FOR *YOU.*
IS THERE ANYTHING YOU NEED--ANYTHING YOU *WANT?* ANYTHING YOU'RE UNHAPPY ABOUT? I CAN FIX PRETTY MUCH... *WHATEVER* AILS YOU.
ARE YOU GOING TO TRY AND TELL ME THIS IS SOMETHING YOU'RE ASKING *EVERYONE* AGAIN?
WHAT WOULD YOU SAY IF I SAID IT *WASN'T*--THAT THIS WAS JUST FOR *YOU?*
I'D SAY THAT YOU'RE A MARRIED MAN AND I'M *EXTREMELY* UNINTERESTED...
...WITH ALL DUE RESPECT.
AND TO THAT I'D SAY THAT IF ME BEING MARRIED IS WHAT'S HOLDING YOU BACK--DON'T LET IT.
I'M IN A PURELY POLITICAL MARRIAGE. MY WIFE DOESN'T CARE WHAT I DO AND I FEEL THE SAME WAY ABOUT HER. IF WE DIDN'T THINK THE KIDS NEEDED THE STABILITY I'D HAVE LEFT HER LONG AGO.
THERE'S *NOTHING* THERE.

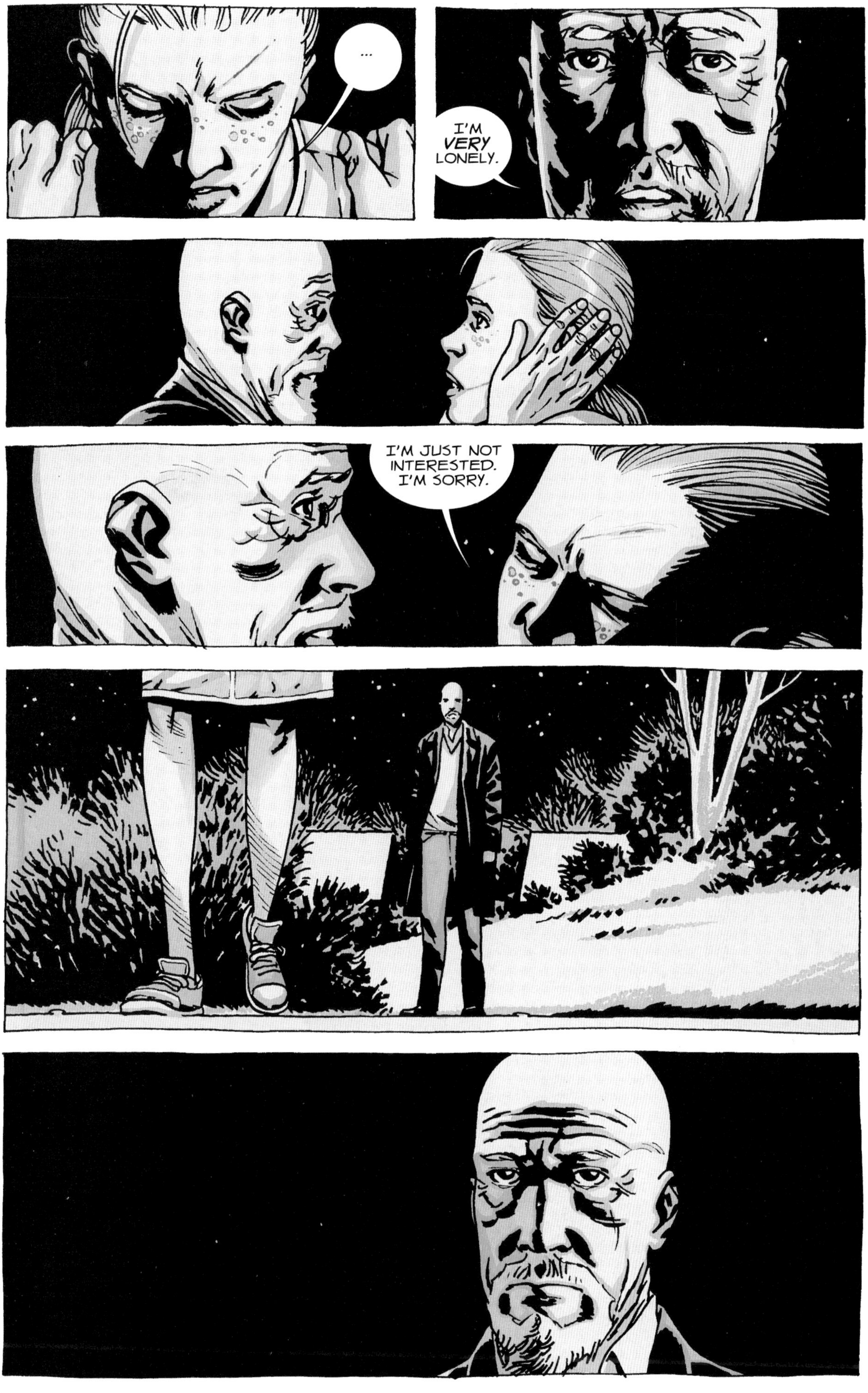
...
I'M VERY LONELY.
I'M JUST NOT INTERESTED. I'M SORRY.

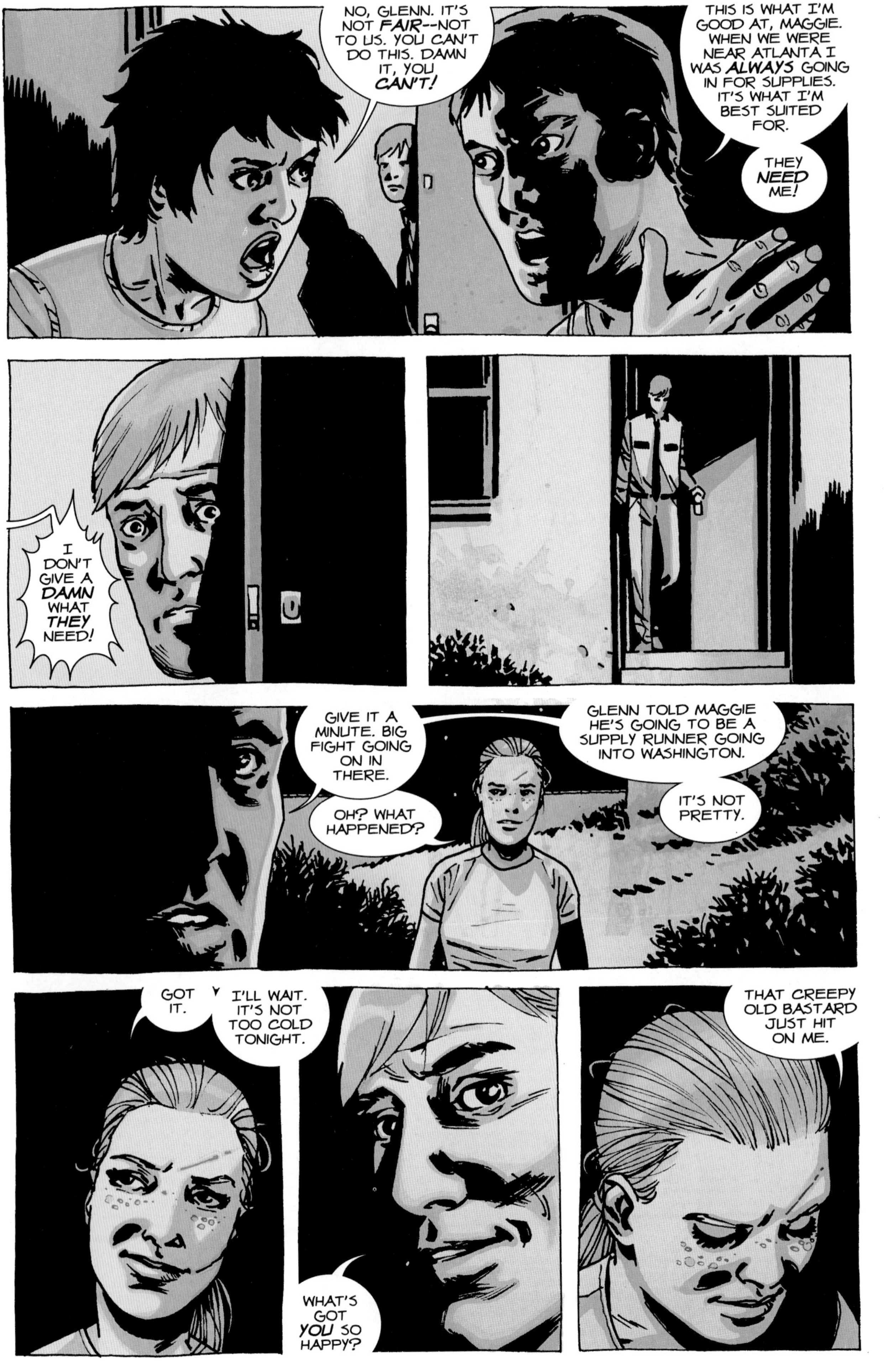

NO, GLENN. IT'S NOT FAIR--NOT TO US. YOU CAN'T DO THIS. DAMN IT, YOU CAN'T!
THIS IS WHAT I'M GOOD AT, MAGGIE. WHEN WE WERE NEAR ATLANTA I WAS ALWAYS GOING IN FOR SUPPLIES. IT'S WHAT I'M BEST SUITED FOR.
THEY NEED ME!
I DON'T GIVE A DAMN WHAT THEY NEED!
GIVE IT A MINUTE. BIG FIGHT GOING ON IN THERE.
OH? WHAT HAPPENED?
GLENN TOLD MAGGIE HE'S GOING TO BE A SUPPLY RUNNER GOING INTO WASHINGTON.
IT'S NOT PRETTY.
GOT IT.
I'LL WAIT. IT'S NOT TOO COLD TONIGHT.
WHAT'S GOT YOU SO HAPPY?
THAT CREEPY OLD BASTARD JUST HIT ON ME.

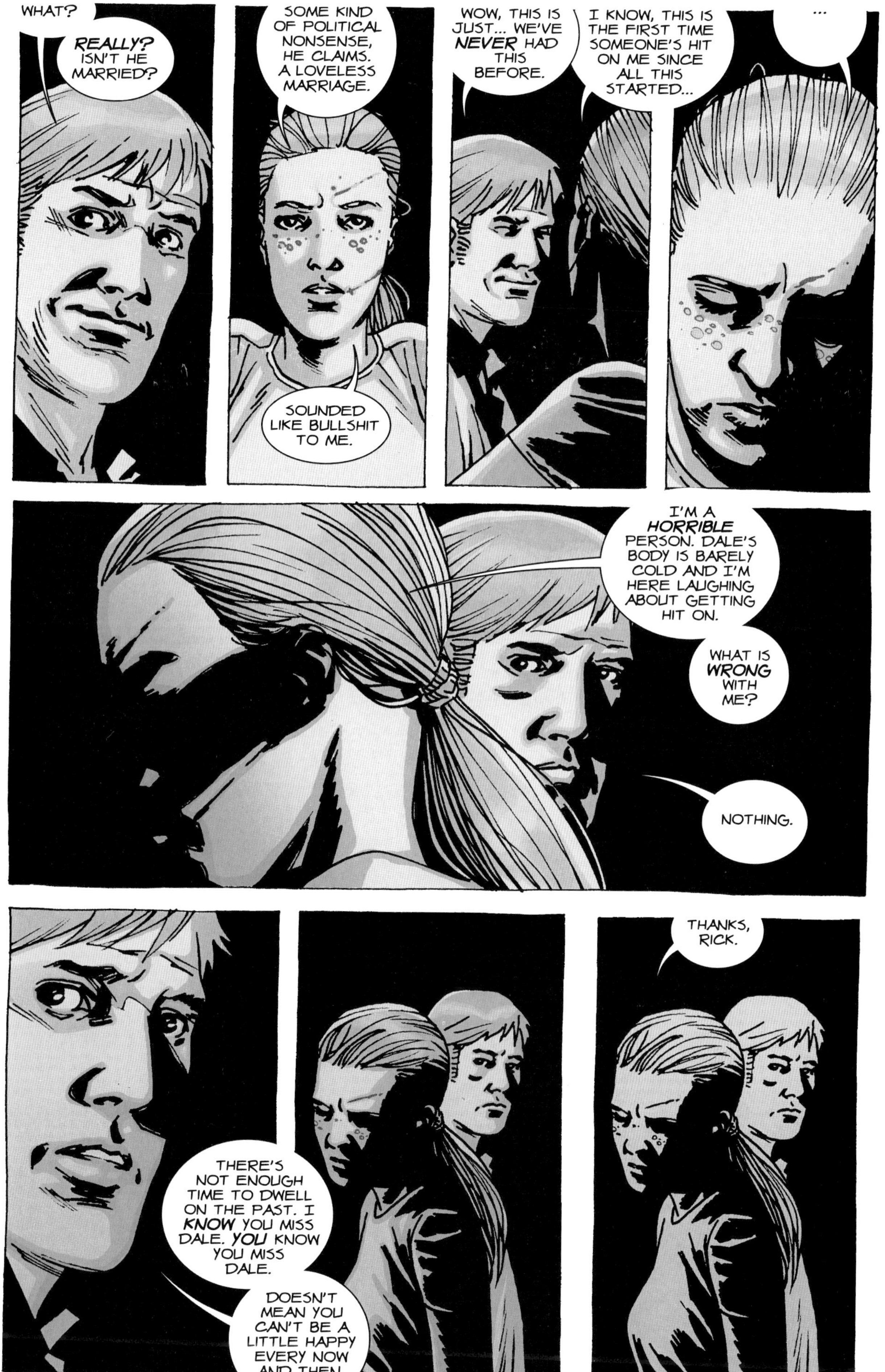

WHAT?
REALLY? ISN'T HE MARRIED?
SOME KIND OF POLITICAL NONSENSE, HE CLAIMS. A LOVELESS MARRIAGE.
SOUNDED LIKE BULLSHIT TO ME.
WOW, THIS IS JUST... WE'VE NEVER HAD THIS BEFORE.
I KNOW, THIS IS THE FIRST TIME SOMEONE'S HIT ON ME SINCE ALL THIS STARTED...
...
I'M A HORRIBLE PERSON. DALE'S BODY IS BARELY COLD AND I'M HERE LAUGHING ABOUT GETTING HIT ON.
WHAT IS WRONG WITH ME?
NOTHING.
THERE'S NOT ENOUGH TIME TO DWELL ON THE PAST. I KNOW YOU MISS DALE. YOU KNOW YOU MISS DALE.
DOESN'T MEAN YOU CAN'T BE A LITTLE HAPPY EVERY NOW AND THEN.
THANKS, RICK.

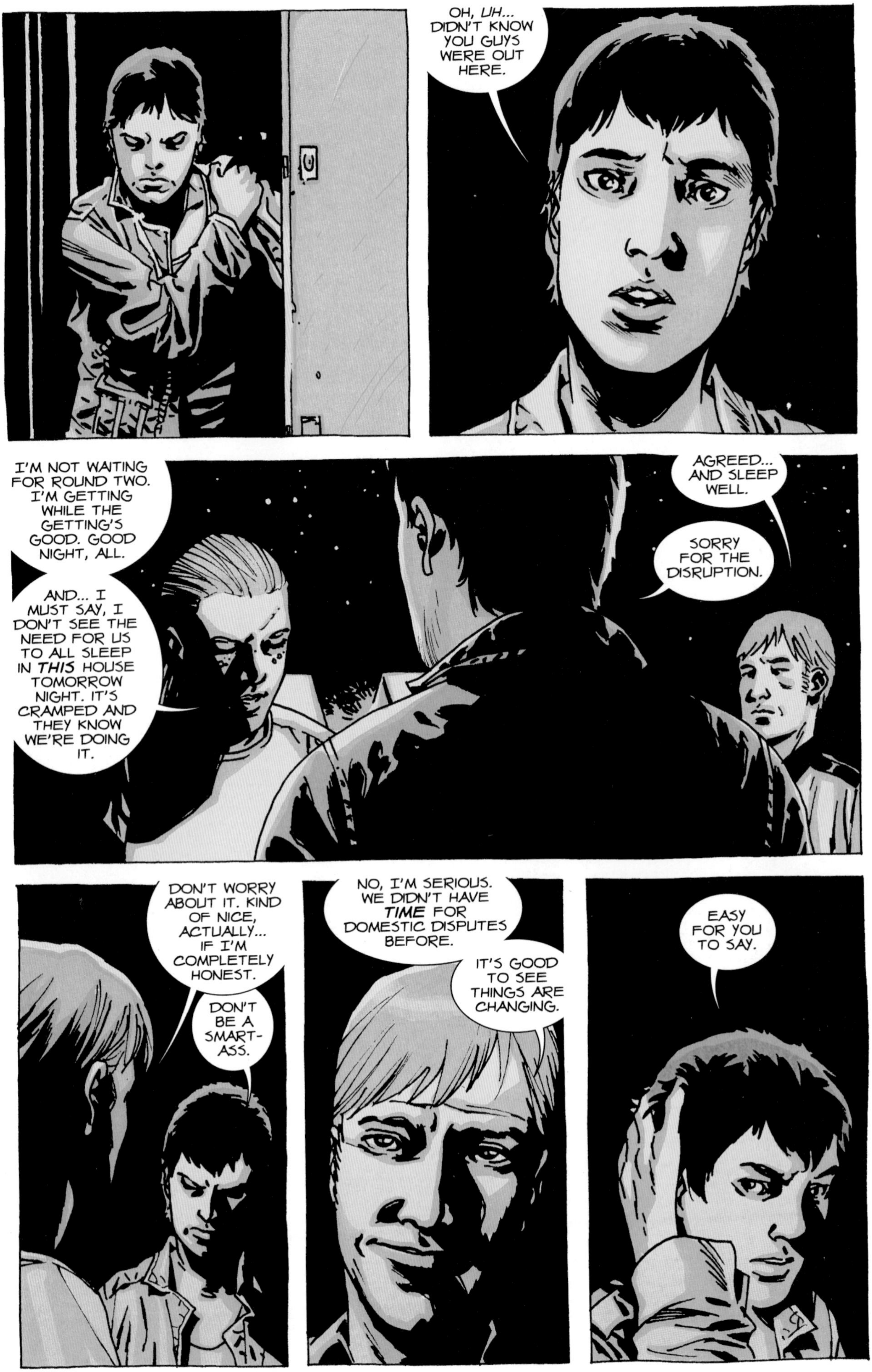
OH, UH... DIDN'T KNOW YOU GUYS WERE OUT HERE.
I'M NOT WAITING FOR ROUND TWO. I'M GETTING WHILE THE GETTING'S GOOD. GOOD NIGHT, ALL.
AND... I MUST SAY, I DON'T SEE THE NEED FOR US TO ALL SLEEP IN *THIS* HOUSE TOMORROW NIGHT. IT'S CRAMPED AND THEY KNOW WE'RE DOING IT.
AGREED... AND SLEEP WELL.
SORRY FOR THE DISRUPTION.
DON'T WORRY ABOUT IT. KIND OF NICE, ACTUALLY... IF I'M COMPLETELY HONEST.
DON'T BE A SMART-ASS.
NO, I'M SERIOUS. WE DIDN'T HAVE *TIME* FOR DOMESTIC DISPUTES BEFORE.
IT'S GOOD TO SEE THINGS ARE CHANGING.
EASY FOR YOU TO SAY.

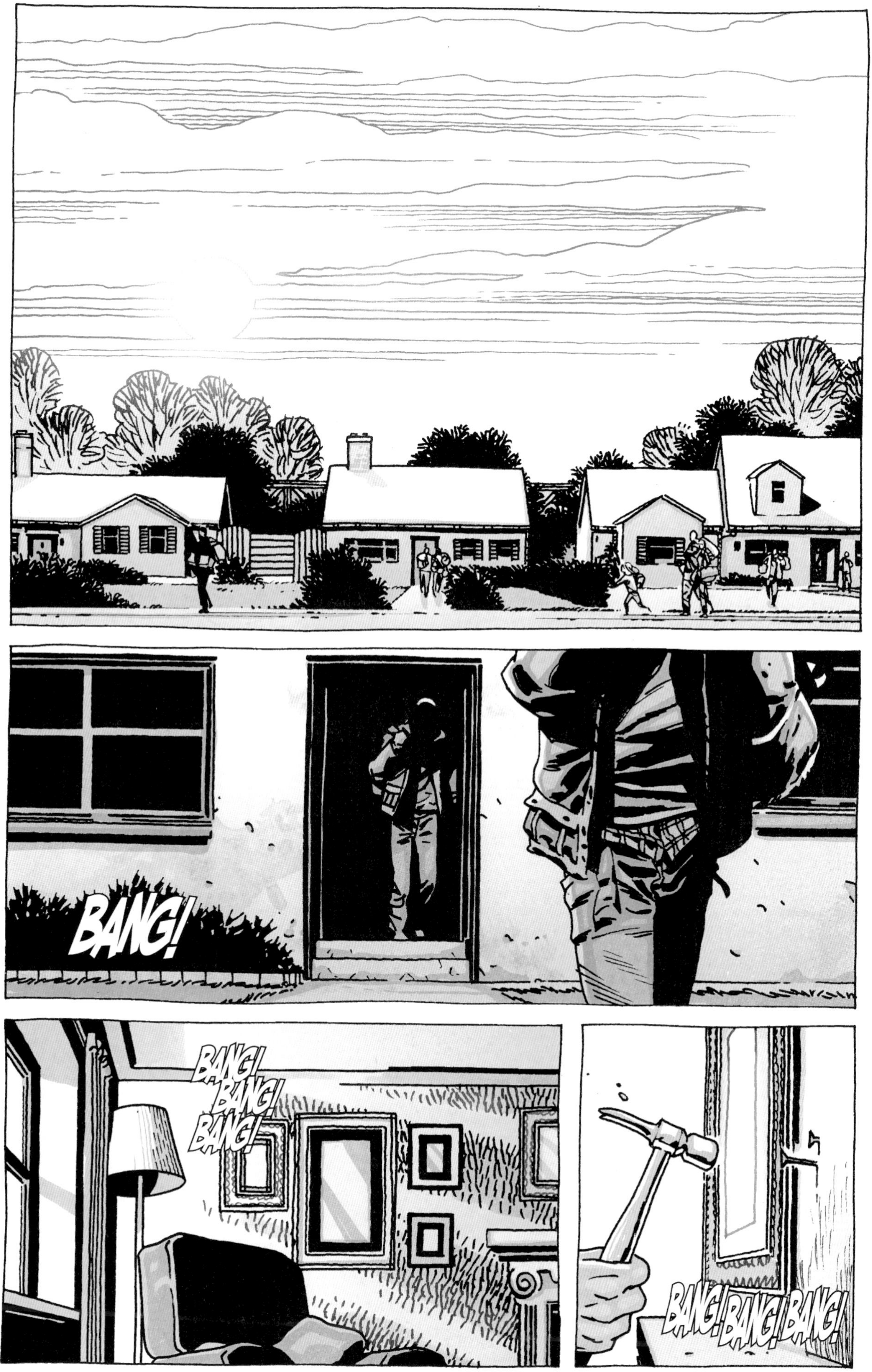
BANG!
BANG! BANG! BANG!
BANG! BANG! BANG!

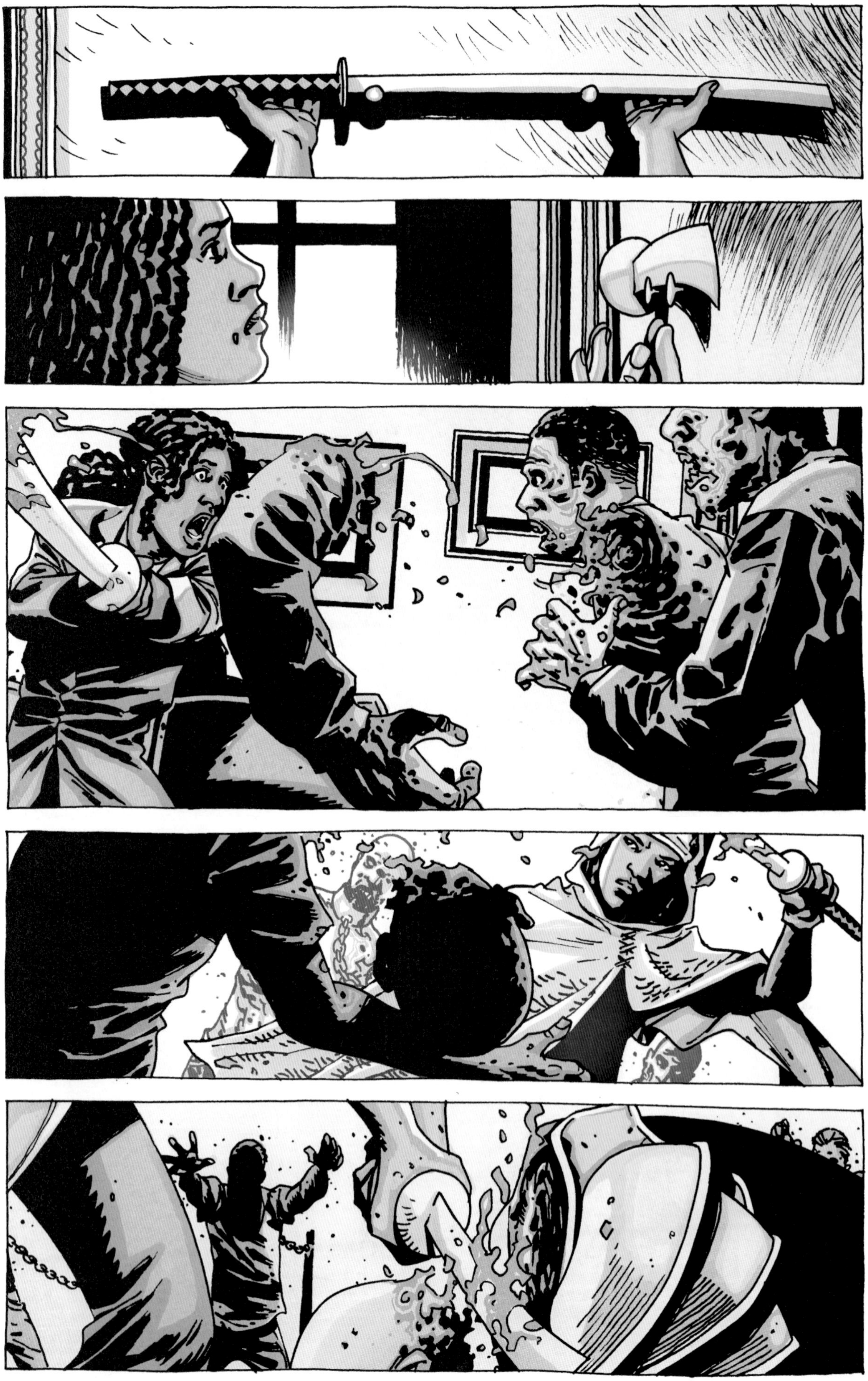

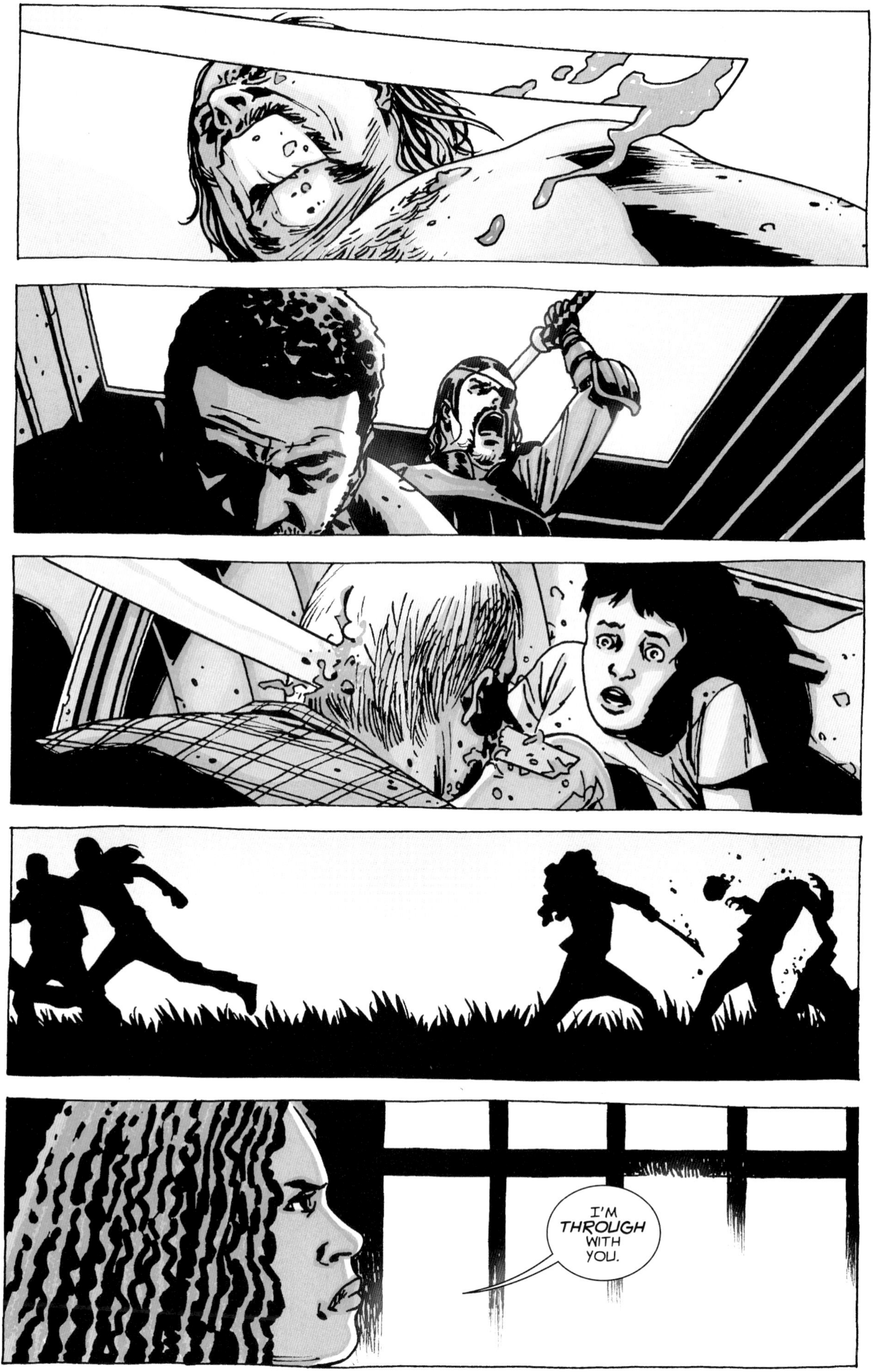
I'M THROUGH WITH YOU.

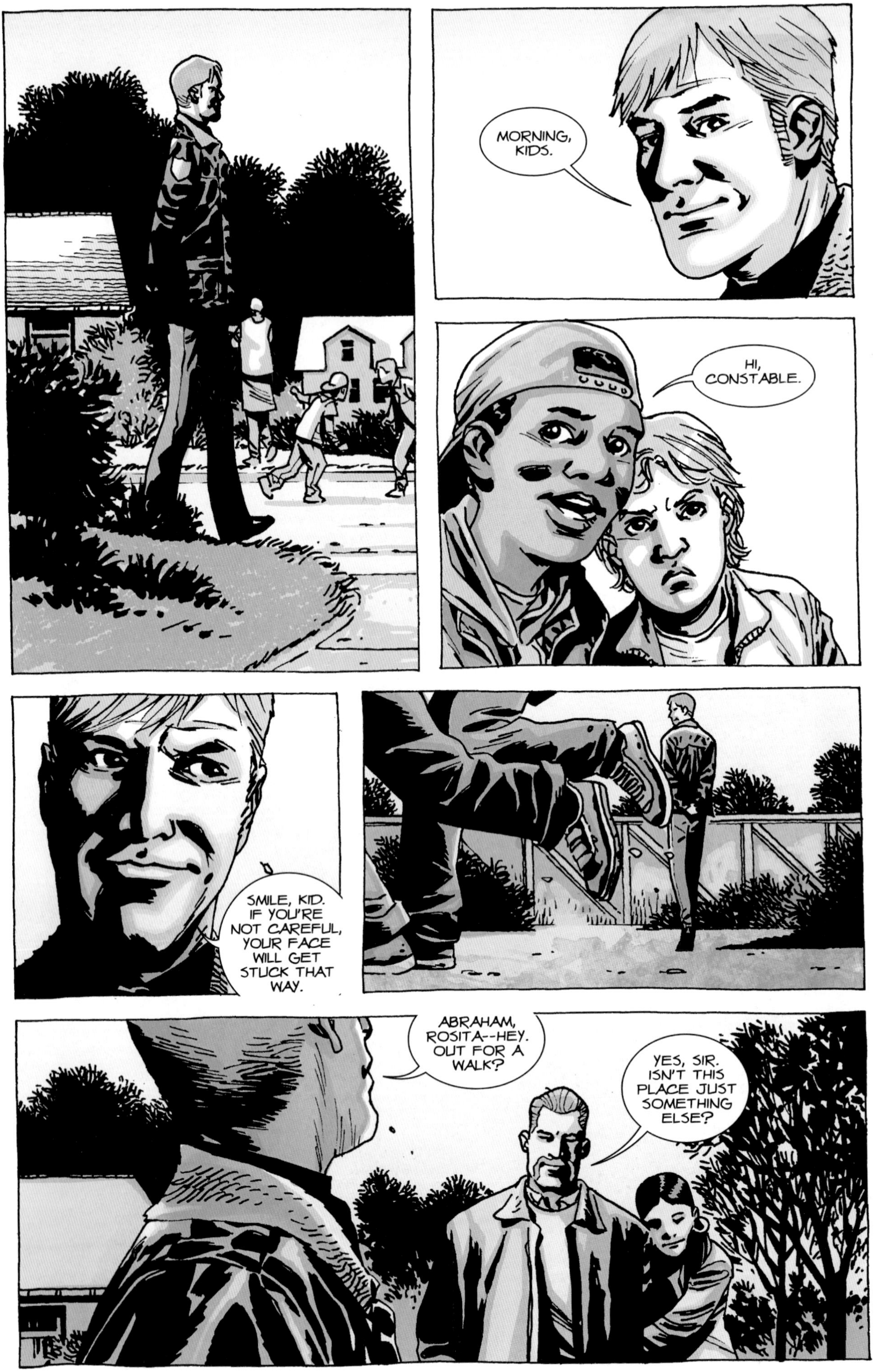
MORNING, KIDS.
HI, CONSTABLE.
SMILE, KID. IF YOU'RE NOT CAREFUL, YOUR FACE WILL GET STUCK THAT WAY.
ABRAHAM, ROSITA--HEY. OUT FOR A WALK?
YES, SIR. ISN'T THIS PLACE JUST SOMETHING ELSE?

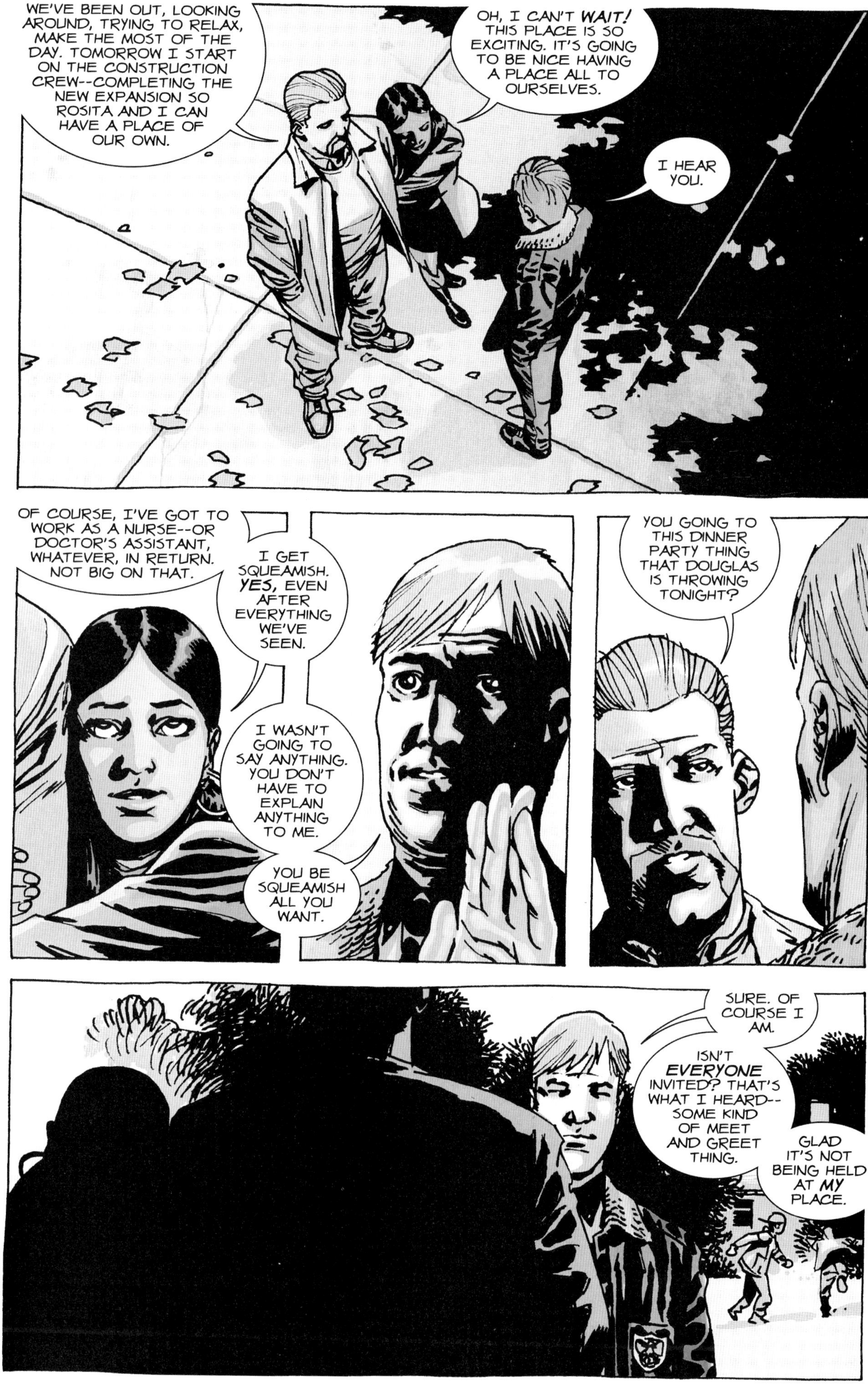
WE'VE BEEN OUT, LOOKING AROUND, TRYING TO RELAX, MAKE THE MOST OF THE DAY. TOMORROW I START ON THE CONSTRUCTION CREW--COMPLETING THE NEW EXPANSION SO ROSITA AND I CAN HAVE A PLACE OF OUR OWN.
OH, I CAN'T WAIT! THIS PLACE IS SO EXCITING. IT'S GOING TO BE NICE HAVING A PLACE ALL TO OURSELVES.
I HEAR YOU.
OF COURSE, I'VE GOT TO WORK AS A NURSE--OR DOCTOR'S ASSISTANT, WHATEVER, IN RETURN. NOT BIG ON THAT.
I GET SQUEAMISH. YES, EVEN AFTER EVERYTHING WE'VE SEEN.
I WASN'T GOING TO SAY ANYTHING. YOU DON'T HAVE TO EXPLAIN ANYTHING TO ME.
YOU BE SQUEAMISH ALL YOU WANT.
YOU GOING TO THIS DINNER PARTY THING THAT DOUGLAS IS THROWING TONIGHT?
SURE. OF COURSE I AM.
ISN'T EVERYONE INVITED? THAT'S WHAT I HEARD--SOME KIND OF MEET AND GREET THING.
GLAD IT'S NOT BEING HELD AT MY PLACE.

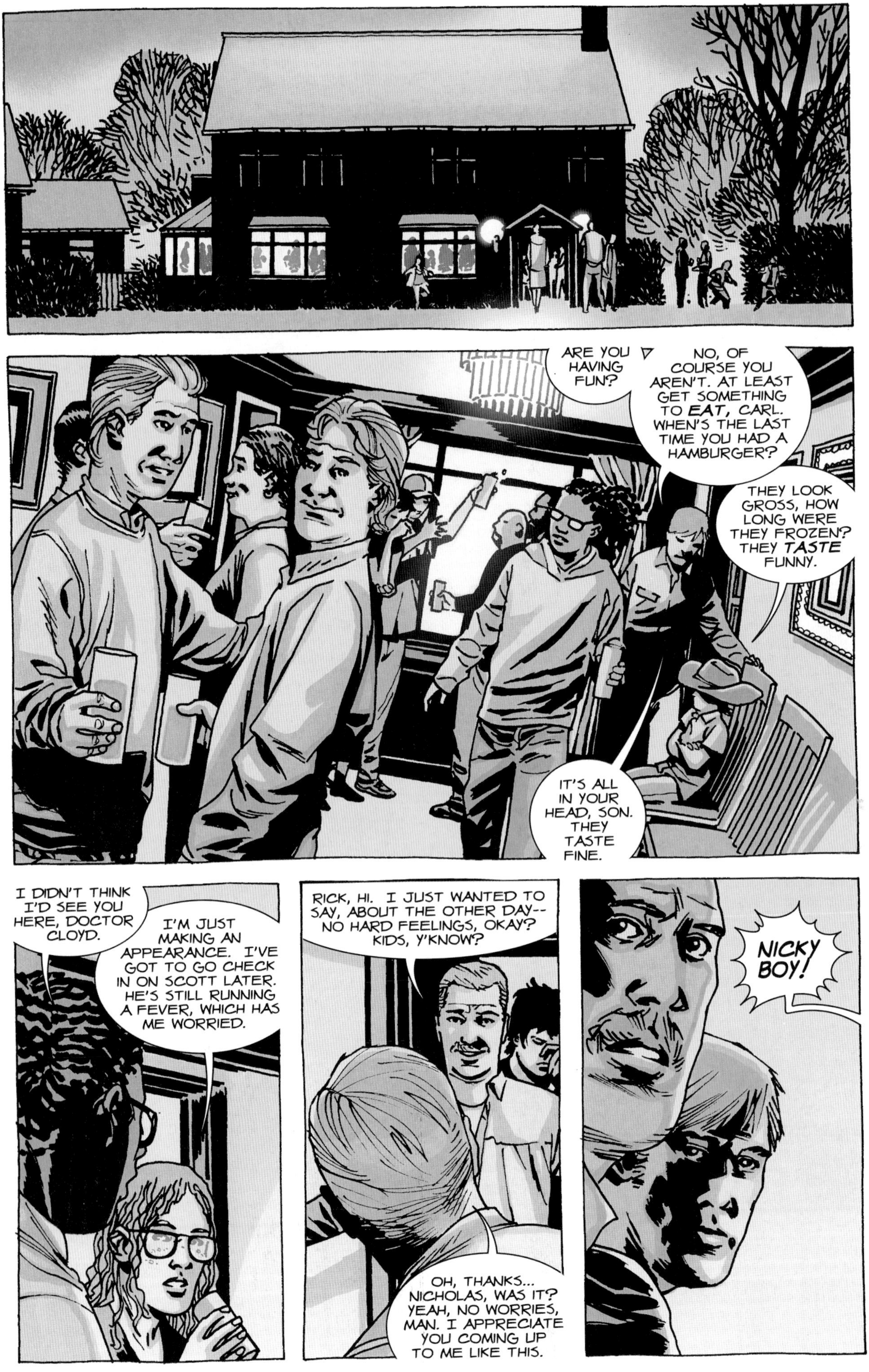
ARE YOU HAVING FUN?
NO, OF COURSE YOU AREN'T. AT LEAST GET SOMETHING TO EAT, CARL. WHEN'S THE LAST TIME YOU HAD A HAMBURGER?
THEY LOOK GROSS, HOW LONG WERE THEY FROZEN? THEY TASTE FUNNY.
IT'S ALL IN YOUR HEAD, SON. THEY TASTE FINE.
I DIDN'T THINK I'D SEE YOU HERE, DOCTOR CLOYD.
I'M JUST MAKING AN APPEARANCE. I'VE GOT TO GO CHECK IN ON SCOTT LATER. HE'S STILL RUNNING A FEVER, WHICH HAS ME WORRIED.
RICK, HI. I JUST WANTED TO SAY, ABOUT THE OTHER DAY-- NO HARD FEELINGS, OKAY? KIDS, Y'KNOW?
OH, THANKS... NICHOLAS, WAS IT? YEAH, NO WORRIES, MAN. I APPRECIATE YOU COMING UP TO ME LIKE THIS.
NICKY BOY!

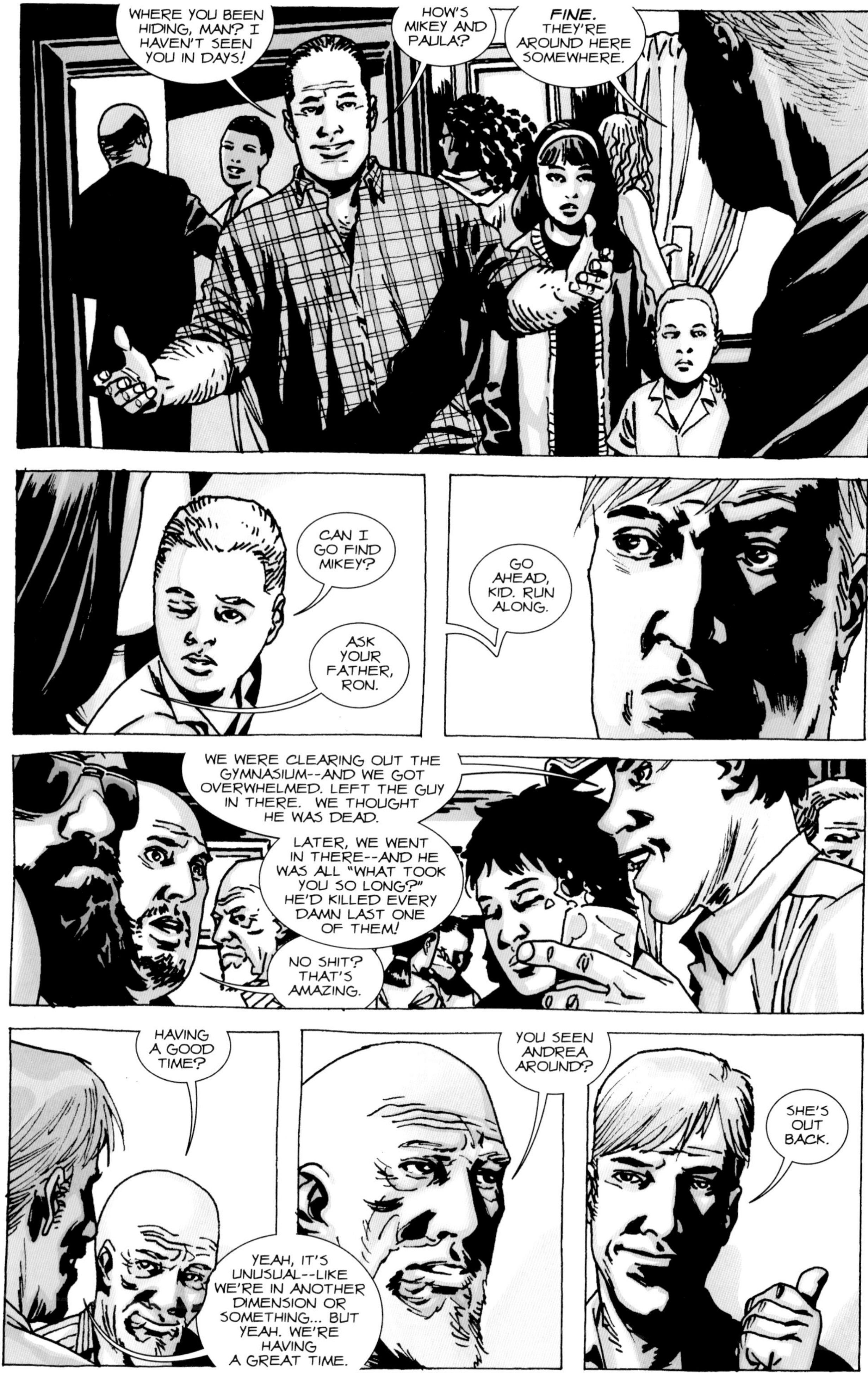
WHERE YOU BEEN HIDING, MAN? I HAVEN'T SEEN YOU IN DAYS!
HOW'S MIKEY AND PAULA?
FINE. THEY'RE AROUND HERE SOMEWHERE.
CAN I GO FIND MIKEY?
ASK YOUR FATHER, RON.
GO AHEAD, KID. RUN ALONG.
WE WERE CLEARING OUT THE GYMNASIUM--AND WE GOT OVERWHELMED. LEFT THE GUY IN THERE. WE THOUGHT HE WAS DEAD.
LATER, WE WENT IN THERE--AND HE WAS ALL "WHAT TOOK YOU SO LONG?" HE'D KILLED EVERY DAMN LAST ONE OF THEM!
NO SHIT? THAT'S AMAZING.
HAVING A GOOD TIME?
YEAH, IT'S UNUSUAL--LIKE WE'RE IN ANOTHER DIMENSION OR SOMETHING... BUT YEAH. WE'RE HAVING A GREAT TIME.
YOU SEEN ANDREA AROUND?
SHE'S OUT BACK.

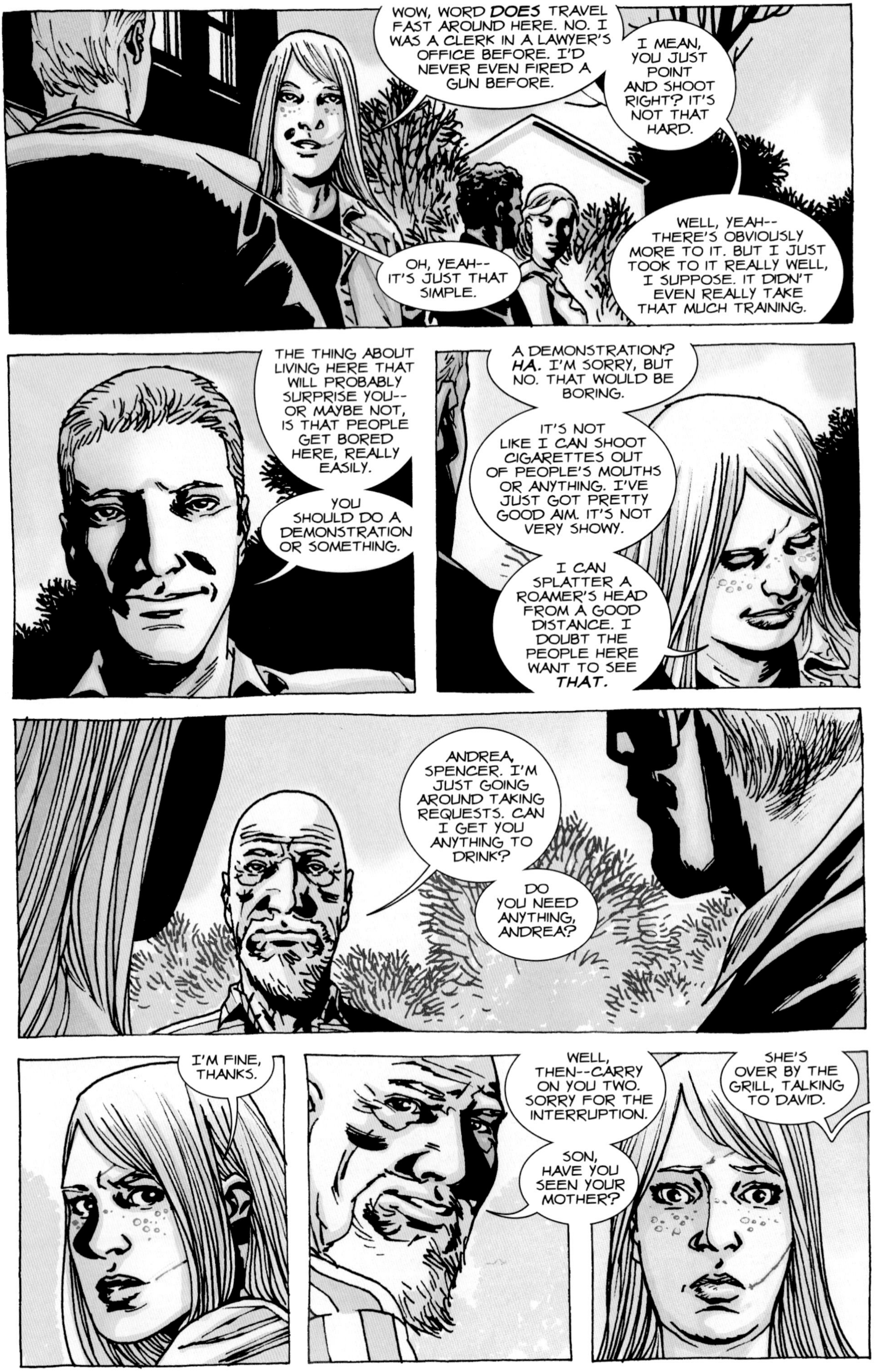
WOW, WORD DOES TRAVEL FAST AROUND HERE. NO. I WAS A CLERK IN A LAWYER'S OFFICE BEFORE. I'D NEVER EVEN FIRED A GUN BEFORE.
I MEAN, YOU JUST POINT AND SHOOT RIGHT? IT'S NOT THAT HARD.
OH, YEAH-- IT'S JUST THAT SIMPLE.
WELL, YEAH-- THERE'S OBVIOUSLY MORE TO IT. BUT I JUST TOOK TO IT REALLY WELL, I SUPPOSE. IT DIDN'T EVEN REALLY TAKE THAT MUCH TRAINING.
THE THING ABOUT LIVING HERE THAT WILL PROBABLY SURPRISE YOU-- OR MAYBE NOT, IS THAT PEOPLE GET BORED HERE, REALLY EASILY.
YOU SHOULD DO A DEMONSTRATION OR SOMETHING.
A DEMONSTRATION? HA. I'M SORRY, BUT NO. THAT WOULD BE BORING.
IT'S NOT LIKE I CAN SHOOT CIGARETTES OUT OF PEOPLE'S MOUTHS OR ANYTHING. I'VE JUST GOT PRETTY GOOD AIM. IT'S NOT VERY SHOWY.
I CAN SPLATTER A ROAMER'S HEAD FROM A GOOD DISTANCE. I DOUBT THE PEOPLE HERE WANT TO SEE THAT.
ANDREA, SPENCER. I'M JUST GOING AROUND TAKING REQUESTS. CAN I GET YOU ANYTHING TO DRINK?
DO YOU NEED ANYTHING, ANDREA?
I'M FINE, THANKS.
WELL, THEN--CARRY ON YOU TWO. SORRY FOR THE INTERRUPTION.
SON, HAVE YOU SEEN YOUR MOTHER?
SHE'S OVER BY THE GRILL, TALKING TO DAVID.

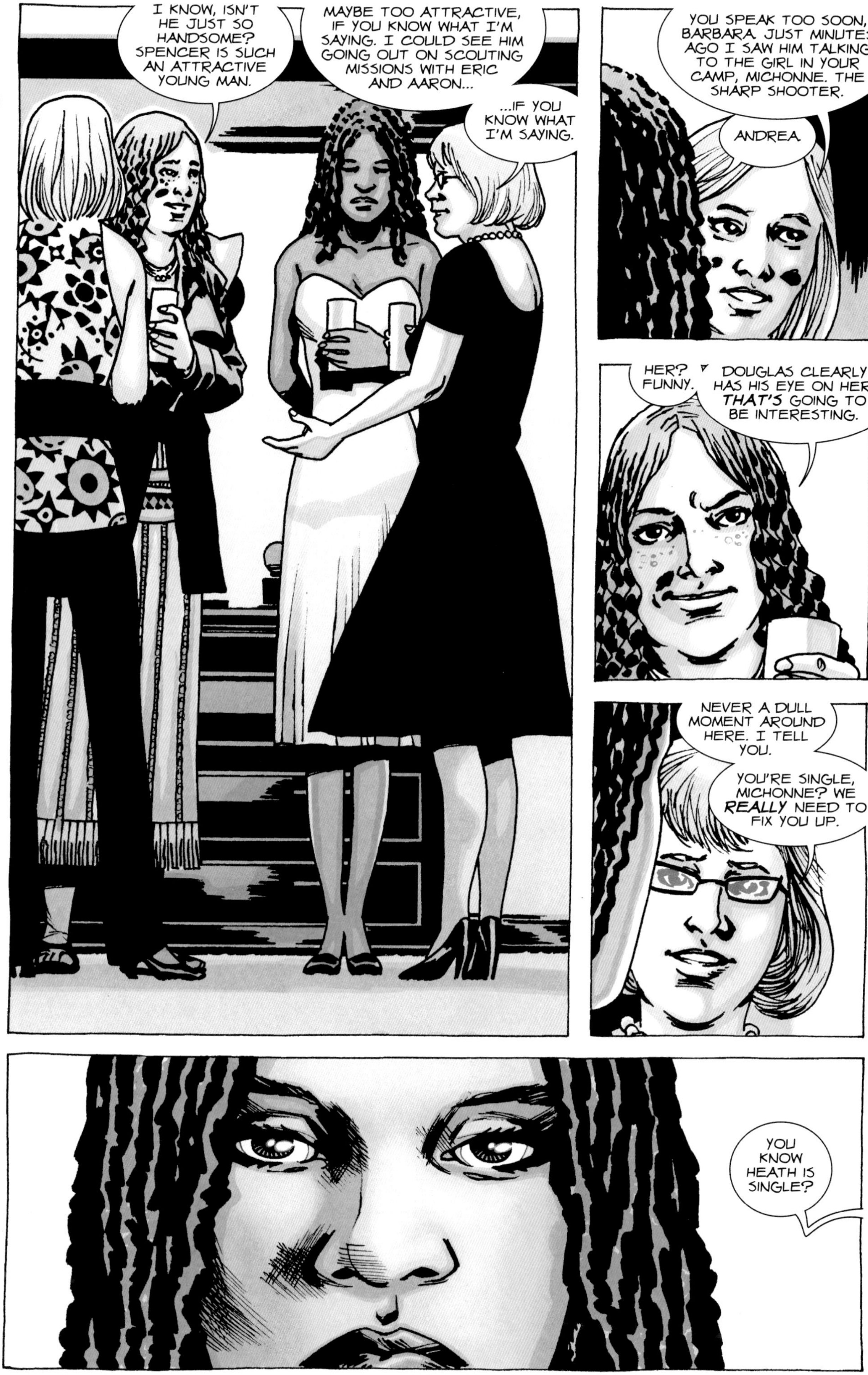
I KNOW, ISN'T HE JUST SO HANDSOME? SPENCER IS SUCH AN ATTRACTIVE YOUNG MAN.
MAYBE TOO ATTRACTIVE, IF YOU KNOW WHAT I'M SAYING. I COULD SEE HIM GOING OUT ON SCOUTING MISSIONS WITH ERIC AND AARON...
...IF YOU KNOW WHAT I'M SAYING.
YOU SPEAK TOO SOON, BARBARA. JUST MINUTES AGO I SAW HIM TALKING TO THE GIRL IN YOUR CAMP, MICHONNE. THE SHARP SHOOTER.
ANDREA.
HER? FUNNY.
DOUGLAS CLEARLY HAS HIS EYE ON HER. *THAT'S* GOING TO BE INTERESTING.
NEVER A DULL MOMENT AROUND HERE. I TELL YOU.
YOU'RE SINGLE, MICHONNE? WE *REALLY* NEED TO FIX YOU UP.
YOU KNOW HEATH IS SINGLE?

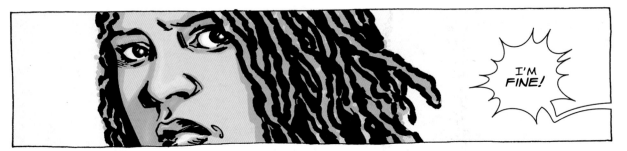

I'M **FINE!**

COME ON, WE'RE LEAVING.

I SAID I'M **FINE!** I'M NOT GOING **ANYWHERE!**

COULD YOU PLEASE--

I'VE GOT IT UNDER CONTROL.

I'LL TAKE CARE OF THIS.

GLENN, C'MON. WE'RE GOING OUTSIDE.

ALL OUR **KIDS** ARE HERE, GLENN. JESUS.

I'M SORRY.

I'M SORRY.

JUST... GET HIM HOME. I'LL MAKE SURE SOPHIA MAKES IT BACK OKAY.

OKAY, THANKS, RICK.

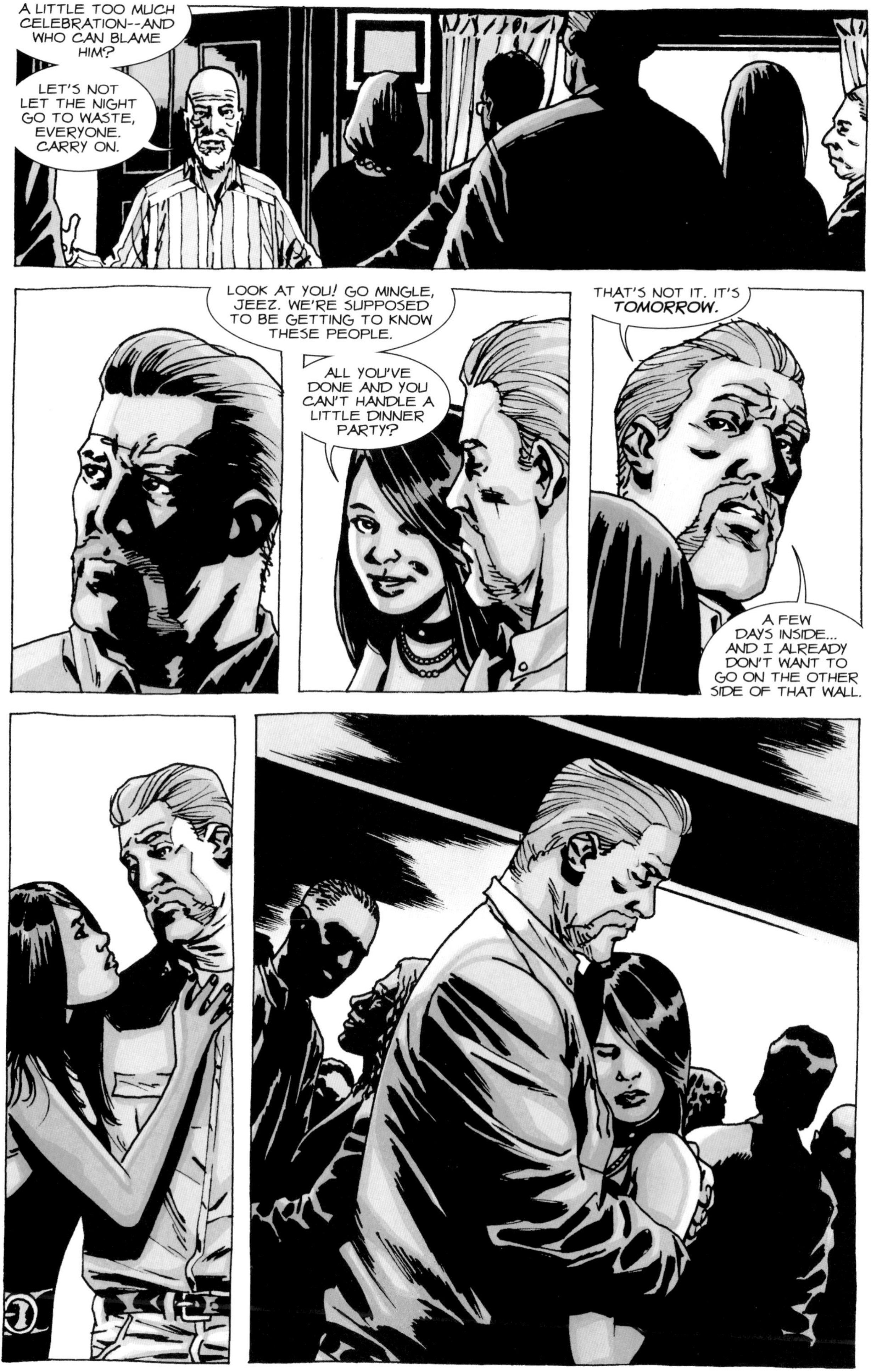
A LITTLE TOO MUCH CELEBRATION--AND WHO CAN BLAME HIM?
LET'S NOT LET THE NIGHT GO TO WASTE, EVERYONE. CARRY ON.
LOOK AT YOU! GO MINGLE, JEEZ. WE'RE SUPPOSED TO BE GETTING TO KNOW THESE PEOPLE.
ALL YOU'VE DONE AND YOU CAN'T HANDLE A LITTLE DINNER PARTY?
THAT'S NOT IT. IT'S *TOMORROW.*
A FEW DAYS INSIDE... AND I ALREADY DON'T WANT TO GO ON THE OTHER SIDE OF THAT WALL.

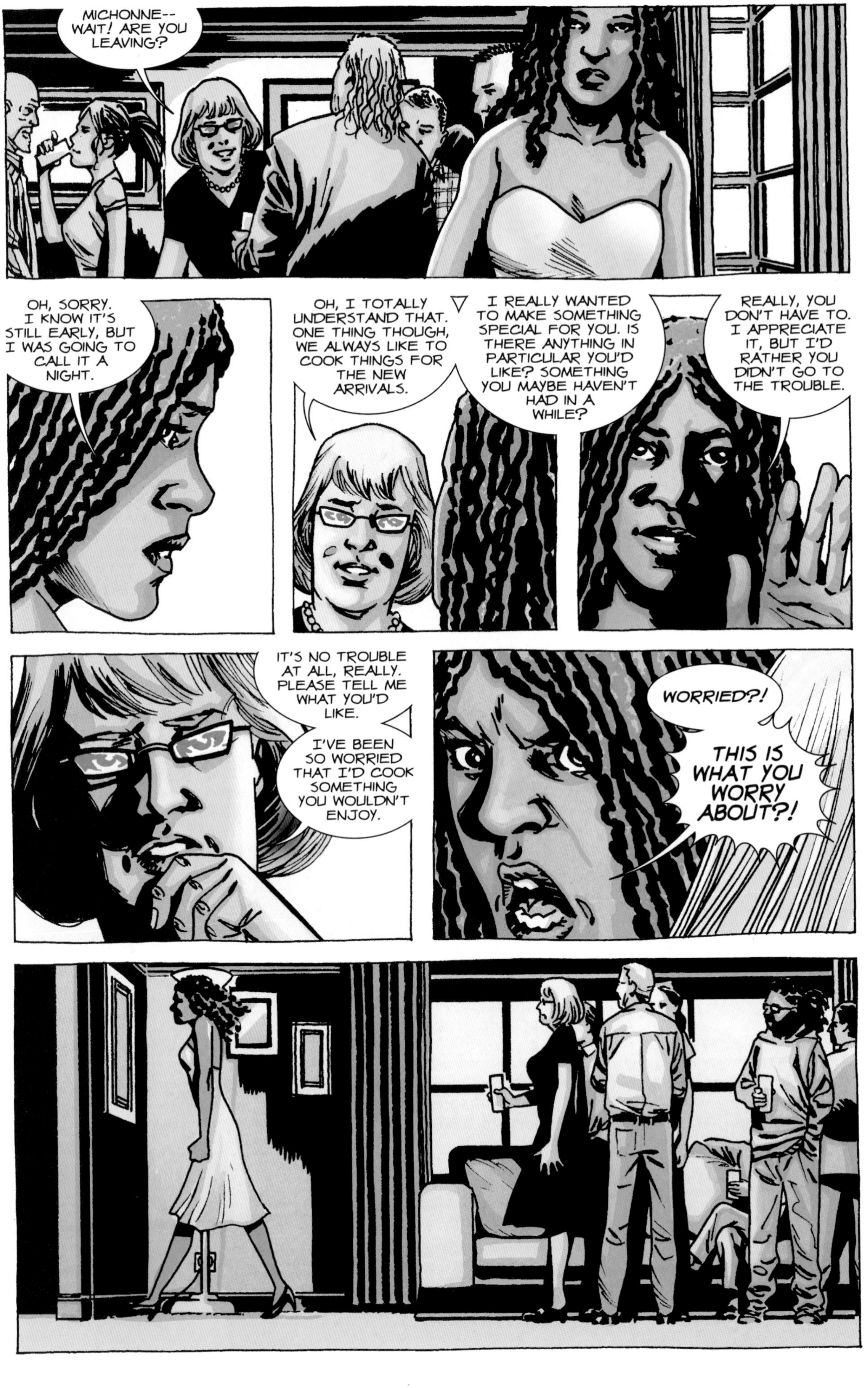
MICHONNE-- WAIT! ARE YOU LEAVING?
OH, SORRY. I KNOW IT'S STILL EARLY, BUT I WAS GOING TO CALL IT A NIGHT.
OH, I TOTALLY UNDERSTAND THAT. ONE THING THOUGH, WE ALWAYS LIKE TO COOK THINGS FOR THE NEW ARRIVALS.
I REALLY WANTED TO MAKE SOMETHING SPECIAL FOR YOU. IS THERE ANYTHING IN PARTICULAR YOU'D LIKE? SOMETHING YOU MAYBE HAVEN'T HAD IN A WHILE?
REALLY, YOU DON'T HAVE TO. I APPRECIATE IT, BUT I'D RATHER YOU DIDN'T GO TO THE TROUBLE.
IT'S NO TROUBLE AT ALL, REALLY. PLEASE TELL ME WHAT YOU'D LIKE.
I'VE BEEN SO WORRIED THAT I'D COOK SOMETHING YOU WOULDN'T ENJOY.
WORRIED?!
THIS IS WHAT YOU WORRY ABOUT?!

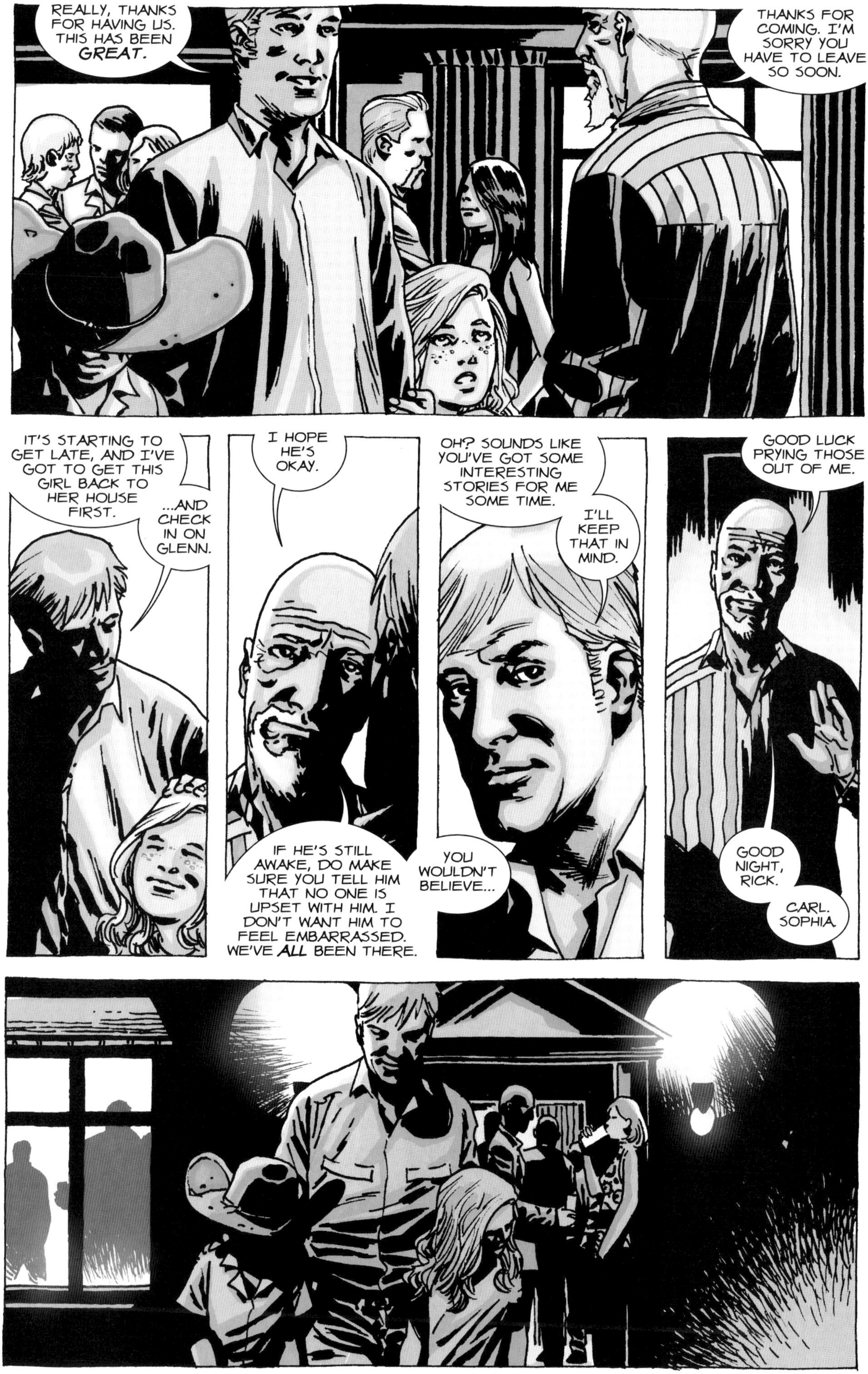
REALLY, THANKS FOR HAVING US. THIS HAS BEEN GREAT.
THANKS FOR COMING. I'M SORRY YOU HAVE TO LEAVE SO SOON.
IT'S STARTING TO GET LATE, AND I'VE GOT TO GET THIS GIRL BACK TO HER HOUSE FIRST.
...AND CHECK IN ON GLENN.
I HOPE HE'S OKAY.
IF HE'S STILL AWAKE, DO MAKE SURE YOU TELL HIM THAT NO ONE IS UPSET WITH HIM. I DON'T WANT HIM TO FEEL EMBARRASSED. WE'VE ALL BEEN THERE.
OH? SOUNDS LIKE YOU'VE GOT SOME INTERESTING STORIES FOR ME SOME TIME.
I'LL KEEP THAT IN MIND.
YOU WOULDN'T BELIEVE...
GOOD LUCK PRYING THOSE OUT OF ME.
GOOD NIGHT, RICK.
CARL. SOPHIA.

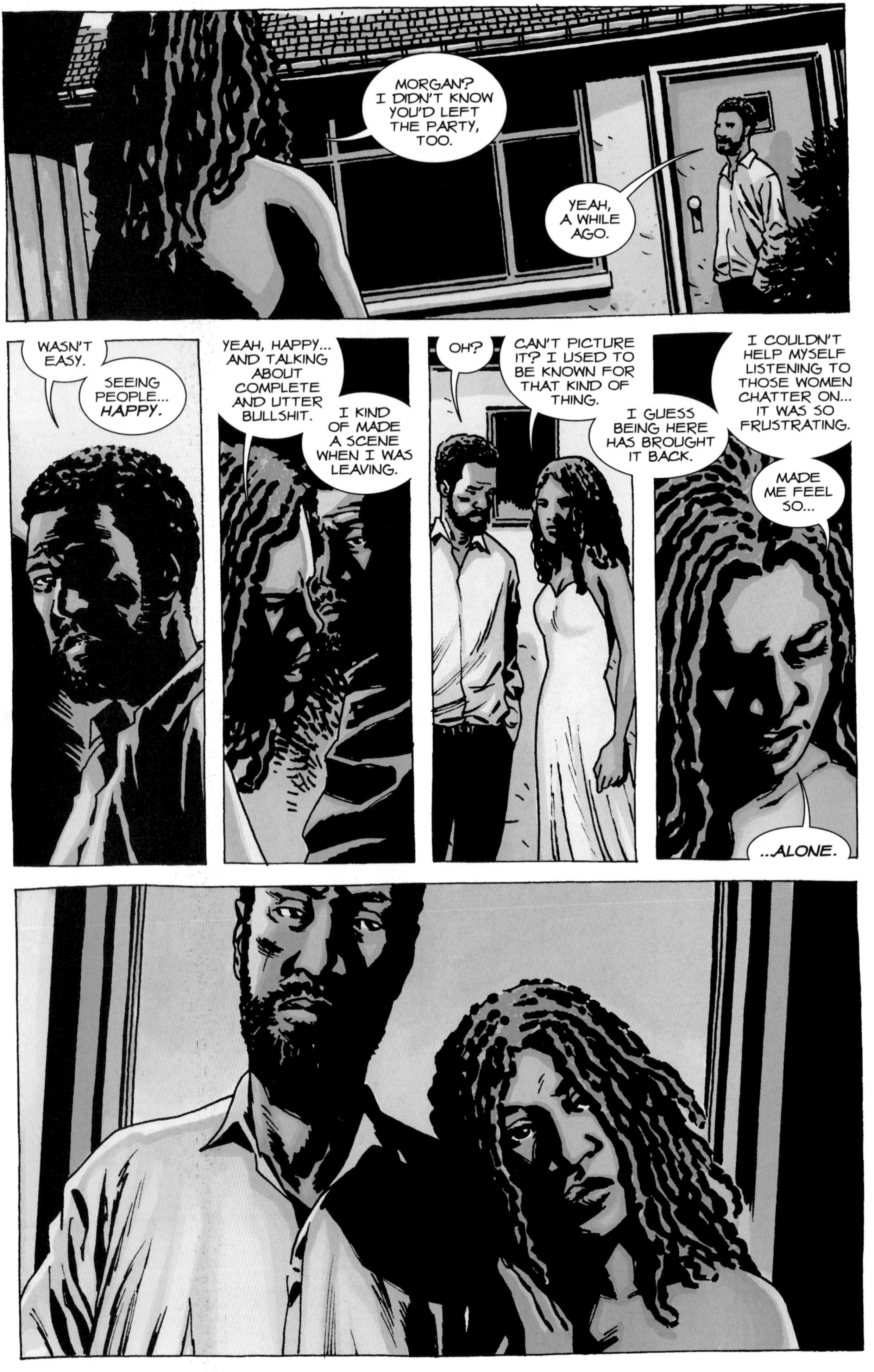

MORGAN? I DIDN'T KNOW YOU'D LEFT THE PARTY, TOO.
YEAH, A WHILE AGO.
WASN'T EASY.
SEEING PEOPLE... *HAPPY.*
YEAH, HAPPY... AND TALKING ABOUT COMPLETE AND UTTER BULLSHIT.
I KIND OF MADE A SCENE WHEN I WAS LEAVING.
OH?
CAN'T PICTURE IT? I USED TO BE KNOWN FOR THAT KIND OF THING.
I GUESS BEING HERE HAS BROUGHT IT BACK.
I COULDN'T HELP MYSELF LISTENING TO THOSE WOMEN CHATTER ON... IT WAS SO FRUSTRATING.
MADE ME FEEL SO...
...ALONE.

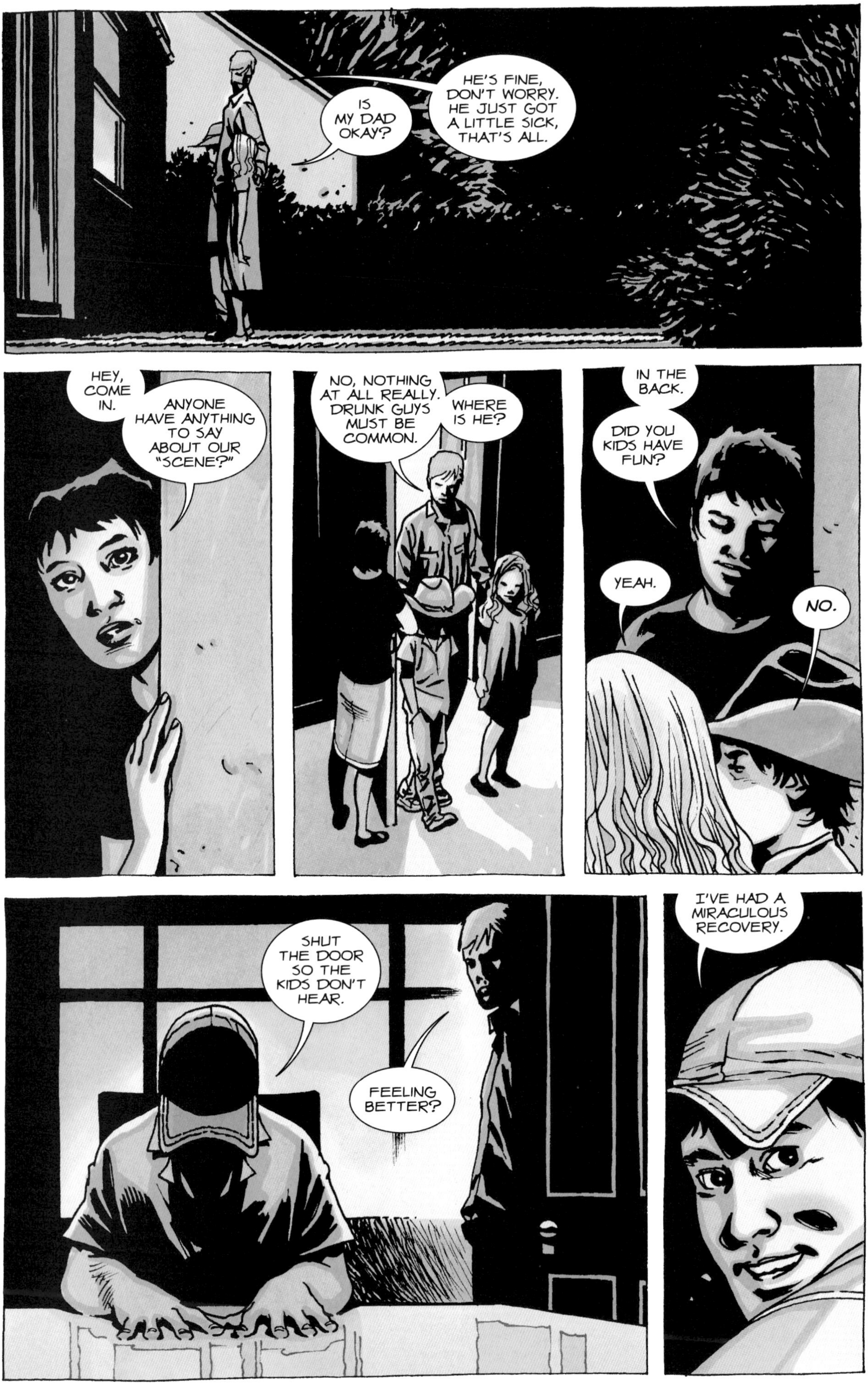
IS MY DAD OKAY?
HE'S FINE, DON'T WORRY. HE JUST GOT A LITTLE SICK, THAT'S ALL.
HEY, COME IN.
ANYONE HAVE ANYTHING TO SAY ABOUT OUR "SCENE?"
NO, NOTHING AT ALL REALLY. DRUNK GUYS MUST BE COMMON.
WHERE IS HE?
IN THE BACK.
DID YOU KIDS HAVE FUN?
YEAH.
NO.
SHUT THE DOOR SO THE KIDS DON'T HEAR.
FEELING BETTER?
I'VE HAD A MIRACULOUS RECOVERY.

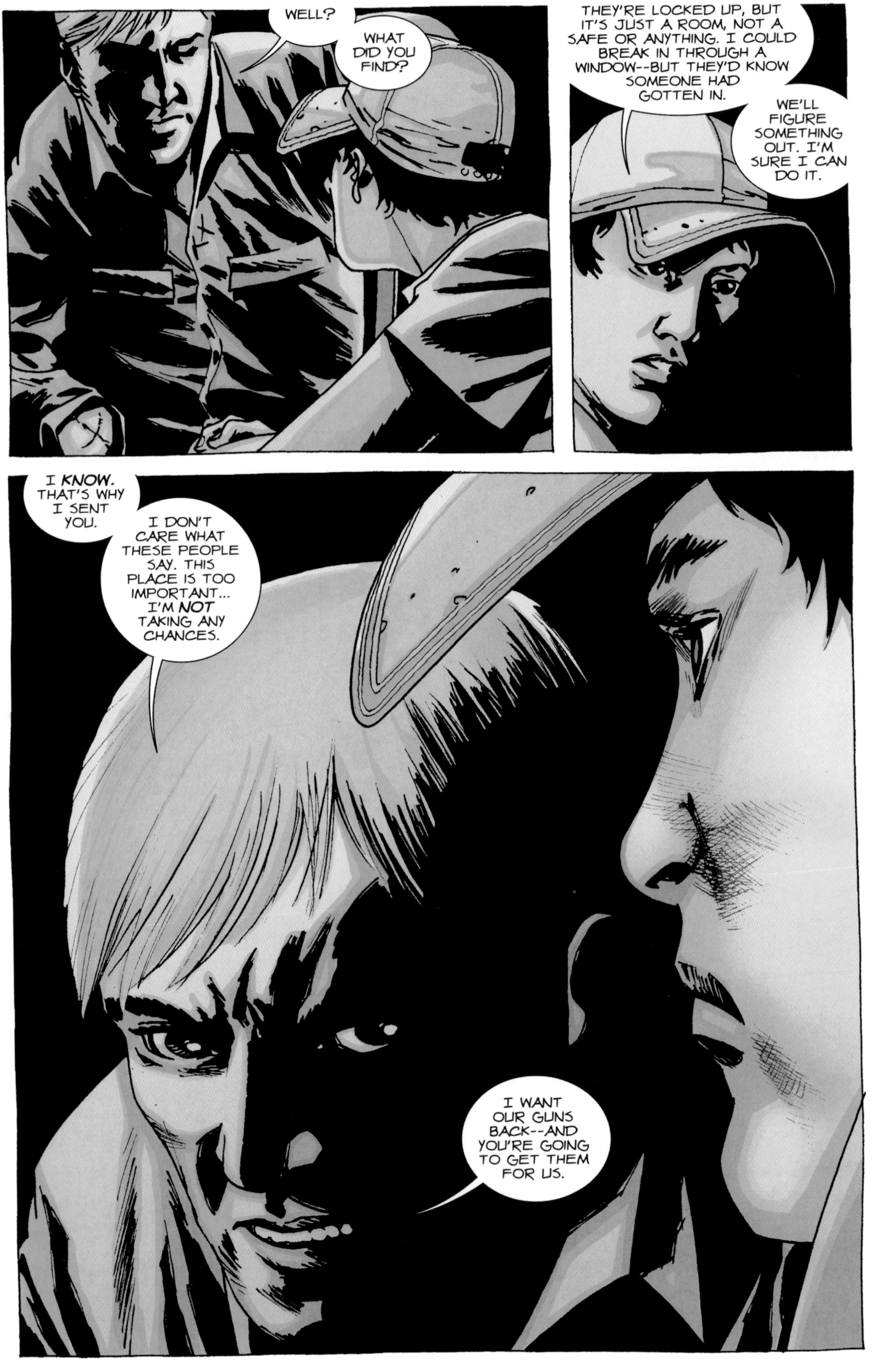

WELL?
WHAT DID YOU FIND?
THEY'RE LOCKED UP, BUT IT'S JUST A ROOM, NOT A SAFE OR ANYTHING. I COULD BREAK IN THROUGH A WINDOW--BUT THEY'D KNOW SOMEONE HAD GOTTEN IN.
WE'LL FIGURE SOMETHING OUT. I'M SURE I CAN DO IT.
I KNOW. THAT'S WHY I SENT YOU.
I DON'T CARE WHAT THESE PEOPLE SAY. THIS PLACE IS TOO IMPORTANT... I'M NOT TAKING ANY CHANCES.
I WANT OUR GUNS BACK--AND YOU'RE GOING TO GET THEM FOR US.

to be continued...

Sketchbook

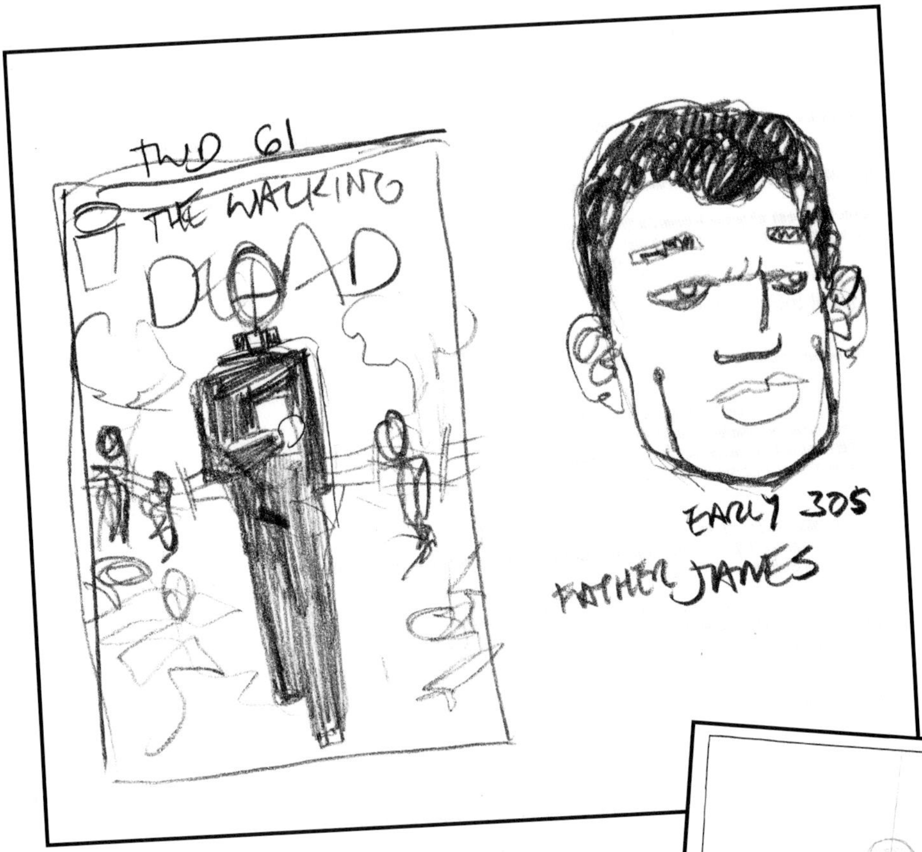
TWD 61
THE WALKING
DEAD
EARLY 30S
FATHER JAMES

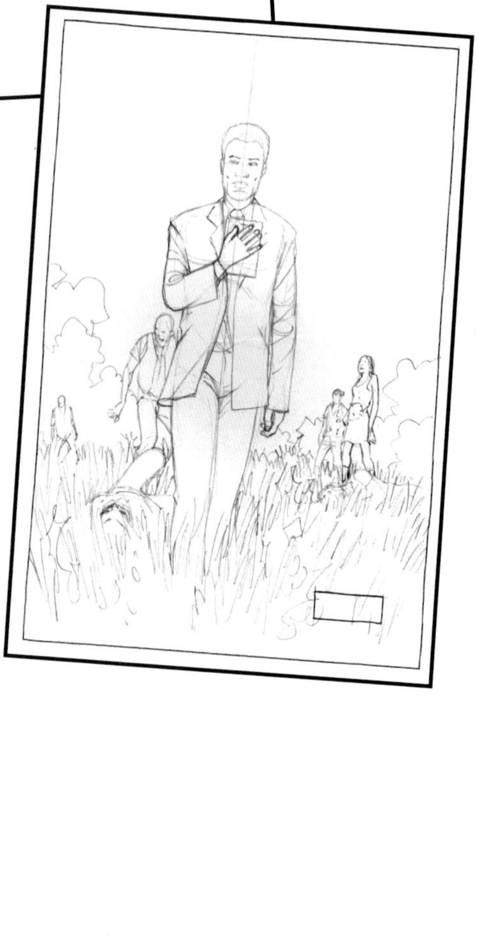

I wanted the cover to issue 61 to mirror the cover to issue 19 a little. The arrival of Michonne flanked by her zombie protectors and the arrival of Father Gabriel (originally Father James) seemed like a cool comparison. Gabriel with no protection, surrounded by more zombies that weren't posing a threat was pretty cool, I thought--and Charlie just knocked it out of the park.

The covers for issues 62 through 66 served dual purposes: aside from being covers, they were also going to be cropped into teaser images. I did up a series of sketches and Charlie dove right in and got to work. It ended up being a pretty successful campaign and really got the book a lot of press. Cool stuff. This cover is just sweet and I love how most people thought it was Glenn who was spying because of the hat.

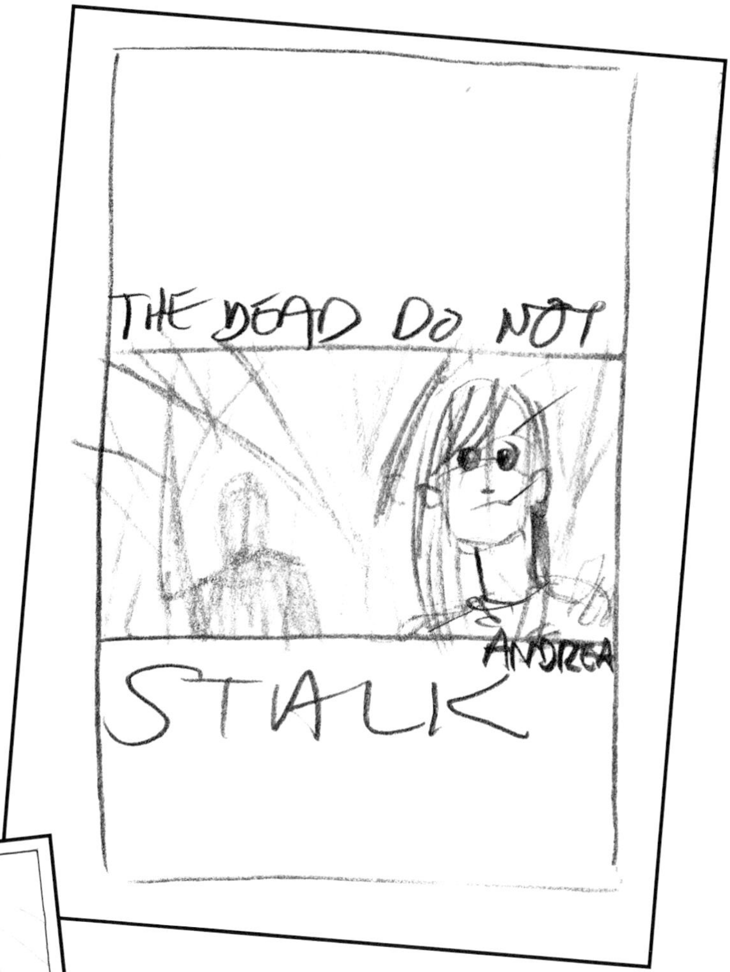
THE DEAD DO NOT
ANDREA
STALK

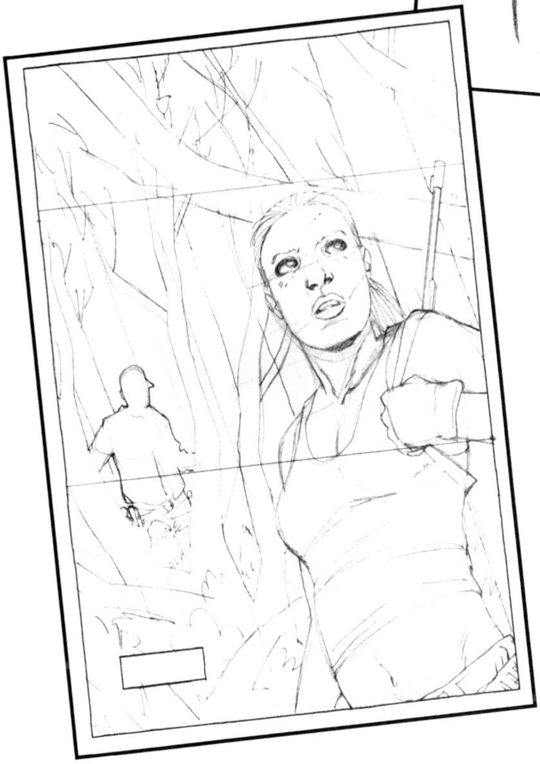

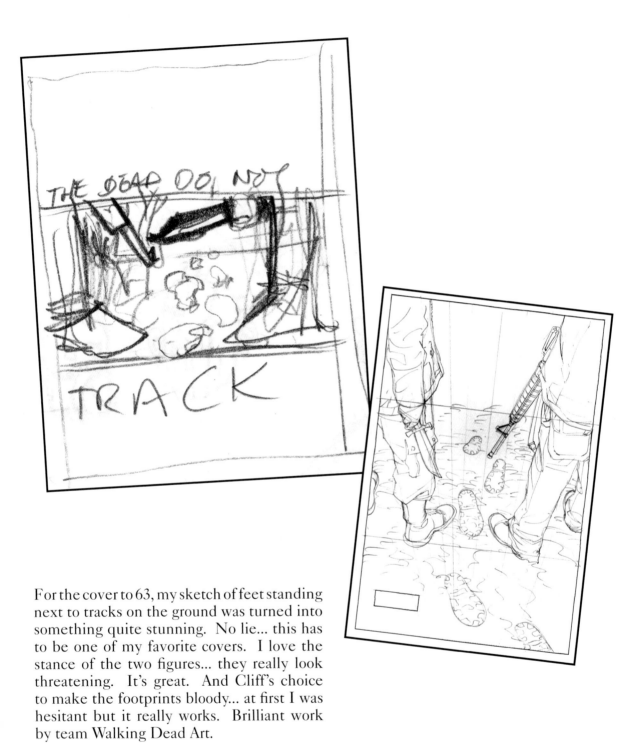

For the cover to 63, my sketch of feet standing next to tracks on the ground was turned into something quite stunning. No lie... this has to be one of my favorite covers. I love the stance of the two figures... they really look threatening. It's great. And Cliff's choice to make the footprints bloody... at first I was hesitant but it really works. Brilliant work by team Walking Dead Art.

I had no idea how to do this. I knew I wanted Rick and Abraham walking through the woods while people in trees spied on them. My sketch is awful, that angle would have never worked. Leave it to Charlie to take something I can't quite wrap my head around and turn it into a masterpiece. The staging on this cover is amazing. It works cropped or un-cropped--it's just brilliant.

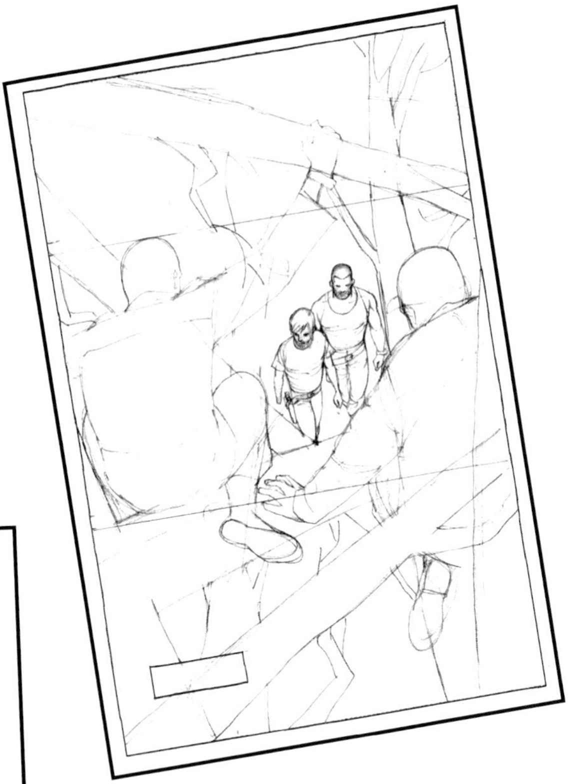

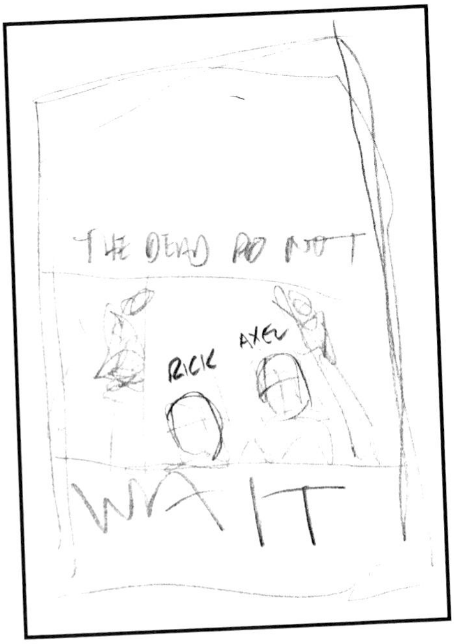
THE DEAD DO NOT
RICK
AXEL
WAIT

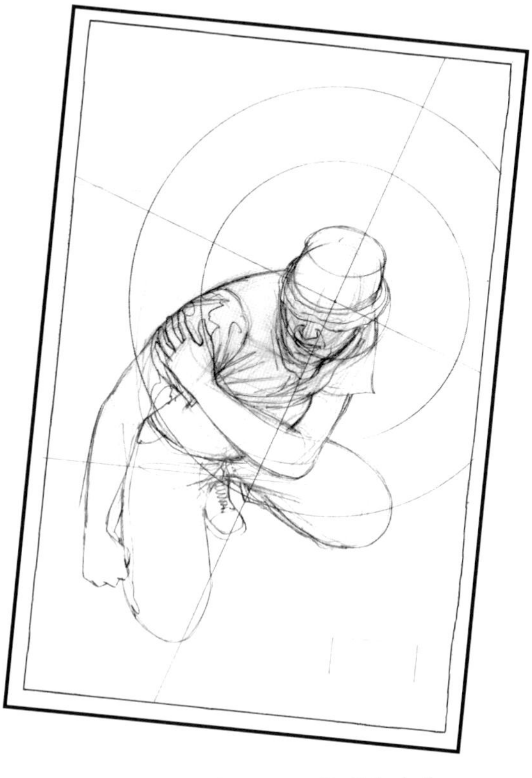

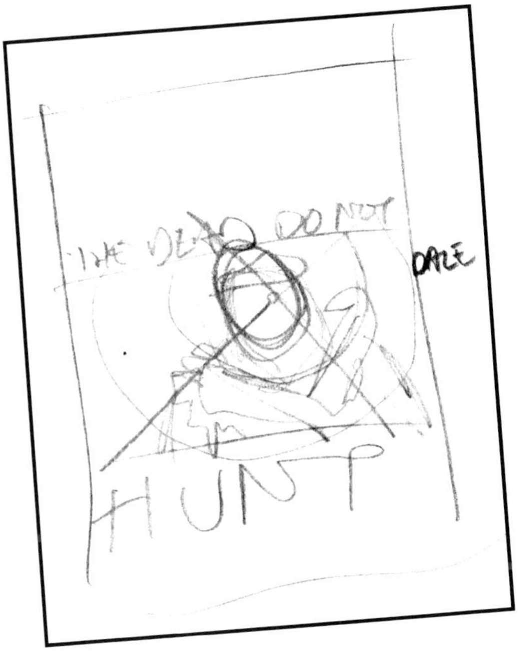
DO NOT
DALE
HUNT

Dale in the sights of a gun. I didn't know how this would work and again, Charlie really pulled it off. Considering Dale did die in this arc... this cover, for my tastes, is a little too literal and spoiler-y but damn, it sure is a cool image.

Some pages that were corrected before seeing print, both from issue 72. On page 8, I was much vaguer with my script than I'd wanted to be. The hanging of the sword wasn't what I wanted and the scene with the zombies, showing Michonne cutting the arm off of her boyfriend and his friend didn't play right. I don't even think I told Charlie where I wanted them to be--which is shameful, and he put them in an alley. All my fault. He changed to be the neighbor's house where Michonne got the sword from her neighbor's son. I picture her running into the house, fleeing her own--zombies in hot pursuit--and finding that sword in the house. It was cool to finally get to show that scene.

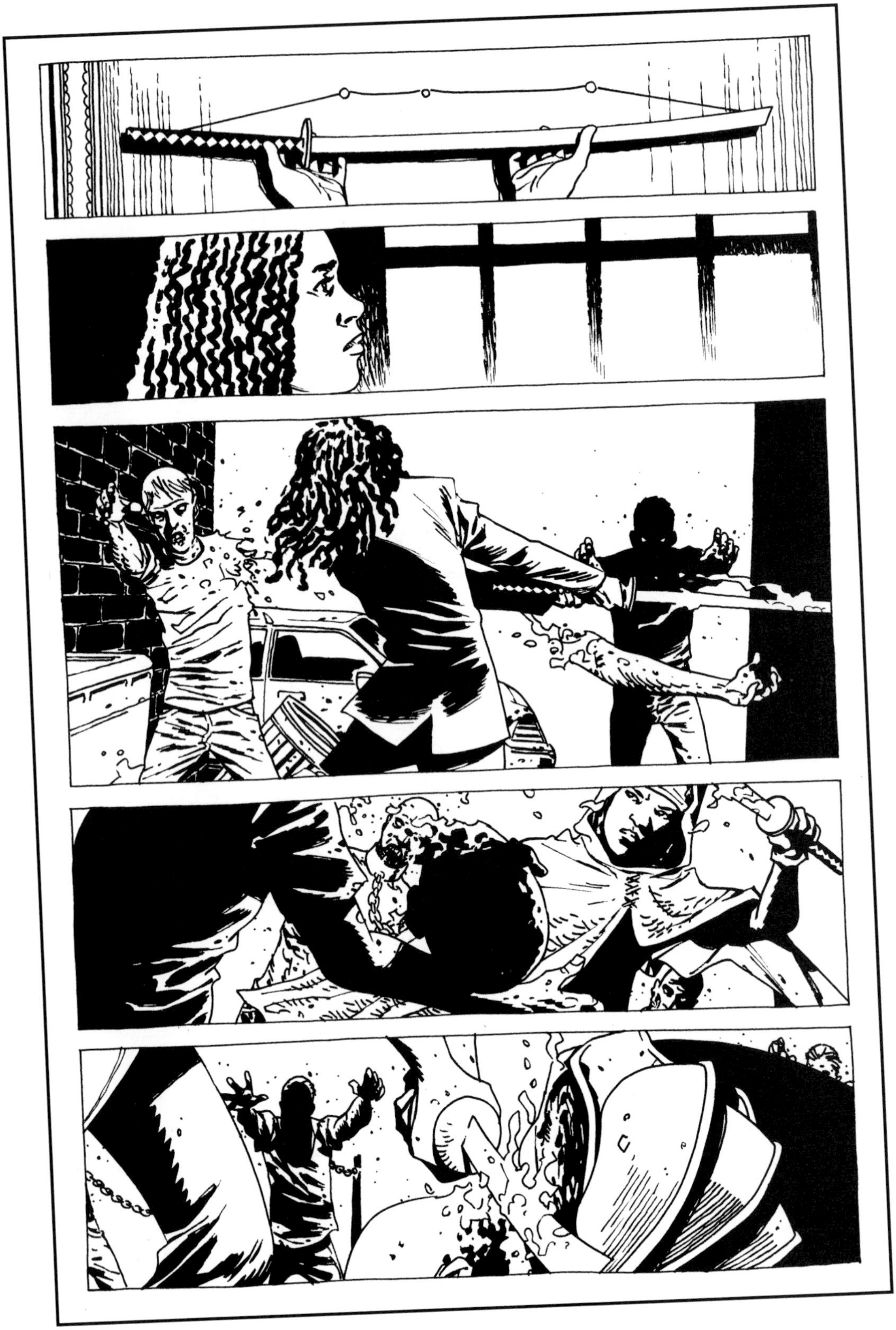

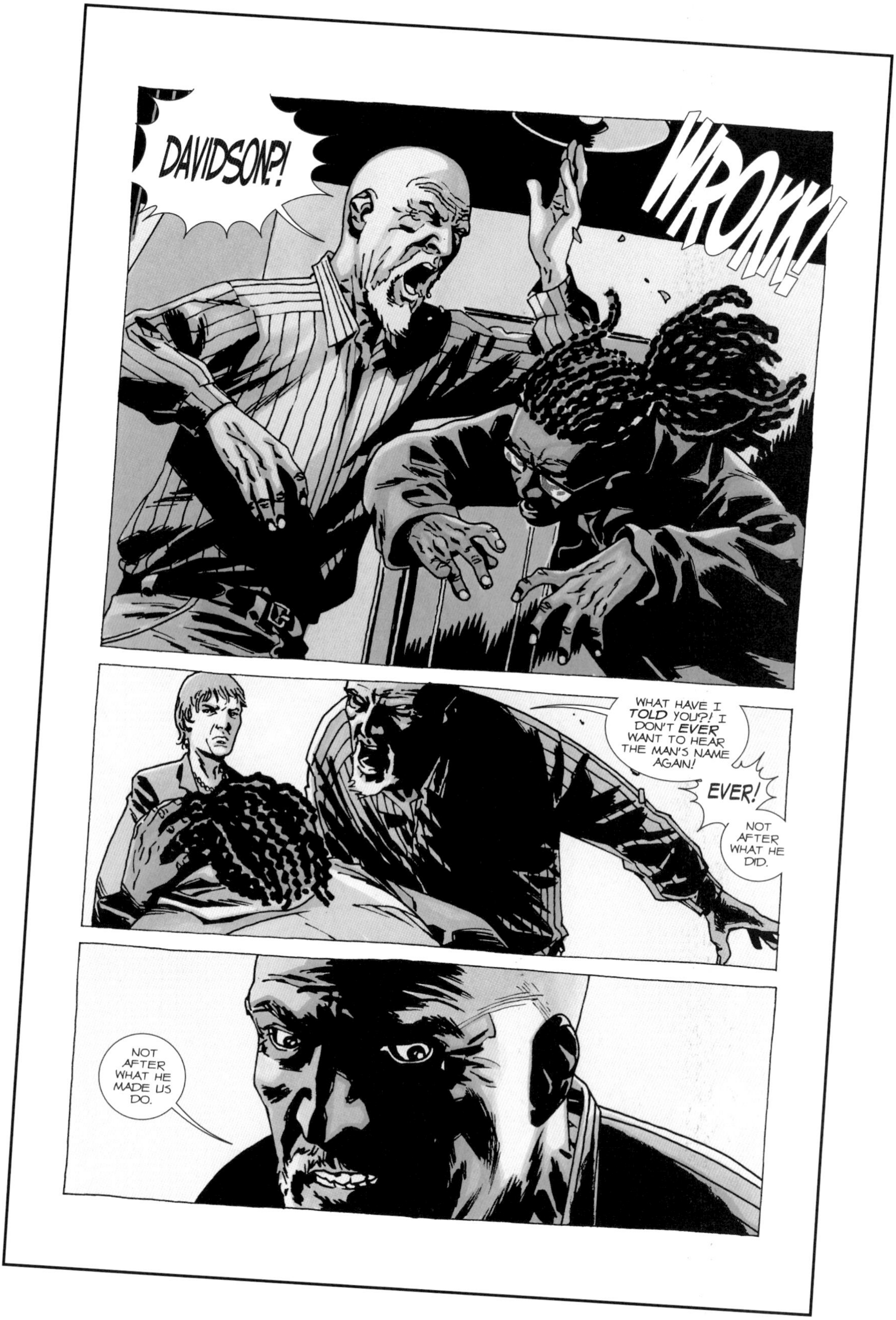
DAVIDSON?!
WROKK!
WHAT HAVE I TOLD YOU?! I DON'T EVER WANT TO HEAR THE MAN'S NAME AGAIN!
EVER!
NOT AFTER WHAT HE DID.
NOT AFTER WHAT HE MADE US DO.

On page 22 we see that Douglas originally did more than yell at Heath. I was going to have him kind of lose it and knock Heath around a bit. When I saw the page, Charlie did exactly what I asked--but seeing it--I didn't want Douglas to be that guy. Douglas is complex, but he's not a violent man. He's no Governor. I wanted him to lose it, but not like this. Thankfully, Charlie happily changed it to have him just yelling.

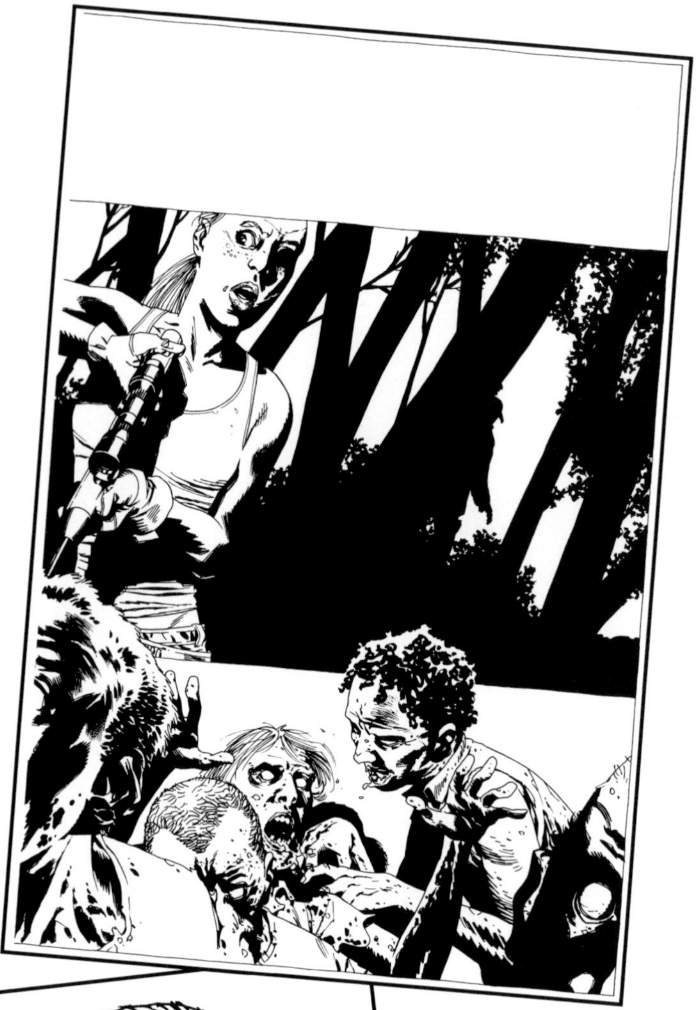

When Charlie originally drew the cover for the volume 11 TPB, he drew Andrea in a way where her head was going to be covered by the logo. Rather than change the dress on the trades (which would bug me for the rest of my life because I'm so anal), I had Charlie draw a new Andrea to patch in.

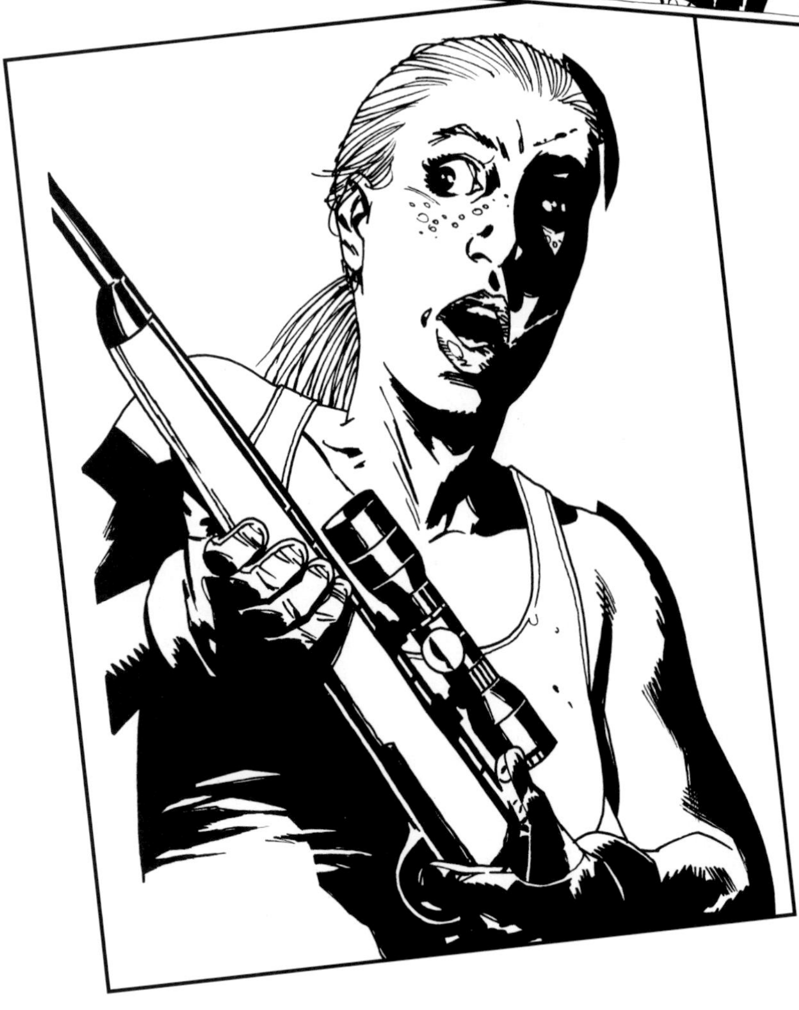

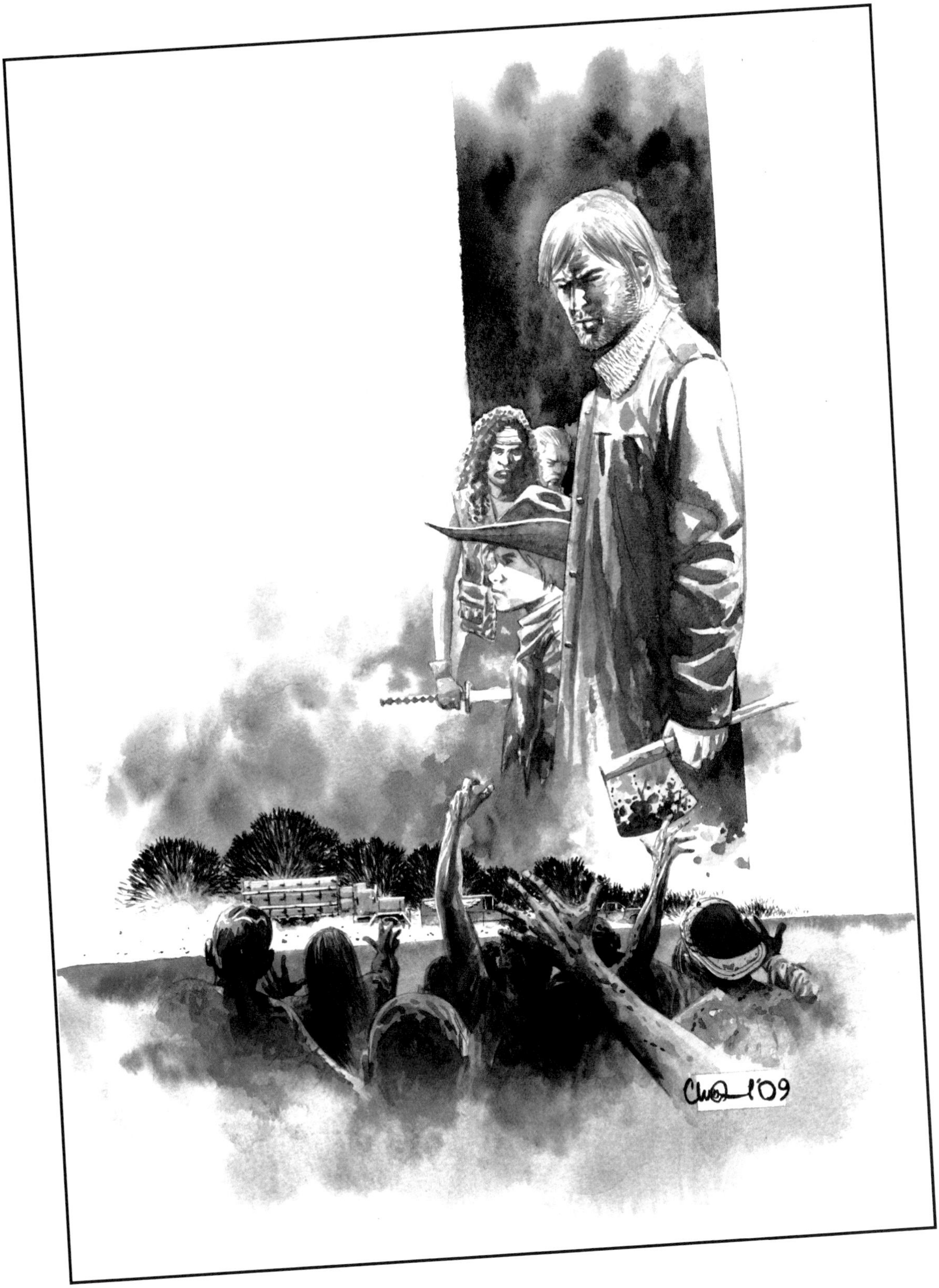

This is the super sweet painting that Charlie did as a promo piece for the Bristol convention. I love this thing; it's so cool seeing Charlie doing a painting of our cast and it looks damn sweet. It also served as the cover to the Image Comics 2010 convention yearbook. Did you get one of those? You should look into it, they're awesome.

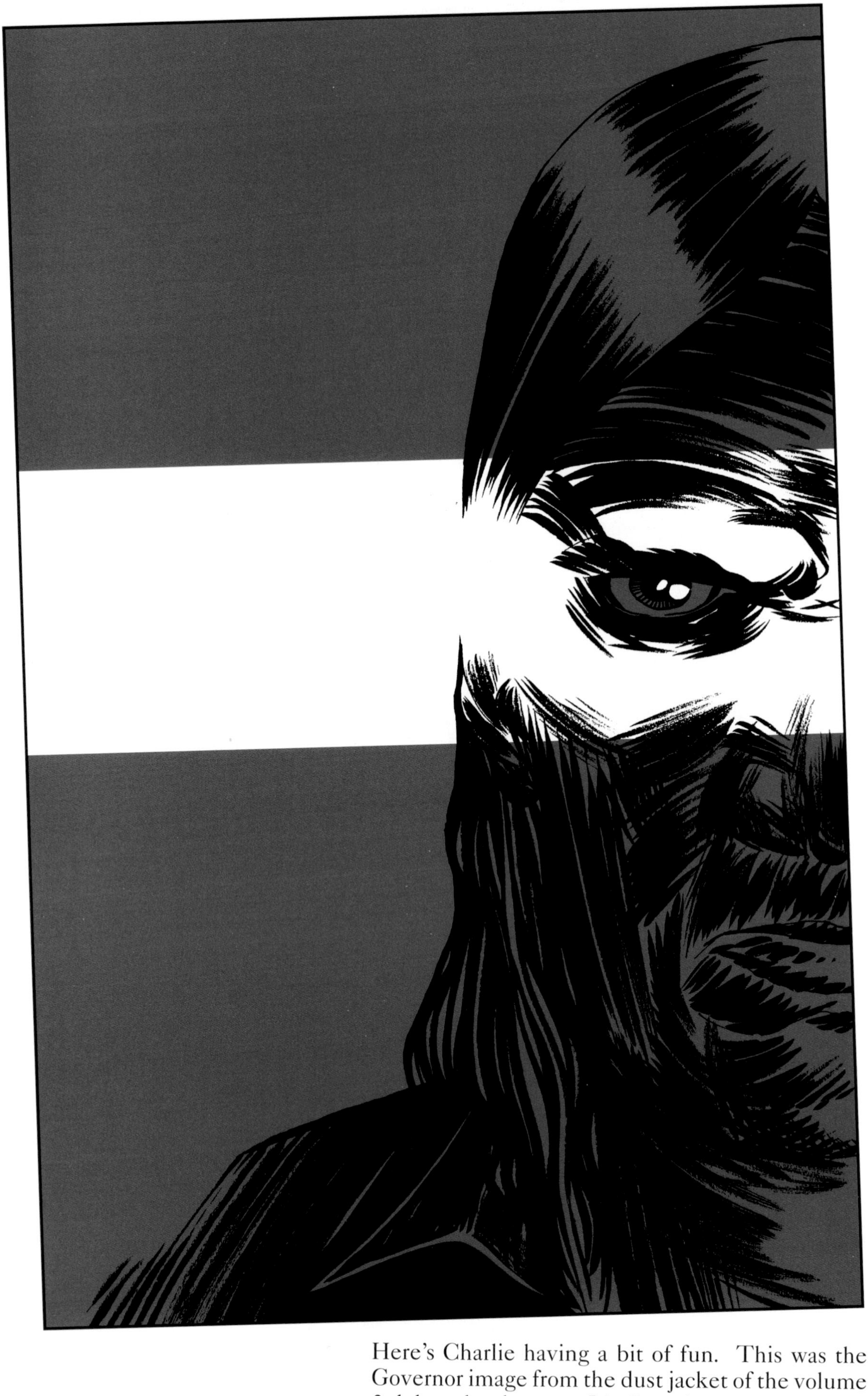

Here's Charlie having a bit of fun. This was the Governor image from the dust jacket of the volume 2 deluxe hard cover. I believe it was colored as a graphic for his website. Looks way cool.

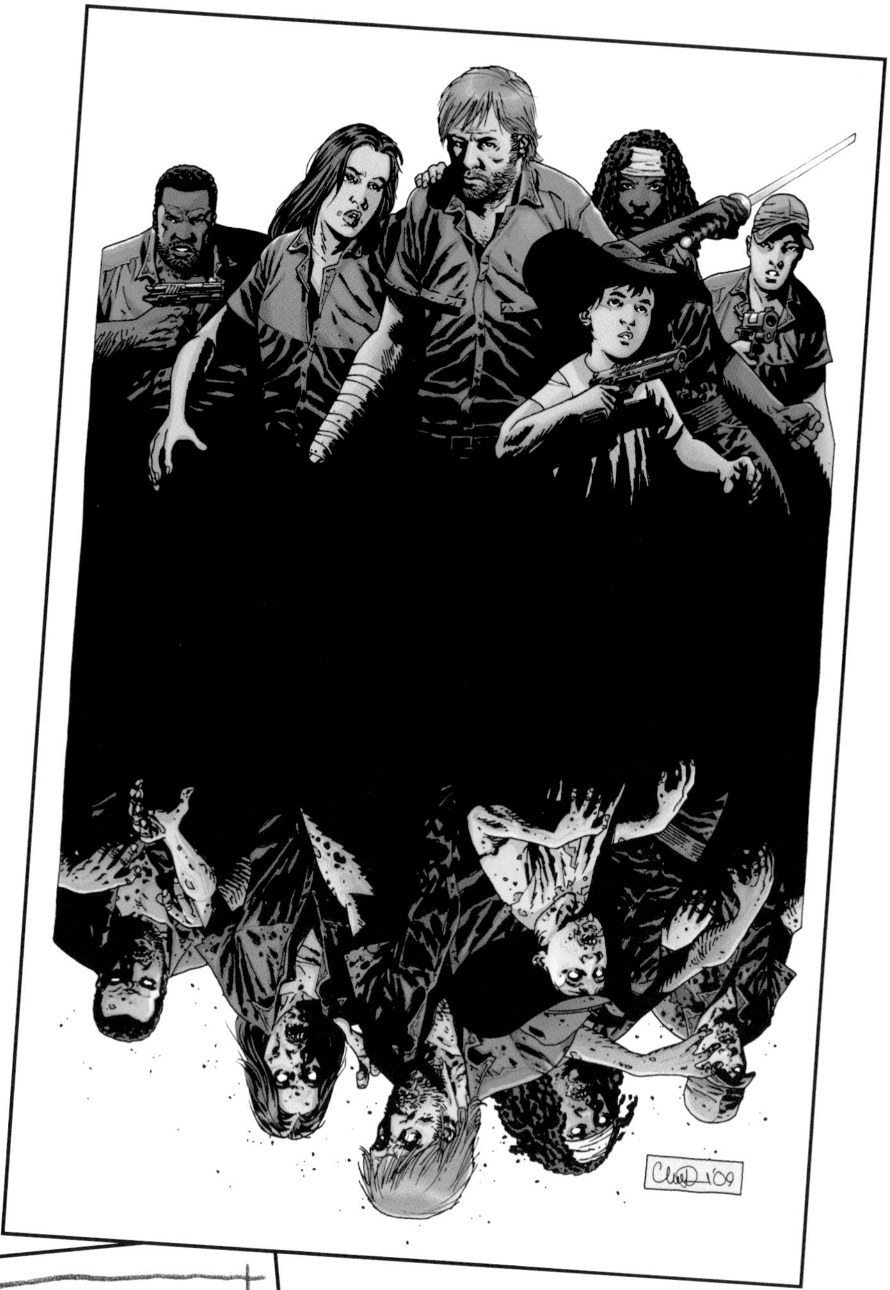

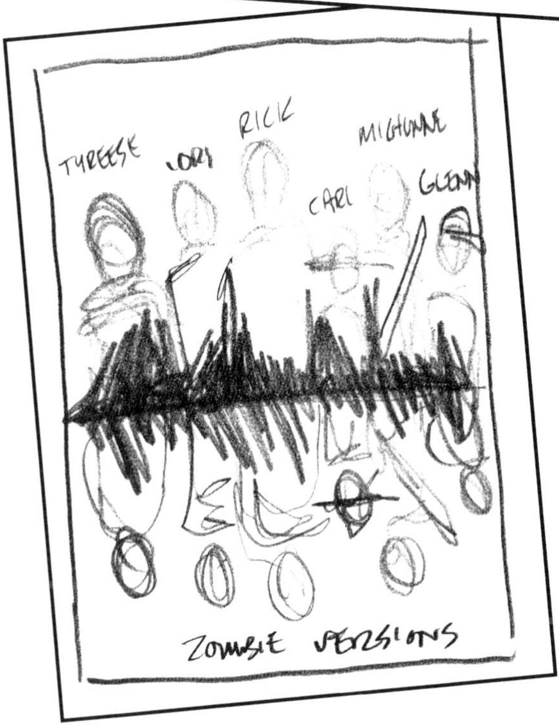
TYREESE
LORI
RICK
MICHONNE
CARL
GLENN
ZOMBIE VERSIONS

Here's my cruddy sketch for the Compendium paperback collecting issues 1-48, and Charlie and Cliff's final version of the cover. I just wanted it to be a mirror image thing, but Charlie came up with the idea of keeping the black area in the middle thick so the logo could run there instead of at the top of the bottom--I think that worked out brilliantly. Way to go, Charlie!

-Robert Kirkman

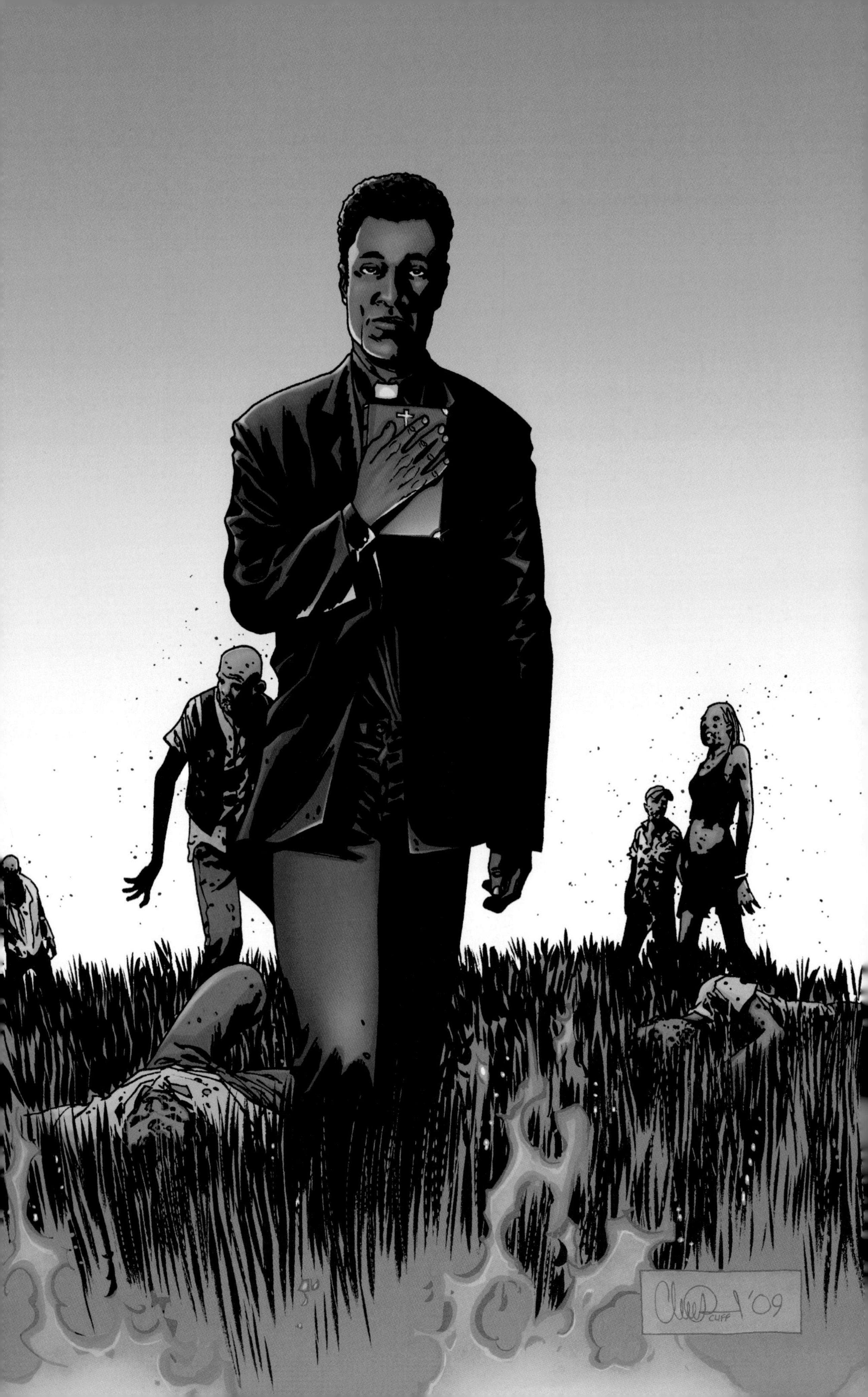

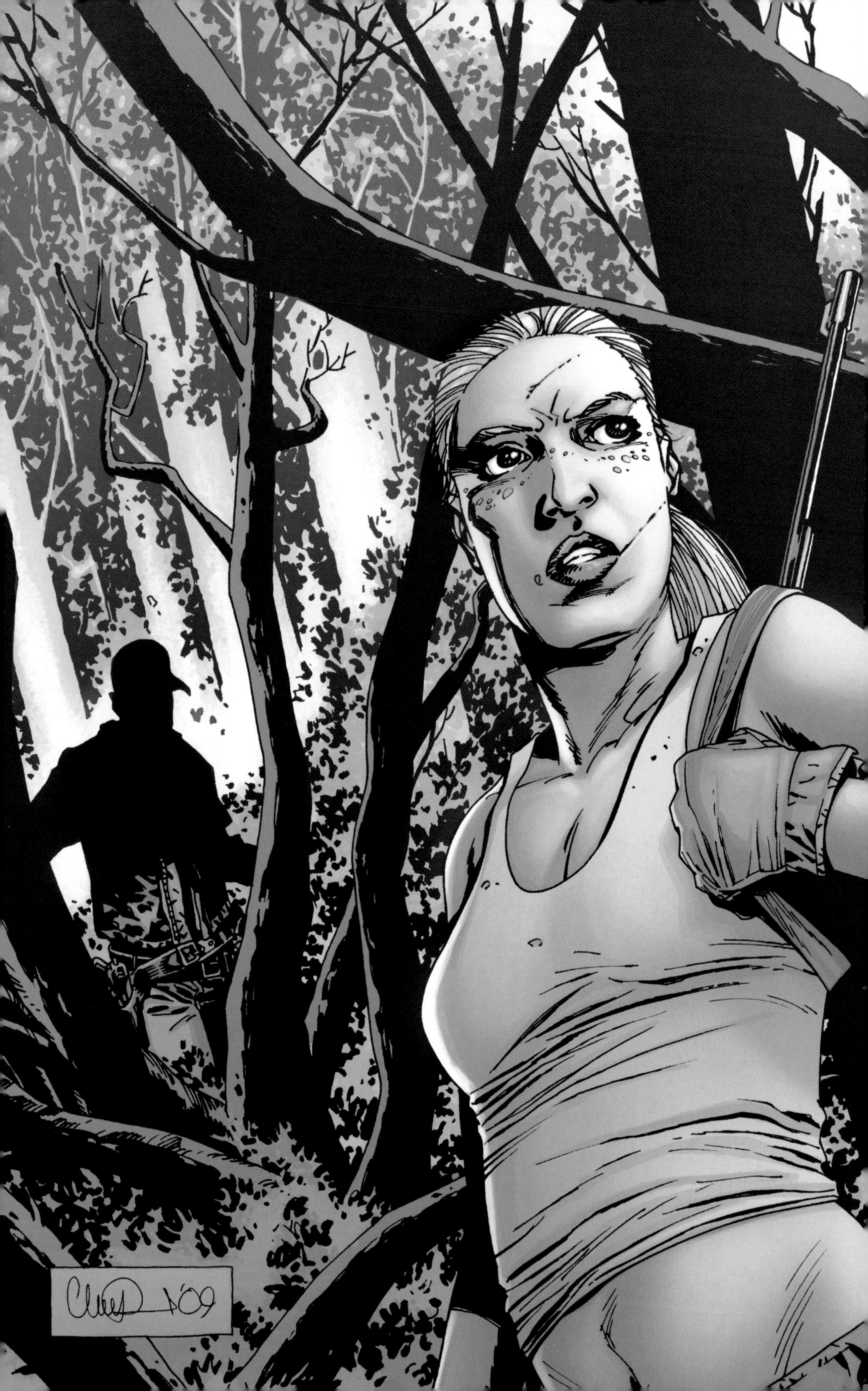

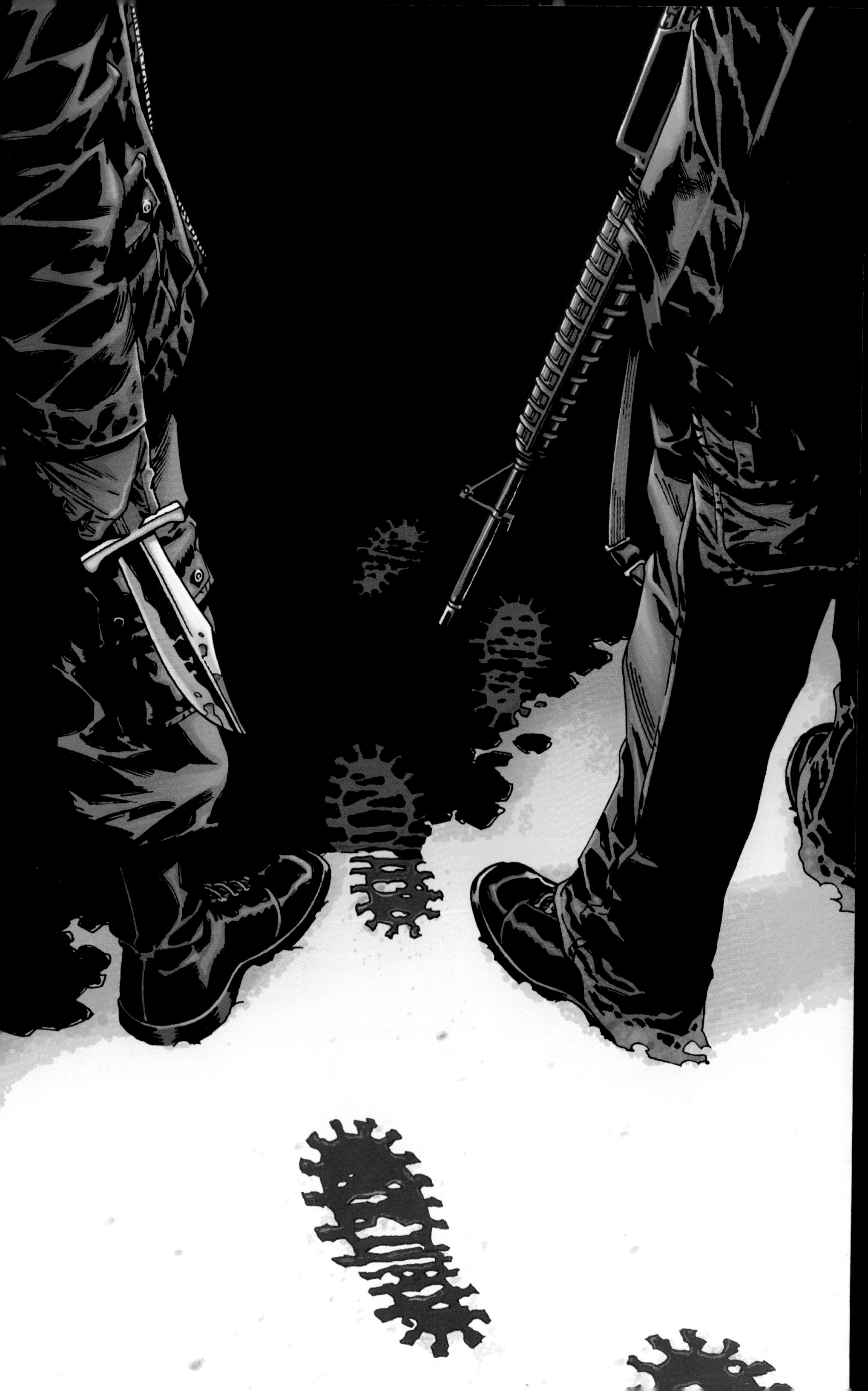

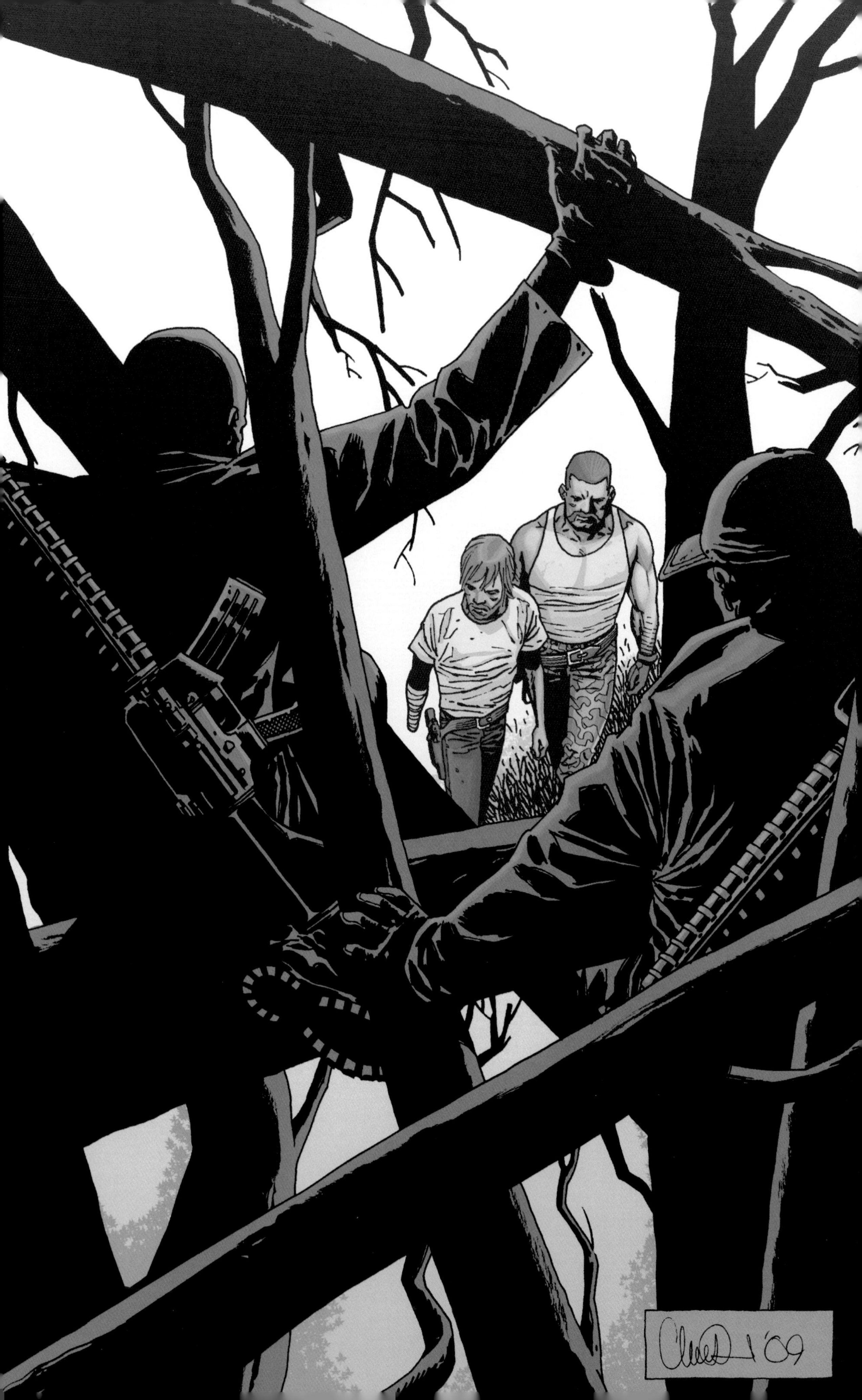

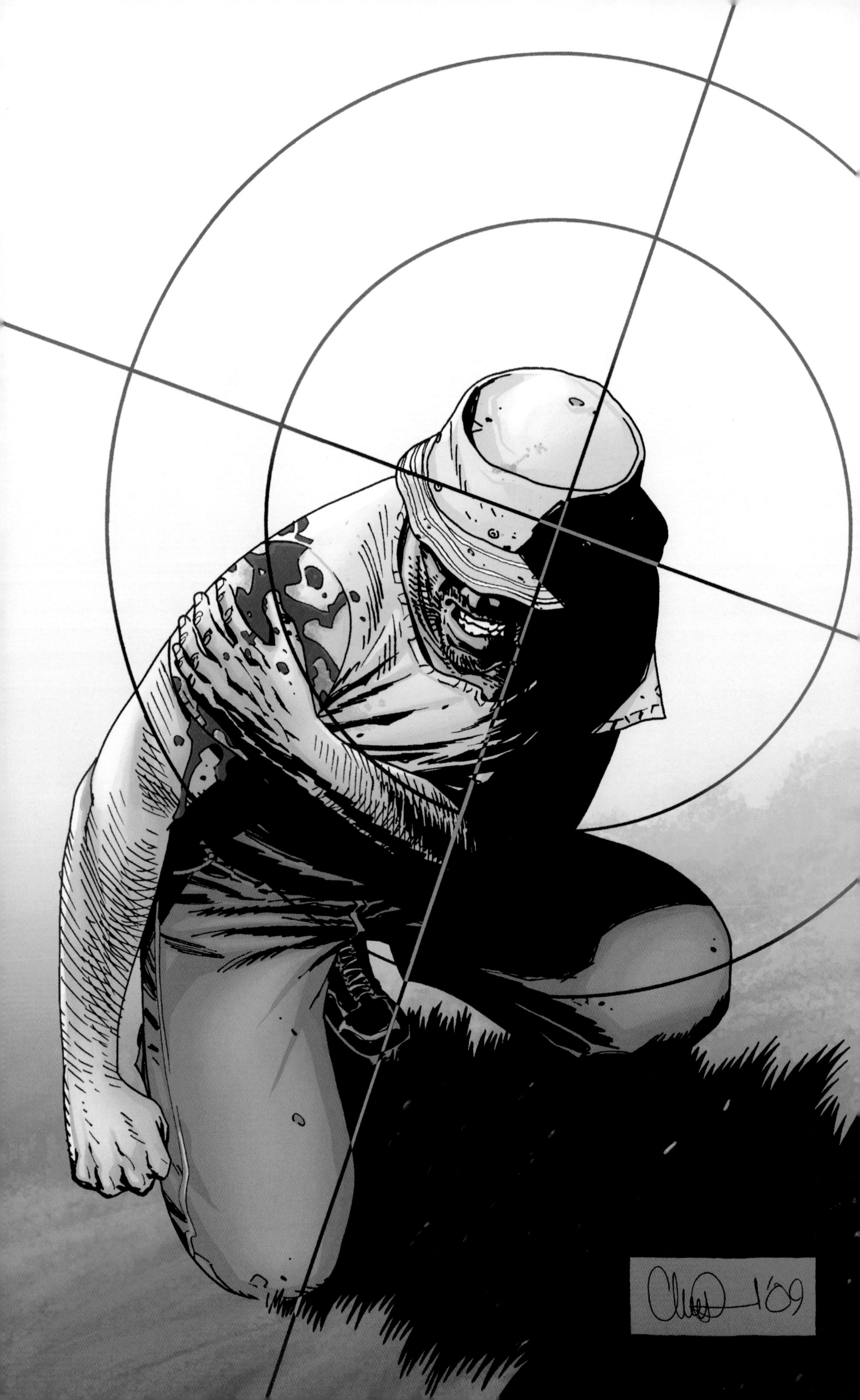

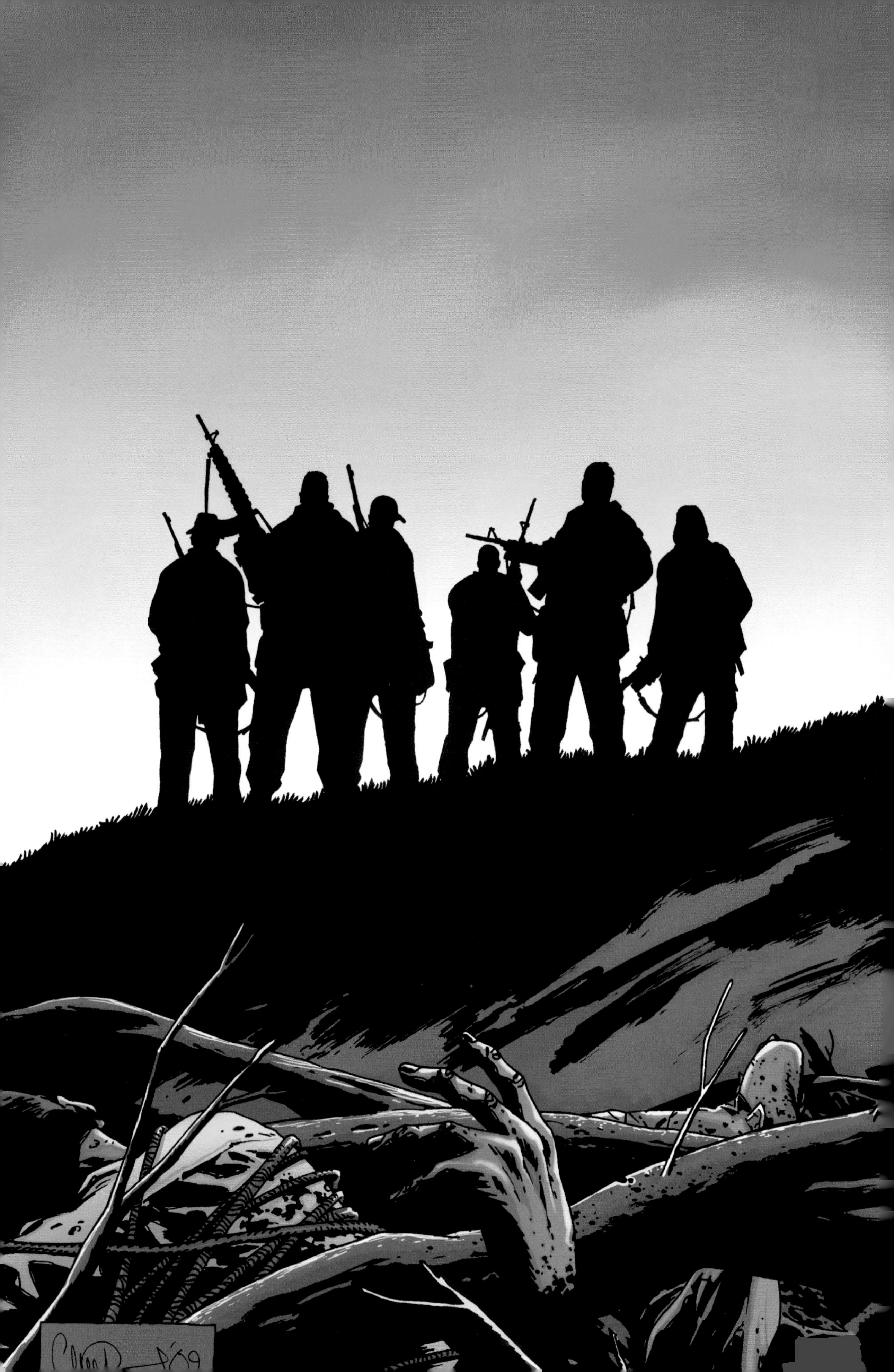

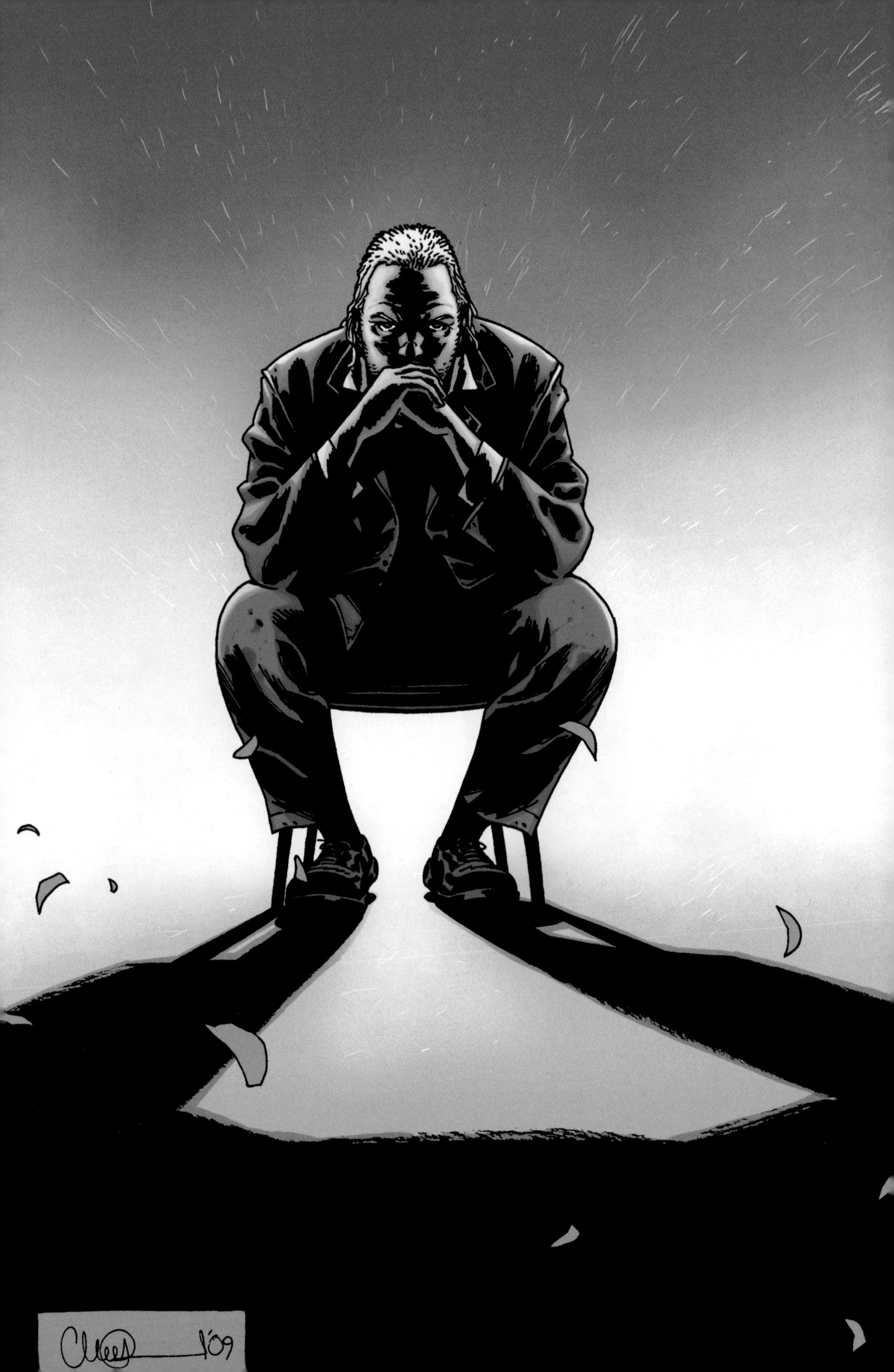

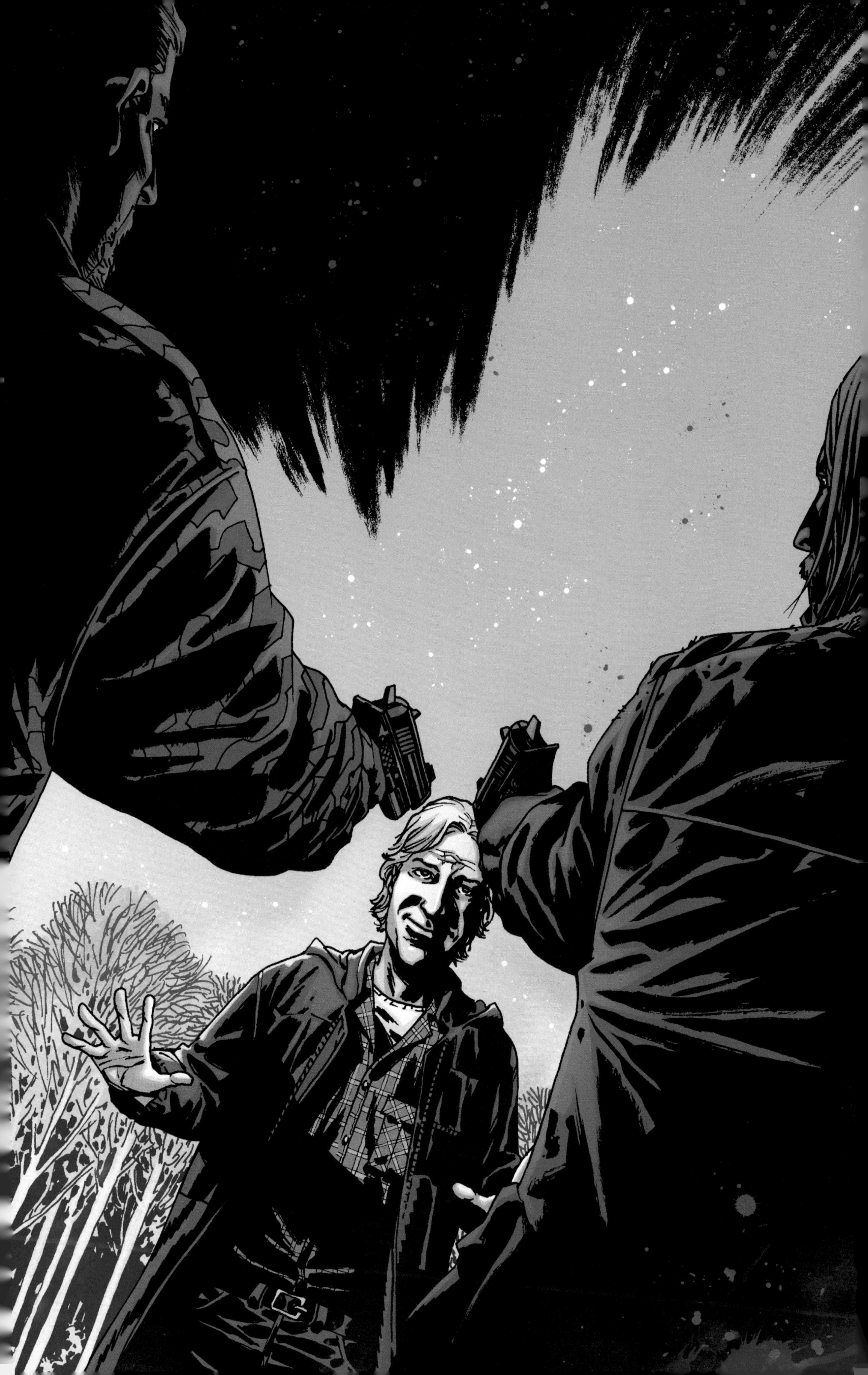

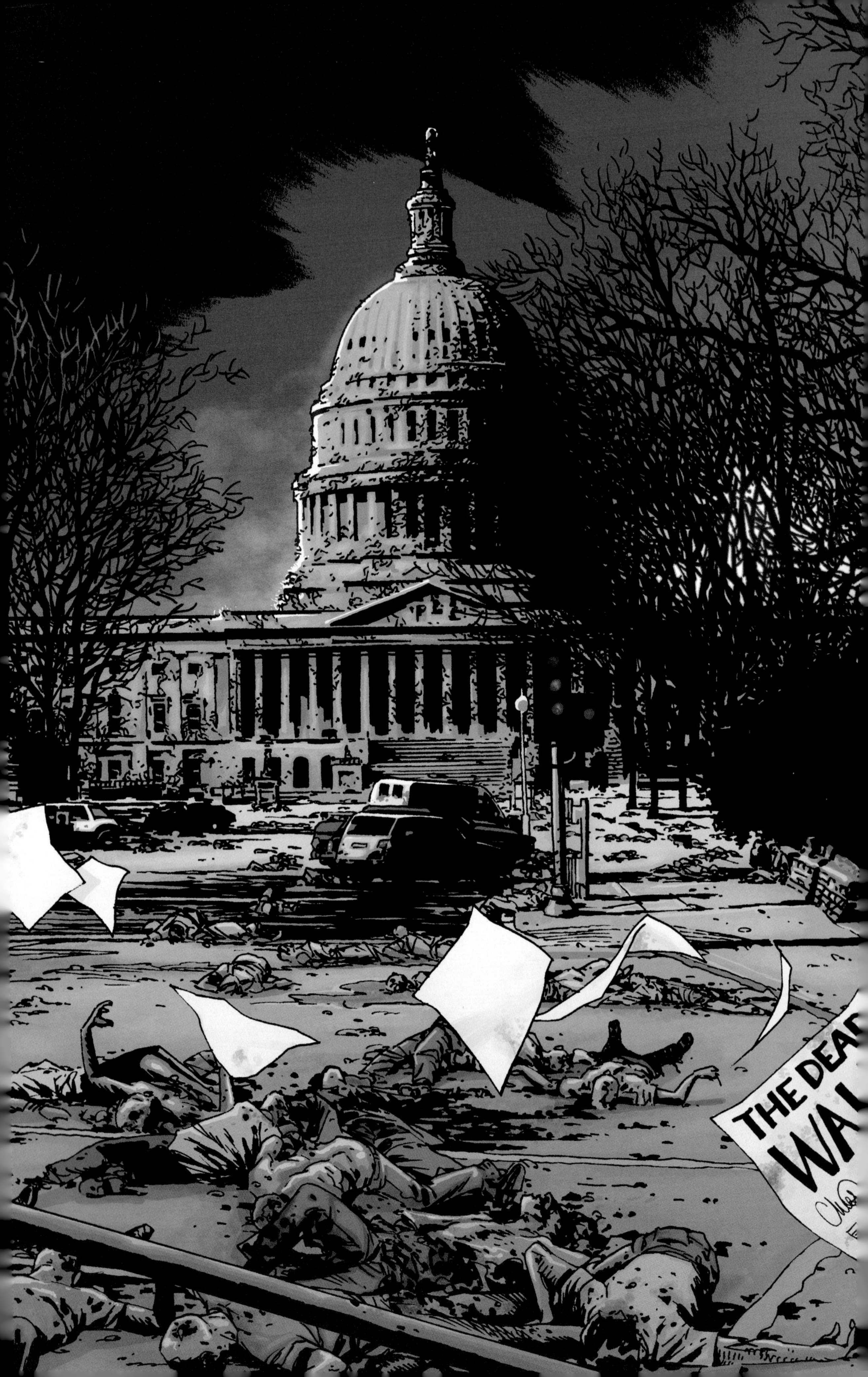

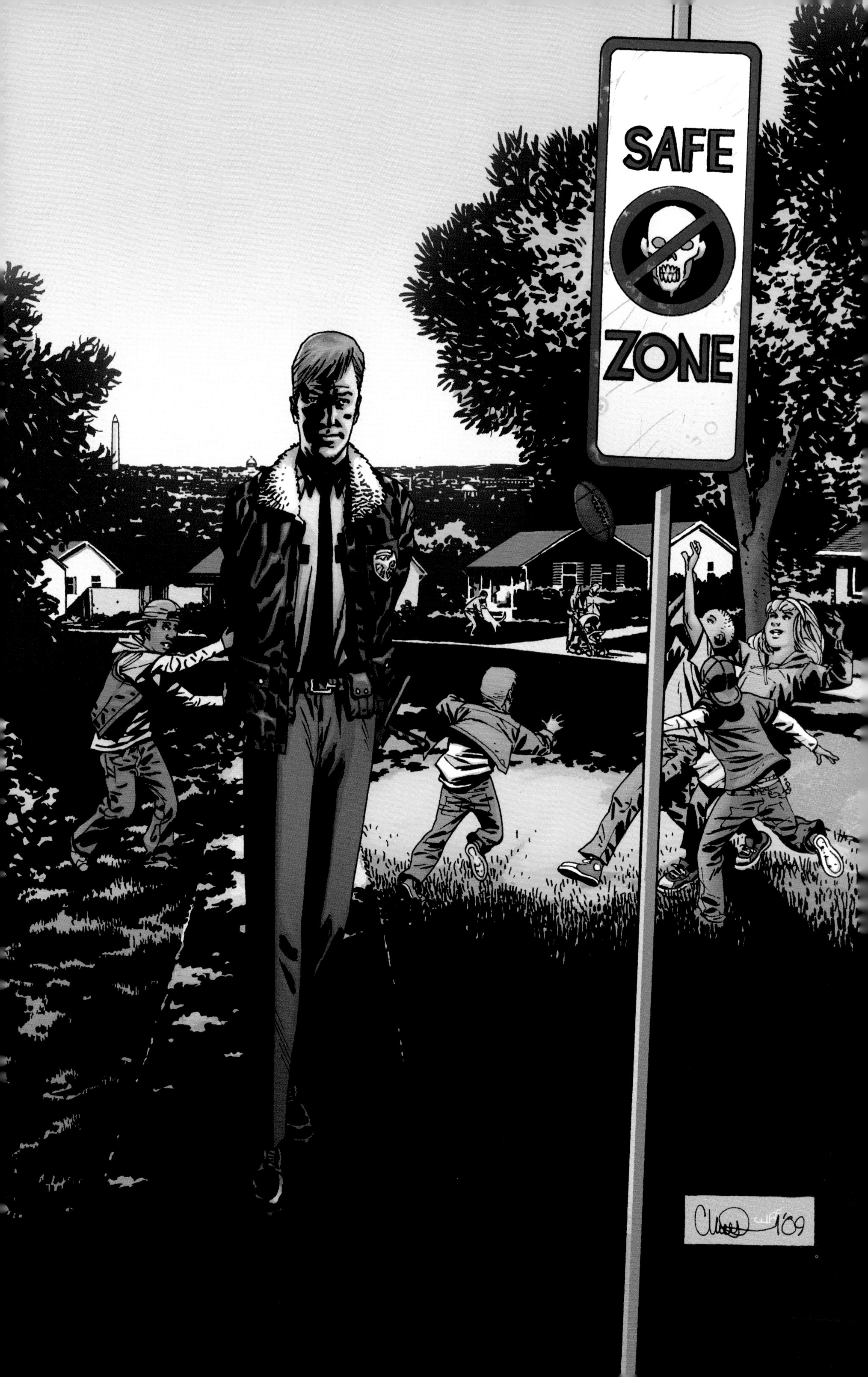
SAFE
ZONE

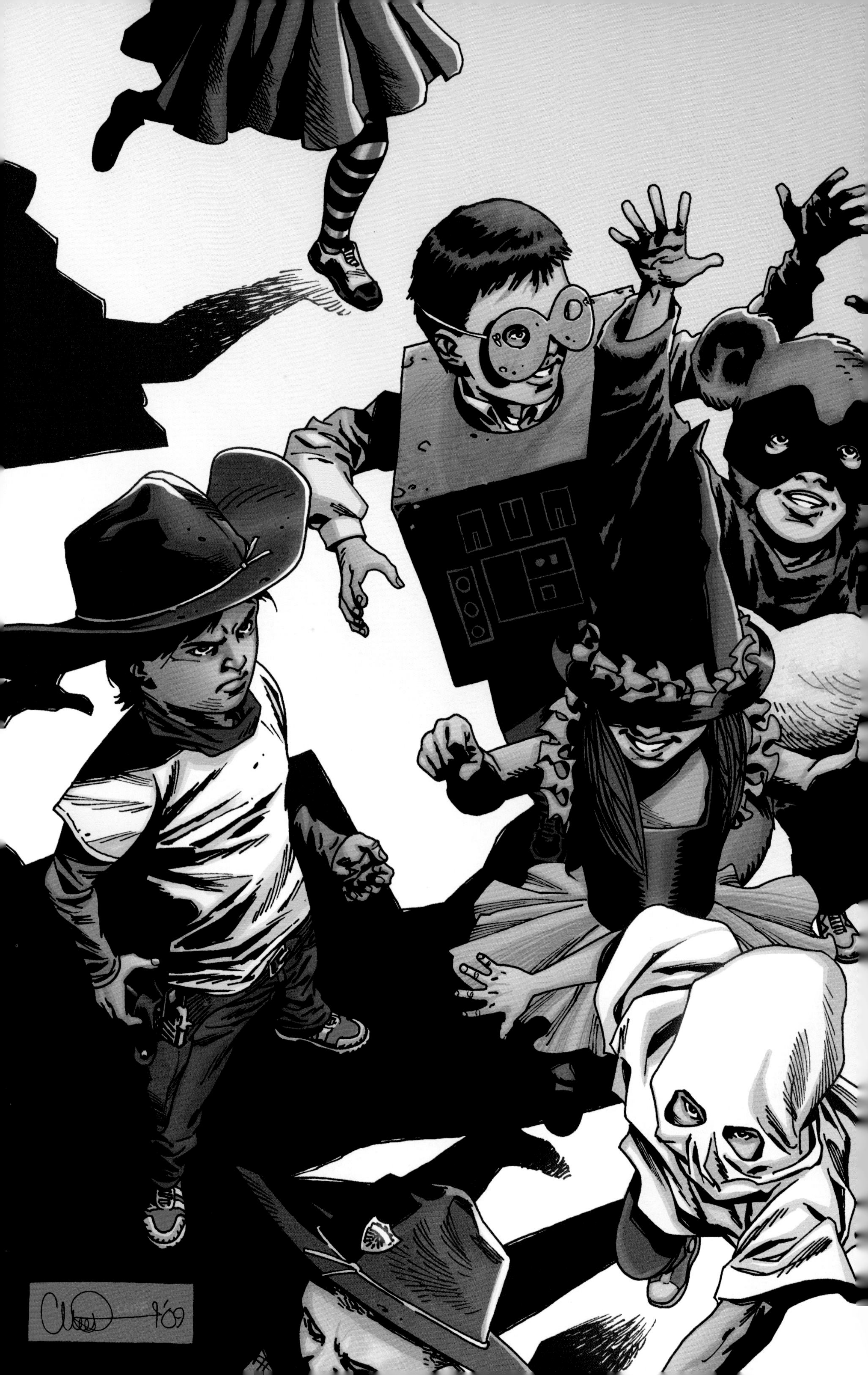
CLIFF '09

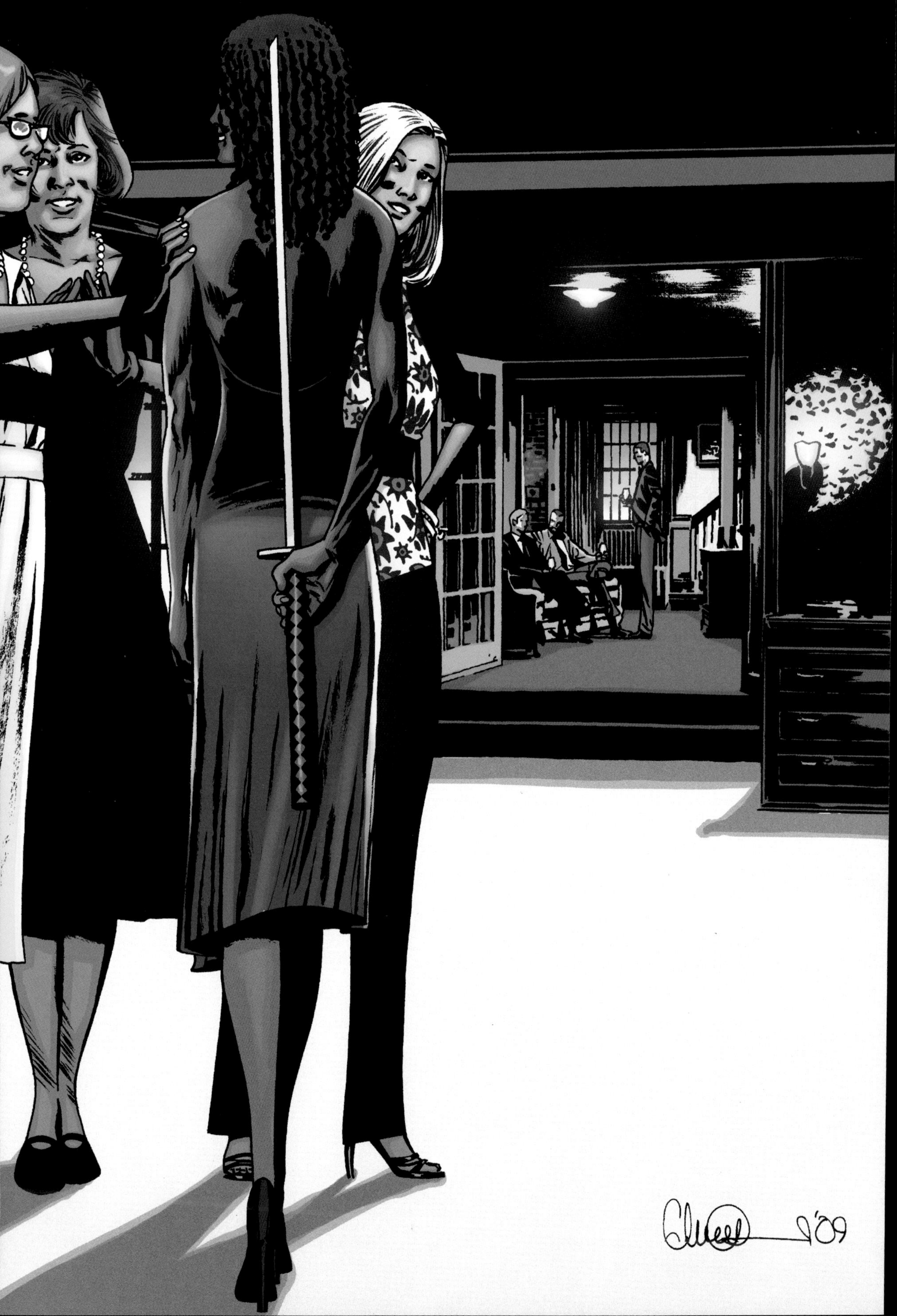

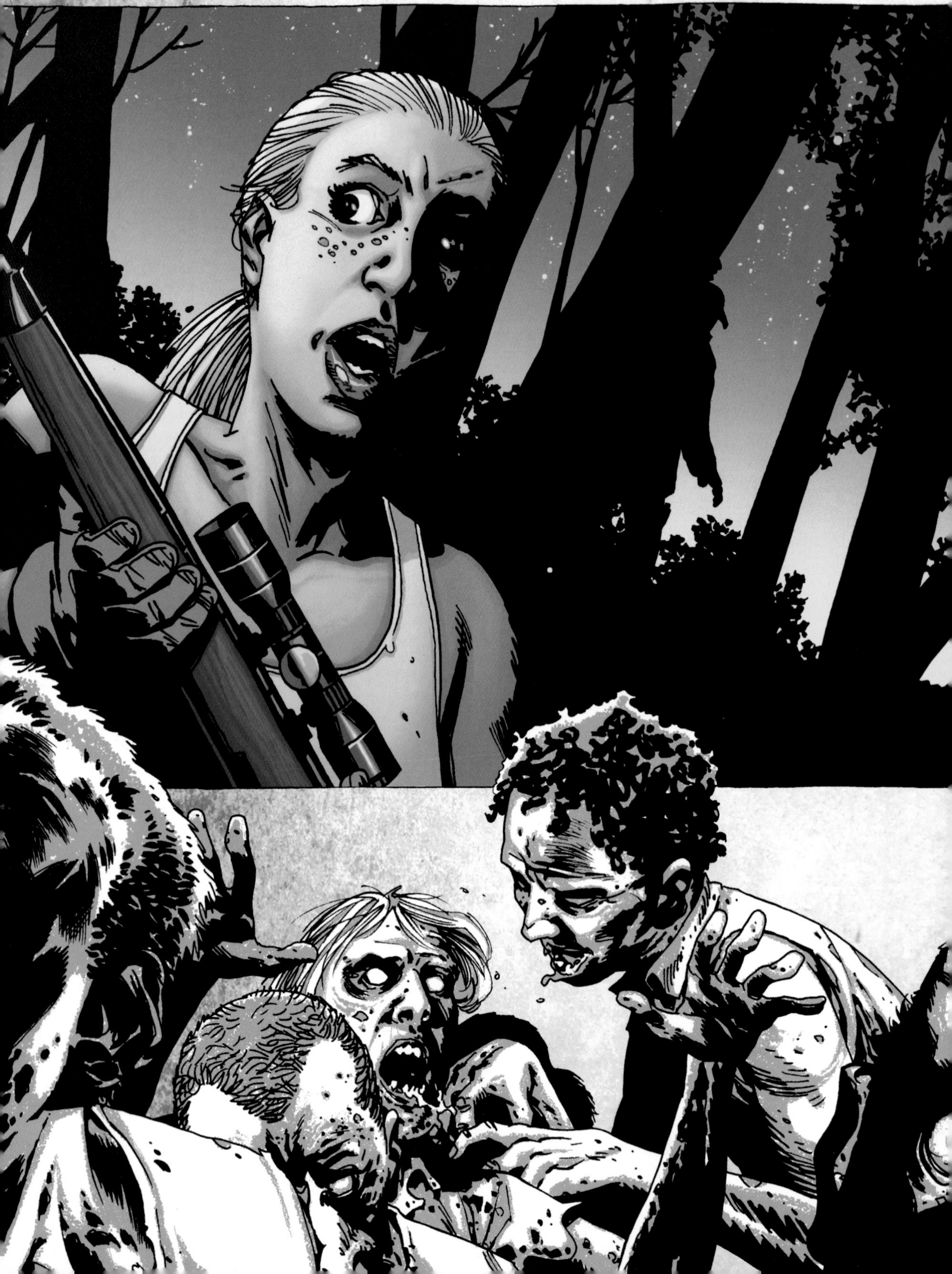

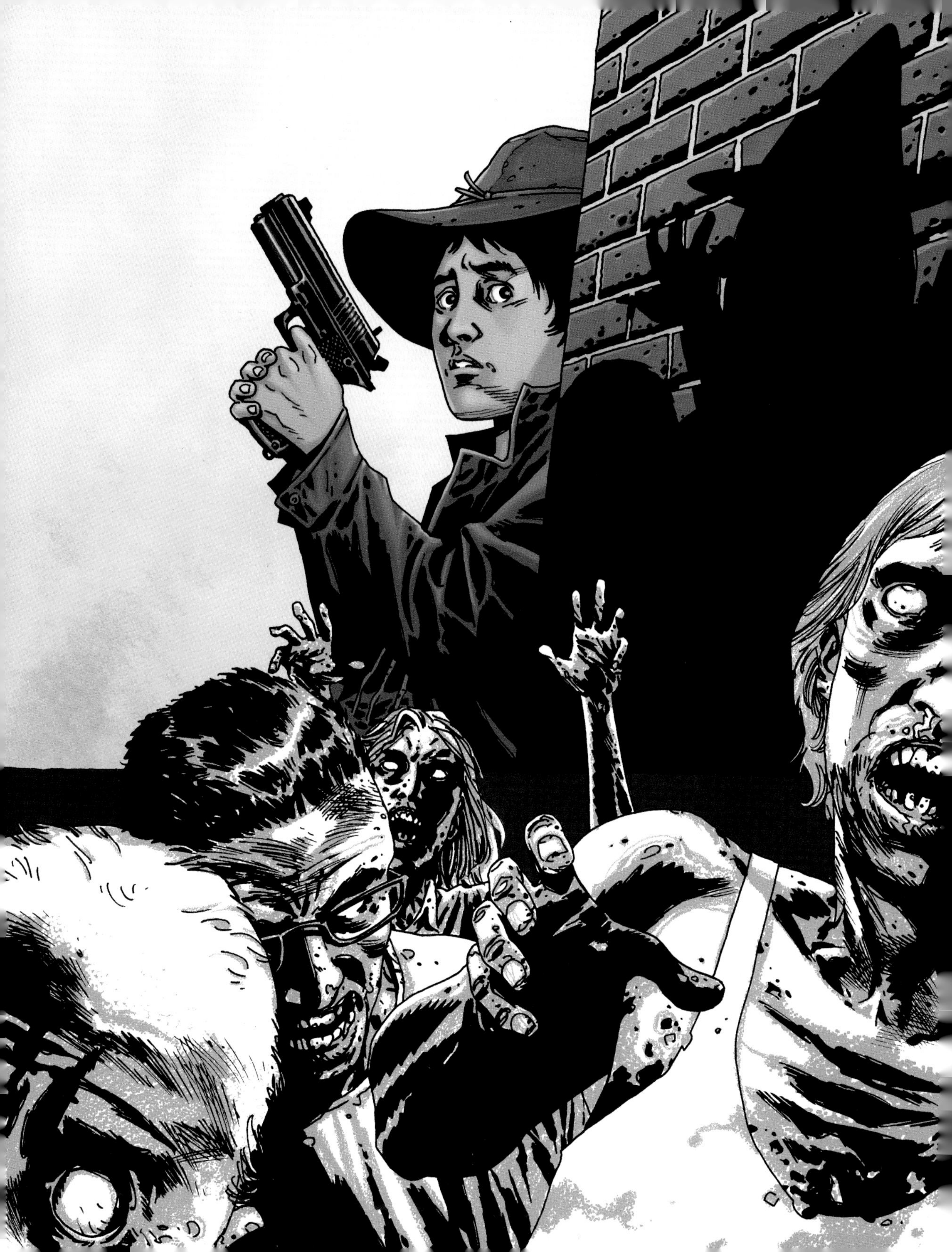

MORE GREAT BOOKS FROM
ROBERT KIRKMAN & IMAGE COMICS!

BRIT
VOLUME THREE: FUBAR

THE COMPLETE
INVINCIBLE
LIBRARY: VOLUME TWO

INVINCIBLE
presents
VOLUME ONE
ATOM EVE & REX SPLODE

THE WALKING
DEAD
BOOK SIX

INVINCIBLE
ULTIMATE COLLECTION
VOLUME
5

REAPER

INVINCIBLE
GROWING PAINS

THE ASTOUNDING WOLF-MAN

VOL. 1 TP
ISBN: 978-1-58240-862-0
$14.99
VOL. 2 TP
ISBN: 978-1-60706-007-9
$14.99
VOL. 3 TP
ISBN: 978-1-60706-111-3
$16.99

BATTLE POPE

VOL. 1: GENESIS TP
ISBN: 978-1-58240-572-8
$14.99
VOL. 2: MAYHEM TP
ISBN: 978-1-58240-529-2
$12.99
VOL. 3: PILLOW TALK TP
ISBN: 978-1-58240-677-0
$12.99
VOL. 4: WRATH OF GOD TP
ISBN: 978-1-58240-751-7
$9.99

BRIT

VOL. 1: OLD SOLDIER TP
ISBN: 978-1-58240-678-7
$14.99
VOL. 2: AWOL
ISBN: 978-1-58240-864-4
$14.99
VOL. 3: FUBAR
ISBN: 978-1-60706-061-1
$16.99

CAPES

VOL. 1: PUNCHING THE CLOCK TP
ISBN: 978-1-58240-756-2
$17.99

HAUNT

VOL. 1 TP
ISBN: 978-1-60706-154-0
$9.99

INVINCIBLE

VOL. 1: FAMILY MATTERS TP
ISBN: 978-1-58240-711-1
$12.99
VOL. 2: EIGHT IS ENOUGH TP
ISBN: 978-1-58240-347-2
$12.99
VOL. 3: PERFECT STRANGERS TP
ISBN: 978-1-58240-793-7
$12.99
VOL. 4: HEAD OF THE CLASS TP
ISBN: 978-1-58240-440-2
$14.95
VOL. 5: THE FACTS OF LIFE TP
ISBN: 978-1-58240-554-4
$14.99
VOL. 6: A DIFFERENT WORLD TP
ISBN: 978-1-58240-579-7
$14.99
VOL. 7: THREE'S COMPANY TP
ISBN: 978-1-58240-656-5
$14.99
VOL. 8: MY FAVORITE MARTIAN TP
ISBN: 978-1-58240-683-1
$14.99
VOL. 9: OUT OF THIS WORLD TP
ISBN: 978-1-58240-827-9
$14.99
VOL. 10: WHO'S THE BOSS TP
ISBN: 978-1-60706-013-0
$16.99
VOL. 11: HAPPY DAYS TP
ISBN: 978-1-60706-062-8
$16.99
VOL. 12: STILL STANDING TP
ISBN: 978-1-60706-166-3
$16.99
VOL. 13: GROWING PAINS TP
ISBN: 978-1-60706-251-6
$16.99
ULTIMATE COLLECTION, VOL. 1 HC
ISBN 978-1-58240-500-1
$34.95
ULTIMATE COLLECTION, VOL. 2 HC
ISBN: 978-1-58240-594-0
$34.99
ULTIMATE COLLECTION, VOL. 3 HC
ISBN: 978-1-58240-763-0
$34.99
ULTIMATE COLLECTION, VOL. 4 HC
ISBN: 978-1-58240-989-4
$34.99
ULTIMATE COLLECTION, VOL. 5 HC
ISBN: 978-1-60706-116-8
$34.99
THE OFFICIAL HANDBOOK OF THE INVINCIBLE UNIVERSE TP
ISBN: 978-1-58240-831-6
$12.99
INVINCIBLE PRESENTS, VOL. 1: ATOM EVE & REX SPLODE TP
ISBN: 978-1-60706-255-4
$14.99
THE COMPLETE INVINCIBLE LIBRARY, VOL. 1 HC
ISBN: 978-1-58240-718-0
$125.00
THE COMPLETE INVINCIBLE LIBRARY, VOL. 2 HC
ISBN: 978-1-60706-112-0
$125.00

THE WALKING DEAD

VOL. 1: DAYS GONE BYE TP
ISBN: 978-1-58240-672-5
$9.99
VOL. 2: MILES BEHIND US TP
ISBN: 978-1-58240-775-3
$14.99
VOL. 3: SAFETY BEHIND BARS TP
ISBN: 978-1-58240-805-7
$14.99
VOL. 4: THE HEART'S DESIRE TP
ISBN: 978-1-58240-530-8
$14.99
VOL. 5: THE BEST DEFENSE TP
ISBN: 978-1-58240-612-1
$14.99
VOL. 6: THIS SORROWFUL LIFE TP
ISBN: 978-1-58240-684-8
$14.99
VOL. 7: THE CALM BEFORE TP
ISBN: 978-1-58240-828-6
$14.99
VOL. 8: MADE TO SUFFER TP
ISBN: 978-1-58240-883-5
$14.99
VOL. 9: HERE WE REMAIN TP
ISBN: 978-1-60706-022-2
$14.99
VOL. 10: WHAT WE BECOME TP
ISBN: 978-1-60706-075-8
$14.99
VOL. 11: FEAR THE HUNTERS TP
ISBN: 978-1-60706-181-6
$14.99
VOL. 12: LIFE AMONG THEM TP
ISBN: 978-1-60706-254-7
$14.99
BOOK ONE HC
ISBN: 978-1-58240-619-0
$34.99
BOOK TWO HC
ISBN: 978-1-58240-698-5
$34.99
BOOK THREE HC
ISBN: 978-1-58240-825-5
$34.99
BOOK FOUR HC
ISBN: 978-1-60706-000-0
$34.99
BOOK FIVE HC
ISBN: 978-1-60706-171-7
$34.99
BOOK SIX HC
ISBN: 978-1-60706-327-8
$34.99
DELUXE HARDCOVER, VOL. 2
ISBN: 978-1-60706-029-7
$100.00
THE WALKING DEAD: THE COVERS, VOL. 1 HC
ISBN: 978-1-60706-002-4
$24.99

REAPER

GRAPHIC NOVEL
ISBN: 978-1-58240-354-2
$6.95

TECH JACKET

VOL. 1: THE BOY FROM EARTH TP
ISBN: 978-1-58240-771-5
$14.99

TALES OF THE REALM

HARDCOVER
ISBN: 978-1-58240-426-0
$34.95
TRADE PAPERBACK
ISBN: 978-1-58240-394-6
$14.95

Battle
POPE
Wrath of God

THE WALKING
DEAD
THE COVERS

TECH JACKET
THE BOY FROM EARTH

BRIT
VOLUME ONE: OLD SOLDIER

HAUNT

THE ASTOUNDING
WOLF-MAN
VOLUME ONE

CAPES

TO FIND YOUR NEAREST COMIC BOOK STORE, CALL:
1-888-COMIC-BOOK

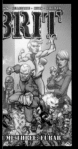

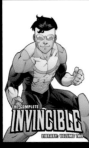

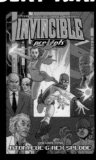

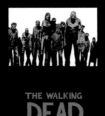

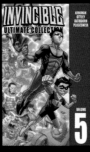

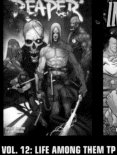

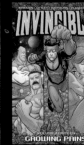

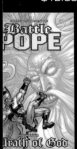

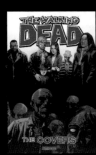

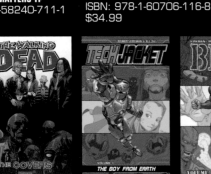

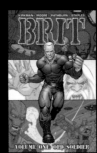

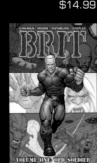

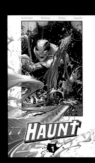

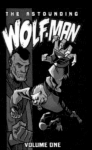

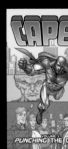